Print, Power, and People in 17th-Century France

by
HENRI-JEAN MARTIN
translated by
David Gerard

The Scarecrow Press, Inc.
Metuchen, N.J., & London
1993

Originally published as *Livre, pouvoirs et société à Paris au 17 siècle (1598–1701)* (Geneva, Switzerland: Librairie Droz S.A.). Copyright © 1969 by Librairie Droz.

Illustration on pp. xii-xiii: Partial street map of Paris from Truchet's map, 1551—called "plan de Bâle") which includes the Rue St. Jacques (the book trade quarter) at the top of the map. Reprinted from *Dictionnaire historique des rues de Paris*, 2nd ed. (Paris: Les Editions de Minuit), 1964, with kind permission from the publishers.

British Library Cataloguing-in-Publication data available

Library of Congress Cataloging-in-Publication Data

Martin, Henri Jean, 1924-
  [Livre, pouvoirs et société à Paris au 17e siècle. English]
  Print, power, and people in 17th-century France / by Henri-Jean Martin ; translated by David Gerard.
    p.   cm.
  Translation of: Livre, pouvoirs et société à Paris au 17e siècle.
  Originally presented as the author's thesis, Paris.
  Includes bibliographical references (p.   ) and indexes.
  ISBN 0-8108-2477-9 (acid-free paper)
  1. Books—France—History—17th-18th centuries.   2. Book industries and trade—France—History—17th century.   3. Books and reading—France—History—17th century.   4. Libraries—France—History—17th-18th centuries.   I. Title.
Z8.F8M37314   1993
381'.45002'0944—dc20   91-39016

CONTENTS

Autant ou plus qu'en Athenes ou *Troye*
Le lieu feiour, & les mufes fçauantes
Font on ce lieu leur demeure remettre,
Plus que iamais ne furent fur le mond
De Aonia, ou par elle femond
Eftoit iadis maint homme pour apprendre,
Aerz & meftiers, apres mon fault comprendre,
Defquelz il vient treigrande vtilité,
An lieu fubdict aumy tranquilite,
Semblablement marchans de toutes guifes
Viennent illec pour toutes marchandiſes
Deſtribuer, & tant de peuple abonde
En celuy lieu qu'il n'y a peuple au monde
Qui foit autant à chafcun gratieufe
Qu'eft ceſte cy, ny autant ſpatieuſe.

✂ Icy eſt le vray pourtraict náturel de la ville, cité, vniue
& Faubourgz de Paris, ou ſont iuſtement figurées toutes les Rues & Ruelles corref
l'vne à l'autre, ainſi qui ſont de préſent ſituées, qui ſont en nôbre deux cens quatre
ſept. Pareillement ſont figurées toutes les Egliſes, & Monaſteres, qui ſont en nom
quatre. Auſſy ſont figuréz tous les Colleges, qui ſont en nôbre quarante neuf. Et p
gnoiſtre icelles Rues, Ruelles, Egliſes, Monaſteres & Colleges, vous trouuerrez le
eſcriptz à chûn ſur ſon propre endroict. Côme plus amplement vous pouez voir d

✂ A Paris, par Oliuier Truſchet, & Germain Hoyau, demourans en
la Rue de Montorgueil, au Chef ſainct Denys.

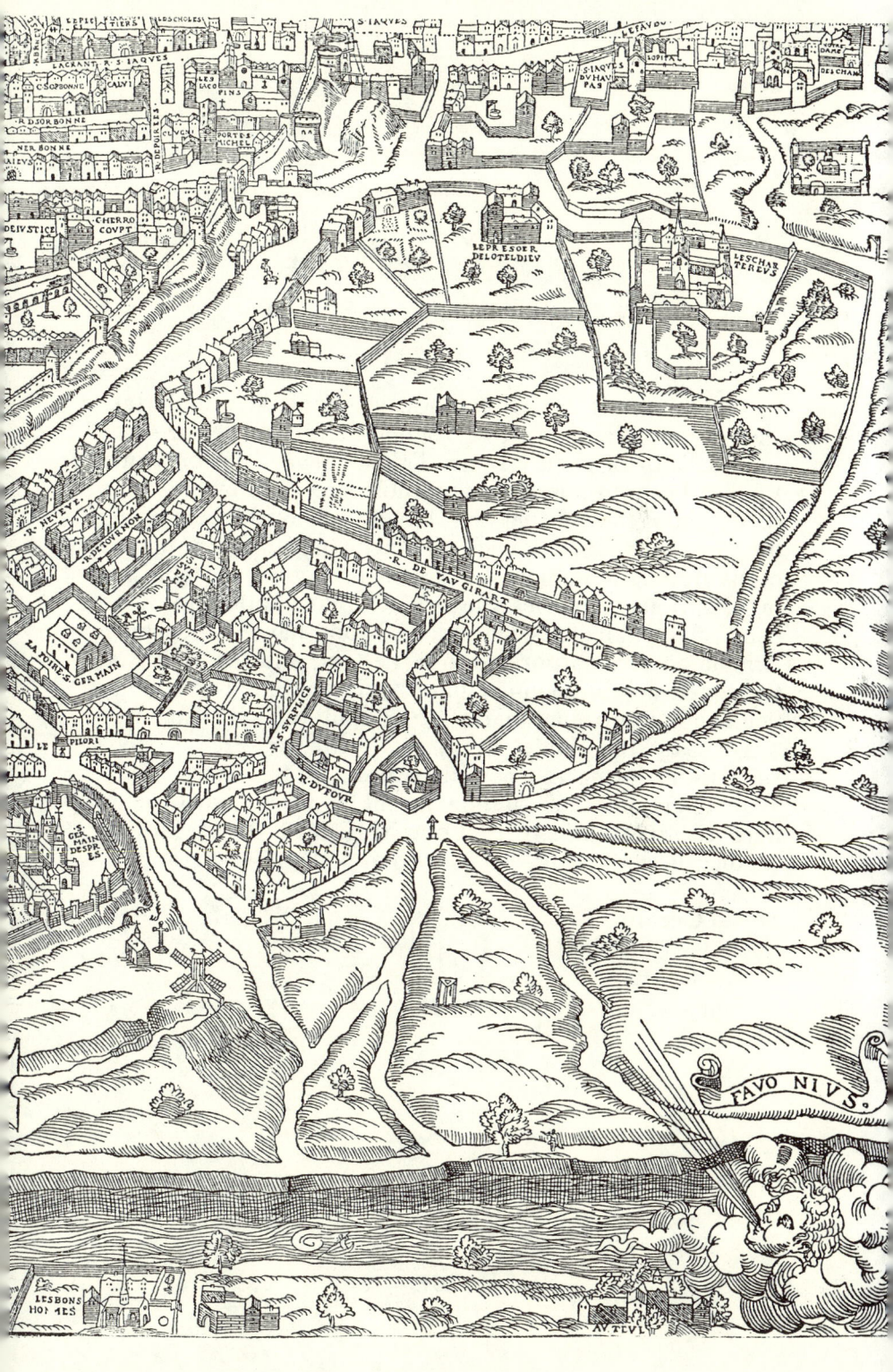

TRANSLATOR'S NOTE

ENRI-JEAN MARTIN'S BOOK was a massive undertaking comprising two volumes and 1091 pages—the labor of twenty years. Translating it—not only into English but into a more manageable size—has meant some reduction of the original text, largely achieved by curtailing the superabundant evidence offered by the author in support of his argument, namely the lengthy lists of works published in the various categories, the products of the book trade he so exhaustively analyzes. Footnotes, too, have either been eliminated or incorporated into the text, and the graphs at the conclusion of volume 2 have been omitted. The aim has been an uninterrupted narrative without loss of substance.

To assist the reader unfamiliar with the French royal succession during the period covered by the book, 1598–1701, the regnal years of the relevant monarchs may be cited here: Henri IV, 1598–1610; Louis XIII, 1610–1643 (Marie de Medici, Regent, 1610–c.1630); Louis XIV, 1643–1715.

David Gerard

INTRODUCTION

L IKE SO MANY OTHERS, this book has a long history. The idea first occurred to me during the dark days of World War II when as a student at the Ecole des Chartes I felt I wanted to devote my career to a study of the greatest period in French history. I began, at Louis André's suggestion, by examining the output of an official propagandist commissioned by Louis XIV to counter the spate of hostile pamphlets directed against Louis from Holland. As I did so I was struck by the complex nature of the pamphlet war in all its manifestations, oral, printed, official and unofficial, and I went on to examine the whole question of public opinion in its wider aspects during that stormy period. My supervisor, Pierre Marot, encouraged me to do this and helped me see very clearly that the history of the book trade above all was directly relevant to the history of ideas and indeed to literary history. A reading of Paul Hazard's *La Crise de conscience européenne* finally convinced me.

It was all too evident that the material aspects of the book trade and printing history had been neglected; to tackle this I realized that I would need a knowledge of economic history, which I sought in Emile Coornaert's course at the Ecole Pratique des Hautes Etudes. There I found that a firm grasp of book trade history would immediately help the student understand how economics influence ideology. At this point I discovered the Minutier Centrale, the national archive depository in Paris, strangely neglected by historians, and I was welcomed by Ernest Coyecque, to whom we owe so much for his efficient organization of that precious storehouse of record. And finally I must pay tribute to my cousin, Gaston Zeller, who lent encouragement when it was most needed.

Anxious to try my skill, I first edited a memoir published in honor of a Parisian printer and publisher, and on the strength of that Lucien Febvre asked me to collaborate with him in a work he felt unable to complete by himself: *L'apparition du livre.* I spent my leisure time on this for the next four years, after my official duties on the staff of the Bibliothèque Nationale. It must be obvious what I learned from such a master, and I regret that he lived to read only a small portion of the manuscript I submitted to him; hence the lessons he had to teach me were never finished and the work was not fully achieved. But at least our brief collaboration showed how fragmentary was the knowledge of the economic history of 17th-century publishing in France. As I examined literally thousands of early printed books in the Bibliothèque Nationale I noticed that research had been concentrated on a small fraction only of the surviving materials, as if the remainder—the majority—was not representative of the past, or hardly so. It seemed that what was badly needed was an inventory of the books, even if the attempt demanded a familiarity with so many subjects that it would expose the many gaps in one's knowledge. At this stage Roland Mousnier agreed to supervise my doctoral thesis. Wisely he advised me to immerse myself in the archives and the great libraries which had been my daily scene for so long, and to use my sabbatical leave to work out a plan of action and develop the line I proposed to pursue. He discussed his own work on the structure of French society in the 17th century at his Sorbonne seminars—work which led directly to some of the chapters in this book—and I am particularly obliged to him for his scientific rigor, an example to me. I could never deceive him!

While I was engaged on this lengthy task, others began to occupy the terrain I fondly imagined was mine alone. Statistical bibliography has by now earned its place in university studies, and the history of ideas now looks to book trade history for support. I am delighted, though somewhat apprehensive, as I offer this first attempt at global interpretation in a field still in need of much research. No one knows the faults of the book better than I. I know I have not always succeeded in condensing the huge mass of bibliographical material: to use only the books that have survived (the only source available) is to court risks, but at least I have the feeling of having reached the limits that a lone student could reach, and I have used actual statistics to support my case. The 150,000 bibliographic citations I gathered during the course of this book will be put at the disposal of the public in the Centre Lyonnais de l'Histoire et Civilisation du Livre, on publication.

I have not made use of computers to exploit the results of the research because I thought it premature to spend government money on them at a time when I was fighting for their use in the project for the union cataloging of the older libraries in France—a real exercise in collaboration if ever there was one—and in that I worked under M. Dupront's direction.

Interpretation of the statistics was even more difficult than assembling them because I had to examine so many books in so many different disciplines, from Theology to Science. Specialists will doubtless criticize this or that interpretation, or bewail some missing factors in the story, but there was no other way to record all the information people had available in one particular age than by reading the varied experience of authors in their works. How can we begin to understand the spirit of an age without a comprehensive idea of its book production? Whatever criticisms are made, I hope at least this is a start, a basis on which later researchers can build, refine and improve. But still, there had to be limits to so vast an area of research. I was often tempted to include an account of illustrations because they illuminate the parallel evolution of the book, but finally I decided to refer to them only when it was indispensable; likewise I omitted chapters on the history of the illustrated book, preferring to leave that subject for a separate work. Again with regret, I did not include maps and atlases or the typography of music, and I have not really dealt with the relationship between authors, publishers and readers, except where it was directly relevant.

And now the pleasurable duty of recording my gratitude to all who lavished their time and attention during the twenty years the book was in the making, and especially for their friendship.

Firstly, Mme Madeleine Jurgens of the Archives Nationales. When I started my research there was no inventory of the holdings—everything depended on the goodwill of the archivists, and Mme Jurgens and Mlle M.-A. Fleury spared no pains. I owe them thanks for many invaluable references and fruitful suggestions. My two old friends, Guy Beaujouan and Michel Fleury, and Father François de Dainville, colleagues at the Ecole Pratique des Hautes Etudes, and that scholarly librarian André Jammes—I owe them all thanks; they gave me much needed encouragement and support. Thanks, too, are due to the audience at my lectures—I will not say pupils because I owe them more than I could ever give them, but rather my friends, particularly Mme J. Veyrin-Forrer, my colleague in the Bibliothèque Nationale, and Mme A. Sauvy, J. Gambier de la Forterie, Mlles E. Bayle, B. Moreau and S. Postal, M. B. Neveu, A. Demoustiers, A. Labarre, Lannette-Claverie, and J. Toulet. Thanks also to my collaborators in the Bibliothèque de Lyon, especially those responsible for organizing the public lectures in Lyons, for those lectures helped me to understand what were the real, concrete issues involved in the study of the sociology of reading. I am a craftsman at heart and therefore practical, not just a theorist, and I would be happy with the thought that I had given the benefit of my skill to a work of scientific value.

As we go to press I must add a further note of thanks: to Professor G. Couton who so willingly read the book in its finished form; to Professor P. Léon who advised on statistical presentation, and to Professor A. Latreille who took a most friendly interest in the book. Without the faithful assistance and constant friendship of my old friend A. Dufour, Managing Director of Librairie Droz, my publishers, the book would never have appeared, and so to him and to the printers, the Presses de Savoie, I offer thanks and repentance for all the labor involved in the typesetting. Finally, loving thanks to my wife, who spent several tedious weeks with me revising proofs; and a word in memory of my parents, who did not live to see the work completed.

PRELIMINARY CHAPTER

A. EUROPEAN PUBLISHING IN THE LATE 16TH CENTURY

A CRISIS IN RELIGION, armed conflict between Catholics and Protestants, a schism which split Christian Europe into two camps, the emergence of Rationalism immediately submerged beneath the groundswell of the Counter Reformation: these, together with a steep rise in prices and various upheavals which altered traditional trading patterns, were the distinctive features of Western European history in the second half of the 16th century.

The book trade faithfully reflected all this, even in the appearance of the books themselves. In the early 16th century a book was a luxury, its typography continually improving as time went by, and the illustrations in books tended to typify the resurgent Humanism of the age. Then come the years 1550–1560. The quality of the paper deteriorates, type design stagnates, the illustrations are merely inferior copies of the earlier period; even a glance at the books shows that the subject matter is changing. The learned editions of Greek and Latin classics, and of Hebrew, the pride of the first Humanist printers, begin to diminish. Cheap, ephemeral books and pamphlets published in huge numbers in Germany now flood into Europe; there is a great quantity of official publication, a sure indication of the growth of administration. Open letters and propaganda in the form of pamphlets are issued by every sect and faction to solicit public opinion and support. Works in modern languages now increase, a sign that national literatures are evolving, a consequence of the systematic use of the

1

vernacular so typically Protestant and of the growth of polemical writings used by both sides to address their followers in their own tongue and help them judge for themselves in the great theological arguments.

New and powerful currents then become visible in the Catholic countries, symbolized by the monumental editions of Scripture. Though often printed on poor paper they were impeccably edited and helped to establish the purest texts as agreed by Catholic theologians. New editions of the Roman liturgy authorized by the Council of Trent; works of the Fathers of the Church with commentaries by scholars at Louvain, Paris and Rome; modern works by Spanish theologians—all these were part of the Counter Reformation publishing program. Huge folios or little devotional booklets (collections of sermons, lives of the saints) were all part of the armory, of that renaissance of religious feeling channeled through publications for the Catholic masses.

This is the general picture of the publishing output during the second half of the 16th century. Certain lines of force are apparent, centers of distribution can be located, some concerted action is visible, and all is witness to a profound process of evolution at work, with conscquences in the following century. To fully understand the situation in the 17th-century book trade we need to know what conditions were like in the late 16th century, and then briefly describe the Paris of that day.

1. Books in the Counter-Reformation

One of the chief features of the book trade in the late 16th century was the efficient distribution of new theological literature. How did this material come to be written? What were the reasons for its widespread marketing in Europe? These are crucial questions if the whole problem of Counter-Reformation policy vis-à-vis publishing is to be faced.

The Catholic Church welcomed printing when it first appeared, but soon it was realized that the new invention also allowed unorthodox texts to penetrate the reading public; some learned editions of the Bible—those by Humanist scholars like Lefèvre d'Etaples, Erasmus or Robert

Estienne—were of an entirely new order and scandalous to traditional theologians. They included prefaces and commentaries hazardous to conventional thought and were soon objects of deep mistrust by the authorities: censure by the ecclesiastical establishment followed as a matter of course. When the printed word was used to appeal to the people to judge for themselves, a common practice among the Reformers, then the orthodox saw this as clear proof that vigilance and systematic control of publishing and reading were essential if the Faith was to be upheld. From this sprang the first attempts at censorship, with church authorities at all levels taking decisions, and eventual codification by the Council of Trent when the first edition of the *Index librorum prohibitorum* was published in 1564. It was the basis of many subsequent editions, and Erasmus, Boccaccio and Machiavelli appear in it side by side with leading heretics. Ten "General Principles" were enunciated, the famous rules of the Index, designed to guide those among the faithful who as part of their professional life were wide readers. Forbidden books were listed in seven classes, and rule 10 referred to publishing, laying down punishments for anyone printing, selling or harboring banned books. All manuscripts had to be submitted for approval by a priest or inspector before publication, and printers' and booksellers' shops were to be inspected regularly.

Heretical works and "wicked" books were not the only ones to come under this ban: vernacular publishing had its dangers, especially the active presses working for Luther. The scandal of free interpretation of the Bible threatened the stability of the Church and its dogmas, and a move was made in Council to ban all translations, to avoid the Holy Book falling into the hands of the semi-educated who might be incapable of understanding it without orthodox aid. This motion was scotched by delegates from countries where Protestantism was well established, but rule 4 specified that no translation of the Bible could be used without authorization by the local Bishop or Inquisitor after due consultation with the parish priest. If this rule is compared with another which confirmed that Latin was to be the language of the Mass and sacraments (though priests could make any needful explanations in the vernacular) then it is clear that Church leaders were anxious to deflect the congregation from the works—the Bible and the Missal—and refer them to the priest or to sermons and homilies recommended for the purpose. The Church went on to require that its teachers and its leaders in contact with heresy must refrain from using their native language unless absolutely indispensable, i.e., in controversy with Protestants, especially in France where there was a marked tendency to use French in theological works and translations of Patristic texts. The return to Latin in dogmatic literature, which the Jansenists rebelled against in the 17th century, prompted those who desired deep spiritual experience to turn to the literature of spirituality, the mystical side of the Counter Reformation opposed to the rationalism inherent in Protestantism.

To win the struggle against heresy, or at least to contain it, the Counter-Reformation had itself to countenance reforms within the Church, and an essential measure was a revision of its authorized texts. Another crying need was a return to fundamentals, to the Scriptures themselves in all their depth, and a study of the writings of the Fathers by the same methods the Humanists were using in their commentaries on the pagan classics. New approaches were necessary, new syntheses to explain the dogmas, new, more positive attitudes in Church apologists. First hints of this fundamental rethinking may be found in the early 16th century, but while the first Catholic scholars worked often in isolation, research in the late 16th century was under the direction of Popes, coordinating the work and arbitrating when there was a conflict of views.

The Council of Trent took fundamental decisions on the whole question of the Bible and Liturgy and their place in Catholic observance, decisions which were to have far-reaching repercussions on the book trade. Catholic scholars declared the Vulgate to be the "authentic" text of the Bible, stressing that a thoroughly revised edition was needed to counter the new, heretical Bibles in circulation. Their pronouncements on this show that the Vulgate was the proper text for an educated Catholic to quote in sermons or other works intended for perusal and study by the faithful. They were not opposed to the Septuagint (the Greek version of the Old Testament) and even made recommendations for its revision. At the same time the Pope somewhat reluctantly authorized Plantin, the great Antwerp printer accredited to the King of Spain, to publish a polyglot Bible. This move suggests that the Church foresaw future needs and felt it important to allow theologians some latitude in their task of interpretation and scope for making corrections in their exegetical works: the polyglot would be a sound basis for this. On the Liturgy the council anticipated much labor ahead, since many traditions evidently rested on doubtful foundations, as both Humanists and Protestants had shown. The duty of revising liturgical practice was placed under the direction of the Pope with the end of securing new service books composed in strict conformity with Roman use. From this began a movement towards unified thought control, the consequences of which were deeply felt in France, and the plan to provide a simple catechism for all believers meant a huge publishing program.

The first work to appear was the Catechism (1564), then the breviary (1568), the missal (1570) and other liturgical works. The official Pontifical edition of the Septuagint followed in 1587, edited by a group of scholars under Cardinal Carafa's direction, one of whom was Pierre Morin, and in 1592 appeared the final, approved version of the Vulgate. Next came the problems of distribution and enforcement of the text, no trifling matter. Dioceses had presses which had to be used for publishing the "correct" version. As early as 1540 Cardinal Cervini was employing a distinguished printer, Antonio Blado, and Paul Manutius was attracted from his publishing firm in Venice by a high fee, to assume direction of the Stamperia del Popolo Romano, publishing catechisms, breviaries, missals, and editions of the Church Fathers. Later on the first official Vatican publisher, the Tipografia Vaticana, was established by Pope Sixtus V with suitable funding, under the direction of Domenico Basa.

The Vatican's favored policy was the creation of monopolies in Bibles and service books which certain publishers could enjoy while keeping a strict surveillance over printers who might be rather less than orthodox to ensure that they did not publish apparently authorized Bibles which yet included altered passages—a common practice after the Reformation. The Pope mandated the Roman rite in all church service books because for at least two hundred years many local usages had crept into services, particularly among monastic orders, and moreover printers were liable to modify parts of the text when asked to do so by local clergy, introducing practices now judged undesirable by the Council of Trent. It can be imagined just how immense was the task of printing and supplying the greater part of Europe in that age with the new materials, and why the Papacy instituted monopolies for publishers they could trust. The idea of a monopoly provoked protests throughout the trade, and even the Kings of France and Spain intervened on behalf of their native printers. Philip II secured an agreement under which Paul Manutius shared the monopoly of breviaries with Plantin of Antwerp, whose presses supplied the Spanish territories in the Low Countries, and Henri III of France secured a similar concession for Kerver, a Paris printer.

A little later the Papacy took some harsh decisions: Sixtus V sponsored the revised version of the Septuagint in 1587 and assigned an exclusive privilege in it to the Tipografia Vaticana which was valid for ten years throughout the Christian world. He did the same when the revised Vulgate came out and in a Bull, *Aeternus ille,* forbade any printer or bookseller to issue any other Scriptures. The Spanish King protested and the Doge's representative did likewise, emphasizing how prejudicial the measure would be to Venetian printers. The Pope died meanwhile and Cardinal Bellarmine persuaded his successor to take no action on the Bull which would only embroil Papal authority in unpredictable situations. At the same time he tried to dissuade the Pontiff from more restrictive measures involving the Bible, saying the decision of the Council of Trent was vague on this issue, but he secured only slight relaxation of policy and in a preface to the definitive edition of the Vulgate Clement VIII specified that publishers must add no footnotes or commentaries, though by some devious process of thought they were allowed to place notes in an appendix printed in a different type face. A later pontifical decree confirmed the rights of the Tipografia Vaticana; quite obviously the Holy Office, despite some contradictory assertions, was determined to keep control over all Bible and liturgical publication, and to use its power in claiming its right to act as the supreme authority over books with a potentially large sale and over all printers and booksellers. Later we will examine the results of this policy in detail.

This period saw much intensive scholarship devoted to matters religious, especially in the subject called Patrology (commentaries on the Early Fathers of the Church) and in studies of the Church's earliest Councils. Unlike the Humanists, Catholic theologians were hesitant to quit their well-trodden paths to engage in a study of Early Christianity, but if they were seeking to authenticate the Church's teaching, then such an investigation was essential. They looked into the early sources even more profoundly than the Protestant scholars did, constructing their case from arguments Erasmus and others had already advanced: the Papacy was anxious to prove with unassailable logic and the help of the Fathers that the Roman Catholic Church had followed the path initiated by the Primitive Church. The case required heavy dependence on the Patristic texts and as the controversy developed it was even maintained that the Scriptures themselves were not sufficient justification of Catholic dogma: the ante-Nicene authorities were brought in, especially the first historians of the Church, to support Rome's claims. Patristic studies assumed enormous proportions, culminating in the proclamation made by the Council of Trent that the Tradition was equally as valid as a source of revealed truth as the Bible.

The great efforts made by the Catholic side benefited from good organization and without going into the history of it mention need only be made of the first edition of the *Index expurgatorius* prepared by Arias Montano (Antwerp, 1570), and a list he made of passages culled from Patristic writings proved of great utility. What we would now call a seminar was held at Louvain, the papers being published later by

Plantin at Antwerp. Teams of scholars and editors were assembled in the Vatican Library and the Tipografia Vaticana was entrusted with the preparation of a vast edition of the Fathers and Decrees of the General Councils, a huge exercise in self-justification. If we were to draw up a balance sheet of various studies done collectively and of individual efforts by scholars, especially the French, it would contain a huge number of works related to the Fathers, although of very variable quality. Not only the Latin Fathers but the Greek Fathers too were included, some of whom had been translated into Latin (though it was difficult to argue theological subtleties at second hand). Athanasius, Gregory of Nyssa, Theodoretus and St. John Chrysostom were the sole Greek Fathers thought appropriate; Origen's *Anti-Celsus* and other Fathers were not published. Though the General Councils had been published at Rome, other national Councils, particularly of France, were not adverted. It was a matter of "chains of thought." But we shall see how French scholars of the 17th century sought to fill those gaps.

This activity meant a revival in the study of theology, though not in the Sorbonne, the traditional center of such scholarship, probably because the authorities there were not keen to rush into print against the Protestants and seemed disinclined to construct those syntheses of doctrine that appeared so vital to Rome. Spain was the country which produced most of the new Catholic thought, in the universities of Salamanca, Alcalá and Coimbra. Dominicans and the newly founded Jesuits were the keenest rivals and adversaries in debate, and the names of the foremost preaching friars are enough to remind us how influential Spanish religious thought was at this time: Caetano, Vittoria, de Soto, Cano, Bartolomeo de Medina, Alvarez, Ledesma, and the Jesuits Salmerón, Maldonado, Francisco de Toledo, Bellarmine, Vasquez, Suarez, Molina and Arriaga. Acquiring their principles of textual criticism from Humanists, the theologians wrote extensive Biblical commentaries expounding the literal meaning to show the validity of Catholic dogmatics, reinforced by extensive quotations from the Early Fathers. New scholastic methods are discernible in Spanish commentaries on Aquinas' *Summa Theologica,* with Jesuits generating controversy on matters of interpretation, often trivial matters like confession, and essential ones like the doctrine of Grace. A new moral theology emerged from the labors of the Jesuits published in countless treatises, ending with the adoption of the doctrine of Probabilism, the belief that certainty is impossible but probability is sufficient to govern one's actions.

The doctrines spread beyond the borders of Spain; in the little world of Theology there was much mobility as teachers traveled about, or were summoned to Rome to account for some of their statements. Jesuits founded colleges and chairs of Theology to promote their thought and combat the evils of Protestantism. Expounding texts, justifying dogmas, interpreting the Scriptures were all key factors in Jesuit strategy and all were posited on Biblical commentary. Maldonado, the Spanish Jesuit, set up courses at Clermont College from 1570 to 1575 and so introduced the new thinking into France despite opposition from the Sorbonne. The conditions at that university have been exaggerated; they were not as abysmal as often painted and valuable commentaries were written by such teachers as Thomas Beauxamis, Antoine Birriet, Francois de Deuardent and Gilbert Genebrard, although none of them served as justification of the Church via textual explication as Maldonado's did. Because he taught with a declared purpose he attracted audiences of five hundred when he lectured, including magistrates and women as well as churchmen, and his sermons were attended by thousands.

One point needs to be remembered: while the exponents of the new thought were preaching with success, the texts on which they based their conclusions were published with great caution; although de Soto's commentaries were widely published they had few readers. The Jesuits were more concerned with their courses than with definitive publication, which was vulnerable to counterattack; hence we find them submitting work for publication only in the final years of the 16th century when Salmerón, Maldonado, Toledo, Ribera and others first saw the light of print. The Catholic riposte to Protestantism came first by preaching and then by the printed word.

2. The Catholic Revival

While the new theology from Spain was sweeping through
Catholic Europe that continent was experiencing what
Lucien Febvre liked to call a "recharge" of sensibility. The
Catholic Renaissance had started, and Spain was of crucial
importance; a few authors and titles will be enough to prove
the vital part played by Spain in the renewal of spirituality. In
the first half of the 16th century the Franciscans led the way:
Alfonso de Seville published his *Arte de servir a Dios* in
response to an appeal by Cardinal Ximenes in 1517 for books
of piety in the vernacular which would appeal to clergy and
laity. Antonio de Guevara, a Franciscan Humanist chaplain
to Charles V, wrote *Oratorio de religiosos* (1541) and *Monte
Calvario* (1528); Francisco de Ossuna, the *Abecedaria spir-
ituales* (1527), and Bernardino de Laredo, the *Montée du
Mont Sion* (French title) in Seville (1535). Thousands of
popular books of Christian living and devotion followed.
Alonzo de Orozco wrote a series of little books of mysticism,
and Luis de Granada was a celebrated author of the day who
consciously used print to combat ignorance with his first
book, *Libro de la oración y meditación* (Salamanca, 1544),
followed by his best work, *Guia de pecatores* (1556), a great
success, and many more tracts on the ascetic life. In the
decade 1550–1560 come works of an outstanding group of
mystics—John of Avila, Pedro of Alcántara, Luis de León
and Ignatius Loyola.

But just when the school of Spanish mystics was in full
flower it was halted. The Grand Inquisitor, Fernando de
Valdez, at the instigation of the Dominican Melchor Cano,
throttled the efforts of a sect called the Alumbrados in a bid
to check any suspected advances by Reformation influence
and to crush both mystical and ascetic publications. He
imprisoned Carrenza, Archbishop of Toledo, for his book
Comentarios al catecismo Christiano (1558) despite its
unassailable orthodoxy. The book is actually on the Index of
1559 along with three tracts of Luis de Granada, one by John
of Avila, one by Francesco Borgia, works by Jorge de
Montemayor, and works by the "Northern mystics." Even
Loyola's famous *Spiritual exercises* only just escaped being

placed on the Index, and in 1566 the Augustinian Luis de Leon was thrown into jail for five years for translating the *Song of Solomon* at a nun's request, and while there he composed his best known devotional works. One can understand the anxiety among mystical writers in Spain under this threat, when St. Teresa herself was the object of suspicion. For about twenty years mystical and ascetic literature virtually ceased in Spain.

A study of the surviving French material from this period suggests that the situation there was not quite the same. There were signs of a revival due largely to Lefèvre d'Etaples and his disciples at Meaux, but from 1540 to 1570 almost nothing. Instead of traditional Catholic works we find more literary works and translations of classical authors; the only religious matter to reach a mass audience was published in Lyons or Geneva, apart from the books of hours which of course were a routine product of publishing houses for centuries. Farther north in Cologne, continuing the work of the Brethren of the Common Life, a group of monks in the Carthusian monastery of St. Barbe composed and translated devotional literature for a popular audience. As early as 1509 the prior, Peter of Leyden, translated Harp's *Spiegel des Volcomheit* into Latin and edited a collection ascribed to Denis the Carthusian between 1530 and 1543. Another Carthusian, Lansperge, wrote a series of tracts on the spiritual life, the best known being the *Enchiridion militiae Christianae* (1538), a copy of Erasmus' book of the same title.

In 1535 Dom Dirk Loer, Nicolaas Van Esch, Pierre de Nijmegen (later a Jesuit taking the name Pierre Canisius) and Surius began systematically translating devotional books by German and Dutch authors into Latin, and ensured a wider readership among the clergy. The program reached its climax with the publication of a collection of saints' lives (1570–75) replacing Jacobus de Voragine's popular *Golden legend.* The Carthusians were also responsible for a far-reaching program of publications including more than a hundred titles by such authors as Tauler, Suso, Harp, Lansperge, Van Esch, St. Gertrude, Catherine of Siena and

the anonymous *Perle évangélique*. A Benedictine, Louis de
Blois, was also published. The whole undertaking marks the
flowering of the German school of mystics and the works
constitute the relatively few texts of first quality in the field to
be published in France. They made their impact later, largely
in the years 1570–80 when the new interest in devotional
literature was sensed and French translations of the Latin
treatises from Cologne appear, some done in Douai and
Louvain, others in convents in Picardy. Jean de Billy, a prior
of Bourgfontaine, translated Louis de Blois' *Miroir* into
French, Nicholas Le Cerf did the same for Suso, and Jean
Jarry rendered St. Gertrude's *Exercises* into the native
language, a work translated also into Latin by Dom Jean
Vesly, the third section including an *Index expurgatorius* of
Harp's works, the intention presumably being to test which
of that author's books were safe, because some of them had
been altered by the Roman censors in 1585.

It has been calculated that of 280 French publications of
foreign titles between 1550 and 1610, 164 were from this
German-Dutch group. Denis the Carthusian was the most
fashionable (34 editions of his various works came out
between 1550 and 1610); Thomas à Kempis' *Imitation of
Christ* was issued at least thirty times, and Louis de Blois
twenty times. Lansperge, Harp, Tauler and Suso followed,
with anything from four to ten editions each, and if Van
Esch, Gérard de Liège, Antoine Van Hemert, St. Gertrude
and Ludolph are counted it is clear that the German school of
mystics was then in the lead. Contacts were established also
with the Italian school of mystics, largely through the
Capuchins, and the Spanish school was kept alive when the
Cardinal of Lorraine encouraged translation of Spanish
devotional literature into French, and Luis de Granada,
Vives and Guevara enjoyed a wide readership in France after
1572, always under threat from Philip II's suspicion of
anything mystical or ascetic as potential heresy. Though
condemned in 1559 de Granada's books were issued with
amendments in 1567. St. Teresa's works were never published in her lifetime, and the *Livre de sa vie* (1575) circulated
only in manuscript and escaped condemnation only through
Banes' intervention. There was some relaxation after 1580,

Luis de Leon's *Way of perfection* being published at Evora
and Teresa's complete *oeuvre* finally seeing publication at
Salamanca. After this, mysticism won the day in Spain, and
classics of the spiritual life came out: St. John of the Cross
(1st ed., 1618 at Alcalá) was the leading spirit but there were
many more, often didactic in the Jesuit manner, as Ribadeneyra's *Flos sanctorum* (1601), Alonzo Rodríguez' *Ejercicio
de perfección y virtudes cristianas* (Seville, 1609), and Luis de
la Puente's *Meditacions de los misterios de la Santa Fe* and *De
la perfección de cristiano* (Valladolid, 1605 and 1612).
Purified by much tribulation, Spanish mysticism was ready to
convey its message to the world. Later we will see how it was
received in France.

3. New Aspects of Humanism

The new currents of religious life prompted a further surge of
Humanist activity. Erasmus' age had completed its revolution—it was now possible to adopt overtly critical positions
and even publish Biblical exegesis with some freedom; even
before the mid-16th century there is evidence of those
practices in France, when Dolet was burned in the Place
Maubert in 1546 and Robert Estienne was forced to flee first
to Lausanne and then to Geneva in 1548, but those examples
naturally discouraged attempts by scholars to interpret
Scripture. Instead they applied their energies to safer
subjects like philology, law and the beginnings of archaeology, and the Greek and Latin classics and French medieval
history. There was certainly much work to be done and more
manuscripts needed, since most of the studies of early texts
extant had been completed. The study of archaeology and of
numismatics was extremely sketchy, the classifying of coins,
medals and inscriptions needed attention as did the scientific
scrutiny of ancient manuscripts and the plotting of relationships between manuscripts. The composition of Latin verse
and even Greek enjoyed a revival, part of a drive to prove
that the classical tongues were not dead. All this was the
work of the second generation of Humanists.

The Germans at Jena, Wittenberg, Leipzig and Heidelberg, and Italians in Rome were interested in archaeol-

ogy, as were French scholars teaching at the Collège Royale or acting as King's Printers. Ramus earned notoriety by his attack on Aristotle but did not lose his place on the staff of the Collège Royal; Turnèbe was immersed in his study of Aeschylus and Sophocles and completed his *Adversaria* (extracts from classical authors with commentaries and corrected readings); Muret was under suspicion on grounds of morality and was forced to leave Paris for Rome; Dorat, the young Ronsard's tutor, composed more than 50,000 lines of verse in Latin and Greek, and edited Aeschylus. Denis Lambin, a fertile Latin scholar, translated Aristotle's *Ethics* and *Politics* and edited scholarly versions of Horace, Lucretius and Cicero; Passerat, his successor at the Collège Royale, edited Catullus, Tibullus and Propertius. Following Budé and Alciat, the jurist Cujas at Bourges University made a fundamental study of Roman law, and pupils of his like Justus Scaliger, Loisel, Pierre Pithou and Etienne Pasquier investigated the legal and constitutional documents of the Middle Ages with scientific rigor.

So great was the interest in classical texts that teams of translators were at work, especially in France, making ancient authors more accessible to a reading public which had little or no knowledge of Greek and Latin. In 1547 Amyot translated Heliodorus' *History of Ethiopia* and Diodorus Siculus' *History* in 1554, *Daphnis and Chloe* in 1559 and Plutarch's *Lives* (1565). Louis Le Roy translated the political and philosophical works of Plato and Aristotle, Xenophon and Demosthenes, and Blaise de Vigenère did the same for Cicero, Lucian, Onomander's *Ars militaris,* Philostratus' *Life of Apollonius of Tyana,* Chalcondyle's *Decline of the Greek Empire,* Tacitus' *Germania* and Livy's *History of Rome.* Contemporary research was becoming accessible to a new readership.

In the last thirty years of the 16th century change was apparent. The Church urged its scholars to concentrate more on the literature of the Early Church and less attention was paid to the classics, except by Protestants or sceptics or those whose faith was in doubt. Heretics suffered severely: Ramus was murdered on St. Bartholomew's Eve in the massacre of 1572, just when he had thought it safe to return to Paris from exile, and his friend Lambin died soon after of grief over the loss. Pierre Pithou, who had narrowly escaped the death penalty, elected to stay within the fold but Doneau, Hotman, Scaliger and others fled to Geneva, the city that was rapidly gaining a reputation for classical scholarship, aided by Henri Estienne II, the established printer there. Son of Robert Estienne, he was the most productive linguistic scholar of his day, devoted his leisure to mastering languages as a recreation from business, and published 58 editions of Latin classics and 74 Greek, including 18 first editions. At the end of his life in 1585 he published his *Thesaurus linguae graecae,* a pioneer dictionary, and later his son-in-law Casaubon continued the work. Yet censorship was just as strict in Calvin's city and the city council (with the honorable exception of Beza) regularly interfered with a zeal to enforce sound moral and religious orthodoxy according to their creed; that was more important than classical scholarship. Henri Estienne was affected by this kind of persecution, charged with atheism and dissolute living, and even tried to re-establish himself at the French court, but he eventually died at Lyons in 1598 a ruined man.

Farther north in the Protestant Low Countries, Spanish troops had to give up their siege of Leyden, and William of Orange granted the city the right to found a university with Janies Dousa, who led the resistance to Philip II's army of occupation, as its head. Lacking scholars of the first rank, Leyden tried hard to attract refugees to the new university, hoping to add luster to the new foundation and rival Catholic learning. The theologian Du Moulin, the botanist Charles de L'Ecluse, Justus Lipsius, and Scaliger, whose *De ratione temporum* had recently been published, were as distinguished as any in the Catholic camp, and new talents quickly emerged, notably Daniel Heinsius, Vossius, Junius and Grotius. Henri IV of France accorded degrees from Leyden the same status as those from French universities and foreigners flocked to the small town where Elzevier had set up his press; Leyden was soon recognized as a center of classical studies.

While in some respects Paris was dethroned by this little Protestant city there was at the same time a kind of détente between what might be called the second Humanist wave and the Catholic world. Behind that stood the figure of Justus Lipsius, and his life and work are worth recalling here. Born in 1547 not far from Brussels, after a Jesuit schooling and further study in the Law Department at the university of Louvain he was appointed secretary to Cardinal de Granvelle at the age of twenty, and went on the Italian grand tour with him. He visited libraries in search of manuscripts and sought out ancient inscriptions, he met Muret in Rome when that scholar was working on his edition of Seneca, and collaborated with him on the text of Tacitus' *Germania*. He made the journey back to his native land in stages before deciding to stay in Jena where he was offered a chair. What made him turn Protestant? It is hard to say, but after several months in Cologne and seeing his great edition of Tacitus through the press at Antwerp he returned to Leyden where he taught from 1579 until 1591 when there was another dramatic move: he left suddenly for Mainz where he abjured Protestantism and joined the university of Louvain. He died there in 1606.

What secret reasons account for his second conversion? Self-interest hardly explains it if he was merely carrying through a decision made five years earlier. Was he simply weary of the rigors of strict Calvinism? A wish to go back to his own country and join his friend Plantin who was faced with the same dilemma and had resolved it in his own interests? Or gradual progression down a long intellectual road? Perhaps all those reasons played their part, but a hint may be found in the texts to which he gave particular attention: they were tinged with Stoicism, and he defended Seneca and Tacitus against admirers of Cicero; certainly their thought informs the two most original of his own works, *De constantia* and *De politica*. In a period of religious and political heartbreak and uncertainty the manliness and detachment of the Stoic faith fascinated him; he uses the Stoic position to show his approval of those who affirm a Providence and insist on the existence of God—constancy for him meant submission to the law of Providence. By this route he would eventually feel bound to respect the rule of obedience and submit to the Catholic principle of authority.

At this time many readers were finding wisdom and solace in Epictetus and Seneca and their works were repeatedly translated. From Du Vair to Montaigne men listened to their teaching and tried to combine prudence and reason with the tenets of orthodoxy. More numerous were readers who looked for justification of Christian virtues in the Stoics while rejecting Stoics' pride. From this movement came Christian Humanism, almost a cult in the early 16th century and given greater impetus by the Jesuits.

4. The Rise of National Literatures

Individual countries were by now developing their own literatures. Though Italy was disunited and entering a period of decline economically and politically, she was still a model for artists and writers. After the golden age of Ariosto, Machiavelli, Aretino, Bembo and Castiglione there was a falling off, yet only in relative terms since the late 16th century was the age of Tasso's *Gerusalemme liberata* and *Aminta,* which worked out principles of modern epic poetry and pastoral drama; then Guarini and Bonarelli added their *Pastor fido* and *Filli di Sciro* to the latter genre, plays which were imitated as models long after, and Marino wrote a 45,000-line epic, *Adonis*, a phenomenon of dazzling, not to say deafening qualities, just when Giordano Bruno paid for his contribution to Rationalism at the stake, and while Galileo was developing his theories.

While the Italian Renaissance was a fading fire, others enjoyed unity under royal protection and encouraged native literature. Under Elizabeth I Shakespeare, Marlowe and Ben Jonson brought the English stage to an unparalleled peak of excellence, as did Spenser and Philip Sidney in poetry, and Sidney was creating something new in English with his *Arcadia.* England was on the way to its classic period in literature. In the Spain of Philip II and Teresa of Avila the literary golden age begins, with Lope de Vega's plays on a par with the English theatre. Inspired by Italian models, Juan Boscán, Garcilaso de la Vega, Hurtado de Mendoza, Herrera and their disciples were laying the foundations of a school of poetry and preparing for Góngora; Jorge de

Montemayor's *Diana* was the prototype of pastoral romance; Cristoval de Figueroa and even Lope de Vega and Cervantes surrendered to the fashion, and the anonymous *Lazarillo de Tormes* and Alemán's *Guzmán de Alfarache* ushered in the picaresque novel, and Cervantes' *Don Quixote* and *Novelas ejemplares* were masterpieces when Quevedo was starting work.

In countries adjoining France a cycle of modern fiction began, and new drama, between 1550 and 1610; baroque poetry and epic is at its peak with Tasso and Camões. France was perhaps more deeply influenced by Italian models than either England or Spain, and the Pleiade group of poets appeared at a time of religious conflict. Ronsard's disciples rekindled the torch after his death, many of them talented but with no genius among them. Du Bartas, a Protestant, tried an epic after Ronsard, and while the work of English dramatists and poets was largely ignored in France, Italian writers were translated widely. Petrarch, Boccaccio, Sannazaro's *Arcadia,* Ariosto's *Orlando Furioso,* and the works of Bembo, Caviceo, Machiavelli, Castiglione and Léon Hébreu were all available; Trissino's *Sophonisba,* Ariosto's *Negremonte* and Tasso's *Aminta* were translated into French as were Bandello's *Tragic histories* and the *Facétieuses nuits de Staparola,* though none were as popular as *Orlando Furioso,* translated by the best French poets of the time, and de Vigenère's rendering of *Gerusalemme liberata* was continually reprinted from 1595.

After *Celestine,* Guevara's *Mots dorés* and some of Vives' novels of Spanish chivalry, from *Amadís* to *Primalon,* were put into French, and *Guzmán,* and *Lazarillo de Tormes.* The Paris publishers Abel Langelier and Nicolas Buon (Ronsard's publisher) were major impresarios in this field, commissioning translators who were often simply incapable of reproducing poetry—only a knowledge of the original could bring real appreciation. The same was true of theoretical works which helped formulate classical views of literature, and indeed for drama the same held true: Italian or Spanish drama was felt to be impossible to translate directly but was adapted in a French version, first for acting and then in printed form, at Paris and Rouen. Which problem brings us to the question of marketing, and may help explain why Lope de Vega was well known in France but not Shakespeare.

5. Business Trends and Contacts with the Intelligentsia: The Main Centers of European Publishing

To judge how important Paris was as a center of new ideas and so of new publications we need to sketch the map of Europe to see just where the rival publishers were located.

Firstly, Spain. A number of printers across the country but no large publishing centers, though a fair number of Spanish books were published in Seville and Toledo; Madrid seems to be of growing importance and there are presses at Alcalà, Salamanca and at Coimbra in Portugal. In Alcalá the firm of Sanchez published books by teachers at the university but only the first edition—after that any further reprinting was done in other European towns. The Salamanca firms of Junta, Gabiano and Portonario were content to import foreign books rather than publish on their own initiative, and Lyons and Venice supplied them principally; the book trade under Philip II was still undeveloped, contrasting with the position vis-à-vis theology and devotional literature, in which Spain led the rest of Europe.

The situation in Italy was very different. While there were few publishers in southern Italy outside Naples, Rome was the home of the Papal Tipografia Vaticana, and Tuscany and the Po valley retained their eminence as traditional centers of the trade, but quality deteriorates. Just as Troyes in France did later, Florence began to specialize in popular literature; Milan can no longer compare with its past; Venice still took the lead and boasted famous houses: Manutius, Giunta, Gabiano, turning out quantities of prayerbooks, though increasingly the once great names withdraw from publishing having made their fortunes and look for more lucrative and prestigious business elsewhere, leaving no successors. So, with Spain now inert, and the Italian trade stagnant, things were very different in the north and east of France, and in Germany Luther and the Wars of Religion prompted new centers of publishing in the Protestant world.

On the Rhine, in Frankfurt and Southwest Germany, in Cologne, Ingolstadt, Augsburg and Munich printing was at the service of the Counter Reformation. In Basel (already past its prime), Heidelberg and Nuremberg it served the Protestant cause. In the far north there was little printing, but in Leipzig, in Jena, Magdeburg, Marburg, Frankfurt-on-Oder and Wittenberg, Luther's base, it was a thriving trade. After Cologne the two most thriving centers were Frankfurt and Leipzig where the major Book Fairs were held—they were the capitals of the trade. For a while Frankfurt was the dominant one, the town where the leading European booksellers gathered to exchange stocks and settle accounts. Thus Germany, hitherto without a particular message to give to the world yet always well supplied with printers and always a prime market for bookselling, now emerges as the heart of the European book trade.

But the most dynamic centers of activity were Geneva and the Low Countries. Publishing was a flourishing industry in Geneva by 1590; for the previous forty years printers and booksellers had been attracted there from Paris and Lyons; Bibles and Psalters and polemical pamphlets poured from the presses and were exported to France where sympathetic Calvinist printers and booksellers sold or reprinted them. Firms like de Tournes, Estienne, Vignon and Chouet published scholarly works with the best type founts from the famous Grecs du Roi matrices which Henri Estienne managed to smuggle out of France when he escaped to Switzerland, and they sold in France, Germany and the Low Countries via Protestant agents in Amsterdam and Leyden.

In England printing was concentrated on London, but it was in the Netherlands that expansion was under way. Amsterdam was never more than of secondary importance, the Commelins being the only large firm, with business connections in Heidelberg and Geneva; Leyden was already showing its potential, and Antwerp had of course been a major center since Plantin's time, his heirs, the Moretus family who were on the side of the Counter Reformation, directing a complex publishing operation with its own typefounding and bookbinding factory. Justus Lipsius was one of its editors and Rubens illustrated books for them. In liturgical books they rivalled Manutius of Venice and marketed their products far beyond the confines of the Spanish dominions in the Netherlands. The best engravers of the day worked for them, turning out thousands of religious pictures ordered by the Jesuits for their evangelizing missions. At Louvain several large firms merged into one company to undertake the publication of heavy and expensive theological treatises and Patristic texts edited by academics at the University of Louvain. Through their agencies in Spain they helped disseminate the works of the theologians of Alcalá and Salamanca in addition to the purely mystical literature of Spain.

Between Protestant Geneva and Catholic Antwerp was Lyons, traditionally the best market for the Paris trade and its keenest rival. Nowhere else, except perhaps Antwerp, did the trade appear so obviously the child of capitalist enterprise as in that city which prospered because of its geographical position and its Book Fairs, yet it was denied a university and a local Parlement because of royal distrust. But to foster book sales all that is required is a readership of lawyers and clergy, and when Barthélemy Buyer established his printing shop in Lyons he soon made it a thriving center for the export trade to Spain and within a huge area of southern France. German printers settled there and later it came under Italian influence tinged with a strong Humanism. The result was a new age of quality printing controlled by a handful of booksellers giving employment to an ever larger work force: French firms like the Vincents, the La Portes, the Frellons and the Sennetons, and branches of Venetian and Florentine publishers—Portonario, Gabiano and Giunta.

Lyons was even busier than Paris, with apprentices and journeymen numbered in thousands, strong enough to start strikes and with leaders to direct them. Most of the labor force was on the side of the Reformers and made their feelings plain, which led to flight in the years 1540–50 to Geneva, where they were joined by master printers from Paris driven out by persecution or the animus of the Sorbonne. The major Lyons booksellers, often converts to Protestantism, were conveniently distant from the center of power in Paris and could aid their cause more effectively, but times grew harder: labor was costly, production more expensive in France than abroad, and Italian business declining. Geneva was more favorably placed since it had access to resources of manpower in its refugees and was close to paper suppliers, and much needed capital left Lyons for Geneva. Antoine Vincent, Lyons' most prosperous publisher and a Protestant, went to Geneva to live but retained his French citizenship, and left his Lyons business to be conducted by his son and other relatives. Claude Senneton did the same in 1558, Barthélemy and Henri de Gabiano in 1571, Barthélemy and Sebastien Honorat in 1572; and Jean de Tournes II transferred his business to Geneva in 1585 and there it remained for a century and a half. Yet, Catholic or Protestant, those who stayed in Lyons all agreed that economics mattered more than religion and preferred to give work to the presses in Geneva. Lyons printers complained that booksellers there only had the imprint and lists of their publications printed in Lyons so as to be able to sell their books in Catholic areas (because they bore a Lyons address); nothing was done to remedy this and many thousands of books were transported via the Rhône and Mediterranean, on the Loire and through Nantes to most of Catholic Spain though produced in Protestant Geneva! But by the end of the 16th century Lyons was in decline and fell from its position as third in rank in the book trade to occupy a humbler position. Meanwhile Paris was entering on a period of prosperity.

B. PARIS IN THE LATE 16TH CENTURY

On 22nd March 1594 Henri IV relieved Saint Denis and entered Paris amid general acclamation. A new era began, following a period in which business and trade had almost been destroyed. About ten years later Francesco d'Ierni, an official in the Italian embassy, described the growing prosperity thus:

"The district of Saint Jacques by which one enters the city is 1740 paces larger than the others, even than St-Marcel; Saint Germain is like a small town, and before the recent wars the population was 18,000. The city has 14 gates, five made of stone. The roads are long and beautiful, well-paved with cobbles; the houses have no gutters, the roofs covered with small black slates and there is very pretty glass in the windows. The facades are not as fair as in Italy, the houses are narrow and mostly of wood, the stairs of stone are narrow and inconvenient, the internal walls of cob and plastered. Some 44 great houses belong to the nobility. You hardly ever see earthenware dishes, but pewter, and brass is the usual substitute for copper.

"There are a great many shops selling merchandise, the women doing the shopping rather than the men, and there are at least three times as many shops here as in Rome: 85 deal in fabrics, all large stores, and in one street alone there are 184 goldsmiths, and about 300 in the town. There are 12 large dress shops selling feathers for the fashionable, and shops selling quills for pens; 22 watchmakers, 45 glass-makers, 110 cooked meat shops, 120 pastrycooks, artists of their kind, 150 butchers, 250 tennis courts well built and maintained, which they say gave employment to 7,000 people before the late wars. In all a huge number of businesses of all kinds.

"The city has 68 parish churches and 31 chapels, 46 colleges, although student numbers are not high—the Sorbonne was at one time the best in Europe. And there are seven hospitals.

"The river Seine divides the city and is busy with barges laden with goods; it flows round an island on which stands the great Cathedral, the Palais and Sainte Chapelle as well as a great many shops and houses. The Palais was the old royal palace and within it is a vast chamber with a floor of black and white marble measuring 112 paces by 45 in the center of which is a colonnade and around the perimeter are statues of French kings, very old. At the end of the chamber is a long black marble table, and in another room nearby paneled with gold the Parlement, Exchequer and city magistrates meet. In a square alongside there are 224 small shops selling a variety of articles attracting customers all day long, men and women, nobles and humbler classes.

"The river is spanned by six bridges, three of stone, three of wood, and another unfinished, with houses on all of them, so built that you cannot see the water beneath unless you enter the shops—you would hardly suspect you were over a river. One of the bridges was recently swept away in floods and with it six woollen mills, accounting for sixteen deaths.

"There are 15 fountains in Paris supplying the inhabitants with river water excellent for drinking. Other needs are supplied by 117 apothecaries, not as attractive as their shops in Rome; 140 druggists; 80 saddlers; 523 shoemakers.

"The city's defences together with the moat measure in all 12,860 paces, tripled if you include the river (the walk round the circuit of the city takes nearly three hours). The King's palace is called the Louvre and is very fair for a French palace, with a number of galleries, some not yet finished, and with three tapestries of gold thread.

"I have heard it said that the King of France enjoys an income of one and a half million écus annually from salt duties. Hares, rabbits and quail are plentiful, thrushes are scarce and warblers hardly exist; pigs are slaughtered all the year round. A runnel of foetid water carries filth from the houses in the streets—the air reeks of it and you need a bouquet to deaden the stink, but they are careful to carry off their excrement in carts. Paris would be a tolerable place to live if some commodities now scarce were more plentiful: for instance melons, cucumbers, figs, peaches, oranges, lemons and other fruits.

"Windmills line the walls outside the city limits, pivoted on a base to let the sails move in the wind. The population is today 350,000 whereas before the late wars it was 600,000. The walls are not strong and there is a fortress called the Bastille, small, quite beautiful and well built, by the English so they say; close to this is the Arsenal which now has few arms in it and lacks a work force."

Such was a foreigner's vivid picture of late 16th century Paris.

1. Topography

Vassalieu's 1609 map of Paris shows that it was hemmed in by its walls built on embankments on which stand the windmills described by d'Ierni. The city is divided into three distinct parts mentioned by every historian: the Ile de la Cité (Roman Lutetia), containing Notre Dame and the Palais, joint symbols of the state religion and royal power; the Montagne Sainte-Geneviève on the left bank, the university quarter; and on the right bank the "Ville," which had recently encroached on what was woodland and marsh where the Seine meanders before reaching the Bièvre. The Left Bank was already densely populated and had many convents inside its boundaries; the Right Bank had not yet spread as far as the hills which surround it: Belleville, Montmartre, and Chaillot were still villages in open country, and Montfauçon, where royal executions took place, was separated from the city walls by a tract of marshy ground, the only suburbs on this side being Saint-Denis and Saint-Laurent with its Fair; the former stretched along the route to royal sanctuary, the latter to Flanders.

The importance to Paris of trade routes and rivers cannot be over-emphasized; it is no accident that its site is close to the confluence of rivers: "A geological feature brings together within a radius of less than 100 kilometres from Notre Dame the convergence of several rivers, the Oise, the Aisne, Marne, Aube, Seine, Yonne and Loing." There was easy access to the East, and also to Normandy and the sea, and the city grew at the point where the river intersects with an ancient route from the Pyrenees to the North Sea via Poitou, Gatinais and Cambrai. To grasp the importance of these facts we have only to glance at the map again: perpendicular to the Seine and carrying an immense traffic, the major routes cross the city from end to end, one by the Rue de la Harpe and Rue St. Denis goes from Porte Saint-Michel to Porte Saint-Denis, and the other via Rue St. Jacquues and Rue St. Martin links Portes Saint Jacques and Saint Martin, Poitiers, Orléans and the Loire region with the northern plains, Flanders and Antwerp, the metropolis of Western Europe.

Bearing these facts in mind it is easy to see why the booksellers settled in the Rue St. Jacques, level with the university on a main axis of commerce guaranteeing a constant flow of business and of news.

2. *The Royal City*

Its role as the capital was the fact of prime importance to
Paris, and in the Paris of the 16th century there were many
reminders of royal power: the Bastille and the Arsenal,
which Sully was soon to enlarge with a park for the royal
artillery, and nearby the grounds around the Hôtel de
Tournelle where tournaments were held until 1559 and
where the King resided, soon to be the Place Royale.
Opposite the Pont aux Changes was the Châtelet, seat of a
powerful tribunal, and on the Ile de la Cité the most
impressive centers of royal power, the Palais and, near the
edge of town, the Louvre. The Palais was the traditional seat
of the monarchy, a city in itself with its own courts and
gardens, town houses, galleries and buildings. There the
Parlement convened, the Court of Aides, the Exchequer and
the Mint were there, the Ministry of Waters and Forests, the
High Constable, the Commander in Chief and the Admiralty
Offices, and the Paris magistracy. In this labyrinth of
bureaucracy the educated classes, and so the reading public,
were to be found, the prop and support of government. In
the galleries and halls of the Palais they promenaded and that
is precisely where the booksellers set up their stalls.

After the death of Henri II the Louvre was the main royal
residence. In 1527 Francis I began to modernize the ancient
feudal palace and demolished the principal tower, and later
architects Pierre Lescot, then Baptiste and Jacques Androuet Du Cerceau rebuilt the west and south wings in
Renaissance style. Catherine de Medici erected the first
portion of the Tuileries (1564–72) and the architects Cham-
biges and Métezeau joined the two wings with the Petite and
Grande Galerie along the river bank, the modern Louvre,
where the first Valois kings held magnificent fetes. In the
16th century the Palais was confined within a narrow
quadrangle occupying only part of the present main square—
two wings still preserve their medieval aspect. Servants and
courtiers bustled about there, the government and Council
met there, the administrative offices were busy and there was
much coming and going. Henri IV's court was predominantly
military and would not be attracted to the Louvre so it did

not come into its own until the later 17th century when the Pont Neuf was completed and so allowed easier access to the Ile de la Cité and the left bank of the Seine.

3. The University

On the opposite side of the river, away from the turbulence of the city center with its government and courts, lay the University quarter.

It retained its ancient traditions. The Rector was at its head, elected in theory for three months, and staff and students were organized in four Faculties: the Faculty of Arts where the Master's degree was taken before continuing to doctorate level, then the three higher Faculties of Theology, Canon Law, and Medicine. The Faculty of Arts as of old was divided into four "nations." In the 16th century changes were slowly coming about and the colleges, originally intended as hostels for poor students, had virtually monopolized the teaching of Arts subjects and Theology. While traditions were maintained in the old schools of the Rue du Fouarre, smaller halls and colleges developed as a teaching body responsible for all or part of the curriculum, and so the modern college evolved out of the ancient university at a time when rival institutions also threatened the status of the ancient seats of learning: the Collège Royal was founded in 1530, and the Jesuits opened Clermont College in an old town house with a modern syllabus designed to attract the best brains among the young. The Reformation had damaged the prestige of the Sorbonne, and while it still collected its dues and maintained its rights in the endowment of livings, its need to raise fees led to fewer students and the bankruptcy of some constituent colleges. Even when Clermont College was closed after the Jesuit plot by Jean Châtel against Henri IV, the Sorbonne did not benefit since parents sent their children to other Jesuit seminaries in Douai or Pont-à-Mousson rather than to the university.

With the return of peace in 1598 order was restored; the King issued new statutes under which the prerogatives of all members of the university were carefully defined: disciplinary regulations, dates of vacations, academic dress and fees were precisely detailed. Though the curriculum was not laid down specifically, a reading list was issued and examination rules determined, and even if the new rules were not always strictly observed, now at least seven or eight colleges offered suitable courses of study.

The Law Faculty was in some difficulties since Canon Law was officially taught only by a small body of professors in buildings that were much decayed, near the Collège de France. The Faculty of Medicine was woefully behind current practice, still teaching Galen and Hippocrates and in constant conflict with the more progressive surgeons of the time, though the evidence of printed medical works of the period suggests that there were innovative teachers in the Faculty. The Faculty of Theology had even more problems: the teaching was confined to two colleges, Navarre and the Sorbonne, the oldest; training was lengthy and the tuition often good, but with the rising tide of Protestantism at their doors they seemed to provide no answers comparable with the profundity of the Spanish theologians—they were more interested in academic studies of the Fathers than with revitalizing Thomist theology, above all with a narrow concern for their own traditions and denunciation of the slightest whiff of "heresy." The ecclesiastical court at Paris was feared more than the Sorbonne itself since it comprised not only Sorbonne professors but members of the Faculty of Theology under the Presidency of the Syndic of the Faculty—ultra conservatism at its most formidable. Booksellers were peculiarly liable to scrutiny since they were distributors of ideas and were nervous of accusations of heresy or bad faith, only too willing to withdraw a suspected book from stock; every new religious work had to be examined by one or more doctors of theology before receiving its imprimatur.

So the university was in effect director of publishing in Paris; it nominated 24 booksellers to whom it gave its custom and who could look for relief from taxation as long as they behaved as servants of the university, living within its precincts. Regents, teachers and students were naturally among the best clients, and only very gradually did booksellers manage to stretch the links that bound them without actually snapping them, thanks finally to other outside influences.

4. Religious Organizations

Teachers and students at university enjoyed the same status as clergy, a role emphasized by their academic dress, and education was seen simply as training for a priestly vocation, unlike that of the Jesuits. A Master of Arts of Paris, and a Doctor of (Canon) Law or of Theology could expect a rewarding career. The Church's grip was also manifested in the great abbeys and convents visible at almost every street corner in Paris. There were three abbeys on the left bank, St. Victoire and St. Germain-des-Prés in the suburbs outside the walls, and St. Geneviève in the Latin quarter. They had lost much of their original spiritual drive: St. Geneviève was governed by abbé Brichanteau of sinister reputation, and at St. Germain-des-Prés the Maurists had not yet begun their reforms. Outside the city were the Franciscans in the St. Marcel district, the Benedictine priory of Notre Dame des Champs which was almost empty, and near the present day Luxembourg gardens was the Charterhouse of Vauvert, faithful to the traditions of an order that had never needed to reform itself and where Dom Beaucousin and his fellows led an exemplary life of contemplation working for a spiritual revival. A little lower down, a convent of the Franciscans, destroyed by a fire in 1580 when Henri III founded the Confrérie du St. Sépulcre, extended as far as the modern Faculty of Medicine. To the east were the Carmelites in the Place Maubert and the Dominicans in the Rue St. Jacques where they preserved St. Thomas Aquinas' pulpit. Opposite St. Benedict's church was the Maturin monastery where Robert Gaguin built a large library where the University Court met, and further east, almost level with the Louvre, the Great Augustinians were established near the spot where Henri III founded the Confrérie des Pénitents Blancs and Order of the Holy Spirit and where Parlement and Excheq-uer held their meetings.

On the right bank many more convents and monasteries were concentrated to the north east of the city: outside the walls was the Cistercian abbey of St. Antoine des Champs, and near the Arsenal the Célestins de l'Annonciation, and in the Marais where later great town houses were erected for

the nobility was the convent of St. Catherine du Val des
Ecoliers. The Clarisses or Cordelières du Tiers Ordre de St.
Francis extended from there to the Rue St. Martin, succes-
sors to the Bégardes near the old gateway of that name in the
15th century. Nearby were the canons regular of Petit St.
Antoine and the Jesuit novitiates established in 1580 on the
site of the present day Lycée Charlemagne. On the Rue St.
Martin itself were Cluniacs (St. Martin des Champs) in
buildings which now abut on to the Conservatoire des Arts et
Métiers, and a Cluniac priory was in the Ile de la Cité, St.
Denis de la Châtre.

Very few religious houses lay between St. Martin des
Champs and the Louvre: Catherine de Medici founded a
Capuchin monastery in the Faubourg St. Honoré in 1574;
Henri III often visited the convent where his favorite Henri
de Joyeuse retired in 1587, the year the Feuillants, a
reformed branch of the Cistercians, took up residence in the
Rue St. Honoré in a monastery bordering the Tuileries. The
foundations of the following century were thus foreshadowed. The picture would not be complete without reference
to the establishments outside the city limits—the royal abbey
of St. Denis, the Priory of St. Victoire near St. Lazare, the
hermits of Mont-Valérien and the great Benedictine monastery of Montmartre, soon to be one of the high points of the
Catholic Reformation.

But the real center of ecclesiastical power was the Ile de la
Cité—Notre Dame. The bishop's palace was just to the right
of the cathedral square on the Rue Neuve Notre Dame: three
buildings, chapel, courts and stables alongside the Hôtel
Dieu, and on the left the cloisters. Churches and chapters
abounded everywhere; the bishopric and canons shared a
common boundary in St. Denis du Pas, and St. Jean le Rond
was alongside one of the towers opposite the great entrance
to the cloister. Between there and the Rue de la Lanterne
and Rue de la Juiverie were the churches of St. Aignan, St.
Christophe, St. Marine, St. Landry, St. Pierre-aux-boeufs,
St. Denis de la Châtre, la Madeleine, St. Geneviève des
Ardents, with St. Germain le Vieil on the other side of the
Rue de la Juiverie.

This lengthy list reveals a striking feature of ecclesiastical organization in Paris: 14 out of 40 parishes were crammed into the Ile de la Cité, the reason being that their limits corresponded with the ancient seigneurial boundaries. The legal status of the churches was equally complex—the parishes of St. Michel, St. Germain l'Auxerrois, St. Honoré and St. Opportune were "daughters" of the bishop, who appointed a vicar to carry out a curé's duties; others were daughters of a chapter which would assign them a chapter of their own. Sometimes the bishop was the patron, sometimes the advowson was the gift of the abbé or of the canons of an abbey or of the University. Ties between all branches of Holy Mother Church were tight and personal in Paris. The clergy were numerous and wealthy, their intellectual quality variable, and they were prone to all the temptations of power—bishops and abbots were often motivated by political ambition, as in the case of the bishop of Paris, a rank held by the Gondi family since 1570; Paul de Gondi's father, later Cardinal de Retz, forced his son to enter a monastery despite his reluctance simply to keep a profitable place within the family. Henri de Verneuil, bastard son of Henry IV though never a priest—in fact a married man—was made bishop of Paris and abbé of St. Germain des Prés, and the newly rich bourgeoisie were keen to secure advancement for their children by means of Bulls issued by influential abbeys.

Most monks ignored the rules of their Orders, and an interesting fact about this sad period is the decay of many monastic libraries. As for the secular clergy, it was common for country priests to be illiterate and to live as debauchés, no example to their flock; many had no understanding of Christian teaching and could not even say Mass correctly. It was obvious that religious education had failed to produce an instructed clergy, and reform was needed. Many varieties of priests were administering the city churches; some simple clerics living as members of different foundations independent of the hierarchy, others the rejects of provincial churches like those seen begging at church doorways. On the whole parish vicars and curés took their duties seriously after their long training at the University and showed piety in their dealings with the flock. A contemporary account by the curé of St. Etienne du Mont tells that when he arrived there the church was without any worshippers, yet many churches were regularly crowded, especially at the time of the Holy League formed by Henri III to drive out Huguenot influence—fanaticism rather than real spirituality. Most religious observance, we must conclude, was no more than pure formality.

Among the higher ranks of the church, from which prelates and the upper echelons of the clergy were drawn, the situation was worse—churches were no more than centers of social intercourse. In a society led from the top the only hope of reformation was groups of enlightened and determined men evangelizing the privileged classes and working down from there.

5. *Population*

Some idea of the population and an analysis by social class would be useful at this point. It is hard to know which figures to accept: do we believe d'Ierni (350,000 in 1594)? Or the author of an official document in 1637 which gives 412,000 as the figure? Or Pierre Petit, who put it at 900,000 a few years later? Roland Mousnier, the leading authority on 17th-century France, has suggested 500,000 for the period, which would make Paris a densely populated city compared with any other French city, none of which reached 100,000, or indeed any other European city except Naples, which was the largest at 300,000.

What social classes made up the 500,000? The royal court was obviously the most influential sector, with the Civil and Military Household. Likewise the royal and municipal administration, the courts of justice from the President to Parlement to the Châtelet's Procurator and his clerks and multitude of lawyers; add the increasing officials of the Treasury and all those organs of state amount to several thousands of people with their families and official households. The clergy were numbered as the sands of the sea in countless churches and parishes; university professors, teachers at the Collège Royal, all the Faculties, the thousands of students went to make up a highly sophisticated citizenry, a perfect market for booksellers. To these educated classes we must add the bourgeoisie, the rentier class and the lesser gentry striving to enter the ranks of the old nobility by purchasing offices, a traditional source of revenue to the French Exchequer and the route to social advancement. Merchants must have formed a large proportion of the middle class but we have few figures, and scarcely any for the working class, the artisans and their apprentices. The document of 1637 does not mention its sources but lists the seven largest trades: drapers, grocers, apothecaries, haberdashers, bonnet-makers, goldsmiths and vintners as having 2,752 masters and 10,000 journeymen; the other 105 guilds accounted for 10,772 masters and about 38,000 journeymen, plus 600 carters and 1200 apprentice carters, 1500 porters, 300 lumbermen and 400 water carriers, which yields a total of 66,000, to which we need to add families.

The Court and royal administration, with the Treasury at the heart of the financial system, meant that the city was a great source of capital, largely through sale of offices and receipts from rents. The consequences of this were that successful businessmen preferred to live off rents from property, and the capital invested from that source ended up in State coffers since they would buy a profitable post and so become ranking officials themselves. This venal system obtained not only in Paris but throughout France and explains why capital investment played little part in the growth of commerce and industry. The country was backward and Paris one huge consumer, absorbing food from the surrounding regions, but attempts to start industries failed: artists and craftsmen preferred to supply the luxury trades on their doorstep, and among those luxury trades since the end of the 15th century had been printing.

6. The Book Trade

After the Wars of Religion in the late 16th century publishing began to prosper. The future of France began to take shape during the upheavals of the years 1560–80; the Catholic League and finally the Massacre of St. Bartholomew were the dividing line after which printers and booksellers had to decide among prison, exile or conformity. The older Humanist printers got out, taking their businesses with them; some handed them over to others who were prepared to stay. Times were hard for the trade and a period of strikes and turbulence lay ahead, though perhaps a dozen firms were doing well at Paris. Morel was the leading publisher, with Fédéric Morel II, King's Printer in 1581, at the helm, which meant steady orders for official publications. Jamet Mettayer and his son Pierre were his collaborators, stout monarchists who turned out propaganda for Henri IV, and Fédéric had the font designed by Garamond, the "Grecs du Roi," for his publications issued in his capacity as Reader in Greek at the Collège Royal. He was the last in the great line of Humanist printers working in Paris, putting his skills at the service of the Catholic League and Counter Reformation. He plunged into current controversies, published many little books on the burning issues of the day and made French translations from the Greek Fathers disputing points of doctrine. He was a man of great enterprise and much in evidence at the Frankfurt Fair every year. Another successful firm was Sebastien Nivelle's, in some ways bolder than Morel; he inherited an old business from Rembolt and Chevallon, was the son of a papermaker and during the time of the Catholic League built up a big business with his son Nicolas, even outstripping the Lyons publishers in their special field of Law. He, too, invested in a monumental edition of the Fathers and organized a consortium to undertake the systematic publication of Patristic texts and prayerbooks of the Roman use, his collaborators, Morel, Drouart and Sonnius, all helping with the huge *Bibliotheca Patrum* edited by Marguerin de la Bigne.

Drouart and Jamet Mettayer were closely involved in the literature of the new spiritual revival, issuing hours, breviaries and devotional works of the Marian cult. Guillaume Chaudière was another bookseller in the same line, appointed to the Cardinal of Lorraine, with a workshop in Rheims. Countless books of piety came from his press, no doubt subsidized by the League, many of them translations of the Rhine school of mystics as well as the Spanish and Italian. Guillaume and Denis La Noue were another firm, possibly the leaders in the spiritual Renaissance that swept France in 1580–90. They issued Guevara's works, Luis de Granada, Ludolph of Chartres' *Vita Christi,* the sermons of Panigarola, Cristi and Feuardent, Crespet and René Benoist's works; they published catechisms, Latin hours, polemical tracts, Marian devotions and, as official publishers to the Carthusians, were responsible for a whole series of mystical works in French translated from originals.

Most of the established publishers were involved in the Catholic Revival, though there were others who while issuing theological works showed a significant interest in literature. The firm of Buon, for example, made its fortune out of Ronsard, the Pleiade poets, Garnier, and other poets and fashionable translators like Belleforest. And Abel Langelier, with a bookshop in the Palais where most of the currently fashionable literature was on display, offered his customers not only controversial authors like Bellarmine but poetry, French translations of the Psalms, of classics, and Boccaccio and Tasso; he stocked books by the contemporary "Neo-Stoic" school (Du Vair, for example) and the brilliant *Essays* of Montaigne—just out.

These, then, were the trends in the trade from 1570 to 1600: a solid base of theology, the arsenal of the Counter Reformation, with new insights into spirituality made available to far more readers through translation. The French taste for "style" in language and literature made translations from both classics and contemporary writers very popular reading matter, and the best epic poets of Italy and France were assured of an audience. Some idea of the make-up of the trade may be gleaned from the fact that a mere eight publishers between them issued 300 titles, more than a third of the entire output, which means high concentration of resources and so ease of regulation from above. And that was to become stricter.

From the time of the stationers in the 13th century regimentation of the trade in books had been liberal, chiefly organized through the University and its appointed scriveners. After printing and the growth of piracy, redress was sought increasingly by aggrieved printers, and jurisdiction inevitably ensued, by way of the Châtelet or Parlement of the King's Privy Council, as printers sought secure monopolies or rights in their publications. Furthermore, unrest in the trade which led to strikes at Lyons and Paris in 1539–44 and 1570–72 forced the authorities to action, passing decrees to regulate the whole business of book production, not simply relations between masters and men. The religious conflicts of the mid-16th century brought in censorship for the first time: Article 23 of the Edict of Gaillon (1571) ordained that two printers each year be elected to act as supervisors with two booksellers as a guarantee that no "libelous" book be issued, and that all books be printed on good paper in a good type. Parlement invited printers to elect a Procureur to implement the law in its name and ensure that there were no violations; the trade was being coerced into self-regulation.

In February 1566, Article 78 of the Edict of Moulin forbade the printing of any book or tract "without our leave and due permission by letters licensing this under the Great Seal." The King was the sole authority, without intervention by other juridical bodies or even the courts. By associating the idea of "permission" to print with rights in a title the monarch could grant advantages to those whose publications he approved and could supervise, and he was able to alter the conditions of the privilege at will: to operate "under the Seal" was therefore to enjoy a powerful patronage, as valuable a perquisite as capital in the period before regular licensing started.

This marked the beginning of State grants of monopolies to printers, and King's Printers were given most of the official work; hence the most lucrative parts of the trade were concentrated in privileged hands, and as royal bureaucracy grew there was ever more need for information and so of proclamations and Acts, which meant steady business. The Papacy and Catholic hierarchy controlled Bible publishing but the King assigned rights in prayerbooks to Kerver and to a guild of Paris booksellers, the Compagnie des Usages; orthodoxy was thus under surveillance. The production and marketing of the Patristic texts led to the creation of another consortium, the Compagnie du Navire, to publish on a regular basis and to ensure retention of privilege in them, which admitted a new principle into the trade—that privileges could be granted in books already long in print as well as new ones, a precedent that was to have far-reaching consequences. The Church played a significant part in all this, authorizing certain booksellers to be official distributors of texts: Mettayer and Morel, Etienne Prévosteau, Pierre Ballard (a music specialist), Nivelle, Michel Sonnius, and Jacques Du Puis were members of the Compagnie du Navire when it was formed in 1585 and Abel Langelier, Barthélemy Macé, Ambroise Drouart and the brothers Sonnius when it was reorganized in 1599. After Kerver's death the Compagnie des Usages consisted of Nivelle, Guillaume Chaudière, Guillaume de la Noue, Michel Sonnius, Claude Chappelet, Jean Corbon and Jamet Mettayer; the same names recur. Quite clearly they were the approved representatives of the trade, favored by Church and State.

What effect did all this have on the spread of ideas?

The authorities' chief objective was to retain printing (a dangerous mystery) firmly in their hands and to suppress anything that smacked of opposition, and one way to achieve this was to organize the entire trade in one guild wherein internal conflicts of interest would guarantee a legal basis for surveillance (to "mend discord") while fostering an oligarchy of established publishing houses acting in the King's interest.

The Edict of Gaillon provided the machinery, with a Procureur as Superintendent, and in 1586 a Code of rules was ratified in Letters Patent by which Paris booksellers and printers were forbidden to have presses outside the city, particularly in the "suburbs." The Article (printed below) reveals the aim—viz., to suppress clandestine presses by its demands before recognizing the status of master printer: there was to be a period of apprenticeship and possession of at least two presses. Again it ensured control by requiring that the imprint of each publisher be on the title page with the imprimatur of royal privilege, secured before going to press. Domino-makers and tapestry manufacturers were forbidden to have presses on which books could be printed—evidently they were a source of clandestine printing. The Procureur and four booksellers and printers appointed as his Assistants in the arduous role of supervisers were assigned very precise duties, and the rules for their nomination changed:

> It is Our will and command that master printers in Our city of Paris do annually elect two of their number and also two licensed booksellers, a Syndic and two Assistants whose duty it will be to ensure that no libel or defamatory work or anything heretical or contrary to the teachings of Holy Mother Church, Apostolic and Roman, do appear. Where such a book is discovered it shall be kept forthwith and reported without delay to Our civil authorities, namely the Civil Lieutenant. To this end the said Syndic with his sworn booksellers, printers and Assistants are to be informed of all books printed henceforth, and no printer may print or cause to be printed any book that has not been previously notified to the said Syndic and his Assistants. The said Syndic and Assistants shall maintain a register of all such books and prepare a summary twice a month for the Civil Lieutenant.

We do not know how strictly the Code was observed. Visits of inspection were certainly carried out because there is evidence of dissension between printing houses, but both printers and booksellers were willing to co-operate out of mutual self-interest against other related trades, domino-makers, haberdashers, papermakers and even cobblers who did some pamphlet selling. The established booksellers were hostile to those who had shown enterprise by quitting the University quarter and setting up in the St. Severin district or on the bridges in defiance of the authorities, and in the interest of keeping down competition they put every impediment in the way of journeymen qualifying as masters.

The imposition of a Code (based on earlier legislation) marks a new stage in the evolution of the trade and is worth discussing in detail here. The first attempt at codification was in 1610 when the Châtelet drafted rules at the request of the King's Procureur. They were ill received since the preamble accused printers and booksellers of responsibility for disorder in the trade. The matter was raised in Parlement and a revised version was agreed in concert with the Guild of

Stationers, but the Rector of the University refused to approve certain Articles. In 1617 Statutes were drawn up for the Guild of Printers, Booksellers and Binders, and in May 1617 the Provost of Paris allowed the Syndic and Wardens of the Company to elect 18 Deputies to help with the administration and legal affairs of the Guild. On 1 June 1618 the King granted Letters Patent referring the proposed Articles to the Provost and Civil Lieutenant. They reported favorably and Parlement registered the Patent although the University was not consulted.

The first Article of the 1618 Ordinance declares that printers, booksellers and bookbinders "were always held in high esteem as ancillaries of the University of Paris, and distinct from the 'mechanic trades'," and that marked the end of a process which had been evolving throughout the 16th century: from now on the 24 recognized booksellers and two binders were no longer the only ones to enjoy University privileges. Every printer, bookseller and binder would enjoy equal prerogatives in law as a fact, as "ancillaries" of the University. This measure thus destroyed University control of the trade and extended ancient prerogatives to booksellers who had no official connections with the University.

In the early 17th century lawsuits about apprenticeship and inheritance were common. The King's motive—suppression of forbidden books and underground pamphlets—coincided with master printers' desire to curtail any competition. Ten of the 37 Articles were devoted to this important question: every apprentice must be able to read and write and had to be unmarried; Articles of apprenticeship were to be properly notarized and entered in the Guild registers, apprenticeship being four years for printers, five for booksellers and binders; masters were forbidden to reduce the period of apprenticeship and if apprentices quit their place of work they were required to serve double the time spent absent— the second time led to their dismissal. The number of apprentices was severely restricted, each master being assigned one, and in the case of masters having two presses, two or three. When out of their time apprentices could not immediately proceed to mastership but had to remain as journeymen (compagnons) with their original master, the period fixed at three years for booksellers and binders, four for printers. After that they could be dubbed master if this was endorsed by two sworn (University) booksellers, two unsworn booksellers, two master printers and two master binders and if a fee of 60 livres was paid to the Guild. Printers had to possess two fully equipped presses of their own to go into business, an expensive undertaking which few journeymen could afford.

The Ordinance made life easier for the sons or relatives of master printers since no apprenticeship was required of masters' sons; they would be accepted by the Syndic and Assistants usually without expense. Otherwise the only path to mastership and a business was through marriage to a master's widow or daughter, though widows often carried on the business alone. Many journeymen out of their time felt frustrated and further aggravated by another measure, introduced to curb the number of masters operating in Paris: "To avoid the many abuses, disorders and confusion which daily grow worse with printing of great numbers of scandalous, defamatory and anonymous books and pamphlets the Guild will henceforth accept no more than one bookseller, printer and binder per year." Measures like this were intended to create a privileged oligarchy in the trade, and any who sought to gain profit from the failure of less fortunate ones were frustrated by a rule which forbade ownership of more than one bookshop or printing shop. Rights in older material were abolished so that in theory it was impossible to monopolize good-selling lines and so become a capitalist with several outlets. Two Articles dealt with relations between masters and men, always a vexed question: the traditional ban on assemblies, on the carrying of offensive weapons, and the swearing of oaths was repeated, and finally books or manuscripts used as copy for printing had to be returned to the owner.

Administration of the Guild and oversight was in the hands of the Syndic, elected annually, and the four Assistants elected for two years, two Assistants changing in rotation each year. The master printers and booksellers assembled for the election at 2 p.m. on the 8th May each year in the Salle des Mathurins at Guild headquarters in the presence of the

Civil Lieutenant and the Procurator-General from the Châtelet, and on election the Syndic and Assistants took the oath. Their overriding duty was to ensure that no book or pamphlet hostile to the State or contrary to the established religion was printed or sold in Paris, and this meant actual inspection of premises and books in progress to see that the imprint of publisher and printer appeared on the title page, with the official imprimatur and author's name; it was also a deterrent to piracy. The Guild officers were also expected to ensure that all parcels and bales of books from abroad were searched by customs officials or dispatched to the Guild headquarters for scrutiny, even books addressed to private individuals, and if any "bad" books were found they were all confiscated and the offender fined. The book trade, which had once thought itself superior to mechanic trades, was now tightly and corporately organized under severe regulations. A new age had arrived.

PART ONE
STATISTICAL DATA

CHAPTER I

THE SOURCES

THE CHIEF AIM OF THIS STUDY is to determine what interested the readers and writers of books, what their social background was, what the psychology of the French intelligentsia was in the 17th century, and what factors conditioned their reading habits. To answer these questions we shall need to examine the book trade in some detail. The historian will have recourse to the *Bibliographie de la France,* the annual monographs on French publishing, using research into the sociology of reading, and exploiting the major bibliographies which deal with book production in general or by specific subject. Two historical sources are vital here: the registers maintained by the Chancellery and by the Stationers' Guild which list records of licenses to print individual books, or records kept by the Royal Library of the books sent there under the system of legal deposit. The other source is the physical evidence of the shelves: books which have survived in the older libraries which have become national libraries. And finally, the earliest catalogs and bibliographies which date from the 17th century. All these materials help us construct a methodology.

1. Archives

Two books by M. R. Estivals are crucial: *Dépôt légal sous l'Ancien Régime* and *Statistique bibliographique sous la Monarchie au XVIII siècle* (which includes references to the 17th century). A list of relevant sources is given below:

   A. *Licensing Registers*
      1. MSS Fr. 16753–16754. Records of the Audience du Sceau. Licenses granted 1635–1664 (no records for 1647–1653).

2. MSS Fr. 21944–21971. Registers of the Paris Guildhall (Chambre Syndicale) listing licenses granted to
authors and booksellers, 1653–1790. For the 17th
century MS Fr. 21944 for the years 1653–1660 is not
in the same form as the others, the license being
grouped under the names of the applicants. From
1660 to 1700 there is a chronological order, then
after a gap in 1701/2 when there was a change in the
legislation there is differentiation between classes of
licence, all of which are recorded.

B. *Legal Deposit Registers*
1. MSS Fr. 21943 and 21845. Lists of books submitted
by printers and booksellers to the Syndic of the
Guild under Legal Deposit rules for resale to help
the finances of the Guildhall; the period: 1626–1689
and 1698–1704.
2. MSS Archives 34–35, 22023–22026, 22032. Books
deposited in the Royal Library under Legal Deposit. Only MS 34 concerns our study, covering the
period 1684–1720.

What do these records tell us?

A. *Licensing Statistics*
1. MS Fr. 16753–4. In each year between 80 and 200
licenses were issued, a mere fraction of total book
production; for example, in 1644, 200 licenses were
issued but over 600 books were published. A quick
check shows that the registers record nothing like
the actual output of books for the appropriate
years. The records are no guide even to the
production of licensed books, and certainly not to
overall output.
2. MS Fr. 21944–21948. These records allow some
idea of book production after 1653 and so are of
great interest. Figures for 1653–1661 are incomplete. Again, the books under licence do not
correspond with books actually published. The
government was tending to offer privileges to a

growing number of books at this time, so that any
study based on this source is inevitably a study of
the efficacy of a system as it was evolving.

B. *Statistics Relating to Legal Deposit*
   1. MS Fr. 21943 and 21845. If the registers had been
      efficiently kept they would be a critical source, but
      after 1626 Legal Deposit was not strictly observed.
      MS Fr. 21943 is proof only that Legal Deposit was
      effective only when the Guilds needed money. The
      average figure of recorded books is very low and
      titles so abbreviated as to defy identification.
   2. Archives 34 etc. are useful. It must be remembered
      that Legal Deposit applied only to licensed books,
      hence the figures relate only to those, and they
      begin only in 1684.

In general manuscript sources are much less satisfactory
for the 17th than for the 18th century, but do have value for
the period after 1661 and particularly 1685–1690, but they
are no substitute for the great catalogs and bibliographies for
a study of the trade from 1601–1700. While they throw some
light on aspects of the Paris book trade in the 17th century
they are quite insufficient as a base for any research
comparable with Furet's study of the 18th century.

2. *Bibliographies*

Printing is the one industry whose products have been
systematically preserved and cataloged, and records fall into
three main categories: booksellers' catalogs, current and
retrospective bibliographies, and library catalogs. How can
we best use these materials?

Booksellers' catalogs tell us what kind of books were
published and which publishers specialized in various fields.
Stock lists tell us about foreign books available to readers in
Paris, but such evidence is still on the slender side since
booksellers issued catalogs only for their own stocks and the
entries are so abridged as to be useless for identification
purposes.

Bibliographies are helpful, especially subject bibliographies. Father Lelong's *Bibliotheca sacra* (4 vols., 1778–85), Dom Ceillier's *Histoire générale des auteurs sacrés et ecclésiastiques* (24 vols., 1729–83) and Quetif and Echard's *Bibliotheca ordinis Predicatorum* (2 vols., 1910–14) contain books long since disappeared. And very valuable modern bibliographies are: Bohatta, *Bibliographie der Breviere* (1939); Weale and Bohatta, *Catalogus missalium* (1928); R. C. Williams, *Bibliography of the 17th century novel in France* (1932); Sommervogel and Backer, *Bibliothèque de la Compagnie de Jésus;* and Cioranescu, *Bibliographie de la littérature française du dix-septième siècle* (3 vols., 1965–8).

Yet even these afford only a partial view. The greatest aids towards a total view are the earliest lists of books published in a given country. Father Louis Jacob produced a catalog for the years 1643–53 annually or every two years, the *Bibliographia parisiana* and the *Bibliographia gallicana*. Although incomplete for the provinces they are quite accurate for Paris, and since they were compiled when the books were new, they are *a priori* evidence for Parisian books in one decade of the 17th century, both as to the kinds of books and the proportion of different subjects, books which have not survived. Still, this does not yield anything like a picture of the century's output, and so we are left with the last category—library catalogs. How far do they correspond with actual books published?

Since Paris is at the heart of our investigations, obviously the catalog of the *Bibliothèque Nationale* is vital. It is not yet complete but it numbers already 17,500 different titles published in Paris from 1601 to 1700 (excluding booklets and ephemera of less than 48 pages). The standard of editing is high, and as successive reprintings are included it is of particular importance to a study of reading habits. The printed author catalog is continued on a card index maintained at the library, and there is an index of anonymous works. Other great libraries' stocks are of immense value: the Bibliothèque Mazarine, the Bibliothèque Sainte Geneviève, and the Arsenal, all in Paris, and there are magnificent provincial collections at Versailles, Rouen, Troyes and Lyons, though all too often their manuscript catalogs, mostly compiled in the 19th century, are not reliable and often incomplete. The British Museum (now the British Library) Catalogue of Printed Books is very rich in 17th-century French material.

Such are our library resources. Of course, the ideal solution would be to compile one massive bibliography of 17th-century French books published in Paris drawn from all the libraries; indeed, Phillippe Renouard began such a task in 1905 for the 16th century and died with it incomplete, but his notes are preserved in the Bibliothèque Nationale and will form the basis of a bibliography in the future. Any attempt by a single scholar to do the same for the 17th century is doomed because the numbers involved are too great and library catalogs incomplete. Even if put into one single list, the hundreds of thousands of entries describing the 60,000 titles would have to be compared with actual copies where they survived, to distinguish between various printings, an impossible task for one person. Instead some kind of production graph might be attempted based on the titles preserved in the Bibliothèque Nationale, if the statistics were used with caution and the necessary controls.

The first question is: how far are the collections in the Bibliothèque Nationale homogenous and how far do they represent an overemphasis on one period rather than another—after all, we seek a balanced picture. To determine this we have to know how the stock was accumulated in the days when it was the Royal Library. Legal Deposit was the original basis, dating from 1537 in the reign of François I, when all new books had to be deposited in the Royal Library. In all probability the term "new" meant at first a text not yet in print. After 1617 it was laid down that books submitted under Legal Deposit were to be licensed books (i.e., those issued "with privilege") and which had not been previously printed, but as the granting of privileges grew apace and the Legal Deposit more efficient, more and more reprints were sent to the Royal Library, especially after 1685 and even to a greater extent after 1701, so that the last years of the 17th century are better represented in the catalog than the early years.

But Legal Deposit was not the only source from which books were acquired for the Royal Library. Gifts were quite common and occasionally the Library could purchase private collections: the brothers Dupuy, King's Librarians, bequeathed their personal collection, and among other libraries donated or confiscated were those of the scholar Trichet du Fresne; Gilbert Gaulmyn, Maître des Requêtes; Chancellor Séguier, who had the right to a copy of every book printed—a right he was jealous of; Fouquet after his fall from grace; Jacques Mentel, a doctor who had acquired some of Gabriel Naudé's books; Falconnet, another doctor, and bibliophiles like Cangé, Fontanier and Thoisy who collected a priceless hoard of pamphlets which might otherwise have been lost.

When the French Revolution broke out there were 153,000 items cataloged in the Royal Library in addition to thousands of other titles in special lists, and some still uncataloged. The expropriation of churches and the libraries of the emigré nobility brought a vast number of books and other materials into public ownership. The Royal Library, renamed the Bibliothèque Nationale, had the lion's share, 250,000 volumes and many other ephemeral publications, mostly from the huge numbers of religious foundations in the Paris region, which explains the heavy emphasis on theology, but since ecclesiastical libraries had also benefited from bequests from nobles, prelates and lay scholars they had many secular publications, too.

Since the early 19th century librarians at the Bibliothèque Nationale have been trying systematically to fill gaps in their stock and on the whole it is a representative collection, but as everyone knows a library is only as good as its administrators, and so the stock in one period is a better cross-section than in another, and particularly in the area of popular literature which is never as well represented as scholarly literature; hence once again the lesson is, if attempting a full and complete picture of reading habits, just as much caution is needed in the case of the Bibliothèque Nationale as with any other evidence.

3. The Books in the Bibliothèque Nationale

A. *Ephemera.* 17th-century printers depended just as much as modern printers on "jobbing" printing, just the kind of matter unlikely to survive. Estimates are futile, and as there was no commonly accepted practice for cataloging "pièces volantes," no stipulated minimum number of pages, only books of more than 48 pages have been included in our statistics, but the minimum for a folio has been fixed at 40 pages, and 44 for a quarto. Anything less is classed as ephemera.

B. *Format.* There is the problem of counting as one work a number of folio volumes of a work in the same way as one would count a small octavo single volume. The problem strikes at the heart of statistical bibliography.
a) Each volume of a work is counted as one.
b) A general figure has been arrived at for the totality of volumes but separate figures given for folios, quartos, octavos, 12mos, 16mos and 32mos. The results have been interpreted from an economic point of view.

C. *New Editions and Reprints.* Two methods are possible: To count only strictly new titles, each book of equal importance whether a best-seller or a privately printed one; this is valid as a pointer to the intellectual life of the time. On the other hand, to count every edition of a work is acceptable in the 17th century when editions ran to no more than 1,200–2,500 copies, and it is also an index to the success of a book as well as to the economic aspects of book production. The latter alternative was therefore preferred.

D. *The Catalog of the Bibliothèque Nationale.* Only the volumes so far completed could be used (A-T); the question was—would this falsify results? Four questions need solution to answer that:
1. Works whose authors are known. It was noticeable that the curve on the graph was the same for the selected 3,000 entries as for all the available entries in the catalog so far; hence it would indicate that results from the incomplete catalog are quite valid.
2. Anonymous works, individual or collective. These include the Bible. Works of this kind have been closely examined in the actual libraries or in bibliographies and

it is clear that the Bible formed only a tiny part of the imprints from Paris in the 17th century.

Church service books. Most of them have vanished; hence it seemed better to exclude them rather than try to base a total on the very few which have survived, yet to keep them in mind as an important element in interpreting the figures.

Official Acts. Numerous, but being of few pages they belong with pamphlets. Ephemeral printing did not evolve in the same way as books; we did not therefore include this class of document with statistics of printed books.

3. Pseudonymous works. No reliable figures are possible, and they have been excluded, but the indications are that they were not numerous and so will not gravely affect the result.

4. Books printed in Paris without place of publication given, and false imprints. At various periods printers were guilty of both practices, and provincial printers and foreigners sometimes used Paris imprints. Clandestine printing means there is bound to be a margin of error in any official statistics since by their nature banned books escape official records, but they must be taken into account in any deductions based on the stocks of the Bibliothèque Nationale.

In sum, the figures must not be taken as definitive but as a point of departure in future research.

CHAPTER II

INTERPRETATION

TWO QUESTIONS HAVE TO BE SOLVED: how far does the stock of the Bibliothèque Nationale reflect the increase in book production? And to what extent does the Library's surviving stock reflect actual book production? A more exact answer might be helped by reference to other libraries beside the Nationale, concomitant with contemporary archives and bibliographies.

1. Other Libraries

Although it has not been possible to analyze the bookstocks of other libraries in the same way as those of the Bibliothèque Nationale, nevertheless some sampling can be made. Cioranescu's *Bibliographie de la littérature française du 17 siècle* makes possible some comparisons:

1. Bibliothèque Sainte Geneviève. Analysis was made of the catalog compiled after the library was requisitioned in the Revolution, which includes the majority of the books but not ephemeral material.
2. Entries relating to 17th-century books published in Paris taken from sales catalogs.
3. The 17th-century books listed in Cioranescu's bibliography.

Cioranescu included only those reprints which had some alteration to the text or a fresh preface or new critical matter. The main emphasis is on literature, but theology, history, medicine and architecture are included, and only technical books and law are excluded. There is a continuous increase to 1640, two peak periods, 1645 and 1665, then a decline to the end of the century: we can therefore generally trust the picture suggested by the surviving books in the Bibliothèque Nationale.

Evidence from sale catalogs indicates a more marked decline around 1651 and at the end of the century, probably because many of the devotional books did not survive. The evidence from the not very reliable catalog of the Sainte Geneviève shows little decline in 1651. To tackle the problem of book production and find out in more detail what did survive we must try other sources.

2. Grouping by Subject and Period

Figures of book production, 1598–1600, 1643–45, and 1699–1700 were examined.

A. 1598–1600. Based on surviving copies but fairly exhaustive since it uses the detailed analysis made by Renouard including books, pamphlets and other ephemera. This helps to:

1. Determine the output of books and pamphlets in each of the years concerned.
2. Specify folios, quartos and smaller sized books; work out Latin and French books; group by subject using traditional classification.
3. Show how many copies for each year are preserved in the Bibliothèque Nationale and trace books known only through early bibliographies or known to Renouard only in single copies.

The table below shows the results of this research, but there are some imponderables. Including everything listed in Renouard, 313 titles were counted for 1598; 274 in 1599, and 338 in 1600, with a ten percent margin of error for the books; distinguishing between books and pamphlets was not always possible because some unique copies were destroyed in World War II and some were mentioned only in abbreviated form in bibliographies. The average for each of the three years was 150, just under one-third of which were religious works. Under the subject heading of Belles Lettres, and much more numerous than Religion, were Classics, books by contemporary moralists (Montaigne, Lipsius, Du Vair in particular), poetry (Desportes, Nervèze, Du Souhait), plays, many novels, and books of courtesy and manners. History was relatively scarce, even when secular and ecclesiastical history were combined. Law and Canon Law were much in evidence, as might be expected in a period of administrative reorganization.

Rather more than one-quarter of the books were in Latin yet there were many translations into French, chiefly from the Classics and Church Fathers, or mystical and casuistical treatises, usually from Spanish, not Latin. Usual size was octavo, folios and quartos being rare, and the small-sized books were of few pages, half of them with fewer than fifty pages. Little booklets of poetry or devotion, usually 30–40 pages, were omitted from the count although they were commoner in the early period. On the whole short books were the favorites, possibly because the trade was recovering from the wars of religion in the late 16th century and could only manage modest publications, or possibly they reflect a contemporary taste for digests and translations.

Renouard. Books Printed in Paris, 1598–1600

	1598	*1599*	*1600*
Bible	6	6	3
Liturgical works	3	5	1
Church fathers	6	3	2
Scholastic theology	4	—	1
Moral theology	3	2	5
Polemical	11	15–17	8
Spiritual literature	7	9–11	13
Sermons	5	4	6
Hagiography	2	1	2
Catechism	—	—	5
Others	2	—	1
Total religious literature	**49**	**45–49**	**47**

	1598	*1599*	*1600*
Classics (Latin and Greek)	8–10	17–20	18
Philosophy and morals	9–10	5	2
Poetry and drama	8	30	15
Novels and manners	12–15	2	13–15

	1598	*1599*	*1600*
Rhetoric, etc.	8–11	8–10	13–14
Total belles lettres	**45–54**	**62–67**	**61–64**
Canon and civil law	14–17	15	22–24
History	25–27	13	14
Arts and sciences	21–22	17	14–15
Folios	18	14	16
Quartos	16	24	18
Octavo, 12mo, etc.	120	116	107
Doubtful	15	7	23
French	112	—	103
Latin	39	—	34
Others	2	—	2
Doubtful	16	—	25
Total	**154–169**	**152–161**	**158–164**

Including ephemera, Renouard gives a total of 925 titles published in the period 1598–1600. In 330 cases he found only one copy (chiefly of pamphlets, about 200); only about 30 books and pamphlets were in bibliographies but 451 titles are in the Bibliothèque Nationale today. Of books alone, Renouard lists 154–169 (1598), 152–161 (1599) and 158–164 (1600), and of these 71 are in the Bibliothèque Nationale for the year 1598, 78 for 1599 and 75 for 1600. Of the 71 in 1598, 27, or more than one-third, are in Latin, 29 out of 78 in 1599, and 26 out of 75 in 1600. More than a third of the books in the Bibliothèque Nationale are in Latin, though Latin titles account for little more than a quarter of those listed in Renouard, which confirms the belief that learned works have survived in greater numbers than the ordinary, run-of-the-mill publications and so are better represented on the shelves today. In some provincial libraries—Amiens and Moulins for instance—unique copies of little devotional books, breviaries, hours and sermons, and of novels, poetry and grammar, and elementary schoolbooks still survive.

B. 1643–1645. This period was more rewarding. The output from Parisian presses was high to judge from

Bibliothèque Nationale stocks, and three other sources offered valuable testimony:

1. *Bibliographia gallicana* (Louis Jacob). Jacob was Cardinal de Retz's librarian, and a friend of Gabriel Naudé. He began his list at a time when European book production was on the increase and the Frankfurt Book Fair had temporarily stopped (the Fair catalogs were main current bibliographies used by the trade). He saw the need for an annual list of books published in France and asked booksellers to send him notices of their publications while he made his own regular count of books in the Paris bookshops. Nine slim volumes appeared from 1645 to 1654, totalling 2,674 titles published in Paris between 1643 and 1653 and about 1,000 more in the provinces. 934 titles were published in Paris 1643–45, a very high figure, more than that arrived at by counting the books in the Bibliothèque Nationale catalog.

2. Surviving Registers of the Seal (Permissions du Sceau). These are licences issued 1643–45 and, though not an exhaustive list, represent titles of several hundred books for which licences were applied for in the offices of the Chancellery.

3. An Inquest of March 1644 conducted by the Stationers' Guild as to books actually in the press.

The three above-mentioned sources yielded these totals when compared with *books actually on the shelves:*

	1643	1644	1645
Bibliothèque Nationale	275	295	202
Bibliothèque Mazarine	155	161	65
Bibliothèque Sainte Geneviéve	109	115	102
Bibliothèque de Lyon	80	63	79
Bibliothèque de Troyes	56	62	53
Bibliothèque de Montpellier	10	17	10
Cioranescu (Author bibliography, A-M)	152	136	140
Other bibliographies	45	52	21
Different editions	499	571	405

These figures are by no means exhaustive but they show three times as many books as Renouard's, confirming the sharp rise in output.

Comparison of Figures with Other Contemporary Sources

	1643	1644	1645
Editions listed by Fr. Jacob*	234	418	282
Editions included in the table above	499	571	405
Editions listed by Fr. Jacob but not in the table above	42	78	46

Missing titles on the shelves can be explained by the fact that the sources are incomplete, but the table is a first attempt to list books hard to find in libraries of the present day.

The Register of the Seal (Permissions du Sceau). Years 1643 and 1644.

Titles listed in the register	419
Titles actually surviving	339
Missing	80

Thirty-nine of the surviving titles were printed in the provinces, and doubtless other provincial books are among the titles which have disappeared. Nor did licence always mean that the book was published immediately: Chapelain's popular *Pucelle,* though licensed in 1643, was not published until 1656. Sometimes it was an application to extend the licence, and that did not necessarily entail an immediate reprint. All doubtful cases were deemed to be books that have vanished; hence the high figure.

The Stationers' Inquest of 1644

Titles mentioned in the text	114
Titles actually surviving	97
Missing	17

Comparatively few missing books here, explained by the fact that scholarly works were in the press for a longer time and have been more carefully preserved than popular books; hence higher survival rates. Furthermore, no account was taken of

---

*There are problems of identification in Jacob's list: his informants altered publication dates in their notes to him, probably with commercial motives; thus Descartes' *Meditations* published by Soly was given as 1643 when there is no evidence that it was reissued then. Discrepancies like this have therefore been ignored. Where copies of the same edition have different dates, the earlier date has been used.

some categories which have almost all disappeared, and which are mentioned in the Inquest: wrappers (4 printers); theses (1 printer); schoolbooks and devotional (1 printer); songs (2 printers); official notices (6 printers); books of hours (7 printers); service books (10 printers).

3. Actual Production

(Surviving books plus Father Jacob's lists and the 1644 Inquest)

	1643	*1644*	*1645*
Bible	13	23	15
Patristics	11	15	10
Scholastic theology	13	19	25
Moral theology	4	5	9
Polemical literature	35	99	18
Sermons	2	4	6
Pastoral and catechisms	9	7	6
Spirituality and devotion	60	89	65
Church service books	20	24	18
Total religious works	**167**	**285**	**172**
Canon law	13	10	15
Civil law	17	18	17
Total law books	**30**	**28**	**32**
Church history	46	39	43
Secular history	125	107	40
Total history	**171**	**146**	**83**
Philosophy	12	8	7
Morals and politics	12	18	10
Philology and rhetoric	21	21	19
Grammar	9	21	17
Poetry	16	25	13
Drama	27	19	29
Novels	16	24	15
Total belles lettres	**113**	**136**	**110**
Medicine	9	13	11
Science	23	31	13
Technology	7	5	10
Total science and technology	**39**	**49**	**34**
Scholar librarians	3	4	5
Heretical works	3	6	20
Grand total	**526**	**646**	**456**

These figures give us the nearest approximation to the actual total of books published in Paris in 1643–45, using Louis Jacob's classification and taking titles, not volumes.

Works listed by Jacob have been counted as full-length books where they have not survived to be checked, although some might have been less than 48 pages; lives of the saints were included in church history and so inflate the figure a little, but funeral orations for Louis XIII have been included in Secular History; hence the high figures for 1643 and 1644. Under Polemical Literature the books are chiefly Catholic controversies which reveal what effect the Jansenist fever had on publishing in 1644.

Vanished Books. Louis Jacob's bibliography also tells us something about books which have disappeared, as far as a title can tell us anything.

Latin works	48	Bible	8
French works	118	Theology and polemics	18
	166	Spirituality	65
Folios	11	Liturgical works	23
Quartos	21	History and Law	19
Small format	116	Medicine	3
Uncertain format	18	Science and technology	7
	166	Belles lettres	11
		Schoolbooks	10
		Others	2
			166

Most of the books that have vanished seem to be French and in the smallest sizes, and those in Latin were class books or liturgical works; the folios were usually liturgies or law books, and the quartos newsbooks which must have been very thin. Some Bibles did not survive, and under the heading Theology a great deal of polemical literature, together with the ephemera or anonymous tracts not recorded in the libraries, has never been traced. Liturgical books and schoolbooks were used until worn out, which explains the high figures. Books listed as History included newsbooks and they too were soon expendable, as were tracts under the heading Spirituality, a fact confirmed by the Register of Licences of the Office of the Seal—two-thirds of them were devotional or lives of the saints, if titles are any guide.

1699–1701. In the closing years of the 17th century more books were submitted for licensing in the authorized way, and from 1684 Legal Deposit records were properly kept. In 1700 an inquiry into books actually in the press was mounted by the government. These records make calculations for the latest period more accurate, and the main objective has been to compare figures derived from those sources with books extant in the Bibliothèque Nationale. That is why we have confined research to the Bibliothèque Sainte Geneviève and Bibliothèque de Lyon outside the Nationale, and not included other libraries as previously. Of course, we have used again major bibliographies like Cioranescu.

Comparisons with the evidence from the Inquiry of 1700. The Government questionnaire asked Paris printers to list the titles they had recently issued and those still in the press. Of 48 printers, ten (with 27 presses between them) stated that they had only ordinary jobbing work in progress— depressing testimony to the current recession. Of 140 titles declared, 96 have been positively identified, only seven of which are not in the Bibliothèque Nationale. The groupings are as follows:

Religion	60 (55 in the Bibliothèque Nat.)
Law	7 (5 in the Bibliothèque Nat.)
Belles lettres	11 (11 in the Bibliothèque Nat.)
Science and arts	9 (9 in the Bibliothèque Nat.)
History	9 (9 in the Bibliothèque Nat.)

In some cases the book reported as in the press is not the same edition as the one in the library. Forty-four titles have not been identified, 39 religious works and five schoolbooks or practical manuals. But the records are so brief that accurate identification is not always possible: if five religious books have disappeared, what about the books of hours which were in the press in five of the workshops without any hint as to their contents? And how can Ordinaries of the Mass, Epistles and the Gospels be identified? Nevertheless only a dozen or so titles actually fail to appear in the records.

Legal Deposit. It was of particular interest to trace the

present whereabouts on the shelves of books sent in under
the terms of Legal Deposit:

	Legal Deposit Copies	In the B.N.	Elsewhere	No Trace
1699	94	76	8	10
1700	101	84	2	15
1701	98	75	9	14
	293	**235**	**19**	**39**

In other words, the Bibliothèque Nationale has preserved
four out of five books received under Legal Deposit for the
past 250 years. Thirty-nine of the 293 titles were untraceable
in the Bibliothèque Sainte Geneviève or the Bibliothèque de
Lyon or the bibliographies, which does not mean they have
disappeared without trace; they may be scattered in a
number of libraries, or even miscataloged in the Bibliothèque Nationale.

Register of Licences. The most interesting of the records
are the Registers held by the Stationers' Guild, the official
record of licences granted to printers before they began
printing. Once again, entries are brief, often omitting
authors' names. For our purposes we pinpointed the year
1699, excluding provincial publications, with the following
result:

Listed in the Register	In the B.N.	Other Libraries	Disappeared
124	81	12	29

The vagueness of many of the entries made identification
difficult even where books still survive, and the physical
impossiblity of analyzing the material bookstocks of the
Mazarine and Arsenal libraries explains why about one-
quarter of the books have not been traced. Possibly some
titles, though licensed, were never printed or may have been
printed outside Paris: in 25 cases out of 29 no trace could be
found in the Legal Deposit registers of books licensed
between 1699 and 1701, which again suggests that many
projected titles were never printed.

The table below shows books printed in Paris 1699–1701
which are still extant:

	Titles	Legal Deposit	B.N.	Other Sources
1699	239	94	177	129
1700	247	101	186	147
1701	228	98	163	73

It is difficult to make exact comparisons with the earlier periods since the Mazarine library was excluded and there were no available figures for the old libraries of Troyes and Montpellier, but Legal Deposit was taken into account. In general it was clearly a time of depression for the trade; if copies of the first edition were always sent under the Legal Deposit rules, then these figures are only a partial reflection of actual production, and provincial printers seem to have ignored Legal Deposit—only a few dozen copies were ever sent to Paris each year.

Below is a table divided by subject:

	1699	1700	1701
Bible	15	13	10
Liturgy	7	5	6
Church fathers	3	8	13
Theology	4	5	5
Sermons	7	9	13
Pastoral literature	5	7	5
Polemical literature	5	9	8
Spiritual literature	39	39	43
Religion totals	**85**	**95**	**103**
Canon law	5	6	6
Civil law	13	10	6
Law totals	**18**	**16**	**12**
Church history	17	14	19
Secular history	22	28	17
Non-European history and travel	4	9	6
History totals	**43**	**51**	**42**
Philosophy	4	3	7
Morals, politics	12	18	18
Philology, rhetoric	12	13	10
Grammar	6	3	3
Poetry	7	9	9
Drama	11	14	9
Novel	13	5	3
Belles lettres totals	**65**	**64**	**59**

	1699	*1700*	*1701*
Medicine	11	3	2
Science	4	5	4
Technology	11	12	5
Science totals	**26**	**20**	**11**
Scholar librarians	2	1	1
Heretical works	0	0	0
Grand total	**239**	**247**	**228**
Folios	7	8	6
Quartos	14	25	33
Octavos and smaller sizes	218	204	199
Latin	13	27	18
French	226	220	210
Others	0	0	0

Compared with the table for 1643–45 the percentage of religious works is about the same (49% compared with 48% if we include Church History and Canon Law) but there is a proportional drop in numbers for the closing years of the century. Theology and Polemical Literature were exceptionally high in the 1643/45 period, which would explain the apparent anomaly here, and in 1699/1701, the age of La Bruyère and Bossuet, moralizing, exhortations and sermons were everyday reading.

CHAPTER III

STATISTICS BY SUBJECT

THE BIBLIOTHÈQUE NATIONALE CALL NUMBERS show History, Science and the Arts holding their own, and Law diminishing. Belles Lettres were at their zenith 1636–40 and 1656–60, the second peak followed by a sharp decline, and religious works went on steadily rising, accounting for nearly 50% after 1670.

It must be emphasized again that results are bound to be tentative and counts based on surviving copies in the Bibliothèque Nationale cannot be regarded as definitive. Some help has been derived from the available specialist bibliographies, based on research in their own fields, and in statistics by subject only books reflecting similar interests for the same public are relevant. It would be misleading to include under the same headings learned and popular works; this factor has moderated our aims somewhat.

1. Religious works

In this very wide field we need to be as specific as possible.

1. Bible. The reading of the Bible, once it was widely available in translation, was a problem for the Church and some churchmen were opposed to the idea of any translation. Lelong's bibliography, *Bibliotheca sacra,* begun in the 17th century and continued by others in the 18th century, is a valuable source, and the catalogs of various Paris libraries under the heading "Bible" were a great help in compiling statistics of Bibles published in Paris 1598–1701, either in French or in the learned languages. In the early 17th century they were usually in Latin, with some Greek and other Oriental languages; French translations are few. In the second half there are more French and fewer Latin, though the latter recovered in the last decade of the century.

2. Liturgy. Some recent bibliographies helped, but with the disappearance of so much of the material and much variation in edition runs it was impossible to draw firm conclusions.

3. Patrology. These great works—library fodder if ever there was—have survived in reasonable numbers and accordingly much research has been done on them; hence statistics of production were possible, distinguishing between folios and the small-sized French versions. The most striking feature is the decline of the heavy folios in favor of the small-sized.

4. Theology. So vast is this subject that it would be too much to attempt *in toto;* thus the statistics are confined to the works, and commentaries on the works, of Thomas Aquinas with the help of Mischelitsch's *Kommentatoren zur Summa Theologiae des Thoma von Aquin.* France was easily the leading publisher in this field, centered on Paris and Lyons, while Lyons published a good deal of foreign material, especially Spanish. Paris was always strongly Gallican.

5. Lives of the saints and sermons. Cioranescu's bibliography was the basis, but again the figures must be accepted with caution since so many of the books have vanished.

6. Spiritual Literature. Spiritual and devotional literature rarely survived and for the purposes of this study only Jesuit literature has been noticed, using Sommervogel's *Bibliography of the Society of Jesus.* Production figures of Jesuit spiritual works reveal that from 1645 their influence waned, a fact confirmed by figures for Jesuit books in the Bibliothèque Nationale for the years 1606–15; 1636–45; 1666–75; 1691–1700.

7. Ecclesiastical Writers. The various sects and orders produced their own writers. The Capuchins decline from 1660 to 1700, again confirmed by the Bibliothèque Nationale material. Batterel's *Mémoires domestiques pour servir à l'histoire de l'Oratoire* and Ingold's *Essai de bibliographie oratorienne* prove that the Oratory shone most brightly at the end of the century. For other orders there is less evidence, and the books in the Bibliothèque Nationale were used as a control for the years 1660–1700 to compare them with the Jesuits. The Carmelites were less and less in evidence, and Franciscans and Dominicans produce less, especially from 1675. The Benedictines, because of Maurist and Augustinian writings, rise steadily. Church dignitaries were always fertile with the pen, especially in mid-century, and there was a plenitude of books signed by people calling themselves "abbé," a qualification which needs to be examined.

2. Science and Geography

This subject is not easy to express statistically because in its early days, Science hardly deserves the modern label. Three fairly distinct categories emerge:

1. Medicine. Remarkably well represented in the Bibliothèque Nationale with a subject catalog specially devoted to it (*Bibliothèque Impériale. Catalogue des Sciences Médicales.* 1857–73). The trend was from early folios in Latin to small French works.

2. Occult Sciences. Caillet's *Manuel bibliographique des sciences psychiques ou occultes* (1913) is a good basis. A steady rise in each five-year period until 1630, after which it declines.

3. Travels. A very interesting subject with a great deal surviving in all the major libraries, enabling a full picture to be drawn of public taste and curiosity anent foreign countries.

3. Literature

Statistics in this field are more dependable and reveal quite vividly the rise and fall in different classes of literature.

1. Drama. The books in the Bibliothèque Nationale are in substantial agreement about the rise of tragedy and tragicomedy during 1630–50, the age of Corneille and his followers, and especially the comedy of Molière in the years 1660–70. One reason for the low figures in the early years of the century is that the sources used were entirely based on Paris, and many plays were printed in the provinces, Rouen in particular.

2. Poetry. Books in the Bibliothèque Nationale and Arsenal show that the popularity of poetry from 1646 to 1650 continues in 1671–75, especially burlesque and heroic verse, while neo-Latin poetry was continuously fashionable.

3. The Novel. R. C. Williams's *Bibliography of the 17th century novel in France* includes first editions of French novels published in the provinces and abroad as well as in Paris, revealing the growth in the publication of novels from Paris on the basis of Bibliothèque Nationale holdings, with reprints.

4. Moralistic Works. Based on Toinet's *Les écrivains moralistes au 17 siècle.*

5. Funeral Orations. Cioranescu was useful, and he includes books with fewer than 48 pages. The popularity of this genre and the one above suggests a France increasingly pietistic and conventionally devout in the late 17th century.

The novel was growing in popularity by 1620–30, tragedy and tragicomedy in 1630–50, poetry and comedy 1645–75, and then in the last years there was a split in taste between those who preferred uplifting tracts and those who liked novels. The first peak coincides with Corneille's plays, the second with Molière and contemporary poets. The fall at the end of the century is due to the exclusion of novels published abroad and of sermons and funeral orations traditionally classed as "Religion" and "Science and Arts."

6. Translations. Cioranescu proves that after 1640 original works were read more in translation, less in their own language, whether Classics or the Church Fathers. But after 1650, Spanish and Italian were less popular as French literature attained its majority, and by the end of the century Latin had lost some of its prestige. It is the start of the Battle of the Books, Ancient and Modern.

Conclusion

From various sources a coherent picture of the growth in the book trade shows two distinct chronological periods, the first up to 1643/45, a peak period in productivity and a time of intellectual crisis, and the second subdivided into two distinct phases, 1645–1661/71, a period of prosperity, and 1670–1700, a period of depression. The trend in physical formats is away from heavy folios and towards light, pocket-sized books, in French.

But can we simply add up the books from all these sources and come to acceptable conclusions? More is needed: from the economic standpoint the statistics would be affected by factors such as size, number of pages, the technical quality, edition sizes; from the sociological standpoint something more definite than merely adding one vaguely defined class of books to another is required when each book's individual conception and its readership will differ so much. Statistics can only be a basis for a hypothesis and still need to be subjected to as thorough a critical analysis as possible using all the documentary aids available. That is the object of the following pages.

PART TWO
THE PARISIAN BOOK TRADE
IN THE AGE OF
CHRISTIAN HUMANISM
1598–1643

FIRST SECTION
STOCKTAKING

CHAPTER I

THE ARSENAL OF THE CATHOLIC REFORMATION

ONE-THIRD OF ALL BOOKS printed in Paris between 1598 and 1643 were connected with religion, so that the first problem was to categorize so wide a field by more specific subjects and investigate the readership. There were three main types of religious literature: the Bible, liturgical texts, and theology, mostly published in huge folio volumes intended for a restricted scholarly public. There was also a large output of "spiritual" works in French, of small size and regularly reprinted, and finally there was a mixed group, chiefly polemical: tracts against Protestants or internal arguments within the Church, or apologetics written to persuade or denounce freethinkers and rationalists. The three main groups reflect the religious preoccupations of the age quite accurately and offer a useful framework for research. This chapter deals with fundamental dogmatics, religious practice and theology—the books which could be described as the arsenal of the Counter Reformation or Catholic Reformation.

1. Official texts: Bibles and liturgical works

The Bible comes first, in its original form, Hebrew, Greek, Latin. The Fathers were concerned to ban any versions which did not uphold orthodoxy, and Pope Sixtus V and Clement VIII forbade any version other than the Vulgate. How far did they manage to have their decrees carried out in France, with the help of the King and Clergy? What consequences did such a strict policy have on the study of the Scriptures in which the French excelled in the 16th century? How far did authorized versions spread? These are the questions we need to answer.

Any study of Bible publication in the early 17th century shows that none of the 16th-century editions were reprinted even in a revised or expurgated form (one exception was a Greek New Testament published in 1642, based on Robert Estienne's, at the Imprimerie Royale). Instead a Polyglot Bible in ten volumes was published, something quite new. Jean Morin, a member of the Oratory congregation of priests, prepared the text, assisted by the Maronites Sionita and Hesronita, Abraham Echellensis and scholars like Godefroi Hermant, Peiresc and Harlay de Sancy. Antoine Vitré completed publication in 1645. The Paris Polyglot was no mere copy of Plantin's Antwerp Polyglot but included Chaldean paraphrases, and was a significant landmark because it received strong support from the French Clergy. They wanted a worthy instrument for use by exegetists, and to show that they were not overawed (as the Preface reveals) by the authority of the Vulgate, which may partly explain why the oriental types cut for the Polyglot were not used in Catholic propaganda in the Middle East.

Jean Morin put out an authorized text of the Septuagint in Greek with a Latin translation, in 1628, and with notes summarizing variants in the Vulgate, an edition not published until 1641. The Vulgate was reprinted twelve times between 1629 and 1658, and the New Testament seven times, the Vulgate widely distributed in France from Lyons and in conformity with Papal ordinances, and in a special edition with glossary for the use of theologians. Only a few privileged publishers were permitted this sanction: Cramoisy, Maturas, Vitré and Huré, all of Paris.

Of the Bibles in French, one-half were Calvinist, allowed under the Edict of Nantes. The Catholic translation followed the Louvain version, a corrected version of the Genevan Bible by Nicolas de Leuze and Francois de Larben, published 1550, and it's odd that the Catholic Church, so urgent for the Vulgate as the authentic text, should use a faulty French translation, rigid and archaic. Pierre de Besse (1608), Jean-Claude Deville (1613), Frizon (1621) and François

Véron (1646) claimed they had improved the text to accord more closely with the Vulgate, and even plumed themselves on having made an entirely new translation, something the evidence of the text contradicts; it only confirms that the translators, all militant churchmen, were anxious to justify Catholic doctrine vis-à-vis Calvinism and took liberties with the text, as for instance in Acts where they speak of the Apostles "saying Mass"!

To appeal to readers from different classes, various formats were used for the Bible. For the upper class reader great folio volumes, richly illustrated, sometimes with a secular flavor to the pictures—what we should call Library Editions, prestige publications. The New Testament was usually in small format, Catholic publishers copying the pocket Bibles favored by Protestants, aiming to reach as many of the faithful as possible. Subsequent work has enabled us to add more to Father Lelong's census of early Bibles: three editions of the Louvain and Vulgate parallel versions, a further eight or nine editions of the Louvain Bible and eight of the New Testament, all published in the first half of the 17th century; altogether there were about thirty complete Louvain Bibles and the same number of New Testaments, more of them from Rouen and Lyons than from Paris. Probably many French Bibles in small sizes have perished, because the *Imitation of Christ* and other popular devotional literature survived in fair numbers, and there is no reason to think that one should survive and the others not, except by chance.

Fewer Bibles were printed in Paris before 1650 than after, and it would seem that translations were uncommon in the France of the Counter Reformation. The very fact that the version available was the Louvain Bible betrays a motive that was simply controversial, yet it would be wrong to conclude that this was mere reactionary policy of the Church to keep the Bible out of the hands of the masses since paraphrases were common. Yet the ordinary Catholic did not study his religion by intensive reading of Scripture alone: one effect of the vicious polemics between Catholic and Protestant over the previous century was to make the pious look to other sources for spiritual refreshment, less severely rational and more emotional.

After the Bible, service books. The Council of Trent instituted reforms in them and Rome decreed that all dioceses and orders must use the revised version unless they had adopted their own for more than two hundred years; for everyone else the Roman use was mandatory. The monastic breviary and missal were revised in 1612 and 1614, the Roman breviary and missal twice revised, first by Clement VIII and the second by Urban VIII, with new editions of the breviary in 1602 and 1631 and the missal in 1604 and 1634, and other liturgical works followed. The Tridentine reforms meant wholesale revision of missals, ceremonials and antiphonars throughout Catholic Europe—so much work for the book trade, as our bibliographies disclose: 11 editions of the reformed breviary were published by Kerver, 1572–85, and five by the Compagnie des Usages, 1586–98. From then until 1617 the second version of the breviary, and another printed by La Noue in 1625, and seven editions of the third version were published by the Compagnie des Usages, 1634–56. Twenty editions of the first revised version were published by Kerver, and after 1585 by the Compagnie des Usages. The second version of the missal appeared in six editions, 1605–33, and the third was published by Soly (1640), d'Hauteville (1647), the Imprimerie Royale (1647) and Clopejeau (1649). The Compagnie des Usages put out a luxury edition of the Ceremonial (1633) and the Antiphonar (1647). Very few service books were printed in the provinces and evidently the Compagnie des Usages enjoyed a monopoly in some prayerbooks as the "cum privilegio Regis et D. N. Pontificis" on the title page proves, for the period before 1614 and after 1631.

The print runs must have been very large, yet most have disappeared. Louis Jacob's bibliography lists several for the period 1643–53 of which no trace remains, and the Inquest of 1644 gives evidence of some haste to print a great quantity of service books because no fewer than four presses were then in process of printing the breviary, and Vitré the printer tells us that the Compagnie des Usages employed between forty and fifty men working on twelve to fifteen presses, so clearly Paris was busy producing the required material although this is not reflected in the pitiful number of copies that survive.

Service books of the Papal (Ultramontane) party and those peculiar to individual dioceses were published in Paris; Paris had its own use and Raulin Thierry and Eustache Foucault published three editions of it (1615–23); Cramoisy and others printed four editions of the breviary and two of the diurnal, two of ritual and one of the missal (1636–55). Provincial clerics ordered their service books from Thierry, Foucault, Cottereau, Février, Béchet, Hénault and Vitré, and the orders from monasteries were even larger. Billaine printed many editions of the Benedictine breviary, and the Cistercians ordered eight editions of their breviary from Cramoisy, and four of the missal, copies of which survive today; Cramoisy also published for the Praemonstratensians. The new regime in prayerbooks resulting from the Tridentine reforms was big business for Paris, though it was not as large a center as Venice or Antwerp (but ahead of Rome and Cologne). The bibliographical evidence is enough to allow a realistic assessment of the volume of business despite the loss of most of the books themselves.

2. The return to tradition: Patrology

The Council of Trent insisted that the Tradition of the Church was as important as the Bible itself as a source of revealed religion, and one consequence was publication of the texts of the Fathers and the whole canon of fundamental theology. French scholars edited and wrote commentaries on the texts and the first systematic collection of Patristic writings came from Paris where a consortium of booksellers was specially licensed to publish or reprint similar material first published in Rome or Antwerp. The scholars of Louvain became immersed in the Molinist controversy, and quit work on the Patristic texts, the Vatican experts gradually dispersed and the Vatican Printing House almost ceased production. Sixtus V's publishing program was unfinished and many of the Greek Fathers went unedited, but Paris was meanwhile issuing hundreds of folio volumes of Patristic studies. It was the main center of such expertise, bigger than Cologne, Antwerp or Venice. The leading Paris publishers specialized in reprints: Du Puis, Sonnius, Chaudière, Soly, Claude

Morel, Sébastien Cramoisy, and the two largest congers, the Compagnie de la Ville and Compagnie du Navire, founded in 1586, published thirty monumental works, perhaps a hundred folio volumes. The Jesuits were the force behind this concentration of effort: Fronton Du Duc, Jacques Sirmond, Denis Petau, Philippe Garnier, Pierre Poussines, Jean Poulain and Balthasar Cordier; all except the last were connected with Clermont College, whose librarian was Fronton Du Duc. A word must be said about their prodigious energy. Fronton Du Duc, despite failing health, made notes and an intensive study of the Greek Fathers, particularly Clement of Alexandria, Basil, Gregory of Nazianza and Gregory of Nyssa; he prepared Byzantine authors for the press and revised a Greek version of John Chrysostom as well as translating it into Latin. Chrysostom's *Opera omnia* was first published in six folio volumes in 1613 and came out at regular intervals from 1609 to 1624, when Du Duc died. The last six volumes appeared in 1636 when the first six were reprinted.

Petau, Garnier, Cordier and Poussines worked on other Greek texts which the Roman Church thought essential to its case. Petau edited Epiphanius with a Latin translation (1622) and an edition of Synesius of Cyrene went into three editions (1612–32), and Cordier produced a Latin edition of Pseudo-Dionysius (1644) which he had published in Antwerp ten years before. Sirmond, Secretary to the General of the Jesuits (Acquaviva), collaborated with Baronius, Bellarmine and Tolet in editing a vast edition of the French Councils of the Church as well as various medieval churchmen. And the Jesuits were equally busy in other fields: Father Fronteau, for instance, a canon-regular of St. Geneviève, edited the works of Yves de Chartres, and Aubert, a canon of the Eglise de Paris, published an edition of Cyril of Alexandria in 1638, while Gabriel de l'Aubespine, bishop of Orleans, and a Capuchin, Georges d'Amiens, brought out an annotated edition of Tertullian.

Little more need be added except to say that laymen were also interested in pure literature, André Du Chesne editing Abelard (1616) and Alcuin (1617); and Nicolas Rigault, the peerless editor of Tertullian, Cyprian and Minucius Felix, was himself a layman, one of the scholarly circle around President de Thou and the brothers Dupuy and an old friend of Casaubon, engaged as a librarian in the Bibliothèque Royale before becoming a councillor in the Parlement and later a high official. His annotations included some dubious opinions on infant baptism and on the relationship between priests and laity; perhaps today we would not grow so indignant at a suggestion that Christ was ugly (he wrote a tract on this subject) but views like this explain the Church's anxiety to keep tight control over studies of this kind and why the Jesuits were involved.

Tertullian was the most favored author: three or four reprints of his huge output appeared between 1580 and 1600 in Paris and continued on into the 17th century. Sonnius in 1608 reprinted Latino's revision of Pamele's edition of 1598 and two folio volumes of commentary on Tertullian by the Spanish Jesuit La Cerda in 1624 and 1630. The Compagnie du Navire reprinted this in 1641 and Nicolas Rigault published a recension in 1634, revised in 1641 and later reprinted four times, 1644–58, which did not prevent Father Georges d'Amiens editing yet more Tertullian in 1646 and 1650. Moreover, individual works of his were published, the *Apologetics* and *De Pallio* separately, and Didier Hérauld's edition of the *Apologetics* was published by Adrian Périer; Marsillius edited the *De Pallio* in 1614 and it was in a recension by Claude Saumaise attacking Petau in 1622. Other titles published were *De Spectaculis* and *Libri duo ad nationes*.

It was probably Tertullian's literary qualities which contributed to this spate of publication, but others of the most prominent Fathers were equally accessible in print—Basil, Gregory of Nazianza, John Chrysostom and Athanasius of the Greeks, and Ambrose, Jerome, and Gregory the Great of the Roman church. Augustine we shall examine later.

Basil first: apart from the 16th-century editions deriving from Erasmus's (Froben, 1532) and the other 17th-century specialists, Graevius, Riscus and Masius, the complete works published in Paris in the early 17th century were a Latin edition from Sonnius (1603) and a Greek edition with Latin translation, the work of Du Duc and Morel (1618), with a reprint in 1638. Two editions of Gregory of Nazianza were published in Paris; two editions of John Chrysostom by Du Duc, and two inferior editions by Nivelle in 1581 and 1588. A Latin translation of Athanasius (1608) incorporating corrections from a Greek version edited by a group of Protestant scholars was reissued in 1612 and reprinted in 1627 with the Greek text revised by Du Duc.

Of the Latin Fathers, Ambrose was issued by the Compagnie du Navire several times between 1603 and 1643. Three reprints of Jerome's works were issued (1608, 1624 and 1643) apart from his *Letters,* all by the Compagnie de la Ville de Paris, and the rival Compagnie du Navire published an edition based on the Rome edition, 1605–19 and again in 1640.

These huge and sprawling works enjoyed wide success, with Clement of Alexandria, Pseudo-Dionysius, Origen, Eusebius, Gregory of Nyssa and Synesius the favorites among the Greek Fathers, and Tertullian, Minucius Felix and Cyprian among the Latin, along with Leo the Great, Gregory the Great, Prosper d'Aquitaine, Anselm and Bernard. In all, the earliest Fathers were of most interest, especially the Latin Fathers, partly because of their Latinity but also because they represented a fusion of Christian and Classical culture, and their apologetics in an age of pagan classical scepticism exactly suited the needs of a church faced in the 17th century with the rise of modern rationalism. The mystics were also of great appeal, as the popularity of Pseudo-Denis, Anselm and St. Bernard testifies; Jerome was much studied and so was John Chrysostom, a pacifying influence after the Council of Chalcedon, soothing to the strife–torn 17th century.

A word about St. Augustine and his immense influence on Jansen, Saint-Cyran and Arnauld, the founders of the Jansenist sect. The authorized edition was edited by scholars of Louvain and published by Plantin, 1576/7, to be reprinted by the Compagnie du Navire several times between 1586 and 1637, the *City of God* and the *Confessions* twice (though this is well below Tertullian). Between 1580 and 1600 translations of the major Patristic texts were published steadily to confute

Protestant arguments, though this was contrary to the later intentions of the Counter Reformation, which sought to cool things, one reason why translations of the Fathers dwindle after 1600; the most exhaustive research has brought to light only a few dozen translations in the period 1598–1643.

Translations from the Greek Fathers continued, notably by Fédéric Morel II, concentrating on dogma, useful in the fight against Protestantism, but apart from Du Perron's translation of some Jerome letters and Father Morin's paraphrase of the *History of the deliverance of the Christian Church by the Emperor Constantine,* and some renderings of Chrysostom and Cyril, French versions become rarer. Augustine was not often put into French, though Saint-Cyran did a translation of *Holy Virginity,* and indeed the paucity of French versions is in striking contrast to the heavy industry invested in the Fathers. A large section of clerical opinion not only sought support from the Fathers but in the early Councils of the Church. Sirmond published a massive edition of the French Councils, and Father Labbe of the General Councils in 44 volumes in 1644 from the Imprimerie Royale. The corpus of canonical writings was published in Paris (1610–24), and two huge editions of the *Bibliotheca patrum,* which illustrates the progress of Patristic scholarship.

The interesting question is: how did Paris booksellers finance such gigantic enterprises? And where was the public rich enough and interested enough to want such bulky folios?

3. Theological Revival: Ultramontane influences

Renewed interest in theology was a concomitant of this basic reappraisal of the Church's validity, notably through the evangelism of the Jesuits, at first chiefly by preaching but later committed to print as manuals which later became classics of the Counter Reformation.

Apart from polemics, Jesuits' writings may be grouped as Biblical commentaries, scholarly works, and Moral Theology. They took the lead in Bible study with books by their most learned men, Francesco de Toledo, Salmerón, Maldonado, Pineda, Ribera, Pereyra, Prado, Luis d'Alcazar. Their works were available all over Europe and were kept

continually in print, particularly Maldonado's, whose commentary on the Gospels was first published at Pont-à-
Mousson in 1598 and reissued in Paris many times from 1617
to 1651. His commentaries on Jeremiah, Baruch, Ezekiel
and Daniel based on lecture notes made at Lyons in 1608
were published in Paris in 1611, and Cramoisy published his
*Commentarii e praecipuis Sacrae Scripturae libris Veteris
Testamenti.* The fact that Maldonado taught at Paris may
explain this output but other presses were also printing
commentaries—*Commentaria in XII capita Sancti Jesu
Christi. D. N. Evangelii secundum Lucam* by Francisco de
Toledo (Rome, 1660) were reprinted by the Compagnie du
Navire; Juan de Pineda's commentaries on Job and Ecclesi-
astes were published by Mathurin Du Puis, Sébastien
Cramoisy and Ambroise Drouart (1619, 1631), and Ribera's
Commentarii in duodecim Prophetarum libros by Denis
Langlois (1611). Two Dominican scholars, Jérome de Azam-
buja and Luis de Sotomayor, were also published currently in
Paris, and in Lyons Spanish theology was widely published.

As the new theology moved outside Spain another generation of scholars went into print, almost all Jesuits, but more
concerned with coordinating than innovating. Cramoisy
issued Bonfrere's commentaries on Joshua, Judges and Ruth
(1631) and Cardon at Lyons published Giustiniani's and
Lorini's works, while Edme Martin, Cramoisy's cousin,
reprinted a whole series of commentaries by the Jesuit
Serarius, first published in Mainz (1609–10). A Fleming,
Cornelius Van den Steen, Saint Cyran's teacher at Louvain,
wrote countless commentaries on virtually the whole Bible,
arranging previous commentators' work and stressing the
allegorical meaning to help preachers preparing sermons and
writers composing books on spiritual themes. His *Commentaria in omnes Sancti Pauli epistolas* (Antwerp, 1614) was
reprinted in Paris several times between 1621 and 1633, and
his *Commentaria in Pentateuchum Moysis* (Antwerp, 1616)
was likewise reissued many times.

With the exception of Bonfrère of Douai and Lorini of
Avignon the French were sadly deficient in such studies.
Rangeuil published two books on Kings (1621 and 1624) and
André Alleret, a colleague, two volumes of notes on the

Bible; Gilles Camart contributed a commentary on Aelian's history, and there were commentaries on individual books of the Bible by the Jesuits Phélippeau and Lombard, Boulduc, a Capuchin, and Jean de la Haye, but nothing comparable to the Spanish school. The French were more interested in philology and textual criticism—the Polyglot Bible is an example—and their scholars at the Sorbonne and Collège Royal, Valérien de Flavigny, Gilles de Muis and Simon Marotte, were expert in Hebrew, preparing the ground for Richard Simon later. Most French scholars in the field of Biblical exegesis were more involved in amplifying Scriptural meaning, aiming to provide paraphrases and commentaries in French for the layman; Pierre Maucorps, Pierre Gorse and Bernardin de Monetreul were actively engaged in this work from 1630 to 1660.

Pierre de Besse included Bible commentary in the sermons he published and did a revised translation of the Louvain Bible; abbé Guillebert edited a Scriptural paraphrase; Antoine Godeau paraphrased St. Paul and the Psalms and planned to translate the New Testament; Pierre Bardin, of the Académie Française, took part in evangelical work by distilling the moral teachings of the Bible into a number of popular books. Paris was busy reprinting this great mass of Jesuit literature in the early 17th century, with Lyons a close second, specializing in Italian and Spanish authors; Paris naturally inclined towards the north, Flanders and Germany. It is interesting that original works of scholarship were fewer in the 17th century than in the late 16th, particularly in France. It seems that the age of the popularizer had arrived.

Works by the great medieval Schoolmen underwent a revival in the 16th century when Rome proclaimed Thomas Aquinas and Bonaventura Doctors of the Church and arranged for the publication of their complete works by the Vatican publishing house. Countless commentaries from Spain appeared, all on Aquinas, and attempts at a total synthesis of Church dogma which immediately provoked controversy. Aquinas was published at Paris (the *Summa theologica* [1608]) and the Douai theologians issued a recension in 1617 and 1639; Pelé published the *Opuscula* in

1634 and although Aquinas' complete works were never published in Paris, Denis Moreau, who had the licence to publish Aquinas, started an edition in 1636, not new but using the best version of existing work. Very few commentaries on Aquinas were published in Paris: Ruiz de Montoya wrote one, published by Cramoisy in 1629, and Rossi, an Italian, and two Flemings, Gilles de Coninck and Gilles Moerasius, wrote others; and there was Martin van den Beek's *Summa theologiae scholasticae,* not strictly on Aquinas' *Summa* but popular because it was a manual and the author a famous controversialist.

A number of new works appeared: Philippe de Gamaches and André Du Val of the University of Paris, and Nicolas Isambert of the Collège Royal published some of their lectures, and Philippe Moncé, a Jesuit, brought out his *Disputationes theologicae in aliquot selectas quaestiones;* Louis Le Mairat, another Jesuit, the *Disputationes in Summam D. Thomas;* and François Penon, a Dominican, the *Hymnus angelicus, sive Doctoris Angelici,* a title which is almost poetic.

Other Schoolmen were studied, too: Estius's commentaries on Peter Lombard's *Sententiae,* Duns Scotus, very little on Bonaventura, some original research by Martin Meurisse, Claude Le Petit, Pierre de Saint-Joseph, Guillaume Gibieuf of the Oratory and Eustache de Saint-Paul, using new critical methods rather than those of the Middle Ages. The arguments about the nature of Grace which split Italy, Spain and Flanders made no impression in Paris, and in commentaries on Aquinas the capital ranked only eighth in volume of work, about the same as Madrid and Coimbra's presses. Lyons was easily first, with twice as many as Venice and far ahead of Mainz, Salamanca or Rome, and if Thomist studies in general are estimated, then Cardon of Lyons was the specialist publisher *par excellence.* Perhaps there were fewer editions of the *Summa* than in Paris but Jammy, a Dominican, did a *Compendium* and then edited 21 folio volumes of Albertus Magnus and the *Bonavantura Bonaventurae,* an attempt to reconcile Bonaventura's and Aquinas's systems by Bonaventura de Langres. Théophile Raynaud published most of his huge output in Lyons, which was the main market for Italy and Spain. Commentaries by the Dominicans Alvarez, Ledesma and Jean de Saint Thomas, the Jesuits Suarez, Vasquez, Molina, Oviedo, Ruiz de Montoya, Lugo and Valentia, and the Italian authorities, Fasolo, Ragusa, Bubalus and Pallavicino, were all published at Lyons, as well as the theology taught at Salamanca University and by Arriaga, a Jesuit teaching at Prague. The Jesuits must have preferred their manuscripts to be published in Lyons, for Suarez personally negotiated with Cardon, and the Jesuits who taught at St. Isidore College in Rome and edited Duns Scotus's complete works under Lucas Wadding's direction employed a Lyons bookseller, Louis Durand. Provincial towns like Rennes, Rouen, Poitiers, Grenoble, Bordeaux and Toulouse also published this kind of material, which depicts a marked difference between the provinces and cautious Paris.

The Counter Reformation made a great contribution to Moral Theology and Casuistry; Aquinas' *Summa* begot many theoretical studies, notably in the delicate area of Penance so heavily attacked by the Protestants. An ignorant priesthood administering sacraments to a superstitious laity was an embarrassment to the Church, and Dominicans, Jesuits and Franciscans began to teach moral theology methodically, the Jesuits founding Chairs in the subject, and by the later 16th century it was an independent subject inspired more by theology than Canon Law. With parish clergy needing more instruction about such things as confession, manuals of practical morality were written which tried to determine matters of conscience more precisely, the beginnings of that branch of study known as Casuistry, the difficult art of judging who is the sinner, and it developed subtleties which shocked traditionalists.

The earliest manual used at Salamanca was Martín de Azpilcueta's *Enchiridion sive Manuale confessariorum et penitentium,* frequently reissued in Paris, and a Franciscan, Jean Benedicti, wrote a book based on it called *Somme des péchés et le remède d'iceux,* reprinted 1539, 1599, 1600 and 1602, an interesting proof that French was used for this type of book, possibly because more and more priests were ignorant of Latin. At a time when Protestantism was stressing the importance of vernacular languages Gregory XIII authorized translations of Azpilcueta's manual. Yet Latin manuals were in circulation, too: Azor, a Spanish Jesuit, was published in Paris a year after he was published in Rome (1600); Laymann, a German, published his *Theologia moralia* in Munich in 1625, and it was reprinted in Paris (1627 and 1630), and Bonacina of Milan likewise in 1634 and 1645. Lessius, author of *De justitia et jure,* on abstract justice and human rights, and other works not in the field of moral theology, found no interest among Paris presses, apart from *Opusculum asceticum,* a devotional tract.

Other little manuals for the use of confessors were available: Manoel Sa's *Aphorismi confessariorum* and Francisco de Toledo's *Compendium Summae casuum conscientiae.* Again, Lyons was much more productive than Paris, with Azor, Laymann, Francesco de Toledo, Sa, Fernandez de Moure and Diana always in print; Tomás Sanchez's *Opus morale in praesenta Decalogi* (1613) appeared the same year in Madrid and was reissued in Lyons seven more times before 1660, and another Lyons publisher, Prost, brought out the same author's *Opuscula sive Concilia moralia* in 1625, probably from student notes. Italian and Spanish authors sent their work to Lyons as its reputation grew in this subject, men like Bonacina, Filliucci, Castro Palao, Lugo and Escobar.

An army of foreign casuistical writers poured into France, causing Pascal to ask in his *Lettres provinciales* if they were Christian, so odd did their names sound to French ears! Lyons and to a lesser extent Paris profited by this invasion, yet French moralists were few, apart from Bauny, Raynaud, and Regnault, whose *Praxis fori poenitentialis confessarii* (Lyons, 1616) was enormously successful.

So by the end of the 16th century most casuistical literature was in French: Benedicti's treatise, *Somme des péchés,* was reissued many times, and the French abridgment of Azpilcueta's manual; Loarte's *Miroir ou l'Instruction des Prêtres et confesseurs* (1605), originally published in Latin at Parma; a translation of Sa's *Aphorismi,* at first condemned by the Holy See, then corrected; and a tract wrongly ascribed to Maldonado, who had condemned Sa's first version. The Franciscan Villalobos and Regnault appeared in French, and many other French manuals for the clergy, but it was a delicate subject vulnerable to condemnation, as Milhard's *Grande guide des curés, vicaires et confesseurs* was by the Faculty of Theology in 1619. Father Bauny's *Somme des péchés qui se commettent en tous estatz* caused difficulties since it was intended for the laity as well as clergy, but it was reissued many times in Paris (1633–43), in Lyons twice, 1636 and 1646, and in Rouen in 1643. Its career was interrupted by a triple condemnation—by the Vatican, by the Sorbonne and by the Assemblée du Clergé de France—this stormy little book which exasperated official critics already outraged by the lax tendencies of other casuists.

As theology grew more profound and esoteric, what provision was there for children and adults in Catholic faith and morals? The Council of Trent emphasized the need for elementary instruction and sponsored a Roman catechism for priests which was not published in French until 1670. The Jesuit Canisius produced a catechism which sold well but was only infrequently reissued in French, and Bellarmine's Great and Little Catechism also appeared in French. The bishops asked for French catechisms but many of the "Institutions of a Christian" and "Instruction for Christians" were for parish priests and curés, teachers' manuals with lessons for reading aloud or homilies with questions and answers; children hardly ever used them, and it was only in the mid-17th century that oral catechism ceased to be the chief source of instruction.

CHAPTER II

THE LITERATURE OF THE CATHOLIC RENAISSANCE

MANY DEVOTIONAL BOOKS and books of "spirituality" were published from 1570 to 90 after a decline from 1540 to 70. The siege of Paris and other political events interrupted the revival in the years 1590–1600 but for fifty years thereafter there was a growing fashion for asceticism, mysticism, meditation, lives of the saints and prayers of all kinds. The 17th century is sometimes called the century of saints and the literature certainly justifies the label—innumerable books of piety and devotion were on sale, material which recent research has been focussing on to add to abbé Bremond's early studies in his *Histoire littéraire du sentiment religieux*. It would be inappropriate to discuss the genesis of this or that doctrine here; rather, we shall survey the literature which came from Paris presses between 1598 and 1643 and, using it as a guide, estimate the depth and vigor of the revival to judge what kinds of books the public for the subject actually read.

1. Authors in the spiritual tradition

Apart from the Bible and the Fathers, French spiritual literature in the first half of the 17th century derived from medieval mysticism, although Ludolph of Chartres *Vita Christi* and Voragine's *Légende dorée* were not issued after 1600. Works by the School of St. Victor, at least Hugues and Richard de Saint-Victor (recommended by Father Joseph, Richelieu's famous *éminence grise,* as good reading for his Capuchins), were reissued in Rouen and the medieval mystics were frequently translated. Denis the Carthusian was

88

not so often in print in the 16th century but some of his writings were translated into French, as were Lansperge and the classics of the Benedictines, Franciscans and Dominicans, particularly St. Gertrude, St. Brigid, Catherine of Siena and St. Vincent Ferrier, and later Catherine of Genoa. At a time when France was covered with monasteries the rules and councils of the great religious orders were all in print. The Rhine-Flemish school of mystics was prominent, more so in Paris than the Italians or Spaniards, though Ruysbroek was not, and Suso was rarely printed. Gerard Groot, Florentius Radewijns, Gerard von Zerbolt and Jan Mombaer were not generally available and Henri d'Harp, once a big influence, was in decline. Thomas à Kempis' *Imitatio Christi* was hugely popular as was Pseudo-Tauler (though under suspicion since Luther expressed admiration of him), but all was well in 1622 when a Latin edition of Louis de Blois' works came out, and he was the Benedictine who secured Tauler's rehabilitation; his *Institutio spiritualis* was put into French with a variety of titles.

Many of the classics of spirituality read in the 16th century retained a readership and others failed to do so, some were known only to a few, some enjoyed a revival in the later 17th century and even in the 19th century. The works most frequently printed are those sponsored by the new orders, the Capuchins or Jesuits that is, in closest affinity with the spirit of the Counter Reformation.

2. St. Teresa and the Spanish tradition: from Luis de Granada to St. John of the Cross

Luis de Granada's writings were tolerated by the Inquisition because he was concerned with the initial experience on the spiritual path, not on the state of the illuminati, and they had much success in France. Cardinal du Perron, Sébastien Hardy, René Gaultier and Simon Martin translated his work afresh and the *Oeuvres spirituelles* appeared in a large folio published in Paris and Rouen many times. French versions of his *Traité de l'oraison et méditation, des Lieux communs et discours spirituels, du Mémorial de la vie chrétienne* and of his *Grande guide des pécheurs* and other works were constantly in demand. John of Avila's *Epître spirituelle* was widely read and, soon after, Pedro de Alcantara summarized Luis de Granada's teaching in his *Traité de l'oraison et méditation,* to which he added his own testimony to the validity of mystical experience.

St. Teresa was the main channel through which the new school of Spanish mystics entered France. She and her companions and advisers helped overcome the doubts expressed by Spanish theologians about mysticism but permission to publish her writings was only given after her death, the most ascetic, *The way of perfection* being the first, at Evora in 1583. The Augustinian Luis de Leon was first published in 1588 when there were a number of reformed Carmelite monasteries in Spain (the first convent of barefoot Carmelites was at Darvelo in 1568) and when they were founded at Genoa in 1590 by Nicolas Doria there was no need to enlist printing to help spread the Teresan reforms in Spain or Italy. In France the case was different, and a Frenchman, Jean de Quintanadoine de Bretigny, in touch with the reformed Carmelites since 1585, financed the first edition of St. Teresa's works and later two translations assisted by Dom Chèvre, a life of Teresa by Ribera, and another edition of her works. In 1605 the first nuns of the reformed Carmelite order were in Paris thanks to Bérulle's diplomacy, but his thought was closer to the Northern school than the Spanish, and Madame Acarie was at first surprised that Teresa's works were read, while the Spanish nuns were shocked by the abstract nature of the prayers offered by their French sisters, and this is where translations become interesting because they were the means by which Teresa's teaching was mediated in France. Ribera's *Vie de la Mère Thérèse de Jésus* was incessantly reprinted between 1601 (2nd ed.) and 1645, and in Brussels, Antwerp, Lyons and Arras; according to L'Estoile it was "the Bible of the bigots." Teresa's own writings were published in Paris in 1601, 1621, 1623 and 1632, and in Lyons (1616, 1629, 1628); in 1630 Elisée de St. Bernard translated them again and Cyprien de la Nativité de la Vierge in 1644, regularly reprinted. Teresa evidently found a wide following in France between 1617 and 1630, which must have led to friction between the more traditional, impersonal disciplines and the highly charged emotional approach of Teresa and her pupils.

St. John of the Cross was known in France before his work appeared in manuscript or print. Madame Acarie had read *Mount Carmel* before she died, while René Gaultier began his translation of it in 1621 before the Spanish version came out, and the *Cantique spirituel* was published in Paris before the Spanish, so that interest was shown in him even though nothing else appeared until 1641 when Cyprian issued a fine edition. Generally speaking, however, St. John did not grip the attention of readers as did Teresa.

3. Capuchin Literature: Benet of Canfield to Yves de Paris

The Capuchins and Jesuits, newly founded orders rather more active than contemplative, also fostered spiritual literature; the Capuchins were introduced to Paris in the reign of Henri III and so were politically suspect in the eyes of Henri IV. Nevertheless they published as much in the latter's reign as in the time of Richelieu and Father Joseph, and from their convent in the Rue St. Honoré they were in touch with their Italian brethren and collaborated in translating Bernardino da Balbano, Mattia Bellintani da Salò and Giovanni da Fano, and after 1600 they published their own work. Father Benet of Canfield was author of a *Rule of perfection* and *The Christian knight,* already published in England after circulating in manuscript and reissued in Paris in French in many editions from 1609 to 1648, and in two Latin editions of 1610 and 1650; it was translated into Italian, German, Flemish and Spanish, a manual for a whole generation of mystics. Another Capuchin was Laurent de Paris, author of *Palais d'amour divin* (1602, 1603 and 1614) and *Tapisseries du divin amour,* much reprinted; Sébastien de Senlis wrote the *Philosophie des contemplatifs* (Paris 1618, 1620) and ascetical books in Latin and French. After 1620 the Capuchins were even busier: Honoré de Champigny wrote *Académie évangelique,* inspired by Bonaventura and David of Augsburg; Philippe d'Angoumois took the story of Ange de Joyeuse as a theme for his books of pietism, and Louis de Paris brought out a *Méthode pour arriver à la perfection*

(1626). Later, Martial d'Etampes published his *Exercise des trois clous amoureux et douloureux pour imiter Jésus-Christ attaché sur la Croix,* and his pupil Jean François de Reims wrote the *Vraye perfection de cette vie dans l'exercise de la présence de Dieu.*

But the most prolific of the Capuchins was Father Joseph. His *Introduction à la vie spirituelle,* a manual of prayer using Father Benet of Canfield's method, first appeared in Poitiers (1616), then in Paris (Fouet, 1620, 1626) and Cramoisy (1634). His *Traité de la perfection séraphique* was published by Fouet in 1624 and the *Pratique intérieure des principaux exercises de la vie chrétienne,* later reissued by Durand in 1638, books designed to aid the ordinary Catholic deepen his faith by prayer and meditation. Finally, his *Exercises des bienheureux* appeared in 1633.

Yet even Father Joseph was not as voluminous as Yves de Paris, who began authorship on Father Joseph's death, was involved in controversy with Camus and wrote an apologetic called *Théologie naturelle* to convert unbelievers. *Morales chrétiennes* came out in 1638 and *Progrès de l'amour divin,* a guide to asceticism, the first in four editions between 1638 and 1645, but the latter only once; two other works, *L'Homme particulier* and *Police générale du christianisme,* went into four editions—his mystical works were not as popular as the books in which he discusses the duties of men in their professions and rank in life.

4. Jesuit activity

Jesuits outnumbered Capuchins as authors in the 17th century in this pietistic genre, almost one-third of the entire output being by Jesuits, whether French or foreign, and the militancy of their posture has attracted criticism ever since Pascal's *Lettres provinciales,* though they had their defenders, too. Their publications are well worth study.

The first Jesuits had been afraid to show sympathy for the Inner Light or any form of Illuminism since Ignatius Loyola's *Spiritual exercises* was attacked, and their emphasis on strict logic in refutation of the Protestant position inhibited their approach to pure spirituality, so for a long time they did not write in that vein; only Louis de Blois and Luis de Granada were somewhat exceptions to this rule. Things changed after 1590 when Acquaviva, General of the Order, urged them to encourage more heightened levels of consciousness in their followers by concentrating on devotional and meditational works. The books that came out of this instruction tended to be produced in Spain or Rome or Flanders where the Society was strongest, but occasional manuals of piety came from Paris presses, like Rosignolo's *De disciplina christianae perfectionis* (translated into French in 1606), Father Sanchez's *Libro del reino de Dios* (1608) and, most popular of all, Rodriguez's *Exercicio de perfeccion,* which went into 11 editions in as many years.

Collections of meditations were well received in Paris, Arias's particularly, and Bellarmine's, and Father Ricci's *Instruttione di meditare* (Rome, 1600) was adapted and published in French by Father Solier in 1609 with the title *Science des saints,* and a further work, Pinelli's *Gersone della perfettione religiosa* was rendered by him into French and published at Douai, Liège, Lyons, Valenciennes and Paris. Father Luis de la Puente's tracts were also popular—René Gaultier translated his *Méditations,* which went into six reprints before 1641, at Douai and Paris, and in many abridged versions. The same author's *Guia espiritual* (Valladolid, 1608) was put into French by François de Rosset and reprinted many times, and his *Perfeccion del Christiano* was translated by René Gaultier and immediately issued in Paris with subsequent new impressions from 1613 to 1621. There was intense Jesuit activity at Douai, Valenciennes and St. Omer, translating Spanish Jesuit books of spirituality; the *Fleur des saints* also saw the light of print at Paris, Lyons, Arras and Douai. Lyons was busy with Jesuit literature in Latin versions, the Flemish Jesuit Busée for example: his *Méditations* were composed for the Congregation of the Virgin, in Latin (Mainz, 1606), and reprinted at Lyons first, then Douai and finally Paris, while a French version was published at Rouen (1616), reprinted at Douai (1617, 1627) but only once at Paris (1644), though much later it was reissued dozens of times. Paris, in short, seems to have been less than zealous for mystical reading matter from abroad.

French Jesuits were also active: Father Richeome the first to score a success with *Adieu de l'âme dévote laissant le corps* (Tournon, 1590, repr. Paris, 1598 and 1602); *Défense des pélerinages* (1604, 1605) and *Sacrée Vierge Marie au pied de la Croix* (Arras, 1603, repr. 1609). Father Solier was not simply a translator but wrote a number of popular tracts: *Imitation de Notre Dame* (Chaudière, 1595, 1596, 1606), *Traité de tribulation* (Douai, 1599; Paris 1600); *Excellent traité de la mortification de nos passions* (Douai, 1595; Paris 1598, 1604); and his *Traité de l'Oraison* and *Histoire de la vie, mort, passion et miracles des saints* were reissued (Paris, 1606). Father Coton's *Intérieure occupation d'une âme dévote* (Paris 1608, 1609) was followed by *Oraisons dévotes pour tous chrestiens catholiques* (1611–1648 in many reprints); *Méditations sur la vie de Nostre Saveur Jesus Christ* (twice in 1614); *Office de la Vierge Marie* (Paris, repr. 1618–1649); Father Loryot's *Secrets moraux* and *Fleurs des secrets moraux* (1614) and *Parallèles de l'Amour divin* (1620).

Father Binet, Rector of the Jesuit college in Rouen, was popular enough for his work to be sought and copyrighted by his publishers, and once the rights expired, Paris booksellers printed him: his *Marque de prédestination,* a book of Marian devotions (Rouen, 1614; 5th ed., 1619) was promptly reprinted in Paris in 1620; his *Consolation* (Rouen, repr. 1616–22; Paris, 1624, 1634); his *Essay des merveilles de nature* (Rouen, 1621; repr. Paris, 1632; 9th ed., 1638; 11th, 1638), and his abridged lives of Loyola, Francis Xavier, Stanislas Kostka and Luis de Gonzaga went into many editions. After them came the *Pratique solide du Saint Amour de Dieu* (Mons, 1623; Paris, 1631–48; Rouen, 1643), a tract called *De l'estat heureux et malheureux* (Paris, 1625, 1627), the *Consolation des âmes désolées* (Paris, 1626–1641), the *Riche sauvé par la porte dorée* (Paris, 1627, 1629) and *Remède souverain contre la peste et mort soudaine* (Paris, 1629).

New titles and reprints multiply after 1620. Father Luzvic wrote three new works: *Mirouers de Philothée, Fiel de la Pénitence* and the *Colloque de l'Amour divin,* and Chappelet brought out three of Father Caussin's *Cour sainte* volumes, aimed at the aristocracy, instructing them in Christian piety and a great success, with 14 editions by 1639 and continuously reprinted until 1669; the *Journée chrétienne* (5th ed., 1628) was followed by *Sagesse évangelique* (Paris, 1635, 1636, 1644) and *Traité de la conduite spirituelle selon l'esprit de bienheureux François de Sales* (Paris, 1637). Father Suffren wrote *Sermons rares et pleins* (Chevalier, 1622), *Testament de Patriarche Jacob;* Father Salian, *De timore Dei* (Cramoisy, 1629), *Ambassade de la Princesse crainte de Dieu* (Chappelet, 1630), *De amore Dei* (Cramoisy, 1631), *Traité de l'Amour de Dieu* (Branchu, 1634), *Ars placendi Dei* (Soly and Josse, 1635). Father de Cresolles published his *Antologia sacra* (1632, repr. 1638), and Fathers Dagonel, Dauxiron, de Barry (one of Pascal's targets) and Poiré all produced similar work, the last-named a wide seller with *Triple couronne de la Bienheureuse Vierge* (Paris, Cramoisy, repr. 1630–1691) and *Science des saints* (Cramoisy, 1638). Father de Cerisiers translated Augustine's *Confessions* and the *Soliloquies and meditations,* ascribed to him.

Books offering spiritual guidance for people in various social classes and professions were in great demand, and the Jesuits provided them. Father Dangles' *Conduite asseurée des âmes à leur perfection* (Lyons, 1636; 2nd ed., Paris, 1638), *Conduite de la jeunesse à son salut* (Paris, 1639), *Conduite assurée des personnes mariées et à marier à leur salut et à leur perfection* (Paris, 1641) were all popular, and for another audience Father Cachet wrote the *Vie de saint Isidore, patron des laboureurs* (Verdun, 1631). Father Jean Cordier and Father Filère took it upon themselves to explain to young girls, women and their husbands, widows and female domestics what their duties and responsibilities were, and Father Bridoul wrote *Boutique sacrée des saints et vertueux artisans* (1650); Father Le Blanc addressed himself to laborers, vine-growers, coachmen and lackeys, stressing the importance of proper conduct in accordance with one's station in life. Yet despite some attention to secular behavior, the Jesuits were all absorbed in the instruction of the priesthood.

The above record of publications proves that their work reached a large public; perhaps the chief difference between Capuchins and Jesuits was that the former produced manuals of piety for people, lay or clergy, already predisposed to such reading matter, while the Jesuits favored propaganda by assimilation, adapting their message to suit a variety of tastes and capacities.

5. Attempts at a synthesis: François de Sales and Bérulle

Parish priests were as involved in the spiritual revival of the times as were the regular clergy, and the three most outstanding authors concerned with pastoral reform were François de Sales, Bérulle and Camus, the first two interested in creating a synthesis of the spiritual life that would help restore French Catholicism and deepen spiritual experience, and Camus more committed to writing that would reach as wide a public as possible.

François de Sales aimed to reconvert Protestants, and his disputes with them had taught him that it was not enough simply to accumulate texts and fling them at opponents to score points; the Church would only triumph if the ordinary worshipper was as well equipped with the sword of the spirit as the heretics appeared to be. The average Catholic did not connect his worship with his everyday life and saw God as a distant figure of awesome magnitude to whom homage was paid at certain prescribed times; François de Sales undertook to convince his readers that life could be dedicated to God without entering a monastery, and that was the message of his *Introduction à la vie dévote.* It was an immediate success, published by Rigaud (1609) with a 2nd and a 3rd edition in the two following years, and more than forty editions before 1620—phenomenal. By 1656 it had been translated into seventeen languages and was head of all the best-selling lists of that kind; there was hardly a confessor or spiritual director who did not quote from it or advise its study and it quite eclipsed other books considered classics in the field. His main aim was to persuade people of the need to keep God at the center of their lives, which was what he meant by "synthesis," and in a new work entitled *Traité de l'amour de Dieu* he ends his first lessons and moves on to a consideration of prayer at a deeper level, though this work was never as popular as his *Introduction,* which parallels the experience of

Yves de Paris whose *Progrès de l'amour divin* was never as popular as his *Morales chrétiennes*. Both examples prove that there was only a very restricted public for the more profound books, a fact which accounts for the different approaches used by Jesuits, secular priests or laity: they had to oversimplify when they were writing for the majority of readers, adapting their material to suit differing capacities.

Nearest in spirit to de Sales was Jean-Pierre Camus, his friend and confidant, among the most prolific of authors with 190 books to his credit, some anti-Protestant polemics, others dealing with the dissension between regular and secular clergy. He wrote a series of little books on pastoral theology for the use of priests, but his priority was the propagation of de Sales' teaching. His *Esprit du Bienheureux François de Sales* was immensely popular even into the 18th and 19th centuries though published only once in the 17th (Paris, 1639), and in his *Panégyrique de l'amour de Dieu* (Paris, 1608) he anticipated de Sales who praised it in a preface to the *Traité de l'amour de Dieu*. Camus suggested practical ways to develop spiritual experience for readers of de Sales' *Introduction* in *Direction à l'oraison mentale,* widely read and often reprinted, and developed his ideas on meditation in *Méditations sur les mystères de la naissance du Sauveur* (1617), *De la foy vive* (1633) and *Spéculations affectives* (1642), in which he dealt with the mystery of the Incarnation and Passion, discussed penance and charity (personified by a heroine called Charity), and propagated the Marian cult.

All this was a mere fraction of his output. Manuals and tracts on prayer, meditations, books of elementary theology, lives of dedicated men and women to serve as models for the aspiring Christian poured from his pen, and he even conceived the idea of writing edifying fiction to improve on the secular romances then in vogue (which in itself signifies a growing public for novels). He employed his lively mind in creating imaginary stories in which high endeavor was mixed with low intrigue, ending not with marriage but entry into a monastery, the hero finally disgusted with the world and vowing to sacrifice worldly pleasures and ambitions in the service of God. Examples of his romances are: *Elise, ou l'innocence coupable* (Paris, 1621), *Dorothée, ou récit de la pitoyable issue d'une volonté violentée* (Paris, 1621); *Parthénice, ou peinture d'une invincible chasteté* (Paris, 1621, 1624, 1637); *Alexis, ou sous la suite de divers pélerinages* (Paris, 1622, 1623) and many others, one of which, *Pieuse Julie* (Paris, 1626) was praised by the abbé Bremond in his literary history as a forerunner of the Tractarian press in the 19th century.

While de Sales and Camus were the most prominent of the devotional humanists, Bérulle was the undoubted master of the peculiarly French school of spirituality, and we might ask how successfully his brand of theocentric teaching and worship penetrated the typical Catholic in the early 17th century. He was of course the founder of the Congregation of the Oratory, and his writings include the following: *Bref discours de l'abnegation intérieure* (his first book, 1597, 1599, repr. 1624); *Elévation à Jesus Notre Seigneur* (1627, repr. 1630); and his most influential, the *Discours des estats et des grandeurs de Jésus* (1623, 1629). After his death in 1629, Bérulle's complete works were not published until 1644, probably for political reasons (they were reprinted, 1657 and 1663), so clearly the press played only a secondary role in disseminating Bérulle's thought. There was opposition to his teaching and some violent polemics, notably between Father Binet and Saint-Cyran, and the fact that none of Bérulle's disciples achieved any success with their writings until after 1643 shows that their hour had not come.

6. Catholic Revival and Traditional Worship

Among all the mass of devotional matter the most popular was what might be called cultist: lives of saints and of the devout, prayers for saints' days, litanies, hours and offices, most of which have vanished, but some sketch of which must be attempted. "Devotional" can mean anything from a guide to religious practice to a tract about a local cult, but most were on themes like the practice of the presence of God, meditations on the Divine or treatises on the nature of divine

Love. Jesuits emphasized the love owed by man to his Savior; the Capuchins, the Passion, wounds and agony of Christ. Much debate broke out, and assertions that before Bérulle worship of Christ was not prominent were refuted, Christ's holy humanity was recognized and the need to follow his example stressed, all this before the French mystics had developed the cult of the child Jesus, the Sacred Heart and Incarnate Word.

The Virgin was the center of worship during the Counter Reformation, thanks largely to Jesuit influence putting Mary at the heart of their devotion before the Oratory invested her with new symbolic and mystical meaning. They preserved relics and images of Mary when so many had been destroyed by the Huguenots; they composed "Imitations" and offices of the Virgin, wove "crowns" of prayers and devised meditations on her life (Arias, Binet, Coton, de Barry, Chiflet and Poiré are names associated with this cult). The Capuchins held aloof from this but other writers (Jean Boucher, Du Val and Serres) and Visitants in the time of de Sales and Camus put Mary at the center of devotion through their books and with images. Dominicans and Jesuits revived devotion to the Rosary, and Father Cavanac wrote a book about it which was very widely read.

Louis XIII ceded his kingdom to the Virgin; many of the books about her were abysmal in their puerility: not only was she the Mother of Christ, and it was not enough to meditate on her role during the Passion, to model oneself on her, or ask her loving and powerful intercession, but she acquired in the eyes of her zealots other adornments portrayed in the absurdly exaggerated Baroque style of art then fashionable. Today, what strikes us is the extraordinary acceptance of such an obsession, the flourishing literature, the alleged miracles in sanctuaries of Our Lady, the pilgrimages to Loreto (even Descartes went on one). Often the cult was purely local—then a pamphlet would be published retelling stories of miracles, most of which have not survived, but Lelong's bibliography lists enough to give us a fair idea of their contents: *Histoire d'un miracle advenu à Notre Dame des Arvilliers à l'arrivée de la Reine-Mère à Saumur, avec le*

rapport de M. Citois, docteur en médecin à Poitiers (Paris,
Sonnius, 1619) or *Origine et fondation de la Chapelle de Notre
Dame des Anges dans le foret de Livry, l'an 1212* (Paris, 1621
and 1672), or *Discours de miracles faits en la Chapelle de
Notre Dame de Bethléem* by Guillaume Morin (Paris, 1605,
repr. 1611–1647). Others read like this: *Merveilles de Notre
Dame de Bethléem de Ferrières* (Paris, before 1651) by Dom
Reinéant of the Maurist Benedictines; *Histoire de l'ancienne
image de Notre Dame de Boulogne* by a Capuchin, Father
Alphonse (Paris, Lamy, 1634 and 1654), or *Parthénie, ou
l'histoire de la très auguste et très dévote Eglise de Chartres* by
Sébastien Rouilliard (Paris, 1609).

The titles are evidence enough of the weight of tradition
and of popular cults underlying the worship of the Virgin, of
the deep penetration into the vulgar mind and emotions of
the age. One illustration of this is the cult of Notre Dame de
Liesse, a village in Picardy which was a pilgrims' shrine in the
16th century. Printed accounts of its miracles already
circulated in the 16th century and were later reprinted in
Lyons, Douai, Rheims and, by 1618, Paris: *Histoire des
miracles de Notre Dame de Liesse* and *Piété francaise vers la
Sainte Vierge Marie, Mère de Dieu, à Notre Dame de Liesse*
by Artus de Moustier (1637); *Vraie trésor de l'histoire sainte
sur le transport miraculeux de l'Image de Notre Dame de
Liesse* (Paris, 1646, repr. 1647–8), and *Histoire miraculeux
de Notre Dame de Liesse* by St-Pérès, a paymaster in the
Royal Gendarmerie. We have also more testimony in the
form of an agreement between Moustier, the Paris printer,
and Claude le Picart, maître d'hôtel to the Prince de Conti,
which reveals that he undertook to supply 36,000 copies of
Histoire et miracles de Notre Dame de Liesse within six
months, evidence of the huge quantities involved.

The Virgin Mary is often represented in the paintings and
engravings of the time as trampling the serpent of heresy
underfoot; the Protestants of course were contemptuous of
the cult and others like it, all of which were enlisted in the
fight against them. A cult of Angels was widespread, and vast
numbers of tracts urged prayers for souls in Purgatory and
intercession for their transit to Paradise. St. Joseph was

venerated as a powerful intercessor and patron of holy dying, and of course as the model for heads of families. The little books glorified Mary Magdalene, who was thought to have brought Christianity to Provence and was a symbol of Penitence— around her and St. Peter an elaborate literature and iconography developed, rich in penitential tears, which inspired Malherbe and other French poets to some of their finest works.

It is a vast area, the literature of hagiography, and developed at an incredible rate. The lives of the saints can be divided into three classes: lives of the apostles and martyrs, biographies of patron saints, and accounts of those only recently dead. The main aim of the first class was not to supply an accurate history of the subject but to exalt the virtues of the saint as a model for sinners, with much emphasis on the power of intercession and indeed of healing. The second category was a faithful account of the life, not only as a model but a psychological study and witness to truth. Patron saints were associated with their shrines, the first of them being St. Denis, patron of the royal abbey and often confused with Dionysus the Areopagite. In Lelong's bibliography there are six hagiographies of Denis, all from the early 17th century. St. Geneviève was held in high honor, too, with five life stories and many books of offices devoted to her for use on the Saint's Day when her body was carried in great pomp in its casket through the streets of Paris. St. Germain and St. Victor, patron saints of abbeys, and St. Roch were the subjects of biographies, and many lesser saints had their stories told by monks whose duty it was to guard their relics. The rules of the various confraternities were a form of literary piety—and a story like that of the miraculous host preserved in the church of St. Jean en Grève was a popular one.

Books about local shrines were published in the locality but sometimes a famous shrine attracted enough publicity to justify a book published in Paris, perhaps a life of the patron saint and his miracle-working powers. St. Martial's pilgrimage to Limoges was a great occasion, and so was St. Anne's to Auray; typical of this class were *Miracles de sainte Restitute, Vierge et martyre* (Paris, 1631) or stories of St.

Godeberte, whose relics were preserved at Noyon; St. Romain, patron of the church of Seure; St. Ulphe, patron of Notre Dame de Parallete, or the *Vie martyre, translation et miracles des saints Cau, Cautian and Cautiane* (Paris, 1610). A life of St. Fiacre by Frère Tristran Rouayr, *Vie et légende de M. St. Fiacre* (Paris, 1617), a saint who healed and was patron saint of gardeners, and another of the same subject, *Vie admirable de Saint Fiacre* by Dom Michel Pirou of the Congregation of the Maurists, were both popular.

Founders of religious orders and early Christian hermits occupied much paper: *Vie de saint Fare, fondatrice et première abbesse de Fare-Moutier-en-Brie* (Paris, 1629) by Augustin Carcat, Provincial of the Reformed Augustinians, and Father Binet's *Vie admirable de la princesse sainte Aldegonde; De la Sainte hierarchie de l'Eglise et de la vie de saint Adérald*, and *Vies et miracles des saincts Peres, hermites d'Egypte, Scithie, Thebaid et autres lieux* (Paris, 1605, and many later reprints). The intention behind some of the books was to promote reforms in religious orders, and to elevate the inner thoughts of readers; presumably some of the nobility were duly edified by Benoît Couronné's *Vie de Saint Eléazar de Sabran et de la bienheureuse comtesse Dauphine sa femme*—he was a King's chaplain and that title went into five editions. A complete cycle of stories was created around Isidore the laborer, patron saint of Madrid, canonized in 1619, but it was intended for priests rather than peasants. The whole corpus was a moralizing mission aimed at clergy and those of equivalent social rank. The more recent orders pursued their fanaticism to the extent of including in the hagiographies bishops, monks, priests and ordinary clerics if their lives were thought worthy enough—for example, Charles Borromée and Philip Neri, not forgetting de Sales, whose life and miracles inspired de la Rochefoucauld. Lives of Spanish saints flooded the market, like Chrysostom Enriquez's *Histoire de la vie, vertue et miracles de la Vénérable Mère Anne de Saint Barthélemy*, a companion of St. Teresa, and the *Vie admirable de sainte Jeanne de la Croix* (Paris, 1614). There was a life of Pedro of Alcantara, a second edition of the *Vie, mort et miracles du Bienheureux Père Gaspar de Bono,* and *La vie admirable de la Soeur de*

Paule, translations from Spanish. Francesco de Castro's *Histoire de la vie de sainte oeuvre de Jean de Dieu* (Paris, 1623) was translated into Italian by Bordini and then into French by François Du Harle. In the year 1633 the abbé de Loyac wrote a new biography of "Jean de Dieu" based on a Spanish life; the life of St. Raymond de Nonnat was in its second edition and a life of St. Marie du Secours was published—both were members of the Order of Notre Dame and the Merci de la Redemption des Captifs—the translator being François Dathia, Commander of their monastery in Paris.

The Jesuits were again most productive, with lives of St. Teresa and John of Avila, of Loyola and Francis Xavier, aimed at the order's novices but clearly of wider appeal, too, especially the story of the three young Jesuits who died in an odor of sanctity, Luis de Gonzaga, Stanislas Kostka and Jean Berchmans. Jesuits martyred on far distant shores were a continual source of interest throughout Europe.

The French soon found exemplary and edifying subjects in their own country: a Capuchin, Philippe d'Angoumois, wrote several works on the life of Ange de Joyeuse, and Jacques Brousse in 1621 dealt with him and with lives of Father Benet of Canfield and the Countess of Pembroke. Funeral orations were a bizarre form of inspiration, widely read, and among them Benedictine abbesses—Jacqueline Bouette de Blémur wrote up their lives, and in 1621, four years after Madam Acarie's death, André Du Val, a well-known writer, published a *Vie de Barbe Aurillot, dite de l'Incarnation, réligieuse carmélite reformée* (9th ed; 1638) and Mother Magdalene de Saint Joseph wrote *Vie de soeur Catherine de Jésus* (3 editions before 1631) as a whole literature of this kind blossomed from the Carmelites.

Other lives were written around men and women who were neither pillars of the church nor miracle-workers, but simply good; for instance, Hilarion de Coste's *Histoire catholique . . . des hommes et dames illustres* (Paris, 1621) and Jacques de la Vallée's *L'Histoire de Catherine de Harley, Dame de la Mailleraye* (Paris, 1616); the *Vie et la mort de Marie de Luxembourg, duchesse de Mercoeur* (Paris, 1625); an account of the illness and death of the same Duchess by her doctor, Bouvard; and two by Nicolas Du Sault, *Amour de la pauvreté descrit en la vie et en la mort de Marthe, marquise d'Oraison* (Paris, 1632) and *Vie de Mademoiselle de Neuvillars, miroir de perfection pour les femmes mariées and les âmes dévôtes* (Paris, 1649). The fact that such edification stemmed from the high-born makes one wonder if the "Catholic Renaissance" was only for the privileged and powerful, like the pompous funeral orations.

Closely allied to this kind of propaganda was the cult of the Virgin and saints, ancient and modern, engineered by the Jesuits as part of their mission to reanimate religion in the nation and using every device—local cults, commemoration of founders of orders, reformers, saints, leaders of the Counter Reformation. There was something revolutionary about their zeal; operating first in isolation and then in cells, they initiated programs of hagiography, in Flanders associated with the Hollandist Movement. The old and much loved *Golden legend* (standard life of the saints) was replaced by the *Flos sanctorum (Fleur des saints),* on sale in Paris bookshops, at Father Ribadeneyra's instigation, and Jesuit activists regularly alluded to saints and their example in their own books, or compiled collections of meditations on the saints and the spiritual and moral lessons to be derived therefrom. They introduced the notion of a Holy Year, and made much play with the symbolic power of saintly life in a bid to give new directions to conventional worship, and significantly to popular worship.

New prayerbooks owed much to the Marian cult and the rosary; the practice of saying the litany led to demand for pocket prayerbooks and illustrated sheets which have not survived, though to judge from booksellers' lists we know they were printed in large numbers. Mettayer, the King's Printer (a fact worth noting), then Marnef and Cavellat after 1584 regularly printed the Office of the Virgin and saints; by 1618, Father Coton's version was constantly in print, and saints' offices were separately printed for use by the regular clergy, particularly Augustinians, Friars Minor and the Benedictines. A canonization was enough to prompt the writing of a life of the saint, with litanies and books of devotions, François de Sales and Vincent de Paul being the favorites. Offices of patron saints associated with various parishes in Paris, and of traditional saints, were on sale everywhere, sometimes separately, sometimes with a biography or litany, the lives often in French, the litanies in Latin with French titles and sub-titles, which makes one wonder who used them.

Books of hours and their public are more of a problem because they have almost entirely disappeared through neglect—they would not have been thought worthy of preservation in libraries since they were so plentiful. Wills and inventories frequently list books of hours as part of a person's effects and they are very common in publisher's stock lists. Rémy Dallin, printer and bookseller, had 906 "saints' daily offices," 690 "holy litanies," 400 "offices of St. Joseph," quantities of litanies illustrated with woodcuts or copper engravings, 1603 "horae concilii" and 2602 "hours of the Queen." Tompère, another printer, owned several thousand hours of all kinds, with many different litanies and saints' lives, and a list of 1647 shows one Claude Calleville with 1650 "heures de concile," in 32mo, 2500 "heures de la noblesse" and 2500 hours of truly minuscule size, 56mo! Pierre Rocollet, a specialist in this field, possessed 5000 copies of hours in all sizes and every conceivable variety in his stockroom, and for his upper-class customers in the Palais precinct he kept richly bound editions with silver corners and clasps.

The 1644 Enquiry into the book trade found that seven printers specialized in books of hours, and the many titles given to this single species—royal, Queen's, Chancellery, nobility, knight's, Capuchin, missionary, black-and-red— clearly testify to a huge output.

7. Uses of illustration

Illustrators, engravers and print sellers, mostly from the Netherlands, began moving to Paris in the hope of better business, and soon Paris was inheriting Antwerp's position as the center of the illustrators' art on copper since engraving had by now almost entirely displaced the woodcut as the medium, even for cheap prints. Wood consorts better with print and there was some loss of effect; for commercial and esthetic reasons only vignettes were used on the same page as letterpress, with only occasional whole-page illustrations on copper. Of course, religious books were attractive to artists, though often the results were poor, and the 17th-century breviaries, missals and books of hours do not compare in range and quality with those of the 16th, being of shoddy quality and often using illustration only at essential points, on grounds of economy. Books where emblems were important received better treatment, and theologians would dictate subjects for treatment by painters, sculptors and engravers, going into great detail to secure, say, an allegorical frontispiece that conveyed the right message. The cult of the Virgin was the subject of abundant iconography, as were catechisms for children, to aid the memory or stimulate the imagination. Catalogs of engravers such as Thomas de Leu, Léonard Gaultier, Firens, Jaspar Isac, Michel Lasne and Claude Mellan impress us today with their pietistic motives and image-making purpose, the fashion of the age. Let us examine illustration as an accessory to the literature, its subject matter, artists, and workshops.

Just as in the 16th century, the Bible was a source of inspiration for a mass readership which could best cope with pictures; the *Histoire de la Sainte Bible* replaced the old *Biblia pauperum,* with large woodcuts page-size and perhaps a line or two of text beneath. But booksellers Richer and Chevalier commissioned Michel Lasne, Melchior Tavernier, Michel Faulte, Van Lochon and Claude Mellan to illustrate a sumptuous edition of the Bible, selecting the main stories from Old and New Testaments, and the Passion was a great favorite, with portraits of the apostles and scenes of martyrdom consonant with contemporary psychology. The iconography of the Virgin kept artists in employment, Béatrizet, Thomas de Leu and Jean Le Clerc in particular doing scenes from the life of Mary and individual prints of famous shrines in Italy and Spain—Loreto was a popular one—as well as "mysteries of the Rosary" and pictures for *Salve Regina* after the Flemish painter Wierix. Father Richeome, a popularizer of the cult, was keen to have such themes in his books, and he was fond of Wierix's engravings from Antwerp, also used by Jesuit propagandists.

So, it was from Flanders and the Low Countries that the new iconography came, to support the objectives of the Counter Reformation by giving publicity to the Virgin cult, showing her standing above the City of Paris or on a crescent moon or in glory as Dürer and Schongauer were wont to represent her. Sometimes she is shown parting the child's swaddling clothes to reveal his face, and she is usually at the center of the picture, not at his side as used to be the case. Other images show her crushing heresy underfoot, or at the foot of the Cross, a posture common in French missals, or on her death bed. In breviaries and books of hours she occupies a place of honor, and her feast days, once proscribed by Rome, were readmitted. In many frontispieces the King and his family or representatives of the nobility are seen praying to the Mother of God.

All the imagery of pietism was enlisted in the fight against Protestantism. St. Peter and the Popes were used as material in theological tomes, an iconography was built around the Sacrament of Penance showing St. Peter and the Magdalene in tears, symbols of the penitent sinner, and the Penitential Psalms would have a picture of David in tears, harp in hand. The Holy Sacrament was even more popular as an illustration than Penitence, probably because it was at the heart of disputes with Protestants: there is a print of 1595 depicting the Pope and the King praying before the host, the vessel containing the host held by two angels. Father Richeome published a book on the Eucharist in 1601, richly illustrated by de Leu, Gaultier and Charles Mallery; Coëffeteau's *Merveilles de la Saint Euchariste* (1606), with a frontispiece of St. Thomas and St. Paul, eyes fixed on the host, which the King and Queen are adoring while underneath David and his companions are receiving shew bread, was reprinted in 1608, 1631 and 1632; and in 1610 Foucault published a book with a significant title, *Sainctes prières et oraisons chrétiennes et catholiques pour se préparer à bien et dévotement recevoir le Saint Sacrement d'Autel avec la confession des péchés pour obtenir pardon et remission d'iceux,* containing twenty-eight plates by Jaspar Isac. In Offices of the Virgin, Mary is depicted taking communion from her Son who holds a pyx in his hand, and in a picture of the Last Supper from the Hours of Louis XIII, Christ is shown like a priest giving communion to his disciples. We get the distinct impression of a deliberate and concerted attempt to promote worship of the Holy Sacrament, and pictures of it—especially those from the religious orders—were plentiful, like the one engraved by Pierre Mariette depicting two angels adoring the host in the pyx whose base is decorated with cherubs and an inscription: "Whoever keeps this in a place where it can be read, whoever reads it or if unable to read, bows in reverence, secures an Indulgence granted by Pope Paul V in 1614 and confirmed by the Holy Father Urban VIII in 1624."

And after the Eucharist, Indulgences. Note how angels are everywhere apparent and how pictures concentrate the mind on the cults of martyrs ancient and modern, with modern saints like Loyola and Francis Xavier figuring in the gallery of hagiography and the image-making process. It could easily be shown how saints' pictures and calendars helped promote popular cults for the masses, but it would need a book; here suffice it to say that a new imagery based on pictures with roots in old traditions grew up as part of the verbal offensives launched in the Counter Reformation and its consequence, the Catholic Renaissance. The frontispieces of so many contemporary books are symbolic of its spirit: Father Coton's *Institution catholique* shows heretics burning in Hell while the Pope, King, Queen and the faithful pray for the souls of the damned; Richeome's *Tableaux sacrés* (Paris, 1601) has a picture of Henri IV and his Queen above a portico, adoring a Virgin who is almost Byzantine in looks, while Paganism is in chains and Heresy overthrown, bottom right, and on either side of the title a statue of Religion holds keys, a tiara and Papal crown. These two examples are of interest since they were written by two successive Principals of the Jesuits in France—the source of the excessive zeal—and indeed most illustrated religious books of the period 1598–1643 were by Jesuits—Richeome, Coton, Binet, Poiré, Barry and Le Moyne. It is no accident that Loyola appears in pictures showing the Assumption of the Saints in a Louvre breviary (he is recognizable by his collar), a role that would follow quite naturally from the importance given to visual imagination in his *Spiritual exercises*. And the most significant fact of all is the sheer volume of production, with pictures (designed all for the cause) multiplied in hundreds of thousands.

CHAPTER III

THE COUNTER-REFORMATION

1. The Counter-Reformation versus Protestantism

W E HAVE SEEN HOW THE EFFORT to vanquish heresy made the Catholic Church go back to its traditions and publish manuals of faith and instruction to justify its dogma and refute Protestant doctrines. In the late 16th century numbers of Catholic theologians, from Paris especially, issued books of all shapes and sizes denouncing Calvinism and upholding Church teaching, but after peace was restored with the Edict of Nantes there followed a period of toleration based on a balance of power, and verbal conflict took the place of armed struggle and the dictatorship of the Catholic League. But it was an unequal conflict: on the Catholic side a vast outpouring of propaganda, and very little from the Protestants because under the terms of the Edict the Huguenots could only publish their works in certain pre-scribed areas, which did not include Paris; any Protestant books or pamphlets actually printed in Paris bore a Charen-ton imprint. Few in number as they were, the Huguenots were not keen to publish material that would invite prosecu-tion, so most of their literature was issued in Geneva or Sedan, safe havens. By the year 1620 there is a decided change of tone in the polemics, in subject, and even the names of authors. Let us look at some typical publications in the two periods 1598–1620 and 1620–1643.

Catholic polemics were commonest from 1598 to 1620. Bellarmine's *Disputations* (repr. 1602, 1608, 1613 and 1619) was much used, and French theologians prepared abridg-ments and adaptations in French, Coton's *Institution catholi-que* being the best known. Militancy was preferred, and the most effective Catholic protagonists were Du Perron, Coton, Richeome and Coëffeteau; on the Protestant side there were Duplessis-Mornay, "the Huguenot Pope"; Du Moulin, the fiery minister of Charenton; Chamier, pastor of Montauban; and Tilenus, a professor at Sedan. A book would be published, a reply would follow and then a further riposte, each writer wanting the last word. Meetings of Catholics and Protestants furnished material, as did a famous confrontation in the King's presence when Duplessis-Mornay debated with Du Perron. The procedure was the same in all cases: a Catholic might choose a subject and issue a challenge to a Protestant minister and, if accepted, the disputation would be published by each side, thus generating further controversy.

Some texts were by converts, at the suggestion of the one who made the conversion, explaining the reasons for the change of faith, and by about 1615 these were almost a literary genre in themselves. Immediately after the Peace of Nantes, Duplessis-Mornay's book on the Mass came out in a second edition, provoking replies by Catholics and this controversy ended up as the Fontainebleu debate. Other confrontations took place in Henri IV's reign, between Du Perron and Tilenus, Coton and Chamier, and Gigord, Cayet and Gontier versus Du Moulin, but the Protestants saw themselves at a disadvantage in open debate, preferring print; hence Du Moulin replied to Coëffeteau's attacks on his *Apologie de la Cène* with a book, and Richeome and Bansillon argued the nature of idolatry; a little later Duplessis–Mornay provoked more reaction with his *Mystère d'iniquité*.

Doctrinal points were disputed endlessly: the Mass (the core of the debate), the Papacy and the Church, apostolic succession, sacraments, Purgatory, prayers for the dead, the cult of the Virgin and saints, images, clerical celibacy, Grace and Predestination. Both sides were ingenious in finding points of disagreement and yet at the same time there is a weariness as traditional arguments are repeated until blunted. The Protestant contention that there was no Scriptural warrant for Catholic dogmas seemed less weighty when the Council of Trent proclaimed the authority of Tradition, and consequent research into Patrology gave their

scholars the edge; in the Fontainebleu debate Duplessis–
Mornay made little appeal to any argument from Tradition
to demonstrate the waywardness of the Church, but the
Protestant stand was essentially on the Bible as bedrock,
which the learned Patrologists and Church historians could
not easily controvert. It might well be asked how much of all
this was comprehended by the public, who would have no
knowledge of Greek or Hebrew, and the answer is that both
sides made much use of quotation from authorities and
quaint devices like the rebus (symbolic illustration) were
used, as when Duplessis Mornay used one to prove that Pope
Paul V was Anti-Christ.

The debate cooled a little in 1610 when King James I of
England, friend and patron of Du Moulin and Casaubon,
entered the lists, in controversy with Du Perron. James
declared that the Church of England was Catholic and Du
Perron pointed out with respect the weakness of that position,
but the tone was courteous on each side as if there was an
underlying wish for reconciliation and to simplify issues. But
when the Thirty Years War broke out in 1618 the tone again
becomes violent and French Catholicism went over to the
offensive. In his inflammatory *Genève plagiaire,* attacking the
Geneva Bible, Coton's successor, Arnoux, took the attack
against the Calvinists a stage further in a fierce sermon
preached before the King and court, provoking four Calvinist
pastors at Charenton—Du Moulin, Durand, Montigny and
Mestrezat—into publishing *Une Défense de la confession des
Eglises réformées de France,* addressed to the King, with a
Charenton imprint. The text was condemned by the Council
and the printer prosecuted; Catholics replied in pamphlets by
Garasse, Frizon, Abra de Raconis, Pitard, Richelieu and
Véron, ranging from provocative to conciliatory. During the
fighting between Protestants and royalist troops the Huguenot
chapel at Charenton was burned down and a leading Protestant, Chamier, killed at the siege of Montauban. Catholic
zealots, eager for converts, planned a wide program of
publication, with Du Perron writing propagandist tracts such
as *Examen du livre du Sieur Du Plessis contre la Masse* (1617),
Traité du Saint Sacrament de l'Euchariste (1622) and *Réfutation
à toutes les objections de St. Augustin.*

The old scholastic apologetics like Bellarmine's *Disputations* gave way gradually to portable little books like Becanus's *Manuale controversiarium,* abridged to tiny size as a 24mo (Paris, 1626, 1628, 1641; Lyons, 1624, 1628, 1636; Rouen, 1632), and similar booklets by priests in Richelieu's circle, especially Véron, who wrote an incredible number of tracts and *opuscula,* one of which, the *Méthode de controverse,* went into 21 editions between 1615 and 1637. Véron left the Jesuits to enter secular life and so gain more freedom of action, and is thus of some interest to this history; like Richelieu and Coton he felt the best way to combat Protestantism was not to emphasize points of contention but to reduce them, focussing on essential articles of faith, and he was well aware of the advantages which came from taking the initiative: if the Calvinists attacked Catholics it was for them to show the grounds of their accusations; in other words, after defining the Catholic position briefly, it was up to their opponents to prove they were in the right and that the Church was not founded on Scripture. Véron challenged them to quote texts justifying Calvinist doctrine.

Brachet de la Milletière was another militant, an agent of Richelieu like Du Laurens and a convert from the Huguenot ministry. He wrote a vast number of tracts aimed to promote unity of the churches and although he irritated some fellow priests and earned a rebuff from the Sorbonne's theologians, he was approved by Richelieu, who made compromise the cornerstone of his policy. In response to the barrage from the Catholics, the Protestants issued only a modest reply: two editions of Drélincourt's *l'Abrégé des controverses* (1624 and 1625) and a tract, *Du jubilé des églises réformées avec le jubilé des églises romaines.* The Protestant booksellers of Charenton were bolder in their use of their imprints and in 1637 Daillé and Drelincourt began the Irenist controversy; La Milletière and Drelincourt in a series of booklets portrayed Camus, bishop of Belley, as a champion of the despised cult of the Virgin, and Daillé's *Apologie pour les églises réformées,* branded as seditious by the Assemblée du Clergé, was part of an increased output in the years 1630–43.

The overwhelming impression from the mass of evidence available is of Protestants reduced to silence, but that might be a rash assumption, as the testimony of their chief protagonists proves: Du Moulin, Aubertin, Daillé, Drelincourt and Mestrezat are all eloquent on the point. Du Moulin in exile continued his attack on Rome; his *Nouveauté du papisme* and *Anatomie de la Masse* (published in Sedan) are suggestive, and the others composed moderate pieces in Paris and had them published in Geneva and Sedan. Recent research proves their study of history and of the Eucharist to have improved their status as experts in a highly technical field, and helped Calvinism regain some of the ground lost in the 16th century. And their case reminds us that we still have to show how books published abroad reached the public they were meant for; that will come later.

2. The Counter-Reformation versus Free Thought: the new apologetics

Quarrels between the rival churches, which had lasted more than a century, eventually led to a kind of Deism ("Christless religion" as it was called) which denied revelation, and the current debate between Aristotelians and Thomists was seen in some quarters as a sign that basic Church dogmatics rested on flimsy foundations. Study of Lucian and Sextus Empiricus encouraged an irreligious spirit and from this came new thought whose godparents were the Classical Revival, Averroist Aristotelianism taught at Padua, and a new scientific rationalism. There was a growing conviction that it was impossible to prove eternal verities purely by logic, and atheism made its first appearance.

The "Christless religion," atheists and others who could be described as nonconformists in religion and morals were known as *libertins* (free-thinkers), a new enemy for the defenders of the faith to deal with, whether Catholic or Protestant, and the main armament against the enemy was reason in a literary form which dates back to Early Christianity, namely Apologetics, the supreme masters of which were at this time Pascal and Bossuet. The first modern work of Apologetics was probably Duplessis-Mornay's *De la vérité de la religion chrestienne* (Plantin, 1581), and excluding books of the old Scholastic type in which the existence of God was proved as an exercise in logic, and the many books in which Apologetics appeared marginally, some thirty titles designed to convert freethinkers were published in Paris from 1598 to 1643, and each religious order supplied its champions: Mersenne on behalf of the Minims, Boucher for the Franciscans, Yves de Paris for the Capuchins, Polycarp de la Rivière for the Carthusians, while the Jesuits flung a whole brigade of writers into the fray—Garasse, Raynaud, Richeome, Antoine Sirmond and Caussin. Grotius led the Protestant attack. Some Catholics like Campanella took an independent line, and secular priests like Du Teil, Silhon and Puget de la Serre, and freethinkers who were anxious to have their lack of caution overlooked all added to the debate, contributing to the cause of enlightenment. While they refuted impiety the defenders did not offer a very positive approach, some discussing a single doctrinal point—whether angels or demons existed—others the immortality of the soul. Some apologists collaborated, as did Duplessis-Mornay, Charron, Garasse, Boucher, Yves de Paris, and Grotius and Jean Macé the Carmelite. Grotius's *De veritate religionis christianae,* based on ten years' travel and research, was published at The Hague in 1627 and went through many reprints in the Netherlands and even by Ruart and the orthodox Cramoisy in Paris; it was published in French by Blaeu in Amsterdam and in Paris again by Pierre Moreau (1644) and Pierre Le Petit (1659).

Some twenty books of this sort have been counted for the years 1622–30, 11 for the period 1600–22, and a further 11 from 1630–40. Some achieved a measure of fame: *Doctrine curieuse des beaux esprits de ce temps* and *Somme théologique* by Garasse (1623–25); Mersenne's *Quaestiones celeberrimae in Genesim* (1623); *De l'impiété des Deistes et des plus subtiles libertins* (1623); and his *Vérité des sciences contre les sceptiques et les pyrrhoniens* (1625); Boucher's *Triomphes de la religion chrétienne* (1628), and de la Rivière's *Excellence et perfection de l'âme* (Lyons, 1626); Grotius' *De veritate religionis christianae* (The Hague, 1627), Du Moulin's *De cognitione Dei tractatus* (Lyons, 1625), translated into French by Drelincourt the same year.

Free thought was under heavy attack and the law's severity

supported the orthodox: Vanini was burned at the stake, Theophilos prosecuted and extremists put down by terror. A new, more sophisticated form of freethinking emerged. But how did such outrageous views gain any kind of foothold when there was almost total opposition to them—how were they published? In fact there were precious few books or pamphlets of this kind in circulation; some erotic or near-pornographic verses, the *Parnasse satyrique,* some poetry by disaffected writers, Gabriel Naudé expressing heterodox opinions here and there in his writings, covertly, and there was more outspokenness during the Fronde rebellion, but on the whole very little; the only works that were strictly speaking free thought were Vanini's *De admirandae Naturae Reginae Deaeque mortalium arcanis Libri IV,* published by the Protestant Périer (Paris, 1616), and perhaps Charron's *De la sagesse,* authorized by the Chancellor after revision in 1604, and widely read. Naturally, most "freethinking" books came from underground presses and were the kind Mersenne refers to in a letter to Descartes of 1630 when he mentions a book which only reached an edition of thirty or forty copies—possibly the *Dialogues d'Orasius Tubero,* published by La Mothe Le Vayer with a false imprint (Sarius of Frankfurt) and under a fanciful date of publication. Or it may have been Pomponazzi's works, again possibly issued by Le Vayer or his friend Naudé. The total of such clandestine works is insignificant, since all the Italian pioneers of free thought were on the Index and not published in France, with the result that the Catholic defenders of orthodoxy could not find any copies on which to base their counterattacks. This is proved by Naudé, himself well placed to find any such material, having to visit Rome to be exposed to such corrupting influences, because only there was the libertine literature to be found actually on library shelves.

Library shelves in France bore no such books, but free thought there developed from a re-reading of classical philosphers, Epicurus, Seneca, Pliny, Lucian and Lucretius, all readily available in Paris bookshops. Protestant publishers occasionally printed Machiavelli or Cardan, but most heterodox or subversive literature never reached print but was privately circulated in manuscript, like Bodin's *Hepta-plomeres,* and other titles we know about only because they were mentioned in opponents' works—the *Quatraine du Déiste* and *Trois imposteurs.* The odd fact about libertine literature is the volume of opposition it provoked despite its paucity, and historians of free thought have to trace its evolution through the pages of its antagonists, which makes us wonder if the new ideas also percolated through to the ordinary reader through the same channels?

3. Contradictions within the Counter-Reformation:
Gallicanism and clerical quarrels

A substantial proportion of the religious press dealt not with spiritual matters but with the administrative and juridical side of church affairs, or what we usually call canon law. The standard works were always in print as were commentaries on judgments of the Roman Curia, which were essential reading for French canon lawyers. Decisions of the General Councils and the major French Councils had to be available for study either as collections or single treatises, and synodical, monastic and conventual statutes and regulations were all in regular demand.

The question of livings was crucial to priests and the source of frequent lawsuits, and the deliberations of the Assemblée du Clergé, decisions of ecclesiastical tribunals and other arms of the Church produced a mass of printed matter defining its jurisdiction and relationship with secular courts. There were also heated controversies of a quasi-political kind, notably between the chauvinistic Gallican wing of the Church in France and the monastic orders. At the time of the Wars of Religion in the 16th century lawyers tried to codify certain principles which would guarantee the independence of the French Church vis-à-vis the Vatican, and Pierre Pithou's *Liberté de l'Eglise gallicane* was the most famous statement of the position. First published in Paris in 1594, it inspired others, like Barclay's *De regno et regali potestate adversus Buchanarum, Brutum, Boucherium et reliquos monarchoma-chos* (1600) and Edmond Richer's edition of Gerson with contributions by Almain, Pierre d'Ailly and Jean Mair, an arsenal of Gallicanism. In 1608 Claude Fauchet's *Traité des libertés de l'Eglise gallicane* was published, though written in 1591, and Pithou's book was reprinted in 1609, with another by Barclay, *De potestate Papae*. With Henry IV on the throne the Gallican versus the Ultramontane (Papal Supremacy) parties slackened, though the odd Jesuit tract put the Vatican case: Stephanus de Avila's *De censuris eccleisasticis tractatus* and the Spaniard Mariana's *De rege et regis institutione* which virtually justified regicide, but without appreciable result until Henry IV's assassination in 1610, which dramatically changed the situation. The Gallican cause was immediately strengthened and the Church in France passionately defended its rights: two documents of an Ultramontane tendency were condemned by the Parlement along with Bellarmine's *Tractatus auctoritatis Summi Pontificis in rebus temporalibus* and Mariana's book. Two pamphlets called *Anti-Mariana* (Paris, 1610) called attention to the Jesuit threat, and Father Coton, Provincial of the Jesuits in France, defended the Society in *Lettre déclamatoire de la doctrine des jésuites conforme à la doctrine du concile de Constance*, denying the complicity of the Jesuits in the plot to kill Henri IV by employing the assassin Ravaillac. There was an instant riposte by an anonymous writer, probably a Protestant, *Anti-Coton*, to which a further *Réponse apologétique* came from a Jesuit, condemned by the Parlement. Pamphlets flew on all sides, with Richelieu, Garasse and Mlle. de Gournay the champions of the Jesuits, and Bellarmine's prompting a riposte from William Barclay's son John.

The argument took another turn when in 1611, Richer, Syndic of the Faculty of Theology, wrote a brief tract entitled *De ecclesiastica et politica potestate*, at first published in only 300 copies but soon reprinted and translated into French in 1612. The Ultramontane party reacted vigorously: Jean Boucher of the Catholic League, an exile in Flanders, attacked Richer from an address in Tournai, though the tract was probably printed in Paris, and Claude Durand, Pierre Pelletier and the Jesuit Jacques Sirmond all defended Ultramontane policy; and André Du Val, a famous Sorbonne theologian, entered the fray to condemn Richer in his

Elenchus libelli de potestate ecclesiastica (1612, repr. 1614). The Faculty of Theology at the Sorbonne was itself divided.

Two further Gallican tracts are worthy of mention: *Grandeur de nos roys et leur souverains puissance* by Jérôme Bignon (1612) and *Apologia de suprema ecclesiae potestate* by Simon Vigor (1613). These were followed by more condemnations in Parlement of two strongly Ultramontane works, a digest of Baronius' *Annales* and Suarez's *Controversia Anglicana,* and when the Estates General met in 1614 there were new developments. While the Clergé de France wanted the decrees of the Council of Trent proclaimed as laws, Parlement wanted the Gallican position to be considered fundamental, which the Clergé deemed unacceptable. Du Perron harangued Parlement explaining their objections, which were supported by the aristocracy, and when put into print, Du Perron's speech provoked further denunciation in which James I of England joined, and another pamphlet war broke out. From 1618 to 1622 the Ultramontane party was in power but in 1622 Richer renewed the struggle with his *Demonstratio libelli de ecclesiastica et politica potestate,* mainly directed against Du Val's *Elenchus,* and one of his opponents, Michel Mauclerc, went into print with *De monarchia divina;* later, in 1625, the Chapter of the Eglise d'Angers, in the course of a quarrel with their bishop Miron of the Ultramontane faction, put out a statement of the Gallican case, *De la puissance royale sur la police de l'Eglise,* provoking a further reply from Miron.

The crisis reached a turning point when Richelieu came to power and made it purely political. Jesuits were disturbed by the new directions of French diplomacy and began a press campaign in Italy with two pamphlets, *Mysteria politica* and *Admonitio ad regem Ludovicum,* which hinted at the eventual deposition of Louis XIII by the Pope and stoked Gallican fury, which was further stirred up by a *Tractatus de haeresi* written by an Italian Jesuit, Santarelli, and ordered to be publicly burned by Parlement. The whole question of relations between the Papacy and French monarchy now came into the open. Richelieu had no wish to see his diplomacy injured by disputes of this sort and Richer had to sign a retraction; from 1630 to 35 hardly anything appeared in print on the Gallican controversy, but in 1636 an anonymous tract, *Nonce du Pape français,* and a new edition of the *Traité des droits et libertés de l'Eglise gallicane* appeared, and since the authors, the brothers Dupuy, were Richelieu's henchmen it is likely that both publications were issued on the orders of the Cardinal—Gallican propaganda was valuable to him. A new pamphlet, *Optati Galli de cavendo schismate liber paraeneticus,* pointed to the imminent danger of schism and was promptly ordered by Parlement to be burned, with the inevitable retorts: *Apotriplius* by Priezac, an Academician; Rigault's *Dissertatio censoria super editione libelli paerenetici De cavendo schismate;* Habert's *De consensu hierarchiae et monarchiae;* Jean Sirmond's *Chimère défaite;* Michel Rabardeau's *Optatus Gallus de cavendo schismate* and Pierre de Marca's *De concordia sacerdotii et imperii,* which summarized and succintly set out the Gallican case.

That Richelieu was behind the affair, recent research has proved, and it was typical of so many other fields in which the Government sought to control opinion through tight censorship of that powerful agency, the printing press, simply banning whatever it disapproved.

The quarrels between the monastic orders and the rest of the clergy may be told briefly. The rise of the Jesuit and Capuchin orders came about at a time when the secular clergy had hardly begun to reform themselves, and the bishops were in a difficult position. New convents and monasteries did not necessarily pose any problems for the bishops but the entry of so many poor young men into orders was a danger because they feared that one day they might have to maintain them if they left their order; moreover, monks who moved from diocese to diocese were reluctant to ask the bishop's permission to preach and hear confession. Secular clergy quoted canon law in support of their contention that church members should make confession with their curé and take regular communion at their parish church.

The Church of England's troubles in this matter kindled a powder keg in France. Civil and ecclesiastical authorities were engaged in delicate negotiations when Camus, de Sales' disciple, led the attack on behalf of the secular clergy, hinting at the dangers of life within a monastery and stressing the value and dignity of parish priests. His *Directeur spirituel désinteressé* had some success in 1631, and Hallier's *Defensio hierarchiae* and St. Cyran's *Vindiciae* gave further impetus to the conflict. Camus made a translation of Augustine's *Opus monachorum* which Richelieu tried to ban but succeeded only in delaying, and the Sorbonne then intervened. Yves de Paris spoke for the Capuchins in *Heureux succès de la piété,* and started another pamphlet debate. From 1625 to 1636 about a hundred pamphlets were written on either side, most of them published openly in Paris by Gervais Alliot under licence, not by the King's censors but by a doctor of theology. Richelieu was unable to suppress the unseemly squabble and could only forbid the sale of books by securing a decree of the Council; it seems probable that portions of a book were circulated as they emerged from the press, a common practice in the 17th century, and false imprints and no mention of the publisher were also frequent, frustrating Government action. But there seems no doubt that the Gallican-Ultramontane affair, which almost led to a schism, made Richelieu consider ways and means to regulate and censor the press with Séguier in the period after 1636.

4. Witchcraft and demons

Of all the Church's enemies the Devil was the favorite target. Prodigies, portents and the doings of Satan and his familiars were of unflagging interest to readers. Newsbooks sound almost comic to us, with titles like *Histoire mémorable et espouvantable arrivée au chasteau de Bissestre prés Paris avec les apparitions des esprits et fantosmes qui on este veux aux caves et du dit chasteau,* or *Vision publique d'un tres horrible et tres espouvantable Démon sur l'Eglise cathedrale de Quimpercorentin Bretagne,* or *Espuvantable et prodigieuse apparition advenue en la personne de Jean Hélian du Sieur Daudiger le premier jour de l'an 1623 au fauxbourg St. Germain.* Sometimes it was an account of a bloody affray: *Histoire espouvantable et véritable arrivee en la ville de Soliere en Provence d'un homme qu s'êtoit voué pour l'Eglise, et qui*

*n'ayant accomply son voeu, le Diable lui a couppe les parties
honteuses, et couppé encore la gorge à une petite fille âgée de
deux ans ou environ.*

This kind of fodder was eagerly wolfed down, and, perhaps
a little more serious, cases of exorcism, for example
*Conjurations faites á un démon possédant le corps d'une
grande dame ensemble les estranges réponses par luy faites
aux sainctes exorcismes en la chapelle de Notre Dame de la
Guarinon au diocèse d'Auch le 19 Novembre 1618 et jours
suivants.* Cases of possession and trickery were publicized,
some of them trivial, some disturbing, some with tragic
consequences, like the case of Elisabeth de Ranfaing,
founder of an order, who accused her doctor of being
responsible for her possession by a demon and had him
burned at the stake. Some cases were famous—Louis
Gaufridi and Madeleine de la Palud, Léonora Galigaï
burned as a witch, Urbain Grandier and the nuns of Loudun,
Madeleine Bavent and the nuns of Louviers. The whole sorry
history is evidence of the sick obsession with witchcraft,
culminating in thousands of trials and the horrible deaths of
men and women at the stake.

Sorcery led to new processes of law, and a sober jurist like
Jean Bodin could write a treatise entitled *De la démonoma-
nie et des sorciers* (Paris, 1581). Another who judged the
stake appropriate as punishment was Pierre de Lancre, a
member of the Parlement of Bordeaux and a friend of
Espagnet, an alchemist who hunted witches in the Pays de
Labour region and wrote books on demonology like *Tableau
de l'inconstance et instabilité de toutes choses* (1610) and
Tableau de l'inconstance des mauvais anges (1612). Another
holder of high office, a councillor in the Présidial at Angers,
Le Loyer published a *Discours et histoire des spectres, visions
et apparitions des esprits, anges, démons et âmes se monstrent
visibles aux hommes;* a judge, Boguet, wrote a *Discours des
sorciers avec six advises faict de sorcellerie,* many times
reprinted; and Martin del Rio, a witchfinder in Flanders,
wrote *Controverses et recherches magiques.* Inquisitors and
churchmen of all ranks contributed to the hysteria: *Pneu-
malogie* by Michaëlis, a Dominican; *Deux livres de la hayne
de Satan* by Father Crespet, a Celestin prior; Pedro de

Valderrama's *Histoire générale du monde*, much of which concerns devils and witches.

While we feel anger and incredulity at these absurdities today, our ancestors believed they were in contact with forces of evil, and had a lively conviction that Satan existed, even in the most sophisticated circles—we need only recall the books about angels and demons written by Maldonado and Huarte, learned theologians, and the "scientists" of the time peopled the universe with spirits and elves in the Neo-Platonist tradition of the Renaissance. Few would dare to express disbelief openly in the face of such concerted conviction and the likelihood of a frightful death, so very few did: Maurice de Mourtrod, Naudé. It was a world and a culture vastly different from ours.

CHAPTER IV

THE HUMAN SCIENCES: FROM CHRISTIAN HUMANISM TO SCHOLARLY FREE-THINKING

THE NEXT SUBJECT OF OUR STUDY is the Greek and Latin classics, a vital source of ideas in the 17th century; then we shall look at history, the witness to men's vision of the past; then geography, in the form of travel books, proof of man's widening knowledge of his planet; and finally, law and politics, the concrete expression of man's need to administer the social order and the means by which he brings in reform.

1. Reprinting the classics

Classical studies enjoyed a brilliant revival in the 16th century but the bloody religious struggles of the later years blocked all progress in Paris so that it was in the Low Countries—Louvain and Leyden—that renewed activity in textual and philological study under Justus Lipsius and the publishers Plantin and the Elzeviers made that region paramount in the field. Paris took second place, although Pierre Pithou and Fédéric Morel II were considerable publishers of classical texts. These tended to be of two kinds: learned editions in large folios with abundant notes and commentaries, and more modest-sized books with few notes and no reference to commentators, designed for everyday use or as student textbooks. The heavy folios, typical of the early 17th century, were from the presses of the Estiennes or Morel or Drouart, who inherited the tradition of the 16th century Humanist printers. The authors most widely issued were Aristotle and Hippocrates, Seneca, the historians Livy, Suetonius, Tacitus, Florus, Velleius Paterculus, Polybius,

Xenophon, Plutarch and the geographer Strabo, with the mathematicians Archimedes and Diophantes. The most popular poets were Persius, Martial, Juvenal, Horace, Catullus, Tibullus, Propertius, Phaedrus and Pindar. One hitherto unpublished text was Diophantes' *Arithmetic*. The new editions were often superior to the earlier ones: Morel's edition of Statius for instance, the work of the German scholar Lindenbrog based on a manuscript of the *Achilleis* which Pithou owned, and with notes by Morel. Casaubon was published by Drouart, notably his *Historiae Augustae scriptores* (1603; new ed. by Saumaise, 1620), Persius' *Satires* (1605) and Polybius with commentary he was working on at his death, published in 1617 by Robert Estienne.

Texts were judged by the number and quality of the commentaries, the learned public having an insatiable appetite for that; Seneca was laden with notes and commentaries by Lipsius, Gruter, Schott and Godefroy as well as older scholars, Erasmus, Beatus Rhenanus and Muret. Martial's *Epigrams* (Paris, 1617) were thought by contemporaries better than anything published earlier simply because there were more notes, by a series of scholars, Hadrianus Junius, Etienne de Clavière, Thierry Marcile, Fédéric Morel, Poelmann and Ramirez de Prado.

Publishers vied with each other in getting out rival versions of texts, and there was fierce competition between European cities. The Paris Seneca was surpassed by a text from Heidelberg by Gruter and another edited by Lipsius in Antwerp (1605), so that Drouart in Paris felt obliged to issue a revised edition in 1607 to include the foreign material. He prided himself on his Tacitus which gathered together the notes of sixteen scholars when the Frankfurt edition had only ten, and that one had eclipsed another Paris text of 1606 which itself had been inspired by a Lipsius edition of 1600. Without substantial collaboration no work was considered definitive, and here in the first years Paris could claim primacy since there were scholars like Casaubon, Passerat, Marcile and Etienne de Claviére to call on, and the Paris booksellers were viewed as specialists in Latin poetry; once equipped with Estienne's alphabet of "Grecs du Roi" they could publish Greek texts as a consortium. Fewer monumental editions emerged after 1620; Casaubon went to London in 1610, Marcile was less productive and Etienne de Clavière and Morel silent, a gap never filled. Two doctors of medicine in Paris edited classical texts at the Collège Royale—Aristotle, Galen, and Hippocrates; a Byzantinist, Henri de Valois, and Bourdelot (of impious inclination), who edited Petronius and Lucian, were the sole representatives.

Thus the classics dwindled at Paris while Patrology flourished, leaving the field to Leyden, where Heinsius, Graevius and Gronovius were at work, and to Protestant scholars in England. Classical studies became a speciality of the Protestant world, especially in Holland.

From about 1630 the pocket-sized formats in good type led the market popularized by Janszoon, Blaeu and the Elzevirs in Leyden and Amsterdam. A flawless text with accurate and adequate notes by the best scholars—that was the recipe, and although Cramoisy and Libert tried to match the Dutch, their books do not stand comparison; they are mere clumsy copies of pirated Dutch texts, even to the frontispiece. They did publish some good material, chiefly the Latin poets Persius, Juvenal, Ovid and Horace, and Libert did several editions of Seneca with and without notes supplied by Giles Farnaby for Elzevier. Caesar, Livy, Florus, Velleius Paterculus, Nepos and Pomponius Mela were also on his list, and for readers of Greek the first books of the *Iliad*, Homer's *Batrachomyomachia*, Hesiod, Theocritus (more than Demosthenes), an edition of Epicurus' *Manual*, Lucian's *Dialogues with the dead*, Aristotle's *Rhetoric* and Hippocrates' *Aphorisms*.

The easiest texts were the most frequently published, and literary texts the most popular. Cramoisy and Libert tell us for whom these books were intended: on the title page is printed "ad usum studiosae juventutis," or sometimes "ad usum collegiorum Societatis Jesu"—so it is obvious why Ovid and Lucian were not on his list. Grammars and vocabularies were in stock, Libert aiming at the University market, Cramoisy and Morel at the Jesuit colleges, Libert and Morel concentrating on Greek grammars (especially

Cleynaert's) while Cramoisy was more general: besides his *Onomasticon latino-graecum in usum gymnasiorum Societatis Jesu* he printed Vigier and Labbe's courses, the *Cornubium adverbiorum* and Father Abram's commentary on Book 3 of Cicero's Speeches, a famous one in its time. He reprinted Father Deschamps-neuf's *Flores latinae locutionis*, a goldmine for any publisher since it was the standard textbook used in all the Jesuit colleges as far as Germany.

Textbooks were an attractive proposition and printers must have been anxious to secure rights in them, not only classical grammars and authors, but history, geography, annals, studies of the sphere, and mathematics. Only a few rudiments of Latin were published in Paris, which is surprising, and very few of the standard texts used in Jesuit colleges; a probable reason for this was the Jesuit practice of sponsoring a press in or near their colleges to print the books their teachers wrote. Many more textbooks were published in Rouen (by Lallemand particularly), Limoges, la Flèche, Bordeaux and Lyons than in Paris, and it can be said generally that the Jesuit order was a big patron of the book trade.

There had been a public for classics ever since the 16th century, and translation of their political and philosophical writers into French was a popular line. In the single year 1600 appeared Aristotle's *Politics*, Plato's *Republic* and *Phaedrus*, the *Phaedo* and parts of the *Gorgias* (Louis le Roy's version), and Etienne de Boétie's *Mesnagerie d'Aristote et de Xénophon*. Aristotle was of continuous interest to the educated reader, and the Stoics: Amyot's *Plutarch* revised by Simon Goulart was in great demand, and Mathieu de Chalvet's Seneca. Ange Cappel's translations of the *De providentia*, *De clementia* and other Stoic works were popular, and the *Letters* was a favorite. Malherbe published the *Bienfaits* in 1630 and the *Letter to Lucilius*, and Jean Baudoin translated Epictetus, Lucian and Aesop. The historians were equally prized: Caesar's *Commentaries*, and Livy especially, and new versions of Tacitus' *Annals* by Colomby, and of the *History* by Rodolphe le Maistre, Polybius and Aelian by Louis Machault, Quintus Curtius by de Soulfour, and Dio Cassius, Suetonius and Tacitus by Baudoin.

Of 149 translations made between 1600 and 1640, 39 were politics and philosophy, 38 history, and 44 poetry, the main staple of a large public of literati in the Humanist camp. Horace, Persius, Juvenal and Pindar were all available in French, though quite two-thirds of classical poetry came from three authors—Virgil translated by Le Chevalier d'Agneaux, La Motte du Tertre and Du Pelliel; and Homer translated by Du Souhait, Certon and Claude Boitel. Ovid was easily the favorite, with ten reprints of the *Metamorphoses* between 1606 and 1645.

Translations of shorter works or parts of longer poems and speeches were made for readers with little or no knowledge of Greek or Latin, almost as exercises in style, and in the decade 1634–45 when French was evolving rapidly, several selections from Cicero were on sale, with a highly polished version of *Eight speeches* in French translated by Perrot d'Ablancourt, Giry and Du Ryer, revised by Conrart; d'Ablancourt had translated Minucius Felix's *Octavius,* and Giry one of Tertullian's *Apologetics,* and others tackled Isocrates, Plato, Tacitus and more Cicero. As the versions of Amyot, Vigenère, Chalvet, Renouard and Baudoin began to sound outdated and almost unreadable, a new generation of translators was coming in, more sensitive to nuances of style and meaning, less awed by precedents, ready to prepare more acceptable versions for contemporary readers.

2. History as a servant of the monarchy: from sacred to secular history

While linguistic study marked time in the first thirty years of the 17th century, there were relatively few new translations, but the history of the ancient world was progressively more studied. From bulky folios to slender octavos there was much variety, but student manuals were coming out in quantities from publishers like Morel, Cramoisy, Sonnius, Chevallier, Libert, Périer and Langelier. Growing pressure from the culture we know as Humanism was felt by all scholars, and ancient history and church history were crucial subjects, especially during the Wars of Religion. Only a few books on pre-Christian antiquity were published from 1598 to 1643, though some interest was shown in Ancient Egypt, land of Hermes-Trismegistus (Thoth), patron of letters, and attempts were made to decipher hieroglyphics, usually by assigning esoteric meanings to the characters. President Brisson's *De regio Persarum principatu* was another work in this genre, but the only book on ancient Greece was Pierre de Marcassus's *Histoire grecque,* compiled from ancient sources. Some histories of Rome for the general reader (Coëffeteau's and Scipion Dupleix's for example) were successful, but apart from Gruter's *De officiis domus Augusti* (Cramoisy, 1628) and Nicolas Bergier's *Histoire des grands chemins de l'Empire romain* (1622) there were few scholarly contributions. The decline of interest in classical philology is reflected in an equal lack of interest in ancient history, as if the public felt the subject already oversubscribed and wanted only general surveys.

Of course great numbers of Old and New Testament commentaries were part of the deep interest in Patrology which characterized the debates of the late 16th and early 17th centuries, but they included those made from a historical viewpoint, too, and once again the Fathers were enlisted. Josephus' *Jewish Antiquities* was in demand, and so was the history of Early Christianity; after 1620 compilations of earlier material were used, particularly Biblical commentaries, evidently for the battling theologians. Tertullian was of perennial interest because of his purity of style, but there was also curiosity about the Greek Fathers and the Byzantine era. As in other fields we can see a gradual shift from heavy, specialist erudition to more practical works suited to the needs of the "general" reader, though that term needs qualification.

Once again Jesuits were the progressive force, not only editing the Fathers and texts of the Early Councils but paying a great deal of attention to secular history, too, especially Byzantine. Fronton Du Duc foresook John Chrysostom for Nicephoros Callistos and edited the first published version of his work in Greek (1630); Father Petau did the same for the *Breviarium* of Patriarch Nicephoros, and Sirmond for the minor works of Eusebius, the chronicles of Anastasius the

Librarian, and Facundus' *Appendix codicis Theodosiani* and *Pro defensione trium capitulorum concilii Chalcedonensis.* Father Labbe edited the Greek text of the *Basilica* of Leo the Wise, and Cramoisy, the publisher of most of these, issued Georgius Codinus' *De officiis et officialibus magnae ecclesiae et aulae Constantinopolitanae,* edited by the German Jesuit Gretser.

Byzantine studies were revived by scholarship of this order, and the work involved foreshadowed the Byzantine Department at the Louvre which later put out prodigious tomes in an ambitious program. This original research the Jesuits hoped would further the reconciliation of the Roman Catholic and Greek Orthodox churches.

History, whether sacred or secular, was inseparable from French history. Sirmond did a great deal of research in all aspects of the subject, histories of the early Councils of the Church in France with documents, and some twenty medieval histories: Sidonius Apollinaris's *Letters,* Fulgentius, Ennodius, St. Avit, Peter the Venerable, Godefroy de Vendôme, Flodoard, Hincmar, Paschase Radbert and *Histoire de saint Charles comte de Flandres.*

French scholars benefited from the work of the Humanists; Pithou, Papire Masson and Claude Fauchet in the 16th century had done much to advance knowledge of the nation's history and were a sound basis for the officials and state functionaries who now started a systematic study of the subject. The brothers Dupuy, librarians in President de Thou's service and later of the Bibliothéque Royale, were in a privileged position, and Pierre, the elder, used the resources to compile an inventory of royal charters, traveling widely to find deeds and records relating to the Crown; this bore fruit in two works of a strong nationalist flavor, *Libertée de l'Eglise gallicane* and *Preuves* (1639), in which they retraced the genesis of French policy in church and state from the time of Philip the Fair, with emphasis on the rights of the French monarchy. Two other brothers, the Sainte-Marthe twins, dedicated their books to the glory of the King, the celebrated *Histoire généalogique de la Maison de France* (Paris, 1628, repr. 1647) and *Histoire généalogique de la*

Maison de Beauvais (Paris, 1646), and a monumental tome supporting Gallican claims, *Gallia christiana.* Théodore Godefroy, diplomat and scholar, put his own specialist knowledge to work in the royal service, followed by his son Denis, who promoted the monarchical cause in *Mémoires concernant la préséance des rois de France sur les rois d'Espagne* (1613), *De la Vraie origine de la Maison d'Autriche contre l'opinion de ceux qui la font déscendre en ligne masculine des rois de France de la race mérovingienne* (1624), *Généalogie des comtes et ducs de Bar* (1627), and *Cérémonial de France* (1619, rev. ed., 1649). His *Histoire du chevalier Bayard* helped create the legend of a great soldier hero, and he initiated a long series of major Chronicles from Charles V to Louis XII, a significant choice of period, just when nationalist sentiment was on the increase and modern France was emerging.

These were examples of early scientific history, though none was comparable with André Du Chesne, called The Father of History, author and editor of many works from the age of eighteen, including Alcuin, Abelard and Alain Chartier. He was largely responsible for the *Bibliotheca Cluniacensis,* a compendium of documents basic to an understanding of Cluniac history which Dom Marrier compiled. Du Chesne was the author of several genealogical histories of the great French families, amply supported by archives he had saved from oblivion, and he made documentalist history a fashion, in works like these: *Antiquités de la grandeur et majesté des rois de France; Antiquités et recherches des villes, chasteaux et places remarquables de toute la France* (repr. seven times from 1610 to 1637, and revised in 1647 and 1668 by François Du Chesne); *Histoire des Papes jusqu'à Paul V* (1616, 1645, 1653) and *Histoire d'Angleterre, d'Ecosse et d'Irlande* (1614, 1634, 1637). He published a *Bibliothèque des auteurs qui ont éscrit l'histoire et topographie de la France,* the first of its kind, in 1618 (repr. 1627), and in 1619 the first volume of a collected edition, *Historiae Normannorum scriptores* which was to provide a complete compilation of the main French historians in 24 volumes. The first came out in 1636, the second in 1641, and volumes 3 and 4, in the press when he died, were supervised by his son

François. The 5th volume was edited by François but lacked the master's touch, and the remainder were continued by the Benedictines as "the historians of France." At the same time Sébastien Cramoisy published an impressive array of huge folios: secular history was now a major attraction to scholars, mostly drawn from the administrative class and all of them devout monarchists in politics and Gallicans in religion. After all, the King and the French Church were their patrons.

Chronicles and annals were the staple of history in the 16th century, but the new form of narrative history, another by-product of Humanism, was modeled on the ancient historians. Early in the 17th century publishers issued old-fashioned history of the annalistic kind for a wider reading public and were evidently trying to supply a fairly complete range. Jesuit scholars compiled universal chronologies, lists of the main events in the history of the world, Petau's *Rationarium temporum* a typical one used by Bossuet when he was private tutor to the Dauphin; another was Torsellini's *Historia ab origine mundi ad annum 1630,* a counterblast to Sleidan's Protestant version of history and a standard textbook for use in Jesuit colleges—the numerous reprints prove it. Baronius's *Annales,* an authoritative but Ultramontane view of the world, was never published in Paris, a point worth noting, but summaries and abridgments tailored for French readers were common. Du Chesne wrote a history of the Papacy and a *Histoire générale d'Angleterre,* Turquet de Mayerne a history of Spain and Fougasse a history of Venice. On the whole foreign countries were of little interest to the French, and their histories were only noticed when they impinged on France, as in the lives of the most recent English sovereigns, Henry VII, Henry VIII and Elizabeth I, all of whom intervened in French affairs. William the Conquerer was a subject of keen interest, so too were the wars between Spain and Holland in the Netherlands.

Whether narrative history or annals, it was of gripping interest to the French reading public to read about France. To a nation still seeking to establish its aristocratic credentials, any study of origins was of passionate concern even if it involved purely legendary matter—Trojan ancestry, for example—and the subject was increasingly a part of school and college curricula. The Oratory used Berthault's *Florus gallicus* and *Florus franciscus,* in Latin and French, as again the multiple reprints prove them to have been a steady diet supplied by the Oratorian monks to their pupils.

For readers who wanted something with more flesh on it there was the old *Rosier historial de France,* with a secular career behind it, and Nicole Gilles's *Annales et chroniques de France,* a traditional source revised and augmented by Denis Sauvage and Belleforest in the 16th century with additional material by Gabriel Chappuys. Belleforest's *Grandes annales et histoire générale de France* was regularly reprinted and updated to 1620 by Chappuys and Savaron. As well as these rather dated histories there was Arnoul Le Férron's *Histoire générale des rois de France,* more modern in concept though by 1600 already a veteran among histories. New histories included: *Inventaire général* by Jean de Serres la, a Protestant, and *Histoire général de France* by Scipion Dupleix, a Catholic; Charles Sorel's *Histoire de la monarchie française, Histoire universelle de toutes nations et spécialement des Gaulois ou Français* by Jacques Charron, and Pierre Aubert's *Histoire ou recueil des gestes . . . et regnes des rois de France.*

History was still the province of scholars, but gradually teachers in academies and professional writers joined in the creation of a nationalistic history for the wider reading public. Propaganda was an obvious theme, and both the general and the elitist public for history were served, latterly by the "Historiographes du Roi," whose style derived from their predecessors in Renaissance Italy.

Just as in our own day readers had a taste for specific periods or personalities: the King most interesting to them in the early medieval period was Clovis, founder of the French royal line, and (not surprising in the age of the Catholic Revival) Saint Louis. The last two hundred years were of absorbing interest, Godefroy for the 15th century, Monstrelet's *Chroniques* and Philippe de Commines' *Mémoires* all selling well in the Paris bookshops, and of course the great national heroine, Joan of Arc. As Royal Historiographer,

Pierre Matthieu wrote histories of the French kings from Louis XI to Henri III, covering the same general time span.

A terrible lesson was underlined by the recent Wars of Religion, showing how destructive civil war could be. Though Protestantism no doubt prompted many histories of heresies that mark the age, and of the Council of Trent (from both sides), the masterpiece of contemporary history was de Thou's *Historia sui temporis*. Though placed on the Index it was frequently reprinted, and likewise memoirs of eminent persons were another profitable line: Du Bellay, de Villeroy, Montluc's *Commentaires*, Cardinal d'Ossat's *Lettres*, though not strictly contemporary were all witnesses to the drama being played out. Most accounts of the Wars of Religion were those of military leaders, statesmen or diplomats of one party or another, and no veteran of the Catholic League failed to tell his story, with the Ultramontane versions of Bentivoglio and Davila giving one view, and the Protestant Agrippa d'Aubigné the other, though his book was ordered to be burned by the Paris Parlement; memoirs of Protestant leaders (La Noue is an example) could only be published outside France. And personal narratives were a new genre, tendentious, and gathering momentum until the historians of Henri IV and Louis XII were more like royal apologists than true historians.

The trail thus begins with an interest in ancient history as an ancillary to classical studies in the Renaissance, leads on to Church history as an arm of the Counter Reformation, flowing into histories of France which ultimately turn into royalist histories. The authors of such works flattered the taste of their readers and their pride in past and present glories, real or imaginary. Their readers were of course the prosperous and educated classes, royal officials, magistrates, lawyers, just like the authors; each would read a monarchist or Gallican interpretation into events, whether of the recent or distant past, and writers were mostly a secure part of the Establishment. In Richelieu's day biographies of Cardinals and Ministers of State were common, and in Suger's time stories of the Mayors of the Palace and of Georges d'Amboise later on, and after him of Ximenes. All this begs the question—to what extent did the King and his advisers encourage historians to write in this way? The answer will be seen later.

3. Voyages and travels

The discoveries of new lands, the extension of commercial communications and a more accurate assessment of classical geography tended to inspire more curiosity about distant countries, with a consequent output of travel books and cosmographies, or what might be called descriptive geography, and new editions of ancient geographers, descriptions of the world and more recent travels. They were in all Paris bookshops and sold well up to the time when the modern science of cartography began.

Classical geographers were the foundation, as in other spheres, and France the center of interest. Strabo on Gaul and Caesar's *Commentaries* were basic texts, along with school books like Father Monet's *Galliae geographia, veteris recentisque* and Father Labbe's *Pharus Galliae antiquae,* Papire Masson's *Descriptio fluminum Galliae quae Francia est* and Louis Coulon's *Rivières de France* or Nicolas Sanson's maps. Descriptions of France, somewhat like modern guides, were more popular with adults: André Du Chesne's *Antiquités et recherches des villes, châteaux et places plus remarquables de toute la France* was a favorite, and others varied from the fanciful to the utilitarian, like Charles Estienne's *Guide des chemins de France.* Individual towns and regions, especially Paris, were covered: Gilles Corrozet's *Fleur des antiquités et singularités de Paris* (1605) followed *Fastes, antiquités et choses les plus remarquables de Paris* by the publisher Bonfons, completed by Jacques Du Breuil, and Du Breul's *Théâtre des antiquités de Paris* (1612) and Claude Malingre's *Annales générales de la ville de Paris* (1640). The first street plans also appeared, to help guide provincials and foreigners round the capital, which now had 400,000 inhabitants.

Once again, a range of materials from the erudite to the popular was available, with a strong nationalist flavor, especially Jesuit books just after Richelieu's death. And an interesting case of early anti-German feeling was over the

Introductio in universam Geographiam by the Protestant
Philip Clüver, infused with a philosophy of a Greater
Germany. It was denounced, though it had been a classbook
used in Jesuit colleges.

Traditional writers on geography were now little read
(Musier, for instance) and a new and comprehensive compendium by a "Gentleman of the Royal Bedchamber," was
published in various formats, and frequently reprinted—
Davity, *Estats, empires, royaumes et principautés du monde*.
There is hardly anything about individual cities, regions or
even countries in most of these early geographies: Ascoli's
book on the British Isles was just such an example, and the
same is true of Sweden and Germany; there seemed to be
little interest in Switzerland or Denmark, and even on the
adjacent territory of Flanders there was nothing to be had in
Paris. Guicciardini's *Description des Pays-Bas* was, however,
a much reprinted work in Antwerp, and Catholic Spain
proved of greater interest to French readers than the
Protestant North, as Ambrosio de Salazar's *Inventaire
général des plus curieuses recherches des royaumes d'Espagne*
proved when its French version was twice reprinted by Du
Breuil (Paris, 1612, 1615). Italian cities were also of interest,
particularly Rome, but on the whole the French were
sublimely indifferent to their neighbors.

Distant countries aroused more interest, and voyages and
travels by individual explorers and missionaries were common, though no one risked formal geographical descriptions
in any scientific sense; the main objective was to describe the
conversion of primitive peoples, but in the process much
precious information about local habits and customs was
gleaned. By the late 1500s the Middle East and Levant had
become a subject of attention; the new discoveries in North
America were not much reported until well into the 17th
century. The charm of the Mediterranean countries was still
strong and one book, Villemont's *Voyages en Italie, Grèce et
Egypte*, though poor in content was a favorite, and Jean
Mocquet's *Voyages* which described the Barbary Coast was
in great demand because of its romantic, almost fictional
flavor. The corsairs of Tunis and Algiers, their Christian

captives, naval battles against them, and diplomatic and missionary activity were assured of a good audience, the most popular account being *Voyages d'Afrique faite par le commandement du Roi . . . les navigations des Français . . . en 1629 et 1631 . . . en côtes occidentales du Royaume de Fez et de Maroc* by a Muslim convert to Christianity, Armand Mustapha, a protégé of Richelieu. It contains a good deal of comment on the attempts by Louis XIII's Ministers to conclude political and commercial treaties with Barbary.

Persia and the Ottoman Empire were other subjects sufficiently exotic to attract readers (notably Pacifique de Provins' *Relation du voyage de Perse*) though Persia was of lesser interest than Turkey—it was nevertheless an ally against the Grand Turk and lay on the route to India. But Turkey was more fascinating. Michel Baudier wrote several descriptive accounts, notably *l'Histoire générale de la Cour et du Sérail du Grand Seigneur,* which went into three successive editions. Jerusalem and the Holy Land and the wars which the Turks prosecuted in Europe were of irresistible interest, with pilgrims' tales at once in demand; one such, *Bousquet sacré, ou le Voyage de la Terre Saincte, composé des roses de calvaire, des lis de Bethléem, des hyacinthes du Mont Olivet* (Paris, 1616; 10th ed., 1623), was a bestseller, perhaps because of its association with pilgrimage, a last whiff of the Crusades. The Far East, Madagascar, Indo-China, China, India and Japan were in Acosta's *Histoire naturelle des Indes tant orientales qu'occidentales,* and Mendoza's *Histoire du royaume de Chine.* Others in the genre were Ferdinand Mendes Pinto's *Voyages adventureux* (1628, 1645), a collection of foreigners' tales translated into French, and straightforward narratives of adventures by French traders and freebooters, like François Martin de Vitré's *Description du premier voyage fait aux Indes orientales par les Français* (1604, 1609) or the *Voyage de Français Pyrard de Laval . . . aux Indes orientales, Maldives et Brésil* (1615, 1619, 1678), an extraordinary story of wanderings from Brazil to Goa and from Madagascar to the Indies, edited by Jérôme Bignon, Librarian of the Bibliothèque Royale.

Missionary activity had been pursued in the Far East with

great vigor by Jesuits and Capuchins (the Capuchins in Tartary) and they left behind narratives of their experiences, often as letters addressed to their superiors at Rome. The Latin originals were translated and were the channels by which discoveries were publicized, whether in Cathay, Tibet or of Catholic missions in Ethiopia or the West Indies, to readers at home, usually emphasizing the persecutions suffered by the missionary priests, especially in China and Japan. The letters by Jesuits were translated into many European languages to help in disseminating knowledge of Oriental cultures, but there was only very limited understanding of the Far East until much later in the 17th century. Baudier and Coulon compiled second-hand accounts, the first published in 1627, the second in 1645, but China remained an enigma for many years.

Apart from some missionary literature there was surprisingly little evidence of the Spanish and Portuguese colonization of America, and even the territories annexed in the name of France, Nouvelle-France, roused little interest, though the explorer Champlain's *Voyages* and Marc Lescarbot's *Histoire de la Nouvelle-France* were read, along with the descriptions by Capuchin and Recollect missionaries of their years among the Indian tribes. Canada shows a steep rise in interest after 1630, largely because Richelieu made that territory the center of his expansionist colonial policy, and the Jesuits who succeeded the Capuchins and Recollects out there were well versed in the art of press publicity; annually from 1632 they published a letter reporting their progress under the aegis of the Superior of the Province of Quebec, Father Paul Le Jeune (1632–39), then Fathers Barthélemy Vimont, Jérôme Lallement, Paul Ragueneau and François-Joseph Le Marcier (1640–70). The pamphlet newsletters were instant best-sellers, encouraging financial and other support from home, but also stimulated business interest under Richelieu's direction, and made Frenchmen more aware of the wide world and its potential for exploitation. The switch of attention from the Far East to the West was all due to the concerting of motive and action by Richelieu and his Jesuit activists, but proved to be a temporary phase.

4. Law and the French State

Given the high esteem in which the profession of law was held in the Ancien Régime it is hardly surprising that legal works formed a high proportion of the output of Parisian publishers. Canon law was of prime importance: canonical texts, general and national, treatises on controversial points, especially the delicate matter of Church-State relations, the legal conflicts between secular and regular clergy, the rules of the various orders, important at a time of monastic revival, and countless technical studies dealing with church bene-fices, livings, and the status of the sacraments, particularly marriage. Without going into the mass of legal publications so typical of this age, we might concentrate on a central topic, Roman law and national law, both public and private. On Roman law Cujas was the fundamental authority, a great master of Humanist legal scholarship, and after him the men who followed in the same tradition, Brisson, Pierre and François Pithou, William Barclay, Thierry Marcile, Nicolas Rigault, Passerat, and Samuel Petit. Two of the most fertile commentators on Roman law were at work on the great Byzantine program of research at the Louvre, namely Charles Annibal Fabrot and Charles Labbe, but very little foreign work was published apart from Grotius and Ber-cholten of Holland. Paris was the acknowledged center of learning and theory in this field and Lyons provided practical textbooks. An interest in purely French law grew alongside other nationalist tendencies, and Paris was the primary producer.

The editing of laws and customaries reached a peak in the 16th century and the growing number of tribunals in all the regions of France meant more customaries. Paris as the ad-ministrative center and the location of its Parlement was the natural home of technical publications in customary law for many districts and bailiwicks near Paris (Chauny, Meaux and Senlis) and even for the provinces (Orléans, Anjou, Berry and Brittany), though the Paris customary was the most important, not a year going by without at least one new reissue. They were edited by celebrated jurists: Argentré for

Brittany—his compilations made Buon the bookseller's fortune—and for Paris there were several, including Du Moulin, Charondas, Choppin, Fortin, Pithou, Tronçon, Tournet and Guérin.

Special mention must be made of the comparative customaries, juridical decisions and precedents in massive syntheses of customary law aimed at providing a general conspectus. Boutillier's *Somme rurale* was the prototype (Paris, 1603, 1611, 1612, 1621; Lyons, 1621); Charondas's *Pandectes, ou Digestes du droit français* (Lyons, 1596, 1597, 1602; Paris 1607–10 and 1637); Guy Coquille's *Institution du droit français* (1607, 1608, 1611, 1637, 1646 in two eds., 1657, 1665, 1668, 1679). Clearly there was much demand in the profession for a synthesis of customary law and public legislation; there were few works on private law.

Yet all this was only a fraction of the huge output in this field. Multitudes of verdicts handed down by the courts, central government and the tribunals throughout the land were circulated, and the legal records of disputes or commentaries on them which sought to influence public opinion, but few survive today. Procedure manuals for the legal fraternity, decrees and decisions of the courts, the growth in royal legislation requiring regular editions of Statutes all meant great profit for the book trade. As a result of discussions at the Estates General assembly at Blois in 1576, a set of royal ordinances, the Code Henri III, was published in 1587 (5th ed., 1621). Rebuffi edited *Edicts et ordonnances des Roys de France;* this and Fontanon's and Pierre Guénois' *Conférence des ordonnances royaux* were standard reference works continually updated. A *Code Louis XIII* was published by Jacques Corbin in 1628, and Néron and Girard published *Les edicts et ordonnances des tres chretiens rois de France,* revised and reissued until the early 18th century.

During the struggle for power between the still comparatively weak central government and the aristocracy in the provinces a great deal of literature about sovereignty of courts, on justice, taxation, public money, military organization, and venality (the sale of offices) was in evidence.

5. Politics

The Spaniard Saavédra Fajardo in the mid-17th century commented with some apprehension that "The northern countries as well as France and Italy are well supplied with books about politics and affairs of state, and with commentaries on Aristotle, Plato's *Republic* and on Tacitus." Not only that but the first bibliographies of politics appeared at this stage, one by Gabriel Naudé. Which books did he think indispensable?

In most Philosophy courses, ethics and economics were considered to be a proper introduction to the subject, and Naudé advises Aristotle's works on moral philosophy as a start, and on economics he suggests Aristotle and Xenophon, adding, "Once the reader has educated himself in morals and economics he can go on to politics." Firstly, he suggested the *Republic* and *Laws* of Plato (Naudé looks for parallels in Christian teaching), the *Politics* of Aristotle, the Bible, Aquinas' *De regimine principum,* Strozza's commentaries on Aristotle, Plutarch, and Cicero (regretting that the second book of the *De divinatione* was lost). He places Bodin high among the moderns, but he does not think Justus Lipsius contributed anything new. In comparative religion he has suggestions; on the subject of treaties and confederations he criticizes Emeric de la Croix; he discusses works on peace and war, praising Grotius, and concludes with a section on administration, books dealing with the education of princes, knowledge of peoples, and a list of "curious and secret history."

The classical tradition is strong in Naudé: Aristotle, Plato, Xenophon, Theophrastus, Seneca, Epictetus and Plutarch, with often foreign commentators who had not been published in France; French authors are well represented: Du Vair, Coëffeteau, Montaigne, Charron; historians such as Matthieu, diplomats like Cardinal Ossat, whose published letters were widely read. For Naudé, the term "Politics" was of wide connotation, a meeting ground of jurists and historians, literary men and philosophers. From so wide a field we can select only the most typical.

The extent of royal power was a subject of continual interest for lawyers, great officers of state and lesser officials. Guy Coquille's *Introduction du droit Français* and Charles Loyseau's *De la Seigneurie* and *Du droit des offices* were in the forefront, with Cardinal Le Bret's *De la souveraincté du Roi, de son domaine et de sa couronne,* and works by bourgeois writers like André Du Chesne, in for example *Antiquités et recherches de la grandeur et majesté des rois de France,* and young Jérôme Bignon whose career was launched with his brilliant *Excellence des roys et du royaume de France,* in which the king was seen as a type of Christian warrior.

As supporters of the King, state officers were interested in the theory of sovereignty but the average citizen was more interested in the effects of the exercise of power. Machiavelli was well known and stimulated argument, and Tacitus was the model for political studies of autocratic power. Despite Machiavelli's infamous reputation his works were all in print at Paris without licence, though with some prudent precautions, a sure sign that he was in demand, unlike Bodin's *République,* which could only be published in exile at Geneva.

Basic works were available on various aspects of Politics— Monchrestien's *Traité de l'Oeconomie politique* (Rouen, 1615), and the works of three foreign refugees. First, Grotius, imprisoned in Holland for his Arminian views, escaped to Paris where he lived till his death in 1645 and wrote the *Apologeticus eorum qui Hollandiae praefuerunt* (1622) and *De jure belli et pacis* (1625), both of which were placed on the Index in 1627 and later published in Frankfurt and Amsterdam. Campanella was the second, a refugee from the prisons of the Inquisition who went to Paris in 1631 and through Peiresc's good offices secured a pension of 3000 livres from Richelieu. He wrote his most famous book there, *Civitas soli,* wherein he views France as the home of a universal monarch under whose protection there would be a unity of all religions. Third, Thomas Hobbes, who published his *De Cive* when an exile in Paris in 1642, and there prepared his great work *Leviathan.*

Richelieu's acts as a promoter of the power and influence of France roused deep passions. Pamphlet wars were waged by protagonists and out of that came theoretical works of great value: *Autorité des roys* by Colomby, Balzac's *Prince* and Silhon's *Ministre d'Etat,* Le Bret's *De la souveraincté,* and *Conseiller d'Etat,* ascribed to Philippe de Béthune, which enjoyed a revival. Baudier worked this rich new seam with his histories of famous statesmen, and Machiavelli was defended by Machon, who based his *Apologie de Machiavel* on the Bible. Naudé even discussed coups d'Etat. Yet although there seems to be an element of free thought in this political arena, most writers were on the side of authority.

CHAPTER V

CLASSICS OF PHILOSOPHY AND SCIENCE: ARISTOTELIANISM TO MECHANISTIC PHILOSOPHY

P HILOSOPHICAL AND SCIENTIFIC WORKS, even if we include technical books, were only a small proportion of the total output from Paris, yet it was in this age that what has been called "the miracle of the 1620s" happened when modern physics, mechanistic and materialist, takes the place of Aristotle's "qualitative" physics. New thought, freeing itself from the obscurantism of church dogmas, was with some difficulty finding a way forward from its first beginnings in the previous century. To grasp the current ideas on science and philosophy we need to look closely at the philosophical and technical books of the day.

1. Philosophy: old traditions and new currents

Aristotle was still the basis of all official science and philosophy despite some recent objections to his theories; the Church and State were still Aristotle's patrons. There had been some blurring of positions when leaders of the Counter Reformation sought support for their theology in Aristotle's thought. Du Vair's edition of the Works came out in 1619, Greek text with a Latin translation in the contemporary fashion, and based on Casaubon's recension (1629, 1639, 1654). Jean Libert, publisher of textbooks for Jesuit colleges, brought out the *Rhetoric* in the Greek with Latin translation; the *Politics* and *Rhetoric* and a treatise on Mechanics were published in French, but Aristotle's works in the original must have been difficult for students, and we may well wonder how many of them ever read and inwardly digested his works.

Spanish commentators were the best known philosophers of the Counter Reformation but their annotated editions rarely appeared in Paris, apart from Arriaga's *Cursus philosophicus,* but Lyons supplied Spanish–inspired textbooks. More common were short handbooks of traditional "Sententiae" and other texts edited for students, sponsored by the University of Paris and often written by its professors. One such was the *Aurea Aristotelis axiomata,* wrongly attributed to the Venerable Bede, which must have been a useful source of quotations at a modest price for the hard-pressed student. François le Roy's *Universae Aristotelis philosophiae brevis epilogus et compendium* was a kind of aide-memoire of the sort traditionally used by students, and another handy little book was put together by Jan Caecilius Frey, a Swiss with a reputation as a brilliant teacher in the colleges of Lisieux, Navarre and Montaigu. In twenty-six years, 6000 pupils went through his hands, including Naudé, who was made a faithful Aristotelian thereby for the rest of his life, although with a tinge of free thought associated with the University of Padua.

There were more voluminous editions, of course. Jean Crassot, Regent of la Marche college, Pierre Padet, François Le Rées, and Eustache de Saint-Paul wrote weighty tomes; Saint-Paul's *Summa philosophica* (1609; 7th ed., 1623) was used by Descartes when writing his *Méditations* as well as by Abra de Raconis' *Totius philosophiae tractatus.* Although the tradition was that philosophy was done in Latin, many books were already appearing in French in that field, for instance Jean de Champeynac's *Sommaire des austre parties de la philosophie* and Bouju's *Corps de toute la philosophie* (1614). On the syllabus for Protestant students taught by Pierre Du Moulin and in Scipion Dupleix's courses for young nobles either in an academy or a private tuition, French works and summaries figured. The central tradition died hard, and authors of student treatises of apologetics supported their argument with a typical Scholastic apparatus, appealing to Aristotle, and mentioning any new theories only to refute them. The only really constructive work to come out of traditional teaching was some logic, and an essay on the humours by Coëffeteau and Cureau de la Chambre, who were in a way early precursors of the modern science of psychology. But generally speaking there was a hardening of the philosophical arteries, a serious impediment to progressive thinking at a time when students in all walks of life were ready for something new.

Other philosophers besides Aristotle were read—Seneca for example, whose tragedies every schoolboy had to learn. Five editions of the complete works in Latin and two in French appeared from 1602 to 1627, quite apart from individual titles. Plutarch and Cicero, and the *Enchiridion* (Manual) of Epictetus were all available in scholarly editions and in translation. Stoicism was thus entrenched in the scholarship of the day, and not seen as heterodox because Christian Humanism approved the Stoic virtues as being close to Christian ideals. The works of the ancient Stoics were quoted by Lipsius, Du Vair and Yves de Paris, and Du Vair's *Coustume et consolation* was reprinted at least 15 times before 1641. The best modern mirrors of Stoicism were the sceptics, Montaigne for instance, whose *Essays* were kept in print by Mlle. de Gournay, and Charron's *Sagesse,* a breviary for brave spirits, though it had to suffer revision by censors. Sextus Empiricus, Lucian, somewhat expurgated (though Bourdelot published a complete edition), and various versions of *Dialogues with the dead* were published by "Orasius Tubero" for clandestine circulation.

The greatest menace to Aristotelian thought in the eyes of orthodox philosophers was the school of Naturalists at Padua, Pomponazzi, Telesio, Bruno, and writers like Paracelcus and Cardan, the inheritors of Renaissance Neo-Platonism. Though not widely known their writings were influential enough to merit reply and even action, as when Vanini was burned for a book that was too clearly anti-religious, and indignation when Campanella openly advocated that Christians should dissociate themselves from moribund official Aristotelianism. The heritage of Neo-Platonism soon spread to critiques of Aristotle's *Physics*. New currents were ever more visible in scientific thought.

2. *Medical and Pharmaceutical Literature*

As Aristotle was to Philosophy so Galen and Hippocrates were to Medicine, and they also suffered from a reaction, if we may judge from books of the time. At first Hippocrates and Galen were unshaken: in 1639 René Chartier published a monumental edition of each, and single titles were constantly reprinted. Galen's masterpiece of physiology, in French, *De l'usage des parties du corps humain,* and Hippocrates' *Coacae praenotiones* were still the standard works, and in surgery they and Oribasius were the authorities. In hygiene, Hippocrates' *De Aere, aquis et locis* and treatises by his lineal descendants, the School of Salerno, were always in print in Paris, in Latin and French versions, and bleeding was still the best therapeutic practice, confirmed by Galen's *Art de guérir par la saignée.* Laxatives were also a sovereign remedy as authorized by Hippocrates' *De pharmacia purgantibus,* and promoted by M. Purgon. Most popular of all were Hippocrates' *Aphorisms,* published by Libert in the Greek with a Latin parallel text, and even in Latin and Greek verses with a rendering in French verse! Yet despite the apparent strength of the Hippocrates-Galen tradition it was all within the circle of a small number of writers who were singularly long-winded.

Firstly, there were the professors of the Faculty of Medicine at Paris. Jean de Gorris made his reputation in the 16th century as a traditionalist and was one of the first to compile a medical dictionary; his books were mostly commentaries on the ancients, in particular Hippocrates. After Gorris was Barthélemy Perdoux, known as "Perdulcis" (died 1610), whose master work was the *Universa medicina ex medicarum principum sententiis consillisque collecta* published by René Chartier (1630; repr. Sauvageon, 1639), the publisher of Hippocrates and Galen. Perdoux's *In Sylvii anatomen et in librum Hippocratis De Natura humana,* from a manuscript belonging to Gabriel Naudé, did not see the light until 1643. The pathology of internal ailments was studied by Duret and Houllier, also followers of Hippocrates and Galen (published by Chartier, 1611) and the Jean

Riolans, father and son, were the most prolific of all in clinical medicine. Jean I wrote many pamphlets against quacks like Libavius, Quercetanus and Israël Harvet, much in vogue by those striving to keep up with modern practice; his *Praelectiones in libros physiologicales et "De abditis rerum causis"* came out in 1601, his *Universae medicinae compendia* appeared first in 1598 and was a classic textbook (4th ed., 1618), and his complete works were published in 1610 and 1638–41. Jean Riolan II specialized in anatomy, with the *Anthropographia, Schola anatomica* and *Osteologia* to his credit, and his complete contributions to that science were published in 1628/9 before his *Encheiridium anatomicum et pathologicum,* which with Harvey's discoveries opened the way to an understanding of the circulation of the blood.

In medicine as in other subjects the Sorbonne was a stronghold of tradition, and exhumed the works of earlier doctors who were of the Hippocratic school, though some newcomers were on the horizon, the King's doctors among them, Du Laurens from Montpellier perhaps the best known, an anatomist of uncanny skill. His *Discours de la conservation de la vue, des maladies mélancoliques et catarrhes et de la vieillesse* was many times reprinted 1597–1630 and his books were published in Latin in 1628 by Guy Patin, in French at Rouen in 1621 and 1661, and in Paris in 1639 and 1646. Another doctor, little known today, La Framboisière, was an industrious compiler of anatomical textbooks, *Scholae medicae ad candidatorum examen pro Laurea impetranda subeundum* (Paris, 1622 and 1630), *Ambrosiopoea* (Paris, 1622), *Canones et consultationes medicinales* (Paris, 1595 and 1619), *Ordonnance sur les médicaments tant simples que composés,* and had his complete *oeuvre* in print by 1633. Probably Du Laurens and La Framboisière owed their reputation to the high offices they held, and Patin would not wish to alienate colleagues; hence the publication of their complete works even when La Framboisière's "chemistry" was of the occult variety. Lazare Rivière introduced chemical medicine, and his *Praxis medica* was published in 1640, his *Methodus curandorum febrium* in 1641; a German, Daniel Sennert's *Institutionum medicinae libri V* (1631), *De febribus* (1633), *De chymicorum cum*

Aristotelicis et Galenicis consensu ac dissensu liber (significant title) in 1633, and his Latin textbooks in 1641. There were plainly two camps in the Faculty of Medicine.

There was an efflorescence of anatomical studies, associated with the names of Riolan, Pardoux, Du Laurens and Charles Guillemeau, and others like Germain Courtin, Jean Vigier, Habicot and Théophile Gelée, probably the result of more experiment by a new generation of surgeons and their apprentices, a fact which would account for contemporary textbooks of surgery and operation techniques. Ambroise Paré was supreme in this skill, his technical manuals going into five editions by 1598 and eight by 1628, highly critical of the conventional approach, by for example Guy de Chauliac, still circulating in the provinces. Jacques Guillemeau's books, *Epitome praeceptorum medicinae chirurgicae* by Pigray, a pupil of Paré, Jacques de Marque's *Méthodique introduction à la chirurgie,* a selection of writings on surgery, and Antoine de Corbye's *Chirurgie française recueillie par Maistre Jacques Daléchamps,* together with another collection called *Fleurs de chirurgie,* were all on sale in Paris. A heavy emphasis on surgical practice. Another work of modernizing tendency was David de Planis' *Traicté des playes faites par les mousquetades* (Paris, Campy, 1642), but on the whole there was little advance since Paré.

In physiology the classical descriptions were still the model but some progress was made in obstetrics thanks to Guillemeau and Louise Boursier, a famous midwife. In pathology syphilis was no longer a fashionable affliction, probably because more efficacious remedies were available, but the plague was a different matter, a menace which regularly decimated the population in the congested capital, and the subject of much speculation in pamphlets describing the symptoms and the awful consequences and offering advice on avoiding contagion. Most of this was sheer ignorance, but in the treatment of fever some progress was made as new remedies were tried.

Therapeutic medicine was always of interest, and we know from the plays of Molière that leeches and purgatives were standard treatments. There is also plenty of contemporary evidence. When new medicines with a chemical basis were introduced their validity was contested and the Faculty split into two camps. Paracelsus was in fashion, a mixture of the esoteric and the practical, and prescriptions flew about that sound like alchemy with their draughts of pure gold, magic and astrology, but there was an attempt to understand the chemistry of the body in such works as Paracelsus' *Les XIV livres des paragraphes* and the *Quatre livres des secrets de médecine et de la philosophie chimique faicte français* by Jean Liébault (Paris and Rouen). The *Pharmacopoea dogmaticorum restituta* by "Quercetanus" (Joseph Du Chesne), a surgeon and doctor of medicine from Basel who became King's doctor and head of a school of "chemists" in Paris, was in regular use, and François Du Soucy and Oswald Croll wrote similar works. Croll, a German disciple of Paracelsus, and a Cabalist, published a *Basilica chymica* in which the art of mummification and the extraction of potions from human skulls is described, but he also described silver chloride, the properties of succinic acid, "sulphuric ether," sulphate of zinc, an emetic, diaphoretic antimony and various compounds of mercury.

The science was at a crossroads, between chemistry and magic. Two English doctors were influential at this time, John Dee, Queen Elizabeth's astrologer, and William Davidson, a protégé of Henrietta Maria, Charles I's Queen, who was later Director of the Royal Gardens. More conventional works of pharmacy were Mattioli's *Commentaires sur les six livres de Pedanius Dioscoride de la Matière médicinale,* Jacques Sylvius' *Pharmacopée* and Bauderon's *Paraphrase sur la Pharmacopée* and *La Pharmacopée.* All the essential knowledge was assembled in Jean de Renou's *Institutionum pharmaceuticarum Libri V,* the vade mecum of apothecaries for generations.

Guy Patin was suspicious of apothecaries, worshippers of strange chemical gods, and sponsored a work by Philbert Guybert which he recommended as practical, without mumbo jumbo, the *Médecin charitable* (1625), a book of receipts giving advice on preparation of the most useful drugs. It reached its 12th edition in 1627 and remained in print until 1680. Guybert was a modern pharmacist, the author of many little manuals and guides for the new race of chemists experimenting with drugs, men who made it possible for a properly authenticated, official list of prescribed drugs to be drawn up by the Faculty of Medicine in Paris, the *Codex,* first published in 1638. It included such items as emetic wine, which angered the Galenists because it was a symbol of the "new" chemical therapy, and when Bauderon's classic *Pharmacopée* included a section on chemistry as an agent in healing, pharmacy as a recognized practice had arrived.

The old bastions of orthodoxy were under attack, whether the Hippocratic school of medicine or the Aristotelian school of philosophy, from new thinkers and practitioners, philosophers and doctors, of the caliber of Paracelsus and Cardan, and in spite of some confusion, some errors and some wild theorizing, experimental science was opening up the route from alchemy to modern chemistry in all its branches.

3. Man and nature

New forces were apparent in other areas, too. The study of "Natural Philosophy" inspired by Francis Bacon's proposals for new scientific method developed into what we call Science and Technology, originally applied to traditional arts and exercises, hunting for instance. The literature of "venery" was extensive, Jacques Du Fouilloux's *Vénerie* and Jean de Franchières' *La Fauconnerie* classics of their kind, and Charles d'Arcussia's small books on wolf hunting were the authority. It was of course an aristocratic society, and horsemanship was of vital concern—the selection, training and riding of mounts was the subject of substantial and sumptuous treatment in large illustrated books like Salomon de la Broue's *Cavalerie française* and Antoine de Pluvinel's *Maneige royal,* part of the furnishings of country houses.

Agronomy as a science dates back to the 16th century. Handy pocket books on the art of the vine or the cultivation of the silkworm were common in the period 1602–06, almost a campaign. Charles Estienne's *Maison rustique* had remained in print since the 16th century, in Paris, Lyons and Rouen, and Elie Vinet and Antoine Mizauld's *Maison champêtre et agriculture* was much followed whereas Olivier de Serres' *Théâtre d'agriculture et mesnage des champs* was not so often reprinted. It looks as if the new manuals of agronomy were for a new class of rural landowners who had recently bought up estates—possibly prosperous city tradesmen with ambitions who needed instruction in the arts of country life and were more willing to learn than the old guard nobility. Collections of tales or verse celebrating country life were popular; Guillaume Bouchet's *Serées* for example, or Claude Gauchet's *Plaisirs des champs*.

Classification of plants and animals now appears on a systematic plan, and botany is well served, though not zoology. Linocier's *Histoire des plantes* was in its 2nd edition, and the first Flora of the Paris region was published. Botanical gardens were created, and the Royal Gardens were a pattern of excellence inspiring illustrated plates of exquisite quality depicting medicinal plants which figured in embroideries and were a feature of herbal remedies. Geology was not yet understood but little books about minerals described their allegedly curative properties and so brought them to the attention of readers as a subject fit for study. Mining and the stratification of rocks was already being advanced as a study in Germany and received its due impetus in France when Richelieu ordered an inquiry into the mineral resources of the country; two books forgotten for half a century were reprinted: *Recepte véritable par laquelle tous les hommes de France pourrent apprendre à multiplier et augmenter leurs trésors* and *Discours admirables de la nature des eaux et fontaines, tant naturelles qu'artificielles, des métaux, des sels et salines, des pierres, des terres, du feu et des émaux* by Bernard Palissy, made into a single volume by Fouet and issued as *Moyen de devenir riche et manière par laquelle tous les hommes de France pourrent apprendre à multiplier leurs trésors et possessions, avec le secret du plusieurs choses naturelles,* a title which betrays a good deal about publishers and buyer. There is more than a hint here that we are in the new age of quick commerical profit as well as the old romantic urge for the philosopher's stone.

It is the increase in technical and utilitarian matter that gives us the clue to the new age. Let us now turn to the corresponding theoretical work, which was vital for an age not fully open to mechanistic doctrines, if it was to make progress. Who were the "new men" busy discrediting received ideas?

While Gassendi was working on his *Exercitationes adversus Aristoteleos* (Grenoble, 1624) a small group of natural philosophers (they are not yet "savants") published theses contradicting Aristotle's *Physics* and the ideas of Paracelsus, which led to further battles with the University of Paris.

Among this audacious group of young scientists were Etienne de Clave, a doctor with a knowledge of chemistry, François Du Soucy, and Antoine de Villon, an astrologer, a mixed bag, but it was still an age of conventional superstition—recently the Rosicrucians had published notices all over Paris about the philosopher's stone, and this had drawn more fire from the progressives. The scene is filled with Occultists (virtually the only tradition of experiment) who nevertheless clear the ground and make further advance possible. Campanella was a name at this time, respected as a scientist yet he cast horoscopes; Jean-Baptiste Morin, who held a chair in the Collège Royal, divided his time between the study of authentic astronomy and astrology, and Mersenne, who was equally at home in "natural magic," "physiognomy" (whatever that was) and a branch of alchemy called Chrysopoea and Argyropoea (the art of making precious metals), was also skilled in astrology. We have to remember that in an age when the Devil, witches and demons were all seen as material facts, Occultism and the Cabala could be accepted as a serious science, and we cannot neatly class them with modern subjects because there were still no "modern" sciences. The kind of obscure and often confused studies typical of this period fit into no framework or syllabus that we would recognize as scientific because the researchers were distracted into so many different sidelines, as in Morestel's *Philosophia occulte des devanciers d'Aristote et Platon* (1607). Porphyry's works were republished, and the sorcerer Maximus of Tyre; even Apuleius's *Golden ass* was seen as hermetic—or at least one must conclude that was a reason for its frequent reprinting. Philo Judaeus, Philostratus, Hermes Trismegistus, Raymond Lulle, Albertus Magnus and Nicolas Flamel were the early masters cited by the occult theorists of the 17th century.

The Cabal was a kind of club based on mystic word arrangements—acrostics—the haunt of devotees of the "mysteries," an early Académie des Sciences, but one which preferred to revive Giorgio's *In Scripturam Sacram . . . problemata,* which Mersenne attacked but Gaffarel supported (his obsession was amulets and talismans). The consuming passion was astrology and forecasting: huge numbers of almanacs, horoscopes and prognostications poured from the presses, scholars devoted much of their time to the subject and Rigault reissued Artemidorus Daldianos' *De interpretatione somniorum.* Gerard of Cremona's *Géomance astronomique* and Spadacine's *Miroir d'astrologie naturelle* (translated from the Italian) sold everywhere.

Alchemy and hermetic chemistry were of consistent appeal: *Lapis philosophicus* by La Paulmier (1609); *Toyson d'or, ou la Fleur des thrésors . . . traicté de la pierre des philosophes* (1612–13), a translation of a work by Trismosin, a German alchemist; *Traicté de la nature de l'oeuf des philosophes* by a nobleman, Bernard, comtc de Trèves (1624, 1659, 1695); *Les douze clefs de philosophie* by Basilius Valentinus; the *Trois livres de la chrysopopée* (1626) by Augurelli, an Italian alchemist; the *Grand esclaircissement de la pierre philosophale* by Nicolas Flamel (1628, 1638) and the *Idée parfaicte de la philosophie hermétique* by Jean Collesson (1630, 2nd ed., 1633).

But the very act of describing experiments, however fanciful, leads to new disciplines, and in Sendivogius' or Valentinus' books there is a hint of something more than a search for traditional abracadabra. What eventually emerged from this curiosity was chemistry, and soon the principles of chemical action and reaction were a part of courses taken by medical students and apothecaries. Etienne de Calve's *Cours de chimie* and Jean Béguin's *Tyrocinium chimicum* are good examples of the new trend, the latter the earliest French chemistry textbook. Modern chemistry was a child of this strange world of alchemists, natural philosophers and disciples of Paracelsus, all of whom made distinct contributions, many of their theories deriving from Aristotle. Hill's *Philosophia Epicurea, Democritiana, Theophrastica,* and d'Espagnet's *Enchiridion physicae restitutae,* the theses of 1624 already referred to, and the work of Lagneau, Clave, Hesteau de Nuisement, and Mersenne owed a lot to ancient atomic theories, denied transmutation of the elements, reduced the number of elements to two (earth and water), and primitive substances to five. Nuisement took ideas from the Neo-Platonists and invested the world with spirits of all kinds; people saw connections between plants and minerals. It was a medley of reason and mumbojumbo, a condition of credulity that makes Mersenne's contempt for Aristotle understandable. Modern science did not emerge from occult practices but from the application of mathematical theories to physics, and the substitution of an entirely new approach to physical phenomena—what is called Mechanistic. And, as always, the proof that new ideas are on the march comes from the evidence of the publishing houses.

4. Mathematical books published in Paris in Descartes' time

In the 16th century Italy was the cradle of new thought. That country saw the birth of modern mathematics and astronomy, and it was there that books in the field were first published, though they were classical texts from the Graeco-Roman world; Paris publishers only reprinted what first came out in Italy. Even by the year 1600 the new thinkers were still Italian, with some from Flanders, but by the turn of the century things had changed. The Greek text of Euclid's *Data* with commentary by Marini, based on three manuscripts supplied by Nicolas Rigault (1625), was a sign of things to come, and was followed by an edition of Archimedes' works in Greek by David le Flurance-Rivault, an artillery expert, and Rigault was considering a series of Greek texts on machines. Viète and his pupils started something new with an attempted reconstruction of a lost work by Apollonius of Perga, *De tractionibus,* and Claude Caspar Bachet de Méziriac published Diophantes' *Arithmetic* in Greek and Latin. Another enterprise was the republication of texts by well-known authors who were not readily accessible, and Mersenne published the *Synopsis mathematica* (1626) as a basic text for students and discussion by academics, a collection of "plus excellents autheurs de mathématiques" reprinted in 1644 with the title *Universae geometriae synposis*. In 1630 Petau published the *Uranologium*, excerpts from Aratus, Hipparchus, Ptolemy and Geminus on the sphere, intended for scholars in Mersenne's circle who were advancing the study of mathematics, physics and astronomy—Roberval, Fermat, Mydorge, Etienne Pascal, Gassendi and Peiresc.

But closer examination of these books tells us something else about the scientific revolution then in progress: we find unexpected features. Problems are called "pleasant and delectable," questions are described as "extraordinary," presumably designed as an entertaining pastime for experts rather than for the average student, a confection for an elite. Some titles at random: *Problèmes plaisans et délectables qui se font par les nombres* by Bachet de Méziriac (1612, 1624); *Problemata duo nobilissima* by Cyriaque de Mangin (1616); *Deux cents questions ingénieuses et récréatives,* arranged and corrected by Didier Henrion; *Récréations mathématiques* by Father Leurechon. Elegant disputes with ever more refined solutions grew with each successive edition: *Questions inouies ou récréation des savants* by Mersenne and *Questions harmoniques* and *Questions théologiques* (1634) by the same author were of this kind. Not unlike chess by correspondence or mathematical problems in our weeklies today, pamphlets and broadsides printed problems and their solution, and even posters issuing a new challenge for the attention of anyone capable of responding.

One typical problem arising out of this kind of approach—mathematics as an amusing diversion—was the squaring of the circle, which some rash amateurs claimed to have done until Mersenne crushed them with proof that it was incapable of solution. The nature of light, optics, the earth's rotation were all hotly debated; Jean Morin, astronomer/astrologer at the Collège Royal, tried to demonstrate that the earth did not move, which Gassendi refuted; the resulting controversy lasted twenty years and ended with the liquidation of "official" astronomy. Sometimes government intervention caused ripples in these closed circles of savants, as when Ramus' Chair at the Collège Royal was put "up for grabs" every three years by competition and the winning one published; or when Richelieu, copying Spanish practice, proposed a prize for the correct determination of longitude at sea: Morin offered a solution that was rejected and another pamphlet war broke out; the proper computation only came with the invention of the compass. Peiresc was able to complete the first map of the moon thanks to more accurate observations; conics developed as a major area of mathematics, and Désargues' work in geometry was followed by the young Blaise Pascal's *Essai sur les coniques*. Désargues' views and proofs were answered through the usual channels, pamphlets and posters which kept those interested informed about the exciting subject. Of course all this was profitable copy for the booksellers.

Viète's work on trigonometry, analytical geometry and algebra was quickly published in a modestly priced series of little textbooks for the general reader with some mathematical ability, a kind of popularizing, but he came of an earlier generation before Galileo was a threat to orthodoxy and Descartes hesitated before publishing his theories. After that, scientific progress tended to be through personal communication or in papers circulated among scholars (cf. Mersenne and his peers), and a little later Descartes, Roberval, Hobbes, Fermat and Gassendi used that channel to announce their findings to the outside world. Mersenne had a French version of Galileo's *Mechanics* published in Paris (1634) before it appeared in Italy, and Rocollet published Galileo's *Nouvelles pensées* in 1639, a year after Elzevier published it in Italian. This very personal method of transmitting new ideas was critical at a moment when the early scientific revolution was stirring in France and was a spur to further thought as well as a source of information to scientists and laymen.

The use of posters prominently fixed to the walls of Paris was a simple and effective form of publicity for the new science (Pascal's *Essai sur les coniques* is the most famous of the posters) and proof of the widespread public interest which was also being catered for in popular formats. Books on the sphere had a long tradition behind them: Johannes de Sacro Bosco's *De sphaere* was the best known, with commentary by Elie Vinet, and next Du Chevreul's *Sphaera,* which was in print until 1640. Others were Georg Peurbach's *Théorique des cieux* and Piccolomini's *Sphère du monde,* more conservative treatments like Boulenger's *Traicté de la sphère du monde,* which defended the official line in astronomy. Until about 1640 views thought to be too novel could not be freely vented; when in 1634 Galileo was condemned, the Jesuits, though admirers of him, compromised by aligning themselves with Tycho Brahe's position, then coming into fashion. This caution is very obvious in the Cosmographies (the ancestors of our geographical manuals), where Didier Henrion avoids the new Copernican theory and Galileo's conclusions, preferring again to support Tycho Brahe, and even invokes Ptolemy, which at least indicates a wide range of authorities!

Further evidence of a new spirit was the huge output of Euclid. The first six books were translated and published in 1598 by Errard, the first nine books in 1604, 1605 and 1629 by Errard, and the complete *Elements* by Dounot in 1609, 1610 and 1613; another translation by Henrion in 1614, 1621 and 1631, another by Le Mardelé in 1622 and 1632, and yet others in 1632, 1639 and 1644. The translators were teachers of mathematics and military engineers seeking to provide textbooks for their pupils, a practice as old as the Greeks. And in the 1620–30 period we see the first modern math textbooks, modeled on Clave's books, already in use in Jesuit colleges, and foreign textbooks on the art of fortification, then the latest strategy in warfare. A typical example was Henrion's *Mémoires mathématiques recueillis et dressez en faveur de la noblesse française* (1613, vol. 1) which comprised "military" arithmetic, sines and cosines, problems in applied geometry, use of the compass and instruction in the art of fortification. An immediate success, it was followed by volume 2 and the two stayed in print for years. In 1621 Fleury Bourriquant, a blatant pirate of math books, published a *Collection ou Recueil de divers traitéz mathématiques,* similar in content and probably based on Henrion's lecture notes without his knowledge. Henrion managed to prevent publication of the material but Bourriquant simply substituted one of Errard's texts. This sort of dealing is sure evidence that a market for such books existed.

Honoré de Meynier published *Paradoxes . . . contre les mathématiciens qui abusent la jeunesse, ensemble les défini-tions, théorèmes et maximes d'Euclide, d'Archimède, de Proclus, de Sacrobosco et d'Aristote* (1624, 1626, 1652), François Besson put out a *Pratique de la géometrie* after Euclid (1626), and Father Bourdin, a teacher at Clermont College, issued his *Prima geometriae elementa* and *Uranie*. But Pierre Hérigone's *Cursus mathematicus* is the book that showed the way ahead: in Latin with French parallel text, it was in six volumes: vol. 1, Geometry; vol. 2, Arithmetic, Calculus and Algebra; vol. 3, Sines and logarithms, with applications in the computing of interest tables, in measuring right-angled triangles, practical geometry, logistics and forti-fication problems; vol. 4, The Sphere, Geography and Navigation; vol. 5, Optics, catoptrics, dioptrics, perspective, trigonometry, the theory of planetary motion in relation to a stationary and moving earth, the sundial, and music. The sixth, a supplementary volume, was devoted to scientific discoveries with a bibliography. The whole compendium was a comprehensive survey of contemporary science.

Mathematics was a unified study, not yet divided between Pure and Applied, so the mathematical theory, the art of fortification, architecture and logistics are seen as one, and indeed that is just how it was seen by the masters of that age—Galileo, Descartes, Pascal and Désargues. They envis-aged some practical application to their speculations, hence the new technical manuals and the beginnings of technology. Accountancy and commercial arithmetic were already well established with their handy tables, since of course it was a business tool, and in general wherever calculations were required there was a market, in navigation, astrology, astronomy, land measurement, all important techniques. More typical titles were *Fabrique et l'usage du radiomètre* by Le Conte (1604, 1605); *Usage du compas de proportion* by Didier Henrion (1618; 5th ed., 1637); *Usage . . . de compas de proportion* by Pierre Petit (1634); *Fleur des pratiques de compas de proportion* by Forest-Duchesne (1639); *Géomet-*

rie reduite en une facile et briefve pratique, and *Tables de direction et perfection* compiled by Regiomontanus, revised and enlarged by Didier Henrion.

After the publication of a Latin version of Aristotle's *Mechanics* (1599) more and newer works on the subject were proposed: treatises on the sundial—a vital instrument in measuring time before clocks were common; optics, which led to experiments explaining optical illusion, and refraction and reflection through mirrors and lenses. But when machinery was made on sound theoretical principles the nation was on the way to a revolution in industry and commerce, though as so often happened, the first applications seem almost frivolous—devices for use in ornamental gardens: *Raisons des forces mouvantes avec diverses machines tant utiles que plaisantes . . . (et) dessins de grottes et de fontaines* (1624) by Salomon de Canus is one example.

A great deal of technical literature was devoted to architecture: Philibert de l'Orme and Androuet du Cerceau, Savot, Le Muet and Bullant were among the new schools of architects, and in the closely allied art of designing fortresses and the construction of defenses the chief authors were Perret, Errard, Henrion, Hume, Ville and Pagan; military needs, then as now, consumed much time and expertise, with Flurance-Rivault and Davelourt the best in gunnery and supply systems. A significant factor is the number of writers who were engineers to the King, which prompts the question—was the teaching of mathematics related to the great reorganization of the army then in train? Royal power and technology serving mutual interest? It is a matter of most important consequence.

CHAPTER VI

NEWS AND INFORMATION: FROM BROADSHEET TO NEWSBOOK

B ROADSHEETS BY THE HUNDREDS OF THOUSANDS—single leaves with a sensational item of news—and newsbooks of perhaps a dozen or so pages, pamphlets reporting a domestic disaster or military success, and posters for display on walls were all features of the communications industry. Since they were all too literally "ephemera," very few of them survive today, but topics ranged from current events and ceremonies, and verses in honor of the royal family to the mathematical problems we have just described in the previous chapter; in short, much the kind of matter so prominent today, especially in the tabloid press, its equivalent. A brief account of the material will help us understand what preoccupied the men and women of the 17th century and judge how well informed they were about current affairs, as well as giving us some idea how public opinion was manipulated in an age lacking our more sophisticated media.

1. General information: Broadsheets and almanacs

Broadsides ("feuilles volantes") dealt with the most trivial events, and the Parisian taste for satire was richly supplied in mock-heroic verses celebrating the installation of a new fountain or a statue or a new public building. Given the Gallic love of gossip, scandal and marital mishaps were all fodder for the grosser palates, a taste recognized for centuries, dating back to the black-letter chapbooks. Squibs and lampoons had intriguing titles like *Cruautés inhumaines d'une femme de Paris nouvellement exercées su la personne de son mari et le sujet pouquoi,* or *Plaisantes ruses et cabales de*

161

trois bourgeoises de Paris, nouvellement découvertes, ensemble tout ce qui s'est passé à son sujet. Pamphleteering was also a political act, and even part of the clerical armory, as when the Dean and Chapter of the church of St. Germain-Auxerrois quarreled in public with a pamphlet, *Réponse de paroissien de St. Germain-de-l'Auxerrois au discours fait par Maistre François Le Charron, doyen de la dite église.*

Murders, sensational confessions and last speeches from the scaffold were the staple of broadsheet literature and a rich source of income to printers—public avidity was insatiable at a time when public hangings were common: *Histoire véritable d'un assassinat commis en la personne d'un jeune gentilhomme de Provence, par un jeune homme qui a été executé en la Place de Grève avec ses accomplices le 19 juin 1627.* In a credulous age portents and monstrosities impressed an eager public: *Naissance d'un monstre ayant la face humaine, la tête et le reste du corps couverte d'une armure façon d'écaille . . . à Lisbon le lundi 10 avril 1628,* or *Discours prodigieux de deux filles nées à Paris le 17 janvier 1605 . . . ayant deux testes, quatre yeux, quatre bras, quatre jambes et deux natures.* (Pamphlets of this kind were also intended for a scientific audience, because they were sometimes in Latin. Dwarfs and giants were of equal interest, and one famous case was the discovery of a large skeleton, thought to have been a Germanic chieftain. Discussion was at a scholarly level, by Riolan, Habicot and Guillemeau, in pamphlets. When ignorance was evenly spread, both cultivated and vulgar readers could be satisfied in print.)

Siamese twins excited attention, as in this famous case in Paris: *Discours sur les jumelles joinctes qui sont nées le dix huictième janvier en la rue de la Bucherie. . . .* And the supernatural was of perennial interest: *Histoire epouvantable de deux magiciens qui ont été estranglés par le Diable dans Paris la Semain Saincte,* and *Histoire prodigieuse du fantôme cavalier soliciteur.* The scenes are all very familiar, with the typical cast including the Devil, demons, and witches, as real as the pious visions of the Virgin Mary and saints. Catastrophes have always been good for sales in the news media, and comets, which presaged disasters, therefore figure largely in the broadsheets—one which passed over France in 1618 prompted a spate of reportage.

Astrology was a natural concomitant of heavenly visitants and was accepted as a science. A humble priest, Jean Belot, gained an international reputation as an astrologer, though he may have been a fictitious character, and the kind of predictions he made were by way of almanacs, a type of publication very profitable as an investment for booksellers and printers, though these too had their dangers, as Morgard, a poet-astrologer from Troyes, discovered when his "predictions" turned out to be too political for the authorities and he was condemned to the galleys. Others had big sales, like the *Grand calendrier et compost des bergers* and Morgard, the astrologer-poet from Troyes, political pamphleteer. Jean Petit, another almanac-maker, called himself "theorist on hidden causes, movements and properties of the stars," and more simply, "professor of mathematics and astrology"; Eustach Noël, self-styled curé of Sainte Marthe claimed to be "professor of mathematical and astrological science," and Sieur Colluch, Mittanour's and Jean Belot's pupil, described himself as "professor in the three departments of philosophy." Almanacs and wall calendars were important parts of the print explosion of the day, pointing towards future journalism.

The power of street journalism was augmented by the political squibs and lampoons like *Estrennes de M. Guillaume,* or ironic tributes to celebrities like Tabarin's *Estrennes universelles.* Eustache Noël's *Almanac ou Ephemeride pour l'an MDCXXXIIII* included an *Almanach du Palais,* "very useful for litigants," which Colluche pirated, and a useful compendium was put together by Fabien Guebet, *Almanach pour l'an de grâce mil six cent quarante deux,* containing a useful list of fairs and markets throughout the kingdom. Religious matters were taken care of by the jobbing press: lists of the confraternities were kept in the churches and convents of Paris, an annual list of preachers in all the churches was issued, and programs of the great processions were regularly published, the kind of information that continues to this day in the form of parish magazines and newsletters.

2. *Administrative and official information*

Official Acts and decrees were in constant currency as the huge bureaucracy kept pace with growing government complexity, and the half a million individual items preserved in the Bibliothèque Nationale from the period 1598–1643 is an indication of the vast output there must once have been. The King, his Ministers, the Council of State, the Parlement of Paris, the Chambre des Comptes, the Cour des Monnaies, and the Châtelet kept printers busy with their orders for the many thousands of decrees, ordinances, enactments and proclamations. And on the Church side of the establishment, the Assemblée du Clergé, the bishops, chapters, guilds and then the lesser departments of state all provided quantities of official information. The public were a force they needed to reach.

These printed pieces mostly relate to public order and the creation and sale of offices, a source of revenue to the Treasury; judgments that would be of professional interest to the multitude of lawyers in Paris, and handwritten notes on surviving copies emphasize points to be kept in mind or confirm that the printed copy is in accordance with the original. To understand the full import of this extensive communications industry, first a word about the institutions themselves and their relationship with the press.

One of the earliest examples of official printing dates from 1500 when 200 copies of an Act were ordered to be printed and sent out to judges so that they would know its relevance at law, but that was exceptional before 1550, to judge by the very few surviving examples. A little later, in a troubled period both Parlement and King made more use of the press to convey their will and publicize their decisions to the French people. Soon the problems of control become evident—a misprint might destroy the sense of an Act, whether it was deliberate or not, and so the custom began of assigning official work to a small group of printers, the King's printers, who were a part of the Royal Household with all the prerogatives and advantages accruing to the office. Not unnaturally they tended to side with the King and his party in power.

By the mid-17th century the King's printers were the most prosperous and well established firms: Morel, Mettayer, Antoine Estienne, Sébastien Cramoisy and Pierre Rocollet. The other power bases, the Parlement, Cour des Monnaies and the Châtelet, had also appointed their own licensed printers, and influential religious bodies and orders did the same. How did this system work in practice?

It would seem that in most cases the secretariat of the various departments prepared copy for the press. In lawsuits the party on the losing side had to defray the expenses of publishing the resulting decree or sentence if it went against them. In the case of royal proclamations and judgments that were of judicial significance, copies would be ordered for lawyers and officials throughout the realm, which meant large printing orders for the already privileged few, the beneficiaries of the system. Copies were available through official channels but also sold on the streets, and since money matters, taxation and prices were subjects of perennial interest to the citizen, the broadsides with their announcements had a wide readership. We know from the bitter rivalries between printers for the privilege of publishing these documents that the business was highly prized, both for its status and its profitability. One interesting feature of the arrangements made for the issue of these publications was the undertaking by printers to supply copies to certain stationers only in the provinces, which suggests there may have been a subscription system, possibly for readers who wished to consult the copies on booksellers' premise, as was done in the case of the official *Gazette*.

The publishing of official communications, originally to alleviate the labor of copyists, was the forerunner of the official journals of our day. The *Journal officiel* was the first such, but with this important difference, that publication of an Act did not make it law. But the whole climate of state control and the employment of printers and publishers with quasi-official duties made for implicit support inside the book trade for royalist policies; entrusted with so large and lucrative a business, the trade would naturally incline towards the monarchy.

3. Royalist propaganda: poetry, narratives, and official image-making

Another feature of press propaganda was the overt glorification of the King and royal family, encomiums about the great traditions of nobility in France, laudatory accounts of official festivals, pompous descriptions of public events and the triumphs of the army. Henri IV was the object of much publicity after his successful entry into Paris in 1594, acclaimed as the national savior in song and epic. Royal marriages encouraged the poetasters and propagandists to extravagant displays of sycophancy and bad verse: the King's marriage to Marie de Medici was an example, when each stage of Marie's journey to Lyons from Italy was marked by fetes and ceremonies, all duly celebrated in poetry or rhetorical prose, to the further profit of the provincial stationers; execrable or not, the verses were printed and circulated at court, often at the expense of the author to help his career. Du Vair produced some gusty rhetorical stuff in honor of the royal pair on their honeymoon, and poets busy at this time included Bertaut and Passerat, La Roque, Deimier, Du Souhait and Malherbe, who used the opportunity to secure the King's attention and be called by Du Perron the best poet in France. His *Ode à la reine* extolled the King, and later he placed his pen at the service of the Regent when Marie de Medici assumed that role, and then of Louis XIII. There was hardly a college principal or dean of a faculty who did not print his deplorable Latin verse in praise of royalty, usually timed to chime with selected state occasions. Appalling examples are the public verse of Jan Caecilius Frey, a philosopher, Georges Critton, and the unreadable Father Le Moyne, all participants in the orchestrated banality. The famous preachers of the day collaborated by printing their sermons in praise of the King, and the historiographers, whether official or not, supplied inflated accounts of ceremonies associated with the court, while any royal progress or entry into a town guaranteed instantaneous publicizing of the event. When Henri IV was assassinated there was a chorus of lamentation, expressing fears for the future, despite the ban on any publication commenting on it, and since the murder was so sensational it prompted a huge trade in pamphlets and illustrations of the bloody deed. Malherbe spoke of funeral orations "mushrooming overnight" and complained that "hawkers tormented citizens on all sides" with their news sheets for sale.

Henri IV was an impressive personality who would attract not just the mere hacks but writers who treated him as a subject worthy of serious attention, but royals of lesser quality also attracted inflationary verse; both the Regent, Marie, and the young Louis XIII from the moment of his birth and baptism received their due, with the astrologers predicting safely a long and memorable reign. His coronation and marriage to Anne of Austria were further milestones attended by more official recognition in verse. Louis was no lover of poetry but his very position as the fount of power and glory meant he was bound to be constantly in the public eye, a position reinforced by the panegyrics: the Queen goes on a pilgrimage to ask God for an heir and the event is the theme for a series of labored narratives; poets rejoice when the royal couple recover from illness, and when the young Louis is reconciled with his mother the Queen Regent, or with the prince of Condé, there is more verse to commemorate the events. The birth of the Dauphin releases a torrent of it, and when Louis XIII dies the occasion is broadcast in pamphlets and broadsides, though fewer in this case than at Henri IV's death.

The public lives of royalty and their successes in war kept the ephemeral press busy. Beginning with the invasion of Italy in the early 16th century, occasional descriptions of campaigns were published as news items, and during the long struggle between the central power and rebel nobles in Louis XIII's reign a good deal of partisanship gave business to the press when a Commander-in-Chief or high-ranking officer wrote their versions of battles. The King had the advantage of massive press support and used it, as in the campaigns in the Protestant areas led by Luynes (1619–21), when every siege, engagement or capture of a town was reported in vainglorious verses. The crowning episode was the capture of La Rochelle and final victory over the Huguenots, which Richelieu exploited in a continuous press offensive, consistent with his policy whether at home or abroad. Victory of the King's arms, success in the Spanish wars, the might of France—these were the themes, and Richelieu never neglected them. He well understood the power of the press.

The rich collections of prints in the Bibliothèque Nationale remind us that pictures were widely used to back up words. The traditional woodcut was employed in the news sheets reporting the Wars of Religion, manufactured in the Rue Montorgueil. Engravers depicted the departure of Spanish troops from Paris with a mocking Henri IV wishing them "bon voyage." Copper engraving eventually ousted the woodcut in the cheap *Histoires* which described current or past events, and to judge by the inventories of the printsellers, prices were kept reasonably low. They were another medium of royalist propaganda, with portraits of Henri IV a favorite in his own lifetime and after, and again when his equestrian statue was officially inaugurated on the Pont Neuf in Paris. Louis XIII and Anne of Austria were shown in a variety of postures, kneeling before an altar, within a medallion, in a chariot yoked to four horses named Might, Prudence, Justice and Moderation, with the figure of Fame at the front, and one print depicts Marie de Medici in a chariot drawn by four women, each representing a virtue; frontispieces in books portray Louis XIII in armor, turning towards his troops.

It is the equivalent of present day photography, reinforcing the printed word pictorially, emphasizing the glamor of royalty. As mirrors of royal glory they take the most spectacular events as their subjects: a betrothal, the tournaments that attended it, a coronation, processions, a cortege, triumphal arches, the iconography of pomp and state. Many images are militarist, emphasizing power and might, with magnificently armored soldiery in plumes and trappings, trumpets and drums, officers and commanders on horseback, scenes of battle, sieges, massive fortifications and battlements. Significantly, it was Richelieu's campaigns that were most systematically imaged, the wars that were the result of his expansionist policy, so that in looking at a picture of the fall of La Rochelle or the Ré fortress or the siege of Casal we are seeing it through his eyes. Callot's prints glorifying Louis

XIII were made by royal command, with pompous dedications in praise of "the most Christian King." That great
importance was ascribed to this vivid propaganda medium is
proved by Marie de Medici ordering the deletion of Richelieu's portrait (she was his arch-enemy) from a scene showing
the siege of Ré.

The feudal aristocracy were markedly less effective than
the monarch when it came to printed propaganda. Perfunc-
tory verse, in praise of dullards and nonentities, fulsome
dedications to the same dreary pattern, the motive so
obvious, the execution mechanical, and genealogies and
catalogs of deceased ancestors—that was the convention.
Often employed to secure the rise to power of a court
favorite, they were a true model of the times, and Richelieu
cultivated the device as part of his general strategy in support
of his own ambitions and, as he saw it, for the country's
benefit. The only ones to reap any benefit were members of
the royal family because they reflected the glory attaching to
the throne and the loyalty that was its due—Condé, for
example, or Soissons, and the Queen Regent. It partly
explains the serious opposition of some of the rebellious
noble families.

4. Political controversy and the appeal to public opinion: Lampoon and libel

The struggle of the monarchy to secure absolute ascendancy
over the old feudal families came to a head in the 17th
century when political pamphleteering provides eloquent
testimony to the struggles of various factions at the center of
power—the Estates General, the Assembly of the Nobility,
Parlement, Protestant synods, all using whatever channels
they could to influence events; one such was the pamphlet
reporting a speech, "a true and faithful account," the usual
method to enlist a following in politics or religion.
Manifestos, political platforms, defence of a policy or an
attack on someone else's were all issued in the form of
"libelles," a term which simply means booklet. They make
fascinating reading today because they are direct evidence of
the extent to which freedom of expression was possible, and

we can trace a distinct evolution in the three historical periods, under Henri IV, Louis XIII, and under Richelieu's ministry.

After the Edict of Nantes (1594) religious conflicts sharpened as the debate was carried into the public domain, as if by tacit permission of the King. The only concerted political campaign concerned France's foreign affairs, notably with Spain, and a famous tract *Soldat français* amused Henri and may be taken as a token of the kind of latitude allowed, a condition that came to an end after his death when there was further instability under Louis. Official or semi-official declarations would be issued, usually addressed to city councillors, heads of guilds, or the President of Parlement, and paid for out of government funds, another arm of propaganda justifying royal actions or interpreting affairs of state in the most favorable light. The King's printers were of course the publishers, and the opposition used the same medium, in extenuation of some political move, sometimes even of revolt (cf. the press supporting Condé's party). Appeals for reconciliation and peace were artfully devised to attract public sympathy by hinting at the horrors of civil war.

Street literature was always a cheap form of persuasion, printed without much style and often lacking printer's or author's name, certainly unlicensed, or with a fictitious name, and often farcical; Guillaume, the King's jester, appears on some surviving pieces, and so does Mathurine, the Queen's fool, and Angoulevent, Prince of Fools. Jacques Bonhomme was the standard Frenchman who appears on many tracts calling for reform or in swashbuckling jingoistic leaflets reviling Spain. When the plebeian element was important the language was a coarse vernacular to flatter the unlettered countryman, and occasionally there would be classical allusions to flatter the bourgeois, who liked to appear educated, but the tone was false and condescending, appealing to the mindless sentimentalist who adored the monarchist confections and the windy rhetoric of ceremonial occasions.

France's relations with neighboring countries was a delicate matter, politically and in religion, and a Frenchman's Catholicism and patriotism suffered from strain at home and abroad. Henri IV's policy towards the Protestants provoked indignation as Catholic pamphleteers saw political danger in the appeasement of the Calvinists. Finance, too, was always a burning question, particularly in a state growing increasingly bureaucratic, and the Treasury was under constant attack for alleged corruption and misappropriation of funds. The sale of offices—venality—was at the heart of state corruption, and along with hated taxes and a multitude of tolls excited rising anger and condemnation, very noticeable after the great assembly of the Estates General in 1614 and of the Nobility in 1617. But on the whole—typical of street literature even in our day—it was personalities rather than principles that interested readers, the struggles for power, the position of favorites at court, political alignments. Pamphlets with titles like *Caton français, Cassandra française, Trompette français* and *Diogène français* caught the eye, condemning Marie de Medici's lover Concini, and when he was murdered there was clear public acclaim, as the pamphlets that followed duly inform us. Incidentally, the use of the word "français" is suggestive, indicating a growing sense of national identity. Luynes, the royal favorite, was the target of another campaign, and princes and Protestants all had their polemicists writing vigorous abuse, a practice which intrigued Gabriel Naudé, who made a special study of it in one of his earliest books, *Marflore*. La Vieuville's turn came next when his relations with a financier came under fire and he fell victim to a press campaign organized by Richelieu using Mathieu de Morgues and Fancan as his verbal assassins.

Satire and sheer buffoonery were employed against the high and the mighty, but we may ask, how were these scurrilous leaflets printed and sold?

Government and quasi-government propaganda was of course given unfettered opportunity to influence the public but the opposition press is harder to define. The nobles and princes in the provinces would arrange for their supporting press to operate with their blessing in their own fiefs, as did the Prince of Condé when he took refuge in Mézières in 1614, or the Protestants at Sedan, and the *Manifesto* issued in the name of the Queen Mother at Angers was probably printed there. It was not difficult to smuggle pamphlets into Paris—hawkers and stationers were always willing to risk penalties for a quick profit, and there is evidence that in the period 1614–1621 libels and other leaflets hostile to the government were actually printed under their noses in Paris, probably because government impotence encouraged risk-taking. The situation changed radically when Richelieu returned to power in 1624.

Reference has already been made to his astuteness in the manipulation of the press through the pens of the most practised pamphleteers of the time—men like Mathieu de Morgues (later Richelieu's enemy) and Fancan, the Cardinal's confidential agent, who was expert at propaganda, especially aimed at Spain, and for various complicated reasons of high policy even composed pieces sympathetic to the Protestants. He eventually fell, and was imprisoned in the Bastille where he died in 1627. From 1625 to 1630 Paul Hay du Chastelet was de Morgues' main rival as a pamphleteer, called "head of the infamous gang" by de Morgues, an Academician like his colleague Sirmond, nephew of the famous Jesuit historiographer. The most famous of all Richelieu's men was Father Joseph, the Grey Eminence, head of what could be called Richelieu's press bureau. Other recruits were Jérémie Ferrier and Du Laurens, converts from Calvinism, and Harlay de Sancy, future bishop of St. Malo, Richelieu's secretaries: Jacques Pelletier, friend of the Jesuits and once Marie de Medici's secretary; Jean de Silhon, a theorist on the subject of Absolution; Daniel de Priezac, a lawyer from Bordeaux; Cureau de la Chambre, doctor and moralist—all three Academicians; Louis Giry, a translator, and scholars of the Académie Putéane who were ready to publish whatever the Cardinal commanded.

Richelieu used the propaganda weapon to promote his policies vigorously, and at the height of his power towards the end of his life he used the same method to create the picture of himself he wished to leave to posterity. Recent research has revealed that there was considerable pamphlet opposition to his foreign policies, as when he went to war with the House of Austria. A storm of pamphlets broke, beginning with two famous attacks, *Mysteria politica* and

Admonitio ad Regem, and continuing with pamphlets in Latin, translated into French, German, Spanish, Flemish and Italian, with titles like *Sapiens franciscus, Scopae Ferreri-anae, Questiones quodlibeticae, Revolutiones magistrales, Veritas odiosa,* and *Vita eminentissimi Domini Cardinalis Richelieu.* It might seem odd that the leaflets bore the imprint of a firm known to be royalist, but it was flagrantly false; they were printed in South Germany, sold by the thousand at the Frankfurt Fair and distributed all over Europe, and possibly smuggled into Paris, though very few seem to have turned up there. Chanteloube and Mathieu de Morgues later attacked Richelieu, acting on behalf of the Queen Mother, using their knowledge of his life and tactics to good effect. But such literature could only be printed outside France, in the Low Countries or Switzerland, any clandestine pamphlet was bought only at a high price, and Richelieu's grip on the press was such that only rarely did any contrary opinion get a chance to be heard. Booksellers who had previously cared little about the court's displeasure were now tamed. We shall see later how he managed this.

5. *The birth of the newspaper*

Parallel with the pamphlet as an effective means of propaganda, the first newsbooks begin their long career. The *Mercure français* was launched by a bookseller. Before that, an annalist called Palma Cayet had published his *Chronologie novennarie* and *Chronologie septennaire,* annual summaries of the events during the reign of Henri IV, whose editor, Jean Richer, had the idea of bringing out "supplements" to those publications, at first irregularly and then each year, which were really news of current affairs. The *Mercure* began in 1603 and lasted until 1648.

The news sheet proper—a periodical—was the product of business enterprise in the great ports of Europe, Venice and Amsterdam. The first French example, short-lived, started in Amsterdam in 1620; ten years later, the *Nouvelles ordinaires de divers endroits* was published by two Calvinists, Martin and Vendosme. The most influential of these early sheets was Théophraste Renaudot's *Gazette,* which began its life on the 1st April 1631. On good terms with the government, he secured an exclusive licence to publish official news, any opposition being banned; thus his only problem was competition from pirate printers. At first a four-page weekly of quarto size, it grew into an eight- then a twelve-page newsbook with a monthly supplement, *Extraordinaire de la Gazette.*

The later history of the *Mercure français* is of consuming interest because it passed into the sinister hands of Father Joseph in 1624, the year Richelieu came to power for good, and the result was improved appearance and better coverage. Instead of a dull recital of unrelieved facts and bald notices of events, it was shaped and edited with a firm object in view, the favorable presentation of government policy, with comment and explanation—in short, a vigorous official line. There was a lot more general information than before and allusions to European politics, writers skilled in presentation were recruited, and often the texts of opponents' pamphlets were printed with refutations. Powerfully assisted by the King and with direct access to the sources of power, Renaudot could only reflect one mind—that of Richelieu, who was well aware how to use the press as an instrument of propaganda.

CHAPTER VII

LITERARY WORKS

L ITERATURE, POETRY, DRAMA, GRAMMARS and dictionaries all figured in the publishing output of the age, accounting for about one-third of the total, to judge by the books preserved in the Bibliothèque Nationale, and if we include the large numbers of individual poems, orations, funeral sermons and official panegyrics which we know were turned out in quantities but which did not survive, then the percentage would be higher.

1. Foreign language and literature

First a look at French and other foreign-language grammars and primers, their publication and distribution. Hardly any German grammars were published, and only a little German devotional literature, in French. Few English grammars were on the market though there were a number of French and Latin-French dictionaries used in teaching French in England. An English and French grammar was published in Rouen in 1595, based on earlier ones by Meurier, Sainliens and Belot, and reprinted in Paris in 1625, the year of Charles I's marriage to Henrietta Maria. The same year, Oursel's *Alphabet anglais contenant la prononciation des lettres avec les déclinaisons et les conjugaisons* saw the light in Rouen, the first of many later reprints and typical of the primers published for the use of Norman merchants trading with Britain, but English was virtually an unknown tongue, as Saint-Amant's verses prove. The English books most likely to reappear in France were those which originally were in Latin, from Buchanan's poetry to Barclay's *Argenis,* Lord Herbert of Cherbury's *De veritate,* and Bacon's works. Some

175

were of sufficient interest to merit translation into French, particularly Joseph Hall's *Characters,* which was translated by Loiseau de Tourval in 1612, and a Calvinist publisher, Jacquemot, put out a popular version of Hall's works in Geneva. Jesuit refugees from England living at Douai were doing the same thing for English Catholic writers, and Marie de Medici was so impressed by Philip Sidney's *Arcadia* that she commissioned Jean Baudoin to translate it into French; *Arcadia* represented the beginnings of pastoral romance in England but this was already an established genre in Italy, as other French translations from the Italian testify. The most surprising feature of this period in publishing history, which coincided with what was perhaps the greatest period of English literature, is that none of the supreme examples of Elizabethan drama were translated into French, including Shakespeare and Ben Jonson, a fact almost certainly due to the bitterness of the religious schism which divided the two nations.

Spain was a different matter. We have already noticed the heavy influence in France of Spanish theology and spirituality; during the Wars of Religion Spanish troops were quartered in many parts of France, helping with military assistance to cement ties between the orthodox clergy and nobility of both countries. Trade was on a big scale with France's southern neighbor and French merchants frequently visited Spain, among them booksellers from Paris and Lyons. The Spanish Marriage made that language fashionable, and the French nobility developed an interest in the literature of the land from which the new Queen came. Grammars and glossaries of Spanish were marketed, Oudin's *Grammaire espagnole* (1597) being the most used (he was "professeur d'espagnol à la cour de France"). It was reissued by his son Antoine in 1658. Other similar grammars did well: *Miroir général de la grammaire en dialogue* by Ambrosio de Salazar (Rouen, 1614, 1615, 1622, 1623, 1627, 1636); primers by Juan de Luna; a *Dictionnaire très ample de la langue espagnole et française de César Oudin.* Extracts in French and Spanish were popular in little pocket books like *Refranes o proverbios castellanos traduzidofs en lengua francesa* by César Oudin; *Diverses leçons de Pierre Messie, gentilhomme de Sévile,* translated by Gruget; *Carcel de Amor* by Diego de San Pedro: *Bouquet de fleurs poétiques* by Alexandre de Luna: *Ephyalte ou Orgueil humilie . . . histoire admirable . . .* or *Rodomuntadas castellanos recopiladas de diversos autores,* and another favorite, *Opposition et conjuction des deux grands luminaires du monde oeuvre: plaisante . . . de l'heureuse alliance de la France et de l'Espagne,* which enjoyed wide circulation, the forerunner of La Mothe Le Vayer's *Discours sur la contrariété d'humeur qui se trouve entre certaines nations, et singulièrement entre la française et l'espagnole.* A taste for all things Spanish was very evident in the second quarter of the 17th century, and the fact that language books were available in Rouen as well as in Paris and Lyons suggests that quite a few Frenchmen knew some words of Spanish and the French writers found subjects in Spanish literature.

New literary works published in Madrid or Seville did not automatically appear in France but if theological they would be imported for sale in specialist stationers; the bookshops in the Palais had no direct links with Spain, only via Rouen, but if there seemed a likely market for new books of spirituality and Spanish devotional literature, translations would be commissioned—Baudoin, Rosset and Audigier were three such translators employed on the work. Poetry was a different matter, a difficult medium to render, which perhaps explains the scarcity of Spanish poetry in French; even Gongora was not attempted, nor any of their playwrights; instead, Spanish plays were freely adapted into French for staging under the name of the adapter. This was the classic period of the Spanish novel and many were translated, though the celebrated *Amadis* was not any longer reprinted in full after 1590, and the novels of chivalry which Cervantes pilloried in *Don Quixote* were no longer as popular, though Montemayor's *Diane* was well received, along with Lope de Vega's pastoral romances and those of Suarez de Figeroa. The new picaresque tale was all the vogue, the premier example of course *Lazarillo de Tormes* (15 reprints), with *Guzman de Alfarache* a good second (12 reprints before 1646). Quevedo's *El Buscon* and *Songes* were popular, and Cervantes' *Novelas exemplares,* translated by Rosset and d'Audigier in 1613, went into its 16th edition in 1646. *Don Quixote* was put into French by César Oudin and Rosset, and reached a 12th reprint by 1665.

One estimate, admittedly incomplete, gives a total of 700 books translated from Spanish in the period 1598–1643, half of them published in Paris. It is hard to estimate a figure for Italian literature because no statistics are available, but the romances, drama, poetry, and language books in the Bibliothèque Nationale indicate that there was a good deal more than was originally thought. Boccaccio's *Decameron* and *Fiametta,* Bandello's *Histoires tragiques,* Petrarch's *De remediis utriusque fortunae,* and Sannazaro's *De partu virginis* were all widely read, and Ariosto's *Orlando Furioso* had been popular for years, first in Jean Martin's version, revised in 1576 by Gabriel Chappuys and popular until 1618, then newly translated by Rosset in 1614 and reprinted in 1625 and 1644. The same enthusiasm for epic made Jean de Vigneau's verse translation of Tasso's *Gerusalemme liberata* (1596) and Blaise de Vigenère's prose version adapted by Jean Baudoin (1626) best-sellers for years. With Léonard Gaultier's illustrations to the first edition and Michel Lasne's in the second, the poem was the supreme literary event of the period, imitations, continuations and partial translations appearing regularly by French poets and dramatists for theatrical recital.

The French reading public also devoured Italian pastoral, especially Tasso's *Aminta* (Tours, 1591), a French version by La Brosse, any many later translations; also Guarini's *Pastor fido* and Bonarelli's *Filli di Sciro,* fanciful modes of faithful nymphs and shepherds that never were. Luigi Groto, Ongaro, Isabella and Francesco Andreini were other writers in the mode.

Italian was probably spoken freely at the court of Marie de Medici and among fashionable aristocratic circles in France, though fewer Italian grammars were available for the beginner than Spanish—César Oudin was active here and his *Grammaire italienne* sold well. The main reason for learning Italian was to make the Grand Tour, an essential part of a gentleman's education. There is no evidence of an Italian theatre in Paris, which might explain the success of the other literary forms, romance and pastoral. Sébastien Cramoisy's brother Claude published some major Italian texts and much theoretical literary criticism which helped mold classical doctrines of drama, poetry and fiction in Europe.

So far as literature was concerned, just as in other fields, the Catholic countries of Southern Europe exercised much more influence in France than the Protestant North, Spain in the religious domain, Italy in literature as in painting and the plastic arts.

2. Poetry

Ovid, Persius, Horace and Juvenal, and Phaedrus' tales were the best-sellers in Latin poetry from 1600 to 1643. Tasso was the hero of the modern school, copied by many lesser French poets who composed epic and rhetorical works, not necessarily full-length but often in pamphlets of a few pages which have long since disappeared so that exact statistical inference is impossible, though it is noticeable that few poets deal with religious or purely "poetic" themes. An exception was the case of Théophile de Viau when he was involved in a lawsuit, and the verse "monuments" published as mementos on the death of fellow poets when a poem would be recited and circulated at court, or possibly read aloud before a performance of a ballet or a tragedy. A poem would be composed to celebrate the marriage or death of an important personage, his family lauded, their exploits duly and flamboyantly versified. Victories won by the army or the King would inspire an encomium, and episodes in the life of the royal family would be commemorated. In short, poetry was simply a form of public propaganda for the monarchy and the aristocracy and preservation of the status quo. The lifeless verse of the age plainly testifies to the grip of stale convention on contemporary literature. Often a work (Malherbe's is an example) would be published at the author's expense to promote himself at court or to secure a pension by advertising his zeal for royalty. It was "official" poetry and gives us only a partial view of the poetry of the age, panegyric and with little sign of love poetry, more suited to public print than private circulation, as dedications prove,

usually to a *grande dame* or a courtier who had hired the poet
to do it.

The printed book was not the chief means by which poetry
was published. In an age when High Fashion was a complete
and artificial way of life for the upper classes, poets wrote for
a patron, usually a courtier, and his immediate circle. Poetry
was for intimate groups of literati who met in taverns or in
salons where the poem would first be recited, then circulated
in manuscript, copied and recopied, criticized by the members of the circle, eventually achieving final shape and
reaching the appropriate quarter at Court, the final arbiter in
the making of reputations. The ultimate ambition was to be
read at Court, preferably in the presence of the King, the
supreme patron and benefactor. It was no longer a sacred,
almost divine, mission (one thinks of Dante and Tasso
crowned with laurel) but an agreeable distraction for cultivated courtiers between military campaigns. In its role as
entertainment and recreation for the tired warrior the poetry
of the period accurately reflects the preoccupations of a
military caste. This is certainly true of the heroic and
religious poetry, and even the love poetry is no longer ornate
and Italianate as in the age of the Valois, but cruder, even a
touch pornographic.

Only a small number of the poems published individually
have survived, and courtiers only wished to preserve the best
versions; outside the court, readers who wished to keep
abreast of current fashions were catered for in a new kind of
book—the anthology, although it had antecedents as far
back as 1530 when poems culled from various sources already
in print might be assembled in haphazard fashion. But now
the deliberate collection comes into fashion, often previously
unpublished verse, sold by booksellers who specialized in
poetry, sometimes by booksellers who were themselves poets
(Du Petit-Vale of Rouen was one). Poets like Rosset and
Jean Baudoin worked as editors or correctors of the press,
and were published at periodic intervals—ancestors of
today's literary reviews.

Two types of anthology coexisted in the early 17th century,
the satirical, which was a term used to include erotic and
pornographic matter, and the "literary," the former enjoying

a great vogue in the years 1597–1623; some fifty-three titles are known from the period, with five new works published 1598–1607 and six in the years 1614–1625. Rouen was the home of this poetry originally, but Paris soon outclassed Rouen when publishers Du Breuil, Estoc, Billaine and Sommaville concentrated on the genre—with profit as standards dropped. What began as spicy verses—the *Muse folâtre* is a typical title—became sheer obscenity in the *Cabinet satirique* and *Parnasse des poètes satiriques.* More and more collections were marketed, often with the anonymous and involuntary aid of the best-known poets. Material of this kind attracted unconventional people and so could soon turn into a current of free thinking dangerous to the authorities, and Jesuit influence was brought to bear with a view to outlawing it. Father Garasse had the *Cabinet satirique* seized, and Théophile de Viau, a blatant purveyor of pornography and himself a poet-rakehell, narrowly escaped death. His work was banned, and the publication and reading of this kind of literature virtually ceased.

The other type of anthology was a truer indication of the way literature was going. Immediately after Henri IV's triumphant entry into Paris a revival in the book trade brought in the fashion for anthologies of unpublished verse. The Rouen publisher Du Petit-Val issued a collection of poems by various hands for sale in the Palais, the most fashionable quarter of Paris. There were 244 poems in his anthology, fifty ascribed to Jean de Sponde (who died in 1595), twenty-seven to Bertaut, and twelve to Du Perron, the last two ranked as the foremost poets of their day after Desportes. Pierre and Nicolas Bonfons published three anthologies drawn from the same source, and Antoine Du Breuil issued the *Académie des modernes français,* then the Guillemots led the field with their *Muses ralliées* (1599 and 1603) and *Parnasse* (1607), containing over a thousand items, mostly by Bertaut and Du Perron, but with a new name appearing more frequently—Malherbe. A rival publisher, Toussaint Du Bray, sought to attract readers his way by introducing a new arrangement in his *Nouveau receuil de plus beaux vers de ce temps* (1609), namely an author sequence instead of poems printed at random. It was an instant success. Du Perron and Bertaut were the most prominent contributors—their reputation and position at Court would guarantee that—then Malherbe, Motin, Forget de la Picardière, Davity and Lingendes. Malherbe held his position for the next ten years in other collections, and though Théophile de Viau seemed to be a threat to him in the *Cabinet des Muses* (Du Petit-Val, 1619) and the second book of the *Délices de la poésie française* (1620), his death removed him from the contest, and when Du Bray, a publisher who vigorously promoted Malherbe's work, put out a *Receuil des plus beaux vers de Messieurs de Malherbe, Monfuron, Maynard, Racan* (1627), Malherbe and the "Parnassian" school were brought firmly to the notice of the discerning public.

Then suddenly there was a change: fewer general anthologies, and instead, collections of poets with similar objectives. Bertault published a volume called *Nouvelles Muses des sieurs Godeau, Chapelain, Mabert, Baro, Racan, L'Estoile, Menard, Desmarets, Malleville et autres,* and, at Boisrobert's prompting, Cramoisy in 1635 published two volumes with the tendentious titles *Le sacrifice des Muses au grand cardinal de Richelieu* and *Parnasse Royale* plainly suggesting their aims. There is little thereafter apart from a collection of rondeaux published by Courbé in Voiture's style, and a volume called *Metamorphoses françaises,* published by Sommaville in 1642, very like Sommaville's *Jardin des Muses,* no more than a reprint of well-known poems by poets of the day. All this in the time of Richelieu's ascendancy, a period of decadence in French poetry that lasted until the years of the Fronde (1648–53) and the factions' fights among the nobles to undo Richelieu's work.

There were of course books by individual poets as well as anthologies, and about thirty have survived from each five-year period up to 1645, exhibiting different kinds of verse: heroic poetry inspired by the example of Ronsard, Du Bartas and Tasso, mostly from the period 1600–30, evidence of the persistence of the old epic; pastoral verse by Honoré d'Urfé, Jean de Lingendes and Maynard; and satire, both the bold, mettlesome kind and the social, moralizing kind. The older gnomic poetry of the 16th century was dying out, though Pibrac's quatrains were still popular, associated with the emblem cult still in vogue, full of dainty "devices" and allegories straight from the classical tradition and Ovid's *Metamorphoses*. Religious poetry had a big following, though the Protestants who had introduced new themes and techniques with Marot and Du Bartas were quieter as the Counter Reformation produced some good Catholic lyric poetry like that of Desportes at the court of Henri III. Anthologies of Catholic poetry appeared from about 1581 in Paris and Lyons, indicative of work in progress. Catholic poets like Baïf, Rapin, Chassignet and Desportes worked to obliterate the heresies of Marot and others, and Capuchin and Italian pietist verse dealt with Penitence (the cult symbols being St. Peter and Mary Magdalene). Malherbe wrote his *Larmes de saint Pierre* after he stayed with the Italian poet Tansillo in Provence. The Psalms, spiritual canticles, odes and sonnets all served religious themes, the favorites being the Passion, lives of the Virgin and Saints, Penitence, and the Eucharist. Meditations in verse were common. Poets, with their fellow artists, painters and engravers, were playing their part in the work of Catholic reconversion.

Some religious poetry was in Latin, a surprising amount of it published in Paris, the last glimmer of the old Humanist school reflected by Passerat and two descendants of a once famous line, Abel de Sainte-Marthe and Nicolas Bourbon. Every royal victory, every national event was celebrated with a noble ode in Latin, heavily academic and encouraged by the newly appointed teachers of Rhetoric in the Jesuit colleges, since Latin was the central discipline (only Malherbe of the moderns achieved definitive form in this field). Teachers considered it important to put new life into the Latin language by encouraging poetry, and Father Caussin (supreme from the time of Des Barreaux to La Flèche) and Father Le Moyne thought it their duty to demonstrate their mastery of Latin (and good publicity for their college courses) by tackling some acceptable subject—a pious exhortation or exaltation of the King. By so doing they were proving that Latin was flexible enough for contemporary use in verse and at the same time instilling Christian ideals and sound monarchist principles into young minds. Latin enjoyed a temporary lease of life through its traditional channel, the Church.

We might ask if poetry was confined to a small circle of readers, perhaps the Court, or if it reached a larger public? Most of the titles quoted above never saw a reprint, but pastoral poetry was the exception, with Lingendes' *Changements de la bergère Iris* going into six editions from 1603 to 1621, and Du Bartas' *Semaines* (very popular in England as *Weeks*), which sold widely in all the Protestant countries. Pibrac's *Quatrains* and Regnier's satires were likewise a continuing success; only Desportes of the religious poets made any impact. To judge by reprints alone, there is no doubt that the most admired French poets were Ronsard, Malherbe and Théophile de Viau. But 17th century taste was mutable. Ronsard was by then of classic stature, and the great folios in which his work was published by Buon were as if Virgil or Seneca were being honored; then, after 1623, the leading spirit of the original Pleiade is no longer in print—a change in fashion or was the market saturated? Malherbe went from strength to strength after his death—his collected works were published by his nephew François d'Arbaud de Porchères in 1630 and went into fifteen successive editions, but even this pales before de Viau's record. Although few editions came out in Paris, the publishers in Lyons and Rouen exploited the demand and his works were reissued *one hundred* times before the end of the century. Libertine he may have been, but he touched a chord, and was a much stronger influence than Malherbe.

3. Drama

Statistics do not show any abrupt change in the amount of poetry published in the first half of the 17th century. In drama the case was different, with a steep rise in plays published between 1630 and 1639, and from then on play books were a common part of stationers' stocks in Paris and Rouen. Until 1620, tragedies, tragicomedies and pastorals were favorites, rarely comedies, and the same held good for the decade 1620–29. From 1630 to 1639 there is an increase in comedy and tragicomedy; from 1640 to 49 pastoral disappears and comedy and tragicomedy are in decline, tragedy alone doing well in the theatres. Corneille was responsible for this, of course, and indeed before 1629 there were no public theatres in Paris, only traveling companies of actors. In the 16th century French drama was patronized solely by the nobility (Robert Garnier's plays were frequently reprinted) but by the next century there was a theatre for the people, and for the lax, free-thinking members of the Court. Plays began to be associated with particular companies and enjoyed no real reputation in good society; playwrights would compose hastily for a specific occasion and presentation, the text not usually thought worth preserving in print. Monchrestien, Hardy and the young Rotrou were all writers of this kind; of the five hundred plays written by Hardy only about forty were ever printed.

Théophile de Viau wrote *Pyrame et Thisbée* (1620); Racan, *Bergeries* (1626); and Mairet, *Sylvie* (1626), signs that new times were coming, and when the royal company took up quarters in the Hôtel de Bourgogne under Bellerose's direction and Mondory's rival company opened a new theatre in the Marais, people flocked to the productions, and Richelieu himself encouraged the best writers to write for the stage. This was the age of bitter controversy about the rules of strict classical drama, culminating in Corneille's *Cid,* and explains why the public wanted to read plays as they were performed, and not wait years until a collected edition came out. So, we find *Sylvie* and *Bergeries* in print coinciding with their staging, to be admired by a reading public as their performance was by a theatre-going public. In January 1637 Courbé had a license to print the *Cid,* which means he had submitted the script weeks before; the first edition came out in March 1637, so that the printing occupied two months, during which Corneille was obliged to revise the text for political as well as literary reasons. After that date its reprinting was assured—1637, 1639, 1644, 1645, 1646, and it suffered countless piracies. Scudéry's attack on the play accelerated publicity for it; his letter to the Académie Française was reprinted three times before exhausting the interest aroused by the affair. The *Cid* was performed many times at Court and at the Palais Cardinal and before the occupants of the boxes at the Marais theatres, to the delight of the *beau monde,* especially the women. To be received with acclamation both on stage and in print tempted dramatists to write too hurriedly and submit work for the press that was not fit for print, so that frequent revisions were needed to make the text coherent, and often these would continue right until the collected edition was being prepared as the definitive one.

The strange thing about play publication was the casual nature of the process, masterpieces being hastily printed to satisfy a quick demand; plays looked very like the newsbooks of the time or the verse *pièces d'occasion,* all with an ephemeral air about them. The typography is abysmal, printers' errors abound, and the poor quality paper of squat octavo or quarto format did nothing to enhance the work, which was obviously produced to make money quickly, using substandard equipment, while the play's popularity lasted.

Another kind of theatrical piece was the Prologue and the Farce, usually featuring before the play proper. Bruscambille sold his prologues in the Hôtel de Bourgogne before the performance, and Tabarin set up a stage for his farces on the Pont Neuf, patronized by city gallants and wits. It was a spectator who first collected them and had them published by Sommaville in 1622 (reprinted more than twenty times)— without any reward for the author, who retaliated with his own collection, *Inventaire universel,* by a printer called Estoc, and oddly enough with far less success. In this way what is usually called Pont Neuf literature developed.

4. The Novel

The habit of novel reading was even more widespread than the reading of poetry or plays. For a time the old romances of chivalry held their public: *Amadis* (called the Bible of Henri IV) was continually in print—Sorel tells us that as a boy he dreamed of heroes in combat, of "infant Gorgiases" and "giants hacked to bits" after he read it, and Chapelain wrote an essay in his youth, "On the reading of old romances." But gradually the old heroic stories sank down to the levels of street literature, hawked about in cheap formats at Lyons and especially at Troyes, the capital of popular publishing where the Gothic lettering and crude woodcuts pandered to the tastes of an unsophisticated public.

By the last years of the 16th century a new kind of novel had begun. By 1640 about five hundred titles had been published, 282 of them in Paris. Novelists came from many different backgrounds, and many novels were anonymous, which may indicate that they were the work of hacks or not well-known writers. Established names include Nervèze, Du Souhait, Des Escuteaux, and Vital d'Audigier, and a number of gentry, civil servants and lawyers tried their hand, often writing for the sheer pleasure it afforded, natives of various regions, Blaise de Saint-Germain from Bourbon, La Rivière from Normandy, Vitelli from Provence, Du Périer, Jean d'Intras and La Mothe from Gascony. Amateurs and professionals were equally influenced by the new elements arriving from Italy or Spain in varieties of pastoral, the Italian style of romance using the novel as a vehicle for Neo-Platonist ideals characteristic of the Renaissance. Translations of classical romances brought readers into contact with novels of the Graeco-Roman age, Apuleius' *Golden ass,* and Heliodorus' *Aethiopica* the two most popular. But the tales of knights and derring-do were fast fading; of new novels in French between 1600 and 1629 only eight feature the knight in his traditional role, fourteen were about princes or imaginary kings, thirteen about heroic warriors, twenty-eight involved travel and picaresque adventures, and thirty-three were love stories employing virtuous terms from a convention of knightly purity: epithets like "chaste," "honnête," "spirituel," "fidèle" and "constante."

And so the long age of the sentimental novel was ushered in. The plot usually involved a pair of lovers separated by unhappy circumstances who eventually emerge from their ordeal with their mutual fidelity unscathed, and the exciting exploits are merely an opportunity for the hero to display aspects of conventional virtues rather than adventures for their own thrilling sake. Often the setting was the Mediterranean and included pirates, then a very real menace, but otherwise no attempt was made to paint a realistic picture of the world. Whether Greek, Turkish, Persian or French, the characters all speak in the fashionable idiom of 17th-century Paris, uttering carefully phrased sentiments expressing the Platonic view of life then so prevalent. Honoré d'Urfé's *Astrée* was the best-seller, a tale of shepherds who speak faultless French of the upper classes and live a life of languid ease amid luxury, without any visible work to do. Such stuff could not satisfy readers with a taste for naturalism, which had always had a place in French literature. *Les caquets de l'accouchée*, while not exactly a novel, made great sport with the bourgeois and their habits, and picaresque novels were in favor with all classes. It was probably the satirical poetry which colored the prose fiction of those authors who favored words like "satiric" or "comic" or "pleasant" in their titles, often reinforced with "of this time" or "real" or "true," as if to advertise their realism. Camus was the most prolific of the realists, using actual events to point his moral, and some of the most interesting novels were by the "libertine" writers, Sorel's *Francion*, Théophile de Viau's *Berger extravagant* and Tristan's *Page disgracié* the most characteristic.

After 1630 realism and satire are more preponderant and the sentimental romance loses its grip. And we can see two currents influencing novel-writing, the aristocratic and the bourgeois, each contributing elements to the new fiction. Adventure increasingly replaces pastoral romance, and new forms of title point to new directions: the words "love" or "lover," common before 1630, cease to appear, and much more stress is laid on historical personalities, something like twenty novels in the 1640–49 period having the names of well-known historical characters in their titles. There is a correlation between the new trend and the troubles of the time, as if in time of war amorous intrigue seems trivial, and adventure more fitting. Novels are full of military engagements, duels, battles, pirate exploits, and the series novel emerges with Mlle. de Scudéry as its prototype.

It is hard to say who were the readers for this mass of fiction. Though many novels only went into one edition, when they did score a success it was a big one. The copies of *Astrée* and of Gomberville's and Scudéry's novels which survive are all in different editions and in volumes of various formats, in the case of *Astrée* more than ten different editions, which suggests a large readership in the tens of thousands, but that is not a scientific test; more research is needed to reach a positive conclusion.

PART TWO

SECOND SECTION
THE STRUCTURE OF
THE BOOK TRADE

CHAPTER I

BOOK DISTRIBUTION: THE ROLE OF PARIS

1. Booksellers' stocks

WITH THE HELP OF INVENTORIES in wills left by booksellers we can reconstruct the little world of bookshops and stalls, beginning with the more modest businesses. In the Rue des Sept-Voies on the slopes of Montagne Sainte-Geneviève was François Rezé whose stock-lines included Guénois's *Conférence des ordonnances,* a traditional law text, the Theodosian Code, a medical work, some classical texts used in the Schools (Aristotle, Homer, Horace, Strabo); and in neighboring premises he kept fifty Latin-Greek dictionaries, Passerat's revised edition of Calepin's standard dictionary, Despautère's grammar, copies of Terence's comedies: total value, 163 livres in 1618. Georges Giffart's stock was different, valued at 600 livres in 1624. He had several hundred books of hours, missals, lives of saints, devotional books. The Widow Dauplet's shop in 1636 was of greater value than this: 2011 livres for a stock of over 5000 books of hours, 1000 ABCs, 16 reams of books of etiquette and several hundred prayerbooks; in a word, all that the devout Catholic or young schoolboy or girl could want.

Other businesses were often attached to a bookshop: Rezé ran a bindery serving other booksellers as well as his own requirements, and they would pay him in kind. Giffart and the Widow Dauplet owned finishing tools to ornament their bindings for the bespoke trade as well as decorating books for other stationers, and Widow Dauplet seems to have financed publication of some of her books of hours, which shows how diversified the trade was—bookselling, bookbinding and

193

publishing could all be done under the same roof. Rémy Dallin is another example of the many-sided tradesman. In 1625 he owned only a small stock, the *Fleur des Saints, Théâtre d'agriculture,* Josephus' *History* and a few other titles, but there were also books he had jointly published, several thousand books of hours, offices, litanies with woodcuts and copper engravings, calendars of saints, and 69 copies of the novel *Astrée.* He had a printing shop and kept his presses working by turning out cheap and rapid-selling lines for the lower end of the market, in collaboration with other booksellers. It was not at all unusual for a bookseller to own a press: Tompère, one of the most affluent printers in Paris, had a bookstock worth 4174 livres, 4 sols in 1643, the usual books of hours, meditational literature, the *Imitation of Christ,* which he partly financed and printed on his own presses. He stocked Luis de Granada's *Mémorial, Catéchisme du bon paroissien, Rules* of St. Augustine and St. Benedict, a *Vie des Saints* and other religious works. Another equally prosperous printer, Calleville, had a bookstock worth 6172 livres in 1647, confined only to books of hours (many thousands of them), and 1137 copies of the *Imitation of Christ* in very tiny format (32mo). Printers evidently traded as wholesale and retail booksellers.

If a reader wanted a bigger selection he would not patronize the bookseller-bookbinder or printer-bookseller but would visit the specialist retail bookseller. The Widow Coulombel in the Rue Saint-Jean-de-Latran had a huge variety in stock: folios of Daléchamp's *Herbarium,* Belon's *Histoire de la nature des oiseaux,* Valturius's *Traité de l'art militaire,* Alberti's *Architecture,* Du Bellay's *Mémoires,* Popelinière's *Histoire de France,* Olaus Magnus's *Histoire,* Pierius's *Hieroglyphica,* Plato, Arnauld de Villeneuve's *Chirurgie* and Vesalius' *Anatomie,* church books, histories, legal textbooks and medical works, editions of the Bible and other sacred works, and the works of Denis the Carthusian; in short, a university bookshop, largely Humanist. In addition to the folios there were 2000 quartos and octavos. The figures indicate a high turnover.

Catherine Delaistre, widow of François Février, a licensed bookseller, was also running a flourishing business: Greek and Latin classics, Plato, Aristotle, Sextus Empiricus, Plutarch, Thucydides, Diodorus Siculus, Caesar, Livy, Tacitus, Columella, Pliny and Strabo. The major works of the leading Humanists were well represented in Erasmus's *Adages* and *Letters,* Lorenzo Valla's *Elegantiae,* Paul Manutius, Budé's *De asse,* Alciat's *De verborum significatione,* modern historians Paul Jove, Paul-Emile, Baronius and the Guicciardini, Hippocrates, Galen, Avicenna and Fernel in medicine, law texts, Estienne's Bible, Church Fathers, church history, the *City of God* in French and other spiritual works, Luis de Granada's *Guide des pécheurs,* and Richeome. The whole of contemporary French literature was represented by just five of Robert Garnier's tragedies. Both Coulombel and Février possessed hundreds of unbound copies of books they helped publish, and the valuation of the former's stock was 565 livres, and 1591 for the latter. Coulombel's would seem to have been undervalued.

The Palais booksellers were on a higher level than this and catered for a different class of reader. Samuel Thiboust had a long narrow shop there in 1635 and stocked students' textbooks although he was some distance from the university: *Flores latinae locutionis,* Behourt's edition of Despautère, Nicot's dictionaries (and Charles Estienne's), Greek and Latin texts. He offered translations of Pliny, Seneca, Plutarch and Aristotle's *Politics,* presumably for a wider public than academics. He also supplied with the tools of their trade the lawyers and government officials who thronged the shops and galleries of the Palais. Religion was represented by the Fathers most in demand, Ambrose and Bernard, The *Gallia christiana, Chronologia temporum,* Sirmond's edition of the French Councils of the Church, Bellarmine, Lessius's *De justicia et jure,* Suarez's *Metaphysics,* and a course in French philosophy. Breviaries and hours he had in quantities, some French, some Spanish, Psalters and missals in fine bindings for his wealthy customers, and the ubiquitous Luis de Granada. For the aristocratic customer he stocked histories of the leading noble families.

That kind of well stocked emporium was typical of the Palais, as the inventories prove: firms such as Guillemot, Quinet and Sommaville were worth anything from 15,000 to

20,000 livres, Rocollet was worth 30,000 and Courbé 90,000
livres. And the bigger firms had trade connections with
provincial booksellers. The headquarters of the trade was the
Rue St. Jacques where the largest bookshops and publishing
houses were situated, capable of producing the huge folio
editions of the Fathers and other voluminous ammunition of
the Counter Reformation for export to Europe.

Robert Fouet was typical of the Rue St. Jacques firms. In
his inventory dated 1642 some 6000 volumes are listed, a
large proportion of them folios of religious works. He
stocked the usual range of hours, service books, Bibles,
especially the version authorized by Pope Sixtus V (Fouet
was an officially appointed publisher of that edition),
Patristic writings, theologians—chiefly French, particularly
Du Perron, Coton and Véron—Canisius's and Richelieu's
catechisms, exegetical works by Jansen, Cornelius a Lapide
and Lorini, Azpilcueta's moral theology and Father Bauny's
works, Sanchez's *De martrimonia,* the Italian and Spanish
theologians, Bellarmine, Canisius, Becanus, Toledo,
Vasquez, Bañes, Suarez, Soto, Arriaga, Pineda, Lugo,
Castro Palao. All the evidence we need for the heavy
penetration of French religious thought by Spain is here.

The literature of spirituality, so much in demand, is also
here: the *Imitation,* Ludolph of Chartres' *Vie de Jésus-Christ,*
St. Francis' *Chroniques,* St. Gertrude's *Insinuations,* Bruno's
Méditations, Lansperge, Suso, Louis de Blois, *Fleur des
Saints,* and lives of the Desert Fathers. More recent authors
include Pierre de Besse, Luis de Granada, Rodriguez and La
Puente, and François de Sales (hundreds of copies), Camus,
Bérulle's *Grandeur de Jésus,* and Boucher's sermons. There
were hundreds of instructions for novices in the religious
orders.

Fouet also stocked textbooks for schools and colleges,
dictionaries and manuals of arithmetic and algebra, Greek
and Latin authors in Elzevier's pocket edition and in
ponderous folios from Germany. History and jurisprudence
were a speciality, and science. He had a great range of
medical books, from Bauderon's *Pharmacopée* and the
Médecin charitable to learned German tomes from Frankfurt, alchemy by Fludd, Béguin and Croll, and *Jours*

caniculaires, published by Fouet, as well as the works of Sieur de la Violette. Humanists from the 16th century, moralists and contemporary writers filled his shelves: Erasmus's *Colloquies,* Scaliger's *Epîtres,* Justus Lipsius, Jean de Marnix's *Résolutions politiques,* Bodin's *République,* Du Vair and Charron's works, Bardin's *Lycée,* and sets of the *Mercure français.* In literature, Ariosto, Ronsard, Montemayor's *Diane,* d'Urfé's *Astrée,* Guillaume Bouchet's *Serées,* Charles Estienne's *Maison rustique,* the Seigneur des Accord's *Bigarrures,* Alemán's *Guzmán de Alfarache,* Barclay's *Argenis,* Sorel's *Berger extravagant,* Heliodorus's *Aethiopica,* and de Viau's poems.

Fouet was valued at 11,052 livres, a modest sum for a Rue St. Jacques establishment. He was a general bookseller, chiefly of Paris publications, with only a small selection of foreign books, probably because he withdrew from the international trade at the end of his long life and had ceased to publish his own material as he had once done. At least a dozen stationers in Paris had stocks worth more than 25,000 livres, and there were three or four whose books were valued in excess of 50,000 livres.

The notaries responsible for drawing up the inventories were understandably discouraged from detailing everything in the case of the largest businesses but we can judge what Morel, for instance, sold in his establishment because when Siméon Piget took over the business from the last of the Morels in 1646 he published a catalog. It runs to 139 quarto pages and gives precious information about the scale and range of subjects, as does another contemporary catalog, *Catalogue des livres arrivés chez Madame Pelé, Rue St. Jacques à la Croix d'or en 1643.* Both catalogs agree in their witness to the large number of 16th and early 17th century books still current, and the country of origin of the Latin books is interesting: 99 from France (74 from Lyons); 86 from the Spanish Netherlands (64 from Antwerp); 429 from the United Provinces; 26 from England; 201 from Germany (53 from Cologne; 42 from Frankfurt); 43 from Italy.

Of course such documents only represent a fraction of the actual books on sale, since they would not include ordinary topical books of little distinction, or pamphlets, either to avoid overloading their lists or simply making the stock seem cheap. Titles evidently remained in print for many years before an edition was exhausted, and others were already very old; hence the conclusion must be that the booksellers just mentioned dealt in new and second-hand books. And those two firms were among the twelve biggest firms in Europe.

A very different world from today's book trade. No clear differentiation among publisher, bookseller, printer and binder. Anyone could sell retail or wholesale once he was in business, could employ printers or binders, and could publish at his own expense or in collaboration with others. Profits from one area of his trade he could reinvest in another, and so each played a vital part in financing the commonest publications, the hours, litanies, offices, prayerbooks, ABCs and primers, staples of the trade. It seems that the more modest booksellers—say those worth less than 5000 livres—possessed a fairly good range of books for retail, and their profits would help pay for the publication of other works at a time when finance had to come from limited sources. The largest bookseller-publishers differed only in scale from their smaller competitors, otherwise trading operations were similar. It was a world still dominated by the craftsman rather than by the entrepreneur, a little like the small publisher of academic books in our day who also does some bookselling.

2. Rivals and partners: the German book fairs

Exchange of stock was common practice throughout the trade; hence a sketch of the major book fairs and other centers of the trade might be helpful before considering the role Paris played. Leipzig and Frankfurt were the most famous fairs and their catalogs afford vital evidence of the output in Europe. Frankfurt was much the bigger, as was Cologne at that time, and Italian firms went to Frankfurt bacause it was nearer. Venice was a major importer of books, Rome far from negligible, Palermo and Naples still active though not so prosperous as the northern Italian towns like Brescia, Verona, Padua and Ferrara while Milan and Florence had passed their zenith. Geneva had replaced Basel as the main trade center of Switzerland and was in close contact with Protestant writers and merchants in France and Germany, as Lyons was for Catholic publishers in France, Spain and Germany. To the north, Antwerp rivaled Venice, Amsterdam was of secondary importance, and London of no importance. Douai sold almost as many books at the fairs as Rome, and in the Protestant world Leyden was rapidly gaining on Geneva.

Firms met twice a year at the fairs, exchanging stock, advertising their lists, settling accounts with each other, and of course selling their wares. The fairs are our best testimony to the essential unity of the trade in Europe, the main shop window especially for the still huge numbers of Latin texts, ancient and modern, the traditional language of learning. Then things changed. On the eve of the Thirty Years War Leipzig eclipsed Frankfurt and Cologne, a foreshadowing of things to come: German emerges as the language of publication in Saxony (but not in the Catholic Rhineland), Antwerp overtakes Venice and the Italian trade disappears from the German fairs, Protestant London, Amsterdam, Leyden and Arnhem increase their dealings with Germany. A schism between northern and Mediterranean Europe was complete, at least for the time being, and though Geneva and Lyons were not much affected by the War, Paris lay only third behind Antwerp and Venice by 1648, the end of that terrible struggle.

The German fairs did less business in the years immediately after the War, with only 5,173 titles listed in the catalogs compared with 8,049 in the years (1613–17) immediately before the conflict; Frankfurt was once more in first place and Cologne was regaining her position for a little longer. Antwerp, Geneva and the English stationers are much in evidence, Paris and Lyons only sporadically, and Venice hardly at all. The book trade's center of gravity was moving from south to north, Italy was being overtaken by the Netherlands, and indeed Paris and Lyons were later to follow Antwerp into decline, and more abruptly. No question but the Thirty Years War was a big factor in the ruin of the European book trade, and booksellers in more distant parts of Europe showed no further interest in a market once so

attractive. Venice, Paris and Lyons all began to desert
Frankfurt when the War was at its height (1630–40), and
when peace was declared in 1648 it is puzzling to know why
Antwerp returned to the German markets while Venice did
not (Antwerp was of course much nearer the great entre-
pots), and Paris and Lyons likewise stayed at home, though
their business must have been badly affected by the War.
Still, there must have been economic and technical reasons as
well as purely military factors for Antwerp's rise to supremacy in the trade. Holland was the great arsenal of book
production, and Italy faded from the scene—one reason for
Venice's decline may have been the higher price of her
books, but the vigor of Protestant enterprise in North
Western Europe was making that whole geographical area a
new center of commercial power; if Venetian woollen
products are compared with the trade in books a similar
picture emerges of a peak in 1600–1610 followed by decline.
Venetian goods were dearer and no longer superior in
quality; the Netherlands were producing better commodities
at lower cost. Culturally, Italian influence and the Italian
language were weakening in their influence concomitantly
with Italian trade abroad. The language and model for
international culture was in future to be French.

3. Rivals and partners: Antwerp and Amsterdam

The Netherlands was divided into the Spanish Low Countries
and the United Provinces, and both halves now enjoyed a
resurgence. Booksellers came to Frankfurt and Leipzig not
only from Antwerp but from Douai, Louvain, Mons,
Brussels, Rotterdam, Arnhem, Franeker, Middelburg and
The Hague, and new firms and townships continually swelled
the volume of trade. Preeminent were Antwerp, Leyden and
Amsterdam; a closer study of their fortunes will help
elucidate reasons why this region should have become so
important in the history of the trade.

Antwerp had been an influential publishing center since
1550 when Plantin established his business there, and grew
more prosperous when it fell into Spanish hands. There
seems to be a kind of principle of reversion at work, since the

arts—and printing is one—have an affection for countries in decline, but Antwerp's case has something to do with the Low Countries' attachment to the Spanish empire, and so immediate connections opened up with southern Europe; though printing in Spain was not of much consequence, the Netherlands were an important outpost of Spanish Catholicism, and Philip II needed a secure base from which to launch counterattacks on neighboring Protestant countries; hence Antwerp booksellers were presented with great opportunities—if they cooperated, and the King offered lucrative monopolies to chosen firms, particularly Plantin-Moretus. Theologians in the Catholic University of Louvain were at the same time engaged on a big program of editing (the Church Fathers), and with the help of the best equipped printers in Europe together with the ancillary arts of engraving and illustration they produced sumptuous books at reasonable prices. Given these advantages it is hardly surprising that the city should be the foremost publishing center of the early 17th century.

Moretus, heir to the Plantin enterprise, was himself a dynamic and imaginative printer in a city of first-class tradesmen, like Nutius, Bellère, Paetius, Van Meurs and Verdussen. Their books were exported to Europe and even beyond—church books, theology, Patristic scholarship, the new criticism of Justus Lipsius, languages—all contributed to the city's reputation, and especially to Plantin–Moretus's fame as the doyen. It is not too much to claim that modern intellectual advance was greatly accelerated by the work of such men. The Plantin–Moretus archives which survive in abundance enable us to reconstruct a detailed picture of the business and are the best source for study of the printing technology and publishing at this period. Let us pause a moment in the Place du Marché du Vendredi near the quayside at Antwerp where the original premises are now a museum, with presses and equipment perfectly preserved. The sign of the Golden Compasses was well-known throughout the Netherlands, each township with an agent or an office in direct contact with Antwerp: at Namur, Bruges, Liège, Armentières, Malines, Cambrai, Ypres. In Brussels Jan Lionart (father of Fédéric Léonard, later of Paris) was the largest firm, bigger than Foppens, Mommaert and Vivien, and acted as Moretus's principal client, agent and wholesaler.

Moretus supplied stationers in the small towns with his own and foreign publications on the usual basis of exchange of stock, and did not confine his trade to the Spanish-occupied territories but traded with the Protestant United Provinces as far as Utrecht, Leyden and Middelburg. The Spanish possessions in Europe and overseas were potential markets, and shipments went by river and sea to Rouen and St. Malo. They traded with German firms and exported to Vienna, Prague, Cracow, Copenhagen, Stockholm, London, Dover, the Duchy of Lorraine, Pont-à-Mousson, Nancy, Toul and Epinal. They had an immense network in France: Amiens, Limoges, Bordeaux, Rouen, Toulouse, Lyons, where they dealt with Arnauld, Borde, Boissat, Cardon, Huguetan, Pillehotte, Anisson and Rigaud, and in Paris they traded with foremost names: Denys Béchet, Pierre Billaine, Widow Buon, Michel Soly, Charles Chastelaine and his partner Biestkens, Jean Jost, Guillaume Pelé, Eustache Foucault, Joseph Cottereau, Thomas Blaise, Denis Moreau, Jean Gobert, Michel Laurent and Claude Sonnius, and of course Sébastien Cramoisy.

The Paris accounts have unfortunately disappeared but a good deal is known about the business methods of large firms. For example, Moretus's speciality was red and black service books for use at church, and it seems they were easy to sell but "black only" were not, so that Moretus would only supply "red and black" for cash or on bills of exchange with a limit of six months, but with a big name like Cramoisy he would operate a barter system since the latter also published prayerbooks saleable in Antwerp. The "black" they sold as they did prayerbooks, for cash with 10% to 25% discounts, but as a rule they exchanged their lines for their rivals' publications. Barter was a vital part of trade practice with large or small firms, a channel through which books from many different places could be supplied to any retail bookshop. Morel and Pelé's stock lists include many foreign books and in fact the trade was organized to secure books from abroad without the transfer of actual money. In any system of exchange, whether of goods or of money, there will inevitably be debtors and creditors, and in the trade between Moretus and Paris, Lyons and Rouen, the French were always in deficit, having to make use of bills of exchange. Cramoisy would deliver books to Brussels and ask booksellers there to pay Moretus, and bills of exchange passed between Antwerp, Rouen and Spain, or Antwerp, Lyons and Spain, with Spain the debtor nation. Lyons and Paris would pay Moretus in kind, sometimes sending him consignments of paper manufactured in France, and Paris and Rouen settled their debts with Antwerp through Flemish bankers in Rouen, the Schott Brothers, who financed the shipments of Moretus books bound for Spain.

The United Provinces, once liberated from the Spanish yoke, soon showed nimble business enterprise. The role of Dutch publishers is too well known to need emphasis but some figures may help: Ledeboer's inventories, revised later by Kruseman (1893), yield valuable information about printers and booksellers in various Dutch towns. Leyden was a busy printing town in the 16th century (44 printer–booksellers from 1551 to 1591) and in the early 17th century (61 names), and rather less active later (55 names). Amsterdam went on steadily rising (38 names from 1550 to 1599; 96 from 1600 to 1624; 154 from 1625 to 1649), and The Hague, Rotterdam, Middelburg and Utrecht were also busy centers. The *Catalogus universalis* complied by Broer Jansz, an Amsterdam bookseller (1640–52), is the Dutch equivalent of Father Jacob's *Bibliographica gallicana* and gives useful statistics for the period 1639–51: 2,380 titles are listed from thirty different places, twenty of them in Holland; Latin publications were concentrated at Leyden among Elzevier, Commelin, Mair and Hackius, and at Amsterdam, Blaeu, Elzevier and Janszoon were the specialists, with Blaeu and Elzevier also specialists in French books.

The chief foreign representatives at the Frankfurt and Leipzig fairs prove that Leyden began to establish a firm hold from 1586 to 1610 and from 1610 to 1620 eclipses Venice, while Amsterdam moves up and is not far short of Lyons in volume of trade. During the stormy years of the Thirty Years War, 1630–50, when the French and Italians virtually disappear, Leyden holds its own, and Amsterdam alone of all the foreign places draws ahead of Antwerp and by 1635–40 is in first place; other smaller firms from the seven Dutch provinces also appear in the tables.

The Netherlands and Geneva were finally the sole regions still in the German market; trade between the Holy Roman Empire and the Latin countries was severed leaving the field to the Netherlands, and their stationers' catalogs confirm this, showing marked activity in Germany, very little in Italy or Spain, and the usual mixture of new and second-hand stocks as the staple of business. French and Latin publications from Paris and Lyons and Geneva figured largely: there was mutual profit, with Dutch books entering the French market on a big scale and French books in Dutch bookshops.

Dutch enterprise soon brought results in the international market, and Leyden was by the last quarter of the 16th century an important depot for Dutch-language books; many new businesses opened, usually Flemish or refugees from the Spanish Netherlands. Guillaume Sylvius was from Antwerp and in 1583 Plantin arrived, invited by Lipsius, his friend, and left two years later after handing over his business to Rapheleng, a relative who specialized in oriental books and so started a Dutch tradition. Louis Elzevier was a Louvain printer who had worked for Plantin in Antwerp and then at Douai, so the conclusion must be that Antwerp was the cradle of later Dutch publishing.

When the University of Leyden was founded in 1575, booksellers, binders and printers flocked there, forming a close bond between the new foundation and the trade. The Calvinist city was a symbol of refuge and its scholars world famous: Lipsius, Scaliger, Du Moulin, Charles de l'Ecluse and Saumaise. Young Protestants made their way there to study (there were 1,735 students on the register from 1575 to 1600), not only from the Low Countries but from Europe, Africa and Asia.

Leyden was foremost in classical studies. Putaneus and Vulcanius (in plain Dutch, Bonaventure de Smet) taught there with Lipsius, Scaliger and Saumaise, and other professors, Vossius, Heinsius, Scriverius, Gronovius and Graevius, a formidable band. Whenever a scholar died, booksellers were at the auction of his personal library, a sure source of profit to the town where the second-hand trade was thriving. It was an advantage to academics to have so many printers in town, and with so much scholarship bursting to publish, the book trade was bound to grow: Rapheleng, Commelin (descendants of Antoine Calvin, John Calvin's brother) and Jean Mair, who published Descartes' *Discours de la méthode,* divided Leyden, Amsterdam and Heidelberg among them. And the Elzeviers were the jewel in the crown.

Louis Elzevier left Douai in 1580, fleeing to Leyden no doubt at the invitation of Vulcanius, Baudius and Heinsius, and probably attracted by the new university. He was a bookbinder who did some bookselling, and was helped by Plantin when he arrived in the city. His old employer had a large stock and supplied Elzevier with books to the value of 1270 florins, which put him in business when he was officially appointed "beadle" (it meant an authorized connection with the university) and quartered in the Rapenburg near the courts, another potential market. By 1592 Elzevier was a publisher with a distinguished list of scholars adding to the city's renown, and his business acumen showed when he appeared at the book fairs, listed in all the catalogs, selling his own and others' books from a range of cities—Utrecht, Amsterdam and Middelburg. He would buy books at the fairs and sell through Paetius, a colleague, and in Paris through Jean Berjon, as well as through his own branch there. As trade expanded he brought in his family, his sons Josse and Louis, the first in Utrecht, the second in The Hague, and Mathieu, a son-in-law, and took premises in the Palais des Etats, The Hague equivalent of the Palais in Paris. At first the Elzeviers did not print their own books but commissioned a printer, but in 1616 Isaac, one of Louis' sons, bought a press, and such was the reputation of this family of scholar-printers that he was appointed Printer to Leyden University in 1620, with authority to erect premises in the university courtyard for his presses and his bookshop— it is there to this day. By 1625 he had completely equipped the new shop with punches, matrices and founts of oriental characters bought from a scholar, Erpenius's widow, whose husband had them from Rapheleng.

But Isaac felt the attraction of life at sea, and sold up 10,000 kilograms of letter sorts, five printing presses, an engraving press, punches and matrices to his brother Abraham and nephew Bonaventure, then joined the navy! It was under the direction of these last two that the firm entered its greatest phase, equipped as they were now with oriental types and of course with Greek fonts. As Holland extended its empire in the Far East, so prospects of a book trade to supply the bookish needs of those countries and Dutch scholars with oriental material ensured prosperity for the Elzeviers. Dutch letter founders supplied them, as did Luther of Frankfurt, giving them an unrivalled lead, and soon they were models for design, illustration, letter forms. Paper was their one weakness since little came from Holland, and most from France which was subject to interruption through war or economic vicissitudes, but Elzevier initiative overcame even that problem—they reduced the size of their books to make the paper go further, and used tiny but still legible types with a special ink to retain a crisp black look on the page. This of course reduced production costs by three-quarters, enabling them to expand business even in the midst of the vicious wars between Catholic and Protestant that were then raging. In 1626 they started their famous "Republic" series (little books, guides to different countries, some thirty-five in all) and in 1629 their most famous line, the Elzevier pocket classics. Their editions of Caesar, Livy and Pliny were masterpieces of their kind when they saw the light in 1633.

Despite the battles ravaging Germany they kept up their visits to Leipzig and Frankfurt, expanding their commercial network and keeping in touch with scholars and other booksellers throughout Europe. Bonaventure presided over the whole concern, Abraham over the printing side, while Louis II was their representative at large. He founded a branch in Copenhagen, and he was in Italy in 1635 where he visited Lucas Holstein at the Papal Court where he had been living since his conversion to Catholicism. He brought samples of the pocket classics to Peiresc in Aix, and suggested a scheme for collaboration in printing to help scholars, when he met Mathurin Du Puis in Paris. Du Puis and the Widow Buon had already been complaining about Elzevier's business methods, but Elzevier believed in personal contact to heal differences, and that personal touch applied also to authors, on whom of course the publishers depended to keep copy flowing in. The French market was assiduously cultivated, and Abraham's son Jean was dispatched to Paris at 16 to complete his education and incidentally make contact with future collaborators, scholars and businessmen. Young Jean lived with Pelé, and his father's reputation and the letters of introduction from scholars like Heinsius at Leyden opened doors—Dupuy's, Chapelain's and Conrart's, for example. But the most important contact was the Chancellor, Séguier, who granted his personal protection to Jean, a huge advantage for the young man when he later returned to Paris with merchandise in competition with French publishers who were very unhappy to see him selling books there when he was also pirating their best lines! But then most booksellers were involved in that sort of sharp practice. It was a matter of survival.

Eventually Amsterdam overtook Leyden. In 1622 it was a city of 200,000 with several established printing firms. Like Leyden they had for years specialized in Bibles, Psalters, navigational manuals, elementary arithmetic books and old-fashioned romances, with some translations; in short, their production was geared to a reading public of merchants, sailors and the bourgeoisie, a vernacular culture. But by the mid-17th century there is evidence of a higher cultural level: Broer Jansz's *Catalogus universalis* gives us some details which indicate that Latin, French and Italian books were part of his stock-in-trade.

Cornelius Claesz was the earliest of the big Amsterdam firms. Founded by a Calvinist from Brabant, the firm published 147 titles between 1581 and 1600, nearly all in Dutch. Travels and atlases were his specialities and with the public interest in voyages growing and skill in map-making fostered by Ortelius's *Theatrum mundi* and Mercator's *Cosmography,* Claesz prospered. The Frankfurt catalogs list Claesz's publications in translation and reveal that he was in the exchange market on a big scale. In exchange for his publications he took other publishers' lines and offered a wide range of books in many subjects, as his 1604 catalog proves; it was the means by which "stockholding" booksellers acquired general lists. Claesz died in 1609 and the business passed into the hands of one of the engravers who worked for him, Joost Hondius. He did some engravings in England and some type-founding, and on his return to Holland bought maps, engravings and equipment used by Mercator to publish his famous atlases in Duisburg. Joost went into partnership with his brother Hendrik and brother-in-law Jan Jansz, son of an Arnhem bookseller who had once partnered Claesz, and in 1638 Jansz assumed control of the business. Between 1602 and 1650 Mercator's atlas was reprinted by Hondius, the Janszoon countless times scrupulously revised and embellished with engravings. It made Janszoon's fortune and enhanced the reputation of the Dutch in the international book trade.

Still more typical was the famous firm of Blaeu, originally Willem Jansz (or Guillaume Jansonius Caesii). Born in 1571, son of a herring merchant—a noble profession in Holland—young Willem was apprenticed to Hooft, a burgomeister of Amsterdam and a famous Dutch writer. Because of a talent for mathematics Willem was sent to Denmark where he spent two years in Tycho Brahe's observatory in Oranienburg. Back in Holland he opened a shop selling mathematical instruments and began publishing engraved maps, the first *Het licht der zee-vaert* (1608), translated into many languages, the foundation of his fame. Next he is visiting the Frankfurt fair and involved in the general trade of book-selling and publishing. His training in mathematical instrument–making meant he knew how to ensure that his equipment was the best, and he bought matrices and punches from Briot, a goldsmith of Gouda, and from Luther of Frankfurt. He improved the working of the hand press and devised a method which ensured more evenness of inking and better type impression on paper, technical advances that made Dutch printing the envy of the world and ultimately made possible the Elzevier pocket editions. Blaeu's shop was one of the sights of Amsterdam, with nine presses and six engraving presses in a building purpose-designed to house them, rooms provided with windows on two sides and a model foundry with cauldrons and tools, punches and materials for cleaning type, the most modern and best equipped in Europe, including Plantin's.

While Leyden depended on the university for its prosperity, Amsterdam owed its reputation to its maps, not unnaturally since the sea was its fortune. Increased experience in the production and marketing of books helped the book trade in both cities, especially in cheaply priced pocket books, the main invention of the great age of Dutch publishing. One of the chief reasons for the profitable increase in trade was the influx of refugees from the south of the country, particularly Antwerp, bringing with them technical and commercial experience and skills. Just as Antwerp had taken the place of Venice, so Amsterdam and Leyden took the place of Antwerp as the foremost center of the trade. The Protestant United Provinces were able to reap benefits from the bloody and divisive war that split north and south in Europe, and like their famous seafarers, the publishers became the great entrepreneurs of the age. Progress in technology went hand in hand with business acumen, so that in France Richelieu takes a hint and founds the Imprimerie Royale to improve standards of printing and book design, with results we shall examine later.

4. *Rivals and partners: Geneva and Lyons*

Although a good proportion of the books published in Paris were in Latin, more French books appear by the mid-17th century, so here a word about the growth of the trade in the French-speaking countries which would have closer connections with Paris than other countries by virtue of the language, either as competitors or partners.

Many studies have been made of regional printing in France and a fairly accurate picture of the distribution of printing is now possible, not only in France but in the Walloons area and French-speaking Switzerland for the years 1550, 1600 and 1650. In 1550 there were 40 printers; in 1600, 60, and 1650, 80. The main printing centers remain constant but whereas in 1550 12 towns had at least two rival printers, by 1600 the number had doubled and by 1650 it had tripled. There were more printers in Northern France than in the South, particularly Normandy, Picardy and Champagne and in the French-speaking regions of Flanders and Lorraine, at least before the Thirty Years War. It is rather like the distribution of elementary schools in France.

Why did printing fail in some areas and not in others? Before 1550 the reasons are clear: printers began work in the largest towns, and usually those with a university—Orléans, Poitiers, Caen, Rennes, Toulouse, Avignon and Louvain, or towns with a Parlement—Poitiers, Rouen, Bordeaux, or with a rich body of clergy—Rheims and Limoges, or in big commercial centers—Lyons, Rouen, Toulouse, Bordeaux. After 1550 other factors entered the picture with gradual increase in local administration and even education, a need for officials and the inevitable growth in official communications, legislation, public notices—all lucrative lines for the average printer. In an age so obsessively concerned with religious dogma and definition, which was an integral part of education, the authorities fostered their appointees, university teachers, college regents, both Catholic and Protestant, and sponsored publishers who turned out the printed matter that made converts. A network of printers and booksellers operated in Protestant regions at Lescar, Die, Orthez, Saumur and Sedan by the academies which taught the new Reformed doctrine, and at Geneva and La Rochelle until the siege of the latter abruptly ended the Protestant grip.

Jesuit fanaticism promoted Catholicism everywhere, in Douai where the King of Spain opened a university, at Pont-à Mousson, and wherever Jesuit colleges were opened new potential markets opened for the book trade. At La Flèche they called in a printer who had been a pupil of theirs and supplied him with equipment to counter the influence of Protestant propaganda coming from nearby Saumur where the Desbordes family were the printers. At Limoges and Tulle, where previously there had only been some local printing, colleges were founded and the trade flourished under tight Jesuit control. It can safely be said that in Catholic France the impact of the Jesuit missions not only affected the religious book trade but also the educational.

So the trade flourished in France and the adjoining French-speaking countries. Important books were published every year in towns and cities, in La Rochelle, Saumur and Sedan, in Douai, Pont-à-Mousson and Brussels on the frontiers, and inland at Dijon, Grenoble, Bordeaux, Limoges, Rennes, Amiens, Rheims and Troyes. The titles current in Paris were quickly copied in other places; Troyes was the home of street literature, and that was all; even Toulouse was only a local trade (the Colomiès, Boude and Bosc families); the French made no mark in the international scene outside Paris, Rouen and Lyons.

Rouen was the home of a very large number of printers and booksellers all registered in the Stationers' Guild (the Communauté) in the early 17th century, and by 1625 there were thirty printers in town, though most had only one press, jobbing printers. Standards were low, as they were at Troyes, printed matter was cheap, the chapbook was king, and they had no competitors elsewhere. But in other Rouen firms more substantial work was done, some educational, some religious for the big Paris market, others for the government and legislature, as well as service books, hours, calendars and almanacs, and clandestine publications, a huge and miscellaneous industry for all classes and tastes. Protestants in Rouen published Bibles and Psalters, controversial material for their preachers, and were specially good in the literary field: anthologies, plays, translations from Spanish romances, novels, new works by Norman and Parisian writers. There was encouragement for local talent as when Raphael Du Petit-Val, the poet, published La Roques' *Premières oeuvres* separately and as a collection. Maurry, another local publisher, brought out the two Corneille brothers, and later Brébeuf, Scarron and Scudéry, sometimes at the author's expense and sometimes as the agent of the Palais publishers.

Rouen was the seat of the ancient Norman aristocracy and so enjoyed prestige, had various courts and a Palais de Justice which was a literary rendezvous of writers and dramatists as was the one in Paris. It could absorb much of its own output while having no trouble marketing its surplus in Paris, Normandy, Picardy and Brittany. Paris was its chief outlet and Rouen booksellers made regular visits, stocking

up their own shops there, or keeping supplies going through
their agents, particularly in the Palais, and bringing stocks of
ballads and chapbooks for the hawkers and pedlars on the
quays, most of it pirated. There were exports abroad, and
imports. Rouen publishers were in correspondence with
Moretus and secured his Spanish debts through their agencies, and there was business to transact with Spain, exchanging new publications for Spanish books to sell in the Palais, at
Rouen or Paris. Books published in Rouen were sold in the
Netherlands and Paris publications were pirated and exported to Flanders and the Low Countries. A flourishing
entrepot and center of primary production, Rouen was
incredibly active and like most businesses had no preju-
dices—Protestant sympathizers there helped facilitate the
import of Dutch books into France and even encouraged
underground traffic in banned literature.

Geneva was already well established as a city of international trade by the late 16th century, and with the coming of
Calvinism a rigid discipline gripped the city, some of the
more unconventional practices ceased and trade was more
tightly organized. In the Catholic world the very name was
regarded with horror and no books with its imprint could
hope to sell outside the Protestant orbit; hence the request
sent from Geneva to Henri IV that books published there
might use the name *Aureliae Allobrogorum* to conceal their
origin and so find their way even into Portugal. With ruses of
that kind, cheap paper, and unimpeded by the stoppage of
work during the multitude of Catholic feast days, no wonder
their Lyons rivals complained about unfair competition,
pointing out that Genevan booksellers were sending consignments along the river Isère and the Rhône to Rome, Spain
and Italy, along the Rhine to Hamburg, Holland and
Denmark, and across to England. Despite this, only two
firms, Chouet and De Tournes, made any impact on the
French market, and they only via fellow Calvinists in the
French book trade. Geneva was simply banned from the
Catholic world and so had to trade with Protestant countries
already well supplied by Leyden and Amsterdam. Competition was keen.

Lyons was the only French city able to rival Paris. Based

on the Lyons books in the Bibliothèque Nationale, a count shows Lyons enjoying comparative prosperity until 1628, then recession for the next twenty years, a slight recovery 1655–70, depression in 1674–75, then affluence interrupted in 1685–86, after which there was total collapse. Ponderous folios were the typical Lyons product, and monumental series, which must have gone well at the German book fairs since Lyons traded there for longer than Paris firms. The picture appears to be of a strained situation in Lyons, always vulnerable to crises yet with a toughness and tenacity which helped it survive better than Paris.

Ancellin, Frellon, de Harsy, Coeursilly and Rigaud were the leading publishers in Lyons, their lists being mostly literary and devotional, which could be expected in a city so close to Spain and Italy, the countries which inspired the spiritual revival in France, mediated through Lyons. Rigaud's *Introduction à la vie mystique* epitomizes the kind of work published for their French customers. As a rule Lyons firms did not travel to the Frankfurt fair; presumably they were content with the French market.

Theology and jurisprudence, massive projects undertaken by zealous Catholic publishers like Pillehotte, Prost, Ravaud and Landry, brought Lyons its fame, and the very nature of such work forced the formation of printing congers: Boissat and Remeus, Prost, Borde and Arnaud; Caffin and Plaignard; Durand, Girin and Rivière. The foremost publisher was Cardon, later absorbed by Laurent Anisson. Horace and Jacques Cardon came from Lucca in Italy (many Lyons booksellers in the 16th century came from Italy), descended from a Spanish army captain of a noble Aragon family. They made a large fortune in publishing theological and juridical works exported abroad, and in theology they specialized in editions of Spanish thinkers, Morales, Valentia, Mendoza, Sanchez, and Vasquez under Jesuit direction, a planned program designed to reinforce Catholic thought and piety in Europe, so that Cardon and Prost played a leading role in the Counter Reformation. A catalog issued by Prost in 1621 reflects their business activity: 828 Latin works published in Lyons; 897 from Paris; 848 from Italy and Spain; 1,540 from Germany, Central Europe and the Netherlands. Of these

4,113 titles, 1,345 are Religion, 931 Law, 383 Medicine, 360 History and Politics, 447 Grammar, Rhetoric and Poetry. Among these, 678 books were in French, 296 Italian, 253 Spanish and 16 German. In 1652 Laurent Anisson, Cardon's successor, issued a catalog listing 1,076 books published in Lyons, 814 in Paris, 624 from Italy, 158 German and Belgian, and 312 Spanish. If we compare the two lists with Dutch equivalents we find that while many books they sold came from Germany and the Netherlands, the majority were Latin works published in Italy and Spain, or Spanish and Italian. Italy and Spain were the main sources of the Lyons trade, in fact their stock-in-trade, and Lyons booksellers channeled Spanish and Italian culture into France as far as Germany; in return they mediated French and German works in Southern Europe. It was the pivot, and like Antwerp it helped keep open communications between north and south Europe at a time when religious and economic conditions made the situation very difficult.

5. *Paris*

We will analyze two moderately-sized businesses by examining their inventories and by so doing arrive at an appreciation of the place occupied by Paris in the trade. Jean Libert, specialist in school books, first. His will is dated 1638, and it is clear that his customers came from northern France. His books went to booksellers in towns with colleges controlled either by the university or by the Jesuits, administered by their Provincial in France, or sometimes in Champagne. Libert's was a regional trade though we know he was in touch with Moretus and the Elzeviers, and he is listed in the German book fair catalogs. Another average-sized publishing firm was that of Toussaint Quinet, a publisher of plays which he sent to various places in northern France, the Netherlands, through Douai to Lyons and Toulouse, and to Montpellier where Du Buisson was his agent. Other firms, Thiboust, Sommaville and Pierre Billaine, for instance, were doing likewise, to judge from documentary evidence. The great firm of Cramoisy traded with northern France and Lorraine and with the South, and with Jesuit colleges and abbeys. Paris was the trade metropolis for a good half of France. In Amiens, Rennes, Vannes, Nantes, Tours, Orléans, Dijon, firms often have the same names as their associates in Paris, having spent their apprenticeship there, and they exchanged stocks with firms in the capital, dealing usually with one bookseller or a small group who could supply what was in demand. A tightly knit world.

South of the Loire Paris was not the automatic center. Poitiers was within its orbit, and one firm, Barbou, in Limoges, applied to Paris for their books but most of his stock came from Pillehotte and colleagues in Lyons. Publishers in Paris had business contacts in Toulouse and Bordeaux, were anxious about rivals in Lyons, but Lyons was predominant in the south, the intermediary between Paris and the stationers of Guyenne, Provence, Languedoc and the Dauphiné, and in Savoy, on the borders of France, Lyons and Geneva each had influence. Further north, in Franche-Comté and Lorraine, the big Paris firms of Cramoisy and Sonnius established branches, first at Dôle then at Pont-à-Mousson, the limits of Parisian influence. The fact that printers were so numerous in the north suggests more opportunities to serve colleges and convents, which all needed libraries, not to mention the army of local and state officials, all requiring reading matter.

The great international firms marketed books published in Paris and in return Paris booksellers sold foreign books. Paris was also well to the fore at the book fairs, more so in the period 1600–20 than 1620–35, after which it disappeared from that scene. The following table indicates which of the Paris publishers were represented at Frankfurt:

Books listed in the fair catalogs

Booksellers	1600–09	1610–19	1620–29	1630–39	1640–49
Beys	17	16			
Buon	7	17	17		
Célerier			16	17	
Chapellet	12	17	10		
Cramoisy	19	176	253	95	1
Drouart	22	34	5	1	
Fouet	1	15			

Booksellers	1600–09	1610–19	1620–29	1630–39	1640–49
Morel-Piget	27	24			
Nivelle	36	2			
Orry	24				
Pacard		44	10		
Sonnius	29	31	5		
All Paris booksellers	354	461	303	159	8

Drouart, Morel, the Widow Nivelle, Orry and Sonnius were most frequent visitors in the early years, then Cramoisy and Pacard, but although probably more books were printed in Paris than either Venice or Antwerp, it was not a great exporter and scarcely more successful than Venice in preventing encroachment by Flemish and Dutch publishers.

The book fairs were apparently in decline in the years 1620–1640. It is as if the growth in vernacular languages as a medium, and the disappearance of Latin, meant the end of the notion of one central market for European book production, which in the history of the book meant the end of the Renaissance. From this time on, the Dutch and French publish their own catalogs, since the book fair catalogs, once the nearest approach to a book trade bibliography, no longer fulfill that role. Between 1640 and 1645 the first national bibliographies were published almost simultaneously in France, the United Provinces and the Spanish Netherlands. Because of the Thirty Years War, relations between France and the German territories were severed, to the advantage of the United Provinces who were able to act as intermediaries between the two contending powers in Europe.

Paris was the arsenal of the Counter Reformation, publishing its monuments of ecclesiastical learning, and although the balance of payments vis-à-vis Antwerp was unfavorable to the French (since Antwerp was also producing similar material) Paris firms recouped some losses by trade with Italy and Spain, either directly or through Lyons. But then war broke out between France and Spain and the repercussions were painful for the trade, as the Moretus correspondence reveals. Trade between Antwerp in the Spanish Netherlands and France was interrupted by the war, so that Paris had to resort to devious means to keep any business, exchanging consignments of books via Dover and Holland. The Compagnie des Usages in Paris, which had the monopoly of prayerbooks and did more than 50,000 écus a year in trade with Spain, had unsold stocks piling up in its warehouses, a setback to international trade which forced Paris publishers to concentrate on the domestic market, and so to publish in French. The weighty folios become redundant, and Latin fades as a medium of international scholarship. Out of a climate of recession a new age is born.

CHAPTER II

PARISIAN BOOKSELLERS

1. Some Statistics

WHEN BARTER WAS AN ACCEPTED book trade practice a bookseller had to be able to exchange books in his own stock, those published by himself or by others, for other firms' publications, and in an age when there was no distinction between bookseller and publisher his standing was measured by the number of books he brought out each year. Below are figures of the volume of trade done by Paris booksellers in the period under review.

Philippe Renouard has researched publishers' business for the years 1598, 1599, and 1600 based on books surviving from those years. Three hundred and thirty titles (more than two-thirds) were published by 17 firms, eight issuing 200 titles among them including most of the large-scale works. Even though the figures depend on survivals and do not include cheap lines and jobbing work, which will have perished, nonetheless it is clear that the Paris trade was in the hands of a small number of families, all related.

Let us see how this came about, and consider book production from 1643 to 1645. Six hundred and ten titles, less than half the total output, were published by 24 firms. If we subtract the eight or nine largest firms from the 24, we find they publish about 350 titles, or less than one-third of the total, which argues involvement by more people in the trade, less concentration. It seems as if publishers did not exceed a certain plateau—about fifteen books a year—but there was an important exception: the Cramoisy brothers, who published more than 100 books, some very large ones, in three years, and this does not include books published by firms controlled by Sébastien Cramoisy, or Claude Cramoisy's output, or the publications of the Imprimerie Royale which was virtually a branch of the Cramoisy family. There seems to be a new factor—the dominance by a single family: the prosperous firms in the early years are not the same as the successful ones at mid-century. Let us look at reasons for success or failure and retrace the development of the book trade in Paris.

2. The Rue St. Jacques: the old firms

Plantin's Paris branch was suffering a recession in Paris. Before 1595 it was managed by Gilles Beys, Madeleine Plantin's first husband, and published some very substantial works: then Beys had to appeal to his father-in-law for money. After Beys' death Madeleine married Adrien Périer of Lyons who was in business throughout Europe and in turn managed the Plantin firm in Paris, but as a Protestant he could not participate in the expanding trade in Counter Reformation books and began to specialize in medicine and scientific works, sometimes distinctly heterodox, which is possibly the reason why none of Madeleine's sons was able to recover the earlier profitability, and the sign of the Golden Compasses passed into other hands while the family emigrated to Rennes, Lille and The Hague in reduced circumstances.

The firm of Mettayer was in similar straits. As King's Printers Pierre and Jamet Mettayer published quantities of official documents as well as fine quality printing for other firms, but only rarely books bearing their own imprint. Perhaps their loyalty to Henri III, to whom they owed their fortune, and to Henri IV, whom they followed to Blois and Tours, only brought a few benefits, but whatever the reason they were outside the profitable pickings in the Counter Reformation program while publishers supporting the Catholic League were given a lot of business by clergy and religious orders. The records suggest that the Mettayers did not have enough capital to engage in large-scale publishing, and after failing to make his bookshop pay in the Palais precinct, Pierre Mettayer tried to turn the services he had rendered to the monarchy into something tangible by requesting the monopoly in Tridentine prayerbooks enjoyed by the Compagnie des Usages, for which he did some printing. This failed, and when his brother-in-law's business went bankrupt in 1615, Pierre had to rely on routine business he acquired as King's Printer with newsbook work, and he even tried to oust Renaudot as proprietor of the famous *Gazette*. When he died in 1638 he owned a fine printing workshop but no bookstock. Was Mettayer's case an isolated one or symptomatic of something deeper? The history of the later Estiennes gives us an answer.

For a long time the Estiennes had been at the head of the Paris book trade, not so much because of Patisson and Robert Estienne III, the poet, printer and translator of Tansillo's *Larmes de St. Pierre* (Father Garasse's opponent who published elegant verses and translations from the classics), but because of Antoine Estienne, son of Paul Estienne of Geneva. Antoine was a vigorous personality; born in Geneva in 1592, he left early and may have finished his education at Lyons but was in Paris by the time he was twenty and formally abjured the Reformed Church before Cardinal Du Perron, who, pleased to have a prominent printer back in the Church, arranged for his appointment as usher in the Assemblée du Clergé at a salary of 500 livres, and secured lucrative printing privileges for him as the Assemblée's official printer. Letters Patent of 1613 granted him the right to open a business in Paris, even though he had not been apprenticed in the city, and later the same year he was appointed printer-in-ordinary to the King.

Favored treatment of this kind naturally provoked protests from other printers, and the Stationers' Guild seized his presses, bringing his work to a halt for months; Mettayer and Morel, the two King's Printers, brought a lawsuit to defend their monopolies and Estienne was unable to publish even routine official matter for a long time. His patrons stood by him, however, and he finally secured a salary of 600 livres, and at Cardinal La Rochefoucauld's request was given premises in the Collège Royal "for his person and his presses." Aided by this kind of powerful support and his own ability, he began a brilliant career, publishing some formidable work, including Greek texts, Du Perron's works, Fronton Du Duc's edition of Chrysostom, Plutarch, a major edition of Aristotle, as well as government publications. His conversion to the Roman faith made him a formidable partisan in the war of words, and he issued many controversial tracts, and devotional and literary works. Later in life he suffered financial hardship—Du Perron's secretary claimed his fees as an author which he had not received from Estienne, and other creditors pursued him for outstanding debts, with the result that he spent some time in prison from 1631 to 36 and was released only after intervention by the King. Later he was the leader of the radical element in the Stationers' Guild.

So despite major advantages Estienne did not escape ruin. One reason was the cost of his paper—most of his creditors were papermakers and evidently Estienne was printing books too ambitious for his resources, while the State was in arrears over their debts to him for official printing; his liabilities exceeded his income, and Estienne suffered the same fate as Mettayer. Clearly it was not enough simply to be a high-class printer, even King's Printer, to stay in business. Yet many firms did prosper as printers and booksellers—the Morels, for instance.

Fédéric Morel II, last of the great Humanist printers, left the firm to teach at the Collège Royale and translate the sacred and secular classics. His sons, Fédéric III and Claude, succeeded him, and then Charles and Gilles, as King's Printers, and managed the family business. A learned family, they produced sound Greek texts and hundreds of standard editions of the Fathers and of classical texts as part of their activities in printing congers, and were prominent on the international scene at Frankfurt, which explains the breadth and range of their bookstock.

Other ranking publishers were Drouart, Chaudière, Du Puis, Chastelain, Chevallier, Robert Fouet, and above all Sonnius, members of publishers' combines in the later 16th century who collaborated on Patristic texts and monumental series. The firm of Sonnius was a close business associate of Plantin-Moretus, who took control of his shop in Paris and his device, the Golden Compasses. Claude Sonnius, Laurent's son, married Marie Buon, herself daughter of a large-scale publisher, and expanded the business. They increased their list impressively, adding popular material to the traditional scholarly works—voyages and travels mainly—and by associating with scholars of prestige, Scipion Dupleix, Davity, author of *Etats et empires du monde,* and Choppin the jurist, their wealth and status also increased. The Jesuits employed them to disseminate their propaganda, and they published the work of Fathers Dauxiron, Binet, Cordier and Suffren in French.

The Buons were another example of publishing enterprise. Nicolas Buon owed his success to the poets of the Pleiade in the late 16th century, and to Ronsard, since some of the glory rubbed off on to the publisher. But being at a distance from the fashionable center in the Palais, in a tiny court on the Montagne Sainte Geneviève, the Buons abandoned topical and modish subjects in favor of religious titles. Like most established firms they went in for joint publishing and brought out exegetical works, classical texts and Abelard. They also benefited from the Catholic revival with their editions of spiritual literature and translations of Granada and Rodriguez, collaborated with Rocollet to issue Guillebert's paraphrases on the Bible, with Richeome, and as official publisher to the Capuchins, with Sébastien de Senlis, Sébastien de Paris, and Louis and Laurent de Paris.

Best known in the field of devotional literature were the brothers La Noue; Guillaume was heavily involved in the Catholic counterattacks of the late 16th century, and they propagated the Spanish mystics. The Carthusians of Bourgfontaine supplied them with a good deal of work and Bretigny's *Vie de la Mère Thérèse de Jésus* was published by Guillaume in 1601. Later Bretigny financed the publication of his and Dom Chèvre's translations of St. Teresa's works. La Noue also published the *Perle évangélique,* French translations of the Jesuit la Puente, Pedro de Alcantara, St. John of the Cross, the *Palais de l'amour divin* by Laurent de Paris, and Richeome's works, Aquinas's *Summa,* Abra de Raconis's manuals on Aristotle, the theologian Isambert of the Sorbonne, Biblical concordances, Sponde's *Historia ecclesiastica* in six volumes, with translations, and prayerbooks for the Compagnie des Usages, all in all a weighty contribution to the Catholic Renaissance.

Clearly some firms were making their fortunes—those who were giving active support to the Catholic League. One such firm was the undoubted leader of the Paris book trade: Sébastien Cramoisy. He deserves special study.

3. King of the Rue St. Jacques: Sébastien Cramoisy

Sébastien Cramoisy was born in 1583 or '84, son of Elisabeth Nivelle and Pierre Cramoisy, a Paris merchant, and he seems to have been apprenticed to the book trade by his grandfather Nivelle. Some years after his grandfather's death in 1603 he was registered as an official bookseller to the Univeristy of Paris, in 1610, head of the family business at the sign of the Three Storks. By 1612 he was one of the most influential booksellers in Paris and in 1621 was official printer to the Duc de Lorraine with an office in Pont-à-Mousson near the Jesuit college, where no doubt he looked for business and reckoned to publish books more cheaply than in Paris, but the Stationers' Guild put an end to that enterprise. Cramoisy was nevertheless prospering and already publishing several dozen books a year. In 1628 he started his official career, a Syndic of the Guild, 1628–30, and in 1629, by a decree of the Cour des Monnaies, secured a monopoly in the publishing of all financial records. By 1633 he was King's Printer and in 1640 Director of the Imprimerie Royale, Guild Syndic again in 1643, not merely as an elected officer this time, but appointed to the post by the King with a commission to reorganize that body. He was an alderman in 1641, a "juge consul" in 1652, a member of the governing body of the Church and Hospital of St. Jacques, and in 1658, when the General Hospital was created from the office for the Mendicant Poor, he was nominated a "director and administrator of the City of Paris in his lifetime." A substantial citizen, and we might with profit look more closely at his business career, 1606–1669, which saw the publication of over 2,500 books, quite apart from the official publications.

The first point to be made is that he was a trusted agent of

the French Jesuits, publisher with his cousin Chappelet of
Jesuit scholars at Clermont, chiefly Fronton Du Duc, Petau,
Sirmond and Labbe. This close connection meant that he
published their schoolbooks, Father Moquot's Greek grammar, the Despautère (a standard Latin grammar used in
Jesuit colleges), Father Coulon's *Lexicon homericon,* Father
Labbe's *Thesaurus prosodicus graeco-latinum,* Father
Deschamps-neuf's Latin phrase books, which he referred to
rather tenderly at the end of his life—and not without cause.
Such fundamental fodder was a sure income, a goldmine,
because the books were used in Germany and the Netherlands as well as France. Yet not only did he print stock
grammars and glossaries, he provided "ad usum collegiorum
Societatis Jesu" texts of all the classics, guaranteed rapid and
regular sales. All those voluminous works of devotion by
Jesuits were Cramoisy's in addition to the extensive travel
literature created by Jesuit missionary work abroad; he was
virtually their official printer and bookseller, and could be of
service to the General of the Order in many little ways. In
return the General would recommend Cramoisy to any of the
order who sought a publisher, and their correspondence is
marked by an extravagant courtesy. Cramoisy's unflagging
support when Jesuit excesses were prompting hostility from
various quarters must have been a comfort, an asset. It was a
delicate mission discharged to the mutual satisfaction of both
parties.

Friend of the Jesuits and compromised more than once, he
owed his escape from punishment to the patronage of
Richelieu and was described in Fancan's *Catalogus mystico-
politicus* as "king of the Jesuits with the soul of Loyola." His
list was by no means confined to Jesuitical works and college
textbooks: he published learned histories and genealogies of
noble families (Du Chesne's collections of historic documents and Du Cange's works) and was responsible for those
monuments of ecclesiastical scholarship with a Gallican and
royalist bias: *Gallia christiana, Histoire généalogique de la
Maison de France* by Ste. Marthe, Godefroy's *Cérémonial,*
and *Preuves des libertés de l'Eglise gallicane* by the brothers
Dupuy. He was the complete sycophant, losing no opportunity as King's Printer and Director of the Imprimerie Royale

to praise the royal family and the King's Ministers, a perfect mirror of the Jesuits and of the monarchy. His title "archetypographer" was well earned, and he enjoyed the protection of the King's Ministers, especially Richelieu, throughtout his long career. He was commissioned to print Richelieu's speech to the Estates General in 1614, the Cardinal's first publication, and from then on he was Richelieu's personal publisher, keeping him in touch with events in Paris. An uncle of Cramoisy (a Nivelle) was appointed to succeed Richelieu as bishop of Luçon, which is proof of family connections reaching back a long time; the Nivelles and Cramoisys were as vassals to Richelieu. From 1630 Richelieu was the power that steered Cramoisy to wealth and high standing, and Richelieu had ambitions for him, as we shall see.

4. Newcomers in the Rue St. Jacques

At about the time Mettayer went out of business and Siméon Piget bought out Morel (1630–40) there was a revival of trade, and Claude's sons Charles and Gilles Morel bought the posts of King's secretary and counsellor in the Châtelet. The Widow Buon retired and her son became a notary in the Châtelet, Denis Thierry assuming control of the business, working for Capuchins and Franciscans. Denys Béchet succeeded to Ambroise Drouart's business and Jacques Quesnel, one of the few cultivated publishers in an age of businessmen, to Eustache Foucault's. A number of small firms started up, some from obscure beginnings, others by merger, and some prospered when they gave up printing for better takings as booksellers. Typical firms of moderate size were Jean Libert and Mathurin Hénault; Bessin; Villery; Taupinart; Petitpas; and Georges Josse and Michel Soly, the two sons-in-law of Jean de Heuqueville. Jean Billaine and Sébastien Huré I were a success when they took over the firm of La Noue as specialists in Spanish devotional writers, issuing a steady stream of saints' lives for the devout reader; in effect they were official publishers to the Dominicans, Minims and barefoot Carmelites, with good business relations with Capuchins and Jesuits. When the Congregation of the Oratory was seeking converts through the writings of Bérulle, Condren and others, they were their publishers, though they were not on a par with Cramoisy.

Another St. Jacques publisher developed in a different way: Jean Camusat, an odd case. He was apprenticed to Thomas Blaise, a second-hand dealer (the biggest firm in the business) whose son was Séguier's librarian, and attained his mastership in 1621. Until 1630 he published nothing, then suddenly put out a number of important books—Bardin (a moralist), Godeau, poet and bishop, and Jesuit and Capuchin work. Bible paraphrases and translations from Christian and pagan classics were his staple, and either his own good taste or the advice of literary men (like Conrart) made him a literary publisher of repute, with Colletet, Baudier, la Mothe le Vayer, Balzac and Chapelain on his list, all of that original circle which was the nucleus of the Académie Française. Tradition has it that his bookshop was the scene of their first meetings, but he was certainly given the job of printing the Académie's formal thanks and compliments, and when he died a solemn service was held just as if he were a member. His business was valued at 40,000 livres at his death. One interesting consequence was Richelieu's pressing the Académie group to appoint Cramoisy as their publisher. They refused out of respect for Camusat and his widow continued to receive their business, but the fact that Richelieu placed his son-in-law Pierre Le Petit in the post shows how important he thought it, and Petit was an ardent Jansenist withal.

In conclusion: it seems clear that the most influential publishing firms in the Rue St. Jacques were most concerned with the great theological works of the Counter Reformation; then, as the older firms passed away or passed to new management, the trade had one supreme representative, Sébastien Cramoisy, specialist in theology not for its own attractions but for the glory of France, not so much a policy of orthodoxy but of chauvinism. The newcomers in the Rue St. Jacques were deep into spiritual and devotional literature in French, or if the originals were from Spain or Italy, then in French translation. This was a change of emphasis, even of direction, for the trade in its traditional stronghold.

5. *The Palais booksellers*

Shopkeepers, especially dealers in fashionable goods, had traded in the precincts of the Palais since the Middle Ages, and booksellers had been in business there since the 15th century, specializing in law and also in French books for a wider reading public than that represented by professionals, whether clergy or university people. The galleries and salons of the 17th century Palais are vividly before us in the engravings that have come down to us, and in satires of the time and Corneille's comedies. It was the very heart of high society and bookshops stocked literary confections, topical best-sellers and pastime literature; Camusat in the Rue St. Jacques was their only rival. Masterpieces and worthless trifles first saw the light in the boutiques of that most fascinating quarter of Paris.

Abel Langelier was the biggest name there, a descendant of an old family long established in the trade, son of Arnoul Langelier, from whom he had inherited the business. Religious poetry was his speciality, so that his clients tended to be ladies of the upper middle class; he also offered them translations from elegant Italian verse and the easier Latin classics. The official publisher of Blaise de Vigènere, Du Vair and Mlle de Gournay, he issued altogether 261 titles between 1572 and 1600 and continued to be as productive until his death in 1610, with editions of poets Desportes and Bertaut, Passerat and Vigènere's translation of Livy's *Décades,* Philippe de Commines' *Mémoires* and Montaigne's *Essays.* With such a good market for law books on his doorstep, of course, he went in for legal works, especially customaries, and for the many gentry in his clientele he supplied books on the military arts, horsemanship and hunting (often illustrated). His was a safe list, catering to demand, with well-tried works, revised editions of older works and a keen eye for the attractions of illustrations.

Guillemot was his next door neighbor at the sign of the Golden Fleur De Lis, a firm established in 1584 by Mathieu I in the Rue St. Jacques but moving on to the Palais in the following year. He left Paris when the Parlement left for Tours, and stayed there unil 1595 when he returned to the

Palais and a new phase of prosperity. Poetry was his speciality: the two-volume *Muses françaises ralliées* (1599 and 1604), two volumes of *Parnasse* (1609), and the *Nouveau Parnasse*. He brought out an illustrated and revised edition of Beroalde de Verville's version of the popular *Dream of Poliphilus*, using the wood engravings which had made its fortune fifty years earlier, but with a copper-engraved frontispiece in keeping with current fashion. He recognized the vogue for Spanish literature and published Pallet's *Diccionario muy copioso de la langue espagnola,* and, well aware of the appeal of faraway places, he offered Margeret's *Estat de l'Empire de Russie et grande duche de Moscovie* (1604 and 1607). Like Langelier he stocked Jean de Vignan's French translation of Ovid's *Metamorphoses* with frontispiece and eleven plates by Léonard Gaultier. Mathieu Guillemot I died in 1610, the same year as Langelier, and his inventory reveals that they were both planning to launch some finely illustrated volumes of the kind so fashionable during Marie de Medici's regency. The *Histoire de la décadence de l'Empire grec et de l'etablissement de celui des turcs* and *Images ou tableaux de platte peinture* were issued by their widows. The copper engravings inaugurated a new phase in the history of French book illustration—hitherto copper had been a Flemish speciality, and some of the plates were cut in Antwerp.

While Langelier and Guillemot published poets of Desportes's generation, a newcomer, Toussaint Du Bray, introduced the next generation: Malherbe and Regnier, and even before Guillemot's death tried to compete with his main strength, poetry anthologies, by bringing out *Nouveau recueil des plus beaux vers de ce temps,* dedicated to the Vicomtesse d'Auchy, Malherbe's patron, a woman of considerable eminence at Court; other poets in Toussaint's stable were Motin and Davity. In 1615 he issued *Délices de la poésie française,* more anthologies in 1617 and 1620, and in 1627, *Receuil des plus beaux vers de Messieurs de Malherbe, Racan, Monfuron, Boisrobert, l'Espile, Lingendes, Touvant, Motin, Mareschal et autres,* with Malherbe enjoying pride of place. Toussaint was the most fashionable publisher in Paris, exhibiting the best in contemporary literature; Honoré

d'Urfé's *Astrée,* Regnier's *Premières oeuvres* and *Satires,*
Malherbe's plays, *Epîtres d'Ovide traduits en français par les
sieurs Du Perron, de la Brosse, de Lingendes et Hédelin,*
Nervèze's *Amours diverses* and *Entretien évangélique de
l'âme dévote,* beautifully illustrated; Racan's *Bergeries* and
Sept Psaumes; Balzac's *Premières lettres* and *Prince,* and
Campanella's *De Sensu rerum* and *Philosophia naturalis.*
Novels and romances were avidly read and Du Bray duly
supplied them, frothy productions for the shallow courtiers,
by D'Audiguier, Molière d'Essertines, Marcassus and
Gomberville. Like his competitors in the neighboring boutiques he offered a wide range of illustration: Du Bartas's
popular emblem book lavishly illustrated by Martin de Vos,
Elie van den Bosc, Henri Le Roy, and Thomas de Leu, and
in 1631 he issued a splendid *Fables d'Esope Phrygien
traduittes et moralisées par Jean Baudoin* with 120 engravings
by Briot. Baudoin's translation of Philip Sidney's *Arcadia*
was illustrated by Léonard Gaultier, Jean de Courbé and
Crispin de Passe, who also designed plates for Marcassus's
translation of *Daphnis et Chloe* and Du Verdier's *Romant des
romans.*

Meanwhile more booksellers were adding to the competition in the Palais, among them Richer (father and son),
founders of the *Mercure Français,* Claude Rigaud, Claude de
Monstroeil, Gilles and Antoine Robinot, François Julliot,
Samuel Thiboust, Gervais Alliot, Rolet Boutonné, Fleury
Bourriquant, Jean Millot, the Collet brothers and Jean
Corrozet. Business was brisk, and some firms had a boutique
in the Palais and a shop in the Rue St. Jacques, but the Guild
put a stop to this and tradesmen were forced to choose their
location. Du Bray made the Rue St. Jacques his main
business premises but craftily traded in the Palais under a
pseudonym, while others divided the business, one brother
operating from the Palais, another from the Rue St. Jacques.

At length fashionable best sellers and illustrated books
were sold even in the sober university quarter, and all the
time a new generation was coming into the trade and scenting
profit in contemporary authors; Augustin Courbé was one
such. He was apprenticed to Jean Gesselin in 1613 and
registered as a qualified bookseller in October 1623 after

serving his time as a journeyman. He opened up in the Galerie des Merciers in the Palais and started a successful career, was appointed authorized bookseller to the brother of the King in 1635, and specialized in supplying literature to the "Précieuses," the fashionable intellectuals of the time, and publishing their work. He made his fortune out of books like *Origines de la langue française* by Ménage, *Remarques de la langue française* by Vaugelas, Chapelain's *Pucelle, Clovis* by Desmarets de Sainte Sorlin, and works by Mlle. de Scudéry, Maynard, Gombauld, Voiture, La Mothe De Vayer, Pierre Corneille's tragedies—the *Cid, Horace, Polyeucte,* the *Comédie des Tuileries,* and *L'aveugle de Smyrna,* a play jointly composed by Corneille, Boisrobert, Colletet, Rotrou and l'Estoile, besides a host of comedies by Chevreau, Tristan, Baudoin, Mairet, La Calprenède and Boisrobert. When his widow sold the business to Thomas Jolly in 1622 it was worth 75,000 livres.

Antoine de Sommaville was another of the modish Palais publishing fraternity. Born in 1597, son of Simon Sommaville, also of the Palais, in 1621 he married Jeanne Le Clerc, the printer Robert Mansion's widow. He began publishing farces, then plays, novels and translations from Italian and Latin poets, plays by Du Ryer, Rotrou, Benserade, La Calprenède and some of Corneille's plays which were the subject of a lawsuit against his old associates Courbé and Quinet. He was also accused of pirating Cyrano de Bergerac's plays, probably because the latter's publisher, Charles de Sercy, would not share his monopoly in them. He published Scarron's *Nouvelles,* a translation of *Pharsale,* Brébeuf's *Entretiens solitaires* and *Poésies diverses,* before selling his rights in them (retaining some copies) to Jean Ribou and Jean-Baptiste Loyson. He helped publish Malherbe's last poems, sold *Moïse sauvé* and St. Amant's poems, paid for by the author. Sommaville's stock was valued at 9,000 livres at his death and he left a great quantity of unbound copies in his shops at Le Mans college, including Corneille, Malherbe, Du Ryer, Cotin, the abbé de Marolles, *Astrée,* the *Decameron,* the *Temple des Muses,* Sully and Rohan's *Mémoires,* Le Moyne's *Galerie des femmes fortes, Introduction à la vie dévote,* and *Imitation du Jesus-Christ,* the Koran, and many other religious and legal works. He sold Montaigne, Froissart, Monstrelet and Ronsard, and Latin and Greek classics, French books, Church Fathers, histories, the *Dream of Poliphilus* in French, the *Gallia christiana,* the *Gallia purpurata* and illustrations of Biblical scenes.

Others in the profitable trade of catering to the whims of the beau monde were Toussaint Quinet, his son Gabriel and son-in-law Guillaume de Luynes. They were Scarron's publishers (*Roman comique* and *Virgile travesti*) and offered a wide choice of plays, more than 20,000 copies of plays and sketches by Boisrobert, Beys, Chevreau and Tristan, a parcel of two hundred copies of Corneille and another of three hundred in which he had been concerned either as publisher or vendor, including *Cinna.* There were in addition several hundred copies of Scarron, Sorel, La Mothe Le Vayer and Amant's works, 92 copies of Montaigne's *Essays,* 92 copies of *Astrée,* 312 copies of *Tolédan* and 372 copies of La Calprenède's *Mort de Mithridate* as well as *Fleurs des saints,* Cardinal d'Ossat's *Letters,* Strada's *Guerres des Flanders* and books on military affairs. Quinet also stocked Seneca, Plutarch, Virgil in Marolles's translation, Lipsius's edition of Tacitus, Godefroy's *Cérémonial,* Martin du Bellay's *Mémoires,* Calvin's works, the *Vie des saints* and other writings by Jesuits (St. Jure, Arriaga and Molina), *Théâtre d'agriculture* by Olivier de Serres, Belleforest's *Cosmographia,* Montaigne's *Essays,* Montluc's *Mémoires,* Monstrelet's *Chronique* and a selection of histories and law books.

Other names in this fiercely competitive field were Nicolas and Charles de Sercy, publishers of Corneille, Cyrano de Bergerac, and Madame De La Fayette; and François Targa, who published Corneille in conjunction with Courbé.

Courbé and Sommaville were very well aware of the physical appeal of the printed book and were at pains to hire the best illustrations. Courbé commissioned Nanteuil, Bosse and Vignon to prepare the plates for Chapelain's *Pucelle* and had Chauveau engrave the pictures in St. Sorlin's *Almonida.* With Antoine de Sommaville he published a new edition of *Astrée* with engravings by Michel Lasne and Rabel, and plays with noble frontispieces by Daret, Chauveau and Michel

Lasne. In Sommaville's magnificent *Galerie des femmes fortes* by Le Moyne (1647), Mariette engraved the plates after Vignon's drawings.

Deluxe editions were Rocollet's speciality. He was Chancellor Séguier's protégé, King's Printer and Printer to the City of Paris, and in his special field the equal of Courbé and Sommaville in theirs. Pierre Rocollet was born in the late 16th century and was in business by 1610, dealing in news sheets and pamphlets, with a few novels; he was one of a group of promising young publishers who were involved in the trial of Théophile de Viau. In his official role he issued various civic documents and local Acts and historical material relating to Paris; *Coutumes de la prévosté et vicomté de Paris* by Cornet; *Antiquités et les annales générales de la ville de Paris* by Malingre, and *Ordonnances royaux sur la jurisdiction de Paris*. Works of that kind would be for the legal fraternity, but he had other irons in the fire: Mareschal's tragicomedy *Généreuse Allemande* and poems by the same author; Mairet's *Sophonisbe;* Alibray's pastoral romance, *Damon et Chloris;* a pastoral idyll by Sieur de Rampalle, *Nymphe Salmacis,* and his *Enclave généreuse;* Coislin de l'Estoile's *Stances sur la mort;* Cureau de la Chambre's *Caractères des passions; Discours sur les principes de la chiromancie;* Balzac's *Oeuvres et lettres* and *Prince* (with Du Bray), and the first annotated edition of Montaigne. As King's Printer, Rocollet issued some histories translated into French, Jean Baudoin's version of *Vindiciae Gallicae* and Davila's *Histoire des guerres civiles de France.* Later, Cousin translated Eusebius's standard history of the Church for Rocollet, and also some Byzantine histories.

Most of Rocollet's clients would be women of fashion—the bluestockings who created a pattern of intellectual refinement and taste, the wits of the leisured classes, not the pedants and scholars. They might lack a weight of erudition typical of the lawyer or cleric but they displayed a lively curiosity about the world, and liked vigorous modern prose enlivened with well chosen pictures in harmony with it. Michel Lasne (possibly with Gallot) did the frontispiece for Balzac's *Prince* and Grégoire Huret the same for Davila's

Histoire des guerres civiles. Abraham Bosse engraved the frontispiece and Melchior Tavernier and Pierre Firens the fifteen plates for Machault's *Eloges et discours sur la triomphale entrée du Roy en sa ville de Paris après la réduction de La Rochelle,* and Crispin de Passe prepared the plates for Pluvinel's *Instruction pour monter à cheval.* With Mellan and Chauveau working for him, the latter in *Histoire de Constantinople* and the former engraving the frontispiece for *Ordonnances royaux sur la jurisdiction de Paris,* Rocollet could be seen as a patron of the foremost illustrators of his day.

The expansion of his business by astute assessment of the market enabled him to buy up several small shops in the Palais, the tenth house, with shop, in the Sainte Chapelle, the eighth bookstall in the Great Hall, the seventh in the Galerie des Prisonniers, and the fifth, which had previously been occupied by Toussaint Du Bray. Without powerful patrons he would not have been so prosperous, but as official publisher (with Chapelain and Balzac) to Cureau de la Chambre, Séguier's doctor, member of the Académie Française and fashionable moralist of the day, Rocollet was an intimate of the Chancellor's and owed his life to Séguier during the troubles with the Fronde.

His estate was valued at 34,125 livres. As well as his own publications he sold books to other booksellers and had a second-hand business, his speciality being church service books and devotions, making profits out of the *Imitation de Jésu-Christ* and the *Introduction à la vie dévote.* Some of the big names in his stock were: Davila and Malingre, Mézeray, d'Aubigné, Scipion Dupleix, Guicciardini, Baronius, Plutarch, Du Perron, Thevet, Commines, Belleforest, Corrozet, Munster, Bodin, Olivier de Serres and Sponde. He dealt in few romances, novels or "pure" literature. He had binders working for him; books bound in velvet and morocco are listed as in his stock, many with silver clasps, for the luxury market. He stocked portfolios of engravings after Raphael, Michelangelo, Rubens and Sadler, prints by Bosse and Gallot, the Bible in pictures, the "Emblems of Horace," maps and plans.

6. *The booksellers on the bridge: colporteurs*

Though most booksellers were to be found in the University quarter or the Palais, other districts had their bookshops, some in the square in front of Notre Dame, some on the bridges, the Pont-aux-changes, Pont-aux-meuniers, Pont Notre Dame or Pont St. Michel. The University quarter lost many of its students during the Wars of Religion and booksellers quit the district for other sites, often the streets themselves, where a living was to be had printing and selling pamphlets and street literature. When trade improved in the 17th century the second-hand book trade revived as never before and the Pont St. Michel was the busiest spot in Paris, David Douceur doing an estimated annual volume of business there of 30,000 écus from the sale of private libraries bought up when their owners died, or from books pillaged in the civil wars. Other businesses were those of Charles Chesnault, who published Loret's *Muse historique;* Christophe Journel and Jean Martin, who specialized in current farces and news sheets. Later the second-hand trade and street literature vendors revolved around the Pont Neuf and the now famous quays on the riverside which sell books to this day. It was to the stationers there that Maître Guillaume and Mathurin, the King's jesters, went to have their squibs and jests put into print. Little booths were opened with trestle tables inside, or the books were often simply laid out on sheets or on the parapet of the bridge. Philippe Gautier, Tabarin's publisher, did good business there, better than in his shop in the Rue des Amandiers near Grassin's college in the University precinct. Further on at corner of the Rue Dauphine, Jean Promé was in business before 1635, Malherbe's printer, whose widow published a *Receuil nouveau des chansons du Savoyard par lui seul chantée dans Paris* and François Commelet's *Almanach français.* Jean Millot was another typical little publisher—he printed Bruscambille and other sketches "On the Ile de Paris," opposite the Quai des Augustins where Nicolas Rousset issued the *Tromperie des charlatans découvertes* (1619).

The Court was unhappy about stallholders, especially the newsbooks and other ephemeral literature, seditious pamphlets and scurrilous "libels" as they were seen, but all attempts to incorporate them into the life of the university failed. When the Guild of Stationers experienced a period of disorganization, many master printers were without funds and tried to make a living on the stalls, so inflating the numbers of unlicensed and uncontrolled businesses. Lacking the powers to ban the trade, the Government tried to discourage it by issuing royal Acts and open letters to local authorities, and by licensing "approved" hawkers and colporteurs. The first official colporteurs had been appointed in the 16th century at the Palais when the Palais Bailiff on 22 September 1578 stipulated which pitches they might occupy by authorization of Parlement. A decree of Parlement dated 30 April 1579 and a further order by the Bailiff (3 July 1579) and later by the Provost (6 April 1594) specifically ordered that colporteurs must sell only almanacs, edicts, official Acts and orders, or any other booklets not banned by the Court, and must keep to their strict pitches on either side of Sainte Chapelle or along the side of the Palais courtyard, each in the place allotted by Parlement. Unauthorized hawking was prosecuted in the early years of the 17th century, and the book trade Regulations of 1618 laid down conditions under which legitimate colporteurs might trade: article 26 stated plainly that they were forbidden to take apprentices, own shops, stalls or a printing establishment, that they must sell their wares from a basket hung round the neck, and sell only almanacs, official pamphlets and publications of fewer than eight pages, in stitched covers, printed by Paris booksellers or printers under permit by a competent judge. Article 27 permitted colporteurs to join the Guild but they had to be chosen from "veteran" master printers, booksellers and binders who could no longer work, nominated by the Syndics and Wardens of the Guild, approved by the Civil Lieutenant of the Châtelet, and they must have been apprenticed in the approved way.

In 1634 colporteurs were even more tightly regulated, though the numbers, limited to a dozen in 1618, were raised to fifty. They had to be nominated by the Syndics and Assistants of the Guild and formally presented to the Provost's Warden, who issued them with an official copper badge. They might sell only official publications or pamphlets of fewer than five or six pages, and any infringement risked corporal punishment and deprivation of their living. Official orders, edicts and newsbooks had to be sold at an agreed price, 12 sols for a complete item or 6 deniers per leaf. They must not trade on Sundays or Feast Days and must not meet outside the Guild.

These, then, were the tough measures taken be Government to try to suppress the clandestine literature it feared. The history of street-printed matter shows it to have been eagerly read, and by 1653 the official hawkers had risen to a total of 100. We are witnessing the growth of a kind of public opinion which, despite every obstacle in the Age of Richelieu, continued to exist.

7. Printing combines and consortia

To finance publication, publishers often resorted to a combine or "conger," which was simply an association of tradesmen, to share costs and have their names at the foot of the title-page. Small firms would even cooperate to publish a small booklet, and the big firms from the Rue St. Jacques of Palais would combine on something more elaborate, as when Charles Hulpeau and Pierre Rocollet jointly published Sieur Aleaume's *Compas de perspective* (1628), each guaranteeing to take 25 copies at any one time to sell, and not to receive further shares until each allocation was exhausted. Joint action was the usual method for expensive projects, say, portfolios of engravings or a heavy series in folio, and many publishers' lists included a majority of jointly published works. On the 10th May 1624 Thomas de la Ruelle, Pierre Rocollet, Guillaume Loyson, Antoine Allazert, Raulin Baragne, Antoine Robinot, Martin, Collet, Jacques Villery and Antoine de Sommaville, Palais booksellers, combined to form a conger by agreement, each owning an equal share in th printing "of all kinds of books," the printer to be chosen by majority vote. Prices and markets were to be regulated and agreed again by a majority, editions would be split up for printing and no one might use more than one press at a time without the consent of the others; books were to be deposited in a central warehouse to which only two members had the key; every quarter the books would be shared out equally and if one sold off his allocation quickly, then other partners might make up a further consignment for an agreed sum, usually at a 20% discount. When the manuscript of a new work came into the hands of one of the partners, or a revised text of an earlier work, then that publisher could only print it with the consent of the others and on condition that the others did not wish to collaborate; and if an author wanted to publish at his own expense and entrusted the book to one of the partners, that publisher had to agree to share out the business with the others.

By modern standards the arrangements were primitive, the aim simply to insure an equal return for each partner. Some congers lasted a long time, others for only a short time, and there must have been conflicts of interest and internal rivalry; we know of one such contest, between Sommaville and Courbé after a conger broke up, a celebrated event in the book world which split into two camps. The most important congers were the two big Associations formed by Henri III, the Compagnie des Usages and Compagnie du Navire, each reorganized at various times in the 17th century. The first used the symbol, the Ship of Lutetia (Roman name for Paris) and started in 1585 with Sébastien Nivelle, Michel Sonnius and Jean-Baptiste and Jacques Du Puis. It lasted ten years, followed by another consortium organized when trade improved again after the siege of Paris, with Abel Langelier, Ambroise Drouart, Barthélemy Macé and the Sonnius brothers as founder members, winding up in 1624. Nivelle was not a partner this time possibly because he was at the end of his long career and might have been thought by the old supporters of the Catholic League to have been compromised for some reason. On his death his three children, the Widow Buon, Claude Chappelet and Sébastien Cramoisy, formed a rival company, the Compagnie de la Ville De Paris, their device a map of Paris with the ship emblem in one corner. Included in the new consortium were some new and enterprising booksellers like Marc Orry, Robert Fouet, Claude Morel, and Pierre Vitré, printer and father of Antoine. It was not quite as productive as the second Compagnie du Navire but published almost as many books until 1624, when both groups ceased business and a new group emerged, specializing in Greek: Claude Sonnius, Claude Morel, Sébastien Cramoisy, the Widow Buon and Antoine Estienne, the largest publishers in Paris, enjoying at least a theoretical monopoly in the use of the famous "Grecs du Roi," as King's Printers.

In 1630, after Antoine Estienne's bankruptcy and the dissolution of the Society of Printers in Greek, and while Richelieu was planning to reorganize the Compagnie des Usages, a third regrouping of the Compagnie du Navire took place with Sébastien Sonnius, Denis Moreau, Jean Branchu, Denis Thierry and Denys Béchet as partners. The Compagnie des Usages, specialists in prayerbooks, comprised three of the Cramoisy family, Robert Fouet, Antoine Vitré, Charles Morel, Etienne Richer, Eustache Foucault, Guillaume Le Bé and the widows Buon, Méjat and Varennes. Clearly Sébastien Cramoisy, in two of the major publishing congers with his brothers and cousins, enjoyed virtual control over two main areas of publishing.

Joint publishing was essential if finance had to be found for major works; no ambitious program was possible without such organization. The Compagnie du Navire owned books valued at 45,000 livres in 1648, a substantial sum when it is recalled that their sole speciality was Patristic studies. The Compagnie des Usages did a huge business in their service books with Spain. All in all, they were powerful commercial facts of life, and their importance to the export trade and as the main communications systems of their day explains the Government's close interest. They were to be continually encouraged and revived by Government help, as we shall see.

CHAPTER III

TECHNOLOGY OF THE BOOK TRADE

L ET US NOW EXAMINE THE WORK of the several craftsmen who actually made the books: type founders,
printers, engravers, print-makers and binders. How
were their trades organized? How did they apportion the
costs that went into the price of the book?

1. Type Founders

These were the men who cut the punches, made the molds
and the individual "sorts" or letters in a fount of type, their
techniques unchanged since the invention of printing. Each
letter or sign was engraved on the tip of a metal punch, the
metal usually steel, then a reverse impression was struck in a
copper matrix and a mixture of lead, tin, copper and
antimony poured into the tiny matrix, fusing at a low
temperature. Placed in a mold, the letters could then be cast.
   Type founding reached a high degree of perfection in the
16th century when gothic letters ("black letter") were giving
way to roman and italic. Artists like Augereau, Garamond,
Guillaume Le Bé I, Granjon and Haultin, all children of the
Renaissance, virtually founded modern typography. By 1580
the major publishing houses in Antwerp, Frankfurt, Rome,
Venice, Lyons and Paris were acquiring and sharing punches
struck by the master founders and trying to acquire matrices
for their more specialized publications. On a smaller scale,
local type founders cast founts for printers in their district,
and by the 17th century foundries were very numerous in
Paris: Etienne Le Blanc's is one such. An inventory of his
goods dated 1635 survives and includes "a furnace for casting
letters, with two benches"; a ladle (to hold the molten

metal); a collection of assorted ladles for each mold, to cool the metal; a "heavy pot" to mix the metal, with two crucibles; 126 composing sticks with flanges (in which the letters were aligned to insure they were of exactly the right size); a "cutting bench" with three planes; a boxwood mallet and five knives to cut and shape the letters. There were other tools: a gauge to set the body size of the type, a table and iron hammers—all the equipment a busy typefounder would require. Le Blanc did not possess any punches and kept only a small collection of matrices, a set of 128 "of an old design," and some matrices of Garamond's pattern together with other sets which he could use as clients ordered, in the common founts of that period, St. Augustin, Cicero, Philosophy, Petit-romain, and Petit-texte.

Other master typefounders were also in business as booksellers and printers, but gradually big firms began to monopolize the trade and in 1610 only three firms in Paris could deal with really large businesses. We find punch cutters like Jacques de Sanlecque and Philippe Cottin buying up small foundries to augment their own punches and matrices, and the firm of Le Bé was one of the largest foundries in Europe. Its story is of considerable technical interest and began with Guillaume I, born in Troyes in 1525, son of a successful papermaker. He learned the art of punch cutting from Robert Estienne, to whom he was apprenticed in 1539–40, probably in association with Garamond who was then cutting his "Grecs du Roi." Two years later he started on his real specialty, Hebrew letters, and went to Venice in 1545 to work with Jewish typographers to perfect his skill; he returned to Rome in 1550 and offered his services to the Pope, then went back to Paris where Garamond was at work, and in 1552, with his father's help, opened one of the first workshops to specialize in the sale of type founts. When Garamond died in 1561, Le Bé bought some of his equipment and formed an impressive range of punches and matrices, later enhanced by his son Guillaume II by further acquisitions and by his own contributions. In Guillaume II's time the foundry had a whole series of roman and italic founts engraved by the finest craftsmen of the previous generation, Guillaume Le Bé I, Garamond, Granjon and

Jacques de Sanlecque II, and matrices struck from punches cut by those artists and others like Haultin. Granjon and Danfrie's "lettres de civiltés" were owned by the firm, and Greek letters designed by Granjon, Haultin and Guillaume Le Bé I, and finally, Granjon's music founts.

It was a treasury of letter types and punches, rivaled only at Antwerp where Plantin had a superb collection, and possibly in Luther's establishment at Frankfurt. The most demanding printer could be supplied with almost anything in roman and italic, although the music characters were possibly inferior, because a cousin of Le Bé's, Pierre Ballard II, enjoyed the monopoly of music printing in France and made all his notation in his own foundry. Guillaume II had a complete set of Greek and Hebrew letters, cut by his father and completed by himself. The Garamond "Grecs de Roi" were the most distinguished Greek types, of exceptionally high caliber, engraved for Francis I, and Robert Estienne was the printer who used them in his famous edition of Greek classical texts. Le Bé could not compete in that field.

Garamond's type fount was generally considered esthetically the best, though his choice of model on which to base them has been criticized. When Estienne fled to Geneva in 1550, the Chambre des Comptes retained his punches and they lay neglected for a century, but some matrices were used, one series given to the King's Printers at the end of the 16th century to produce some Greek texts, and others taken to Frankfurt by André Wechel, a refugee printer from Paris, while yet another set, struck for Henri Estienne II, ended up in Geneva.

Materials of this quality were of fundamental importance for the scholars who turned to the Fathers to substantiate Catholic doctrines, publishing those massive sets of Patristic texts. They were used regularly by Morel and by the Compagnie du Navire. When Paul Estienne came back to Paris from Geneva to escape his creditors he pointed out that the matrices he had inherited from Henri Estienne II were in the hands of the Calvinists at Geneva and would probably be used to further the Protestant cause. The King authorized him to try to buy them back. He was successful and when they returned to Paris their custody was entrusted to Antoine

Estienne, who was made an associate publisher of Cramoisy, Sonnius, Widow Buon and Claude Morel in the Society of Printers in Greek, the founder members of which included the partners in the Campagnie du Navire and Compagnie de la Ville De Paris. Together they made good use of the "Grecs du Roi," working in effective collaboration.

Oriental founts were also available thanks to the initiative shown by François Savary de Brèves, who had collected eastern manuscripts when he was Henri IV's ambassador. While in Rome he had Guillaume Le Bé engrave oriental letters and commissioned Antoine Vitré to print some copies of books with the types. Savary's heirs were keen to make money out of the precious punches and matrices, and offered them to other countries, including England and Holland, which prompted the French court to act out of fear that they would fall into heretical hands. Vitré was ordered to buy them, and for only 4,300 livres, while he commissioned Sanlecque to complete the set on the King's orders. Richelieu wanted to make use of the types for books intended to aid his policy of conversion in that part of the Middle East, but he did not pay Vitré the promised sum. Instead, the Clergé de France financed the project, and more help was given by Michel Le Jay, a Parisian lawyer who augmented the numbers of types still further and published a Polyglot Bible even more comprehensive than the one Plantin published for Philip II.

Private patronage like this, and the support of the official body, the Clergé de France, insured that the typographical tradition begun under Francis I would continue, and the subsequent history of the punches cut for the oriental letters proves that in Guillaume Le Bé II, Philippe de Sanlecque and Philippe Cottin, France had type designers and founders worthy of her traditions. In the art of roman and italic designs they made no great personal contribution, though they maintained high standards, the only original craftsman being Jean Janon and Pierre Moreau. Janon was a Calvinist, probably born in 1580 in Switzerland. A scholar in Greek, Latin and Hebrew, he was trained as a printer in Geneva, Basel and Mainz, and worked with Robert Estienne III in Paris before starting his own business. He ran into difficulties with the authorities when he issued a book by a converted Protestant minister, and was forbidden to open a shop in Charenton in 1610, but he appealed successfully (possibly at Robert Estienne's suggestion) to the authorities in the Calvinist University of Sedan, and was reinstated as official printer to the Prince and the Academy there. He was a punctilious craftsman and when the foundries either could not or would not supply him with the founts he wanted— probably because he was a Protestant—he used knowledge he had picked up on his travels to produce his own types and issued a sheet of type specimens in roman and italic (1615–21), of a size smaller than any that had been obtainable previously, the "Sedan" types, still in use today. He also announced his intention of designing Greek and Oriental type founts and promised the printers that he would supply them with whatever they needed from his own workshop, including printing presses, which were usually made by carpenters. Janon also invented a steel gauge for measuring letters accurately. With all this to his credit, surely he can be ranked with his predecessors.

The Imprimerie Royale bought matrices struck from his punches, and his founts were used in their finest publications, yet what was his reward? Sublet de Noyers and Cramoisy gave him 1,000 livres for his matrices but later a decree of the Council forbade him to export punches or matrices of founts outside France, and so deprived him of large orders, from Moretus at Antwerp for example. He later left Sedan to join Ballard and worked as an ordinary punch cutter for 25 livres a month, then did some engraving of oriental founts for a Caen resident who was an amateur of such typography. The next we hear of him is on a charge of printing illegally, and eventually he returned to Sedan where he ended his days as a recipient of the Consistory's charity.

The other innovator was Pierre Moreau who made cursive letters and secured a license to engrave punches with combinations of letters, but he had to give this up when the Guild attacked him on various charges and he sold his foundry to Thierry. Despite the good reception accorded his books, the time was not ripe for innovations except in propaganda by the State or the Clergé de France.

Estimates of the value of founts and other materials in a type foundry are of interest, as are the prices charged by founders. Le Blanc's business was valued at 223 livres, 4 sols in 1635, including matrices, and that was a modest foundry. Yet Pierre Ballard I, who owned an almost unique collection of matrices and music notation, was valued at 2,308 livres, 5 sols (foundry and printing shop) in 1639, and his bookstock at 13,582 livres, 16 sols. Guillaume Le Bé's foundry was not valued at his death but it is interesting that on Guillaume III's death in 1655 the whole foundry was valued at a mere 4,853 livres, while the bookstock, not large, was valued at 4,257 livres. Basic materials were obviously considered of slight value compared with books, even though punch cutting was expensive, as we can judge from the accounts of various patrons and state authorities who paid high prices for sets of punches.

As to the prices asked by letter founders, we have some evidence. On 23 December 1637, Nicolas De La Forge, a founder living in the Rue Bordelle, promised Jean Camusat a fount of roman Petit-texte consisting of 150,000 letters, 25,000 leads, 5,000 quoins, with two pounds weight of 2-point letters, the order to be delivered before 15 April 1638 at the following prices: for the making of the letters at 25 sols per 1,000—225 livres; for the material—35 livres per hundredweight (which would work out at 14 livres in this case); for the manufacture and materials in the 2-point letters—7 livres. Total, 372 livres. Another case is Jacques Cottin, who had orders for a fount of Nonpareil (very small letters) to print Richelieu's Bible. On 6 March 1656 he was commissioned to supply 100,000 letters in roman and 45,000 in italic in three months, at 40 sols per hundred (roman) and 45 sols per hundred (italic) plus 4 livres the hundredweight of type, which came to 340 livres for casting and 80 livres for the materials. Total: 420 livres.

To cast a fount of good quality in new metal, not re-using old metal, producing enough letters represented an outlay of several hundred livres; the type alloys of tin, copper, lead and antimony were much rarer then and each letter had to be cast individually and was cut by hand. The regulations required every printing shop to have five founts in good condition, and letters were worn out more quickly than today; hence there was heavy expense for the printers who tended to order founts with a limited number of letter sorts, perhaps a few tens of thousands, or even a few thousands made from reused metal, which was less costly. Rapid wear resulted in frequent recasting of types if a decent impression was wanted, and this prompts a close inquiry into the numbers, size and general condition of the type founts used in the printing workshops of Paris.

2. *Printers*

We might begin with a description of Rémy Dallin's press after his death in 1625. It was not in a specially constructed building but in his own home on Montagne St. Geneviève, probably in one room or two, a little larger than the others. He owned two printing presses, one more modern than the other, equipped with a screw thread, not a brass platen, while on the first press they were of wood. A third press, called an "estanconnière," was for printing engravings and had an iron plate, screw and platen. The presses were in the center of the workshop, affixed to floor and ceiling by massive wooden beams. In the window recesses and along the walls the cases of type stood with drawers beneath holding dozens of founts of great range, from Petit Canon and Gros Roman to Cicero, Petit-Texte and St. Augustin. Nearby were his ornaments, fleurons, headbands, Dallin's own device, leads, letters in 2-point, open letters for use as initials in chapter-headings, and twenty-two illustrations used in standard books of hours.

There is evidence in the archives of many other such printing shops: Denis Langlois I owned two presses in 1635, one a rack and pinion press, the other an older model which employed a rope to move the carriage back and forward. There were 14 founts of type in his shop, 100 ornaments and some open letters. Mettayer's workshop had four presses in 1639, all in good condition, 22 founts, cases filled with 2-point letters, numbers, fleurons, printers, flowers, some Hebrew letters and music notation. Claude Calleville left four presses in his will, and forty different founts. Jean

Tompère's was the largest concern, with four working presses and two dismantled, fifty founts and plates and designs for books of hours, in which Tompère specialized, as Dallin did.

We can estimate the value from figures in the inventories: Rémy Dallin's was valued at 770 livres in 1625, Langlois's at 710 livres in 1635, and Michel Brunet's, which included two presses, at 746 livres. Less than 1,000 livres would buy a workshop with two presses and a good assortment of type. On a larger scale, Robert Estienne III's shop employed five presses in good working order and was sold for 1800 livres in 1631, Pierre Mettayer's for 1,455 livres in 1639, Tompère's was valued at 2,500 livres in 1643 and Calleville's at 3,177 livres in 1647. Printing presses could cost anything from 50 to 100 livres and letter founts were costlier: Dallin's 2,859 pounds weight of type was valued at 490 livres, 9 sols, 1 denier; Langlois's 2,643 pounds at 524 livres, 4 sols, 6 deniers; and Calleville's 8,599 pounds at 2,778 livres tournois. When these quantities are compared with Plantin's much earlier figures (1589) they are modest. He had 44,000 pounds of type and even within a given fount the actual number of letters was not very great in Paris printing shops, usually less than 10,000, so we can deduce that printers used the same letters over and over again. Only when completely worn out were letters replaced, and that is why so many 17th century books are only just legible. Even if it was still less costly to be in business as a printer than as a bookseller, the printing of good quality books required frequent replacement of type in excess of what most printers could afford.

It is known how many printers there were in Paris in 1644 because a document dated February and March of that year gives the following figures:

    1 workshop had 7 presses
    5 workshops had 5 presses
    8 workshops had 4 presses
   11 workshops had 3 presses
  35 workshops had 2 presses
  16 workshops had 1 press

In all, 183 presses were scattered throughout 76 different workshops. Most firms had fewer than four presses, the majority (51) had two or only one, which was contrary to the Statute of 1618. The same source gives a figure of 257 freemen and 94 apprentices in the trade, and in only 15 firms were there more than eight workmen, and in only two were there more than 15 workmen. Since the proprietors themselves also operated the presses, clearly all the presses in the city were not working at full strength when the document was prepared. Returns made by various master printers in answer to this inquiry reveal that several small workshops had no work at all in terms of books actually going through the press, or were operating with a much reduced labor force. Little wonder there was so much anger at the excessive number of printers when so few could actually secure regular work, the rest having to scrape a living on jobbing printing or clandestine publications. There is evidence that the increase in presses was recent—Vitré confirmed that there were only 15 or 16 printing shops in Paris at the beginning of the 17th century—and the number of presses probably fluctuated between 100 and 150, while the number of freemen and apprentices was between 400 and 500. We can also tell from the same source who the printers worked for—very few were publishers as well. Apart from some who specialized in books of hours, only five or six master printers were also publishers: Louis Sevestre, Jean Guillemot, François Targa, Antoine Estienne and Antoine Vitré. Most of the others worked for the major booksellers—Quinet, Rocollet, Sommaville and Courbé at the Palais, and Camusat, Thierry, Le Beau, the Widow Buon, Denis Moreau, Claude Sonnius or Denys Béchet in the Rue St. Jacques. Sébastien Cramoisy had a dozen presses in six different printers' shops working for him, without counting the Imprimerie Royale, also under his direction.

Most printers were simply wage earners, and their equipment was for the most part scanty: they could not afford to employ correctors, so the master did this himself even where his education was limited, hence the many errors in the books of the period; an example that comes to mind is the

Mort de Pompée (1644), printed by Denis Houssaye in an apothecary's apartment, with four workmen.

Nevertheless, a host of learned works was published in the first half of the 17th century with print of high quality and of impeccable correctness, for the most part in a few workshops where standards were of the highest. Morel was the best of these, last of a long line of Humanist printers, with the Mettayers and Robert and Antoine Estienne, all of equal merit and active partners in the congers, as we saw. To these we could add Raulin Thierry, Jean Libert, Edme Martin and Antoine Vitré.

Martin was an apprentice of Morel's and printed the scholarly Greek texts published by Cramoisy, La Noue and others, a cultivated man and meticulous press corrector at a time when they were scarce. He knew Greek and Latin and was the natural successor to Morel and Antoine Estienne as the premier French printer, equally absorbed in the "shape and spirit" as someone put it, of the French language, a rare interest then. Men of letters rushing into print sought his services, and the Jesuits, who were putting out masses of material, praised him highly. Sébastien Cramoisy, who commissioned so much work from him, eventually made him printer to the Imprimerie Royale and encouraged his own niece to marry Edme Martin II. Yet he does not perhaps stand as high as Antoine Vitré, son of Pierre Vitré, one of the better printers of the late 16th century. Antoine began modestly enough, with news sheets and political pamphlets and was mixed up in the *Parnasse satyrique* affair as one of de Viau's accusers. Later he printed Savary de Brèves's oriental texts, becoming a specialist in that arcane branch and producing books (as King's Printer) for the conversion of Muslims in the Levant. In 1635 he succeeded Antoine Estienne as printer to the Clergé de France, and in 1645 he published his masterpiece, the French Polyglot Bible.

Vitré attained eminence as a typographer and with Chancellor Séguier's aid was influential in Guild affairs. He was what might now be called a trouble-shooter, negotiating with troublesome workmen, the strong man called in by the authorities to restore order in the trade when necessary, no longer the Humanist scholar-printer respected for his learn-

ing but a skilled technician producing good physical specimens of books even when he did not understand their
contents. In his career we see the embodiment of quite
significant changes in the evolution of printers and printing.

Let us now try to reconstruct the detailed operations in a
typical printer's. Each press needed two workmen, one to
pull the handle which operated the platen, the other to place
the blank sheets of paper between frisket and tympan, keep
the formes inked and pull off the printed sheets. Paper had to
be damped before printing and hung out to dry afterwards,
preferably by a third hand—usually the youngest apprentice.
The compositor was at his case, setting up the print in formes
of standing type; thus, to ensure smooth operation, there had
to be four people in a chain working at full stretch to keep the
press going. We know what rate of work was accomplished
by this relatively small labor force because a regulation of
1654 lays down what was supposed to be finished each day by
the compositors:

Non-pareil (6 pt.)	2/7 forme daily
Mignon (7 pt.)	1/3 forme daily
Petit-texte (7½ pt.)	1/2 forme daily
Petit-romain (9 pt.)	2/3 forme daily
Cicero (11 pt.)	1 forme daily
St. Augustin (12–13 pt.)	1½ formes daily
Gros romain (18 pt.)	2 formes daily

In normal circumstances a compositor would complete one
forme per day in Cicero, and if we exclude the smallest type
size used for breviaries and hours, and the largest, used in the
big service books like Missals and Antiphonaries, the daily
output averaged between one and two formes.

The rate of work expected of pressmen was fixed in the
late 16th century at 3,000 sheets a day for normal-sized type
and 2,500 for red and black; by 1649 these figures had been
lowered slightly to 2,700 sheets a day in black from Gros
Canon to Petit Canon, 2,600 in black for smaller letters,
2,500 red and black in large letters, 2,400 for the same in
average-sized letters and 2,200 for minuscules.

In a 14-hour day the old hand press had to turn out 200
sheets an hour or 3–4 a minute, and since the press bar

needed two pulls for each sheet, that meant printing one sheet *every ten seconds* while another man was releasing the frisket and tympan, taking out the printed sheet, substituting a fresh sheet and, when necessary, inking the forme every twenty seconds—a dizzying rhythm to keep up and rewarded with a high wage in contemporary terms: in 1618, fixed at 18 livres a month, and in 1654, at 27 livres a month. Compositors were also hard pressed and though their training was more demanding they did not earn any higher wage than pressmen even if they were setting a complicated Latin text (Greek did earn them more money), and this may explain the many typographical errors and fantastic spelling variations.

A word now about the numbers of books in a typical edition, the time needed to print a book,and prices of books.

Three of Corneille's tragedies, *Nicomède, Andromède* and *Pertharite,* came out in editions of between 1,200 and 1,250 copies. Brébeuf's *Pharsale,* printed in Rouen, was an edition of 1,200 copies, and Lamy's translations of Ovid in 1,350 copies (1660). Chamhoudry promised Chaulmer that he would publish his *Tableaux des différentes parties du monde* (1653) in 1,350 copies, and in the same year Sébastien Martin published Maigron's *Dieudonné* in 1,500 copies. Pascal's *Lettres provinciales* was in 1,500 copies, and Jean de Chevallier's *Philosophe abrégé en vers* (1655) was issued by the printer Le Cointe in 1,000 copies. Bouillerot undertook to publish Lescalopier's *Judith* (1644) in 1,000 copies and Rivière printed 1,500 copies of the Jesuit Le Blanc's *Direction et consolation des personnes mariées* (1663). In 1642 Michel Brunet printed 1,000 copies of a controversial work by Gaspard Cordier called *Rang des abbés en la hierarchie de l'Eglise,* and schoolbooks were usually in editions of 1,000 to 1,500, the *Apparatus elegantiarum,* for instance, printed by Bénard and Julien (1,000 copies) in 1652, and the standard *Gradus ad Parnassum* (1660) in 1,500 copies, printed by Julien. Other works of the time which we would call popular varied from 1,000 to 1,500 copies as a rule: *Emblèmes d'Horace* (1637), published by Courbé in 1,000 copies, Baudoin's translations of Aesop with illustrations (1630) in 1,500 copies, and Louet's *Arrète* in 1,500.

From such figures we may deduce the average at 1,350,

and when we recall that the number of sheets printed daily varied between 2,500 and 3,000 we might wonder if there is any correlation between the figures and if the rule was to turn out one sheet, recto and verso, per day as the norm to make best use of manpower and minimize unproductive "dead" time. We can deduce the output: taking an ordinary octavo book of about 240 pages printed in an edition of 1,350 copies, the actual printing would be completed in a fortnight but the composing would take thirty days if the letters were in Cicero, a typical size. That is quite fast by contemporary standards. The great folios were another matter: a typical 1,200 page folio, not unusual, would require a year to print and nearly two years to compose if done by one compositor, which meant that many lengthy works were shared between several printers to reduce delivery dates.

A document dated 4 September 1641 offers useful information on these matters. The contract concerned "red and black" (i.e., church service books) and was between Vaudran, a printer, and Mathieu Guillemot, commissioned to publish service books for the church in Angers, one a Processional, the other a Missal after the Use of the Angers church. It was specified that the Missal was to be in Gros Romain and that 1,300 copies were to be printed, estimated at "two days per sheet" at a cost of 7 livres a day; the folio Missal was to be in an edition of 850 copies in Petit Paragon, and other founts assessed at 8 livres per sheet. Guillemot agreed to pay transport costs and to pay Vaudran 20 livres a week in wages plus 24 livres a month for hire of plant, and to pay the two workmen while the books were in transit; Vaudran would pay them for their work at a rate of 30 livres a month.

So for a month's work on the Processional, say 13 to 15 sheets, recto and verso, resulting in 1,300 copies in red and black, Vaudran received less than 200 livres from Guillemot, out of which 60 went in wages to his pressmen, 80 to himself, and 24 livres for the hire of his equipment. The fruits of his labor brought in nearly 250 livres, out of which he had to allow traveling expenses and food and lodging for his apprentice, part of the food for his two journeymen, ink and depreciation of his press, all of which reduced his profit margin. If the Processional required, say, 20–25 sheets, then Vaudran would have had to spend two months in Angers to print it, and he would have probably received 400 livres for the job. If the Missal involved 150 sheets, the 850 copies in red and black would need about two and a half months to finish and would bring in about 1,000 livres after he had paid his workmen, but not allowing for the other charges included above.

The printer and his two journeymen would appear to have made a nice little profit from the deal, but this was exceptional. More usual was the case of Bouillerot's printing of Lescalopier's *Judith,* 50 leaves octavo, in St. Augustin type, 1,000 copies at 6 livres a sheet. Lescalopier supplied the paper and Bouillerot received 300 livres for the work. If the two pressmen completed the job in just over a month, that would mean 50–60 livres in wages, so Bouillerot's profit came from whatever was left after allowing for depreciation of equipment, cost of ink and other overheads including hire of premises.

This evidence is proof that the cost of printing was worked out per sheet and varied according to the type size used and the number of copies in the edition. As a general rule the state of the book trade in the years 1640–1660 would probably allow for the sort of profit Bouillerot made, and a typical printer might expect to make 1,500 livres a year from his press if continually employed, which was a good income. Most presses were not in continuous use, however, and most printers were chronically unemployed; they almost invariably worked for booksellers and occasionally for authors, and their wages depended on what they could negotiate with the bookseller on whom they depended. Until we know more about the individual wealth of printers we must be cautious about firm conclusions respecting actual profits from printing.

3. Book illustration: engravers and printers

Paris in the late 16th century saw the gradual displacement of woodcuts by copper engraved plates, a pity in some ways since the sharp black and white of wood harmonized better with black print, and the wood block could be easily inserted in the forme along with the letterpress, inked and printed on the same press at the same time. Copper had to be inked with special ink and printed on a special press; after copper engraving became fashionable two related crafts—the book and the engraving—began a long period of close collaboration. The art of engraving on copper came to France with Italian masters attracted to Fontainebleau by the decorative painters working there, and soon workshops were employing French craftsmen who began to rival their teachers. This was the origin of the first French school of etchers and engravers, which excelled in decorative and architectural motifs, but it was at Antwerp that copper attained its greatest reputation in the hands of Jérome Cock, Philip Galle and the Wierix family. Many thousands of prints were produced there and Plantin earned some of his reputation on the finely illustrated books he commissioned. When he opened a branch in the Rue St. Jacques, Paris could hardly ignore the new technique. Melchior Tavernier, a Fleming, set up as an engraver and printseller in Paris, and the Jesuits were making great use of pious pictures as part of their crusade, mostly produced in the Wierix studios. The French were still sending orders for engravings to Antwerp in the late 16th century, and Antwerp engravers had their eye on the French market, but gradually Flemings and engravers from northern France established themselves in the Rue St. Jacques as the last of the old domino makers were fading from the scene in the Rue Montorgueil, decorating fabrics when there was less and less call for the old-fashioned woodcuts. The earliest of the new engravers included Mallery, Jaspar Isac, Firens, Crispin de Passe and Thomas de Leu and Léonard Gaultier; after 1630 the next generation included Michel Lasne, Grégoire Huret, Rousselet, Bosse, Mellan, Nanteuil and Chauveau. They turned out their own works in proof and complete portfolios, sold prints, their own and by fellow-artists, and supplied the taste for albums and single prints. It was a new era in visual communications. Publishers commissioned work and whole books were made up for sale to a market greedy for them in France and abroad. François Langlois was a successful name in this market, as was the Mariette family, which continued in business for two hundred years.

Publishers of illustrated books and printsellers would sometimes clash, especially when print specialists encroached on what ordinary booksellers considered their territory. The Guild instituted proceedings against any print publisher who included prints in a text already published, and eventually engravers and printsellers were forbidden to add texts of more than a fixed number of lines to their plates, and only booksellers were allowed to publish illustrated books, which meant that to publish a work of that kind the bookseller had to negotiate with two people: the printer of the text and the plate-maker, since ordinary printers rarely owned the special type of press used for printing plates. Moreover, the printing of the plates was usually the job of the artist who engraved them.

We have figures related to costs of publishing woodcuts and copper engravings, from Mathieu Guillemot's inventory of 1610:

Copper

18 designs and plates for Ovid's *Metamorphoses*	72 livres
33 plates for Nicolas Nicolay's *Voyages en Turquie*	109 livres
18 plates for *Philostrate*	324 livres

Wood

15 woodcuts—portraits of Ottomans	45 livres
13 woodcuts for the *Songe de Poliphile*	10 livres

By a happy accident the woodcuts made for the *Songe de Poliphile,* the most popular illustrated book of the 16th century, were listed against the copper plates for Philostrate's *Tableaux de platte peinture,* the most famous early 17th century illustrated work, and even after allowing for wear of the wood blocks, the difference in the two sets of figures is striking, and clear proof of contemporary taste. If copper does not seem too high in price, we know that sixteen years later when Mathieu Guillemot's widow went into partnership with her son Mathieu II, she obtained 300 livres from him for the right to use of the plates (not to own them) by the Guild.

Samuel Thiboust's inventory of 1635 gives more details:

11 pictures for the *Milice françoise*	11 livres
8 pictures for Ovid's *Metamorphoses*	108 livres
53 pictures for *Théogène et Chariolée*	318 livres
18 for the *Ane d'or*	85 livres
5 for the *Mythologie des dieux*	60 livres
7 for Ronsard's *Works*	6 livres

It is clear that plates cut by skilled craftsmen after famous paintings, even when part-worn, were worth a good deal, and works of lesser artists worth less—Rocollet's and Sommaville's inventories tell us that much. We also have evidence of the price a publisher would pay for plates: Abraham Bosse in 1635 agreed to supply Guy de La Brosse with 1,000 illustrations of plants for a big book on the Royal Garden, each plate about 16 "thumbs" in height and a foot wide. The price agreed was 25 livres, increased by 5 livres when La Brosse asked to improve the density by hatching. The artist was to receive 2,000 livres for the frontispiece and two plans, and if the death of La Brosse had not interrupted the work, this unusually big order would have brought the engraver 32,000 livres.

We do not have the contract for illustrating Chapelain's *Pucelle* but we know that Bosse received 1,300 livres for 13 plates, or 100 livres a plate in 1654, to be shared with the painter Vignon who supplied the designs. A letter from Valdor, the engraver, asks Séguier for a salary of 400 écus a year while he was engaged on the illustrations for a great work celebrating the military triumphs of Louis XIII. The book, *Triomphes de Louis le Juste,* appeared in 1649 after six years' work; evidently Valdor was well paid for it. Another contract dated 31 July 1630 is an agreement between four publishers, Du Bray, Guillemot, Rocollet and Sommaville, an engraver, Briot, and Jean Baudoin, the translator for an illustrated edition of Aesop in French. Briot was to deliver 100–120 plates with designs he had submitted to the publishers and which they had passed, each plate costing 11 livres. The edition was 1,500 copies, Briot to receive 10 sols for the proofs of each plate. He would be paid 60 livres a month and the plates would be the property of the publisher, who had invested 2,000 livres in the work, and this did not include translator's rights, cost of paper and the actual printing.

Obviously a lot of capital was needed to finance a book of engravings and this explains why, instead of buying plates, publishers resorted to other means, as Rocollet did when he published *Elogée et discours sur la triumphante réception du Roi en ceste ville de Paris après la prise et reduction de la ville de La Rochelle* (1629). He received 1,000 livres from the Provost in charge of Commerce in return for a guarantee to deliver 200 copies of the book, and then he entered into partnership with the engraver Firens and Tavernier, who printed the plates while Rocollet printed the text; income from sales was divided equally among the three associates. Apart from the Provost's 200 copies, Rocollet sold 500 at 3 livres, 15 sols apiece.

Still more interesting is a contract of 7 August 1637 between Courbé the bookseller and Daret, an engraver, about publication of the *Emblèmes d'Horace* in 1,000 copies, sharing costs. Daret had already cut 103 plates and was to be paid 22 livres for each before the books were sold; in addition he would receive 13 sols per hundred for the plates he printed. Courbé supplied the paper and paid the printer and translator, and the plates were to be divided between the two parties to the agreement, and costs shared. They reckoned the engraving and printing of the plates made up nearly half the cost of the book, further proof of how expensive illustrations were.

The engraver was an artist in copper, not just an anonymous craftsman like the men who made woodcuts, and demanded high rewards, although for more commonplace subjects, books of piety with stock pictures of second-rate quality, the designers earned less. Books with ornamental vignettes, head and tailpieces and like decoration were problems because they required separate presses; because of cost this discouraged publishers from using more than a frontispiece, which could be sold as a separate.

4. Bookbinders and finishers

Vellum was the usual binding for pocket-sized or slim volumes; calf or morocco, with or without gold tooling, for bigger books. Hundreds of thousands were bound in this way. How did the binders cope with this huge market?

We have a description of a typical bindery, the workshop of Gilles Dubois, a craftsman of some distinction, binder-in-ordinary to the King. It was his job to bind the new additions to the Royal Library, many of which passed into the Bibliothèque Nationale. His raw material consisted of 10 skins of red morocco, cost 32 livres, and 106 pounds of vellum, cost 306 livres, 4 sols; boards—53 livres, and finally, marbled paper for his endpapers. The great press used by binders cost 15 livres, and his other presses, one for backing and the other for trimming, were valued at 20 livres together. About 250 pairs of boards (made of wood, either walnut or pear) cost anything from one sol to one livre the pair. A rack placed against the wall held his tools, hammers, chisels, and "stones for pounding books." In the shop at the time this inventory was taken, there were 160 folios in process of binding—in the words used in the document, "pounded, sewn and backed," representing work valued at 110 livres.

The material was modest in range; a few hundred books of fine quality. Dubois used boards and other materials of rather better quality than his competitors and was a high-class binder, but the relatively small number of presses and tools shows it was a small-scale business, as a rule. There were no bookbinding factories employing large numbers of workmen. Dubois does not seem to have possessed any more finishing tools than other binders despite his eminence, and would have worked in collaboration with the other half of the craft, the "finishers" or "leather gilders," a separate skill. One such finisher, Georges Giffart, in 1624 had a stock of books numbering 853, and an impressive collection of finishing tools, double fillets, lace fillets, point fillets, small chain, serrated ornaments, branches, grotesques, laurels, Capuchin crosses, memorials and other ornaments, which must mean that he was in the luxury trade, working for aristocrats and wealthy bourgeoisie, producing exquisite bindings later sought after by bibliophiles like those in Chancellor Séguier's circle. Yet even this stock was valued at no more than 200 livres, and we know that an order for a complete set of finishing tools in 1624 came to 74 livres. Tools were easy to come by, and finishers and gilders were traditionally thought to be the proletariat of the trade in the Guild, which is probably the reason why so many were denied mastership despite their increasing numbers in the trade.

It would be interesting to know how much the various styles of binding cost and how far this was reflected in the price of books, but of course most books were sold unbound, and booksellers would display only a small number of bound books in their windows; a customer would have a book bound to order, perhaps in a uniform binding for inclusion on the shelves of his private library. A document of 1650, signed by the 28 leading binders of Paris, offers an insight into the trade: to avoid excessive competition when work was scarce and cost of materials (skins, board, gilt) was rising, they fixed a scale of minimum prices for service books, agreeing not to undercut or poach upon each other's business. The agreement stipulated that a folio binding should be priced at 2 livres, 15 sols; a quarto at 1 livre, 15 sols; an octavo at 1 livre; a 12mo at 12 sols. This suggests that with a price of 10 livres for an octavo breviary and 20 for a folio breviary, and 12 for an ordinary folio, a good quality binding accounted for between one-third and one-quarter of the cost of a book, a quite considerable proportion.

5. Papermakers

Paper was of course absolutely fundamental to the trade. Troyes had played a crucial role as a source of paper in earlier days, and the paper made in Champagne had always enjoyed a reputation for good quality, though its rising prices caused complaint. Plantin ordered paper from Troyes for his major works, including the Polyglot Bible, and in the 17th century Paris got most of its paper from Troyes, particularly from a papermaker called Sébastien Gouault, whose name appears in countless inventories. Yet already Troyes was in decline as a center of papermaking. Good quality rags were hard to find and the materials from which to make paper became shoddier and the product poorer, with the result that printers and booksellers looked elsewhere for supplies—to Normandy, Auvergne and Poitou. At Thiers, Pierre Ferrier supplied paper to the Compagnie du Navire and the Imprimerie Royale, and at Limoges Léonard de Bloye and Jean Poylevé were the main producers.

When orders were large, booksellers dealt directly with provincial suppliers who were in touch with local manufacturers, and sometimes they traded through middlemen in Paris, firms like Melun, Androuet and Le Goux. The last named left inventories which again give us an insight into a trade: in 1627 Pierre Le Goux owned a large stock of paper valued at 2,696 livres, and among his customers were Noël, a printseller, and Ballard and Rollet Le Duc, printers and stationers. Among his creditors is Léonard de Bloye of Limoges, Boisneux of Thiers, and Aymon and Nicolas Denise of Troyes, which is big business, yet Le Goux tells us he did not keep a day book "because I could not read or write." In 1655 a Pierre Le Goux died in possession of an even bigger concern, because his stock is valued at 40,612 and among his customers he numbers several dozen printers and stationers in Paris including the biggest names, Cramoisy, Vitré and Huré, who were in debt to him for thousands of livres. We also hear of other big names, Sonnius and Béchet for instance, who made agreements with Le Goux to pay off arrears of debt. The evidence shows the chain of dependence in the trade: just as printers were dependent on booksellers, so booksellers were dependent on papermakers.

CHAPTER IV

THE SOCIAL BACKGROUND

W E HAVE EXAMINED THE TECHNICAL and industrial aspects of the trade, so now let us look into the social environment of this little world, try to estimate their numbers, analyze their daily lives, private, public, professional, define their status at the heart of the nation's capital, and thus perhaps better understand their metier.

1. Masters and men

The Guild of Stationers, Printers and Binders has left a complete record for the period under review and from it we can draw the following table which shows the numbers and origins of the new masters admitted:

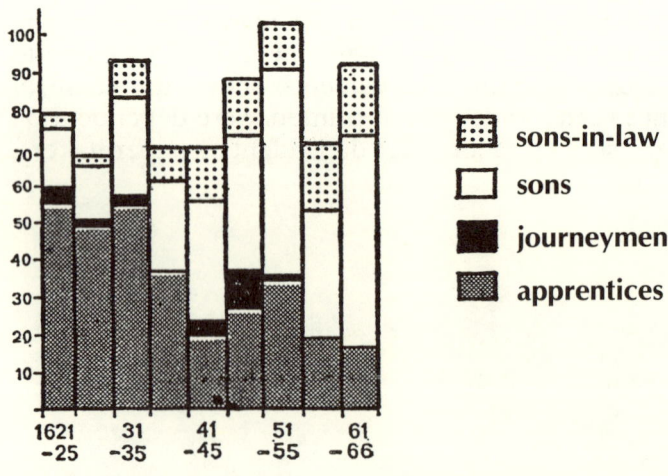

Note that until 1640 there was a fairly large percentage of senior journeymen among the new masters, and that 404 freemen were admitted to the Guild between 1618 and 1645, a yearly average of 14. But how many actually owned a bookshop or workshop? We can draw a graph of the numbers of freemen (i.e. "masters") between the years 1610 and 1700:

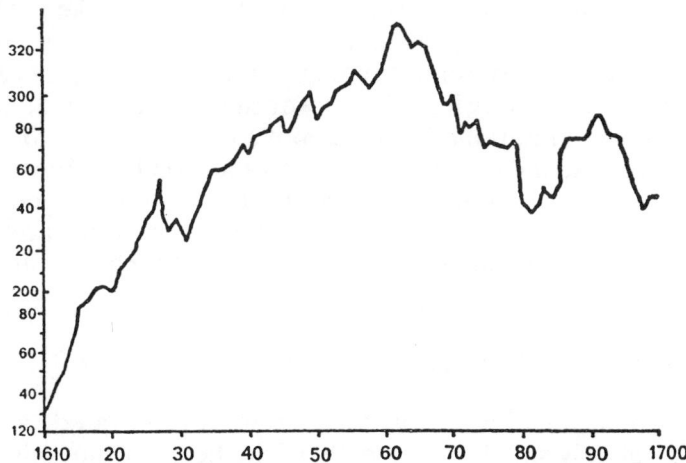

Between 1610–1620 and 1640–1650 masters increased by more than 50%. It is known that there were 200–225 masters or widows of masters in 1625, representing 200 businesses, and 250–300 in 1643–44, a number which rose sharply during the Fronde troubles, when even keepers of bookstalls were admitted freemen of the Guild; later the State moved against them and kept a close surveillance on entry into the trade.

The Guild registers can be used to determine numbers of apprentices and liverymen: 543 finished apprenticeships begun before 1643. Of fifty apprenticeship indentures surviving, only eighteen can be traced in the registers, an indication that the registers must be incomplete even when we allow for those who failed to finish their time, so that once again firm conclusions about precise numbers of workmen in the trade are impossible.

The Inquiry of 1644 showed that 257 journeymen (*compagnons*) and 94 apprentices were on the register, fewer than actual apprentices in work; in printing alone 424 people were employed, including the proprietors. For stationers and binders, the indentures are revealing: 42 signatures of master printers appear on 75 apprenticeship documents dated 1600–1615, and 33 stationers; and on 75 documents for the period 1635–45, 30 are signed by master printers and 45 by stationers, most of whom seem to be stationer-binders. The figures seem to suggest that apprentice stationers and journeymen and apprentice binders were at least as plentiful as printers, especially if unskilled workmen are included, and women, who traditionally carried out some of the bookbinding processes, and of course the colporteurs on the streets. A reasonable total would be about 1,000 people engaged in printing, bookselling, binding and gilding books in Paris, a substantial proportion of the city's population when it stood at 400,000.

2. The book trade quarter

The whole of this work force was concentrated in a comparatively small area, mostly in the heart of the university quarter as the regulations prescribed. The Rue St. Jacques was the main artery, traditionally the street of the stationers. Between the high tower of the church of St. Séverin and the chapel of St. Yves almost every house had a sign outside, the printer's or stationer's device. Opposite the chapel was the Chastelain's sign, Constance, and Boulanger's St. Louis (1620–46), then Thomas Blaise's St. Thomas, and Estienne's famous olive tree (he had already lived near the Collège du Plessis and then near the Marmourests before he sought asylum in the Collège Royale, protected by powerful patrons and the great prestige of his name). After crossing the Rue du Foin and the Rue des Noyers we pass further along the Rue St. Jacques past the Golden Tower of Abraham Pacard, then the sign of the Buons, St. Claude, and then Chevallier's shop, rebuilt in 1611 at the sign of St. Peter. Opposite were David Douceur's

Mercury, Du Puis's Golden Crown and Robert Fouet's Time and Chance.

Crossing the Rue des Mathurins we arrive a little higher up where the Rue des Ecoles now stands and where La Noue sold devotional works at the sign of the Name of Jesus, Regnault Chaudière's Ecu de Florence, his relative Guillaume's Time and the Savage, and next door, at the sign of the Fountain, the Morels lived where Joost Bade and Vascosan had lived in earlier times. Further on, just before the Benedictine monastery, was the sign of St. Martin and the Solar Ecu where the Drouarts did business, later occupied by Jean Gesselin and Denys Béchet, and close by Claude Rigaud was at the sign of the Green Oak Tree (he also had a stall in the Palais) before he returned to Lyons. Opposite the Sorbonne by the Benedictine hospital was Clovis Eve, stationer and binder to the King, at the sign of the Silver Lion (1601–21), and next door at the Columns of Hercules a picturesque character, François Langlois, a bookseller and printer who specialized in prints after Van Dyck, one of the leading picture dealers in Paris and adviser to Charles I of England; his premises were occupied by the Mariettes after his death. Other famous names lived nearby: Claude Cramoisy at the sign of the Licorne, once the Kervers' shop, and just below Plantin's old branch establishment at the Golden Compasses the Sonnius family were in business in succession to Adrien Périer and took over the house next door, the Ecu de Bâle, where Reformation propaganda was published in the 16th century and later, quite the reverse, when Flemish and French Jesuits published their Counter-Reformation material from the same address.

Next door to Sonnius and just as orthodox was Sébastien Chappelet at the sign of the Olive Tree (1615), then St. Sébastien (1625) and finally St. Rosair (1633). Just across a tiny alleyway was his cousin Sébastien Cramoisy at the sign of St. Christopher, king of the Rue St. Jacques, who adopted his grandfather Nivelle's sign, the Three Swans when he acquired his stock. He had the house rebuilt with a wide courtyard in front to allow access to his wealthy clients arriving in their carriages. Passing the Rue St. Jean de Latran and beyond the Benedictine cemetery on the site of the present Collège de France was the sign of the Salamander where the Moreau family lived, and on the opposite side of the Rue St. Jacques between the church of St. Benedict and the walls of the present-day Sorbonne was Martin Du Breuil, a binder; below what is now the Ecole Pratique des Hautes Etudes, at the higher end of the street, were Gering at the sign of the Golden Sun, Edme Martin, a printer of great repute, and Langlois, another printer.

In the same part of the Rue St. Jacques, now cut off by the Boulevard St. Germain and the lower precincts of the Sorbonne, Antoine Berthier lived at the Fortune, the Cottereau family at the Prudence, Camusat and later Le Petit at the Golden Fleece, the firms of Branchu and Coignard at the Golden Bible, Michel Soly at the Phoenix, Guillaume Pelé at the Golden Cross, Jean Orry at the Lion Rampant, Jean Germont and Jean Billaine at the St. Augustin and St. Benedict, Sébastien Huré at the Good Heart, and many others. It was the great street of the trade, both sides a series of narrow houses extending up and down, with all the well-known names trading near each other, apart from those who were at the Palais. Add a large population of engravers and printsellers, students, theologians and teachers, and that was the university quarter.

Many other small printers and bookseller-binders lived not actually in the Rue St. Jacques but in the side streets, some in the Rue des Cordiers between the Jacobin convent and the Rue de la Sorbonne; the other side of the Rue de la Harpe between the Sorbonne, the Collège d'Harcourt (now the Lycée St. Louis) and the Mathurin convent was the home of yet other tradesmen. François Piot, a bookseller and binder, lived in this area with contacts as far afield as Grenoble and Avignon, his bookshop and bindery in the Rue des Mathurins near the College of Surgeons, at the sign of St. Côme and St. Damien. In the Rue des Maçons near the College des Trésoriers, Julien Jacquin, official printer to the University, had a house, and Robert Sara (1627–49), Edme Pépingué (1631–50), Deshayes (1625–38), and Jean Julien, who printed for Harcourt College from 1644 to 51, all lived on the

Rue de la Harpe. And near the gates which marked the limits of the University quarter and Paris—the Porte St. Jacques, Porte St. Paul and Porte St. Victor—many little groups of printers and binders had their modest premises.

The book trade was confined within a tight perimeter between the Rue St. Jacques, Rue des Noyers, Rue St. Etienne des Grès and Rue de la Montagne St. Geneviève. Many small workshops and bookstalls were crowded into the maze of streets, the Rue des Sept Voies, Rue Carmes, St. Jean de Beauvais and St. Jean de Latran, some quite famous. The Mettayers were in the Rue de la Montagne St. Geneviève, not far from the Place Maubert and the Collège de Laon, near the Boucherie St. Geneviève, and Jacques Langlois I was a little higher up, opposite the St. Geneviève fountain, in 1634. Antoine Vitré was in the Rue des Carmes from 1629 to 45, near the gates of the Collège des Lombards. Binders were well represented in the Rue des Sept Voies, a continuation of the Rue des Carmes, and printers like Dallin in 1625, and later Louis Feugé, Jacques Bessin and Jacques Guillery were there too. In the Rue St. Jean de Beauvais, Rue St. Jean de Latran, Rue Chartière and Rue Fromentelle leading to Puits-Certain there was a heavy presence: Ballard at the sign of Mont-Parnasse, Robert Estienne III and Jacques Dugast at the sign of the Olive Tree opposite the Medical School, and Le Bé, the type founder, had his works at the Grosse Escritoire at the corner of the Rue St. Jean de Latran and St. Jean de Beauvais; and a little lower down, Jean Libert printed and sold schoolbooks. Flanking the premises of the well-known firms were innumerable little men making a precarious living in sheds and wretched lean-to dwellings in obscure courts or on the ground floors of tiny houses.

In this kind of tight living space it is easy to imagine what life must have been like for the artisans and craftsmen. Crammed together in dark and narrow alleys, living in almost continual gloom, light only penetrating through college courtyards, with just an occasional open space like the wide Rue des Amandiers opposite the Collège de Navarre, they rose early and worked late. Men and women were equally involved in the trade and women often carried on a business;

everyone went to the same wells for water, lived in each other's laps, could not escape from neighbors, fought, quarreled, married among themselves, were frequently in the hands of the law for misdemeanors or settling accounts before a notary. They were a tightly knit community, bound closely by family ties and by the very street they lived in, a village within the city. Everyone suffered from the same lack of economic security or the plague which cut down their numbers from time to time. The market was unsure, a sudden economic crisis meant unemployment, lack of orders from their patrons, the booksellers of the Rue St. Jacques or the Palais, and so ruin and starvation. High prices discouraged less affluent clients from book-buying, and the multitude of competitors made life hard. Little wonder that so many freemen and journeymen quit the district to look for employment in less crowded areas of the city where they could print fugitive reading matter, risking punishment but working somehow to bring in a little money.

Another problem was the shifting population in the university quarter. Although the colleges and University still attracted large numbers of students from Paris and elsewhere, there were not the great numbers that used to be in residence before the Wars of Religion in the 16th century. Colleges had scanty revenues to support them and were often abandoned and their premises used by booksellers to store their books. There was a move towards the fashionable and residential quarters where more customers might be found, and some of the de luxe publishers set up near the Capelle St. Yves at the bottom end of the Rue St. Jacques—Mathieu Guillemot and Toussaint Du Bray are examples—to the indignation of their rivals because they attracted more passing trade by their displays and so tempted customers into their shops before they had penetrated far into the district. Others established shops on the Petit-Pont and Pont St. Michel—bridges were for obvious reasons good places for business—and in booths in front of Notre Dame, while others were scattered throughout the town, some in the Rue Tiquetonne and others near the old woodcut artists in the Rue Montorgueil.

The Palais was fast becoming the fashionable quarter for

respectable booksellers. It was being rebuilt and the Pont Neuf was under construction, so that a new development area was in being, naturally attracting trade all around the Place Dauphine. Shops and smaller booths opened in the long galleries within the Palais complex where bookshops had been in business many years, and here came tradesmen from the university quarter hoping to find new business in a new environment. Guignard and others were in the Rue de la Pelleterie, Courbé and Lamy in the Rue de la Calende, Sommaville elected to open in the Rue St. Anne and Rocollet in the Rue St. Pierre des Arcs. Printers were likewise drawn there by the presence of so many big booksellers who might be good for orders, and workshops on the ground floors of houses were common.

The Pont Neuf was the home of bookshops specializing in what we would call best-sellers, entertainment literature, political lampoons, or the *dernier cri* in the literary world. The Pont Neuf was started in Henri III's reign and completed under Henri IV, and was a direct channel between Les Halles, the commercial district, and the Rue St. Honoré, and so to the Louvre, the Ile du Palais and the Left Bank. It was a wide bridge and not lined with houses like the others, a promenade to walk along and be seen. Among the crowds hawkers and pedlars circulated, stallholders sold goods overlooked by the new bronze statue of Henri IV, and everywhere was the stir and bustle of busy life in the Rue Dauphine where the famous Cormier extracted teeth; the whole area a magnet for tradesmen. Needier members of the Guild left Mont St. Hilaire and Puits-Certain in search of business on the Pont Neuf, and when work was scarce their colleagues from the Palais joined them on the street selling cheap pamphlets, the bane of government officials.

3. Social background

The book trade was essentially on "open" trade, that is, open to people of all ranks and backgrounds, and promotion from apprentice to journeyman to mastership was quite regular. From the hundred or so indentures that survive we can gain some knowledge of the backgrounds of typical apprentices:

many came from the provinces, of course, sons of laborers or minor officials in country towns, petty tradesmen, even from the unskilled, day laborers and casual laborers; very rarely from the merchant class. Often they were the sons of journeymen or of masters in other trades, and in practice entry into printing or bookselling depended on family contacts or friends in the trade, parents placing a boy with a printer they knew who was perhaps related to them or to a neighbor in the trade; in that way he would still be within reach of his family, a convenient arrangement. Quite often an uncle or stepfather who was himself a master printer or binder would apprentice his stepson or nephew to a colleague.

If we compare such generalizations with the evidence from some 90 surviving marriage contracts we find that in more than half the cases (48) marriage was between people in the trade; twenty daughters of printers, binders and booksellers married outside the trade, out of a total of 68, and 22 men out of 70 married outside the trade. Husbands and fathers were from many walks of life: laborers, journeymen, street pedlars, merchants, artists, petty officials, lawyers, surgeons, skilled artisans, ordinary citizens and, in one case, the captain of an infantry regiment. The table below gives the background of witnesses to contracts:

	Journeymen	*Masters*	
		Dowry less than 2,000 livres	More than 2,000
Number of contracts	18	47	25
Number of witnesses	94	308	274
Average no. of witnesses per contract	5.2	6.5	10.9
Occupations			
Casual workers, craftsmen, servants	7	17	—
Masters and merchants	20	71	49
Book trade journeymen	14	11	—
Master printers, booksellers and binders	26	138	75

	Journeymen	Masters	
		Dowry less than 2,000 livres	More than 2,000
Artists	2	4	4
Principals of colleges, professors	—	5	5
Petty officials	6	14	32
Citizens	6	17	20
Surgeons, barristers	—	6	14
Doctors, lawyers	—	7	28
Nobles and gentry	4	8	34
Clergy	5	3	10
Laborers	3	1	3
Various	1	6	—

The evidence shows the book trade to be pretty much the same in social makeup as other trades. Some printers and booksellers climbed the social pyramid by marriage to minor officials in government, and it is noticeable that the few from the higher ranks of society were connected with families at the top end of the book trade, like Cramoisy and Blaise. Writers and men of letters never honor the occasion with their presence—a very different picture from the days of their predecessors a century earlier, when Joost Bade, Estienne and Vascosan were alive. The trade has fallen from the hands of literary artists and scholars into the arms of petty tradesmen and shopkeepers.

4. Career: from apprenticeship to mastership

In the years 1600–1675 we have 75 marriage contracts which tell us something about careers and family advancement. At the bottom of the ladder, with dowries of 100–160 livres, are nine journeymen, one of whom had recently attained the rank of master, and the picture varies greatly: there is Jacques Le Comte, a journeyman printer living in the Rue St. Etienne des Grès, married to Guillemette Besse, a laborer's daughter in 1622, with three witnesses only: Robert Olivier, a canon of St. Etienne des Grès, for Le Comte (in the absence of Le Comte's family), and for Guillemet, her uncle Le Sueur, a second-hand dealer living in the same street as Le Comte. The dowry, administered in accordance with Paris customs (each partner having no responsibility for debts contracted by the other before marriage), amounted to 100 livres in money, clothes and utensils, to which Uncle Le Sueur added another 50 livres, giving it to his niece to celebrate the union. A modest dowry in all, 150 livres, typical of the artisan class. Le Comte worked for a long time as a journeyman before presenting himself in 1632 as a candidate for the mastership. The Guild Syndics questioned his application, perhaps a technical objection connected with his apprenticeship, and deferred his case for a year. It was never granted officially but this did not deter Le Comte from describing himself as "A master printer and bookseller and citizen of Paris" on a document at the time of his wife's death in 1642. His furniture was worth very little—169 livres for the contents of kitchen and living room; his clothes and linen, 55 livres; and his silver, two table spoons, 6 livres. The goods were those of an ordinary workman, though they did have a house in the Rue St. Etienne des Grès, one floor of which Le Comte's wife had inherited; the other two they bought later. In 1642 Le Comte had a number of promissory notes totalling 350 livres and owned six silver spoons, which proves he was not destitute. It is impossible to say if this was because of an inheritance, remuneration for his work as a skilled printer, or clandestine business on the bridges or the quays. His son was apprenticed to Desdin, a bookseller, on 24 August 1632 for four years, married in 1648 a locksmith's daughter with a dowry of 600 livres of which 200 was cash, and ended up as a bookbinder in the Rue Chartière in 1653, founding a dynasty of binders which lasted well into the 18th century.

Another case is Charles Dubourg, admitted master in 1655, and so advancing a stage beyond his father, as the younger Le Comte did—their upward progression was made without difficulty, and the same was true of Noël Bordier, a bookseller and binder employed by Clovis Eve, the King's binder, who married one Geneviève Charpentier in 1614 and secured with her a dowry of 300 livres. Her father was a stationer and finisher. Robert Sara's wife was not a master's daughter but he nevertheless rose to the rank of Assistant in the Guild, and Edme Martin's career is also instructive: he came from Chateauvillain-en-Champagne, a simple journey-man until his marriage in 1608 to Michelle, daughter of André Eschart, a bookseller/binder of modest means. The witnesses included his two uncles, Jean Le Duc, a perfume manufacturer, and Claude Eschart, a merchant of Paris, and a cousin, Jean Le Clerc, an engraver. Claude Morel, Martin's patron, was his witness, a friend of Guillaume Belet, an officer of the Châtelet. With a dowry of 600 livres from the sale of a house Martin was in a favored position, and with his own high standard of skill and a smattering of culture, probably picked up when he worked for Morel, he was set for a promising career. In 1610, two years after his marriage, he was appointed official University bookseller and opened a shop. At the sign of the Golden Sun his printing works prospered and later he was Cramoisy's printer and Technical Director of the Imprimerie Royale. He died in 1646, leaving a fortune.

Martin was exceptional. Most journeymen, as many as four out of five, never attained master's status and in old age many of them were obliged to work as colporteurs to eke out a living and died in poverty with nothing to declare in their wills. The way to financial success was through a fortunate alliance or profitable inheritance, though opportunities were fewer in the 17th century, and soon the position grew worse.

Master printers were often the inheritors of small dowries, sometimes the reason for bankruptcy of apparently sound businesses. One such misfortune befell Adrien Périer, bookseller, and Pierre Mettayer, the King's Printer, experi-enced similar hardship. Périer left for The Hague and his sons found it difficult to be accepted as masters in their trade, while Mettayer's wife had to sell a cloak to defray expenses during her husband's fatal illness, after having parted with her silverware because she was short of ready money. Dowries in the period 1600–25 varied from 600 livres to 3,000 livres and even in the best families (Clopejau, Houzé, Sevestre, Rezé, Sommaville and Ballard) they were less than 1,200 livres. Next come firms like Boulanger, Quinet, Février, Celérier, Prévosteau, Libert, Thierry, Robinot,

Rocollet, Chaudiére, Fouet, and even Sébastien Cramoisy at the outset of his career; dowries here varied from 1,500 to 3,000 livres, and this was the elite of the trade, only exceeded by a few exceptionally rich men—Sonnius, Buon, Douceur and Morel, who were in some cases thinking of quitting for more lucrative careers elsewhere. Widows or widowers could sometimes improve their financial standing by remarriage, the men often looking for a rich old dame of the kind satirized in poems and dramas of the day.

But now a closer look at the inventories of some tradesmen, documents that will give us a precise description of their effects and so help us fill up a picture of their life style, still fragmentary perhaps but better than nothing.

Firstly, booksellers. A document dated March 1648 concerns Denis Moreau at the sign of the Salamander, one of the most prosperous men in the trade. His house in the Rue St. Jacques was narrow, two or three floors, Moreau's family sharing part of the ground floor with his shop, and occupying all the rooms on the first floor. The shop had two counters and behind it was a room furnished with a walnut table and two benches, two stools, some small cupboards, and on the walls a dozen bookshelves; in the kitchen were the usual cooking pots, stewpans and stove, and behind was a small court with a copper fountain. Above the shop were the family rooms, three in all, the front room the best furnished, with a tapestry worth eight livres on the wall, two pictures, one of the Conversion of St. Paul, the other of Tobias, together valued at six livres. In the room was a four-poster bed, a table, six chairs of walnut, some high stools, another smaller bed, a cupboard and cabinet; there was similar furniture in the other two rooms and an attic with two wooden tables and rough shelving. In total, furniture and fittings were worth 487 livres. Some clothes in a chest were valued at 11 livres, a good deal of linen at 356 livres, silver at 162 livres and coins of various denominations, 1,078 livres. A quite modest household.

Among his papers were promissory notes from booksellers, churchmen and middlemen in the trade, totaling nearly 1,200 livres, and his debts included 1,256 livres to a papermaker, Androuet, and to other papermakers,

Gaouault, 305 livres, and Nicolas Denise, 100 livres. He owed 800 to a printer (Blageart) and 850 to Piot the bookbinder, 330 livres, 1 sol to someone called Pépin for "arrears" of interest on a capital sum, and to Marie Moreau, daughter of the deceased, 11 livres, 2 sols, 6 deniers— interest on a capital sum of 2,000 livres loaned by the mother; there was also interest owed to Antoine Noyers, Maître des Requêtes to the Queen Mother.

There was no sign of any real estate owned by Moreau, or of income from annuities or shares, but he did possess a considerable stock valued at 39,776 livres in 1647, and a further 6,034 books in which he held shares in the Compagnie du Navire, which tells us that at the time of his death Moreau had important works in progress on his presses and was an enterprising businessman reinvesting his profits in new publications. Marie, his elder daughter, brought a dowry of 5,400 livres when she married Etienne Dauguy, bookseller, and books worth 4,200 livres. Nicole, the younger daughter, married her father's journeyman, Edme Couterot, son of a laborer from Bire-sur-Marne who later rose to master, and her dowry was books worth 4,500 livres on the understanding that she and her husband lived for two years with her widowed mother, continuing Denis Moreau's business and receiving one sol for every pound (money) of merchandise sold.

There is in all these cases a shortage of liquidity, which must have been acute at times. Moreau was possibly among the firms that suffered during the economic crisis of 1630–35 when his father-in-law, Antoine Estienne, crashed through failure to find markets for the unsold stocks in his warehouse; certainly Moreau was on the international scene, specializing in massive series of religious works for export abroad.

Jean Libert was in business on a more modest scale. He ran a shop and lived in a small room and kitchen with a kind of cubby-hole on the ground floor of a house in the Rue Jean de Beauvais, with a small apartment of two rooms on the first floor. His furniture and fittings were valued at 735 livres, his clothes and those of his wife, all of serge or black broadcloth, at 36 livres, 10 sols, linen in a chest, 410 livres, and jewelry and plate, 1,200 livres. He had money (gold écus, pistolles and Spanish quadruples) worth 2,818 livres—valuable reserve funds. Libert went blind and was forced to restrict his business activities but his bookstock was valued at 11,685 livres, while his debts and the promissory notes recorded in his ledgers amounted to several thousand livres. He was in better financial shape than Moreau because his stock-in-trade was schoolbooks, which meant a steady income from trade in Paris and the provinces, unaffected by the wars that so often ruined international trade.

Pierre Ballard was another prosperous tradesman. His inventory of 1,639 shows that in addition to his furniture, including linen and plate worth 1,268 livres, his bookstock was worth 13,582 livres and his printing shop 2,308 livres. Ballard owned a little house in Cormeilles-en-Parisis with a garden and a vine which he bought for 600 livres in 1628; its furnishings were worth 400 livres. Ballard was later Commissioner for Artillery, which may mean that he intended to quit and leave the business to his son, especially the profitable monopoly in music publishing which descended from father to son for some time after. It is rare to find a bookseller continuing in the trade once he has bought a sinecure that yields a profit (every citizen's objective in 17th-century France), but many bought a nice little property in the country (still every French citizen's objective today). Few owned much property in Paris, as Mathieu Guillemot did. Son of an affluent stationer who had done well out of de luxe books, he became a Syndic during the Fronde, and his possessions prove him to have been very rich. Though his furniture was worth only 700 livres, his clothes, 100 livres, linen, 275 livres and jewelry, 255 livres, he had 2,644 livres in silver coins, a bookstock worth 13,795 livres, a house at Clamart worth 800 livres in 1647, and some land. He owned a shop in the Palais and he bought two houses in Paris for 20,000 livres, the one he lived in at the corner of the Rue St. Jacques and Rue de la Parcheminerie, and the house next door which he had repaired. He had to sell some of his shares to make these purchases but he had promissory notes in hand, and his day book would no doubt show his assets to be far more than his debts.

The wealthiest publishers—Cramoisy, Sonnius, Courbé—

bought property in Paris, but this was unusual because most of them could not afford it, unlike their predecessors, who owned the houses in which they lived. In the 17th century they were more likely to sell any property they had inherited and invest in shares of books and copyrights; economically, the climate made hard cash harder to come by, and was a serious obstacle to expansion.

Bookbinders were not in the same category as printers and booksellers, though they often sold books. We can divide their craft into the forwarders and finishers (i.e., those who bound books and those who decorated the covers). Jean Nicod was a finisher living in just two rooms in 1624, the first room a kitchen cum workshop, and the second a bedroom and living room. His furniture was worth only 183 livres, his equipment a few dozen livres, his clothes 17 livres, 10 sols, all made of cheap serge. His wife's wardrobe was a little better, her petticoats of black serge, pink and green, lined with velour, valued at 62 livres, 10 sols, which would square with the likely fact that she owned one of the shops her husband let out to rent under the Palais clock, a fashionable rendezvous. The linen chest was valued at 131 livres, some silver at 73 livres and jewelry at 35 livres, in total a value of 800 livres. Nicod owned 4,340 books in sheets of very small format, probably hours or litanies, and 1,667 others decorated with tiny fillets, the first lot valued at 800 livres, the second at 487 livres. He was in debt to Perrière, a printer, to the tune of 20 livres for goods delivered, and 30 livres in rent on the two shops. The whole of his property did not exceed 1,500 livres, well below a bookseller's.

Salvian Pigoreau, another finisher, left nearly 500 livres in furniture in 1636, including linen and clothes plus 800 livres in ready money and silver, finishing tools worth 100 livres and a bookstock of 4,412 livres. Michel Balagny had furniture, clothes and linen worth 824 livres in 1647, silver plate worth 70 livres, and his books—offices, litanies and primers—worth 5,729 livres. His assets were worth 3,256 livres and liabilities 3,280—debts to printers and papermakers.

The forwarders were in much the same state as the finishers. Guillaume Bénard lived in a spacious house of five rooms, but when Anne Pelé, his wife, died in 1628 the furniture was valued at only 226 livres, clothes 126 livres, linen 106 livres, plate 132 livres. Bénard's bindery was one of the largest in the city, with five presses, a good supply of calfskins, vellum and paper, 300 books bound and unbound, all ordered by booksellers—forwarders were less directly involved with bookselling than finishers. Occasionally Bénard published a book—a stock service book, or a schoolbook, not unusual with binders. At his death his bindery and equipment were valued at 4,000 livres.

Many binders were close to poverty. Pierre Auger, a forwarder, and Martin Du Breuil, a finisher, were near-paupers, as we know from documents, and this class was the proletariat of the trade, with the equipment and skills of leatherworkers. They were often illiterate. In 1620 hostility between finishers and leatherworks came to a head in a riot, a sure indication of instability in the trade, as economic conditions in Paris became acute and work scarce.

Master printers, another branch of the trade. Edme Martin was one of the richest, yet his home was a modest one: a shop, room and kitchen at street level and a room on the first floor, with furniture valued at 402 livres, which means he was pretty comfortable. His clothes were valued at 62 livres, linen at 476 livres, silver plate at 396 livres, and ready money, 5,263 livres. The printing shop next to his apartment was well equipped, and valued at 4,230 livres, and his books and papers at 1,635 livres, a total of 5,865 livres. His debtors, that is, the publishers for whom he worked, owed him 13,557 livres, and he had 3,538 livres income from investments. His assets amounted to 35,038 livres, his debts less than 1,000, yet even Martin was unable to invest much in bookstocks or fittings and equipment when so many of his publishers were tardy payers; the evidence suggests that they delayed payment until they had sold sufficient copies of their books to recoup the initial outlay—even Cramoisy would postpone payment for decades, relying on the power of his name and fortune. Printers were in a less profitable business than booksellers, but required less capital, and they always seemed to have good reasons for suspending payments or failing to renew orders, except on credit. Martin's prosperity was by printers' standards unusual. Some printers (Gasse, for instance, or Tompère) had big reserves, but we do not know what those reserves were.

Claude Calleville lived in three rooms, his furniture valued at 185 livres, his clothes at only 28 livres, his linen at 51 livres, with no silver plate, and cash (in louis d'ors) at 244 livres. He owned a printing shop well equipped and estimated at 3,177 livres and a bookstock valued at 3,000 livres, mostly books of hours, and he was reckoned to be one of the leading printers of Paris, playing an important part in Guild affairs. Dallin, Denis Langlois, Pierre Mettayer, Challemaigne and Brunet were all less wealthy than Challeville, and their difficulties were apparent—they made no attempt to renew outworn equipment because they could not afford it. Others were in wretched circumstances. Antoine Coulon's printing shop was valued at 1,699 livres in 1649, and the rest of his goods at 300 livres; Pierre Durand's workshop at 2,370 livres, his goods at a mere 163 livres in 1642 (Sébastien Chappelet, a bookseller, owed him 1,590 livres for work done); Claude Prudhomme, the printer of the very popular *Mort de Pompée* (1644), lived in one room of an apothecary's house, his press and ancillary equipment valued at 1,140 livres and the rest of his goods at 423 livres.

When orders ceased, printers were in dire straits, looking to any avenue, legitimate or illegitimate, for work, whatever the risks. When men are struggling to earn their bread, it is going to be difficult for agents of the State to control their activities and keep them policed. As the years went by, the different trades in the book world become more demarcated—printer, binder and finisher—and also less profitable as competition grows, offering cheaper and cheaper rates. For evidence of a depression in the trade, marriage settlements are valuable. Nine of the 75 contracts mention a dowry of less than 600 livres in the years 1600–25, all of them journeymen. In a similar number of contracts for the years 1635–50, twenty dowries of the same value are cited, only seven of which belong to journeymen, the rest to binders (forwarders and finishers) and printers. One Marie Trouvain, daughter of a bookseller-binder, brought only 100 livres as dowry, and marks on the document show all present to have been illiterate. Louis Barbote, a well-known master printer, received only 300 livres from his future wife, Anne François, whose father was a master dyer, and Florimond Badier, a binder of considerable artistry, had only 600 livres as dowry for his wife Marie, daughter of Jean Gillède, a master binder.

Other settlements prove to have been under 1,200 livres, even those of master printers like Langlois and King's Binders like Du Bois. The aristocracy of the trade afforded more, as did Edme Martin when he gave away his daughter Jeanne to Bookseller Robert Denain with a dowry of 2,500 livres; and, maintaining the intermarriage system, when Claude Cramoisy married his daughter Marie off to Edme Martin II, she brought with her a dowry of 2,500 livres from her father and 500 from her uncle Sébastien. Anne Thiboust, daughter of a Palais bookseller and stepdaughter of Jean Libert, brought 3,000 livres as her dowry in 1637 when she married Nicholas Cochon, a pastrycook. The two daughters of Denis Moreau I were given 4,500 livres, though largely in books, and when Pierre Guillemot and Jean Libert married, the dowries were in the 10,000 livres class, like Sébastien Cramoisy's children on their marriage. And Denys Béchet, son of a bookseller, picked up 16,000 livres when he married the rich widow of a deceased goldsmith, using it to buy back his father's bookstock.

The figures reveal two distinct tendencies: increasing poverty for the majority and increasing wealth for the few whose children made prudent alliances.

5. Social Mobility

Some book trade dynasties die out, some suffer financial ruin, some enjoy unparalleled prosperity, others find new careers—the upwardly mobile in search of enhanced status in one of the proliferating government departments. By hard work or shrewd marriages, our tradesmen were ever alert to possibilities to advantage themselves. The Blaise family is an example: Thomas Blaise was the son of a Mons stationer who came to Paris, was admitted master and married the daughter of a bookbinder, Marie Rezé, who brought a dowry of only 600 livres; after her death he made a more profitable marriage with Gilette Humeau, who was worth 2,000 livres. His elder son Valéran married Alix Pescheux in 1630, with a dowry of 24,000 livres and a host of important people as witnesses, this due to Valéran's position as first President Chevalier's and later a Queen's secretary—powerful patrons, an example not lost on the family because his younger brother Pierre changed career and joined the influential Capuchin order. A sudden sense of vocation? Not at all, to judge from subsequent events. Supported by his brother Valéran and his publisher father who was respected at Court, Pierre was soon appointed Librarian to Chancellor Séguier and then canon of the church at Langres and chaplain of Sainte Chapelle.

Likewise Thomas Blaise's two daughters reveal ambitions to marry someone better than a mere binder; one found a doctor of some eminence, François Blondel, and the other an infantry captain, Louis de Blois, Sieur de St. André, to whom she brought a dowry of 10,000 livres. Though relatively modest, the marriages enabled Blaise to quit business, an escape route achieved by astute tactics rather than commercial brilliance, but as if exhausted by his efforts to secure improved social status for his children, he died in 1658 with no very large estate. Another tradesman, Jean Orry, steward to the Princesse des Ursins, escaped from his class with the help of aristocratic patronage. But what happened to the families who stayed in the same profession for several generations, like the Chaudières?

Guillaume Chaudière I was one of the most considerable publishers in Paris in the 16th century, descended from a long line. When he died in 1601 his widow took control of the firm, and nine years later ended joint ownership of the business shared between herself and children. Guillaume Chaudière owned two large houses in the Rue St. Jacques, the sign of the Savage and one next door, the first worth 6,500 livres, the second 5,000 livres, besides a twelfth part of a house in the Rue St. Jean de Beauvais worth 500 livres. His widow acquired another house in the Rue des Lombards valued at 9,000 livres, bringing the total value of all the property to 21,000 livres, plus the bookstock at 30,663 livres and shares in the Compagnie des Usages worth 9,794 livres. A very large fortune. After the widow's death the property went to her three daughters and a grandson. The first daughter, Blanche, married Nicolas Buon, one of the foremost publishers of the day, taking a dowry of 1,000 écus, but she died prematurely, leaving an only daughter, Marie, who also married a publisher. With her legacy Marie was an eligible girl, and with a dowry of 6,000 livres could choose her husband. He was Claude Sonnius, sole heir with his sister (who married a collector of tolls) of his father Laurent and uncles Michel and Jean. Claude attained high office in city government, bought property and invested widely, and dying childless, bequeathed a large house to a religious order as a hospital. By alignment with administrators, lawyers and notaries, the daughter and granddaughter of Guillaume Chaudière kept up their position in society and in the book trade.

Gilette, Blanche's sister, married Robert Fouet, bookseller, in 1594, bringing a dowry of 1,000 écus. Fouet had just opened a bookshop and when his mother-in-law retired, he took over nearly all the Chaudière stock through inheritance or purchase. Like his brother-in-law Buon and nephew Claude Sonnius, he was one of the leading publishers and could place his children to greatest advantage: his son was of the rank of "bourgeois," his daughter Marguerite, married Charles Chastelain II, and his other daughter, Marie, married a doctor, Claude Liénard. Nevertheless he had to sell the property his wife had inherited to keep his business going, and when he died his assets were not all that impressive—an estimated 11,000 livres, with no ready cash or silver plate. This was probably due to debts because his son Pierre had a deed drawn up renouncing his inheritance as more of a burden than an asset. Once again it looks as if the economic depression of 1630–40 hit Fouet as it did Denis Moreau and Antoine Estienne.

But it did not prevent Marie Fouet from enjoying ample prosperity. Her husband became King's doctor and her son Liénard, Sieur des Bruyères, gentleman usher to the King, with a consequent career at Court. Nor did this social triumph make him forget his family because when Margaret

Chastelain wanted to marry one of her father's apprentices, a Dutchman named Nicolas Biestkens, the Guild had to admit him despite his nationality, by order of the Queen, and when Biestkens died, Marie's son (the courtier) was tutor to their son. Influence was important in this tight trade. Michel Soly was son of the third of Guillaume Chaudière's daughters by Pierre Soly, a bookseller in partnership with Fouet who failed and died poor in 1661. The families that prospered generally had the right connections, while those who continued simply as tradesmen did less well.

Booksellers like Charles and Gilles Morel, last of their clan, used up their inheritance buying offices, one of them as a royal secretary, and venality was a way of life. Robert Estienne IV, the last of the Paris branch of the family, bought the post of Superintendent of Irrigation, was a lawyer in the Parlement and ended as Treasurer of the King's Works.

The most outstanding example of social elevation is the career of Sébastien Cramoisy. In 1613, after running the business for five years, he married Marie Chaillou, daughter of a Parisian and granddaughter of Jean de Riberolles. His keen business acumen counted for much, of course, but not everything. For the rest we look to Richelieu and the Jesuits, because as a grandson of one of the heroes of the Catholic League Cramoisy was naturally favored by them, and there may have been a link with Richelieu's family through his grandfather, Sébastien Nivelle, and Pierre Nivelle, Cramoisy's cousin, was General of the Cistercians and Bishop of Luçon in 1649. Whatever the connection was, Cramoisy started his climb when he was nominated as King's Printer and a Syndic of the Guild, 1628–31, and his appointment as Director of the Imprimerie Royale reinforced his status, resulting in his election to the Echevinage, the ruling city council, in 1649; at one bound he passed from being a respected official to the rank of a nobleman. He was meanwhile planning the best possible alliances for his children—there is a story that Boileau wished to marry one of Cramoisy's girls but retired in favor of a gallant musketeer. The elder daughter married Pierre Mabre in 1635, a King's Messenger in Flanders, bringing a dowry of 12,000 livres; his second daughter (her dowry 20,000 livres) married a high-ranking officer of the Châtelet, Jean de la Rue, later usher to the King and an intimate of the Chancellor; and the third daughter brought a dowry of 25,000 livres when she married a merchant, Jean-Jacques Forne.

Cramoisy paid particular attention to his sons' careers. Jean, the youngest, went into a monastery, the Congregation of the Oratory, and soon enjoyed preferment as canon of Luçon, then King's almoner in 1669, and canon of the church of St. Jacques de l'Hôpital. The elder son, Louis, was bought the post of King's secretary, and later became a lawyer in the Council of State and Privy Council, where he secured privileges and monopolies for his father in the book trade almost as a routine by-product of his official duties. When Louis died without issue the business went to a grandson, Sébastien Mabre-Cramoisy, whom we shall meet later.

CHAPTER V

THE AUTHOR

THE MOST ESSENTIAL FIGURE in the world of the printed book is of course the author. With the aid of the *Bibliographia parisiana* for the year 1643/44, we can list the backgrounds and occupations of writers, lay and ecclesiastical:

Ecclesiastical		*Laymen*	
Churchmen of senior rank	49	Members of the high court	5
Lay priests	16	Lawyers	5
Congregation of the Oratory	4	Professors	10
Jesuits	69	Merchants	2
Dominicans	10	Gentry	8
Minims	10	Courtiers	8
Carmelites	18	King's historiographers and librarians	12
Other monks	21	Doctors	18
Theologians	39	Architects	3
Almoners and king's chaplains	6	Mathematicians	13
Abbés	4	Unclassified	85
	246		169

Churchmen are in the majority, just what we would expect when organized religion was so dominant in everyday life and religious publication a large part of the output of the trade, though bishops and clergy often wrote on subjects other than religion, and many were simply professional writers. A career in the church was the best way to combine a taste for learning with a flair for writing, as Du Perron, Bertaut, Camus and Father Le Moyne proved. There were fewer

283

lawyers than we might have expected, and writers on technical subjects were very few, apart from professional teachers; the Court is well represented with its chaplains and almoners, while the 85 "Unclassified," whose names appear in present-day works of literary criticism, had no precise title or were so well known as not to require identification. The phrase "gens de lettres" was coined at this time to describe the new kind of writer who was then beginning to make a career of it and who usually came from the gentry-legal-courtier classes. Let us look at the ways by which they made a living if they had no private income or were not in holy orders.

1. The early history of authors' rights

Most contracts with authors have been lost because they were of a private nature, so that our evidence comes not from them but from the records of notaries and the private papers of scholars, together with authors' wills and book trade documents.

There were three main categories of payment. Firstly, the author would be given a certain number of free copies of his book. The Duchess of Aiguillon asked for 100 copies of the *Perfection du Chrétien,* written by her uncle, Cardinal Richelieu, as his heir when she assigned the monopoly in that work to Cramoisy. Hippolyte de Béthune specified that 50 copies of his father's book (of volume 1, in fact), *Ambassade,* be sent to him, and the poet Du Bois-Hus, an equerry, requested 50 copies of his collected poems, *Nuit des nuits,* on fine paper. Véron, the controversialist, likewise asked for 50 copies of his translation of the New Testament, as did the brothers Sainte-Marthe for the third edition of their *Histoire généalogique de la Maison de France,* Gilbert Du Plessis for his *Histoire des terres australes,* and Denis Challine, a Parlement lawyer, for a translation of Juvenal.

Often an author would sell his manuscript or the copyright he had secured in it to a bookseller, or he might come to an agreement with a bookseller to write a book for a fixed sum. Playwrights who wrote for a particular company would often sell their manuscripts. Benserade sold his tragedy *Cléopatre* to Sommaville in 1636 for 150 livres, and the same Sommaville gave Rotrou 750 livres for four plays, *Ménechmes, Céline, Célimène* and *Emilie,* and bought ten more plays for 1,500 livres. La Calprenède received 200 livres for *Mithridate.* Though no documentary evidence survives for Pierre Corneille, we know he was engaged in deals over copyrights in his plays, not always scrupulously. Other evidence comes from a promissory note for 600 livres signed by Courbé and Billaine in exchange for three collections of poems which Tristan agreed to let them have, 400 livres for his *Amours,* 100 for *Oeuvres chrétiennes,* and 100 for *Vers héroïques.* Claude Malingre, King's Historiographer, promised to deliver the manuscripts of short histories of Spain, England, Italy, Poland, Hungary, Denmark, Germany and Sweden, each to consist of twenty pages, 12mo in Cicero roman, for only 25 livres.

Translators fared better than Malingre: Du Bosc was paid 150 livres for a translation of Narni's sermons, and Urbain Chevreau could reckon on 300 livres in louis d'ors and silver, one copy in morocco, six in calf and thirty vellum copies of his *Ecole de sage,* a book he translated partly from Joseph Hall's original and partly wrote himself. Jean Baudoin's contracts were a model of what a good translator might expect from his publisher: when he began work on the translation of *Police de dieu* from the Italian (3 volumes), Fouet, his publisher, gave him more than 60 livres for the manuscript of a portion of Part One, and of Parts Two and Three in their entirety. Marie de Medici sent him to England to work on a translation of Philip Sidney's *Arcadia* on very good terms—six livres a week until the work was completed. But when he translated Bacon's works the conditions were harder: he had to supply one page of Gros roman per day (Sundays and feast days excepted) at 3 livres the page, which meant he could earn up to 80 livres a month if he kept up the pace. In 1630 he was still working by the page—3 livres, 4 sols per page in Gros roman for translating a text of Aesop to accompany illustrations. Another translator, Du Ryer, produced copy for a scale of one écu per page, but few writers could earn more than 1,000 or at most 2,000 livres a year by the pen, a very modest sum when we consider the life style they would have to keep up if they were to gain access to the kind of people they needed to consult in order to write.

Teachers were little better off. The compiler of a textbook, *Apparatus elegantiarum latinum locutionum,* was paid by the page, 30 sols per sheet, and even for great legal works authors were paid at the same low rates. In the case of those ever-popular devotional books it is hard to estimate the income their authors might expect, but Yves de Paris, author of the best-selling *Morales chrétiennes,* signed a contract with Denis Thierry in 1638 by which his sister received 800 livres for each volume. Ogier, an established writer, was paid 2,000 livres every quarter by Louis de Villac, Camusat's successor, for a collection of his sermons, funeral orations and panegyrics, plus 30 copies of the whole work.

Novelists, always popular with the middle-class readership, usually made profitable agreements, especially if they were well known, like Honoré d'Urfé. Far too aristocratic to touch filthy lucre, he sent his valet to collect the 1,000 livres he earned for the third part of *Astrée.* In 1646 La Calprenède, then at the height of her fame, was paid 3,000 livres by Sommaville for the second and third parts of *Cléopatre,* each part consisting of four books of 40 or 50 pages; and Toussaint Quinet paid Scarron 1,000 livres for his *Roman comique* and 11,000 livres for the last eleven books of *Virgile travesti,* no mean reward.

Those more impressive figures should not obscure the real facts of literary life for most writers, who were very badly paid by publishers; the tale of the poets Musidore and Musigène in Sorel's satire *Francion* is a fairly accurate picture. Any author who had enough money to pay for his own work to be published did so at some risk, because he first had to pay the printer and then find a bookseller who would take the books, often a complicated matter because of Guild regulations. Authors were forbidden to sell their own books, at least in theory, and so had to chance their luck; while Corneille managed it, St. Amant did not. It was all quite fortuitous.

2. Patronage

One solution for a literary man with inadequate financial means was to become a member of a noble household, perhaps the poet or official historian, even a pamphleteer, or to seek work as a secretary or in some official capacity which would enable him to dine at the lord's table and so possibly find his way into the Court where the right contacts would be of inestimable value. The hero of the novel *Francion* was typical of the aspiring writer of the day, a young gentleman of good background but no money who decides to seek his fortune in Paris, and learns how to make the right kind of poetry from two threadbare poets, Musidore and Musigène, who borrow the books they need from the stocks which booksellers cannot sell. He makes a dismal start in his poor clothes and is abused by the page in the baron's family when he accidentally finds himself in the Louvre. When at last he does manage to compose something he fails to get it into the right hands, namely the great personage to whom he addresses his Epistle Dedicatory. When he hears that a ballet is to be staged, he writes some verses to put in the Queen's mouth, although he was not commanded to do so, and his highest reward is to be allowed to help with the stage management; he is somewhat wilting by this time, and has a violin score stuffed in his mouth. His luck turns when his mother sends him money and he buys some clothes to cut a decent figure, attends various salons and meets a VIP, Clérante, who tells Francion that he is worried by a satirical piece circulating at Court which makes him look a fool. Francion tells him how to rebuff such an attack and the two men join forces when Clérante asks after Francion's circumstances and Francion paints a black picture, at which the nobleman suggests that he come to live in his establishment for a salary. Francion accepts but reserves his right to freedom of action, and not to be hired as a servant, to which Clérante agrees. Soon our hero is riding a horse worth 200 pistoles, has personal servants and is the master's favorite. He disdains his friends from the days of his poverty and addresses himself to his real task in life, as befits a true satirist, "to punish folly, humble the proud, and ridicule man's ignorance," laying the blame on the rich, the legal profession and the phony aristocracy.

Francion's career was not unlike Théophile de Viau's, a lawyer's son who later secured the patronage of the Duc de Candale, whom he followed in the rebellion and through all his amours from 1615 to 1619. He was involved in the Rohan faction through Marguerite de Béthune, the Duke's mistress, and wrote verses in praise of Concini at the close of that statesman's career, and survived Concini's assassination only to rally round Luynes, favorite of the hour, and managed to enter the Court circle. But then he made a mistake. After suffering Candale's contempt at some point, Théophile joined Lozières, Luynes' enemy, and was promptly banished by him for his laxity of conduct; it was a time when loose morality was again subject to censure. Luynes, however, came increasingly under fire and needed skilled pens to counter the attacks—Théophile was an obvious choice. Once more he was recalled to serve a Minister, once more he showed himself a practiced flatterer, singing the praises of Luynes, the one-time favorite. He reaped his reward as propagandist to the royal cause in 1621—a royal pension; then there was another about-turn when Luynes died in December 1621. Théophile nimbly attached himself to another patron, Montmorency, who although a Duke was unable to protect him against the wave of hostility that broke out around him in resentment against his dissolute life, his friends at Court and in the city—a bad example during the period of Catholic Renaissance. What is important to our story is the value assigned to writing skills at Court, clearly demonstrated by de Viau's career. Literary talent was a force to be reckoned with, and was sought after by the many factions which made up a monarch's Court.

That generation of writers, the emergence of literary "schools" and the clients for whom writers were recruited to support were all crucial factors in the history of authorship and the rise of their influence in politics, and importance to our culture generally. Earlier we can detect the germs of the same spirit in Henri IV's reign and the part played by writers like Motin, Sigogne and Regnier in the plots hatched by the Comte d'Auvergne and the Marquise de Verneuil.

In the early years of Louis XIII, pamphleteers included most of the writers of the time. An interesting study could be made of the adventurers and free lances in Queen Marguerite's household: poets like Vital d'Audiguier, Maynard, Lingendes, Deimier, Pitard, and a future saint who was much involved in politics, Vincent de Paul; historians, too, like Victor Cayet, Scipion Dupleix, President Savaron, Baudoin, and others like Mathieu de Morgues, who went from sermons to pamphleteering. It would be useful to know more about Clairville's work, or Meynier and Nervèze, allies of the Prince of Condé, or about Du Lorens, de Nevers's associate, or Charles de Besançon, Tristan, Patrix, Neufgermain and Voiture, all close friends of Gaston d'Orléans. We would like to follow the tracks of the Gondi, whose pens were influential from the late 16th century to the time of the Fronde; to define precisely what Besançon or Scipion Guillet's role was in working for Lesgiduière, or Balzac and the Girards for Epernon, or Tristan, Vaugelas and their cronies composing broadsides for the Duc de Guise, or Serizay for La Rochefoucauld. It would help historians to know more about Théophile de Viau's own circle, his friends and fellow debauchees—Bassompière, for instance, and of course patrons like Montmorency and Cramail, or details of the careers of men like Molière d'Essertines, Maynard, Boissat, Mairet, Hardy and Malleville, not forgetting brave Vanini. And then of course, St. Amant in the comte d'Harcourt's entourage, and Faret, who reconciled Richelieu with his patron.

All of them were creators of the political history and propaganda of the period 1610–1630, and the most striking feature of all of them is their affinity with rebel aristocrats, then in a permanent condition of unrest, rather than in the royal cause. They were free spirits, natural Bohemians, contemptuous of conventional morality and restraints, ultimately faithful only to their own impulses. They might sometimes flatter the Court, but in their hearts they were chronic opponents of authority, especially religious sanctions, and that was probably why they were such evident admirers and supporters of political adventurers. From 1625 to 1630 the center re-established itself under the monarch, various dissident noblemen were executed, exiled or killed in battle, and their literary spokesmen lost their patrons and so their occupation. After Théophile's banishment, opposition to the legitimate monarchy was silenced, the Catholic recovery made itself felt, and literature finds expression in devotional and pietistic books: in literature as in morals and politics, the impact of firm rule, a return to household piety. The Age of Richelieu had come.

3. Royal historiographers and official propaganda

The royalists appeared to be indifferent to the benefits of press support at this time. Unlike the Valois, Henri IV had no interest in literature. Du Perron, Bertaut, Desportes and Vauquelin des Yvetaux functioned at Court, but theirs were merely inherited rewards for earlier services; they did not seek preferment with the pen. When Malherbe was received at Court in the Louvre, it was a nobleman, the Duc de Bellegarde, who did the necessary negotiating, and even if he was not as unhappy as he claims (he was after all a member of the Royal Household and patronized by the Royal Equerry), he failed to secure the pension he wanted, even though he was the authorized celebrant of Henri IV's victories in arms and of the royal amours. Marie de Medici was more generous towards Malherbe and Gombauld, but it is hard to see any policy behind her actions. Though Luynes, a typical aristocratic rebel, gave Théophile and others pensions in return for their work in defence of his policies, Louis XIII had only Bordier the Court poet, and thought him sufficient. But royalty, by virtue of its prestige and power, never lacked support, and every history officially sanctioned from the 16th century onwards contains conventional panegyrics in support of King and country. There is no doubt that if the records of the Chambre des Comptes had survived, there would be plenty of evidence of financial emoluments paid out for poems saying the right things, if not of actual pensions. Treasury accounts do survive which refer to historical works, royalist pamphlets and other official propaganda commissioned by the government, and they reveal the mechanisms by which monarchist propaganda was created, especially through the work of royal historiographers.

Ever since the early medieval Chronicles of St. Denis, French kings had employed annalists and historians, and by the time of Catherine de Medici systematic use of official history was patent. In 1560 Pierre Paschal was commissioned to write Catherine's life and reign, and was given the title Royal Historiographer with a salary of 1,200 livres a year, from 1564. Charles IX encouraged his Secretaries of State to write histories of his reign, possibly as a deterrent to attacks on him in print, and he required their memoirs to be written "bien et fidèlement," in return for a pension. When Henri III established the first Royal Academy in 1572, an official royal historiographer was appointed at a salary—the institution was made definitive. Its first occupants were Pierre Mathieu (1571–1610), Bernard Du Haillan (1610–1620), Charles Bernard (1621–1636) and his nephew Charles Sorel, and others were appointed concurrently as state funds permitted: Nicolas Vignier and Gabriel Chappuys until the end of the 16th century, then Nicolas Prou des Carneaux (1610–1634), Julien Peleus (1611–1622), Jacob Badouère (1613–14), Théodore Godefroy (from 1613), Jérémie Ferrier (1619), Nicolas Renouard (1621–1628), Scipion Dupleix (1620–1643), the Sainte Marthe brothers (from 1620). When Richelieu came to power it was the turn of Balzac (from 1627), Gollefer (1630), Sirmond (1633–34), Bréville (1638), Billion (1643), Baudoin (1644) and Brisacier (1646). Nor does the list end there: Pierre Beaunis de Chanterain, Sieur de Viettes, Claude Malingre and Puget de la Serre were also engaged. Most historians of proved capacity wrote for the royalists, so not surprisingly that was the thrust of all the history published in the first half of the 17th century—monarchist, Gallican and Government-slanted.

Geographers and "cosmographers" were also recruited to the cause. In the 16th century Nicolas de Nicolai, a famous traveler, was official artist and geographer to the King, and was later made a valet de chambre. André Thevet was granted a salary as royal cosmographer from 1576 to 1585, as was Antoine de Laval (1577–1610), Pierre de Nautonnier,

Sieur de Castellane (1604–1613), Louis de Chaban, Sieur de Maine (in the Council of State, 1619–21), Pierre de Montmort (1621–22), Jérôme Badot (1620–28), Jehan Cavelier in 1621, Pierre Berhus (1620–23), and Andrê Du Chesne from 1618 to 1640, succeeded by his son François.

Other scholars were employed in the same cause: the directors, keepers and writers in the royal libraries, philologists like Casaubon and Rigault, great names like Jérôme Bignon, and men of learning like the Dupuy brothers, who were in charge of the archives and whose main task was to provide diplomats with arguments in favor of France's territorial ambitions. Official publications presenting the royal case all bear the names of the writers mentioned above, and no doubt the many anonymous pieces in print were also theirs. The names of these writers, combined with that of the King's Printer on the title page, make it abundantly clear that they were a corps engaged on propaganda designed to promote the monarch and his program.

4. Richelieu and the Founding of the Académie Française

With Richelieu in power, official propaganda changed significantly. Political and religious polemics were simplified, and the office was reorganized. Véron and La Milletière dealt with anti-Protestant propaganda, Marca and the Dupuy brothers with the Gallican material, and in the political field Richelieu's famous "greyhounds" were put to work. Richelieu patronized the *Gazette* newsbook, using it to woo public opinion to his side in the crisis of 1615. By offering big rewards—a bishopric, control of a monastery, even a red hat—he secured the service of very competent adjutants.

Richelieu looked beyond mere polemics and plumed himself on his literary gifts, ordering his staff to engage in imaginative writing, plays for example, and had the faithful Boisrobert and Chapelain draw up a list of writers who had fallen on evil days, with a view to finding people worthy to receive largesse from the Minister. Aubéry, Richelieu's first biographer, listed 26 authors on his pension list, and Séguier followed suit, enlisting writers and paying them out of his own funds. A list survives, in his own hand, which gives the names of writers employed in 1636, including two theologians, Morel and Grandin, and Baudoin, Conrart, Colletet, l'Estoile, La Chambre and Blaise.

The Government propaganda ministry was most efficient from 1630 to 40; salaries multiplied as more writers were recruited and more support bought. There is nothing disinterested in this policy, though it must be admitted that Richelieu had genuine cultural inclinations.

At this point it would be appropriate to say something about the founding of the Académie Française. In 1636 Boisrobert, Richelieu's devoted ally, heard that a group of literati were in the habit of meeting at Conrart's residence, home of the King's Secretary. He was interested enough to ask for an invitation to join them, liked what he heard, and reported back to Richelieu. From this modest beginning the idea of an Academy sprang, and although enthusiasm was not general, who could resist the Cardinal once he was convinced of something? The founder members were Conrart, responsible for vetting publishing monopolies and licences, and himself a kind of literary director to the firm of Camusat; Chapelain, a notary's son, typical of the new generation of bourgeois literary men; Gombauld, Marie de Medici's old protégé, who no doubt hoped to recover the pension he enjoyed during the Regency; Godeau, Conrart's cousin, soon to be made Bishop of Grasse by Richelieu; Giry, a translator and Parlement lawyer, later on the Privy Council; Habert, Commissioner for War, and his brother, the abbé de Cerizy, a close friend of Chancellor Séguier; and finally, two recalcitrant characters, Malleville, Bassompière's secretary, still in the Bastille and still faithful to his master who visited him in prison, and Serizay, La Rochefoucauld's steward, both of them in retirement at Poitou. They were both enrolled.

Others joined the original nucleus with Richelieu's approval as the Académie's patron. Other writers Richelieu appreciated included: Desmarets de Saint Sorlin, l'Estoile and Mlle. de Scudéry; the pamphleteers Silhon and Sirmond; a Councillor of State, Paul Hay du Chastelet, and his brother, the abbé of Chambon; Maynard and Colletet, needy and greedy, ostensibly reformed from their lives of debauchery, and not well treated by Richelieu or Séguier; Bautru, a diplomat and writer whom Richelieu had commissioned to keep watch on Gaston d'Orléans; the abbé Colomby, Malherbe's nephew and a vile poet who still had his uses—had not the title of King's Orator been created for him in return for his speeches on State occasions? And Séguier's protégés also joined: Jacques Esprit, a boon companion, Cureau de la Chambre (his doctor), Baudoin, who entered the Chancellery after service for Queen Marguerite, and Marchal de Marillac. And finally, Auger de Granier de Mauléon, another of Séguier's pensioners, who specialized in writing scandalous memoirs, and was the first member to be banned from the Académie, for reasons not now clear.

The main body of members was therefore pretty clearly of the Establishment, with a small minority in league with other factions, people like St. Amant and Faret, allies of Henri de Lorraine, comte d'Harcourt; Balzac, whose apparent haughty independence was supported by a pension as a royal historiographer; Tristan l'Hermite, Voiture, Master of the King's Household; Vaugelas, whose pension was quashed while he was in opposition but later reinstated; Baro, a close acquaintance of the Duchesse de Chevreuse, and Patru, a client of the de Retz clan.

According to its Statutes the Académie might not debate any religious questions except within the laws of the Church, and neither morals nor politics could be discussed unless in conformity with royal authority. Articles 24 and 26 specify that the principal object of the Académie is promotion of the French language, and to that end it was enjoined to compile a grammar, to codify principles of rhetoric and poetry, and above all to create an official dictionary. In a series of articles the function of the Academicians as guardians of the purity of the French language was widely canvassed, and they took this responsibility seriously, keeping standard examples of approved styles and even awarding authors diplomas, duly sealed, for "correct" pieces of writing. There was an interesting parallel here, inasmuch as the Académie's censorship of literary style was rather like the Faculty of Theology's censorship of religion and morals. This could have been why the Parlement delayed ratification of its Statutes for so long, and only granted their passage when Richelieu demanded it, asserting that the Académie's role was not that which was imputed but that it would concern itself only with books submitted by the authors themselves. We will examine Parlement's quite justified fears a little later.

The condition of authorship can be summed up like this: if writers tried to live by their work, they found that publishers would not pay them enough, so they were haunted by fears of making a proper livelihood, and place-seeking seemed a legitimate way. Until about 1625, authors could earn a pension or a post in the service of some noble family, clients of the ruling class, and after that date the same rewards are open on a much larger, better organized scale by the authorities under Richelieu's command—just so long as the recipients were willing to serve without question and reflect only orthodoxy in religion, morals and literary matters. By its system of guaranteed pensions the State gave purpose to writers within the framework of the newly founded Académie, and in so doing extended the power of absolute monarchy even into the life of the mind.

CHAPTER VI

THE AUTHORITIES AND THE BOOK TRADE

W E HAVE EMPHASIZED THE MEANS by which the civil and religious power sought to keep control of all aspects of publication and, further, to exercise direction in an attempt to mold public opinion. This leads us naturally into an account of the actual methods used to muzzle the book trade.

1. The Government and the trade: licensing and censorship

The licensing system and government control of the monopolies issued to printers and publishers gave the State power over everything that was published, theoretically. It was given definitive form in 1563 when every new text had to be submitted before publication to the Chancellor, who granted a permit by Letters Patent, a temporary monopoly in its publication, to the applicant, usually either the bookseller-publisher or the author. The sole right to print and publish was what we mean by "privilege."

It was an ingenious method because the advantage gained by the applicant would be enough to encourage him to comply with the regulations governing the licence and even pay the duty imposed on Letters Patent, though in theory they were granted freely. Hence the notion of "sole privilege" was introduced as a royal favor, the implication being that anything in print appeared by dint of royal grace, which at the same time explicitly endorsed it as fit to print, and all was dependent on the applicant's docility and the good will of the Chancellery. It was a powerful weapon by which the King and his Ministers brought pressure to bear on authors and publishers.

Yet although simple in principle it was not easy to apply in practice. If the King reserved the right to grant exclusive privileges, even to the exclusion of the courts, he still had to enforce this on various regional Parlements, and they were far less pliable than the Paris Parlement. In the field of religion, always delicate, to claim the right to approve or condemn books, not only religious but philosophical, moral and scientific, was not lightly recognized by the traditional home of theological studies, the Faculty of the Sorbonne. They represented orthodoxy in the eyes of the vast body of churchmen and students, and they would not hesitate to make the lay Chancellery look foolish if necessary, should the officials there pass anything of doubtful quality. The Faculty of Theology exercised this right until 1623, when anyone hoping to publish could submit his manuscript to two doctors of theology in the approved Faculty, failing which the Chancellery could seek authentication elsewhere. It was a turbulent time in religion, with the battle for the soul of Europe actually being fought on the ground, and all too easy for dangerous doctrines to be circulated and licensed, especially if the theologians were too overwhelmed with work to cope. Richelieu acted, therefore, and in 1623 a Board of four official censors was set up, consisting of André Du Val, Pierre Quedarne, Jacques Messier and François de St Père.

The Faculty was, of course, incensed at this intrusion into its ancient privileges, and so began a long struggle between its theologians and the Crown. The Faculty passed a resolution to restore its function as censor and the King did little at first, but then on 26 August 1624 he issued an Edict officially assigning the four-man Board a salary of 2,000 livres. The Faculty opposed ratification of the Edict by Parlement and found allies in Parlement who were equally opposed to the usurpation by the Crown of their own powers relating to censorship. The affair ended in anti-climax when the Keeper of the Seal temporized, delaying submission of the Edict before Parlement, and made reassuring noises to quiet the newly appointed Board, who solemnly renounced their intention of exercising their new powers.

A few years later the Crown returned to the attack. In

January 1629, article 52 of what was called the Code Michaux alluded to a great increase in clandestine publications, and proposed the following remedy:

> . . . We forbid printers to print or booksellers to sell any books or other writings without the name of the author or printer and without prior permission granted by Letters under our Great Seal which will not be granted before the text shall have been submitted to our Chancellor or to the Keeper of the Seal. They will commission whomsoever they think proper, according to the subject of the book, to read and examine it and then to release it in accordance with the requisite procedure, at which stage a licence will be granted. Two copies of the manuscript will be made, and one of them bearing the original certificate licensing it is to be kept by the bookseller or printer in whose name the said licence is granted.

This was the first official document to formalize censorship. The Chancellor chose the censors from the Faculty of Theology (which indicates a form of compromise). A document of 1633 reveals that Morel and Grandin, doctors of theology, received salaries from the Office of the Seal which suggests that Chancellor Séguier had taken censorship back into his own hands, a theory supported by the fact that in the Jansenist controversy and in the early days of the Fronde uprising a statement by the Faculty accuses the two men by name of having accepted the Chancellor's commission verbally (that is, secretly) and taken a salary for carrying out duties to the detriment of the Faculty's traditional prerogatives.

Were secular books scrutinized in the same way? We know that in the 16th century the Maîtres des Requêtes had duties of this kind, even to the surveillance of theological censors, but loss of the Chancellery archives makes it impossible to know for certain. The names of the King's secretaries who signed the licences are often those of specialists in various fields: Nicolas Renouard, a cousin and patron of the translator, Claude Binet, a poet in the Ronsard tradition; Olier, son of a high official in the Chancellery and brother of the Oratory's founder; Conrart and Pellisson, King's secretaries and of the Académie Française—no coincidence, that—and Louis Cramoisy, brother of the publisher, and Beaugrand, mathematician and friend of Mersenne. Descartes in one of his letters writes that Beaugrand was specifically ordered by Séguier to examine his *Dioptrique* and two other treatises, and that Séguier himself read the *Discours de la méthode*. Obviously the Chancellor had people capable of giving an opinion on a variety of subjects, mostly secretaries to the Crown, and in cases which might prove difficult he read himself or called in specialists. A 1633 list of pensioners' names, in addition to scrutineers of theological works, Baudoin, Colletet, l'Estoile and Pierre Blaise, must mean they were censors.

A letter from Mersenne to Descartes in 1637 gives us an idea how censorship was organized: "At no time has there ever been such strict watch on books. The Chancellor employs trusted agents to pass judgment on works of theology or politics, and the Académie is his instrument for censorship of verse and literary prose; for sciences he employs mathematicians." Fears about the real purpose of the Académie Française would appear to be justified. Séguier was acting pragmatically all the time, with the expediency that characterizes holders of high office, deflecting opposition he could not overcome directly, and in the secrecy of his Department laying the foundations of a powerful agency of censorship that would flourish later under Colbert. Recent investigation by French scholars reveals his deep distrust of anything emanating from Italy.

2. Licensing and privilege

The assigning of exclusive rights and privilege in the printing and sale of a book for a specified period, so preventing others from printing and profiting from the same work, was another aspect of the control system, in France and abroad. Royal policy differed in the periods 1598–1630 and 1630–1643 when Richelieu came to power, and Letters Patent granting monopolies reveal a variety of different kinds: firstly, but less usual, a blanket privilege to authors who were deemed trustworthy, for all their works, past, present and future; secondly, privileges in new books, and, rarest of all, privileges in new impressions.

The monopoly was usually granted in new books for a period of five to ten years, rarely longer, but there was evidently no definite rule. The size and importance of the work was taken into consideration as well as its potential public. The large and learned folios intended for the international market, orthodox and scholarly, were favored especially when they were costly to produce and hard to sell; illustrated books fell into this category because they were also costly to produce.

The period of privilege was not usually long. The *Introduction à la vie dévote* went into what might be called the public domain after only six years; Benet of Canfield's *Rule of perfection* and Binet's *Essai des merveilles de la nature* after ten, and Camus's devotional books after six or eight years, without any prolongation. The same applied to plays and novels. Booksellers tended to print the words "Avec privilège du Roi" on the title page to discourage pirated versions, but with only a temporary right in their publications they could not afford to pay their authors much, with the results we have seen—authors seeking patronage of aristocrats or the Crown. Sometimes licences were granted for older works, and the State extended licensing beyond the limits embodied in the Edicts of 1563 and 1566, an important question which we need to examine further.

Two different categories of books were affected: church books and books already in the public domain, or whose authors were revising with a new edition in mind for which they wanted an extension of the privilege. In the case of church service books it is instructive to trace the history of those revised according to the Roman use after the Council of Trent—the "Rome prayerbooks" as they were called. The King granted a privilege to French publishers, giving them a better chance in competition with foreigners through protection, and at the same time insuring control of liturgical practice. For the beneficiaries, the Compagnie des Usages (The Prayerbook Society), there were clear advantages, but naturally those who were excluded from such blessings were in furious opposition; e.g., the University Faculty of Theology and the Parlement of Paris, which was hostile on principle to printing regulations coming from the royal Court. They hated monopolies and were chauvinist about the liturgy, hostile to the introduction of Roman use in France. Every time the privileges enjoyed by the Compagnie des Usages came up for renewal, they questioned the basis on which they were granted. In 1596 the King's Council hesitated over renewal, and in 1603 Henri IV refused to renew it beyond 1st January 1605 when the Vatican was revising the liturgy again, which meant changing the prayerbooks. This was a temporary victory for the opponents of privilege, but in 1614 the Estates General again won confirmation of the privilege in conditions that are of some interest.

The Assemblé du Clergé was planning to reissue Plantin's Polyglot Bible and sponsor publication of the Greek and Latin Fathers, and forced the government to go back on its decision of twelve years before. They offered any publisher who would undertake to issue the learned works of the Fathers a thirty-year privilege in the Roman prayerbooks. Four companies were formed and a contract signed with the largest of them—the leading Paris firms and Cardon of Lyons. This was the second Compagnie des Usages, and the constituent parties sought ratification by Parlement on so important an agreement; it was made a condition of it. To facilitate its passage they voted the sum of 8,000 livres to defray De La Mothe's expenses in securing Parlement's support, but the jingoists in Parlement did not yield an inch, and eventually what remained of the 8,000 livres was returned to the partners in the Compagnie, and the contract was never carried out.

There were two clearly opposed viewpoints in the fight over the Roman prayerbooks: Parlement's, supported by the book trade acting in accordance with medieval concepts of corporate principles and proper division of labor, and the Crown's, which took a broader view of the national interest in planning the best possible standards in the home product and obstructing foreign imports which would be a drain on available resources of money, even if it meant that a monopoly made missals and breviaries dearer. However, though the Clergé's scheme failed, it sowed the seeds of new ideas, namely that in exchange for a privilege in one field booksellers might agree to publish books of general interest more readily. We shall see how Richelieu and Colbert took up this idea and made it a cornerstone of their policy vis-à-vis the book trade.

The question of books in print and extension of privilege was more complicated. Parlement again tried to restrict the application of principles laid down by royal edicts in the 16th century, or at least to block any further developments on those lines, and by a decree of 1578 forbade any extension in the case of a new edition unless that edition had been considerably revised. In 1586 the booksellers Du Puis and Beys were authorized to publish Seneca's works revised by Muret, for which their colleague Nicolas Nivelle had a patent even though the works had already appeared in Rome; thus it was established that it was not lawful to seek a privilege in a book published abroad, even if it had not been previously published in France.

The Crown resisted extension of privilege or licensing of books in print and in 1595 did not renew the monopoly granted in 1586 to the Compagnie du Navire to publish Patristic texts which had already been published in Rome and Antwerp; the same restrictive tendencies are apparent here as in the case of the Roman prayerbooks. But if an author or publisher sought an extension of copyright for a new edition or revision of a book, the same restrictions did not apply, and a patent was issued without objection. Parlement was quite willing to support legally any applicant anxious to secure his rights. In this way Mlle. de Gournay secured a series of privileges in Montaigne's *Essays* even before each one had expired, so keeping the entire text in her hands in successive editions. Ronsard's friend Jean Galland was granted a perpetual monopoly in the poet's works "for certain considerations and as a special favor," and another bookseller, Jean de Bordeaux, secured the copyright of Du Bartas's *Works* in folio in 1609, a project that had not hitherto been attempted.

Extensions of privilege in collections of legal precedents or

Statutes were quite normal: Charondas Le Caron, Louet and Bacquet, for instance, and for revised editions of Ambroise Paré or Calepin's *Dictionarium octo linguarum;* and the same was true in the case of new translations of existing works and revisions of old translations, from French versions of the catechism and the works of Luis de Granada to Renouard's translation of Ovid's *Metamorphoses.* None of this was strictly logical since the privilege tended to protect a revised version of an earlier work rather than a new one. Sometimes copyright in a new version proscribed earlier ones if they were felt to be inimical, as the case of Mettayer, the King's Printer and a zealous monarchist, clearly shows: he published a translation of Du Laurens's works by Théophile Gelée, and not only was the translation made Mettayer's sole property but any other versions of the same author's works in Latin or French were forbidden. In the case of legal precedents and Statutes the same ban applied—no earlier versions might be reprinted, and though the Letters Patent are not precise on this point, Parlement appears to have deemed it unlawful to put out editions that might rival those already enjoying a monopoly assigned by the Crown. It was an equivocal situation, with some publishers securing lucrative privileges despite the atmosphere of restriction.

Although in theory there was to be no abuse of privilege, and most books, usually the smallest sizes, were hardly ever granted any extensions, the royal will was inclined to hinder foreign imports on sound mercantilist principles, and the government acted against common practices in the trade that they thought harmful. When Pierre de Besse informed the King that some of his titles in the public domain were being reprinted abroad at Douai in Spanish territory and exported to France, he promptly received an exclusive privilege covering his early books as well as his new titles; and when Lipsius was about to entrust his great edition of Seneca to his friend Plantin in 1605, the King issued a patent to Chevallier in respect of that work, to avoid "money being diverted from the kingdom."

Among all these conflicting cases it may be wondered how far publishers sought personal favors or took advantage of any lack of vigilance by the Chancellery. Those who felt themselves disadvantaged by the regulations naturally turned to piracy, especially in areas distant from Paris. Lawsuits multiplied significantly from 1610 to 1620, and more decrees were issued to establish new legal status. The popular *Astrée* of Honoré d'Urfé was a case in point. After he had written the first two parts, d'Urfé, a Gentleman in Ordinary of the King's Bedchamber, was granted a ten-year privilege which he transferred to his publisher Du Bray. Shortly before it expired, d'Urfé completed the third part of the work and Du Bray obtained a licence for the entire work for a further ten years, ratified by Parlement. The instant success of *Astrée* prompted Ouyn, a Rouen bookseller, to anticipate the expiry of the first licence and, without waiting for any further developments, he reissued the first two parts. The Guild wanted to make an example and were happy to make things awkward for d'Urfé when he complained about the reprints (he demanded high prices for his manuscripts). He took his complaint to the Court of Requests, the highest authority in such matters, but his licence was confirmed only in the case of the first two parts of the novel, not the third.

Attempts to restore the monopoly in Roman prayerbooks also failed, and Parlement ratified a licence granted the Superior of the Célestin order in France for the publication of their own prayerbooks, but denied a request for an extension by Langelier's widow for Seneca's works. A general attack on abuses of privilege was launched, and restraints imposed under Article 33 of the 1618 Statutes of the Guild were repealed. The Chancellor presumably had either the public interest in mind in wishing to see better editions in print, or was aiming to check imports of foreign books. Specially advantageous conditions were sometimes granted, but on the whole he sought to enforce the law, and resisted the practice of extending licences without a great deal of revision of the original text. When the Chancellery deviated from this principle without valid reasons, the Parlement or the Court of Requests invariably quashed the decision, with the eventual result that most new books came into the public domain within five or ten years, quite a short time.

It prompts the conclusion that book trade regulation was

liberal, and that seems to harmonize with a slow but general improvement in the intellectual climate of Europe at that time. The international book trade and the interchange of ideas between nations was not so fatally damaged as before by the old barriers of language, censorship and wars. There was considerable optimism in the book trade and hopes of good business ahead as a result of the many new libraries created in the religious orders, old and new, and the Jesuit colleges needed huge supplies of books. In the case of current publications, and especially French books, there was a buoyant market when privileges ran out, and new works could expect a promising future with such limitations on monopoly and copyright. There was little for the trade to complain about. Paris was particularly well placed to supply the export trade, and the good faith and reliability of businessmen made up for the law's delays and deficiencies, since with an encouraging atmosphere for trade most publishers shunned the pirating of colleagues' property, in the common interest.

The period of the Catholic Revival, the last phase of the Renaissance, could be said to be a time when the Crown was prudent about intervention in the trade, preferring to act strictly through the law, and not yet motivated by political expediency.

A change in the Crown's attitude is evident a little later, if we examine the licences issued from 1630 to 1635. The still delicate question of the Roman prayerbooks came up again when Pope Urban VIII ordered another revision—it meant that all the dioceses would have to change their service books yet again. Richelieu issued a patent by which publishers of the new prayerbook would be granted an exclusive monopoly for thirty years, and in November 1631 he specified who those publishers would be: Claude and Sébastien Chappelet, Michel and Jean Sonnius, Sébastien and Gabriel Cramoisy, Robert Fouet, Antoine Vitré, Charles Morel, Etienne Richer, Eustache Foucault, Guillaume Le Bé, and the widows Méjat, Buon and de Varennes. As a *quid pro quo* the partners in this, the third Compagnie des Usages, would undertake to publish books in a number of oriental languages, for use in the Eastern missions planned by Richelieu and Father Joseph, an echo of the idea first proposed by the Assemblée du Clergé in 1614, as Richelieu's own publisher, Sébastien Cramoisy, no doubt reminded him.

From publishers not on the favored list, thirty altogether, there came opposition, declaring the patent illegal and the licence invalid and pointing out in their deposition that there were five widows, six childless sexagenarians, eight people drawn from three families owning three bookshops, and three relatives of the Sonnius clan, three of Cramoisy and two of the Chappelet families. If the scheme went through, they declared, "10,000 families will be in despair." In a shrewd plan to divide the opposition the Compagnie gave a share to its leader, Cottereau, and secured a decree of Privy Council affirming the patent valid. From then on it was a matter of conciliating Parlement, but Parlement refused to ratify. The Crown was by this time much stronger than in the days of the Regency, and the Privy Council allowed the Compagnie to institute proceedings if necessary. This is probably why Blaisot went ahead and published a Roman breviary to test the validity of the patent. Parlement backed down, found Blaisot guilty of infringing the monopoly, but did reduce the licence period to nine years.

Despite Richelieu's power, the Compagnie's grip was loosened even more by having to make concessions to Lyons publishers to secure their compliance. The really significant factor in all these vicissitudes is the favor shown by the King to the publishers—the most prosperous firms in the trade in fact—who were his supporters. They gained sweeping profits from the most lucrative area of publishing—books used in church.

From 1635 licences were granted for longer periods, which might imply pressure from the literary lions around Séguier—Conrart, Cureau de la Chambre, and perhaps Corneille and Gomberville, the only writers to gain from such a move. But not so. Cramoisy had a twenty-year patent on *Anthologia latinarum locutionum* and obtained another on *Concilia Galliae;* moreover, the period allowed for Cornelius a Lapide's *Commentaries* was increased from six to fifteen years. In 1636 Jean Billaine secured a patent for the offices of the Benedictines which effectively put the monopoly of missals and probably of breviaries into his hands. After this there is much bending of rules, and the Chancellor adopts new tactics: in 1641 Séguier resumed a policy which had been in abeyance for fifteen years and granted Cramoisy, acting for the monopoly Compagnie du Navire, all rights in five of the most important Fathers—Augustine, Bernard, Ambrose, Gregory and Jerome. Gervais Alliot was granted exclusive rights in a popular work, Marchant's *Hortus pastorum,* and Billaine's patent in Benedictine service books was reaffirmed. Pierre Blaise, son of Thomas Blaise, Séguier's librarian, was granted rights for twenty years in Ribadeneyra's *Fleur des saints,* Sébastien Huré in Luis de Granada's works, and Michel Soly was granted rights in Daniel Sennert's works; other lesser concessions were granted to La Peirère, Chastelain, Chaudière and Guédois.

All the books mentioned above were in the public domain or were just about to be generally available, and all were best-sellers, so it is not hard to imagine the feelings of the disadvantaged brethren at this change in policy, a change that was the prelude to a long sequel.

Richelieu and Séguier made good use of publishing privileges in 1630 and in 1643; the facts are plain. After 1635 the Thirty Years War badly disrupted the old commercial networks and compounded a crisis in the trade, already inflamed by economic depression. In these circumstances the French Crown adopted quite clear policies, to give all-out support to the publishers it trusted most, the influential and prosperous firms, those in short most intimately bound up with power, and—in the literal sense—privilege.

3. Publishers' rights and privilege

Meanwhile the civil and religious powers had their own official printers and publishers, and collaborated closely with them. The King's Printers, though in some cases they did not have their own printing shop, were a part of the royal household with all the prerogatives. They enjoyed a monopoly of all government and official publications, and the accruing profits, which the surviving accounts of the time prove to have been high; the ceaseless government publishing machine ensured them their fortunes. The firms were often owed many thousands of livres by the Crown, and sale of royal proclamations, a desirable source of income, stirred the anger and jealousy of less favored publishers. Who were the Kings' Printers? Ballard was official music publisher to His Majesty, and the others were Pierre l'Huillier, Jamet Mettayer and his son Pierre, Féderic Morel II and III. After l'Huillier's death in 1611, Mettayer and Morel kept official publishing in their own hands, and in 1613 Antoine Estienne was appointed King's Printer, though he was unable to act in this capacity until 1619. In 1629 Sébastien Cramoisy, by dint of family connections and government favors, was sole printer of the royal mint, and from 1633 was King's Printer when Mettayer and Morel disappeared from the scene.

Chancellor Séguier granted exclusive rights in the printing of royal Acts to Antoine Estienne, Sébastien Cramoisy, Pierre Rocollet, Sébastien Chappelet and Antoine Vitré, by now all too familar names. Antoine Estienne was especially favored and was saved from bankruptcy several times by timely intervention of the Privy Council (he was under the special protection of Cardinal Du Perron), and Cramoisy, Vitré and Rocollet were in regular correspondence with the Chancellor. Cramoisy was personal publisher to Richelieu, and like Rocollet lost no opportunity to court favor of the Cardinal. The Crown was creating an elite which in return for marked financial advantage could assure support in a sensitive field, communications; a policy was ripening that was to have consequences in later years.

The Church, the other arm of the Establishment, also intervened in the affairs of the trade, through the medium of its Assemblée du Clergé. As the chief representative of the body of the Church in France the Assemblée was wealthy and influential, employing many printers and publishers to disseminate its official documents and multifarious litera-ture. Antoine Estienne, with Cardinal Du Perron's support, was appointed official printer to the Assemblée and, after his bankruptcy, Vitré, who ousted Cramoisy—all of them fighting for the juicy bone. The Assemblée's printer was not only responsible for their publishing but curiously enough was also steward and butler, and so must have known these worldly prelates intimately. Vitré seems to have been in the confidence of the Jansenist faction, and in effect their publisher, and he issued the second edition of Petrus Aurelius on the orders of the Assemblée.

The Clergé de France kept a close watch on publishing and financed favored firms. They loaned 3,000 francs to the first Compagnie des Usages and played an important part in creating the second; they opposed the plan to form the third Compagnie when it was clear that the monopoly would raise the price of prayerbooks. They were behind the big program of Counter-Reformation propaganda and underwrote the best publishers, ensuring that their equipment was of the highest class, bringing back the famous Grecs du Roi from Geneva, and preventing the export of Savary de Brèves's oriental founts. They supported the weighty publication of the Fathers' ancient texts, especially the Greek Fathers, to replace what they called the "faulty" Protestant editions from Geneva, London and Frankfurt. They loaned Morel 8,000 livres, free of interest, to help publish a monumental edition of St. John Chrysostom, and renewed it several times as costs spiraled, in face of bids from other publishers, and they commissioned Morin of the Oratory and Aubert, Canon of Paris, to edit scholarly works. They were a looming influence on the publishing world. Cramoisy was not so keen to get involved in the huge series of Patrology and instead sponsored a collected edition of the French historians edited by Du Chesne, a sign of the times, but the Clergé, urged on by Montchal, archbishop of Toulouse, determined to launch the Fathers and commissioned Vitré to undertake publica-tion, with Henri de Valois as editor. This type of massive publications program was only possible through public bodies; no individual publisher could afford the huge outlay.

The Clergé de France also paid salaries to writers for work done on their behalf and gave liberally to authors whose work they approved. Diocesan clergy and religious orders were on good terms with publishers, the former being particularly concerned with prayerbooks, and they would have a local printer issue a prayerbook with modifications based on local use if they did not agree with the Roman use. This would be a lucky windfall for a local printer because a breviary or missal meant several months' work with good remuneration, since the bishop or local chapter would advance him the price of the paper or pay for part of the edition in exchange for a certain number of copies. The Clergé were responsible for most of the large orders and employed two technically fine printers, though not very good editors, Raulin Thierry and Eustache Foucault. From 1634 we find the old firms, Cramoisy and Vitré, carrying out the same orders for the Paris diocese, with Clopejau specializing in "red" prayerbooks. The contracts (for 1634, 1650 and 1660) stipulate very large orders, with the attendant profits on guaranteed sales and slight risk.

Cramoisy again took the lion's share of work for religious houses. He had been the Cistercians' publisher since 1612, helped to this prize by his cousin Pierre Nivelle, and later he published for the Cluniacs and Praemonstratensians, exporting their service books abroad and in France, as his correspondence with Moretus shows. He was in receipt of big orders from Cluniac, Cistercian and Praemonstratensian abbeys.

The Billaine family also did well out of profitable contracts for the religious: Jean was sole printer to the Benedictine order and enjoyed a monopoly in their prayerbooks; in addition to this he published the Maurist scholars, and when the Benedictines founded libraries in their monasteries he was the one who furnished them with books. His fortune was made.

But above all it was the Jesuits who prosecuted a full publishing program, for their numerous colleges and missions; the writing of textbooks and grammars, and a plethora of devotional literature kept the presses busy. Usually the printer nearest their colleges received orders for the textbooks, and this, coupled with new sciences and new interest in history and geography, brought prosperity to the trade. The Jesuits had a very definite book policy, and Parlement as early as 1608 granted Jesuits the right to choose their own printers and forbade others to print for them—in a way a kind of decentralization by recruiting local printers who were often former pupils of Jesuit schools. For major theological studies they looked elsewhere, and since most leading theologians were Italian or Spanish, it was in those countries that such material was published, with emphasis on spiritual-ity and relations between spiritual and temporal powers, a delicate subject in the newly emergent nation-states of Europe. The Provincials of the Order turned to publishers in Cologne, Antwerp and Lyons, especially the last because of its geographical position and welcome absence of a Parle-ment or university which might have resisted their publica-tion methods. In Paris the Jesuits employed leading firms to publish accounts of their foreign missions and books by members of the circle close to Fronton Du Duc and Sirmond of Clermont College, and were cautious about books which might give offense to the Parlement or the University Faculty of Theology. The more orthodox booksellers, Cramoisy, Sonnius and Chappelet, were given plenty of work—they were, after all, descendants of the publishers who had worked for the Catholic League—and the correspondence between Cramoisy and the General of the Order reveals the degree of esteem the Jesuits had for Cramoisy.

4. Policing the book trade

Every new book had to be licensed to see the light of day. At first, censors were not appointed by the King; any doctor of theology could certify approval and a privilege would automatically be granted, though some books were pub-lished even without that formality. No permit was needed for a book less than forty pages long, which colporteurs would sell, and there was no real control over books imported from abroad. Preventive censorship hardly existed in early days, as L'Estoile's *Journal,* written in Henri IV's reign, suggests: books and pamphlets were hawked about the Palais and city streets, and newsbooks printed in Frankfurt and elsewhere circulated in Paris; anyone wishing to keep up to date with affairs in England, or the Low Countries or Venice, could do so at little risk. Indeed Henri IV is said to have relished the satires and lampoons published about his courtiers, though he was not amused when he saw a piece called *Henri's incestuous marriage to Marie de Medicis,* published in Rouen by Adrien de Launay. Bold or offensive pamphlets had to be circulated covertly, of course.

Henri IV was careful not to stir up the religious passions of an earlier generation which had torn France apart. He prevented Parlement from proceeding against a book called *Amphitheatrum honoris* by Siribanus, an Antwerp Jesuit, and he had a printer imprisoned who was suspected of publishing a pamphlet against Jesuits, but far more typical of that period was the action of the Châtelet or Parlement in refraining from interference in publishing, though punishment for misdemeanors in that trade was their prerogative.

Things changed after Henri's assassination. On 8 June 1610, Parlement condemned Mariana's *De rege et regis institutione,* but the Regent Mother intervened to quash the charge at the request of the Papal Nuncio. A decree was issued against Bellarmine's *Tractatus summi Pontificis* and the Chancellor ordered a stay of proceedings following further pressure by the Nuncio. Parlement forbade publication of Father Coton's *Requête à la Reyne Mère et Régente de France* in its original form, and Coton's friends persuaded the Lieutenant of the Châtelet to seize *Anticoton* and some Gallican pamphlets from a bookseller called Du Carroy, occupied his house after he fled, and hounded both him and his son.

The Faculty of Theology and Parlement, staunchly chauvinist, were quick to outlaw any books with Ultramontane tendencies, including: *Réponse apologétique à l'Anticoton* and *Troise très excellentes prédications* by Spanish Dominicans, Sponde's *Annales ecclesiastici,* Becanus's *Controversia Anglicana* and Suarez's *Defensio fidei catholicae . . . adversus Anglicanos.* The situation was explosive and the Faculty even censored a book by one of its own, Edmond Richer, the *De ecclesiastica et politica potestate,* the action duly confirmed by Parlement. Controversy with Protestants began again; the Faculty vainly tried to suppress unrest after Henri's murder and imprisoned Gilles Robinot for publishing *Triomphes du Roi* despite a royal license, a book by the abbé de La Frenade which contained "vengeful slanders" against the State. In 1611 Duplessis-Mornay published *Mysterium iniquitatis,* which was immediately condemned, but when Berjon published a tract by Du Moulin against the King of England, the Regent Mother only advised more moderation; it was only after 1613 that vigorous measures were taken against this Calvinist bookseller who was protected by an influential faction at Court. The Châtelet and Parlement tried and failed to make an example of five Paris booksellers and made little headway with their list of undesirable books presented to the Guild with a request for their confiscation. Jean Richer, editor of the *Mercure français,* was prosecuted without result. Among the powers that be it was recognized that reform of the book trade was overdue.

The Statute of 1618 was the result, whereby the Guild of Stationers was subject to corporate control by new regulations, some to regulate the activities of hawkers and others relating to books imported from abroad—no such book was to be sold without prior inspection by a member of the Guild Council. This was passed when de Luynes was in power, despite the opposition from pamphleteers, three of whom (the Siti brothers and the poet Etienne Durand) were sentenced to a flogging for "libels" and one hanged, but hostility to the Queen Regent's favorite deepened and more severe measures were imposed, ordering the Civil Lieutenant to bring to justice any who "print, publish and sell defamatory libels." Stronger measures were also taken against banned books, and hawkers caught with them were threatened with flogging. Berjon and Petit were in trouble for "printing libels" and Berjon was given 24 hours to dismantle his press. After another case Parlement decreed that no printer, bookseller or colporteur could print or sell or otherwise distribute any publication failing to include the name of printer and author. Handwritten newsletters were banned and booksellers and printers encouraged to have their premises in the university quarter.

Such measures infallibly testify to disorder in the trade and the helplessness of the authorities in the face of disobedience. The clique of courtiers who surrounded the monarch were outraged by the activities of the "libelers" and satirists who flourished in the Regency period, when Vanini went to the stake for his freethinking in Toulouse and de Viau's contests with the State began through his evasion of the regulation about submission of manuscripts before publication. He certainly would not have shown the compromising passages in his *Parnasse satyrique* to Estoc and Sommaville before it was published, and it is worth noting that the two wealthy supporters of the Establishment who appeared for the prosecution at his trial, Rocollet and Vitré, went on to enjoy the fruits of such collaboration in high places for years afterwards.

The Théophile affair, and the episode of Fontanier's torture in the Place de Grève in 1621, mark a new phase in the struggle for free thought just as Richelieu's rise to power is another chapter in the story of the underground press, when even authors of some social eminence found that they were not beyond the law, as Ossat's *Letters* (referring to delicate negotiations conducted by Henri IV) clearly proved. The iron hand of censorship is now heavy on France, and when political pamphlets and ribald songs circulated in the civil wars of the Regency period there is immediate muzzling of the press by a string of decrees, edicts and judgments in court making it ever more hazardous to attempt illegal publishing: no publication without authorization is the watchword. Yet even Richelieu, with all his powers and his agents, found it hard to keep total control of the press. The Chancellery under Séguier was continually reviewing the situation, and in 1636 a systematic censorship was imposed, still without much effect. Not for another thirty years was control at all effective.

5. *The Imprimerie Royale*

No study of royal policy and the book trade can ignore the Imprimerie Royale. When it was founded in 1640 Richelieu was at the height of his power and the trade in a critical state after complete disruption by the Thirty Years War and its ruinous effect on the export of big-scale publications which were so costly to produce. The great editions of the Fathers were a matter of pride to the government, not only as part of their Catholic heritage but as examples of French scholarship, and the crowning achievement was the Polyglot Bible, seen as a rival to Plantin's. One way to establish national standards for such enterprises was by the creation of a Crown Printing and Publishing Office, and here the guiding spirit was Sublet de Noyers, Superintendent of Public Works, whose brief was to encourage new industry. If the highest standards of skill in book production could be combined with the finest scholarship, that would surely be the best way to restore France's position as cultural leader of Europe, and at the same time the most efficient way to raise the standard of the printers' art.

Two plans were submitted, the first proposing a workshop of twenty presses, and two official bookshops (like Her Majesty's Stationery Office, UK) in the Rue St. Jacques and the Palais. The workshop would be called the "Manufacture Royale d'Imprimerie," and would publish new works and reprint old ones, would have the monopoly of official publications, and instead of a King's Printer there would be a corps of authorized printers stationed in the new "Manufacture." The second plan, possibly coming from Estienne, was for a plant with thirty presses, a room for proof correctors, a library for use by scholars and specialist advisers to the press, a workshop for type founders, stores, and bookshops. This plan also envisaged a foundry for the making of "new Greek, Hebrew, Latin, French and Arab types," recalling that there were as many skilled type founders in Paris as there had been in the 16th century. The cost was estimated at 100,000 livres. To make it viable the King was to grant the Imprimerie Royale exclusive monopoly in dictionaries and lexicons in Greek, Latin and French, and in the Bible, decrees of the Church Councils and civil courts, and in the works of St. Thomas Aquinas.

The legal basis of the Imprimerie is a mystery. No official Act was passed nor was Parlement's ratification sought. Perhaps Richelieu or his Minister responsible for it were anxious to avoid open confrontation with the Stationers' Guild, anticipating protests from the King's Printers (prominent members of the Guild), who would naturally fear the loss of their lucrative monopolies to the new Imprimerie. But a decision was taken and in 1639 the new institution created and staff appointed; Tanneguy Le Fèvre, a Protestant scholar, was made Director of Printing, and Raphael Trichet du Fresne was in charge of proof correcting. Sébastien Cramoisy was technical director but, possibly out of delicacy, did not assume the official title of Director, perhaps not wishing to upset his rivals, especially Antoine Estienne, who was probably involved in the initial planning. Edme Martin was given the post of Chief Printer, and Claude Cramoisy was general administrator, with Gabriel Cramoisy his deputy, the kind of neat family takeover under Sébastien that was so dear to Sébastien's own heart.

Assembling all the necessary equipment and installing it in the new premises occupied most of 1640. The Minister, Sublet de Noyers, was impatient at the (as he saw it) calculated delay in supplying paper—he suspected papermakers of conspiring to raise prices, and the Privy Council passed a decree denouncing "cabals and monopolies" formed with that objective, no doubt at the instigation of Paris publishers who did not enjoy any of the privileges of the Imprimerie's cosy coterie. Papermakers were making contracts with foreign buyers to sell them supplies as a priority, which meant precious paper was being diverted from France, just the very material needed by the new publishing house. The decree forbade owners and tenants of paper mills to export any paper before the Imprimerie Royale had been supplied. Eventually paper supplies came from the Auvergne and Limoges.

Cramoisy and de Noyers were supplying the new type founts, and gathered an impressive array of letter faces of 16th century masters—Garamond, Granjon and Le Bé—and Jean Janon, the only letter engraver of merit in the 17th century, was given the task of cutting six sets of Gros and Petit Canon in roman and italic. When Balthasar Moretus in Antwerp learned about the new type, he asked Cramoisy quite civilly if he might purchase the letter punches; Cramoisy's reply was to secure another Privy Council decree forbidding the unauthorized export of punches, matrices or founts, an act which only shows how aware of the Plantin-Moretus firm the French were, how jealous of them, and how ready to keep their own expertise at home. And they were quite willing to indulge in industrial espionage to discover the trade secrets of their rivals in the Low Countries: in June 1640 de Noyers wrote to the French ambassador there, asking him to find out the recipe for the black printer's ink used by the Dutch. Furthermore, the Ambassador was asked to recruit four pressmen and compositors locally who might be willing to come to France, terms reasonable, "on a private basis" (no mention of the Imprimerie Royale), but negotiated in Sébastien Cramoisy's name as if it were a private arrangement with an ordinary printing firm.

The Imprimerie opened in November 1640 and immediately began work on seven presses. The first book was a de luxe edition of the *Imitation of Christ* with a frontispiece depicting Louis XIII on his knees before a crucifix. After this came a Latin New Testament, then one in Greek, a Latin Bible in eight volumes, and monumental editions of Virgil, Horace, Suetonius, Terence, Juvenal and Persius, to show off the varieties of type in their armory. Richelieu's own works on religion were soon put into the new program as if to reflect some of the glory from his new brainchild.

There was a clear commitment to titles pleasing to the leading warriors in the Catholic Revival, massive luxury editions in folio, all splendid advertisements of French orthodoxy and French culture to show to the world. Nor was the new Imprimerie content to leave the Church Fathers to the existing experts at the Compagnie du Navire, but issued its own celebrated Byzantine series of the Greek Fathers, begun in 1645 under the direction of a Jesuit, Father Labbe, and then a collection of 37 volumes of Church Councils. The mountains labored, and there is no doubt about the high standard reached, the printing impeccable and illustrations fine, with Poussin tempted back from Rome temporarily to take charge of the art side and to design some frontispieces. The pity is that he did not stay longer and make his contribution as great as Rubens's was to Plantin's projects at Antwerp, but other painters and engravers were involved— Mellan (the best engraver of his day), and Duret, another engraver, Stella, a painter, Bosse, Nicolas Cochin and Le Brun all helped with the illustrations and decoration of the Imprimerie's books.

It was not a question of profitable monopolies—that was not the point. It was rather a matter of prestige and national pride, since there is little doubt the enterprise was run at a loss, the books being very costly to produce, occupying much time and selling very slowly. The King was probably the best customer, asking Cramoisy to furnish him with a presentation copy of this or that work to hand to visiting royalty or bestow as a mark of favor. In 1670 the emporia which were part of the Imprimerie still had copies in stock of books published twenty and thirty years earlier in unrealistic editions of 1,000 or 1,500. Losses to the Treasury were considerable, the outlay between 1640 and 1646 being 354,000 livres and sales only 60,000 livres. After Richelieu's death and de Noyers' departure, it fell into discredit, and Cramoisy had to fund expenses from his own pocket. In short, the venture was obviously a propaganda machine for the French Crown, in part an answer to Plantin-Moretus, Richelieu's bête-noire, because that firm had supported Marie de Medici's and Mathieu de Morgues' campaigns against him. Richelieu hoped to provide the King with great publications which would enhance the Crown and help with its public relations in dealing with the rest of Europe.

Other matters that were to affect the future of publishing in France can be associated with these years: censorship grew more stringent, the *Gazette* began its long history, and the Académie Française was founded. The Imprimerie was yet another factor in the aggrandizement of France.

PART TWO

THIRD SECTION
SOCIETY AND THE BOOK

It has to be remembered that even in these early days of the printed book, in the 16th century they poured from the presses in hundreds of millions. Nor was the book, in the words of a 17th-century Paris bookseller, a "consumable" product; most of the books published continued to be used and reused, passing through many hands, circulating through the trade. About 25,000 new titles were published in Paris between 1598 and 1643, and totals of books published in other towns of France and in the major centers abroad added huge quantities to the international output. Which begs some questions: For whom were the books intended? From what social classes did the readers come? What issues of the day were of concern to them? What forms of culture did the books reflect? What was the proportion of old and new books in the libraries—will their holdings tell us anything about reading tastes? What intellectual and religious interests did readers have? Which books banned during the Counter Reformation were still available from earlier times? How was the reading public in Paris affected by the new directions in publishing? And foreign books—how far did they influence new and heterodox thought in France? Can we trace evidence of reactionary or progressive attitudes in readers?

Fascinating questions to which some answers can be attempted.

One way to assess the reading taste of that distant age is by a scrutiny of extant library catalogs, which in general record two kinds of collections, either the library of a religious foundation or the private library of a bibliophile or scholar—after all, there were no public libraries to supply research needs. Other information can be gleaned from the inventories and wills which list the personal collections of some deceased individuals, and they come from all classes, sometimes recording only a handful of books, sometimes numbered in hundreds and even thousands, but in every case direct testimony to the actual reading habits of our ancestors.

CHAPTER I

LIBRARIES

BIBLIOGRAPHICAL RECORDS improved in the first half of the 17th century to cope with the increased output of books. The Renaissance had been the age of the "amateur," like Montaigne who described his tastes at length in his essays. Justus Lipsius traced the history of libraries in the Classical period in the hope of encouraging his contemporaries to follow their illustrious predecessors, and there were even manuals of library economy. Guides to books often included some account of libraries and we have a precious glimpse of some Parisian and other French libraries in Father Jacob's *Traité des plus belles bibliothèques* (1644). He claimed that "the kingdom of France excels all others in its learning and its libraries," chiefly to be found in Paris, and interestingly he took the figure of 4,000 volumes as minimum for a good library, reckoning that there were 90 such in Paris. In 1651 La Fizelière mentioned 76 "large" libraries in his *Rymailles des plus célèbres bibliothèques de Paris,* from which we may infer that Jacob's figure was correct.

1. Ecclesiastical libraries

The history of church libraries shows them quickly making good the losses in the Wars of Religion, when they were often simply abandoned or became ruinous, while libraries unaffected by the troubles started a new phase of growth, as the Célestins, the Carmelites of the Place Maubert and the St. Victoire Abbey did. Monks were busy restocking libraries that had suffered damage, repairing books and restoring buildings, compiling catalogs, searching for new additions to stock or encouraging donations from vanity or piety. The St.

Germain des Prés library was restored by Luc d'Achery, and Richelieu ordered a new building for the growing library of the Sorbonne, which received big bequests from Claude Morel, Claude Héméré and Michel Le Masle, as well as a major share of the Cardinal's own books. The Franciscan library, destroyed by fire in 1580, was reorganized and rebuilt with a stock of 4,000 in 1643, and grew to 7,000 a few years later. Having lost all its books St. Geneviève Abbey was replenished by Cardinal de la Rochefoucauld as part of his reform of the old place, and eventually had a stock of 8,000. The old wounds were healed. Architects made provision for libraries in their plans for new religious foundations, often with well equipped quarters. The Little Augustines, founded in 1612 by Queen Marguerite in the Faubourg St. Germain, had 4,000 books by 1644 and the Barefoot Augustinians had a fine library by mid-century. The three Capuchin convents (in the Rue St. Honoré, Faubourg St. Jacques and the Marais) between them pos-sessed "a large number of books" in 1644; the Barefoot Carmelites' library in the Rue Vaugirard was famous; the Jacobins in the Rue St. Honoré had 4,000 volumes; while the Minims, thanks to Mersenne and his friends, included an outstanding scientific collection in their 8,000-volume library in the Place Royale.

The University colleges did little to restore their collec-tions, apart from Navarre and Harcourt, but of course the real renaissance was in the Jesuit and Oratory colleges. The latter were the inspiration of Bérulle in 1611, specializing in the literature of controversy, of which they had a collection of 6,000 books with a rare treasury of Eastern manuscripts bequeathed by Harlay de Sancy. The Jesuits were well aware of the value of a good library and their Clermont College library was probably the finest in Paris. After an unfortunate episode when some of their order were expelled, the library was besieged and virtually pillaged by collectors and book-sellers anxious for the spoils. It was poor consolation for them to have the Royal Library housed at Clermont for a time, but once they had returned to their college they set to work to rebuild the collection, with impressive results. Their school for novices was rebuilt on land given them by Louis

XIII opposite St. Paul's church, and books were bought from their funds; by 1643 they had a new library of 4,000 volumes and the new Clermont College, alongside the old one, had a very large library, soon to be one of the most important in Paris.

So after a period of poor provision compared with the Protestant libraries, so rich in science and new kinds of exegesis, the Catholic Church was rearming itself and soon had an arsenal from which to draw, all in aid of faith and scholarship in defence of the true religion.

2. *Personal collections*

In Father Jacob's bibliography of libraries, in addition to some twenty church libraries in Paris there are seventy private libraries, each of between 3,000 and 4,000 books, belonging to six Princes of the Blood, Ministers, Councillors of State, five Maîtres des Requêtes, eight Presidents of the courts, seven court officers, nine lawyers, two financiers, seven doctors and a score of theologians. We know many of their names: André Du Chesne and the brothers Sainte-Marthe; René Moreau, a doctor; Riolan, famous anatomist; Guy Patin and Jacques Mentel, Pierre Frizon, and Jean de Launoy. Scholars had their own collections, often better than the libraries they sometimes administered on behalf of aristocrats. Gabriel Naudé's personal library was of greater scope than President de Mesmes', for whom he acted as librarian, or indeed than those of a number of cardinals whom he served, including Mazarin. Other scholar-librarians with fine personal collections were the Dupuy brothers; the Royal Librarian, Jérôme Bignon, Director of the Royal publishing house, whose library argues a progressive spirit; Jean-Baptiste Haultin; and Jean Tilleman Stella, Richelieu's librarian. What we might call the first special libraries were started by enthusiastic amateurs, people like Claude Martin, a humble bachelor of medicine, Metz, Commissioner for War, and Claude Hardy, a mathematician and friend of Mersenne, all of whom had good collections of mathematics and related subjects. Oriental manuscripts were collected in the Far East and Middle East by bibliophiles like Claude

Hardy, Claude Chrestien and Gilbert Gaulmyn—free spirits, all of them, like Jean Bourdelot, doctor to the Prince of Condé, and indeed in all these amateurs there was (as there usually is) a touch of the free-thinker, the liberal and unorthodox. It is to them that we owe the preservation of the precious chain of challenging new thought deriving from the Italian Renaissance, which lay deep in their bookshelves when reaction was at its most virulent in France.

It is surprising how so many personal collectors afforded their books—the Dupuys were not wealthy, yet they owned a huge library of luxuriously bound volumes estimated at 20,000 écus. Others amassed collections at small expense, like Naudé, who seems to have had a collector's nose for rare items at low cost found in the bookstalls on the Pont Neuf, some from the early 16th century and now among the treasures of the Mazarin Library today, others picked up from libraries stripped during the Civil Wars. A happy time for bibliophiles! Many other names can be cited, all zealous collectors: de Mesmes and de Thou, the first Presidents of the Paris Parlement; Hurault de l'Hospital; Michel, the Chancellor's heir; Amelot de Beaulieu, first President of the Cour des Aides; Molé, Lauson, Longeuil, Phélypeaux, Harlay, Hector de Marle, Versigny, Faye d'Espeisses, and Du Tillet: a roll call of the upper echelon of state officials.

The nobility were not bookmen. Only one could be called a bibliophile, the Maréchal de Bassompière, but the royal princes inherited large libraries—from the Duc d'Angoulème, the natural son of Charles IX, to Gaston d'Orlèans, who did actively collect books and had them bound in rich calf with his monogram stamped on them. Richelieu, Chancellor Séguier and Cardinal Mazarin were all keen book collectors, and Richelieu employed distinguished scholars as his librarians, notably the Orientalist Gaffarel, Stella, the mathematician and diplomat, a Reader in the Collège Royale, and Hémeré, a Sorbonne theologian.

But why these private libraries? Was it a family tradition in the upper ranks of the Civil Service? It was. Unlike many aristocratic patrons they were genuine booklovers and scholars like Peiresc, and Du Tillet, one of the best historians, and of course many of the foundation members of the Académie Française (Molé, de Thou, the Comte d'Avaux, or the L'Hospital family). True, a demonstrable respect for conventional Humanist culture helped ambitions for promotion or a rise in social status, and we can observe vanity at work, a search for glory. In Naudé's pioneer manual of librarianship, *Avis pour dresser une bibliothèque,* written for his patron, President de Mesmes, "desire for fame" is listed as one of the motives for founding a book collection, and it is obvious that many of the books were what we would call "choice," that is, objects for display, the wealthy parvenu being more interested in the value of the binding than of the contents. Gaston d'Orléans was that rare bird, a prince of the royal line who was genuinely a bibliomane, ceaselessly searching for new additions to his library or his "cabinet of curiosities," a typical creation of the age, which of course later grew into our modern museums, now in public ownership. Séguier was a collector long before he attained high office, and once said, "if anyone wants to buy me he has only to offer me a book," which was literally true. During his advance through Normandy at the head of the royalist troops against the rebel magnates, he would often visit private collections in the vicinity and discuss their treasures, and no doubt terms. Richelieu was not quite so fanatical but did amass a large collection, partly from a sense of the prestige it conferred but also as a resource to supply his propaganda machine in the fight against Protestant heresies, and he availed himself of a big acquisition when La Rochelle fell. Most of the scientific and specialist theological works in that city's private hands went into Richelieu's private library, a profitable transfer.

Many factors, therefore, went into the making of these extensive and priceless (as it turned out) personal collections: zeal for learning, self-glorification, *noblesse oblige,* bookish traditions in the ranks of civil servants and the new interest in science. The King's Library, curiously enough, was not the largest or the most luxurious, with only a few thousand printed books (but a good collection of 4,500 manuscripts) despite the regulations governing Legal Deposit. Even his own librarians had better private collections than their master, but when the librarian Dupuy's own library was bequeathed to the King, it improved immediately and began to occupy a position worthy of the sovereign, annexing other libraries as they became available. Even in this highly personal field the State was imposing its sanctions.

3. Libraries for the use of scholars

Anyone of the twentieth century entering a typical private library of the 17th century would have been struck by the almost theatrical setting of extravagance. The Duc d'Or-léans' books in the Luxembourg were at the end of an enormous gallery hung with paintings by Rubens depicting the life of Marie de Medici, the shelves trimmed with green velvet. Séguier had two large salons painted by Vouet and other smaller apartments for his manuscripts. Cardinal Mazarin kept his library in a handsome gallery painted throughout with brilliant pictures; it is now part of the Bibliothèque Nationale. Even in religious houses artists contributed to their decoration, as in Clermont College whose library was paneled and with frescoes and monumen-tal Baroque wall and ceiling paintings, often used as a pictorial catalog. Libraries were often the repository of other materials: cases of medals and coins, curios, antiques, shells, and it was peculiarly the age of medallions, the basis of much antiquarian study, along with inscriptions. The house of the Minims in the Place Royale had cupboards full of medallions, and we know that in addition to his huge library, the Duc d'Orléans collected precious stones, engravings, bronzes, statues, bird and flower paintings on vellum—all without any system, shells next to marine instruments—the whole enter-prise being intended to dazzle the visitor.

Yet these were valuable for later generations and none more so than the books. On the library walls were pictures which were an iconography, a key to both contents and to the taste of the collectors; how they saw themselves and which writers they most approved. Naudé asserted that "we can judge the soul of an author from his books and his appearance from his picture," and Patin surrounded himself with what he called his "tutelary deities"—Erasmus, the two Scaligers, Montaigne, Muret, Charron, Paolo Sarpi, de Thou and Rabelais from the past, and Saumaise, Grotius, Naudé and Gassendi from his contemporaries. In Clermont College portraits of college patrons were hung—Richelieu and Fouquet by Le Brun, the great Jesuits Loyola and Francis Xavier (four pictures by Poussin), and the illustrious alumni of Clermont, Maldonado, Fronton Du Duc, Petau, Sirmond and Caussin. When the Sorbonne inherited Richelieu's library it included portraits of Platina, Bembo, Sadolet, Sigogne, Cujas, Filelfo, Petrus Victorius, Bessarion, Petrarch, Pithou, Bartole, Montaigne, Ermalao Barbaro, Boccaccio, Balde, Baronius, Charles d'Angennes, William Allen, Thomas More, Henry VIII and John Fisher.

In convents and monasteries theology and church history were the predominant subjects and at St. Germain des Prés, where the library was considered to be an "all-round collection," fifteen of the twenty-one classes were devoted to aspects of religion. Only in the late 17th century, when scholars and others anxious about their souls bequeathed books to convents, did the libraries of religious orders include literature and history, the Minims acquiring Father Nicéron and Mersenne's scientific collections, and the Jesuits always strong on the Humanities as part of their curricula.

Private libraries tended to be similar in composition, with on the whole wider scope. Naudé's library manual, *Avis pour dresser une bibliothèque,* appeared in 1627 and was reprinted in 1644, laying down principles to be adopted in creating a good library, following Montaigne's dictum that a heap of books is not a library. He recommended a wide range of books, ancient and modern, "chosen from the best current editions either in single volumes or sets with the best commentators in each subject." Of course it is assumed that "ancient" and "modern" authors will be in the original tongues, the Bible and Torah in Hebrew, the Fathers in Greek and Latin, Avicenna in Arabic, Dante, Petrarch and Boccaccio in Italian, but if a knowledge of Italian is lacking, then a translation in French is acceptable, an interesting sidelight on contemporary valuations of scholarship—while Hebrew is essential, it is no shame to be ignorant of a modern language like Italian. Dividing knowledge into Aristotle's main classes, Naudé counsels the acquisition of "the best work" in each subject field ("faculté"), with the best commentaries, and the "thinkers who have written on specific subjects" or who "put a contrary view most felicitously" or who "brought new ideas into the realms of knowledge" or who has opposed a theory with "proper cogency and reasoning," because "it encourages a timid and a servile spirit" if a writer is overlooked "simply because he is opposed to traditional authorities." There speaks the new age.

A library must embrace all human knowledge, in Naudé's view, meaning theology, medicine, jurisprudence, history and mathematics, but if a choice has to be made, then he advises the old masters in theology, law and the traditional sciences, but is happy to include recent writers and has a marked preference for the unorthodox, possibly due to his clear delight in Renaissance thought. Poets and historians are oddly excluded, no doubt a personal whim, because he was primarily a learned man of liberal mind steeped in a venerable classical tradition which tended to emphasize the permanent values and to see contemporary imaginative literature as frivolous. We find the same spirit in the private libraries, which were themselves the foundation of modern thought and the places where dissidents might find material for their controversial books.

The average bookseller could not meet the demands of the rare book collectors who ranged over Europe for their prizes—their letters are full of allusions to exciting discoveries or requests for their recipients to look out for this or that obscure item. Scholars were in constant correspondence, the early equivalent of *Transactions* and *Proceedings,* in journals, and discussion about books and the exchange of books made for strong bonds between them. Manuscripts were a source of particular interest, again a consequence of the Renaissance when manuscripts had revitalized classical studies. Bourdelot had 370 manuscripts, Tileman Stella 300, Trichet du Fresne 100, Mentel 136, and Naudé, Du Tillet and Bouillau each had a respectable number. Richelieu, Mazarin, Petau (a member of Parlement) and Séguier were all manuscript-fanciers, ever ready to deal with a fence (as at Fleury-sur-Loire) for the possible spoils of a ruined abbey or, like the Maurist monks, to offer a new printed book in exchange for a manuscript from a neglected corner of a monastic chest. The dispersal of the Clermont library after the Jesuits' expulsion, or the same fate which overtook Mazarin's library in the Fronde troubles, might seem like vandalism to us, but it was a passionate age, and unscrupulous. Ismaël Bouillau visited Italy on behalf of the Dupuys looking for manuscripts, and reported that convents were ill-guarded, with no impediments to his work on the collation of manuscripts he could not bring out.

The Levant was another source of manuscripts from the old Byzantine monasteries, Boulliau dreaming that he might come across "a complete comedy by Menander or the four lost books of Appolonius of Pergamum." Ambassadors and merchants were told to watch out for possible treasures, and Savary de Brèves brought back hundreds of manuscripts from Turkish hands when he was ambassador in Constantinople, booty which found its way into Richelieu's library. Séguier had no scruples about accepting manuscripts from merchants in exchange for trading facilities in the East, and he sponsored a Greek monk, Father Anastasius, in his travels in the Turkish Empire, including Mount Athos, in search of hidden treasures. It was a thorough mission. He took away 116 manuscripts from Athos, paid for at his own expense (he received nothing from Séguier), and even demanded as "treasure trove" others which Athanasius had hidden, two years after the good Greek priest had died! It was by this kind of assiduous blackmail, theft and pillage that the great collections of Greek and Eastern manuscripts were created, which were the basis for the massive series of Byzantine studies and the editions of the Greek Fathers emanating from the Louvre in the mid-17th century.

Collectors like L'Estoile specialized in ephemera, newsbooks and pamphlets, of inestimable value to social historians, finding them among family papers left untouched for years; Philippe de Béthune had a collection of 1,935 manuscripts, half of which were political papers and correspondence, very precious to researchers in later years. In an age when precedent was a cardinal principle of the law, the preservation of authorities from the past was vital, and armies of copyists were at work preserving and recording the necessary documentation which enabled, say, the Cour des Aides or Chambre de Comptes to function. Dupuy and Godefroy, as part of their duties as librarian/archivists, supervised the compilation of such records, the registers of the Parlement, Chambres des Comptes, the Châtelet and Hôtel de Ville for use in Séguier's Chancellery, and Jacques Dupuy was responsible for a weighty piece of scholarship, *Preuves des libertés de l'Eglise gallicane,* an important arm in the defence of the French Church against Papal assertions. Probably the most important source was a collection of basic documents compiled by Loménie de Brienne, a Secretary of State, which was immediately in demand, everyone wanting a copy. Richelieu made de Brienne's son sell him the original for 30,000 livres; it then passed into Mazarin's hands and thence to the Bibliothèque Nationale, priceless material for the study of French law and custom, and all of it the result of private initiative by statesmen anxious only to justify some action or establish a case.

Both ecclesiastical and private libraries were open to the *bona fide* researcher even though there was no access to the public. Among the scholars who created and made good use of these treasuries was Eustache de Blémur, librarian of the St. Victoire abbey and later of St. Geneviève under Cardinal de la Rochefoucauld, where Father Fronteau built up the stock, taught philosophy, learned nine languages, studied history, published the works of Yves de Chartres and became Chancellor of the University. Another indefatigable user was Jean de la Haye, chaplain to Anne of Austria, Procurator General of the Cordeliers, who owned a valuable personal library and supervised the reorganization of the convent library. He deposited the basic materials for his *Biblia magna* and other exegetical works, and for the scientific work of writers like Jean de St. François, Pierre de St. Joseph and Eustache de St. Paul. They owed a great deal to the books and records in the convent on the Rue St. Honoré. The Sorbonne, of course, had its share of scholarly librarians: Marguerin de la Bigne, editor of the *Bibliotheca Patrum;* theologians Gamaches, Filesac, Morel, Héméré; and Du Boullay, historian to the University. On the opposite side of the Rue St. Jacques in Clermont College was the circle associated with the librarian Fronton Du Duc, who edited John Chrysostom, and lecturers of the caliber of Father Sirmond, Father Petau and Father Caussin. In St. Germain-des-Prés the Maurists were eclipsing even the Jesuits in academic work—Luc d'Achery wrote his *Spicilegium* and worked ceaselessly on medieval texts. His efforts were the mainspring of the later Benedictine scholarship for which the Maurists were famous.

Church history and theology was a prodigious industry; Jesuits were writing devotional tracts for the faithful and Carthusians were communicating their mysticism. The last named had a policy to reserve for books one of the three cells assigned to each monk, and from those tiny corners, backed by well-stocked libraries, they turned out their translations of the Spanish, German and Italian mystics. The Minim order had a reputation for science (Mersenne's influence) and their aim was to deepen an understanding of the divine purpose by the study of mathematics, replacing official Aristotelianism with a new scientific philosophy, yet one that was not influenced by dangerous "modern" critics. Mersenne stimulated an interest in research from his cell, which was a kind of center for advanced study, visited by thinkers and philosophers with whom he was in regular correspondence. New problems would be discussed, books exchanged with other men of scientific bent who had their own libraries, and under Mersenne's direction it enjoyed great prestige as a seminary. Among his correspondents were Descartes, Pascal (father and son), Roberval, Fermat and Gassendi—the first modern scientists.

The aristocrats' libraries were also centers of vigorous intellectual life. Henri de Mesmes welcomed Turnèbe and Lambin at his magnificent mansion to borrow books and work with scholars like Claude Fauchet, Léger Du Chesne, Thomas Sébillet, Théodore de Bèze (Beza), Dorat and Claude Dupuy. The same house was just as welcoming fifty years later when Naudé was librarian there, though the habitués never attained the glittering eminence of the group which met every evening in the Hôtel de Thou and later in the Bibliothèque Royale: Sirmond, Rigault, Keeper of the

Royal Library who edited Tertullian, Naudé, Luillier, Diodati and La Mothe le Vayer, all of the freethinking fraternity, and Gassendi, Henri and Adrien de Valois, the historians, Guyet, a noted philologist, and Chapelain, whose general knowledge and grasp of Latin poetry was appreciated in this group, which was more academic than literary.

Presidents of the Parlement were valuable aides to the Crown when they boasted good private libraries, because their interests were legal and constitutional, so that their libraries were more like documentation centers—useful to Kings seeking support for their pretensions in various expansionist adventures. So, there was an astonishing variety of libraries, which must account for the powerful surge of curiosity and research that put France at the head of European thought and awakening scientific and administrative life at this time. There is not a lawyer, historian or textual editor who did not make use of them, and the center of it all was Paris, the favored capital city. The provinces felt ever more alienated. The centralizing tendencies of the age were therefore increased at the political, the social and, now most obviously, the intellectual level.

CHAPTER II

SMALL AND MEDIUM-SIZED LIBRARIES: BOOKSTOCKS

ALTHOUGH SO NUMEROUS, the collections just described were for the well-to-do or the comparatively small class of scholar-gentlemen; they tell us nothing about the reading habits of the man-in-the-street. Our only source of information or clues as to his reading matter comes in wills when a list of books was part of the estate. Often difficult to read, cramped and hard to interpret, sometimes deceptive, the titles often enigmatic, they are still our only source.

1. The Evidence

The lists from wills are buried in the millions of documents in the state archives and the analysis that follows is based on 190 inventories, from three periods: 1601–41; 1642–70; 1671–1700, only a tiny fraction of the whole, but it may help to give us an idea of what books were read. About 15,000 titles were examined and we will leave the last period (1671–1700) for later mention. The lists refer to books actually bought and read decades before, of course, in the owner's youth or middle age; hence a list made out at death in 1645 will more likely reflect life and times in Henri IV's reign than in Louis XIII's; the latter will be reflected in the inventories of 1660–70.

Let us look at the sources for the years 1601–41 and 1642–70. The interest lies in the size of the collection and the owner's social position, and we find that they came from three classes, the bourgeois, artisans, and tradesmen, with a small number of priests. Lawyers, doctors and academics had fairly

good collections, and so did government officers and bureaucrats of all kinds, often owning books numbered in hundreds.
With ever more bloated bureaucracy under the Ancien
Regime office-holders, placemen, courtiers, army officers and
secretaries of every sort multiplied, all concentrated in Paris.
In the earliest years of our period, large personal libraries are
rare (1601–11), but they grow quickly in the years afterwards.

1601–41

	Fewer than 28 books	28–100	101–500	501–1,000	1,000 +	Total
Priests	2	5	1			8
Abbés, prelates			2	3	1	6
Artisans, merchants	10	5	1			16
Citizens	1	6	6			13
Attorneys	1	5	1			7
Barristers	1	9	20	3	1	34
Members of Parliament		4	10	1		15
Members of Chambre des Comptes or Cour des Aides			1	1		2
Officials of the Judicature		3	4			7
Treasury officials		3	2	1		6
King's secretaries	1	2	2			5
Councillors		3	2	1		6
Ministers of State			2			2
Courtiers	1	3	7			11
Gentry	1	4	7			12
Army officers	0	0	0	0		0
Commissioners of War	1	2	2			5
Scholars and teachers				4		4
Architects, artists	3					3
Doctors and surgeons	1	2	7	5		15
Others	3	3	5	2		13
Total	**26**	**59**	**82**	**21**	**2**	**190**

1642–70

	Fewer than 28 books	28–100	101–500	501–1,000	1,000 +	Total
Priests	2	3	5	1	1	12
Abbés, priests			2			2
Artisans, merchants	7	3	3			13
Citizens	2	3	4	2		11
Attorneys			1			1
Barristers		1	7		2	10
Members of Parliament		1	7		2	10
Members of Chambre des Comptes	2	2	8	1		13
Members of the Cour des Aides			2	1		3
Treasurers of France		1		1	1	3
Officials of the Judicature	1	3	1		1	6
Officials of the Treasury		1				1
King's secretaries		1	15	3		19
Councillors	1	1	5	3		10
Ministers of State			1	1		2
Courtiers	2	1	3	4		10
Gentry	4	2	7	1		14
Army officers		5	1			6
Commissioners of War		1				1
Scholars, teachers				3		3
Architects, artists	2	2				4
Doctors and surgeons		2	7	2		11
Others	4	4	15	1	1	25
Total	**27**	**37**	**94**	**24**	**8**	**190**

We are frustrated when we attempt to analyze the tastes and interests revealed in the lists by the scribes' habit (bored no doubt with their task) of referring to books as "a parcel"; they were only interested in single titles if they thought them of value. Two-thirds of the books cannot be identified in the

1601–41 period, and even more in the 1642–70 group. Since to us the most interesting information would be in those "parcels," we know that any conclusions have to be modified since they are based only on ponderous folios and quartos, yet some listings were done so scrupulously that with some care we can come to a more balanced result than one based solely on the weighty tomes. Booksellers' stock lists help since they include many "ordinary" books not mentioned in last wills and testaments. With prudence the 15,000 titles can yield evidence unobtainable in any other way.

2. Religion

In a priest-dominated society religious publications were in the majority and may be used to determine 17th-century readers' knowledge of the Bible and the Church Fathers, how theology penetrated down to the average reader, how interested people were in the religious controversies of the day, and what kind of people were attracted to devotional and mystical writings. The following table helps towards a more complete picture:

	1601–41	*1642–70*	*Total*
Bibles (Vulgate or Benoist's translation)	117	95	212
Exegetical works	22	30	52
Books of hours	12	12	24
Breviaries	23	11	34
Missals	12	8	20
St. Augustine	38	40	78
St. Bernard	23	28	51
St. Dionysius the Areopagite	9	10	19
St. Ambrose	17	15	32
St. Cyprian	14	26	40
St. Gregory the Great	14	10	24
St. Hilary	4	8	12
St. Jerome	20	18	38
St. Basil	12	15	27
St. Clement of Alexandria	10	5	15
St. Cyril	7	8	15
St. Dionysius of Alexandria	4	7	11
St. Gregory of Nazianza	10	7	17

	1601–41	1642–70	Total
St. Gregory of Nyssa	5	8	13
St. John Chrysostom	13	12	25
Tertullian	18	23	41
Bibliotheca Pauperum	5	11	16
Flavius Josephus	45	32	77
Nicephoros	18	8	26
Zonaras	12	8	20
Eusebius	16	16	32
Chronologies	14	13	27
Baronius	26	41	67
History of the Popes	11	15	26
History of the Council of Trent	10	9	19
Church Councils (Collections)	10	21	31
Casuistical works	12	8	20
St. Thomas Aquinas	24	19	43
Albertus Magnus	2	2	4
Bellarmine	11	8	19
Canisius	11	8	19
Becanus	2	3	5
Suarez	6	10	16
Vasquez	2	3	5
Hosius	8	2	10
Coeffeteau	8	8	16
Du Perron	24	28	52
Richelieu	1	6	7
Petau		14	14
Anti-Protestant works	12	10	22
Duplessis-Mornay	8	6	14
Libertés Eglise gallicane	2	18	20
Gallia purpurata et Gallia christiana	2	9	11
Augustine	2	2	4
St. Cyran		10	10
Fréquente communion (Jansenist)		12	12
Other Jansenist literature		5	5
Arnauld d'Andilly		5	5
Lives of saints	54	61	115
Imitation of Christ	1	6	7
Denis the Carthusian	7	3	10
Luis de Granada	27	33	60
La Puente	13	8	21
Rodriguez	2	8	10
St. Teresa	1	3	4
St. François de Sales	6	18	24
Camus	2	7	9

	1601–41	*1642–70*	*Total*
Richeome	5	6	11
Coton	11	7	18
Caussin	1	14	15
Hayneuve		7	7
Talon		7	7
Le Moyne		9	9
Suffren		7	7
St. Jure		9	9
Bérulle		6	6
Senault		7	7
Lives of Jesus	9	12	21
Devotion to Mary	5	11	16
Other devotional works	19	26	45
Besse	3	3	6
Panigarola	5	1	6

It is no surprise to find the Vulgate and Benoist's translation of the Bible well represented, or in a Humanist age so many of the Greek and Hebrew versions of Scripture, especially Erasmus, Pagnino and Estienne's versions. No copy of the Plantin or the Paris Polyglot Bible, but a number of concordances and commentaries, particularly Jansen, Maldonado and Cornelius a Lapide. Study of the Fathers was a consuming passion—Jerome was a favorite but it is surprising to come across 40 examples of Cyprian and 32 of Ambrose, presumably because Counter Reformation leaders admired his organizational ability at a time when the early Church was threatened. The subtlety, literary finesse and capacity to argue a case, so characteristic of the Greek Fathers, evidently impressed readers at a time of bitter controversy with the Protestants, while Tertullian's purity of style in Latin would account for his appearance in 41 collections. Bernard was the most popular, and of course his has always been a strong influence on French spiritual life, like Augustine. The *Bibliotheca Patrum* was the Complete Library of the Fathers, and it is interesting how many readers equipped themselves with sets of the Church Councils, the decrees and doctrines promulgated therein being vital to the defence of Catholicism during the Counter Reformation. Josephus' *Jewish antiquities* appears in 77 cases, Nicephoros and Zonaras (chroniclers) in 26 and 20 respectively, and

Eusebius 32 times; clearly chronology and church history appealed to the scholarly public—witness Baronius's monumental histories and their large following.

The evidence underlines the urgency with which Catholic theologians were returning to their roots in a period of stress and turmoil, a regular tendency in the religious history of France. An analysis by occupation of the owners of Bibles, collections of the Fathers and Church Councils and Church history yields the following:

	1601–41	1642–70	Total
Ministers and other churchmen	5	6	11
Merchants	1		1
Citizens	2	3	5
Lawyers	8	5	13
Members of Parliament	3	4	7
King's ministers	1	8	9
Courtiers	1	2	3
Others	2	1	3

The table is based on 52 collections containing the basic works of Church dogmatics. Others besides churchmen appear to have had an interest, especially lawyers and statesmen, who shared the same world since religion and politics were one, but there is no sign of doctors of medicine, gentry or courtiers. The legal mind was the very stuff of the ecclesiastical and political systems in France, what we would call the power structure, trained to give the expected support by appeal to precedent and authorities. Without a set of the Fathers and Church Councils the lawyer-ecclesiastic would have lacked a library in the sense he would have understood, and indeed lacked "culture." This was still the Renaissance, when new philological approaches to old texts were reinforcing tradition, but we may be forgiven for wondering if those ponderous folios in the lawyers' studies were really read, marked and inwardly digested? Were they the answer to some deep spiritual need, or merely a traditional legacy? And what of theology? Did the old Scholastic theology keep its grip? Was new work eagerly read? How were the writings of French theologians received?

While Aquinas was still a respected authority, names from the past who were not still on shelves included Peter Lombard, Occam, Albertus Magnus (he did appear twice), St. Bonaventura and St. Anselm, all of whom were to hand a century before. We would expect to see Bellarmine, Canisius, Suarez, Vasquez, Maldonado, Cornelius a Lapide and Jansen, and a good representation of anti-Protestant polemics along with a battery of Biblical exegesis and commentary, but there is little interest in Vatican history and a marked reticence about new and, particularly, foreign literature. What foreign books there were came from Germany and the Netherlands rather than Italy or Spain; thus it would seem that the Ultramontane school of theology (emphasizing Rome's supremacy) came into France via Catholic areas like Cologne and the Spanish-occupied Low Countries, which fits in with the picture of the international book trade at the time.

French theologians are plentiful, which endorses the picture we have of a chauvinist France long before Chauvin. Though there is nothing by Du Val and Gamaches, which is surprising, Petau's *Théologie dogmatique* and Coton's *Institution chrétienne* were much read, and of course the massive restatements of doctrine by each side in the Catholic-Calvinist controversy, the two main Catholic apologists, Du Perron and Coëffeteau, ranged against Duplessis-Mornay at Fontainebleu and the arguments of King Charles of England at Charenton. It is hard to avoid the impression that the heavy folios published by the doughty champions on both sides were main reference sources of appeal by either professionals or personal combatants interested in the debate. And the rising tide of nationalism is plainly illustrated by the many titles defending the Gallican Church, as in the *Libertés de l'Eglise gallicane* and *Preuves*, and then the first signs of the bitter Jansenist controversy in the challenging new book *Fréquente communion*.

Once more, favorite writers in the 16th century have disappeared in the field we know as "spiritual" writings; there are hardly any Flemish or German mystics in our lists. Lives of the saints and the *Fleurs des saints* were still common, but Benoist's and Ribadeneyra's, not the *Golden legend;* the *Imitation of Christ* is quite rare now, but Denis the Carthusian and Father Talon's *Histoire sainte* fairly common; Luis de Granada's works were for some reason immensely fashionable, as were La Puente and Rodriguez, again the Spanish connection, but before 1642 there are few French writers in that tradition. Then come François de Sales, Camus, and the Jesuits Caussin, Richeome, Hayneuve, St-Jure, Le Moyne and Suffren, joined by the first writers from the new Oratory, Bérulle, Senault and Bourgoing. The Marian cult is typified by *La triple couronne de la Vierge Marie.* If we are to trust the evidence of the inventories, the new spirituality came little and late to Paris, but of course there are gaps in our evidence, and many small devotional books would be in those "parcels" where there is no hint of their contents. They were felt to be of little value financially, and are only named in exceptional cases: St. Teresa, the *Livre du Mont-Calvaire,* John of Avila, Panigarola, Pierre de Besse's sermons, Benet of Canfield and Laurent de Paris. And even the *Imitation of Christ* is mentioned only if in a luxury format.

Despite the sparsity of evidence, the large proportion of Patristic texts, the collections of Church Councils and all the theology in the booksellers' catalogs point to conventional interest in controversy—and to the speed with which Camus and Yves de Paris were stocked and sold. There is not much interest in the new literature of piety, which suggests that the Carmelite and Capuchin tracts were intended for consumption by their brethren; this would explain the success of the Jesuit program of publishing for laymen in the 1630–40 period, and possibly the hostility to Jesuit influence in the following decade—flow and counterflow.

Among readers who did possess spiritual literature:

	1601–41	1642–70	Total
Churchmen	1	5	6
Merchants	2	2	4
Lawyers		3	3
Officials of the Law Courts	2		2
Members of Parliament	1	2	3
King's secretaries		3	3

	1601–41	1642–70	Total
Ministers	1	1	2
Nobility	6	8	14
Others		3	3
	13	**27**	**40**

If we compare this table with the list of those who owned books on Patrology and theology, we find that only very few of those with an interest in theology read devotional books. Lawyers were indifferent to recent works of that genre but courtiers and the nobility, who had a lot of Spanish and Italian material, read foreign books of devotion. So the first faint signs are seen of that split between the interests and preoccupations of professional people (lawyers and clerics) and the Court, the former faithful to intellectual traditions, the latter beguiled by new fashions in reading. But we must not exaggerate interest in religious affairs outside professional circles: the Bible and various lives of the saints (to take the most characteristic material) were included in only 212 and 115 lists out of 400 inventories examined. Parisians were not particularly interested in religion, and we can tabulate this lack of interest under various professional occupations:

	1601–41	1642–70	Total
Doctors	8	6	14
Apothecaries	1		1
Lawyers	7	4	11
Barristers	2	1	3
Officials of the Court of Justice	1		1
Officials of the Treasury	4		4
Members of Parliament	3	1	4
King's secretaries		2	2
Maîtres des Requêtes	1	1	2
Nobility	1	1	2
Others		4	4
	28	**20**	**48**

Doctors head the list—a profession considered impious from time immemorial—but it's perhaps surprising that lawyers come second. An absence of religious works does not mean that their owners were freethinkers, only that professionals tended to buy textbooks of use to them at work, but there is evidence of a passionate interest in the question of man and the universe when we find both religious works and books of an atheistic or deistic tendency on the same shelves. If we are to arrive at definite conclusions we must have other evidence of indifference to religion, not simply incomplete statistics of books owned.

3. The Classics

Classical texts were second only to religion:

	1601–41	1642–70	Total
Seneca	49	78	127
Cicero	36	38	74
Virgil	34	29	63
Horace	26	11	37
Ovid	16	27	43
Martial	8	8	16
Juvenal	9	6	15
Catullus	7	8	15
Persius	2	2	4
Lucan	3	4	7
Ausonius	5	1	6
Lucretius		3	3
Plautus	15	12	27
Terence	5	6	11
Caesar	22	13	35
Sallust	5	4	9
Livy	42	42	84
Tacitus	39	43	82
Quintilian	6	4	10
Pliny	52	39	91
Vitruvius	4	2	6
Columella		1	1
Galen	13	10	23
Vegetius	3	1	4
Boethius	2	6	8
Cassiodorus	10	10	20
Sidonius Apollinaris	3	2	5
Aristotle	44	44	88
Plato	38	26	64
Xenophon	18	29	47
Lucian	18	14	32

	1601–41	1642–70	Total
Sextus Empiricus	3	5	8
Plutarch	80	87	167
Demosthenes	12	24	36
Isocrates	7	6	13
Homer	16	7	23
Theocritus	3		3
Pindar	4	4	8
Aeschylus	1		1
Sophocles	4	2	6
Euripides	5	1	6
Aristophanes	8	9	17
Herodotus	11	16	27
Thucydides	17	13	30
Polybius	7	4	11
Hippocrates	14	8	22
Euclid	8	9	17
Archimedes	3	5	8
Diophantes	2	2	4
Ptolemy	9	8	17
Strabo	9	7	16
Diodorus Siculus	12	6	18
Appian	4	3	7
Dio Cassius	4	6	10
Heliodorus	3	3	6
Philostratus	15	22	37
Aelian	4	2	6

The list above makes it plain that this was an age imbued with the Humanist spirit. Plutarch's *Lives* were commoner than the Lives of the Saints and Seneca was read more widely than Augustine, while Plato, Aristotle, Pliny and Cicero were of more interest to readers than the Fathers. On the whole, philosophers and moralists—the intellectuals of the Classical period—were the favorites; secular influences were at work. Next came the historians, Herodotus and Thucydides, Livy and Tacitus (in two out of five libraries), Diodorus Siculus, Dio Cassius and Appian, and Plutarch and Xenophon were most probably read for their historical rather than their philosophical content.

Orators still exerted their spell, Demosthenes, Isocrates and Cicero appealing to lawyers who wanted models for their own advocacy. Of the poets, Homer, Horace, Virgil and Ovid were the exemplars, and though in the drama there was a carbon-copy classicist in Corneille, readers preferred not tragedy but comedy—Plautus, Terence and Aristophanes are far commoner on the shelves than the Greek tragedians, though Seneca was always a hit.

The following table shows occupations of those with a substantial number of Classical texts in their libraries:

	1601–41	*1642–70*	*Total*
Merchants	3		3
Citizens	2	1	3
Lawyers	7	4	11
Officials of the Judicature	1		1
Members of Parliament	8	6	14
Treasurers of France		2	2
State Councillors	1	2	3
King's secretaries		1	1
Ministers		1	1
Courtiers, nobility	4	3	7
Doctors	2	1	3
Ecclesiastics	3	1	4
Others	2	2	4

The keenest students of the Classics prove to be lawyers and administrators, who preferred them to the learned Fathers.

4. Philosophy and Science: Scepticism and Stoicism

The Classical world evidently still had much to teach the educated classes in the 17th century, but it is this century which saw the birth of modern scientific method and so philosophy and science had an influence from the past in the Sceptic and Stoic Schools with Seneca, Plutarch, Lucian and Sextus Empiricus, the Platonists and Neo-Aristotelians. The new element was the growth of an interest in natural science and empiricism in astronomy and mathematics. Ancient and modern men of science are listed below as they appeared in surviving inventories; these confirm Seneca and Plutarch as pre-eminent (the Neo-Stoics), with a modernist, Du Vair, and Justus Lipsius, particularly his *De constantia*. Scepticism is represented by Montaigne, Lucian and Charron, and Machiavelli in the latter part of the century, possibly via the translations coming from Holland. There is a glimpse of scandalous free thought in Giordano Bruno, Vanini, La Mothe le Vayer, the *Cabinet satyrique* and even the Koran—most unusual. And even in unimpeachable sources like Aquinas's *Summa,* Garasse's *Doctrine curieuse* and other apologetics, there is a suspicion that they were collected by a "liberal" because in their refutation of ideas writers give heretical views an airing.

	1601–41	*1642–70*	*Total*
Seneca	49	78	127
Plutarch	80	87	167
Lucian	18	24	42
Sextus Empiricus	3	5	8
Erasmus	20	28	48
Justus Lipsius	4	11	15
Du Vair	13	25	38
Montaigne	11	29	40
Charron	10	8	18
Garasse	4	12	16
Other apologetics	2	4	6
Koran	3	8	11
Plato	38	26	64
Philo Judaeus	16	15	31
Marsilio Ficino	5	8	13
Pico della Mirandola	3	6	9
Giorgio (*Harmonia*)	2	8	10
Pierius (*Hieroglyphica*)	14	19	33
Hermes Trismegistus	4	3	7
Simon Maiole d'Ast (*Jours caniculaires*)	5	6	11
Demonology	6	9	15
Libavius	4	4	8
Chemistry, alchemy	4	7	11
La Primaudaye	4	10	14
Binet (*Essai*)	4	8	12
Bacon	2	14	16
Hippocrates	14	8	22
Galen	13	10	23
Avicenna	7	4	11
Fer	4	5	9
Sylvius	6	1	7
Gorris	6	7	13
La Framboisière		6	6

	1601–41	1642–70	Total
Mercuriali	4	5	9
Cardan	10	10	20
Vesalius	6	2	8
Du Laurens	8	10	18
Paré	8	12	20
Aristotle	44	44	88
Various modern philosophers	19	12	31
Pliny	35	32	67
Mattioli	17	18	35
L'Obel	4	2	6
Histoire des plantes	8	13	21
De Natura Stirpium	2	5	7
Rondelet	4	3	7
Belon	5	5	10
Maison rustique	4	7	11
Théâtre de l'agriculture	1	6	7
Vénerie	3	3	6
Ptolemy	9	8	17
Strabo	9	7	16
Traité de la sphère	4	6	10
Copernicus	1	3	4
Galileo		2	2
Kepler		2	2
Ancient architecture	3	5	8
Modern architecture		5	5
Military art (ancient)	3	5	8
Military art (modern)	8	11	19
Mathematical works	3	7	10
Euclid	8	9	17
Archimedes	3	5	8
Diophantes	2	2	4
Gassendi		3	3
Descartes		4	4

The new literature of free thought tended to be in the most comprehensive collections, arguing tolerance on the owner's part, or in those which were significantly weak in religion, but we cannot tell who actually owned this unorthodox material, still less who read it, and the picture is puzzling when Lucian, a noted sceptic in all things, is found next to pious lives of saints or Luis de Granada. It is as if we have not two distinct categories of readers, the pious and the free-thinker, but rather a case of vacillating interests, changing states of mind. Certain it is that the old unreflecting conventional piety is being infiltrated by newer views of the world.

Seneca and Plutarch were paramount, as they had been for a century, and Platonism was in vogue, a strong current in contemporary thought, reinforced by Philo Judaeus, the "Christian Platonist," Marsilio Ficino and Pico della Mirandola. A curiosity about the occult and allegory is typical of the late Renaissance awareness of Nature in books like Pierius's *Hieroglyphica* (in 33 libraries), and the emblematic lore in Giorgio's *Harmonia* (in 10 libraries), Hermes Trismegistus (in 7 libraries) and other Cabalists. The books of Lancre, Le Loyer and Bodin were on demonology, another current obsession, read as avidly as purely scientific works like Simon Maiole d'Ast's *Jours caniculaires* and Binet's *Essai des merveilles de nature.* Alchemy was turning into chemistry in authors like Libavius, Croll, Fludd and Béguin, as the titles in the personal libraries adequately prove, and the presence of Bacon reminds us that contrary to received opinions, he was clearly well known in Paris when Descartes was writing his *Discours de la méthode,* to be published in Leyden.

Plato was in 64 of the inventories, Aristotle in 83, and philosophers in the Aristotelian mode figure in 31 cases. Medicine is well represented by Hippocrates, Galen, and more recent books by Cardan and Paré, and we can record some 16th-century books on botany and zoology. Finally there was even a hint of psychological moralizing done in a scientific way (probably due to the influence of the recently founded Académie Française), in "treatises on the passions" by Coëffeteau and Cureau de la Chambre.

What does it all mean? Was there much interest in the exact sciences? One thing is clear: Galileo, Kepler, Gassendi and Descartes are conspicuous by their almost total absence, though a few specialists had Copernicus and Clavius. Diophantes' *Arithmetic* and Archimedes hardly figure at all, but Euclid is a standby, along with books on the sphere (another legacy from the Middle Ages) and some geometry and elementary algebra. Mathematics seems to have been of interest for practical reasons, namely the construction of fortifications or in architecture. Altogether, then, a mixed public of diverse interests ready to follow scientific theories if they subserve practical ends.

5. The Taste for History

Quite obviously history was of absorbing interest, and is massively present in the libraries under review: ancient history, church history, and many editions of 16th- and 17th-century annals and chronicles, as the following table shows:

	1601–41	1642–70	Total
Chronicles (Mer des histoires and Chroniques de France)	19	9	28
Thevet (Vie des hommes illustres)	3	6	9
Munster (Cosmographia)	4	7	11
Vignier (Bibliothèque historiale)		11	11
Sleidan (Histoire entière)	8	5	13
Paul-Emile (De rebus gestis Francorum)	12	15	27
Nicole Gilles (Annales de France)	14	11	25
Belleforest	27	47	74
Fauchet (Antiquités)	5	2	7
Du Tillet	26	16	42
Pasquier (Recherches)	16	35	51
Serres (Inventaire de la France)	11	25	36
Du Haillan	18	15	33
Dupleix (Histoire de France)	11	25	36
Du Chesne	2	7	9
Paul Jove	12	11	23
De Thou	15	18	33
Davila	1	16	17
Froissart	15	12	27
Commines	21	16	37
Monstrelet	10	18	28
Martin Du Bellay	23	13	36
Ossat (Lettres)	22	37	59
Histories of Louis XI	6	14	20
Histories of Henry IV	9	8	17
Histories of Louis XIII	5	11	16
Godefroy (Cérémonial)	2	4	6

	1601–41	1642–70	Total
Sainte-Marthe	5	17	22
Histoire de Bretagne	9	15	24
Antiquités de Paris	5	11	16
Histories of The Catholic League	2	3	5
Histories of Mare de Medicis, Richelieu and Louis XIII	1	16	17
Mercure français	4	9	13
Histories of ministers		15	15
History of Richelieu's Ministry		15	15
Davity (*Etats et empires*)	22	44	66
Collections of "republics"		6	6
Coëffeteau (*Histoire romaine*)	9	25	34
Other ancient histories	9	20	29
Guicciardini	13	16	29
Other histories of Italy	6	10	16
History of England	5	20	25
History of Spain	15	22	37
Strada, *De bello belgico*	4	7	11
Histories of Holland	4	4	8
History of the Turks	19	25	44
History of Malta	3	6	9
History of Portugal	3	1	4
Machiavelli	2	12	14
Bodin	22	18	40
Balzac (*Le Prince*)		7	7
Grotius (*De jure belli*)		6	6
Other political works	3	9	12
Voyages and travels: Levant	4	10	14
Voyages and travels: Asia	9	9	18
Voyages and travels: Africa	4	6	10
Voyages and travels: America	7	4	11
Voyages and travels: Muscovy	1	4	5

Occupations of Owners

	1601–41	1642–70	Total
Merchants		1	1
Citizens		1	1
Lawyers	2	4	6
Members of Parliament	7	8	15
Treasurers of France		2	2
King's secretaries	1	2	3
Councillors of State	2	5	7
Ministers	1	1	2
Courtiers, nobility	4	4	8
Churchmen	1		1
Others	3	2	5

History, then, and especially modern history, is read by all classes, with evidence of a decline in ancient history, except Coëffeteau's *History of Rome,* read for its purity of style. Foreign countries are of more interest, Guicciardini's *History of Italy* in 30 libraries, and there were histories of England, The Netherlands (especially the struggle against Spain) and of Spain itself, always of interest as France's chief rival. Germany and Eastern Europe had little appeal, though exotic Turkey was featured in 30 libraries, and a book of Far Eastern travels published in Holland, *Histoire de la navigation de J. H. de Linschot et de son voyage ès Indes orientales.*

Davity's huge compilation, *Etats et empires du monde,* was in 66 libraries, and modern histories of the Dutch Republic were in dozens of others, and this, with the other countries in the list above, suggests a widening of curiosity about the world beyond France, though then as now the French were primarily interested in France. Foundation narratives, Munster's *Cosmographie universelle,* Sleidan's *Histoire entière* and Belleforest's *Histoire universelle,* were almost obligatory, and then come the books centered on France: Fauchet, Pasquier, Du Tillet, all staunchly Gallican, and others by Du Haillan, Jean de Serres, Dupleix, and Du Chesne, sponsored by the government and Richelieu; Godefroy's *Cérémonial* and the Sainte-Marthe brothers' *Histoire généalogique de la Maison de France,* the *Gallia purpurata* and *Gallia christiana,* all emphasized the glories of the French monarchy and Church. Above all, the crises of recent nationalist struggles gripped their imagination, either through Italian historians putting the Papal (Ultramontane) view, the Wars of Religion or the Catholic League, or the French standpoint via De Thou. And the legend of the good King Henri IV begins its career here with accounts by Palma Cayet and dramatic stories of his violent end, and even before Louis XIII's reign ended, the histories of that reign had begun.

A new consciousness of current affairs is evident—the newsbook *Mercure française* was taken by many collectors, and the vogue for biography (Richelieu compared with other Ministers) could be seen in books like Silhon's *Ministres d'Etat* and Mathieu de Morgues' commentaries, always flattering. In the political field there is more secular bias: Aristotle, Plato, Machiavelli and Jean Bodin's *République*.

As French law evolved out of feudalism, more treatises on French institutions are published. So, many strands combine to present a strong thread of nascent nationalism, very marked in politics and religion. Given the evidence published in the tables above, the emergence of France as a militant and expansionist nation-state becomes credible.

6. Literature

The table below illustrates the favorite reading in the field of pure literature, poetry, drama and novels:

	1601–41	1642–70	Total
Ronsard	18	14	32
Alain Chartier	2		2
Du Bartas	6	17	23
d'Urfé (*Astrée*)	2	4	6
Chapelain (*Pucelle*)		3	3
Stories	1	13	14
Comedies		6	6
Coëffeteau (*Caractère des passions*)	1	1	2
La Chambre (*Traité des passions*)		8	8
Balzac		5	5
Vaugelas		2	2
Spanish stories	8	3	11
Italian stories	12	7	19
Petrarch	7	3	10
Boccaccio	5	5	10
Ariosto (*Orlando Furioso*)	9	4	13
Tasso (*Gerusalemme liberata*)	1	2	3

Perhaps the main conclusion from these figures is the attraction that Spanish and Italian romances had for French readers, but again, we have few details since literature had little monetary value and the notaries were content to label as mere "parcels" what would have been of considerable interest to us if itemized. We will have to turn to other sources if we are to gain any reasonable understanding of what readers enjoyed reading.

CHAPTER III

TYPES OF LIBRARIES

S TATISTICS WILL TAKE US only so far in any study of ideas and the ways in which they were diffused through the printed word, as when we come across two opposing philosophies or cosmogonies on those old library shelves— they immediately give us pause, and tell us more about the mixed influences that went into the making of 17th-century people than mere bald figures. Likewise, a description of the many kinds of libraries in Paris should help us round out the picture of a reading public.

1. Libraries of modest scale

Humbler but no less interesting collections were often more influential in disseminating new ideas than the grandiose libraries because they were bought purposively to inform and stimulate minds of some acuteness in the bourgeoisie. Typical owners of modest collections, of perhaps at most a few dozen volumes, were business people, Masters of Guilds, shopkeepers and ordinary citizens. A glazier in the Place Maubert, for instance, had a copy of *Chroniques de France* and *Mer des histoires,* a copy of Josephus and a French Bible, which bespeaks an individual of the artisan class who had wide interests within his modest means, the kind of craftsman who would think his way to revolution some generations later. In 1646, Pasquier Léger, a master baker and a man of similar interests, owned de Serres's *Inventaire de la France* and a *Vie des saints.* Even prosperous merchants had little more—Gobelin, a wholesale draper, had only four books, worth 7 livres in 1606, a Bible, a Plutarch, a History of France and Josephus' *Jewish antiqui-*

ties; Jacques Conrart, a Protestant, owned a *History of the martyrs* by Jean Crespin, a *Mystère d'iniquité,* Duplessis-Mornay's *Réponses* and a French Bible. A goldsmith's widow, Anne Hirondelle, had a copy of Rodriguez' *Pratique de la perfection* and Luis de Granada's works, together with nine prayerbooks and other devotional books, proof that the literature of the Catholic Revival had reached the humbler levels of society.

The paltry inventories of some—lawyers, priests, military men and courtiers—show little interest in reading, while others—a grocer, some clerks, lesser administrators and doctors—had a genuine interest, as their wills testify. If we omit twenty collections which contained only legal or medical textbooks, the rest could be called libraries, consisting of books which have the clearly defined stamp of personal choice. These are the ones to study.

2. The Closed World of Traditional Humanism

Again it must be stressed that our evidence is imperfect, and any alleged description of reading habits must be tentative. Actual examples are probably the most trustworthy indicators of taste.

Take King's Councillor Antoine Le Féron's books as a sample of personal choice. His inventory bears the date 1646 and lists 1,000 books. Among them were very recent Bibles, chiefly Plantin's versions, a New Testament printed at the Imprimerie Royale, a concordance and exegetical works by Maldonado and Father Noël, a set of the *Bibliotheca Patrum* and individual works by both Greek and Latin Fathers. He had a set of the Church Councils, both General and French, and ecclesiastical histories by Eusebius, Josephus, Nicephoros's *Chronicles,* Gaultier's *Annales* with an epitome of a Gallican tendency, and the *Gallia purpurata* and *Gallia christiana.* Only Aquinas and Occam remain of the medieval Schoolmen, and in their place are the warriors of the Counter Reformation, Bellarmine, Medina, Canisius's *Catechism,* Becanus's *Somme,* and the writings of Du Val, Coëffeteau, and Petau. Spiritual books included the old *Vitae Patrum eremitarum,* Surius's *Vie des saints,* Louis de Blois, Luis de

Granada's *Catéchisme*, Rodriguez' *Traité de la perfection chrétienne*, La Puente's *Meditations*, John of Avila, Busée's works, Coton's *Année chrétienne* and St. Jure's *Traité de l'amour de Dieu*. The high percentage of devotional literature is unusual in the circles in which Le Féron moved.

We may assume that the anonymous "parcels" contained many of the Classics in modern editions, with Greek texts and parallel Latin translation, and occasionally a French version; and the standard dictionaries would be there, Nicot and Calepin, with the modern Humanist scholars, Polydore Virgil, Lipsius, Pico della Mirandola, Du Vair and Montaigne. We could expect a high state official to be interested in history, and so it was: Belleforest's *Cosmographie*, Dupleix's *Histoire romaine*, de Serres's *Inventaire général de l'Histoire de France*, a *Hispania illustrata* and a history of Germany, Guicciardini's *Histoire de l'Italie*, a history of the Turks and Paul Jove, Davila, and de Thou's more recent histories, Cardinal Ossat's *Lettres* and *Chroniques des ducs de Brabant*.

There is very little science apart from Belon's *Histoire des oiseaux*, Pierius's *Hieroglyphica* and Giorgio's *Harmonie du monde* (if the last two can be called "science"), which confirms the entrenched Humanist education of the upper classes, traditionalist and reactionary. Le Féron read the strictly conventional Humanist literature deriving from antiquity, pagan and Christian, which was the armory of the Counter Reformation. Féron's shelves bear the imprint of 16th-century literary Humanism when it was taking shape, and in that he was typical of the men who occupied posts as administrators and bureaucrats in the Ancien Regime; they felt a natural affinity with the spirit of the Renaissance, a movement which had raised their families to social eminence and to which they were correspondingly loyal.

There were many like Le Féron: Antoine Feydeau, a councillor in the Paris Parlement whose family had been in the civil service since the 16th century, and Nicolas de Nicolaï, Sieur de Goussainville, whose origins are traceable to the late 15th century and whose ancestors had occupied the post of First President of the Chambre des Comptes since 1506 and continued therein until 1791. He specialized in jurisprudence, with a large number of textbooks and legal classics appropriate to his profession, typical of those whose families were like dynasties in the various high offices of state. Another case is Charles Dolet, whose father, son and grandson were all lawyers; Dolet himself was a jurist, a theoretician, as his personal library testifies. Customaries, codes and precedents, all imbued with Humanist/ Renaissance principles, and of course monumental editions of Classical authors and the Humanist thinkers of the previous century; the jurists Budé, Alciat, Pithou, the philosophers Turnèbe and Casaubon; Erasmus and Cardan, patterns of classical Humanism, and the more recent writers in the tradition, Montaigne, Charron, Bodin and Grotius (*de jure belli*). In short, he was a collector in the mainstream of approved thought whose world view reflected Neo-Platonist thought of the Italian Renaissance.

Again, like Féron, Dolet is strong on history: Villehardouin, Froissart, Monstrelet, Martin Du Bellay, Sleidan, Paul-Emile, Paradin, Belleforest and Ossat were all on his shelves, but not many Fathers. He bought all the major Counter Reformation literature, Bellarmine's *Apologia,* Toledo's *Somme,* Bouju's *Corps de philosophie,* and a little devotional literature too, Rodriguez, Busée, and Suffren. Again we note the nationalist bias in that he owns that pillar of Gallicanism, the *Libertés de l'Eglise gallicane,* and Jansen's most popular work, *Fréquente communion.*

Claude Pucelle, another lawyer, owned a collection like the foregoing except that there were rather more Patristic works and more on the Jansenist debate, with scarcely any devotional matter. Pucelle's family had been lawyers for many generations and again the orthodoxy is absolute, completely typical of the legal-administrative class, devoted to the maintenance of traditional culture. One wonders how much of these laborious works they actually read, how many of those ponderous folios they opened, or if their shelves were status symbols? But that is another question.

3. Modernist Tendencies

Some personal collections did have a different emphasis. Jacques Le Coigneux, President of the Chambre des

Comptes (after the death of his wife, Marie de Cerisiers) in 1624, had a huge law collection, a really professional, special library of Roman law, Humanist legal theory, sets of customaries with commentaries, royal codes and collections of ordinances, modern commentaries on Aristotle (Pitard, Carpentier), histories, annals and memoirs, and on the same shelf a Bible, works by Du Perron and Lucian. Nothing of the conventional religious kind—did it mean he was indifferent? Was he secularly minded? Impossible to say, but intriguing.

Louis Phélypeaux de Pontchartrain, President of the Cour des Comptes and father of the Chancellor, had only 400 books but all were so new and of such good quality that they were valued at 5,693 livres, a high figure. It would seem to be the collection of a *nouveau riche,* with the usual Bibles and recent editions of the Fathers but no foreign Counter Reformation theologians; Petau's *Théologie dogmatique,* the Church Councils, and *Libertés de l'Eglise gallicane,* no devotional literature and few Greek or Latin classics. Customaries and ordinances and twelve volumes of the Register of Parlement (MSS), fourteen manuscript copies of the Registers of the Chambre des Comptes, eight of the archives, and diplomatic manuscripts, the working tools of a high state officer. History was there in quantity, chiefly of Germany and Italy, and Ortelius's *Theatrum orbis terrarum,* some illustrated descriptions of European countries, *Roma mediterranea,* Gruter's *Inscriptiones antiquae,* and books on Italian architecture.

It looks as if the old order, based on classical literature and flowering in the Italian Renaissance with the discovery of new manuscripts of the ancient texts, was subtly changing and on the verge of disappearing as the paramount influence. The tendency grew stronger as it moved from the City of Paris, bastion of tradition, and closer to the Court. Anne Mangot, Sieur de Villarceau, doyen of Maîtres des Requêtes, had lawbooks, histories, pamphlets defending the Queen Mother, du Chastelet's broadsides, Bodin's *République,* but only three Bibles, one Estienne, one Latin Bible with French translation, some Fathers, Eusebius's history, some devotional works, St. Jure, Bérulle, and Rodriguez' *Perfection chrétienne.* There was Biblical criticism and theology—Maldonado, Toledo, Bellarmine, Canisius, Du

Perron—and Counter Reformation literature was plentiful, the *Libertés* again, and *Fréquente communion* as well as Petau's rejection of the Jansenist doctrine of grace. There is altogether less Humanism in this collection and more contemporary religious and political controversy.

Jean Fabry's is another typical example. A King's Councillor in matters of finance, not one of the great officers of state but related to Séguier, he lived lavishly in a large household, his library new and luxuriously appointed. He had a Plantin Bible with superb engravings, a Psalter printed at the Imprimerie Royale, the 37-volume set of the Church Councils, six titles by St. Bernard, but apart from Irenaeus no other representatives of the Fathers. Of the Classics he had Seneca, Plutarch, Cicero, Pliny, Livy and Caesar, mostly in French, and there was a good deal of recent history, Coëffeteau and Dupleix, Guicciardini's history of Italy, histories of England and of Portugal, Mathieu's *Histoire de Louis XI,* the *Annales et antiquités de Paris,* a history of the Council of Trent, local histories (Berry and Brittany), some heraldry, Dupleix's *Histoire de France.* Books about recent events included *Histoire du Maréchal de Toiras,* on the siege of Breda and Bois-le-Duc, a copy of the *Histoire des Ministres d'Etat,* and more pamphlets anent Richelieu and the Queen Mother.

This owner seems a little more devout than our previous examples, having Luis de Granada, Rodriguez, lives of Marie de l'Incarnation and Sainte Chantal, literature of the Jansenist controversy, and books by Petau, Camus, and St. Cyran. New thought was represented by Bouju's *Corps de philosophie,* de la Chambre's *Caractère des passions* and *Caractère des animaux, Astrée, Polexandre, Amadis de Gaule,* and twenty volumes of "poetry, history and 'republics' " printed in Holland. We have here a keen interest in current affairs and a leaning towards modern literature and thought.

Sometimes an interest in contemporary affairs goes with a concern for knowledge outside traditional Humanism—Eustache de Refuge's books are a good example of this. He was of Breton extraction and in 1592 a Member of Parlement, Maître des Requêtes in 1600, Ambassador to Switzerland, Holland and Flanders, and wrote a *Traité de la Cour* in

1617, the year he died. In his 1,000-volume collection was a *Bibliotheca Patrum* set, several Bibles, works by Counter Reformation theologians and juridical books, with a large selection of Classics. There was much more besides: a good many histories, as might be expected in a diplomat's home, with an impressive range of politics, Catholic and Protestant, and the same curiosity about witchcraft and demonology, Spanish and Italian books in great numbers, literary works by Tasso, Petrarch, Montemayor and Cervantes, and the conventional textbooks of military science, fortification, mechanics and the like. An avant-garde flavor was introduced by his considerable collection of mathematical and astronomical treatises, recent voyages and travels, and a whole series of maps of European countries, with surveying and mathematical instruments. This was a diplomat who began his career in the Paris Parlement, the heart of the career Civil Service, and had a later career as a diplomat traveling in Europe, an original spirit in many ways, breaking out of the old framework of culture and tradition, still willing to learn from Italian experience while venturing into new versions of history and politics, and wider horizons of travel and contemporary geographical exploration then opening up the New World.

Nor was he an isolated case. Science was a source of fascination to many other than professional mathematicians and astronomers (like Hérigone and Boulanger). Jean-François Le Grand, an ordinary lawyer, author of *Dissertationes philosophiae et criticae*, without the same reasons as Refuge, the international statesman, to enlarge his knowledge of the world, nevertheless had a useful collection of Neo-Platonist and mathematical works among his alchemy and Cabalistic lore: Pistorius's *Ars cabalistica,* Pierius's *Hieroglyphica,* Le Loyer's *Traité des spectres,* a *Lexicon alchimiae Arbor Lulli,* Campanella's *De magia,* and Fludd's works. He also had Cardan's *De subtilitate,* Cornelius Agrippa, *De ortu et causis subterraneorum,* Rondelet's *Traité des poissons,* Cureau de la Chambre's books, Du Laurens's *Anatomie,* and Hippocrates. In the literary field he owned Balzac, St. Amant, Voiture, and Vaugelas's *Remarques,* Montaigne's *Essays,* Campanella, Charron and La

Mothe Le Vayer. And, again in the van of new thought he had Descartes, Gassendi, Mersenne's *Harmonie universelle* and Clavius on the astrolabe. He thus stands in sharp contrast with Le Féron, if we compare the two libraries. There is nothing in common between traditionalists and moderns.

4. Priests and Freethinkers

After the lawyers we might consider the two other main professions of the day, equally traditional, namely the church and medicine. Priests came from very different backgrounds and we should expect a wide variety of reading taste among the dignitaries and prelates in the upper ranks. Nicolas Coëffeteau concentrated on the Fathers, church and secular history and Classics, as did Potier, bishop of Beauvais, who had a library of exegesis, theology, church history, law and medicine, forty scientific books, and standard works in Italian and Spanish—a typical Humanist of the privileged classes, nurtured in the only school they knew. Not in the forefront of the Counter Reformation, more an intellectual (for the church was their natural habitat), and like Cardinal de la Valette, Potier refreshed his leisure with reading more fitted for a statesman than an ecclesiastic.

Examples could be multiplied. The books belonging to the professors in the Faculty of Theology reveal their owners' predispositions clearly, but again far more interesting is the reading matter of the humble parish priest. Jean Raizin, a priest in the Church of the Madeleine, owned five books, an Old Testament, a Virgil "in old letters," a Calepin and a Greek lexicon. Was this poverty or lack of interest? It was common for many ordinary clerics to possess only a Bible, some of the Fathers and a little church history. The inventories tell the same tale of sparse provision, possibly because the routine devotional and pastoral books were passed over as of minimal value. Jean Picart in 1625 was better equipped, with Benedicti's *Somme des péchés,* twenty volumes of sermons and thirty devotional manuals. Pierre Matissart, a priest of the parish of St. Lieu St. Gilles, owned a Benedicti, a Council of Trent Catechism, a Bible, a breviary, and a *Vie des saints,* and appeared to have some interest in the Catholic-Protestant conflict. He collected Pierre de Besse's sermons, and meditated on the *Palais de Miséricorde* and *Imitation of Christ* as well as Horace, Plutarch, Montaigne, Pibrac and the *Antiquités de Paris.*

The evidence suggests an age of transition, though it was very gradual. In Jean Cospéan's inventory of 1646 only two-thirds of the 150 books are specified by title, and most are predictably devotional-theological: the Bible, classic commentaries by Cornelius a Lapide and Lorini, Bonacina's *Théologie morale* and Vasquez's commentary on Aquinas, Marchant's *Hortus pastorum,* Turlot's catechism, Cordier's *Famille sainte,* La Puente's *Méditations,* St. François de Sales' *Sermons* and St. Jure's *Connaissance de l'amour du fils de Dieu.* Perhaps the devotional and strictly theological appear side by side more than was the case previously, but on the whole the new type of evangelical literature was still not readily bought by either priests or laity.

Doctors' book needs did not extend towards religion. We have a list of a certain Basile, a Regent doctor at the Sorbonne's Faculty of Medicine. Unsurprisingly it includes Hippocrates and Galen, with commentaries by Houllier, Duret and Gorris, and the good doctor read Aristotle, Plato and their disciples. Vesalius was there and Pliny, and Belon and Rondelet testify to an interest in natural science, but outside that subject his horizons were limited: a few classics, Plutarch, Aristophanes, Sophocles and Theocritus, and a dictionary or two (one in Hebrew, something of a surprise). Not a trace of religion, though that all-purpose label "parcel" might have covered something in that field.

Other doctors were in much the same case: Marescot, Lescaillon and some others whose lists survive show no more inclination to the faith, but one Jean Piètre had a broader outlook and among his medical textbooks and his zoology and botany were a Horace, Cicero, Plutarch, Homer and Sophocles, Erasmus' *Adages,* Commines' *Mémoires,* Michel de l'Hospital's *Lettres,* a mythology and a Bible in French. Duret had all the classics of medical science in Greek and Latin, and the major literature, as well as French poets, Ronsard, Erasmus, law books, the Fathers (rare in the medical profession), and maps of France. Guénault, another doctor, had over 700 books, of which only 150 were itemized, with some interesting titles: Budé, Serres' *Inventaires, Histoire de Cardinal de Richelieu,* Talon's *Histoire sainte,* Coton's *Institution catholique,* Richelieu's *Perfection du chrétien,* Du Perron's *Invocation des saints,* Petau's *Traité de la penitence publique,* a life of St. Bernard, Jansen's *Première et Seconde apologie,* Arnauld's *Traité de la fréquente communion,* Andilly's *Lettres,* St. Cyran's *Lettres,* the *Milleloquium Sancti Augustini,* and Latin and French Bibles.

So the doctors, brilliantly caricatured by Molière and satirized by Boileau, were of differing intellectual complexions, like other mortals. Some were immersed in the Jansenist controversy, others keen students of theology, yet others seemed to be agnostic, even atheistic, like the next two: Ponce Prévost (1640) had an exceptionally fine collection of medical works, including anatomy, surgery, pharmacy, natural history; and chemistry, arithmetic and astrology were all well attested. Petronius was a significant presence, and so was the *Ouvrage des moynes,* a hint that this doctor was interested in the controversies between the parish priests and the regulars, whose side he was on. Bodin's *République,* Pagnino's *Paraphrasis in Dyonisium,* Charron's *Sagesse,* Vanini's *Temple de Salomon,* and the *Amphitheatrum mundi* betray his sympathies.

Another doctor was Nicolas Cappon, all of whose books were listed in detail (1651), an unusual event. Aristotle, Pliny, Cicero, Suetonius, and Plutarch stood alongside his professional textbooks, and Erasmus's *Adages* (a favorite with the medical profession), Joseph Lange's *Polyanthea,* Le Moyne's *Peintures morales,* Rabelais, the *Decameron,* Charron's *Sagesse,* Vanini's *Amphitheatrum mundi* and *Dialogi,* and geographical tables.

Again, not a great deal to base definitive judgments on, and we would be more confident if we knew whether or not the notaries omitted titles they knew were of ill repute. Why did a notary leave a blank in Maréchal d'Hocquincourt's inventory, then change his mind and fill the page with other titles? But where there is no evidence of religion on the shelves, but instead books of a scientific bias or sceptical tendency, we know we are dealing with unbelievers who must have scandalized their contemporaries.

5. The Upper Classes

Only some thirty inventories relating to the aristocracy or to members of the Court circles actually survive, and they raise interesting questions. Most of this group had only moderate-sized collections, like the Duc de Luynes, who owned devotional manuals (Granada's *Catechism* in Spanish, Le-gar's *Cantiques spirituels*), some homilies, two controversial books, Coton's *Genève plagiaire* and Du Perron's *Réplique*. No Patristic works, few classics (Tacitus, Ovid's *Metamorphoses* in French, Bénévent's translation of Aristotle's *Politics* and Vigenère's translation of Livy). Coëffeteau's *Histoire romaine* and Renouard's *Doctrine de l'Antiquité* were there, and some modern history: Guicciardini's *Histoire d'Italie,* histories of Louis XII and Charles VI, Paul Jove's *Histoire,* Du Tillet's *Mémoires,* the *Histoire du Chevalier Bayard,* Henri le Grand's *Décades,* a *Cérémonial français,* a copy of *Histoire généalogique de la Maison de France,* and a list of the Constables of France, all in expensive binding, but of minimal value compared with the rest of his estate.

Another nobleman, the Maréchal de Schomberg, read very few books, and the Duc de Candale few more. The duc d'Orléans and Bassompière were unusually bookish and Philippe de Béthune's library was extensive. The brother of Sully, he was a diplomat of much experience, widely traveled on missions for Henri IV and Louis XIII, and built up a large collection of manuscripts and official papers of considerable importance to students of diplomacy and foreign affairs. When he was 47 he had an inventory made of his library, then numbering fewer than 100 and valued at 234 livres, 10 sols, a very low sum for someone of his rank, but the contents were choice: Pseudo-Dionysius, a *Rosaria de la Vierge,* Richeome's *Tableaux sacrés* and *Défense de pélérinage,* Desportes' *Psalmes,* Bellarmine's reply to seven theologians, some devotional works, a missal and breviary; no theology or Patristics. He had only a Tacitus and a Lucian (Rome, 1591) in Classical texts, and only a few law books; in geography,

Ortelius's *Theatrum orbis terrarum,* the atlas that was in most inventories, and *Histoire des Indes occidentales et orientales.* He had several good histories, including Monstrelet's *Chroniques,* Froissart, Commines, Du Bellay, Du Tillet, Pasquier's Gallican *Recherches,* and others with an Ultramontane slant—Baronius's *Annales,* Platina's *Historia Pontificum,* Ciacconius's *Vie des Papes et des Cardinaux* (engraved portraits of the Popes) and another volume devoted to Holy Roman Emperors; histories of Spain and the Kingdom of Naples figured in his list and souvenirs of Rome—*Antiquités des familles romains, Romanae urbis topographia,* and *Promptuario della medoglia,* which is an account of the transportation of the great Egyptian obelisk to Rome in 1590. Finally, there were some books indispensable to a gentleman of his superior rank: Du Cerceau's *Bâtiments de France,* Gabriel Muscu's *Architecture militaire,* Evrard's *Traité de fortification,* medical works by a doctor then in favor at Court, Joseph Du Chesne, and finally, Bertaut's poetry. Here then was a library not made to a preconceived pattern established by convention but a spontaneous creation, born of his own personal interest and experience of the world as a statesman. He was a genuine book lover.

Other book lovers did exist in the upper ranks: Charles Thiersault, a Gentleman of the Bedchamber, owned a Plutarch, Seneca, Pliny (the Elder), Suetonius, Livy and Tacitus, mostly in French, and a good collection of law (the Pandects, customaries, Louêt's decrees, and Loysau's *Traité des offices*). History was in good supply—Belleforest, Froissart, Paul Jove, de Thou, Du Tillet, Fauchet's *Antiquités gauloises,* many histories of foreign countries and local histories of Brittany and Provence, Davity's *Etats et empires,* and Ortelius's map. He was interested in architecture, French and Italian, and had two emblem books, Salomon de la Broue's *Cavalerie française,* Ovid's *Metamorphoses* in French, Erasmus's *Adages, Genève plagiaire* and La Puente's *Méditations.* History was (typically) this courtier's favorite reading, the imaginative escape equivalent to fiction today.

Religion, hardly in evidence, is usually left to the wives of the courtiers. Louise de Bourbon-Soissons, the first wife of the Duke, died in 1618 and in her great chateau at

Longueville she had *Histoire généalogique de la Maison de France*, Chalcondyle's *Histoire des Turcs*, Mathieu's *Histoire de Louis XI*, Mariana's *Histoire d'Espagne*, a History of Navarre, Baudoin's *Histoire des rois de Pérou*, Coëffeteau's *Histoire romaine*, all appropriate to her position. She also read a great deal of piety—Luis de Granada; a Life of St. Francis (a manuscript on vellum bound in red morocco and another with a "quantity" of pictures in a gold-tooled red morocco binding, which probably means the *Fioretti* of St. Francis); an edition of St. Bernard in French, a *Vie des saints*, La Puente's *Méditations*, Rodriguez's *Perfection chrétienne*, five volumes of devotions, and fifty-eight other little books of the spiritual life. Henriette de Joyeuse, widow of Charles de Guise, Prince de Joinville, left in her room three cupboards full of books including a French Bible (illustrated), a Roman missal, a book of Hours, an Office of the Virgin in Latin, a *Vie des saints*, St. Jure's *Connaissance du monde*, Luis de Granada's *Catechism* and other works, a life of Bérulle, René Benoist's *Vie du Christ*, Suffren's *Année chrétienne*, Hayneuve's *Méditations*, Godeau's *Paraphrase des psaumes*, Coton's *Cérémonies de la vraie religion*, Rodriguez's *Traité de la perfection chrétienne*, St. Teresa's works, and "fifty devotional books" in a parcel. Clearly a most devout woman.

Marie Leschevin was the wife of Pierre Sopite, First Valet of the Bedchamber, and owned in 1620 a French Bible, a breviary, a *Vie des saints*, Luis de Granada, a Story of the Virgin, Panigarola's works in one volume (a famous preacher called the "Christian Demosthenes"), a volume of sermons by the Archbishop of Rouen, several book of hours, the Psalms, a vellum prayerbook, and another twenty volumes with no details.

The last and most typical example of the taste of high-born ladies is Catherine Habert, wife of Charles Dujardin, another of the King's Valets de Chambre. Of her it was said that she "retired in 1615 to the convent of Notre Dame des Grèves to practice piety and virtue." Her inventory is dated 1633: a breviary, a New Testament, the Psalms in Greek and Latin, Ribera's and Lorini's commentaries on the Bible, Aquinas (the *Somme* and the *Opuscules*), Valentia's commentary on the *Somme*, Gamaches's theological works,

Bellarmine, Gregory the Great, St. Bernard and St. Bonaventure, Aristotle in Greek and Latin, Toledo's commentary on *De anima,* Conimbres's commentaries on *De coelo* and *De anima,* Clavius's book on the sphere, Aristotle's *Rhetoric,* Plutarch's *Lives* in French, Dante, a Calepin in eight languages, a Greek-Latin dictionary, a Spanish-French dictionary, an Italian-French dictionary, the *Maison rustique* and a number of philosophical books. Her devotional literature consisted of François de Sales's *Traité de l'amour de Dieu,* a *Paradis des contemplatifs* in Italian, a "Maker of the world" in Italian, a life of Granada in Spanish, a life of St. Albert in Latin, a life of Angelo da Foligno in Latin, and the works of Richeome, with a collection of controversial literature studded with the leading names in the field, Coëffeteau, Du Perron and Delrio.

A veritable library of theology! Did Catherine Habert—again one asks the question—actually read all those tomes in Latin, Greek, Spanish, Italian? It seems hardly credible, and yet her action in withdrawing from the Court into retreat, to meditate and experience a quite different life style, was in some ways symptomatic of the age. Women of the highest social rank not uncommonly did just that.

6. Bluestockings

This was the age of the original bluestockings, intellectual women, and if ever there was a characteristic example of the species it was Marie Aragonnès, daughter of Madame Aragonnès, whose salon was famous for its madrigals. She was most gently bred and a close friend of Mlle. de Scudéry, Pellisson, Conrart, Ysarn and others of that breed. Her personal library is an interesting reflection of what a woman of high culture read. She had some history and some Classical texts: a history of Spain and a history of the Turks, the *Histoire romaine* and *Histoire de France* by Simon Dupleix, the *Cérémonial français* and a book on fortifications! She had some law, a Fontanon, a Cujas, a commentary by Charondas on the Paris customary, and a *Bibliothèque du droit français* which may have been for her husband, son of a magistrate. In Classics she had Plutarch, Seneca and Cicero, the great triple favorites, and for church history, Josephus and Baronius's *Annales.* In the religious field she had a French Bible, a *Vie des saints,* Granada and Aquinas. In science there was a book on the natural history of plants, a 12-volume set in folio of Aldrovandi's *Histoire naturelle,* and the other standby, *Etats et empires du monde,* Sanson's maps, Scapula's Lexicon, Della Crusca's Dictionary and *Alaric.* This was a library of basic texts but no literary works, and no philosophy. As usual there were several "parcels" of books in quarto and octavo, yet the titles we have do not suggest an unusually learned woman.

And Voiture—what was his library like? A few classics, Aristotle in Greek and Latin, odd volumes of Plutarch, Plautus, Cicero, Seneca, some Latin historians, a commentary on Virgil, Mariana's History of Spain in Spanish, Hérigone's *Cosmographie,* and Bacon's works in English. She also had three Gothic romances: *La chasse et départ de l'amour,* the *Roman de la rose* and the *Roman de Perceforest,* and Balzac's *Lettres,* valued at 60 livres the lot, a modest sum. At the end was a note of "44 little books of various kinds of stories" valued at 10 livres.

Not an unusual collection. Scarron, the playwright and novelist, had a library very little bigger than this. It is here, in the literary and "arty" circles of the day, that we miss knowing what was in the "parcels," because the fashionable writings of their contemporaries, which we must conclude they bought, are rarely listed. This does not mean they were not read—they must have been—but were probably not thought to be suitable for shelving among the "serious" works.

CHAPTER IV

WHAT THE INVENTORIES DO NOT SAY

OST READERS WERE EITHER CLERICS or belonged to the class known as the *noblesse de la robe,* the army of civil servants who kept the growing bureaucratic machine going. A library was part of their reflected glory, a function of their position, the sinecures they had bought for money, and the whole tone of their collections is orthodoxy, both pagan and Christian. The ambitious careerist would surround himself with books appropriate to his office, a scholarly Humanism typical of the late Renaissance.

But the inventories do not tell the whole story because of those anonymous parcels, never identified, but which whet the appetite. One suspects that they contained the very staple of the book trade, and if we ignore this evidence we make the same mistake that modern sociologists make when they research contemporary reading habits and draw their conclusions from "prestige" libraries of a quality that is proof of only one section of the reading public, the intellectuals. The vast mass of popular literature, thrillers, paperbacks, periodicals and newspapers is read to tatters and disappears without trace, leaving little evidence of our present-day mass culture. So it was with the equivalent reading matter of the 17th century. Unfortunately we cannot send out our questionnaires to those readers, so we are obliged to interrogate what scanty evidence we have from other sources, local references and other testimony, which is rare in the age of Louis XIII. We can only ask questions and try to formulate answers.

1. *The humblest readers*

Some idea of the size of the reading public in Paris is essential if we are to identify the readers and decide who read what. The registers of occupations were destroyed in the fire which burned down the Hôtel de Ville in Paris in 1871, so any exact information has been lost forever. A knowledge of the elementary education system in the early 17th century helps, and we do know that the recommendations of the Council of Trent which relate to the instruction of children were carried out at least in theory, so we can be sure that vigorous effort was put into Catholic education at basic levels. Schools were opened in Paris under the auspices of the Chantry of Notre Dame, but with little organization and illiterate teachers. Reading, writing and arithmetic, with elementary French grammar, were, in some sense, taught, but the methods were medieval, chiefly rote learning of prayers and catechism, because one of the aims was a regular supply of simple parish priests. A child would read and learn (in Latin) the Magnificat, Nunc Dimittis, Salve Regina, and "verses and responses of the Mass." To this would be added the Offices of Our Lady, Holy Cross and Holy Spirit, the Penitential Psalms, the Office of Trespasses, Vespers and hymns. After this he went on to his "Civilité," a little French book in type designed by Granjon and which gave its name to that type fount. Once that was mastered he went on to writing and some simple arithmetic. He could improve his writing ability by taking lessons from a writing master who specialized in legal text hand or in a commercial hand for those hoping to enter business, and he might also learn some accounting.

In the little parish schools there would be too many children for a teacher to cope with, and with a roomful of boys and girls from different backgrounds and of all ages the quality of the education may be doubted. Teachers were paid and so would tend to choose sons and daughters of well-to-do families, hence the value of Vincent de Paul's work in founding charity schools. But by the early 17th century the system was just not adequate to the demands made on it.

People were flocking into Paris from the countryside and few were receiving even basic instruction—only those whose work required it would bother to master reading and writing; ordinary laborers, servants and apprentices could at most manage their name, decipher a short sentence with some difficulty, and count their wages. Masters in the various trades and crafts could probably manage more than that, and the average merchant could read and write without much difficulty and do the calculations necessary to his business.

Given these conditions it would be unrealistic to expect many (or even any) books in the paltry belongings left by the poor, and a comment in the *Fortune des gens de qualité* confirms what we suspected about the gaps in the inventories (i.e., that they would prove to be the real popular literature), for it avers that the average tradesman had only "his book of hours for praying and an almanac for the dates of Fairs." But even if they were not intimately acquainted with books, they were accustomed to print on the posters which covered nearly every wall with sale notices, regulations about tolls and taxes, or official decrees. Colporteurs, whether authorized or not, moved about the labyrinth of mean streets in the densely packed city hawking their pamphlets and broadsheets. A few survive but the vast majority perished long ago; we can have only a faint idea of the volume of traffic they represented. Stories were always popular, in the humblest as well as the noblest dwellings. Aesop and the old "Gothic" romances and heroic tales in verse mostly came from Troyes, headquarters of the street literature trade. A surviving chapbook depicts two peasants from St. Ouen and Montmorency discussing in their dialect various stories they have been reading, a tale from Aesop, a "Mirour" of some fanciful history (usually this kind of metrical tale related the fall of some great personage), and a story called "John of Paris." Sales of this kind of reading matter probably went on ceaselessly at the city gates.

As for the propaganda generated by the Counter Reformation, it is hard to say how far it penetrated down to these social inferiors. Modern literature, romances and poetry would not appeal, and the satires and political squibs probably only to, say, law clerks, pages, and barbers' apprentices, so numerous in the Latin quarter, Ile de la Cité, Louvre and Pont Neuf.

2. *Cavaliers and Courtiers*

The clergy, doctors, civil servants and lawyers formed the bulk of the reading public; the aristocracy was less interested. The attitude of the gentry towards the art of reading was formed long ago in the "courtesy" books written to advise on the ideal education of a gentleman or courtier. They originated in Italy, the best known being Castiglione's *Cortegiano,* a manual of breeding, the author of which was a courtier to the Duke of Urbino, one of the most cultured dukedoms in Europe. Literary culture gets special emphasis and the Duke of Urbino is fulsomely praised for creating one of the great libraries of the world to house "a large number of excellent books in Greek, Latin and Hebrew," ornamented in gold and silver, which he considered "the greatest treasure in his palace." According to Castiglione, the gentleman must be "above average in what is called the Humanities, knowledgeable not only in Latin but in Greek because of the many subjects sublimely treated in that language. He should be well versed in poetry, rhetoric and history and should be able to write prose and verse in his own language. Apart from the contentment this brings for its own sake, it will greatly increase his influence with the ladies, who love such accomplishment." Music, too, was an indispensable part of a gentleman's training. Such cultivation was not primarily designed to provide a firm moral or intellectual groundwork but rather to help him cut a good figure at Court; hence his studies must have practical application, desirably in modern languages (French, Spanish, Italian) rather than the dead ones because they will be of assistance to him in his travels.

Montaigne dealt with this subject in his *Institution des enfants,* written at the request of the Comtesse de Gurson on the birth of her son. He was aware of the problems of educating a gentleman in the new mode, and though a voracious reader himself, adopted a swashbuckling, cavalier attitude towards the pedants and arid academics of his day. He condemned some subjects as of no use, the aim being "not to produce dry logicians but young gentlemen." It was the beginning of a new era in education which enlists practical skills and talents to help form judgment and character: the private tutor in a household should mold the mind of his young charges by close contact with the material world, to learn with a view to practical efficacy. Latin should be learned not from grammar books but as a living language through which educated equals might converse. Above all they should "learn the great open book of the world." The gentleman at Court should not be a scholar or an expert, but a man of broad general culture—a lesson which all future educational theorists took to heart and transmitted to posterity.

The other side of a courtier's life was the military, the notion of the "officer and gentleman." The implication was that the only proper career for a gentleman was as a well-trained soldier commanding men, and such training began at 15 or 16, so that any theoretical course of study of the traditional kind was of short duration. He is not expected to encumber himself with useless learning at university—a private tutor will see to all that. The youth may acquire some Latin and Greek, but only enough, and will not waste time arguing the subtleties of Plato and Aristotle but study the moralists instead, and the historians, keeping aware at all times of the lessons of "courtesy," conduct and political behavior. In poetry he will acquire enough technique to shine in his sovereign's presence, and will learn the best diplomatic French so that he can draft correspondence for his King; and other foreign languages will be useful on campaigns (which were a form of aristocratic game). Mathematics and geometry were important in the construction of fortifications and their theoretical basis gave a good grounding in the art of reasoning. Now let us examine what happened in reality.

The French nobility had a reputation as dashing cavaliers but short on intellect, and in Castiglione's book they are praised for their valor but criticized for their scorn of education. After the French King Francis I's invasion of Italy in 1520 the French Court was imbued with Italian influence, as it was again in the time of Catherine de Medici, with a corresponding rise in the general level of culture and external elegance; some even of the "quality" were sent to college. Famous Italian military academies attracted Frenchmen of the upper classes who learned horsemanship and weaponry—a civilization in decline was handing on its traditions to another nation in the ascendant. This contact was later severed by the Wars of Religion in France; children of high birth then were placed with a friend's household or a patron and received their military education that way, soon experiencing bloody war in reality on the Catholic or Protestant side. In an atmosphere of almost continuous warfare the bravos spent their lives on military operations, and when peace returned under Henri IV they retained the habits of professional soldiers at Court while in all other matters they were virtually illiterate. Dashing swordsmen made Philistinism fashionable.

In his *Desseins et professions nobles et publiques* Antoine de Laval has left us an intriguing tale. He welcomed into his chateau near Moulins some travelers who were passing by, and during their brief stay showed them his library. Later on they described their experience to a local landowner who said, "If he had some books he must have been a real gentleman," probably a typical reaction. And again Maréchal de Biron was one day explaining the meaning of some Greek poetry at Court to a group of officials, saying he felt "ashamed to know more than lawyers did." Culture at Court (a tradition deriving from the Valois) had more to do with the stage, where ballet and masques and fêtes of great brilliance were composed and performed, based on classical mythology, so that it must be assumed that the young blades had enough background knowledge to follow the plots as spectators and participants. Tapestries and magnificent portfolios of engravings, as well as illustrated books, were the background at Court, as we know from such productions as the *Temple des Muses* and *Tableaux de plates peintures* which circulated and were admired as much for their illustrations as their narratives. Emblems were a cult and the closely related study of genealogy, family history and armorials was catered for in many books devoted to them, replete with superb pictures and designs, with titles like *Science héroïque* and *Vray théâtre d'honneur*. Equitation was another indispensable art, and again the inventories give us proofs of this in the titles of books by specialists on the subject.

Literary taste is hard to judge if we rely solely on the wills, but we know that poets and dramatists gravitated to Court, and their work must have reflected their patrons' taste. *Astrée* was the work of a cavalier, and other lesser books by authors like Du Souhait and Nervèze interpreted the cult of good breeding for the bourgeoisie. The rakes at Court were responsible for satirical, salacious and often witty verse, though they were scornful of hallowed subjects like Classics, knew hardly any Latin (the badge of the scholar), despised book-learning, and thought it honorable to be ignorant. When they felt a need to acquire a smattering of culture they had recourse to a hack manual or a romance with a thinly "classical" theme. In a book called *Banquet des Muses*, Jean Auvray deplores courtiers' lack of culture but adds that at least they have a smattering of Ovid's *Ars amatoria,* Ronsard, Bembo, *Amadis* (a very old and simple fairy tale), Belleau and *Astrée.* Court poets presented dedicatory epistles to courtiers and verses were circulated; the Court was the first to appreciate new schools of writing (Théophile de Viau, Tristan and St. Amant were first read at Court) and there was criticism as a form of conversation, with often sound judgment and a more liberal and sensitive approach than that of the traditional clerics steeped in Latinity and an outmoded pedantry based on principles of Classical verse.

There *was* an improvement in the education of the officer class even before the close of the 16th century; those who dismissed education as something unbecoming to officers and gentlemen of the King's armed forces were only reacting against the tide of social evolution. The Jesuit colleges aimed to produce a well educated Christian laity without making a charge (no small matter for the lesser gentry), and when universities showed more flexibility in their curricula the prejudice against their dusty traditions began to disappear. Noblemen's sons entered Jesuit seminaries with a private tutor, who was often a needy friend, completed the course with this help more quickly, then left to continue their military career, having acquired enough tuition to hold their own with a member of the legal fraternity or a priest without pursuing their studies into the last years of specialization.

And there was more. This was the time when the French army was in process of reorganization, due largely to the example of Italy. Though we do not know a great deal about the details it is evident that more than simply horsemanship or arms drill was included—Benjamin's or Pluvinel's courses in geometry were mandatory because a knowledge of Euclid was required to plan complex fortifications. Meanwhile individual teachers of mathematics offered courses in Paris and the Jesuits put the subject into their curriculum, which explains the sudden growth in math textbooks. As they deepened their knowledge the more gifted of the young officer class helped increase the public involved in solving the problems circulated as posters on city walls by such as Pascal. Here too we are witnessing the start of the Cartesian revolution as the last vestiges of the old oral culture fade away.

3. Women

Despite the difficulties they encountered in securing an education, women played an important part in the literary life of the 17th century. No provision was made for young women's schooling, though some private tuition was available. Girls were sent to school reluctantly and usually left to the care of their mothers, to be taught how to manage a household or recite a few prayers.

The governess was a familiar figure in upper-class households, women who were sketchily educated, could memorize a few pieces by rote and instill them into their pupils who would mindlessly recite them in turn. Women were seen simply as the weaker sex; in Montaigne's words, "the most useful and honorable occupation for the mother of a family is the management of a home," but if women wished to enjoy books, "then poetry is more suited to their emotional needs" and "they might find comfort in history." He accepted that they might read a little elementary philosophy, "the part that relates to life," to help them "judge temperaments and humors and so defend themselves from slanders," and to learn "to tolerate deceitful servants with equanimity, to bear the uncouthness of the slattern, the pains of increasing age and other afflictions." He preferred to leave his daughter Eléanore's education to his wife and governesses and not to interfere himself to avoid disturbing her feelings, even when he disapproved of her methods.

Convents were the only places where girls could be properly educated—the answer to the problem as far as the upper middle and aristocratic classes were concerned. Their daughters would attend there from age 10 to 15, but we have no idea how good the teaching was—much depended on how much the family could afford. Standards must have varied greatly. The case of Louise de Marillac, a pupil at the abbey St. Louis de Poissy, was probably exceptional: she learned some Latin. Another girl, Anne de Gonzague at Faremoutière under the care of abbess Françoise de la Châtre, learned Latin and other fundamental subjects with a view to a career of responsibility in the abbey. Most girls were trained only to be pious Catholics and good (i.e., submissive) wives. In 1674 Poullain de la Barre, in a book about the education of women, deplored the fact that the old tradition persisted, little changed since Agnes in the play *Ecole des femmes* (early 16th century) who could read and write and so was ahead of her other women friends who were totally illiterate.

Most women learned practically nothing in their childhood, like Madame de Maintenon, whose aunt brought her up with her own daughter. The two girls preserved the delicate whiteness of their cheeks by wearing a mask and had to carry a copy of Pibrac's *Quatrains* in their luncheon basket, to memorize a few lines at a time. Molière's character Gorgibus in *Sganarelle* is only a little dated when he urges her to give up reading *Clélie* and instead to read "Pibrac's *Quatrains* and Mathieu's learned *Tablettes*, a most worthy book full of wise sayings to be learned by heart." And it was not only women of good family or the bourgeoisie who spent their time learning how to please, because the same happened in the lower ranks. Mother Changny was not exaggerating when she wrote in 1643, "A woman is thought well bred if she can read, write, play an instrument and is skilled in needlework" (*Vie de la bienheureuse Mère de Chantal*). She makes it plain therein that the primary aim is marriage—education can if necessary come later.

It is hardly surprising in these circumstances if most books portrayed women as frail creatures, if not actually vicious, with limited intelligence, as in Jacques Olivier's *Alphabet de l'imperfection et malices des femmes*. The sketch, *Caquets de l'accouchée,* where women neighbors gossip around the bedside of an expectant mother, was intended to convey an idea of the banalities of women's conversation and cultural deficiencies. In fact the sketches are an acute rendering of daily life and the lying-in scenes are an opportunity to present a vivid picture of a typical Paris neighborhood. The hero is shown hiding behind a tapestry with paper and ink given him by an accomplice, a female cousin who has just had her seventh child, so that he can note down what is said. The women are all conventional housewives of the middle class with husbands in good positions, a Treasurer angling to marry his daughter into the nobility, a King's secretary, a lawyer, a doctor, an attorney, a bookseller, a draper; the women's problems are all to do with money or with the regular confinements they had to suffer. Topics of conversation range across the gossip of the town, the various amours and scandals in the aristocracy, or news of happenings at Court. Books are sometimes mentioned but never anything substantial, perhaps a trifle bought by their husbands to amuse them or a newsbook or almanac with astrological predictions in it. The secretary and doctor's wives discuss the merits of Tabarin and Mondory, and Mathurin's exploits are a favorite subject; a councillor's wife complains that something she read recently called *Discours du courtisan à la mode* was stolen from another book called *Espadon satyrique*. Other literature was outside their experience. A Protestant lady knows Calvin, Marot and Beza besides "an infinity of great philosophers" (which was probably boasting), and a Catholic who occasionally read the Bible wonders "if it isn't a dangerous book because it caused the deaths of so many people who interpreted it indiscreetly." The only other reference to books was to St. Teresa's works (she had just been canonized); one of the women had just bought a copy at an auction to gain an Indulgence, and a doctor's wife observes that there are two versions of Teresa's life, each ascribing a different father to the saint.

Rabelais is occasionally mentioned, and women, like many young students of the day, were great readers of romances, with *Amadis* the favorite. From hostile sources we learn that *Astrée* and other amorous adventure tales were thought to have a disastrous effect on naive readers. Middle class women can only have had very limited access to real culture and the titles mentioned in memoirs like l'Estoile's and in Sorel's *Francion* prove that romantic novelettes were the staple reading of most bourgeois women.

When the literary salons reopened after the Wars of Religion there was an improvement, at least in the higher social echelons, when poets and writers were admitted to the *conversazioni*. Morals and personal behavior which had been gross and violent grew more refined, and those same currents of thought and elegant expression which irrigated the lives of soldierly courtiers were also working in the feminine sphere. Some reservations must be made: the most famous salon, in the Marquise de Rambouillet's town house, conducted its discussions verbally and not by correspondence. Men and women met in the Blue Room, exchanged ideas and aired their minds and curiosity by conversation and debate in an atmosphere congenial to the arts and with a view to refining judgment and critical awareness. Poetry was a living, spoken expression of art, often composed spontaneously or recited without reading a line, which may account for the comparatively poor library owned by Madame Voiture and Arténice, and even Marie d'Aligre. Literature was for utterance, not reading.

Most of that high culture was for a very limited circle of "précieuses," privileged noblewomen. For others the Counter Reformation proved to be a force for good, illustrated in Orcibal's life of St. Cyran where he describes life in late 16th century Paris as a spiritual desert. A little later Acarie, seeing his wife reading *Amadis* and other romances, buys her devotional books, and soon we are to believe that she was transported through prayer and proper reading to higher concerns; he asks for more books of mysticism and arranges for Angelo da Foligno's work to be translated for her. Madame Acarie was so carried away by the experience that she could not read the books but had others read them to her, and she instructed her daughters to read her a passage from some saint's life every evening after supper. She gave her servants good books to read and inwardly digest, and according to her biographer, St. Teresa's works and Ribadeneyra's life of the saint were read aloud in the French translation by Dom Chèvre. Eventually Teresa appeared to her in a vision and she promptly founded the reformed Carmelite order in 1604.

That was perhaps a case of unusual piety, and that kind of inspiration was slower to infiltrate into the lives of Paris matrons; more often it would be a nominal piety, but an impetus is at work nevertheless. New convents were being opened all the time during the Catholic Revival and there was a good following for Spanish and Italian mystical writings as the literature was prescribed for gently bred women by their spiritual instructors. If we want to trace the evolution in reading which took place in the years 1600–1645 we have only to glance at the books published on women's rights. The tone after about 1630 is very different from what had gone before, and Mlle. de Gournay was not alone in defending the principle of sexual equality. Du Bosc, a Franciscan, published a book on the subject of the *honnête femme,* discussing the status of women and pointing out that the best way to help women attain "perfection" is through study, and he controverts Montaigne on that point. According to Du Bosc the study of good literature aids the critical faculty and is the best antidote to idleness and frivolity; more, it is French books that are recommended. He regrets that more women prefer *Amadis* to the *Cour Sainte* and prefer a play to a sermon, but he urges them to read philosophy, even classic pagan philosophers, while taking precautions analogous to those taken by the Israelites when they cut off the hair and nails of foreign women they wished to marry! He advises history as well as poetry so that they could improve their mental state while shining in conversation.

Du Bosc's work was a positive step forward. Stories of

famous women were published, and "galleries" of portraits of celebrated women with accounts of their lives; the Sieur de Grenaille edited a compendium of advice from Tertullian and other Fathers for the instruction of women, with the alluring title, *Bibliotheques dès dames*. Books written in defence of women began to multiply in the 1640s: Du Bosc's *Femme généreuse* and *Femme héroïque* and Du Soucy's *Triomphe des dames*. And the role played by women during the Fronde troubles encouraged more cognition of them in books like Couvay's *Honnête maîtresse* and St. Gabriel's *Mérite des dames;* and when the best-selling poem *Pucelle* came out in 1656, Chapelain, its author, put at its center not a hero—but a heroine. The age of the bluestocking had reached its apogee.

PART THREE
THE PARIS BOOK TRADE IN
THE CLASSICAL PERIOD
1643–1701

The 17th century is neatly divided into two, corresponding to the reigns of two successive kings, Louis XIII and Louis XIV; the first period (1598–1643) is the age of the Catholic Revival, and the second (1643–1701) the Classical Period. But 1643 was not just the year when one king died and another began his reign, or the year when Richelieu died, leaving the mark of his personality deeply imprinted on the country, or the year when authority was vested in a monarch only five years old. Beneath these surface events powerful new forces were ready to explode and they cannot be conveniently bracketed within regnal years or political boundaries since they were symptoms of new tendencies internationally, and of the breakdown of entrenched traditions. The book trade is one most important manifestation of the deeper change that was, in effect, the end of the Renaissance and the beginning of a new economic phase. As we chart the history of books and reading in the second half of the 17th century we shall be measuring not only material transformations but that profound evolution which the book trade helped to engineer in the intellectual, religious and the political life of the age.

FIRST SECTION
THE CHANGING CENTURY
1643–65

CHAPTER I

CRISIS IN THE BOOK TRADE:
EXTERNAL FACTORS

THE FACT THAT STANDS OUT above all else to a student of the 17th century book trade is the number of crises which followed one after the other in the years 1643–1667. If we try to isolate the factors behind the crises we might better understand the consequences.

1. Crisis in the Stationers' Guild, 1638–43

The Guild of Booksellers, Printers and Binders was in a state of almost perpetual turbulence from 1638 to 1644. The rules of admission to mastership were not so strictly applied prior to those dates, and from 1632 to 1637, 123 new masters were accepted. In 1637 and 1638, Cottereau, a Guild Syndic, seemed to give up bothering to register the new freemen, possibly through negligence but more likely because they were not seeking admission through the normal channels. There were too many competitors in the trade and many of the newly qualified printers or booksellers could not afford to open a proper bookshop or printing workshop and simply set up a stall anywhere in the city. The election of Cottereau's successor in 1638 was clearly of concern to the trade because on their way to preside at the voting for the new Syndic the Civil Lieutenant and Procurator of the Châtelet were stoned. The riot was provoked by the poorer brethren in the Guild, those who had most to fear from any reforming of the rules to enforce stricter regulation, since that would mean a real threat to their livelihood. The authorities reacted vigorously to the riot and in June 1639 changed the election procedures, specifying that office-holders were to be nominated by senior Syndics and Assistants, whose numbers were increased to 18 (6 printers, 6 booksellers, 6 bookbinders), all the most senior members. The choice was no longer to lie with the membership as a whole. The following September general reorganization took place based on the new rules, with Antoine Vitré the new Syndic. He was close to the seat of political power in Paris and was joined in office by Jacques Quesnel, one of the richest booksellers in the Rue St. Jacques, Jean Guillemot, proprietor of one of the biggest bookshops in Paris, Claude Calleville, a prosperous printer, and Thomas de Neuville, a bookbinder.

Vitré set to work promptly. He regularized the procedures to deal with those who had opened a bookshop or print workshop without having registered officially, enforced the rule which forbade printers to employ more than two apprentices, and required that they could at least read and write, which had not always been the case. He was responsible for a Châtelet decree of September 1641 by which only three new freemen a year could be admitted, other than sons of existing freemen, and nominations had to be submitted in March each year. After a period when journeymen out of their time could practice without much fear of penalty, suddenly they were strictly bound by tight rules. There was certain to be resentment.

The problem of copyright, the exclusive right to publish certain titles, was also tackled, and hostility came to a head when Vitré was due for re-election. His supporters wanted him to remain for a further year but his opponents managed to persuade the Civil Lieutenant to let them designate the 18 freemen who would be authorized to choose the new Guild Council, and so maneuvered into the vacancy their own nominee, Quesnel, a known opponent of Vitré on the subject of the monopolies granted to the Compagnie des Usages, a profitable branch of publishing. But Quesnel was somehow displaced by the forces of the Establishment, and Estienne, who had come second, was elected in his place, a situation that is itself revealing.

Estienne was an excellent printer, though heavily in debt,

and a worthy successor to his more famous forebears. After a number of prison terms, a bankruptcy, and an alcohol problem, he still remained popular with the humbler members. An eminence in the printing world, known as "the first of the King's Printers," he was jealous of Cramoisy, another eminence in the trade, king of the bookselling and publishing side and Director of the Imprimerie Royale; and so we have two opposite poles, with Estienne symbolizing opposition to the reigning powers. A manifesto issued by Estienne's opponents incidentally throws light on Estienne's faction:

> About 20 years ago there were only 17 or 18 printers' workshops, and they all produced good work. At present there are more than 26 workshops, and for that reason printing is of much poorer quality . . . it is apprentices who account for the increase in numbers . . . there are far too many members of the Guild who have no right to be and more than two-thirds are mere stall-holders on the bridges or quays or are hucksters at street corners. Everyone is at odds with everyone else. The booksellers in properly established businesses want conditions to be restored as they were in their fathers' day instead of the present low standards which cheapen the dignity of the trade. We urge that the art of printing be restored to its former position of prestige using a good letter without errors, on good quality paper, and that we be encouraged to produce well printed books without the great expense of employing foreign printers. The people in business on bridges or at street corners have no such worries and take any kind of stock, good or bad. They will pirate a book, thirty or forty of them, which someone else has taken pains with before they stole it. Any decent printer or bookseller is bound to feel frustrated.

Estienne's group was supported by the lesser fry, binders and gilders, yet a list of his allies shows that most printers, even the largest firms, were for him. Hénault, who had no grievances against Vitré, was an Estienne supporter and so was Quesnel, though he was foiled of a coveted copyright. The faction was a coalition of opposite interests, a microcosm of the trade as a whole, in a state of unrest arising out of deep economic and social factors. The authorities knew which side to support since from their point of view the main responsibility of the Guild was to prevent publication of undesirable literature, and so it was imperative to maintain proper order in the Guild through the power and influence of the most influential members, which they did by a decree of October 1643. Under the Council of State they nominated Cramoisy, Vitré and Blaise as joint Syndics, with a fourth, Claude Sonnius, appointed later, and four Assistants, Jean Jost, Nicolas Frémiot, Jean de la Coste and Jacques Langlois. The four Syndics were notorious favorites of the Crown and the Chancellor, who benefited from copyrights and various sinecures he could sell, and the Council's decisive action proves the importance they placed on the proper direction of the trade in the interests of the ruling caste. For the guidance of the newly appointed syndics the Council issued a detailed program:

> The Syndics will take responsibility for proper regulation of the trade, and the rules must be strictly observed. They will visit printing establishments and inspect all books in the press; the sheets already printed, together with the MS copy, will be taken away for scrutiny and a report made to the Chancellor. In order that the said Syndics named in the present decree might be informed of the places where books are printed, all printers and booksellers in Paris must submit a statement to the Syndics listing the titles of books in the press, the number of presses, and their address.

We cannot tell if printers did furnish the information demanded but in February 1644 a general inspection of premises did take place because we still have the report. To understand the gravity of the situation and the difficulties inherent in any remedy for the abuses of the trade, we have to examine two reports sent to the chancellor which seek to propose solutions and restore order in the Guild and in the trade at a crucial moment in its history.

Sébastien Cramoisy was almost certainly the author of the first report and he begins by complaining about the superabundance of presses in Paris, many workshops having only a single press, which was contrary to the regulations, and 35 printers with only two. Of 183 known printers in Paris, only 80 have regular work, while the rest "make do with ephemeral matter, occasional Acts, speeches, songs or political squibs," and Cramoisy adds, "the kind of material that is most subject to censorship is invariably the work of those shops with only one press and which lack regular work." A radical solution was proposed: "To recommend that the very small workshops be combined into one or two larger premises in colleges, with perhaps eight big rooms, 13 metres x 8 metres, or in sixteen rooms made by dividing the eight rooms into halves, with ten presses in each half, five along each wall with cases in front of the windows." This was an old dream, to replace individual printing shops with a factory and so turn the printers into a consortium which could then be more easily controlled. But the report appears to have rejected this plan as impracticable: "It would be fraught with difficulties and impossible to implement," for reasons which are most revealing and throw fascinating light on the contemporary trade:

"The proprietors are often masters of colleges and writers of seditious pamphlets, or hacks employed by colleges as teachers, or friends of the Principal or other teachers, hence if it is proposed that printers be lodged in colleges they will corrupt the staff that much more easily." The report went on to say that if 10 or 20 presses were installed in each room, there would be so much traffic that proper surveillance would be impossible; moreover, the more printers there were in close contact, the more likelihood of concerted action and even riots when the premises were inspected. Workmen would have a bad effect on each other, there would be more subversion, and they would be more likely to quit their jobs for various reasons. There would certainly be more quarrelling over copy and accusations of stealing each other's rightful work. Far better, the report concludes, to apply existing rules more stringently, suppress printers with only one press or force them to join a small concern. By this means the number of printing firms could be reduced to fifty, and a strict watch could be kept that the figure was not exceeded. Any printer with fewer than three presses would be denied master's status, the annual admission of new freemen would be drastically curtailed, and printers and apprentices required to know Latin and thus raise professional standards.

This was a characteristic 17th century solution to the problem. No attempt to analyze underlying causes and the distress. The second report (like the first, preserved in Chancellor Séguier's papers) recommends the creation of three posts, "Councillors, Superintendents and a Comptroller-General of Printing." They would have to be expert in the law relating to the press, would authorize all manuscripts submitted for publication, or even reprints, make regular inspections of printers' and booksellers' premises, forbid the sale of unauthorized publications, and supervise books imported from abroad. In short, bring tight control and order into every aspect of permits, privileges, and copyright. The Guild was clearly not considered tough enough at self-regulation, and more powerful state officials would take over. An ingenious idea was mooted to provide the necessary salaries: a small committee of mathematicians would be formed to examine the manuscripts of almanacs submitted for publication, the best two being awarded 2,000 livres and enjoying exclusive rights to publication, the profits from the sale supplying the officials' salaries. Fees for the registration of books when permits were issued were to be paid either in money or in kind, i.e., books.

Soon after the reports were published, the Fronde uprisings began and the Chancellor decreed that *all* books were to be authorized, even reprints of existing titles—further evidence of the alarm felt by government, and the Fronde was indeed partly blamed on the spread of seditious literature which led to active rebellion. We also possess an important document illustrating conditions in the trade, a report on an inspection carried out in February 1644, in Cramoisy's handwriting. It appears that 75 printers employed 281 journeymen and 110 apprentices; if we assume four pressmen to a press (as a contemporary document indicates), then only just over 100 presses were working effectively, but to have a clear idea how busy the presses were we need to know if the work was seasonal. The inspection report suggests that most printers employed either two or three persons, so some twenty presses were critically short of work, and we can tell what kind of work they turned out because printers had to declare what they had in the press. If the statements are trustworthy, about 150 presses were printing books openly for sale, though every one might not have been legal. Twenty presses were printing books of hours, sixty were engaged on religious books (theology, devotions, and controversy), fifty specialized in general and current affairs and fashionable publications beloved by the Palais clientele, and a further dozen or so printed official publications, and legal and political texts. The rest provided medical, scientific and school textbooks.

Of the remaining thirty presses, twelve were not in use, and in some cases the inspector must have observed a discreet silence in order not to compromise the printer: about a score of them were printing only stationery, packets for needles, covers for song books—what we would call the winkle-bag trade. It was the printers in obscure cellars far from the university precincts that prompted official suspicion, employing their families rather than properly indentured apprentices, and often ready to earn their bread printing dangerous and subversive matter. Pierre Angueran was one such, described as "one who employed a press though he was not registered as a master printer," who had set up his press in the Rue St. Anne, printing "ribald verses against the recently deceased Cardinal (i.e., Richelieu)." Richelieu was a main target of the dissidents of the Fronde.

Of course Authority felt it had to suppress this perpetual insurrection in print, but was it the most threatening or dangerous? After all, these little men in their cellar workshops were hardly men of influence in society. Was not a well established printer like Julien Jacquin, who published "by command of the University Rector" a Petition "concerning pernicious doctrine taught at the College of Clermont," a more difficult case? He was protected by the Sorbonne but was unlucky to be caught printing a pamphlet against Cramoisy's friends, the Jesuits. Presses were quite legitimately publishing controversial matter, though not only about Protestantism, as Cramoisy found on his inspection: two books, by Petau and Camus, were on Grace and Penitence, which meant they were about Jansenism, which was to split the Catholic church. And more was found on this distressing internal quarrel—a book of excerpts from St. Augustine (the theology which lay behind Jansenism), a book called *Augustine pauperus* which Calleville had on his press, declaring he had "two volumes of Augustine's works, otherwise known as *Augustinus pauperum*"—proof of a systematic program of publication by Jansenist supporters; on a neighboring press was an edition of Antoine Arnauld's *Traité de la fréquente communion.* The inspectors had come upon evidence of the debate within the Church which would have appeared more widespread if printers had declared everything. Here was the beginning of the schismatic arguments on Grace and the taking of Communion orchestrated by the press in the years 1643–46.

There was a severe crisis, far from settled. Firstly, there were the attempts to limit the number of master printers concurrent with complaints that too many printers and booksellers lived precariously. Secondly, the Guild was torn by a serious conflict between the booksellers, mostly the affluent ones under the Chancellor's protection, and the rest. Thirdly, the Crown was deeply concerned about unlicensed printing when so many were making a living out of underground literature, and even respectable publishers were involved in disturbing controversies, notably Jansenism.

2. The First Outbreak of Jansenism, 1643–47

The inspection revealed that the Jansenist question was a source of unauthorized but profitable income, even to the more favored publishers. Father Jacob's *Bibliographia Parisiana* lists nearly 100 works on the subject from 1643 to 1645, but the actual number of books published on the subject was far greater, as extant copies prove. The affair of the two most notorious titles, *Augustinus* and *Fréquente communion,* and their huge readership came like an explosion. Jansenism had arrived with sudden force on the French ecclesiastical scene, and largely through the medium of print.

Only a bare summary of the Jansenist controversy is possible, and our concern will be to discuss its impact on publishing and the way that medium helped mold public opinion. The debate was about the definition of Grace, beginning with *De auxiliis,* a Pontifical decree of 1610, stocked by a printer called Coulombel, who had hundreds of copies—a sign of the urgency felt by the Vatican over the spread of new doctrines about Grace. Jansen's chief supporters, St. Cyran, Arnauld and Port-Royal, were already preaching Jansenist doctrine, while Jansen was making intelligent use of the printed word to reprint an edition of Augustine, originally issued at Louvain in 1555, on the subject of Grace, for distribution to a chosen few by St. Cyran. For a long time the discussion was confined to a small circle, but two years after Jansen's death his friends had a work of his, *Augustinus,* published posthumously. In that tract Jansen used Augustine's denunciation of the Pelagians as a cover for attacking the Jesuits on the grounds that they distorted Augustine's teaching on Grace. The result was the decree *De auxiliis,* which forbade any further discussion without special dispensation. The attempt to gag failed. The Paris publishers Soly and Guillemot reprinted the *Augustinus* and Calleville printed two further tracts by Conrius, another Jansenist. The tracts were presumably intended to shock, because the first set out to prove that unbaptized children would suffer in Hell, and the second used the parable of the Good Samaritan to show that free will is subject to the lusts of the flesh (carnality was much digested at this time) until saved by Grace.

It was a concerted offensive, using the press very skillfully. The three tracts were in Latin, to appeal to the widest possible educated public within and without the Church, and the printers were carefully selected: Soly was one of the most fashionable in the Rue St. Jacques and had business contacts in Flanders, and Guillemot had a shop in the Palais patronized by the modish intellectuals of the day. It was a bold thing to be a Jansenist in such an age: St. Cyran, leader of the French Jansenists, incurred Richelieu's hatred and suffered imprisonment for several years, and Arnauld, his disciple, was refused his doctorate in theology by the

Sorbonne. Richelieu, of course, mistrusted any theological conflict, and the injury he sustained from Jansen's pamphlet *Optatus Gallus* was enough to make him an implacable opponent of the new doctrine, especially when it was seen to be so attactive to the livelier young minds at the University. Rome stepped in by banning not only *Augustinus* but any other pamphlets in support of it, too; Jansen's publications were carefully scrutinized, with the inevitable result that the controversy spread. Rome lost vital support in France when Richelieu died in December 1642, and in 1643 a Papal bull condemned *Augustinus*. The Jesuits had printed it even before it was officially promulgated, a move which risked antagonizing the very nationalist French church. Arnauld and his fellow Jansenists immediately responded with another tract, *Difficulties,* rejecting the bull. The bitter struggle was launched.

At first the rebuff to Jansenism was hesitant. Pierre de St. Joseph published *A defense of Augustine of Hippo against Augustine of Ypres* (i.e., St. Cyran), printed by Josse (1643), followed by an anonymous tract, *Extrait de quelques propositions de Jansenius . . . ,* but at this point someone calling himself Irenaeus appealed for peace in the Church, and a counterblast appeared in the form of a reprint of *Censure de la Faculte de Théologie de Paris de 1560 contre Baius.* Preliminary skirmishes. The Jesuits were embarrassed at finding the University of Paris rejecting their demand that their college at Clermont should be integrated into the university and award university degrees. They were relying on support at Court and playing for time, while the Sorbonne mounted its own attack on them. The Rector, St. Amour, sent a letter to the Pope passionately condemning Jesuit scheming, and a young theologian, Godefroy Hermant, wrote a succession of pamphlets accusing them of moral turpitude; Hallier, a professor, collaborated with Arnauld in a polemic, *Théologie morale des Jesuites,* the forerunner of Pascal's *Provinciales.*

Arnauld now judged the time ripe to publish his most uncompromising work, the *Traité de le fréquente communion,* printed on Vitré's press—and Vitré, be it noted, was official printer to the Assemblée du Clergé de France. The matter was now far beyond mere theological disputation, since it involved the Princesse de Guémenée and was written as an attack on one of her friends associated with Sesmaisons, a Jesuit. The object of this famous essay was clear—to publicize the Jansenist position and demonstrate its superiority by addressing itself to all thinking Catholics and enlist their support. It was a success: five reprints were called for within a few months and the Jesuits had to recruit their keenest brains to refute it. Sirmond was first, with a tract, *Praedestinatus,* condemning the heresy of predestation, published by the orthodox Cramoisy (the manuscript is in the Barberini Library). More books flew from Cramoisy's presses: *De libero arbitrio* by Petau, and three volumes of his *Théologie domestique,* revised to meet the new heresies. Father Lombard weighed in with *Lettres d'Eusèbe à Polémarque sur le livre de M. Arnauld,* published by Jean and Mathurin Hénault, zealous supporters of the Jesuits, like Cramoisy, but not so well known as he. The decisive attack on Jansenism came with Father Petau's *Traité de la pénitence publique à la communion,* after which the quarrel became personalized and vicious rather than objectively theological. Cramoisy put out *Remarques judicieuses sur le livre de la fréquente communion* and was promptly prosecuted by the University Rector, who wanted revenge for the jailing of his own printer, Julien. Cramoisy was no stranger to prison; and another work that would have cost the publisher a prison sentence had he been caught was *Sommaire de la théologie de Sieur Arnauld,* which was published without an imprint (the author was the Jesuit Father Séguin).

Arnauld and his disciples retorted to these attacks with a *Lettre d'un docteur de théologie à question de ses amis sur un livre intitulé 'Sentimens sincères et charitables sur les questions de la prédestination et de la fréquente communion.'* More anonymous tracts came from the Jansenist camp: *Extrait de quelques propositions de Jansenius* and a *Censure* against Baius. St. Cyran's nephew wrote a *Censure* against Sirmond's *Praedestinatus,* and Godefroy Hermant was the probable author of *Réflexions du Sieur Dubois, docteur en théologie,* in answer to Petau's *Traité de la pénitence publique.*

So it continued, blow and counterblow through the

medium of the press until the date of that Inspection of Paris printers, one of whose objects we might suspect was the uncovering of Jansenist books and pamphlets from whichever side. Arnauld's opponents called on the government to intervene to suppress Jansenism, but Mazarin was not inclined to get embroiled and suggested that the two main adversaries go to Rome to argue the question. This was rejected as contrary to the usual practice of the French Church, and the controversy dragged on, with Arnauld writing a fresh polemic, *Apologie de M. Jansenius,* in reply to Habert, whose further riposte, published by Blaise, Séguier's publisher, only served to emphasize the difference in class between the two antagonists. Habert suffered disastrously, was disowned by the Sorbonne and annihilated in a most elegant way by Arnauld in a tract, *Seconde apologie de M. Jansenius,* written in impeccable French, in contrast to Habert's ponderous Latin. Another work of Arnauld's, *Tradition de l'Eglise sur le sujet de la pénitence et de la fréquente communion,* was dedicated to the Queen and directed against Jesuit casuistry in a style of effortless grace and pellucid reason, which made a formidable impression on the public. In his *Lettres de Polémarque à Eusèbe* he uses irony with great effect to destroy Jesuit arguments and undermine their authority in France, which was threatened still more when bishops and university professors joined the Jansenist cause. Skill with the pen was proving a mighty force to bring in adherents.

Yet opposition was also growing as the Jesuits skilfully defused some of the hatred they aroused, and as always the Court feared any destabilizing movements. Using its influence, it sought to cool passions. An ex-Protestant, La Milletière, thought he saw a way to reconcile Calvinism and Catholicism in the *Traité de la fréquente communion,* but this only roused suspicions, which were cleverly exploited by the orthodox. Arnauld found he had sudden enemies, notably Father Deschamps, who argued effectively in *Defensio Censurae Facultatis Parisiensis latae XXVII junii MDLX* against the *Augustinus.* Though in Latin (decreasingly the language of theology), it went into three impressions. And other anti-Jansenist tracts appeared: Charles Hersent of the

Oratory, Prince Henri de Bourbon, the abbé of St. Germain des Prés (a heavy folio), bishop Abra de Raconis, Father Bourgoing, and Jean de Launoy, none of whom were Jesuits. Camus then contributed four titles on penance, and the Jansenists replied with two more, *Apologie de M. Arnauld* and *Apologie de M. St. Cyran*. The debate soon spread to the provinces.

The clash between the two sides had shown the Jansenists strong and demonstrated the skill of that party in exploiting print to publicize its message and enlarge its following in France. Moreover, the battle of the books brought theology out of the cloister and into the public mind, using French in preference to Latin to reach the ordinary reader, and the vernacular proved a winning trump in the game, particularly in Arnauld's hands. The second lesson learned from the struggle, even more crucial, was this: the powers-that-be were unable to cope. The dull and abstract pedantries that constituted the official statements were no answer, nor could the government prevent the "pernicious" new theories being openly peddled in the streets and bookshops, an unhappy augury for any future clashes between rebel groups and the State if the State was helpless to suppress new thought. Although Jesuits and other anti-Jansenists had the support of the most important publishers in Paris, Cramoisy, Blaise and Hénault in particular, the Jansenists could count on one very big name, Vitré, as well as a number of others willing to take risks on their behalf. Though forced underground, they had a network of agents and distributors and knew which printers they could trust. If this had not been the case, how were they able to take on the authorities and continually surprise them for more than ten years?

3. The Fronde: privilege and trade regulation, 1649–50

The Fronde rising was even more alarming to government, and happened when the Stationers' Guild was split into two camps, the privileged and the unprivileged, and just about the time when the Church (which was the State in another form) was badly shaken by the Jansenist controversy. The grievances about monopolies and copyrights for loyal publishers created resentment, none more so than the prayer-book monopoly, the most profitable of all.

Richelieu had granted a 30-year monopoly to the Compagnie des Usages, which he himself had founded for the purpose of printing prayerbooks under Cramoisy's direction; Parlement had reduced the term to six years, expiring in 1640. The situation seemed favorable enough for the Compagnie to hope for an extension of its privilege, but then Vitré approved a new regulation which had a bearing on the question of this much-prized monopoly. As Syndic he submitted a memoir to the Guild suggesting certain compromises and offering his resignation—the reason for that being the lack of support from his Assistants, especially Quesnel. The Guild passed a resolution asking Vitré to remain as Syndic with his Assistants, with the request that if he did not accept their propositions, it be left to him "to do whatever seems good to him to bring relief." It is hard to say what then happened but Vitré's "compromise" was rejected, and after 1640 the Compagnie des Usages did not have the prayerbook monopoly, though other booksellers were slow to avail themselves of the new liberty through fear of reprisals from the privileged booksellers, who were mostly the bigger fish in the trade. The Chancellor, Séguier, took the opportunity to grant outrageous monopolies to his favorites: Cramoisy had it for Augustine, Ambrose, Jerome and Bernard, a substantial part of Patristic publication, and Blaise received a 20-year exclusive monopoly in Ribadeneyra's ever-selling *Fleurs des saints* as compensation for expenses he incurred in revising the translation. Alliot and Soly acquired a joint monopoly in *Hortus pastorum*, till then in the public domain; Huré, the monopoly in Luis de Granada's works. All the powerful in the trade enjoyed even more copyright privileges: Rocollet, La Peirère, Jean Jost, Billaine, Vitré, Chaudière and Guédois.

Nothing may have been new in such flagrant privilege-mongering but it aroused virulent resistance, and when two monopolies were assigned in one day they were challenged in the courts. Cramoisy had no difficulty in disposing of Alliot's objection to his retaining the monopoly in Ambrose's works, but Rocollet had a great deal of trouble when his rights were challenged. He had an interest in the prayerbook of the Paris Use, subtitled "the layman's breviary," which gives us a hint of the vast potential market, one traditionally outside the exclusive monopoly of any publishers—and Rocollet's patent specified that it was only for the revised edition. He wanted to forbid his rivals to publish any earlier editions, and secured Séguier's support for this. When the Archbishop of Paris was appealed to, he authorized Clopejeau, the diocesan printer, to print the old version only, upholding Rocollet and partners' exclusive rights to the new edition. The dispossessed printers, Tompère and Soubron, referred the case to the Council, eventuating in a decree confirming Rocollet's copyright in the revised prayerbook, but for a reduced duration, and inviting rival printers to collaborate in its publication. Estienne then questioned the decree's validity, and we find Rocollet supported by Calleville, one of Syndic Vitré's Assistants, while Quesnel, who had opposed Vitré on the question of the Compagnie's prayerbook monopoly, now sides with Estienne. The whole case illustrates the divided self-interests of the Guild in the face of a government which pursued its policy of overt favoritism in return for support.

Estienne, recognized as Syndic by a majority of the Guild, began a major offensive against abuse of privilege, and since this meant attacking the Chancellor he needed the support of Parlement, which was traditionally hostile to printing monopolies. He seized his opportunity when Hénault was accused of ignoring someone's monopoly in "an old book," urging him to appeal before Parlement against the charge. As the leader of the "Interventionist" group in the Guild he obtained a warrant to summon to his support all who had contravened regulations on privileges, in direct contempt of the Chancellor who issued a decree forbidding Estienne to appeal before the Parlement. Estienne was later removed from office and replaced by three more malleable Syndics.

Vitré in 1641 persuaded the Guild to accept revision of its Statutes in principle but his "new regulations" came to nothing simply because he had no power base in the Guild strong enough to challenge the influential master printers, and they would tolerate no infringement of their substantial advantages. Matters stagnated for a time until the outbreak of the Fronde disturbances in 1649, but two events just beforehand were of significance in the struggle against monopolies. A new set of regulations passed by the Lyons Guild alarmed the ruling clique in the Paris Guild because it set a precedent for reform, and they feared the Chancellor might favor Lyons printers if they did not reform themselves in Paris. In 1647 an order came from the Chancellor to Guild Syndic Huré stating that it was the King's will that nothing be printed except by an authorized patent; the date is significant because the Jansenist quarrel was at its peak and the first rumblings of the Fronde troubles were heard. The Crown was seeking to assert its power over the press. The same order had in fact been repeatedly reissued for years, but Séguier had not sought to enforce it in the case of "old books." This time it was different. Before a delegation of the chief publishers (Cramoisy and Blaise, his favorites), two printers from the opposing faction (Estienne and Blaisot) and two binders, he emphasized that the King wished to include old editions within the regulations governing monopolies. In other words, nothing was to escape the net; everything was to be submitted for government validation. In 1649 a document was issued, called by its supporters, *Edit du Roy contenant les nouveaux status et règlements pour le faict de l'imprimerie,* and by its enemies, *Lettres obtenues par aucun des imprimeurs et libraires.* It is most instructive.

The preamble to its 37 Articles gives a "summary of intent," no doubt a partisan view, but revealing nevertheless. It begins by declaring that the Paris book trade is in decline:

"Few good books are published in Paris. Most of them are manifestly poor, slovenly, printed on cheap paper, full of textual errors which are a disgrace to the trade, and do injury to the State. More, it is outrageous that our literary men have to use old and out of date editions for their research, which are often expensive as well." After pointing out that apprentices suffer from "masters indifferent to their training, with consequent apathy on the part of the youngsters and lack of good will," it continues, "For every printer and publisher who shows care for his work and produces books worthy to see the light, there are a thousand ready to print and reprint the same book in a cheap and nasty form full of errors." It adds ominously, "Such disorder in the trade can only bring advantage to our foreign competitors because they manage their own affairs so much better than we, and publish a better product. They advance all the time, their bookshops and their agents in all our fair cities, encouraging our people to buy their books and attracting money out of the kingdom, or else they reprint our books in a far superior style, and resell them even using our paper."

Having established that these evils were due to a surplus of printers who lack proper training, the legislator proposes a miracle cure: stricter regulation, primarily by restricting admissions to mastership. The old clause forbidding more than three new masters per year was endorsed, with a suggestion that 300 livres be required instead of 30 as the registration fee. Once more the idea of limits to the number of apprentices was mooted, and a proper knowledge of Latin and Greek—though the number of masters knowing Greek could be counted on one hand. Apprentices who married their masters' widows were to be admitted masters only if they fulfilled certain conditions relating to the date of their apprenticeship, which in effect made it almost impossible for them to become masters. Other Articles forbade any assembly of apprentices, the carrying of arms, or the practice of asking remuneration for the copy turned in after the text was printed.

With the suggested reduction in the number of masters went a corresponding endorsement of monopolies enjoyed by the traditional names. Pedlars were forced to open their packs in the presence of a Syndic or his Assistants and were allowed into Paris only once a year, for three weeks; they would not be able to sell their books through an agent or bookshop. Regular visits by Syndic and Assistants were prescribed to ensure that printers were obeying the regulations.

The most crucial Articles pertained to the thorny subject of copyrights and privileges. A new ruling was proposed:

> To encourage those printers and booksellers desirous of printing and publishing the Fathers of the Church in Greek or Latin, or any estimable authors of antiquity in

whatever language, and to help them recover their costs and improve their standards of work, We will that they secure a licence to print under the Great Seal for such time as We deem proper and in accordance with the author's merits, and in one format, be it folio, quarto or octavo, while permitting other printers to secure a patent under the Great Seal in the form of Letters of Privilege (Licence) to print the said books in a different format. During which time and until it expires no other printers or booksellers may pirate, print or sell in Our Kingdom under the pretext that it came from abroad any copies of the said books, notwithstanding Letters or Regulations to the contrary. The paper must be of good quality, the letter good, and it must be correct. Two proofs will be printed, one to be sent to the Chancellor, the other will be attached to Our Seal as its warrant in case another version is eventually published, in which case the privilege will be annulled. This does not apply to Lives of the saints unless in a revised version or translation, or to the reformed prayerbook, missals, breviaries, diurnals, psalters, graduals, antiphonaries and catechisms which must nevertheless be printed on good paper with a good letter correctly set. . . . Old grammars and dictionaries of established use may be printed by any bookseller or University printer provided the Rector or one of the Regents issues a certificate of approval. Almanacs may be published under the same conditions but there must be no predictions under pain of corporal punishment.

Letters Patent published the same month legalized licensing of older books, so despite a little easing of the situation in the case of prayerbooks and a few schoolbooks, grievances were not likely to be mollified by this kind of legislation. It was more likely to exacerbate the differences existing between the prosperous and privileged booksellers enjoying considerable monopolies, and the rest. When the next stage was reached—ratification by Parlement—determined opposition to the new law was organized by Estienne as spokesman for the dissidents. Not only were apprentices and the masters without lucrative privileges opposed but the University had been unhappy about the new regime ever since it lost its traditional control via its own official booksellers. The dispute was really about privilege—copyright—and when Parlement ratified the Royal Edict in September 1650 it did not include Article 26, which related to old books and extension of the licence after expiry, but instead submitted it to "twelve men of letters" for consideration, with the result that for nearly twenty years there was no legal basis for action on the licensing of older books or for extension of any rights in their exclusive publication.

The crisis deepened in this atmosphere of uncertainty as to rights in titles, old and new, and manifestos and memoirs flew about, putting the case for and against the orthodox view. Estienne, representing about 300 Guild members, outlined reasons for their opposition to the new Edict. It amounts to a denunciation of those who sought to extend their rights in a title after expiry by currying favor with the Chancellor, especially by trying to maintain monopolies on older books which should be free for publication by any practicing printer:

> It can be said that if the new system of granting monopolies is extended to cover older books and those in the public domain it will cause more misery in the book trade than would a war with its pillage and looting because if favored individuals can enjoy retrospective privileges it will exclude most Guild members from their right to print what has always been virtually the only kind of book they could earn their living by, namely the reissue of a title in the public domain. If such a privilege is granted to only a small number of our membership then some 900 people will suffer. Breviaries and other service books account for half the work done by printers, the Bible and other fundamental works the other half. These are our daily bread and are now the object of new monopolies which the leading booksellers hope to acquire, to our detriment. Their names are well known. They have invested 40,000 livres in the Guild to secure its acquiescence. As for the other fifty types of service books, when fifty members have rights in only one (though one leading member has no fewer than fifteen titles to himself) how will the other

900 fare when they have nothing and no regular source of income? It is no use saying that prayerbooks are excepted—that is only a bait to secure privileges in fifty other kinds of books. They pretend that if they are to publish scholarly or Humanist works and other traditional material on good paper and in a good letter they must be granted monopolies in them. By the same token should not the Crown have to do the same thing in the case of service books like breviaries and prayerbooks according to that reasoning?

There is some force in the argument, and it goes on to assert that only in free competition can there be improved standards, an early example of that liberal profession of faith. Another passage is interesting as a shrewd comment on the effect a strictly uniform regime will have on book prices: "Nothing is more certain than that books printed freely and without restrictions costing a sou will cost much more when they are published by exclusive licence, a tacit form of taxation on the public." All good *laissez-faire* doctrine.

The contrary view appears in a document entitled *Mémoire d'un ancien imprimeur et libraire pour conserver l'employ des impressions aux maistres et compagnons imprimeurs de la Ville de Paris,* probably composed by Vitré, and though written twelve years after the law of 1649, it explains the bitterness about extension of privileges:

> The first Statute to regulate the Guild was passed in 1618 when it was impossible to foresee the competition from other places which has since worked to the great disadvantage of the Paris trade. In olden times there was no Parlement or university in even moderate sized towns, with unfortunate consequences for the Crown about which I say nothing, but I do claim that many excellent books printed in Paris are boldly pirated in other provincial towns.
>
> At the time the Statute was passed no other town had engaged in pirating Paris books—Rouen printed its own but now has a thriving trade in piracies. Troyes once concentrated on chapbooks and almanacs but now duplicates Paris publications. Lyons published good quality books without infringing the rights of Paris

publishers—not so now. Orléans, Limoges, Tours and Poitiers were once content to publish their own works but now pirate what is published at great cost and risk by Paris booksellers.

This was not a wholly accurate picture; Rouen was pirating Paris books long before 1645 and the provinces were quick to reprint the more promising titles from Paris the moment a copyright expired, but this caused little reaction. In 1644 the Rouen Parlement passed a decree confirming a ruling made forty years earlier, which seems to prove they were trying to regularize the position with regard to reprints: it ordered that to avoid internal squabbling, the title of any book they planned to publish which had not already been published in Rouen had to be registered for licence; books of less than forty pages had to be registered six weeks before the licence expired; forty to eighty pages, three months before; eighty to one hundred and twenty pages, four months before; and over one hundred and twenty pages, six months before.

With this in mind we can better understand the attitude of the Keeper of the Great Seal, Mathieu Molé, when he declared himself in favor of an extension of the licensing system, if indeed it was he who delivered the speech ascribed to him by the author of the following memoir. Even if it was not he, it eloquently summarizes the case for monopolies:

Those who oppose the notion of monopolies in older works and further monopolies in new books think they are working for the good of the Guild but in fact are inviting its destruction. Only by strict licensing can the presses of Paris be kept working and the provincial presses discouraged from unfairly stealing Paris books. Rouen, Troyes, Lyons, Limoges, Orléans and other towns in France and abroad can publish books at 4 francs which Paris cannot produce for 10; booksellers in the capital are hampered by high prices for rents, and cost of living is high, wages are high, paper costs more than in the provinces. If we abolish privileges our trade will be ruined, piracy rife and the Paris trade seriously undermined. The licensing system is the only insurance we have of steady employment. Let there be no suggestion that this noble city which has published so many superb books, with pain and expense, should abandon its old safeguards to fill other people's pockets. Our competitors in the provinces and abroad hope to reap a harvest, and half of the Paris production would find no buyers if the pirates could do as they please. It is only right that the city which published the books in the first place should reap the profits rather than let them pass to others who have sown nothing and taken no risks.

The scene in 1650 is therefore of an increasingly crowded trade with more and more printers tempted to find a living in dangerous political and religious underground literature. At the same time the high costs in Paris drive the established firms to seek royal protection in return for loyal support in a joint ambition to suppress "undesirable books."

4. Print Workers' Demands

While the masters in the trade were arguing about privileges, their journeymen had their own troubles. The Edict of 1649 made it far less likely that they would ever be admitted masters, and they pressed for improvement in conditions which the Guild thought it politic to concede. A reduction in working hours was granted "on condition that they worked with greater application and interest than they had formerly shown . . . and that they were at work by 5 a.m. and continued till 8 p.m. without leaving the premises for meals, and that they agreed to complete the work now in the press at the rates in force when it was begun." The new rules ratified in September 1650 stipulated that the volume of work done "shall be 2,500 sheets a day for books in black print, 2,200 for red and black, without reductions in wages and daily rates." So pressmen gained some alleviation of their workload; no mention is made of compositors. Journeymen were feeling more independent (possibly during the political unrest at the time of the Fronde), the cost of living had risen during the civil dissension and there was general unrest among working men at the drastic cut in employment opportunities caused by the restrictions on apprentices entering the craft, who were obliged to have a knowledge of Greek and Latin. Masters tried to attract men from rival establishments and used any unskilled boy at the press (he had only to pull on a bar), while journeymen tried to enhance their wages and keep down the numbers of apprentices, to their own advantage.

In the years 1653–55 there were many incidents, journeymen pointing to abuses and warning that skilled manpower would evaporate if that continued, the masters complaining to the Guild Council that the situation was intolerable. The Guild appointed a Committee of Twelve to find an equitable solution, and interestingly, their report was placed before the Parlement, not the Privy Council. Parlement issued a decree in 1654 confirming the Committee's proposals, a compromise. The masters secured their demands on the apprenticeship issue—they could employ apprentices who were able only to read and write; the ticket–of–leave system was adopted, by which a journeyman could only be taken on if his former employer supplied him with a reference certifying that he had completed the work assigned to him; journeymen were expected to complete fixed daily quotas, and wage scales were strictly regulated, often to their advantage.

Journeymen were still not satisfied. There was further trouble in the printing shops in 1654 and a lock-out was organized by the masters to try to smash the resistance; early in 1655 a fruitless attempt was made to bargain—essentially the journeymen opposed new measures which made the employment of apprentices easier, and they wanted the right to quit their masters at eight days' notice even without completing work in hand. They further demanded that something be done about "the high cost of living in Paris" and wanted compositors' wages raised to 50 livres per month, although the 1654 decree stipulated 27 livres (in 1618 it had been 18 livres per month). That figure was for "ordinary" work. For extraordinary work they considered wages should be negotiable, depending on the varying qualities of the manuscripts they handled. They voiced their opposition to the employment certificates, a system by which they carried a docket bearing the name of their master, making it impossible to obtain a change of master if they wished.

Parlement met these objections with a fresh decree in 1658 which confirmed previous regulations about working conditions. It prohibited the issue of employment certificates but allowed the re-engagement of a journeyman if a previous employer supplied a reference affirming that he had completed his work there and kept the rules. Both parties agreed to eight days' notice before dismissal or voluntarily quitting a job. It permitted journeymen of an agreed age to request promotion to mastership if they were certified as capable workmen by two sworn booksellers, two non-sworn booksellers, two master printers and two bookbinders, with a registration fee of 30 livres instead of the 300 laid down in 1649. The decree granted the principle of negotiation for extraordinary work, a victory for compositors, and to study fair rates for regular work a Commission was set up consisting of four booksellers and four "worthy citizens" chosen by the Procurator General. The Commission was also to consider what reply to give the journeymen who wanted their representatives to meet the masters "to settle outstanding differences in the trade" according to traditional usage. Clearly the Parlement was taking workmen's grievances very seriously.

Never had the Guild been so busy or so active in promoting progressive causes, and churchmen belonging to the Commanderie de St. Jean de Latran gave it their support; for once the ordinary membership appeared to have a voice and were meeting freely. But this did not last. The masters affirmed that journeymen had never had the right of assembly "or to take an oath, celebrate Mass or organize a benevolent fund," and this time Parlement allowed the masters to act as they saw fit.

It is hard to judge how many of the rights demanded by the men were actually met by the decree of 1658, but there was little sign of unrest among the journeymen. Parlement seems to have been resolute in opposing Séguier's reactionary policy—that much can be said.

5. The high cost of paper

Meanwhile the cost of publishing books was seriously affected by the sharp rise in paper prices. Vitré left a record for the year 1668/69 which clearly illustrates the rise:

Place of manufacture and grade of paper	1630 price	1669 price
Auvergne		
Nom de Jésus	1 livre 12 sols	1 livre 5 sols
Pot	2 livres 5 sols	5 livres 10 sols
Cornet fin	2 livres 12 sols	5 livres 10 sols
Couronné fin	2 livres 12 sols	5 livres 10 sols
Petit êcu	3 livres 5 sols	5 livres 10 sols
Grand écu	4 livres	6 livres 10 sols
Carré au raisin	4 livres	7 livres
Grand raisin	7 livres 10 sols	13 livres
Angoulême		
Carré à fleur de lys	3 livres 5 sols	4 livres 10 sols
Grand cornet fin	4 livres	6 livres
Lombard	4 livres	6 livres
Petit compte	2 livres 10 sols	3 livres 10 sols
Normandy		
Petit couronne et petit carré	1 livre 12 sols	2 livres 10 sols
Joseph	2 livres	3 livres 5 sols
Pot	2 livres 5 sols	3 livres 5 sols
Champagne		
Volume de Brie	2 livres 10 sols	4 livres 10 sols
Volume de Segon	3 livres 10 sols	6 livres
Bâtard	2 livres	3 livres 5 sols
Omessier	3 livres	4 livres 10 sols

Vitré blamed the price rise on Richelieu's policy of taxation. In 1633 the Chancellor imposed a duty of 5–9 sols per ream when paper had always been free of duty, in the interests of students. The trade was naturally up in arms against the tax but failed to get it abolished, and by 1669 nearly half of the price of a sheet of paper selling for 20–25 sols was tax of one sort or another. This is how it was made up:

Paper duty	7 sols
Toll	1 sol
Paris customs duty	1 sol
Permit	1 sol
Registration	1 sol
Trading tax	1 sol
Total	12 sols

A press which used three reams a day paid 48 sols a day in taxes, which yielded 100,000 livres a year from the whole book trade. This made competition with foreign countries difficult because Angoulême paper, for instance, the finest in France, was 3 livres 15 sols per ream plus taxes, and Paris had to give up using it, while the Dutch publishers were hardly affected because they were not taxed anything like this, and their transport costs were lower. Vitré adds, "They [the Dutch] had only to send it by the river Charente to the sea." For these and many other reasons the cost of Paris-published books rose sharply; consequently formats were much reduced to the smaller sizes, and in general slim pocket volumes were the preferred style.

6. The Crisis Continues: Theological Quarrels and the Power of the Press

In 1650 the Jansenist quarrel broke out again. Nicolas Cornet of the Faculty of Theology published five Propositions on the subject of Grace, aimed at the Jansenists, and Parlement forbade any further pronouncements by the Faculty, at which Cornet appealed to the Assemblée du Clergé who promptly appealed to the Pope. The Jesuits joined the Faculty and the Assemblée in a press campaign against Arnauld and his Jansenist disciples, and for three years a vigorous program of anti-Jansenist polemics was mounted in books and pamphlets published by their arch-sympathizer Cramoisy and other more prudent but sympathetic publishers who did not print their names. All the old doughty combatants were fighting the verbal fight again: Petau, Marandé, Sirmond, Deschamps, Brisacier, Vavasseur and Morel on behalf of orthodoxy, and on the other side the abbé de Bourzeis, a member of the Académie Française, Godefroy Hermant, the belligerent canon of Beauvais, and Noël de La Lane, abbé of Valcroissant, with Arnauld the master-mind behind the campaign. He came out of a semi-retirement during which he had been translating St. Augustine and plunged into frenzied pamphleteering with titles like *Avis* or *Considérations*, rather like open letters in which he replied to attacks on him and publicly debated questions of the hour, and at the same time worked on serious apologetics rebutting charges of heresy; a typical title: *Apologie pour les saints Pères de l'Eglise défenseurs de la grâce de Jésus Christ.*

Both sides addressed their case to the man-in-the-street, and passions and personalities were locked in combat and calumny. A Bill of Innocent X condemned a Jansenist manifesto and the Jesuits quickly arranged for its sale on the streets, delighted to have a powerful weapon and propaganda for their politico-religious ends. One of their most telling pieces of ammunition was an almanac entitled *Déroute et confusion des Jansénistes,* with an illustration by Mellan showing Jansen in a sinister cloak, holding a book called "Jansen and Augustine"; wings sprout from his shoulders and he is being struck by lightning as he cowers among a group of Calvinist ministers. Arnauld's answer was to refrain from an immediate reply, and to intimate that he would reserve the right to reply when the Jesuits showed more sense and some restraint. The almanac drew a counterblast from M. de Sacy called *Enluminures du fameux almanach des Jésuites.* The warfare was intense, and even Arnauld was discouraged when he found his letters condemned by the theologians of the Sorbonne. But then a famous name came to his aid: Pascal, aided by a small group of courageous publishers, helped to give encouragement by publishing tracts in defence of the Jansenist position.

Print was the decisive medium in this prolonged war of words. Ever since 1647 the Jansenists had moved on the fringe of legitimacy, but it was only a question of time. During the Fronde troubles the royal censors in theology were opposed by the professionals of the Faculty of Theology at the Sorbonne, the traditional authorities in that field, and in the political sphere the ultimate censor, the Keeper of the Seal, exerted his authority. Chancellor Séguier and Molé, the Keeper of the Seal, assumed control of the book trade, and in 1656 judged the time ripe for action against Jansenism when the Sorbonne comprehensively and definitively condemned Arnauld. The highest theological authority in France was condemning Jansenism as a heresy. Then came Pascal's *Lettres provinciales,* simple yet profound essays couched in everyday language and human terms which made a deep impression on the readers who obtained them mainly from colporteurs anywhere in Paris. Arnauld had a document drawn up declaring his condemnation null and void, and Séguier thundered against the pamphleteers, demanding that they be found and punished. Camuset was the Commissioner vested with the task of finding the culprits, something he did quickly, catching a printer, Charles Savreux, red-handed at home with a large stock of Jansenist literature. Savreux and his two assistants, Migeot and Jean Houzé, were committed to the Bastille. More copies of Arnauld's *Protestation* (against his condemnation for heresy) were seized, with Pascal's *Lettres provinciales,* but Camuset was not prompt enough to catch another offending printer, Le Petit, who was actually setting up the first *Lettre provinciale,* and who ironically was a member of the Académie Française, regularly attending meetings with other Academicians at Séguier's official residence. He was probably forewarned of Camuset's search and put emergency plans into operation— by the time the police arrived the offending formes containing the text of the First and Second Letters had been safely secreted, incredible as it seems, under his wife's apron! She left the house under the noses of the police, taking the formes to a neighboring printer who ran off 1,500 copies from them the next day.

The struggle continued. Le Petit's workshop was sealed by the police but the seals were removed a day later; Desprez, a bookseller who sympathized with the Jansenists, was searched and some of Arnauld's pamphlets confiscated; the trio in the Bastille were liberated and soon back at work, and the *Provinciales* continued to appear; nos. 3, 4 and 5 were printed by Denis Langlois, which diverted suspicion because he normally worked for the anti-Jansenist faction.

The story of the publication of Pascal's seminal work is full of anomalies and puzzles: while the third *Letter* was being printed, Camuset visited the printer, who was also in the act of printing Arnauld's first *Lettre apologétique*. He merely asked for a sample page of the *Letter*, and took it to Séguier, who asked to see the complete work—and took no action. Later, Langlois became alarmed at the stir caused by the *Provinciales,* and when printing no. 9 made a clean breast of it to Pierre Ballard, Guild Syndic. Séguier discussed the matter with his colleague Fouquet but then simply assured Langlois that there was no need for alarm. In these circumstances it can hardly be said that the Pascal *Letters* were published illicitly. A contemporary note by Baudry d'Asson throws an interesting light on the methods used to sell them:

> Instead of giving the *Letters* to our booksellers Savreux and Desprez to sell, we have 6,000 copies printed, 3,000 of which we keep, the other 3,000 we sell to the two booksellers at one sol apiece, which they then sell at 2 sols 6 deniers. In this way we make 50 écus which covers our printing costs and our 3,000 copies cost us nothing. Everyone benefits.

Jesuits were the prime target in the *Lettres Provinciales* and naturally wanted them suppressed. They put their case in a pamphlet signed "The Paris booksellers," pressure which forced the Civil Lieutenant to reaffirm the decree which forbade any printing without permission, and after further ripostes from Port-Royal (headquarters of the Jansenist party) Séguier asserted that it was perfectly normal for permission to be granted to publish anything that defended the truth, but that he was well aware who was responsible for Jansenist propaganda and would make an example. Pascal's *Letters* ceased at no. 18. But the struggle dragged on and infected the Stationers' Guild itself, some of whose Assistants were Jansenists voted into office in the election of 1657.

Gradually the government gained the upper hand. Desprez and Langlois were arrested and blamed St. Gilles as the author of wicked books. St. Gilles was indicted and found a powerful protector in the person of the Bishop of Coutances, who hinted to the Civil Lieutenant that St. Gilles' arrest would not please Mazarin. Desprez was later released and, with support in the Parlement, had his sentence of 5 years' banishment annulled. Port-Royal eventually found the State too much for them despite reaching a wide readership through the press, and were forced into exile in the Netherlands. They now looked for help to foreign publishers, who were always willing to accept business, and so added to the menace of competition to the Paris trade.

7. Foreign competition: the Elzeviers

The Flemish book trade had close commercial relations with France, exporting books of high quality, the products of an energetic and rapidly expanding economy. Leyden and Amsterdam were prolific centers of book publishing and the Elzeviers the leading publishers, observing the rules and not blatantly seeking direct competition with French publishing houses. French books were published by Flemish and Dutch houses but most of their output was Dutch or Latin and intended for readers in the Netherlands. The pattern began to change around 1640 when Corneille's success as a playwright tempted the Elzeviers to piracy; Leyden followed suit and some of Paris's best-sellers appeared in the Netherlands under home imprints. Regnier's *Satyres* was published in an unauthorized edition in 1642 and soon all the well-known French writers were available: Charron's *Works*, Commines' *Mémoires*, Brébeuf's translation of Lucan's *Pharsalia*, Balzac's *Oeuvres diverses* and *Lettres choisis*, Scarron, d'Assoucy, Richelieu, Tristan, Quinault and Furetière. The Elzevier branch in Amsterdam replied with Serre's *Secrétaire à la mode*, Philippe de Mornay's *Mémoires*, Hardoin de Péréfixe's *Histoire du Roi Henri le Grand*, all openly published. Others appeared either with false imprints or with no imprints: Somaize's *Véritables précieuses,* Molière's *Précieuses ridicules* and other comedies, St. Amant's *Dame ridicule,* Rabelais, Cureau de la Chambre, Bassompière's *Mémoires,* Cardinal de Retz's *Conjuration de Comte Jean-Louis de Fiesque,* La Fontaine's *Contes,* Father Bouhours's *Entretiens entre d'Ariste et d'Eugène* and Nicole's *Essais de morale.*

Systematic piracy of the best-known and universally admired French authors became a fact of life for the Paris book trade when the Elzeviers opened offices there, and other firms began to profit from the illicit trade practice. The trick was to reprint an established author who would sell anywhere, in one of the small, pocket-sized formats on which the Elzeviers made their reputation, modified craftily using the original publisher's imprint but with the words "according to the text of" in minuscule letters on the title page immediately before the publisher. Often an imaginary publisher's name and place of publication was used. Impudent, but it reaped rich rewards for the Elzeviers, and for a while there was no reaction. The French authorities were helpless to prevent the printing of illicit literature in their own country and could not stop overt piracy from abroad; some Paris booksellers openly traded as agents for the Elzeviers. French authors were not averse to a larger audience by this means, legal or not, and indeed accepted selection by Elzevier as a compliment. Balzac wrote a eulogistic letter to the Elzeviers when they published his *Lettres choisis,* although it went hard with his own publisher, Rocollet. Chapelain prepared an edition of Montaigne for the Elzeviers. They were secure in their fame as publishers.

But the important link was with the Jansenists of Port-Royal. St. Gilles was a proof-reader at Port-Royal and while it is known that he was in touch with Daniel Elzevier, St. Amour certainly was. Elzevier wanted to publish a good French grammar, and St. Amour promised to negotiate with Claude Lancelot about such a project. The Elzeviers had already published Pascal's *Provinciales* in 1657 and followed it with a Latin version designed for the clerical reading public outside France. This was the start of close collaboration between Jansenists and the Flemish publishers—the Protestant connection, it could be called. Jansenist tracts printed by Flemings were imported into France via Rouen and thence to Paris, and in 1667 Ponchateau smuggled Sacy's translation of the New Testament into Amsterdam when the French refused to allow it in. It enjoyed a wide readership under a quite false imprint, that of Gaspard Migeot, a Mons publisher, though in fact it was a Protestant who published it.

8. *The Early Years of Louis XIV: the Trade Wars of the Booksellers*

Trade was stagnant in Paris in the decade 1650–60, a recession exacerbated by the internal divisions within the Guild and the Jansenist controversy which drove trade underground, and finally the blow from foreign competitors taking advantage of the political and economic situation to infiltrate the French market. Control over seditious publishing was made more difficult. Inside the trade the big firms were securing monopolies and acting against any infringements by the small men trying to make a livelihood. Cramoisy acted against Berthelin of Rouen (most piracy was carried out in provincial towns) and secured two decrees from the Privy Council confirming an extension of his privilege in a new and enlarged edition of *Histoire de la décadence de l'Empire grec et établissement de celui des Turcs.* He took action against Lyons stationers, too: Jérôme de La Garde, Jean-Antoine Huguetan and Marc-Antoine Ravaud, the last-named for having pirated Sponde's *Epitome Annalium Baronii.* Later he restrained La Garde with a decree relating to an edition of St. Bernard, the property of the Compagnie du Navire, and invoked the copyright privileges enjoyed by the Compagnie des Usages against other Lyons booksellers who published a breviary. But in this precarious trade business was a matter of profit and loss and sheer survival, despite Cramoisy's bullying lawsuits, and Lyons continued to be a nest of pirates in a flourishing state of trade. Avignon, Grenoble, Rouen and Lyons all ignored the claims of Paris big business as to their rightful monopolies, and once an initial term had expired took no cognizance

of any extensions of copyright but went ahead and published
their own editions of books likely to sell, fighting objections
from Paris in their local courts or Parlements, which were
generally partial to their case. Paris publishers could not
afford lengthy lawsuits individually, and, unwilling to risk a
verdict so far from home and with local ill-will, they banded
together to found a company to share the expenses of legal
actions.

Disputes over coveted lines which had a guaranteed
demand over the years (notably prayerbooks and other
service books) flared up whenever these appeared to fall into
the public domain. Rocollet had his monopoly of this very
desirable material renewed in 1659 but Loyson was granted
a patent for the same prayerbook with a slightly different
title. Rocollet was accused of making "huge sums" out of his
monopoly, and everyone took up the cry "Liberty to Print!"
It was simply a fight for a decent living, always menaced by
the power of the Crown and its absolutism in domestic and
foreign affairs. The political scene was tense, the book trade
in a critical condition. In such circumstances underground
publishing flourished, and although France had known
periods of anarchy in the 16th and early 17th centuries there
had never been such an outburst of seditious and scurrilous
literature. In religion a systematic, intelligently led press
campaign had been proved successful in putting across the
message of Jansenism, creating a readership which no
previous party had ever matched, a triumph of collaboration
between a determined group of believers and the press. And
in addition to these significant political-religious movements
there was the bread-and-butter question of the cost of living.
Faced with a growing threat to trade from the Netherlands,
Paris seemed helpless to remedy anything; the only response
central government was capable of was further grants of
monopolies, in the teeth of resistance from the provinces and
from within the Paris trade itself, which was in a hopelessly
divided state. France in the mid-17th century is a scene of
political, religious and economic dissension and divisions.

CHAPTER II

BOOK PRODUCTION

W**AS THERE A CORRESPONDING CHANGE** in production during the crisis years, 1643–67? It rose to a maximum in 1643, declined from 1644 to 1657, and rose again between 1664 and 1671, when it reached the highest figure for the whole century. Folios decreased after 1645 in favor of quartos, and by the end of the century books of small format are the norm, an inevitable result of recession, when books expensive to produce in the largest sizes will be abandoned in favor of more cost-effective products. There was no significant change in the crisis period, but one interesting trend is the output of Latin publications: one-quarter of the entire production in 1641/45, less than one-sixth in 1666/70. The Guild registers of copyright applications already reveal Latin to be exceptional, even in theology; the Bible, the Fathers, even Classical texts were usually in French translations. Two clear trends, then: small formats and less Latin, which portend a change in reading habits and the very culture of French society. The old Humanist pedantry whose natural language was Latin is being replaced by a more worldly spirit, ushering in the classical age of French literature and the "honnête homme," civilized, urbane, reading and writing with a new clarity, elegance and simplicity.

1. Christian Humanism: New Directions

After the age of heavy Classical scholarship characterized by Casaubon, there comes a change when Rigault turns away from that kind of heavy erudition, and only François Guyet continues his dogged collation of Cicero's manuscripts yet is in constant touch with collaborators in Holland. Those massive folios of Classical texts gradually give way to working texts for scholars in handier formats published by Elzevier and others, models of textual accuracy and with a minimum of notes. The intention was to provide students with readable texts rather than to pursue every single grammatical point to exhaustion, a trend which reflects a different mood. Utility will henceforth be the keynote, rather than respect for rigid precedent. The mood was noticeable in other fields: there were fewer of those excruciatingly learned works on jurisprudence, once typical of the Renaissance, and the daunting commentaries on the traditional customaries (d'Argentré, Du Moulin), which gradually disappear from publishers' lists. Only Guignard, a specialist in this subject, was still supplying his customers with it in the mid-1600s, but most of his stock was pre-1640. Medicine was also in process of change: René Chartier's huge edition of Hippocrates and Galen came out in 1670–72 but it had been started forty years earlier and was no longer typical of its age. Gorris, Pardoux and Jean Riolan I, the main French medical authorities of the Renaissance, were no longer in print; instead, new treatments were coming in from Germany with more emphasis on drugs, early modern pharmacy. New manuals of anatomy embodied new knowledge, and the first little books of advice on self-help in illness found many readers; one such, entitled *Médecin charitable,* was a best- seller until 1680.

The Council of Trent encouraged Catholic scholars to spread more knowledge of the Faith among the middle classes and educated professional people. Spanish, Italian and French devotional writers published work for the instruction and edification of laymen. Official Papal editions of the Scriptures were issued, and commentaries by Maldonado, Vasquez, Serres, Toledo, Perez, Pineda, Ribera, Lorini, Cornelius a Lapide and countless other moralists whose names often sounded strange and barbarous to French ears. Counter Reformation propaganda poured from Paris and Lyons without fear of objections from the Faculty of Theology or the Parlement, but texts with any political bias favoring the Holy See were avoided—Gallican sentiments were in the ascendant. Spanish theology made great impact on France, a safe and secure scholastic brand, though Escobar, a moral theologian, was attacked for his "laxity," which might have meant a hint of new tendencies which traditionalists would condemn.

New theology from foreign sources begins to make its impact, of which Jansenism was only the most spectacular. From about 1645 the Vulgate or the Louvain Bible are no longer kept in print, and although Cramoisy put out some of Maldonado's and Lapide's work he gave up publishing texts in that very subject from which he had made his fortune. Fewer of the standard theological authorities were published and the old unity of the Catholic world was breaking up, even in the special field of Patrology when the nationalist Assemblée du Clergé de France sponsored its own edition of the Fathers. Jansenism led to a re-examination of St. Augustine, with consequent new editions slanted from both sides of the argument. The major split was the Protestant-Catholic one, of course, but Protestant thinking was not far removed in one respect from the views of the French church, namely on the question of St. Peter and the See of Rome. The Clergé de France encouraged the scholarly Benedictines of St. Maur to continue their huge history of the French Church, the *Gallia Christiana,* and there was a revival in Thomist studies at the Sorbonne (published by Denis Moreau and his son Denis, and by Edme Couterot), especially Jean Nicolai's work.

The Bible received more attention, no doubt a reaction to Protestant freedom in this field. Jean de la Haye published various books of the Bible with commentaries and in 1645 a *Biblia magna* with notes by Jean de Gagny, Sa, Menochio and Tirin, followed by a 19-volume *Biblia maxima* in folio, under Mazarin's aegis, an encyclopedia of Bible studies. It was the age of the Polyglot Bible. In 1615 the Clergé de France planned to commission a multilingual Bible to rival Plantin's, and with the help of a distinguished printer, Vitré, a new set of oriental types, and financial help from Michel Le Jay, Séguier's wealthy friend, the work began. Philippe d'Aquin, a Jewish convert, revised the Hebrew text, and Syriac and Arabic texts were edited by a Lebanese, Sionita, who lapsed in his labors and was confined in the castle of Vincennes by Richelieu to force him to finish the task. In 1645 the 10-volume Polyglot was ready, a majestic work on fine paper with impeccable typography, a tribute to Paris printers, but unfortunately lacking in scholarship. The first four volumes were little more than a reprint of the Antwerp Polyglot, and the last five volumes in Syriac and Arabic were scamped by Sionita. The preface was a vindication of the Vulgate, which would be orthodox State policy, and makes one wonder why so much energy was put into what is essentially a superfluous piece of work. The reason was plain: like Jean de la Haye's *Biblia maxima* it was the late expression of an outmoded school, no longer appropriate to the new age, a semi-official work published with government approval which was not entirely profitless because it provoked reactions from scholars which marked a new departure in Biblical exegesis. The chronology of the Bible was discussed, so too was the validity of the original texts. Some championed the Vulgate, others questioned it. And when Hobbes published his *Leviathan* (1651), a number of Protestant commentaries were actually published in Paris; even so orthodox a publisher as Cramoisy published Grotius's *Annotata ad Novum et Vetus Testamentum,* and Cappel, a Protestant minister at the University of Saumur, published his *Criticae sacrae* under Cramoisy's imprint on Mersenne's recommendation, prompting a reply from Arnold Boodius, a Protestant. This work laid the foundations of modern Biblical criticism as Cappel compared various recensions to establish the Hebrew original as authentically as possible, studying the grammar in a historical context, questioning, for example, Solomon's alleged authorship of Ecclesiastes.

There was a more positive, scientific spirit abroad, Catholics and Protestants even collaborating on textual problems, and once released, the new spirit of inquiry unfettered by Authority and past precedent flowed into religious history and historiography. There was a willingness to confront problems with a fresh eye—the discussion of the authorship of *The Imitation of Christ* (Jean Gersen or à Kempis?) was one such. Historical events and personalities were re-examined in the same critical spirit: Jean de Launoy tried to show that St. Dionysius the Areopagite was not the apostle to France, that St. Victorinus, bishop and martyr, was not bishop of Poitiers but of Petaw in Pannonia, that St. Bruno was not converted after seeing a vision of a canon in Paris telling him he was damned, and that St. Lazarus, Maximinus, St. Martha and the Madeleine did not evangelize Provence.

Adrien de Valois began the serious study of chartularies. It was an age when Cartesian objectivity was the new tool: research and synthesis, verification and proof were the criteria of late 17th-century scholarship. Copernicus and Galileo were now heroes; a book published in 1655 on the "Pre-Adamites" provoked only scorn. By today's rigorous standards the science and the scholarship might seem elementary, but it was a beginning.

In matters theological the Clergé de France had traditionally been the coordinating body but there was now increasing intervention by the Crown, which made the royal purse available for projects that would enhance the prestige of France. In the world of the printed book the Imprimerie Royale was the obvious symbol of royal dignity and influence, expressed, for instance, by the 37 volumes of Conciliar Decrees. Likewise, the huge enterprise of the Byzantine History (texts of the obscure Byzantine historians unknown in the West), conceived as a gesture of reconciliation between the Eastern and Western Churches and as an affirmation of French scholarship. Such worthies as Agathias, Manassès, Anne Commène, Theophanes, Leo the Grammarian (Combefis, 1655), George Syncellius and Joel saw the light of day (Allatius, 1651), thanks to the Imprimerie. Later, Labbe published the first correct edition of Michael Glycas, and when Du Cange published the Chronicle of Pascale in 1668 the whole cycle of Byzantine chronicles from the 5th to the 15th century was completed. In spirit and in expertise the project was thoroughly modern.

The Maurists began to issue their studies of monastic history and hagiography with Dom Ménard's *Martyrologium sanctorum ordinis divi Benedictini* (1629), and Dom Tarisse's work on the library of St. Germaine des Prés was a pioneer of its kind. In 1648 Dom Luc d'Achery edited Lanfranc's works and a 12-volume series of unpublished Patristic texts, the *Spicilegium,* and Dom Chantelou edited an 8-volume *Bibliotheca Patrum ascetica* (1661), St. Bernard's sermons (1662), then his complete works, and the Rules of St. Basil (1664). Other scholars, like the Maurists Mabillon and Montfaucon, worked yet again on St. Augustine.

There appear to be two main currents active at this time: firstly, the traditional transmission of the basic authorities, the old habit of reliance on precedence for authentic doctrine, giving way to the second, a more scientific spirit and greater specialization with royal support, in the interests of national prestige. It marked the end of one world, the age of Humanism, and the beginning of a new age, which attained its majority at the century's close.

2. *The Age of Translations*

Latin texts by mid-century had declined to the point where they were largely textbooks for school use, although the Aldine classics had reached a large, classically educated public. In spite of the high standard of work put into the Elzevier pocket classics, the public for Latin was not increasing. French was replacing Latin as the staple tongue, spoken and written, and French was replacing Latin in school. Predictably of course, traditionalists like the Jesuits taught through the medium of Latin, but the new Jansenist movement at Port-Royal taught their pupils in French, whether history or languages, classical or modern, and the existing manuals are proof of its success. The Congregation of the Oratory also used French. And the revolution in teaching methods was only one aspect of a change reflected in the many new translations. Within a twenty-year period we can count translations of Tacitus, Caesar, Lucian, Thucydides and Xenophon, by Perrot d'Ablancourt; Tacitus, Cicero, Tertullian, Isocrates and Plato, by Du Ryer; Phaedrus and Terence by Lemaistre de Sacy; Quintus Curtius by Vaugelas; Horace, Virgil, Juvenal, Persius, Catullus, Tibullus, Propertius, Lucan, Statius, Plautus, Terence and Seneca, by Michel de Marolles. Stoic authors were somewhat neglected but the historians were prominent—

Livy, Caesar, Suetonius, Sallust, Quintus Curtius, Herodotus and Thucydides all won new readers once the language barrier was removed. The Greek tragedians still proved too big an obstacle for translators, possibly because they feared rivalry from contemporary dramatists already writing their own versions of classical drama.

As early as 1550, in the age of Amyot and Vigenère, translations began, but they were only a by-product of the new critical study of classical texts. In Vaugelas' day there is a marked difference—far less study of classical texts in the original. Translation is an end in itself, a new literary genre, the Latin or Greek merely a model on which to devise a new, French, model. It is the *form* that is important in 17th-century translations, not the deeper implications; hence the translator was inclined to render his material in the spirit of the age—his age—even at the expense of anachronisms and distortion of the original. The Classics were no longer a revered object of pious study and restoration, but rather patterns of style to be first imitated and then if possible surpassed.

The same change of emphasis is visible in Christian literature written in traditional Latin. Even the Jesuits' translations of Augustine and Boethius had novel features, and the Jansenists as part of their quarrel with orthodoxy did just what Calvin did a century before—used French. Their translation of Augustine into French was a notable success, and in their search for support for their doctrines on Grace they put St. Chrysostom into French, too. The only permitted French Bible was the Louvain version, known to be faulty; the only other authorized way to communicate Scripture was by Paraphrases, a compromise which Catholic orthodoxy thought safer than a new French version of the Bible. Maucorps' Paraphrases were popular, and Godeau's, based on the Pauline epistles, and Hector Le Breton's Proverbs. Numerous versions of the beloved Psalms were circulating and new Lives of Christ in French replaced Latin, not only to meet popular demand but to meet a need for greater accuracy and faithfulness to the original. Bernardin de Montereul wrote a *Vie du Sauveur de monde Jésus-Christ*, Talon a lengthy *Histoire sainte* (1640–54), and Bralion (of the

Oratory) composed *Histoire chrétienne*. A whole new literature on the Jews and the story of Christ was now available.

The pressure for a new Catholic French Bible to rival the
Calvinist and help win back converts from the Protestant
camp forced Louis XIII to sanction a translation late in his
reign, a version by Jacques Corbin published by Huré in 1643
and challenged by the Faculty at the Sorbonne despite its
royal patronage. Richelieu appointed three theologians to
prepare another translation—a sign of a new dispensation—
but his and Louis' death put an end to the plan. Corbin's
Bible was actually withdrawn from sale, to reappear in 1661
with a new title page, and readers with no Latin were invited
to use the revised Louvain done by Véron in 1647. But the
demand for a completely new French Bible was irresistible,
and work on various Books of the Bible began in haste: Job,
Ecclesiastes, Proverbs and the Song of Songs, by Philippe
Corduc, a minister, and in 1644 a French version of
Erasmus's New Testament was allowed. Séguier, however,
refused an appeal to publish a French Old Testament. The
fight for the liberty to read Scripture in the vernacular was
joined. Cardinal de Retz consulted Poncet, a Benedictine
theologian, and issued an edict endorsing the traditional ban
on Bible reading by the laity in the vernacular, with support
from Cramoisy who published a book patronized by de Retz,
*Sanctuaire fermé aux prophanes ou le Bible défendue au
vulgaire* by Le Maire, King's chaplain.

Marolles, translator of the New Testament, gave up
further attempts to produce a complete Bible in the face of
this powerful opposition, and the attack was switched to
prayerbooks, which might not bring the same objections;
Father Coton had set an example with an Office of the Virgin
(1634) which made a fortune. Baudoin published the hymns
in the breviary in a French version (1640) and the Compagnie
des Usages itself employed French titles in its breviaries to
make things easier for the user with no knowledge of Latin.
Rocollet sold a prayerbook in French, Marolles published a
French Office for Holy Week, and in 1650 a French and
Latin Office of the Church appeared with Rules of a
Christian life, the Psalms, and Hymns for Sundays and Feast
Days. But that little book came from Port-Royal, the seat of

Jansenism, and a storm blew up around it. Despite its condemnation by the Congregation of the Index (1651), it sold nearly 15,000 copies in eighteen months, and Arnauld claimed that 60,000 copies were sold in 1688. Marolles, leading the new offensive on behalf of a French liturgy, secured a licence to translate the breviary in 1659, and a year later there was the affair of the "Missel de Voisin."

Joseph Voisin was chaplain to the Princesse de Conti and was asked by her to translate the missal; his translation appeared in 1660, dedicated to the Princess and with the approval of the bishops and professors of the University of Paris. Then high politics entered when Mazarin, anxious to dissuade Pope Alexander VII from granting protection to Cardinal de Retz after the Fronde troubles, intimated that the intention of the translation was to convey the spirit of the Mass into French. The Pope then asked the Clergé de France, then in session, to condemn the new translation, which they did with the approval of the Faculty of Theology in January 1661. The Privy Council ordered its suppression and the Lieutenant of Police was instructed to seize all copies, at which the Grand Vicaire of the Paris diocese issued a statement declaring their approval of the new missal. A pamphlet war broke out and the Parlement acted equivocally, first issuing Letters Patent endorsing the Pope's ban, then licensing a translation of the Office for Holy Week, including the text of the Mass with a dedication to the Queen Mother. The Princesse de Conti had hidden copies of the missal, but now they were on open sale and bought by thousands of worshippers. The innovators had won.

Once the Mass was in French, the Bible could no longer be delayed, first of all the New Testament. The Assemblée du Clergé assigned two men, Marca and Berthier, to the task of finding men capable, while Le Maistre de Sacy was coordinating work on the same project at Port-Royal. Amelote was the publisher of the Port-Royal Bible, and was the first with a licence because the rival translation had to apply to the Spanish monarch for their licence to print in the Netherlands on the Elzevier presses (though with Migeot's imprint). The long struggle for a vernacular Bible was over, and French had triumphed over the Latin tradition.

3. Religious Instruction and Propaganda

By now nearly all religious and devotional manuals were in French, pocket size for the general reader, amounting in volume to one-fifth of all books printed in Paris. Jesuits wrote more than one-tenth of them, the Capuchins contributed a good proportion, and in the last years of the 17th century ordinary parish priests wrote a good many. The classics of the spiritual life were now at last available in French, too, and found a much wider readership. St. Brigid, St. Gertrude, Catherine of Siena, Catherine of Genoa, a manual of meditation ascribed to St. Augustine, Tauler's *Divines institutions* (1650 and 1658) in Chardon's translation and in Loménie de Brienne's in 1665, the first published by Huré, the second by Savreux, and in 1681 another by Talon published by Le Petit. The cult of the Sacred Heart, a peculiarly French obsession, gave rise to Lansperge's work on this theme, newly translated as *Discours en forme de lettre de Notre-Seigneur Jésus-Christ à l'âme dévote* (Savreux, 1657), which reached the 7th edition in 1666, and Louis de Blois's *Institution spirituelle,* translated by Girard, a Jesuit, was reprinted in 1642, 1650, 1658 and 1673. A few lesser known works were also put into circulation, notably Jean Climaque's *Echelle sainte,* which thanks to Arnauld's championing was in great demand.

Some authors, though less than a century old, enjoyed classic status: Luis de Granada, St. Teresa (translated by Arnauld and others), François de Sales (especially *Introduction à la vie dévote*)—a great influence on 17th-century Catholicism. Best sellers in this field were Ribadeneyra's *Life of St. Teresa* and other works of the Carmelite school; Camus; Benet of Canfield's *Rule of perfection;* Jesuit writings, especially Father Poiré's *Triple couronne de la bienheureuse Vierge Marie;* Busée's *Méditations,* used as a manual by the Congregation of the Virgin, a contemporary phenomenon, and by the Priests of Mission; and above all the *Imitation of Christ,* translated by Girard, Le Maistre de Sacy and Corneille, with fifteen editions in Paris alone between 1610–1645, and fifty more in the next 25 years.

Translation was therefore a powerful transmitter of traditional Catholic devotions and the books of the period display a clear didacticism, a sense of earnest purpose that is evangelical. The literature was in the form of spiritual exercises, prayers, meditations, catechisms or canticles, in handy pocket sizes from octavo to duodecimo, with some such title as "Simple Method," "Short Way," "Summary," suitable to the lay reader who would be deterred by more substantial theology. The retreat was fashionable, enabling clerics and the more devout laity to withdraw from the world, equipped with a book of devotions. The market was assured. Cults were a popular distraction and books about them in demand, whether the Passion or the stigmata, the Sacred Heart or the Christ Child, the Sacrament of the Altar, and always of course, Mary. A form of Mariolatry was universal, inspiring verse, Hours and Offices of the Virgin, all in French. Catholicism and a national spirit were nicely fused. Lives of the saints, their pictures and prayers in their honor were printed in hundreds of thousands, nearly all now vanished, and the stories of recently canonized men and women were cheaply printed as chapbooks and devoured by the hungry devotees. Anyone dying in an odor of sanctity would be written about, and if he or she were in an Order, they would publicize it. There was a veritable industry in these tracts for the times. And today scarcely a trace of them remains.

Pastoral theology was also popular. Bonacina's *Cursus theologiae moralis* (1645) was reprinted in Lyons and Rouen, along with its rival, Bonal's *Cours de théologie morale.* From Germany and Flanders came Binsfeld's *Enchiridion theologia pastoralis* and Jacques Marchant's *Hortus pastorum,* and for the average parish priest there were pastoral manuals instead of the old heavy folios for theologians; examples: Charles Borromée's *Instruction . . . au confesseur,* Barthélemy des Martyrs' *Stimulus pastorum* or Molina's *Instruction des prêtres.* Guides for the use of confessors were used by all priests, and catechisms to instruct the flock or booklets of advice on administration of the sacraments like the "little Sa" (named after the Spanish Jesuit) were recommended reading "for all good curés" in the Lyons region. Bertin Bertault's *Directoire des confesseurs en forme de catéchisme,* condemned by the Sorbonne in 1635, when revised was in its 25th reissue by 1669.

Seminaries were being founded to turn out priests worthy of the name, and were stocked with practical manuals giving useful advice to priests in their livings and reminding them of the dignity of their office, all in handy-sized form, octavos, duodecimos and even tiny 32mos. The Oratory was turning out sermons and instructions with titles like *Instructions sur le manuel sous forme de demandes et résponses* . . . , or *Conduits pour les principaux exercises qui se font dans les séminaires ecclésiastiques* . . . , or *Méditations sur les principaux vérités chrétiennes et ecclésiastiques,* or the *Vraie et solide dévotion* by Beuvelet (1652–56). Others in continuous print were *Sentences chrétiennes,* the *Idée d'un ecclésiastique* and the *Parfait ecclésiastique* by Claude de la Croix. In the Mazarin Library there are a few surviving titles—an anonymous *Instructions familières pour bien disposer et ayder un malade à mourir chrétiennement,* a little book of 48 pages, 12 mo, bound with a *Discours enseignant les places en l'Eglise pour les clercs et pour les laïcs* and *Avis donné aux confesseurs* by Charles Borromée. The two masters in this genre were Olier *[Catéchisme chrétien pour la vie intérieure* (1656), *Journée chrétienne* (1665) and *Introduction à la vie et aux vertus chrétiennes],* and Jean Eudes, whose manuals for priests sold in their thousands.

So many books of this kind have vanished that we must conclude they had enormous influence in their time, and we can glean some idea of their market from the publicity. One little 32mo entitled *Miroir des prestres et autres ecclésiastiques* published by Trichard "near the church of St. Nicholas de Chardonnet," advertised itself plainly as "A little mirror for clerics to use and thereby see themselves more clearly than in a large and scarcely portable volume—there are enough of them in libraries. This little book can be your own property and can be consulted quickly." The publisher adds that he has other copies in sheets, and even of placard size "for easy display in church halls and sacristies," evidence of a growing public for this type of book.

Sermons and homilies for the priest to use as source material were plentiful; Jean-François de Reims wrote a

Directeur pacifique for spiritual directors and penitents, and in Jacob's bibliography there is a large number of catechisms for the years 1643–53, and we know that Jacob is incomplete. Among them are Bellarmine, Luis de Granada, Camus's *Enseignements catéchistiques* (1643), Du Chesne's *Sainte curiosité* (1643), Turlot's *Vray trésor de la doctrine chrétienne* (1645), Bonnefons's *Dévôt paroissien répondant à un curé* (1643), *La science du chrétien,* the *Catéchisme et instruction sur la Sainte Masse* by Hyacinthe de Paris (1646), the *Catéchisme royal en vers* by Pierre Le Blanc (1646), *Instruction familière en forme de catéchisme* by Louis de la Bresse (1647), Louis Abelly's *Instruction chrétienne* (1644) and *La science du Prince très chrétien* by Sieur de Loyse (1644).

It was the kind of literature that played a decisive part in the Catholic response to the Protestant threat, and was organized systematically through groups of clergy and individual priests. When St. Cyran and Port-Royal on the one hand and the Jesuits on the other made such heavy use of French and depended for their impact on unpretentious books for the mass of believers, French society was steeped in a wave of evangelism at a time of intense devotion. Jean Eudes, de Renty, Bernières-Louvigny and Boudon were using the printed word to preach to a wide public in Normandy and Brittany; Boudon's little books published by Michallet were very popular, but at this distance in time it is hard to judge fashion because all the evidence has disappeared. The Jesuits had traditionally been reserved about mysticism but now entered the field under the inspired direction of Lallemant, with Father Surin perhaps the most dynamic. His *Cantiques spirituels* (1657), *Catéchisme spirituel* (1659) and *Fondements de la vie spirituelle* (1667) enjoyed a great vogue, and Father Crasset's *Méthode d'oraison* was an aid to those who found praying difficult. Leaflets and simple woodcuts were all part of the Jesuit armory as they preached their way through France and the rest of the known world. Very few copies survive. Vast quantities of pious literature reached simple readers in the form of chapbooks, naive and edifying without any complicating theology and with titles like *Exercices et considérations très utiles en temps de guerre* (1648), no doubt helpful among the miseries of the

Thirty Years War, like *Elévations des âmes dévotes à Dieu pour demander la paix* (1652) and *Entretiens spirituels pour adorer le Très Saint Sacrement de l'autel* (1657).

Hymns were popular and collections of carols were printed in Troyes for the Paris market; little illustrated books with pictures of the Passion, like the *Fontayne des playes du Sauveur où se puise le pur amour avec toutes les vertues* (published by an engraver, Weyen); the *Perpetuelle croix* by Andries, which sold 50,000 copies in Flanders in one year; the *Emblèmes de l'amour divin*; *Tableau de la croix,* and the life of Christ in pictures.

This was also the age of the "Confrérie," or brotherhood of believers attached to convents and churches, with an organization, rules, prayerbooks and pictures studied by their members. One such, the Confrérie de la Vierge had Rocollet publish its own little book of devotions in 1644, proof of a high degree of prosperity. Other woodcuts and leaflets commend devotion to the Holy Sacrement, and a booklet of 40 pages, 12mo, called *Douleurs de Jésus,* was printed in 1663 for the "Association des filles et des femmes dévouées au Père Eternel," who unite in suffering with the Son. It was an age when images of piety and intense devotion were of almost neurotic intensity.

The book, the pamphlet, the cheap tract and the crude woodcut all played their part in this great movement toward spiritual revival. The important point is that the press was the medium deliberately exploited to promote what the evangelists sought so passionately, that dimension of mysticism which is normally a private matter, not committed to writing and certainly not to publication on this scale. Once more it betokens a new impulse, a sign that another class is more widely visible. The books were addressed specifically to this class—monks, contemplatives, the gentry, officials, military officers, and of course their wives. The "bon alboureur," the "bon laquais" or the "soldats chrétiens" who appear in titles and prefaces should not mislead us. Works of this kind were not designed for the direct use of the lower orders, who would have made little sense of print, but for their masters. Books were the tools of the upper classes for the instruction of their social inferiors; it was the proper responsibility of the privileged class to admit their servants to an orthodox presentation of the faith. There is some evidence that occasionally books must have got into the hands of humble folk: Abelly's *Couronne de l'année chrétienne* (1660) was donated to the Hospital for Incurables by the Chevalier de St. Maurice, to be read by the pauper inmates and the servants. A choice little work by Father Cyprien, *Livre des pauvres* (1652), may have been glanced at by the uneducated or illiterate—it was a 24-page quarto with three splendid and moving impressions in woodcut of Calvary, the soul in a state of mortal sin, attacked by a demon while the Guardian Angel hides her face, and a glowing Hell in flames; one section was devoted to prayers, and there was an illustrated elementary catechism prefaced by a note inviting better-off readers to explain the pictures to the poor and recommending that a copy be given to a poor person in lieu of alms.

Readings from approved spiritual works were duties devolving upon heads of households, as a pastoral letter from the Archbishop of Paris pointed out; it also enjoined them to keep a file on the family reading (it was rather like a modern questionnaire) to show which books were read weekly, if not daily and on Feast Days. The single extant copy of that letter is addressed to a carpenter. Again there is a sense of new energy and purpose in all this huge output; not only is it in French, but it has precise objectives—citizens, people—not simply other coteries of scholars or ecclesiastics, and is written to a formula, succinctly, for a lay public. In any study of the late 17th century and its ideological evolution, this class of reading matter is of central importance.

4. *The Bibliothèque Française*

The early years of Louis XIV's long personal rule saw the creation of modern French culture, original, native, irrigated by the classical tradition and inspired by a strong national self-consciousness. The men of the time were clear about this, and Charles Sorel made it explicit in his preface to the *Bibliothèque française,* itself a symbolic work: "Our language is perfectly adaptable for expressing any thought—no subject is beyond our capacities. Hebrew, Latin and Greek are perfectly translatable into French, and our own native writers are now composing original works as translations. Anyone can be educated without needing to know any language but French."

The purpose of his *Bibliothèque française* was to list essential French books in all subjects, an annotated bibliography first published in 1664, revised 1667. It was a slender book, but it tells us what our "honnête homme"— the cultured man—was expected to encompass in his reading. Essentially the intellectual revolution of the previous hundred years was *linguistic,* and Sorel begins his bibliography logically with a survey of "Books dealing with the Correct Way to Speak French," meaning aids to translations. There were few German-French or English-French dictionaries but several glossaries and manuals of Spanish and Italian, safe Catholic countries, Oudin's probably the best. In Latin-French dictionaries Sorel selects Estienne, Morel, Nicet and Pajot for special mention and points out that Latin in the Port-Royal schools is taught through the medium of French—the first hint that Latin was a dead language.

Sorel was an enthusiast for his native tongue. He lists books which emphasize the superiority and nobility of French: *La conformité du langage françois avec le Grec, Traité de la précellence du langage françois sur le toscan,* and *Dialogues du langage françois italianisé.* Then he follows with contemporary philological works: Ménage's *Harmonie etymologique des langues* and *Origines de la langue française,* Father Labbe's *Etymologie des plusieurs mots françois,* Borel's *Antiquités gauloises et françoises,* rhyming dictionaries and special subject vocabularies. Grammars, too: Ramus, Maupas, Oudin's grammar for foreigners, and his *Curiosités françoises,* and an anonymous *Grammaire françoise.* Pasquier's *Palais des curieux,* Vaugelas's *Remarques sur la langue françoise,* with critiques of the book, and Scipion Dupleix's *Petits traités en forme de lettres à diverses personnes studieuses* and *Libertés de la langue françoise* were next. New books expounding principles of phonetic spelling he lists with a note explaining that "he links writing and spelling with books on grammar because the latter explains pronunciation and, because of its precision, makes talk more refined and agreeable." It was on this foundation that the work which eventually led to the great Académie Française Dictionary first took shape.

In a society dominated by the priest and the lawyer, rhetoric was bound to play an important part, and Sorel follows his section on Language with one on Public Speaking. Aristotle first—the *Rhetoric* translated by Estienne and Cassandre, then Quintilian's *Institutions oratoires* translated by the abbé de Pure, then French treatises: *Rhétorique* (Du Perron), Sieur d'Epy's *Addresse assurée pour acquérir la facilité de persuader,* Dom Charles de St. Paul's *Lumières de l'Eloquence* and *Tableau de l'Eloquence françoise,* and La Mothe Le Vayer's *Rhétorique du Prince.* To these were added Du Vair's *Eloquence françoise,* Balzac's *Discours de la grande éloquence,* Father Léon de St. Jean's *De l'éloquence chrétienne,* Richesource's *Eloquence de la chaire,* Panigarola's *Art de faire un sermon,* and Sieur de Hauteville's *Art de bien discourir.*

Logic was next. A French translation of Aristotle's *Organon,* a work by Fresne-Canaye called *Organone,* Scipion Dupleix's *Logique,* Du Moulin's work of the same name, and Jean Salabert's *Addresse du parfait raisonnement.* Other titles were Scipion de Gramont's *Rationelle,* Jacques Himbert Durant's *Instrument logique,* St. Ange's *Conduit de jugement naturel,* Hugues de Picou's *Usage de la logique,* a *Logique sans espines* and a *Logique* used at Port-Royal "with new observations outside the scope of Scholastic logic."

Other branches of philosophy were represented, but Sorel preferred French translations, e.g., Fougerolles's *Opinions des divers philosophes,* Plutarch's *Opinion des anciens philosophes,* Seneca's *Questions naturelles,* Lucretius's *De rerum natura* translated by de Marolles. In addition, Cotin's *Théoclée,* a refutation of Epicurean doctrine, Lactantius, Augustine, Salvian and Theodoretus's *De providence divine,* Raymond de Sebond's *Théologie naturelle* and Yves de Paris. Plato and Aristotle were of course fundamental to the educated person's reading, and Sorel lists various translations, followed by philosophical surveys in French, *Epitome des livres d'Aristote* by Noël Taillepied, *Principauté de l'homme* by La Framboisière, François de Gravelles's *Abrégé de philosophie* and Sieur de Dampmartin's *Connaissance des merveilles du monde et de la nature*, Marandé's *Clef des philosophes* and Bary's *Fine philosophie*. Readers are advised to consult Jean de Champeynac, Scipion Dupleix, Du Moulin and d'Abillon to deepen their understanding of philosophy, and there is a word of praise for Louis de Lesclache, "who has taught philosophy for many years in French," and Savigny, who tried to put philosophy into tabular form, is recommended.

The insistence on French distinguishes the bibliography from any others; when he lists individual works in various branches of science he is at pains to point out that "not every subject has books in French," but those included are all in French. Jean Bodin's *Théâtre de la nature*, Sacro Bosco's treatise on the sphere, Wilkins's *Monde dans la lune*, Pascal's *Traité de l'Equilibre des liqueurs* and on the nature of the vacuum, Petit's *Dissertation sur la nature des comètes*, Etienne de Clave's *Des elements et des principes* and *Des pierres et des pierreries*, Claude Duret's *Saleure de la mer* and *Du flux et reflux de la mer*, Bernard Palissy's *Discours admirable des eaux et des fontaines* and Guy Patin's *Des tourbes*.

Under Botany and Zoology he includes *Théâtre d'agriculture*, *Maison rustique*, *Jardinière françois*, the *Livre de la nature et des plantes* by Guy de la Brosse, and after Rondelet's and Belon's works on birds and fishes he ends with Pliny's *Histoire naturelle*.

Sorel groups together "books which appertain to Nature," and among the works which "discuss philosophical aspects of that subject" he lists Cardan's *De la subtilité*, Bacon's *Histoire naturelle*, Pierre Bailly's *Songes de Phestion* and *Paradoxes historiques*, and Mersenne's *Questions curieuses et inouyes*. Books on Man he groups with works on anatomy and Coëffeteau's and La Chambre's books on humors. The question of the immortality of the soul is dealt with in a number of other listed titles under Morals and Apologetics, and on "spiritual matters" he advises the *Pimandre* of Hermes Trismegistus, and Pseudo-Dionysius who deals with

God and the orders of angels. On Magic and Demons he recommends Gabriel Naudé's *Apologie pour tous les grands hommes qui sont estez accusez de magie.*

Sorel's comments on the "new sects" is worth quoting in full:

> In the Philosophy Section you will find authors who have made their own way without recourse to Plato or Aristotle, and of course we do not need to confine our reading to one doctrine only. Here are some examples of books dedicated to new ideas: *La philosophie naturelle retablie en sa pureté,* a translation of Despagnet's *Enchiridion,* considered to be paramount in its field which goes beyond conventional philosophy. We also have several works by M. Descartes—*Méditations métaphysiques, Livre des principes, Discours de la méthode,* the *Dioptrique, Météores, Géometrie,* the *Monde,* the *Traité de la lumière, Traité de l'homme et la formation du foetus,* the *Traité des passions,* and two volumes of his letters. His works are generally agreed to be masterpieces, and the Sieur de Roure's philosophy is in harmony with M. Descartes's, giving rise to a new school based on their theories. I might also mention another new treatise, *Esprit de l'homme, de ses facultés et de ses fonctions et de son union avec le corps* by M. de la Forge, on Cartesian principles. Other new thought is so far only available in Latin, so I would recommend two little anthologies, *Des méthodes des sciences* and *De la perfection de l'homme.*

Sorel is prudent when discussing the new theories: "As to the profit to be derived from all this new thinking, be advised that there can be no point in studying novel and extraordinary theories without a thorough grounding in the traditional systems, especially the fundamental work of Plato and Aristotle. If you feel sympathy for the new ideas you need not fear for the future peace of the world—often the new schools differ from the old only in terminology."

There is hardly a mention of Mathematics, probably because Sorel did not fully understand the Mechanistic revolution going on before his eyes. Most contemporaries thought Descartes only another version of d'Espagnet, and though they were attracted by the new approach, still saw Aristotle as the unquestioned master, a fact that is plain in all the philosophical manuals.

The bibliography is not particularly strong in Medicine and Law, readers being referred to other specialist sources; the reason is fairly clear—Sorel had the general reader in mind, the man or woman with wide cultural interests. On the subject of Religious Instruction he lists only the standard guides: Bellarmine's *Doctrine chrestienne* and Richelieu's *Instruction du chrestien;* for Bible study he cites Father Talon's *Histoire sainte,* Father Girard's *Peintures sacrées,* the standard Paraphrases and de Marolles' translation of the New Testament. Of Patristic authors he includes Augustine's *City of God,* St. Ambrose's *Offices,* St. Gregory's *Morales,* Justin, St. Cyprian, Lactantius's *Institutions chrétiennes* and some Tertullian. In Apologetics he suggests Charron, Duplessis-Mornay, Mersenne, the abbé de Loyse and St. Sorlin's *Délices de l'esprit,* and for "advanced students" he offers Aquinas, Coëffeteau, the *Théologien françois,* Marandé's *Morales* and *Réflexions chrestiennes, Theologie des Pères* and abbe Quentin's *Théologie françois.*

Devotional literature has a section, beginning with the *Imitation of Christ* in a number of different French versions, then François de Sales's *Introduction à la vie dévote* and *Traité de l'amour de Dieu,* and Camus's *Esprit du Bienheureu François de Sales.* Then follows this revealing comment on devotional books:

> Many people are content to read traditional books of piety although so many new books come out every day. Some confine their reading to Luis de Granada and similar manuals of religious instruction urging us to shun sin and seek only God and good works. Rodriguez's *Sur la perfection de la vie réligieuse* is valuable for secular thinkers as well as the religious, and the same is true of Richelieu's *De la perfection du chrestien.* Father Senault's *Homme criminel* is in this category, and we can learn much from the *Eschelle sainte de St. Jean Damascène* which describes the various steps which lead us to Heaven. For those who wish to meditate on the deep mysteries of the spiritual life there is du Pont's

Méditations, Father Suffren's *Année sainte,* Father
Hayneuve's *Méditations,* and others. Books on Prayer
will help those who seek fruitful results from their
reflections. In short, there should be no difficulty in
finding help appropriate to everyone's needs.

On Morals he cites only Nicolas de St. Martin's *Morales
chrétiennes,* Caussin's *Cour sainte* and Yves de Paris, yet in
what we might call the social sciences he shows much more
interest, something symptomatic of this new age. He starts
with the ancient authorities, Plutarch, Diogenes Laertius,
Cicero, Epictetus, Valerius Maximus, Cato, Boethius, followed by La Mothe le Vayer's *De la vertu des payens* and
Justus Lipsius's *De la constance.* He recommends Petrarch's
Remèdes pour la bonne et la mauvaise fortune and the French
writers influenced by it—Marandé's *Jugement des actions
humains,* Le Moyne's *Peintures morals,* Senault's *Usage des
passions.* On morals he singles out Jean de l'Espine's
Discours du repos et du contentement de l'esprit, Bary's
Morale, Videl's *Conduite de la volonté* and Gomberville's
Doctrine des moeurs.

Manners rather than abstract morality interest Sorel, and
here of course his basic sources are Italian: the *Galatée* by
Giovanni della Casa, Guazzo's *Art de plaire dans les
compagnies* and *Conversation civile,* Matteo Palmieri's *Vie
civile* and a book by Fabrice Campani; note that all are in
French. They were somewhat passé already in Sorel's day,
and he prefers home-grown French works on the subject:
Grenaille's *Honneste garçon,* Faret's *Honneste homme,*
Bardin's *Lycée,* and books designed for women—Grenaille's
Honnête fille, Du Bosc's *Honnête femme* and *Femmes
heroïques,* Le Moyne's *Galerie des femmes fortes* and
Conseils d'Ariste à Célimène.

This of course was the age of the "honnête homme," and
the art of social cultivation, the Courtier, the Gentleman, the
Man of Quality, all models of civilized behavior. There was
no lack of handbooks on the subject: Castiglione's *Courtisan,*
Peregrini's *Sage en cour,* Guevara's *Avertissement aux
courtisans et aux favoris du Prince,* and French classics of the
genre: *Traité de la Cour,* attributed to Eustache de Refuge,

Balzac's *Aristippe,* Sieur de Neuville's *Fortune de Cour,* Callières's *Fortune des personnes de qualité.* Sorel himself was the author of a guide for the upwardly mobile: *Chemins de la fortune . . . pour acquérir des richesses en toutes sortes de conditions et pour obtenir les faveurs de la Cour, les honneurs et le crédit,* a pretty shameless piece of self-interest. He also thought well of Du Val's *Dessin des professions nobles et particulières,* Fortin de la Hoguette's *Testament ou conseils d'un Père à ses enfants* (a very fashionable work), Pelletier's *Nourritures de la noblesse,* and Pasquier's *Gentilhomme* and *Gentilhomme parfait.*

As Sorel put it: "Although we dwell on earth we observe the heavens and the stars; so, from a study of the Gentleman we go on to the Prince, and from the Prince to the King." Every since Osorio, the "Institution of the Prince" was a favorite topic among the upper classes, and we can date the French cult of "honneur" from the mid-17th century. The more socially ambitious reader in Louis XIV's reign, by studying the works of De Lancre, Héroard, Badoin, Fortin, Senault and others like them, could easily imagine that their wordly hopes could be achieved.

Next, Politics. Aristotle's *Politics* is the natural foundation, together with Plato's *Republic,* here in a translation by Louis Le Roy. François Patrice's *République* is listed but Machiavelli's *Prince,* then by no means new, was dubbed "somewhat dangerous," to be read "with care" and in conjunction with a *Discours d'estat contre Machiavel* (remember, the bibliographer was a Huguenot), and with *Fragments contre Machiavel.* Bodin's *République* is "a solid and practical book," and he recommends Lipsius's *Politiques,* Molinier's *Politiques chrestiennes,* Paul Paruta's *Perfections de la vie politique,* Tacitus's *Discours politiques et militaires,* Mellier's *Discours politiques et militaires sur Corneille Tacite,* and works by Ammirato translated by Baudoin. Jean de Marnix, Jacques Hurault, and Coignet's *Discours politiques sur la vérité et le mensonge pour garder la foy promise* are all, according to Sorel, "full of instances and authorities from the past as well as many new topics introduced by the authors." He praises the *Conseiller d'Estat* by Eustache de Refuge, Priezac's *Discours politiques* and

Silhon's *Ministre d'Estat.* Thomas More's *Utopia* is in this section with Turquet de Mayerne's *Monarchie aristo-démocratique* and *Défense de la monarchie.* He prefers "works of practical value" like Montchrestien's *Occonomie politique,* René de Lucinge's *Accroisement des Estats,* "which is concerned with beating the Turks," and La Noue's *Discours politiques et militaires,* "a book that speaks from experience."

The last paragraphs in his chapter on Politics are worth quoting:

> The science of Politics has been much studied of late. Thomas Hobbes, an Englishman, has written a book entitled (in French) *Les fondemens de la politique* in which he lays down certain principles for a State very different from ours. His views are innovatory and I cannot entirely agree with him. M. de le Hoguette is generally more approved in his *Elémens de la politique,* wherein he shows that the proper ordering of a State rests on natural laws.
>
> Of our French authors, M. de Scudéry's *Discours politiques des rois* is a dialogue with Princes and their public utterances on various subjects. A recent work we have high hopes of is *La politique des conquérans,* if it lives up to its title. Otherwise Politics is best understood by reading the Memoirs of Statesmen, Lives, Letters, Treaties and accounts of negotiations. A few other books could have been included here, but they are no loss.

5. *Literary Works*

The last ten years of Richelieu's Ministry (1633–43) were a fertile period in literature. Descartes published his *Discours de la méthode* in Leyden, Corneille's best work was staged in Paris and the Académie Française was founded. It was indeed a remarkable phase. The years following, from 1643 to 1660, were fraught with political and social crises and tension, and unproductive from a literary standpoint; only Pascal's *Lettres provinciales* and Molière's *Précieuses ridicules* were of first rank.

The theatre was high fashion, no fewer than 136 plays (mostly tragedies and tragicomedies) appearing between 1640 and 1649, compared with 112 in the previous decade. From 1643 to 1648, 36 tragedies and 32 tragicomedies were published. Corneille was the leading dramatist; a one-volume folio edition of his collected plays was reissued several times, in 1644, 1648, 1654, 1656, 1660 and 1664, an achievement previously equalled only by Ronsard. Taste was for high tragedy, inflated, bombastic, in heroic verse extolling the search for "Grandeur," a kind of Holy Grail, a theme which befitted the age in which the swashbuckling Prince Condé lived. During the Fronde, subjects tended to be more strictly historical or political, though heroes were still drawn on a Baroque scale, speaking in grandiose rhetoric, the theatre the French nobility most relished. Plays were usually published in editions of 1,250–1,500 copies and reached a small public in print—they rarely went into a second edition but on stage the author's reputation was quickly made and his work was a never-ending topic of discussion in the literary salons. The *beau monde* who constituted the audience were as theatre-conscious as we are television-conscious today. Molière made comedy a fashion through his genius (52 comedies by various playwrights were published between 1660 and 1669). It was a vogue that did not last.

The novel lost some of its grip in mid-century but La Calprenède wrote multi-volume sagas: *Cassandra* (10 vols.) and *Cléopatra* (12 vols.), and Mlle. de Scudéry used her brother's name when she published *Ibrahim ou l'illustre Bassa* (1641) and her famous *Grand Cyrus* (10 vols., 1649–53) followed by *Clélie* (1654–60). They were enormously successful, the first volumes of *Grand Cyrus* were sold out before the last ones were published, forcing the later print-runs to be increased to meet the demand and the earlier ones to be reprinted. We should like to know more about the marketing and distribution of these popular titles but the surviving copies in the Bibliothèque Nationale give little help since they include eight different editions of volume 1 of *Cassandra* and seven of volume 2, and seven different editions of volume 1 of *Cléopatra* and eight of volume 2, which at least demonstrates a wide diffusion.

If we ask what was the great attraction of these now unreadable novels, the titles give an indication of changing expectations: after about 1650, love stories have less appeal, and the words "love," "lover," and "loving" are very much rarer in titles (about ten cases from 1640 to 1660). The new keywords are "gallant" or "magnificent," anything suggestive of vainglorious war or Romanized glamor. The warfare is wholly absurd and unreal, the heroes, like Vercingetorix, merely insipid Platonists mouthing philosophical platitudes. The background is contemporary, steeped in the *mores* of French militarism; the characters in *Cyrus,* for example, mere cardboard cutouts of Prince Condé and his captains or Madame de Longueville, stars of their day whom readers loved to recognize. The hero in fiction is the exhausted figure of the *grand seigneur,* loyal at all times to his sovereign lord, by implication sanctifying the King. There was a change of tone during the Fronde (which jolted the aristocracy badly), reflected in *Cyrus* after volume 5, and more so in *Clélie,* where there is emphasis on a credible psychology, less on the stock responses to unreal situations, and less of the aristocratic pose. La Calprenède's later novels had fewer admirers and they too showed subtler treatment of character and sentiment, just at the time when Molière's unsentimental, devastating mockery was in performance on the stage.

A taste for poetry is on the increase, especially heroic and comic verse, the former appealing to aristocratic taste and worship of an ideal leader; esthetic taste was satisfied by masques and ballet, popular at Court and in the great houses. Epic was the supreme form in poetry, *La Pucelle* a good example, though most poems in this vein did not appear until the late 1650s and into the Sixties. The quickest way to fame and money was by writing plays. Most of the poetry was abysmal, with Virgil as a model, but lacking entirely his power or purpose, the poetasters could only manage feeble copies. Like Homer and Tasso, Virgil was read in translation, though Christian and Biblical themes were preferred, as in Du Bartas's *Semaines.* In most of the epics there was a confused melee of heroes—Moses, Job, Paul, Mary

Magdalene, Clovis, St. Louis, Hildebrand, with national saviors like Charles Martel and Charlemagne. The interesting point in all this is the physical product. While fiction and plays were published as cheaply as possible, small-sized and almost grudgingly produced, no expense was spared in the printing of an epic, no matter how appalling. Bosse was commissoned to do the engravings for Perrin's translation of the *Aeneid,* Chauveau and his pupils designed the plates for Tasso's *Gerusalemme liberata* and Scudéry's *Alaric,* and Bosse, Chauveau and Bourdon collaborated on the plates for St. Sorlin's *Clovis* and *Pucelle.*

The engravings tell us more about the absurd contemporary cliché of the hero and his posturing than any printed page; they are all plumes, sword thrusts and clashing armor, with a vaguely theatrical backdrop of knightly tournaments, but no research at all into actual events or local color. All the characters are dressed as if for an entrance on stage. The reaction to this tedious and artificial world was burlesque, popular in the Forties and Fifties. The last category to mention in poetry is the Latin, chiefly religious, verse for which there seems to have been a steady public. In all, a varied literary scene.

CHAPTER III

PUBLISHERS AND PUBLIC

1. The Paris Book Trade, 1643–67

DESPITE EFFORTS TO REFORM IT, the trade suffered during the period covered by this chapter. There were more master printers, booksellers and binders than ever, but production lagged, there was a good deal of unemployment and standards of workmanship fell, with bitter competition for orders among the poorer printers who did not share in the monopolies and other privileges of the better-off. A census of books published and a careful study of the licenses issued by the Chancellor's office gives us a fairly accurate picture of trends in publishing.

For the Palais publishers, Quinet, Sommaville and Courbé, it was a prosperous time because they dealt in drama, fiction and fashionable literature. Henri Le Gras, Charles de Sercy, Guillaume and Etienne Loyson and Guillaume de Luynes were also doing well; Guignard, a law specialist, would have a steady clientele, and Rocollet (history, devotional books and engravings) was a well established firm. De luxe editions were a feature of the Palais emporiums but their staple—what brought in the steady revenue—was the newly fashionable pocket-sized book. Bookstocks consisting largely of that class of book would rarely be valued at more than 20,000 livres (Rocollet and Courbé were exceptions, valued at 34,000 and 90,000 livres respectively).

Some of the grand old firms in the Rue St. Jacques were now not so successful but other well-known names were still doing well: the Widow Buon, Siméon Piget (successor to the Morels), Denys Béchet, and Antoine Berthier, Sonnius's

442

agent, were still in the international trade, singly or in collaboration. With Sébastien Cramoisy they were the leading publishers but they showed no signs of expansion, Cramoisy excepted. He was the Establishment personified. His influence in the Compagnie du Navire and Compagnie des Usages, his role as principal King's Printer and printer to the Archbishop of Paris, his publishing monopolies in Cistercian and Praemonstratensian liturgical books, his position of official publisher to the Jesuits, the anti-Jansenist, pro-Gallican publishing and the host of devotional books made him impregnable. Yet even Cramoisy was affected by the religious and political conflicts of the time, as other big names were. Moretus in Antwerp complained of high prices charged by Cramoisy for his publications; new issues of the prayerbook published by the Compagnie des Usages were not selling well, and when the frontier with Spain was closed, the Compagnie could not export its breviaries or missals, and 200,000 livres worth of unsold stock mounted up in its warehouses. When Chancellor Séguier renewed the Compagnie du Navire's licences there was uproar among the excluded publishers. Cramoisy was forced to suspend payment for a time, and even to quit business; Moretus writes from Antwerp in some anxiety, urging Cramoisy to keep his promises and not tarnish his good name. Cramoisy was in financial difficulties and though he managed to stave off disaster with the help of creditors, he later gave up the business, referring clients to his brother Claude and his nephew Edme Martin. He had enough wealth to retire on, and died leaving a fortune of one million livres and a stock of 400,000 books.

He was the last of the generation of publishers brought up in the Counter Reformation. Another age brought new names: Jean and Mathurin Hénault, Gaspar Méturas, Pierre de Bresche, Georges Josse, Jean de Heuqueville, and Edme Coutereau, Denis Moreau's son-in-law, who built a thriving business on devotional books and ecclesiastical history. Other successful firms included Sébastien Huré, who gained by La Noue's bankruptcy and profited from the current thirst for spiritual literature, lives of saints, and authors like de Sales, Catherine of Siena and the like. An example of the precarious state of trade is Thomas Jolly, who had bought up Courbé's stock in 1660, adding Courbé's device, a plum tree, to his own, the arms of the Netherlands. He was in business with his brother-in-law Simon Besnard, trading with Lyons and with Holland. Somewhere along the line there must have been bad judgment or a failure of some kind, because quite suddenly Jolly went to prison, in debt to the tune of 202,557 livres while his assets amounted only to 125,000 livres, big enough sums but not enough to guarantee stability.

2. Monastic Orders and their Publishers

As we know too well by now, a large part of Paris publishing was for religious houses wanting books for their newly founded libraries or restocking with a fresh collection after reform or reorganization. Many new Orders started in the 17th century, and that was good for trade. Convents in St. Teresa's name were founded in 1604 in the Faubourg St. Jacques; in 1611 Madame Acarie's cousin opened the first Ursuline convent and Bérulle the first Oratory in the Rue St. Honoré, and in 1619 the Visitants came to the Faubourg St. Michel. In 1608 Angélique Arnauld refounded a closed order at Port-Royal, and Henri IV encouraged the Pénitents de la Miséricorde in Picpus and the Recollects in the Faubourg St. Martin (1603); in 1605 Louise de Lorraine, Henri III's widow, endowed a convent of Capuchines opposite the Capuchins of St. Honoré, and in 1608 Margot honored a vow made during the recent troubles and founded a company of Augustines near her residence. Marie de Medici laid the foundation stone of the Church of the Minims and brought a Spanish Order, the Freres de la Merci de la Redemption des Captifs to the Marais. There were so many started that only a few can be mentioned here.

Paris had three abbeys, St. Victor, St. Geneviève (reformed by Cardinal de la Rochefoucauld) and St. Germain des Prés, all for men. For women there was the abbey of St. Antoine des Champs, Montmartre, near the present Madeleine, a priory under the direction of Marguerite d'Arbouze; the abbey of Port-Royal, which came to the Faubourg St. Jacques from Chevreuse; and the Val-de-Grace from Val-

Profond near Bièvres. Other religious communities multiplied: two Augustinian foundations, one called the Little Augustinians, the other settled in the Rue Notre Dame des Victoires. New Orders swarmed all over Paris: the Third Order of Franciscans, the Nazarene Fathers, the Sisters of St. Elizabeth, the Visitants, Ursulines, Brothers of Christian Doctrine in the Place Maubert and Rue St. Martin, the Barnabites in the Cité, and the Théatins who came in 1644. The Jesuits opened a novitiate school as well as their college, the Oratorians opened a seminary, as did Vincent de Paul at the Mission at St. Lazare, where Louise de Marillac launched her Daughters of Charity. According to the *Description de la ville et des fauxbourgs de Paris en vingt planches* (Jean de la Caille, 1714), 28 abbeys, priories and convents were in being before 1600, and 61 were founded in the first half of the 17th century. The age of piety indeed!

This frenzy of reform and reconstruction had its effect on the book trade, since naturally books had to be provided in the libraries which were integral parts of the new foundations. The regular and secular clergy were deeply involved in teaching and evangelization, and gradually an increasingly better educated laity was emerging.

3. The Beginnings of Modern Education

The Council of Trent made strong recommendations about elementary education as part of its strategy to re-educate Catholics, only to be frustrated by the Wars of Religion, which destroyed many existing establishments. When peace returned, schools were started again, usually run by the parish priest or sometimes a layman, all in very haphazard fashion, and occasionally with help from the municipality or individual bequests and charities which allowed free schooling to the poorest children. Then we begin to hear of "congregations" set up to provide instruction, especially for girls. In 1537 Angela da Brescia founded the Ursulines, and in 1592 César de Bus, founder of the Brothers of Christian Doctrine, introduced them into Avignon, then in Isle-sur-Sogne and later throughout the Midi, and by the end of the 17th century nearly 400 schools had been established for the education of girls. Pierre Fourrier started the Filles de la Congregation de Notre Dame, with 100 schools in the next hundred years. In 1606, one of Montaigne's nieces, the Blessed Jeanne de Lestonnac, started the Filles de Notre Dame in Bordeaux, and an Order called the Visitation, founded by François de Sales and Jeanne de Chantal in 1610 at Annecy, ran 86 establishments for children of the upper classes. Others were the Sisters of the Good Shepherd, the Sisters of Sainte Geneviève, and the Calvariennes (Filles de la Providence), and in 1625 Vincent de Paul founded the Filles de la Croix in Picardy.

The charitable movement prompted action in Paris and some free charity schools were opened, conducted by pious women from the convent schools. One Françoise de Blosset, "after consulting with experienced persons," started a school near St. Nicolas-du-Chardonnet and another in the Fossés St. Victor district, continued by a curé, Bourdoise, "in the basic subjects." M. Vincent's Filles de la Croix came to Paris from Picardy to be welcomed by Madame Lhuillier, who opened what was in effect the first school to train women teachers, and in 1639 M. Vincent opened a school for boys and one for girls near the church of St. Laurent. Louise Bellanger was teaching 40 poor girls with assistance from the Confrérie de Notre Dame-du-Bon-Secours in 1642, and the curé of that parish, Pierre Martin, opened three schools for boys and three for girls in 1646.

The Precentor of Notre Dame (who had been studiously ignored by the founders of the free schools) started a campaign against them, claiming they were not confined to poor children, but he failed to stop the schools; they were approved by Parlement and they developed rapidly, the parish of St. Sulpice (thanks to Jean-Baptiste de la Salle) having 14 classes numbering 4,000 children in 1693. Nicolas Barré in Rouen, M. Démia in Lyons, and LaSalle in Rheims opened schools, and especially in Paris good progress was made; the Precentor himself was moved to reorganize elementary education under a better system. All elementary schools were based on the Catholic religion with Latin a fundamental part of it, but religion was tackled in a less purely formal way, as an exract from the 1654 *Parish school,* a manual for directors of schools, makes clear:

> *School books.* On the second shelf of the book cupboard there will be devotional literature, Ribadeneyra's *Lives of the saints* (4to), and Lion in two volumes (price 1 écu), a necessary part of children's reading. If he wishes the teacher may keep the two volumes of the *Fleur des exemples* to find stories for his catechism, a copy of the diocesan catechism, some abridged versions of Mysteries of the Faith, Confirmation, Confession, Baptism and Communion which he may even hand out to the children if he thinks they can comprehend them. These little books may be had of Maistre Pierre Targa, Rue St. Victor, at the Sign of the Golden Sun. *Paradisus puerorum,* printed at Douai, is an excellent story book and the teacher should have a good supply because children learn by example rather than precept. The *Méditations* of St. Bonaventura ought to be available during Holy Week. The *Pédagogue Crestien,* printed in a small octavo (Mons and Rouen), is sold in Paris, a most excellent book on doctrine and with some good stories. Father Bonnefons' *Enfant catéchismé* is also an excellent work, and other good books are Granada's *Guide des Pécheurs,* the *Catéchisme paroissial des Festes,* the *Première communion,* all to be had of Maistre Pierre Targa.
>
> *Books for the Teacher, and other items.* As well as books of piety and instruction there should also be a Despautère (grammar), a Donatus (Latin grammar) and some little Greek grammar, in case there are any children learning Latin or Greek.

The teacher was expected to keep a stock of pictures, and beads to reward the children. We can deduce from this that although the principles in the manual might not always have been carried out to the letter, nevertheless they must have fostered the habit of devotional reading, or how else can we account for the huge consumption?

College education was a different matter. After the Edict of Nantes the Protestants opened schools and colleges south of the Loire, and the Jesuits founded their colleges in most large towns. By 1610 there were forty such, and by 1627, 40,000 pupils, 12,000 in Paris alone. By 1640 there were seventy colleges, and shortly after that there was hardly a town without its college, however small, teaching Latin and Rhetoric. The various municipalities were pleased to allow the Jesuits this freedom because it meant that education was available at small cost, and it was good for business. Some colleges were administered by secular priests, others by officials known as Regents, usually laymen appointed by the University. Other Orders played their part in the educational renaissance: Oratorians, Eudists in Normandy, Benedictines, Carmelites and Augustinians, in the precincts of their monasteries, all teaching in their "Latin schools."

Individual benefaction was also a factor: in Sorel's *Francion* the Lisieux college is described as having been founded by a "pedagogue" with five or six assistants. Harcourt College (the modern Lycée St. Louis) numbered St.-Evremond, Nicole, Boileau and Racine among its students, and Clermont College set the pace in Jesuit education. Princes of the Blood and nobles sent their children there for a sound education, rubbing shoulders with the offspring of ordinary tradesmen and artisans of Paris. In 1621 Clermont had 1,650 pupils and in 1645, 3,000. The University opened "Latin schools" under its aegis and reformed its own colleges, employing properly salaried staff. In North Eastern France some colleges had between 1,000 and 1,500 pupils; the Jesuits had 12,565 scholars in their Paris schools in 1627, 6,940 at Toulouse, in Champagne 5,578, and in the three other provinces about 15,000: some 40,000 young men altogether. This was the start of organized curricular teaching.

A word about the social background of the students. Evidence from class registers seems to show that until mid-century children of the upper classes were in the minority—fewer than 10% were the sons of gentry, even where there was a substantial community of petty landowners. Children of the rentier class, whose fathers drew their incomes from investments, were scarcely more numerous;

children of civil servants and other officials accounted for 20%–30%, the majority being merchants' and artisans' children, even some laborers'. The presence of lower social ranks was offensive to some parents who wanted nothing to do with crafts but planned the traditional schooling in the Humanities with a view to a future career for their children in the huge administrative bureaucracy of State, adding to the crowded and unproductive classes already burdening society. In an environment of venality—the sale of offices—the highest ambition was to be a placeman. Future choice would need to be made between an education for its own sake or with an eye to a niche in some paying profession. Did they want training for law or for the life of a gentleman?

4. The cavalier, the professional, and the well-bred man

The dashing cavaliers were of the type immortalized by Frans Hals—fond of plumes and finery, mettlesome, feckless, brave soldiers but in no sense cultivated; indeed, ignorance of academic subjects was a point of honor with them. They flaunted themselves as a class, flouting common morality, viewing life with cynical, worldly-wise tolerance. When Louis XIV came to the throne they were already notorious as an amoral, pleasure-seeking, boorish nobility, "les hommes d'épés." As a historian put it: "They belonged in a brazen, heartless world, bent on pleasure and power formed around the incipient dictatorship close to the Crown." They were the men of the Fronde, of Tallemant des Réaux's *Historiettes* and the *Histoire amoureuse des Gaules*.

In the early 17th century they began to lose their grosser qualities, even sent their sons to college (or hired private tutors). The Prince of Condé has been mentioned in this narrative before and he was typical of this class, vain, vindictive, choleric, but educated by Jesuits and completed his rigorous course of studies at an early age, including Advanced Philosophy and Fortification, modern military science. Neither was he a stranger to the Paris literary scene; he often went slumming with other gallants, tried his hand at verse, and was a patron of letters.

The next generation was more cultured and not afraid to be seen to be part of the literary life. Bussy-Rabutin, St. Evremond, La Rochefoucauld, Turenne, Maréchal de Gramont, the Duc de Crequy, the Comte de Fiesque, the Chevallier de Nantouillet, the Duc de St. Aignan, who studied two hours a day to please the King, and others of the same stripe all had cultural affiliations with Paris; some, like the Duc de Montausier, were a standing joke among their peers. The reformation of aristocratic manners was to some extent due to Jesuit influence in education—which even included theatrical evenings in college to attract a threatre–loving class to a closer study of serious drama. Young women of the highest rank were also present, and debates were a feature of college life, tackling subjects of current concern—during the Jansenist controversy, for instance, Grace was on the agenda. Of course the young blades still affected to despise the studious and men of inferior social origins, with whom they inevitably had to mix in college. Any form of pedantry was bad taste, whether the legal drudge, the dreary classical scholar or the trainee priest, symbol of excruciatingly dull Latinity. To the young aristo whose future depended on his swordsmanship, bookish pursuits were nonsense. He was aware that a degree of training was needed, and that some introduction to history or ethics was desirable if he was to serve his country or his monarch—the feudal spirit of loyalty to the sovereign power was endemic to this type of mind. Family, the code of "honor," counted above everything else for this Quixote figure, emphasized by his concern for outward appearance and extravagance in dress.

To the average cavalier a good book meant one with plenty of fine-looking pictures in it, and that would take a fine binding with his arms emblazoned on the cover. Books were for display: *Caractères de Philostrate* is a fair sample, and the more scenery there was between the covers, the happier he was. Heroic epics, military exploits with glamorous battle scenes, family pedigrees, genealogy, armorials were the basic reading for this class, and there was a fashion for mythology, emblem books, and books illustrating themes he would encounter at the ballet or masques; it was the age of allegory. He would read anything on hunting or horsemanship, weaponry or warfare, recent ideas on tactics or siege strategy and fortification, which involved some mathematics. Young officers who had gained experience in the Thirty Years War applied themselves to studies which involved the new Cartesian theories, and an interesting sidelight on that is Descartes's own career, which was originally planned to be a military one, in which case he would have ended up a captain of a regiment. His education at La Flèche College, a seminary for officers, ensured that he acquired the mentality of the officer and gentleman. There was always a streak of contempt in him for old-fashioned pedantry.

Finally, the young cavalier was as much a worshipper of precedent as any stuffy professor of theology. The Court in Mazarin's and Anne of Austria's time was influenced by Italian models, ruled by principles formulated by Castiglione, with emphasis on the art of conversation and a capacity to amuse, a route to higher office. Vivacity, "esprit," good judgment and approved taste were essential faculties, and a knowledge of affairs marked out the young man of promise; hence the great demand for translations and summaries of information. There was an increased need for precision, in facts, in style of address ("points"). In a curious way this increased sophistication was a return to an oral culture, at Court at least, when knowledge and judgment were communicated in conversation within the groups and circles which met for recreation and amusement, and also in the elegant soirées at the town houses of the great in the capital. Concomitant with the more strict organization of formal education in the colleges, a new kind of refined verbal intercourse was developing in aristocratic circles.

The salons of the capital were famous, where poets and literary folk gathered, and where the first bluestockings or précieuses lent their talents (though in French the word also includes men). A *Dictionnaire des précieuses* identified the social rank and occupations of the men and women engaged in the cultural and artistic life of the period:

Princes and dukes 32
Marquises 43
Counts 35
Barons 5
Knights 7
Court officials 17
Gentlemen and "hommes d'épées" 34
Financiers 23
Maîtres de requêtes 10
Members of Parliament 15
Members of the Cour des Aides 1
Members of the Chambre des Comptes 2
Councillors of State 3
Lawyers 1
Clerks 1
Citizens of various occupations 22
Abbés 13
Literary people 62

Civil servants (*gens de robe*) are least in evidence; most are from the aristocracy or upper middle class with money, and the milieu is strongly reminiscent of today's fashionable world of politicians, diplomats, millionaires, actors and sportsmen. In the 17th century it was a small world of Court and rich bourgeoisie, the kind mocked by Molière (though he was a favorite of theirs), later anatomized by La Bruyère, and like the 18th-century world of the "Cognoscenti" which Voltaire reckoned to number between 2,000 and 3,000. The Précieuses were a complete social entity and their women members more than a little like coquettes, with a high grade of wit and worldliness though without much formal education, most of which came from social intercourse and the reading of fashionable novels. But there was a serious literary component, and a lot of good criticism emerged in the form of essays as well as high-toned gossip. It was from the *conversazione* that the journal of ideas and discussion developed, the ancestor of our Reviews, more or less invented by Renaudot, a born journalist who launched the *Gazette* in his office, which was a clearing house for correspondents who supplied much of the earliest material for the paper in the form of questions to the editor and contributions on a variety of topics. It was essentially a social age when the "conférence" (discussion group) was the natural habitat, in print or in person. Originally the notion of a meeting or seminar was to allow young professionals and academics to discuss rather specialized subjects, but anyone with a genuine curiosity would be attracted to them, and soon the "conférence" or "séance" was a type of higher education, prototype of the Académie or, later in England, the Royal Society.

The range of subjects was impressive: the earth's motion, comets, Greek atomic theory, the nature of language, equality of the sexes. We know that regular meetings took place on Mondays, conducted in French, whereas hitherto the language of serious debate had been Latin; a paper would be followed by lively discussion in a congenial auditorium where ideas and social behavior could evolve together. One salon was known as the "Palais Précieux," where "every diversion could be found to amuse men and women of intellect and curiosity." Louis de Leslache arranged lavish gatherings of men and women of the aristocracy where philosophical and modern political theories were discussed, and these lasted from 1635 to 1669. Bary, Isnard, Vaflart and St. Ange taught at these assemblies. Jean le Soudier launched his "Conférences académiques et oratoires," meeting three times a week, a mixture of the religious and worldly. Rohault expounded Descartes in private and public, as a tutor and lecturer to audiences of "prelates, abbés, professors, courtiers, philosophers, artisans, college governors, students, foreigners, in a word to people of all degrees and professions and to both sexes."

Another vital ingredient of this life style was the précis or abstract (hence the word "précieuse"), which set out schematically and in convenient form new propositions or theories in a scientific way; it was a product of Cartesian method. This supplanted the ponderous folio. French takes the place of Latin, and gradually a wider and wider circle of readers is drawn in, and popular texts begin to be written to help make abstruse subjects palatable to lay readers. In the provinces we hear of literary or scientific groups from all educated classes with an interest in "cultural progress" meeting in Grenoble, Lyons, Provence, at Châlons-sur-Marne, where a list of members survives, and in country chateaux where the latest thought and newest ideas from Paris were eagerly debated. This was the provincial society that wished to keep in close contact with Paris and made the fortune of the *Mercure galant*. And humbler citizens were becoming involved, too, as Furetière's *Roman bourgeois* tells us. The story is set in the Place Maubert, a bourgeois district, where Lucrèce, a lawyer's niece, helps her aunt run a house where a lot of entertaining is done. The author provides a lively picture of middle-class life, and evidence that there was some social mixing when a Marquis gets himself introduced to the spirited and attractive Lucrèce. To judge by the conversation, there seemed to be no barriers between the classes as they mixed on these occasions, especially if they were of the opposite sex. A character speaks about "an ambitious man" who was "a lawyer in the morning and a courtier in the evening." He would be pleading in court at the Palais in the morning, and in the evening engaged in dalliance with an alluring young woman who hoped to deceive him into thinking she was from a noble family, "convinced that if someone was dressed in the height of fashion they must be of the *bon ton* and a cut above ordinary humanity."

Ordinary humanity patterned itself on the Court, and an ambitious person would keep in the swim by reading the "right" novels to gain some idea of acceptable conduct. Furetière's young Nicodème is of this type, while his rival, Jean Bedout, is more like the old-fashioned bourgeois, niggardly in dress, uncouth in manner, and though generally mean, he assiduously attends "conférences," which he dimly perceives are the places to see and to be seen in. Both of them seek the hand of Procurator Vollichon's daughter, the lovely Javotte, of whom Furetière says, "If she had only been born outside the bourgeoisie—I mean if she had been raised in the *beau monde*—she might have been worthy of a really well-bred husband." Alas, poor Javotte was raised in a very humble household and has only ever read the *Civilité puérile*, so that she has no idea how to respond to gallantry. Her responses to Nicodème are flat and dull. After weighing the pros and cons, Vollichon decides on Bedout, and hoping for a marriage soon, he plans to let his daughter mix in high society and meet the précieuses, but not to excess because he doesn't want to lose his daughter to their kind altogether. A cousin introduces Javotte into a typical group "where poetry and prose is discussed to extinction and all contemporary writing comes under minute scrutiny." Here she takes up with one Angélique from a higher class, whose dowry is worth 50,000 écus, and through her she meets Hippolyte, an unbearable prig who knows Italian and takes an interest in science, and a man called Charroselles (an anagram on Charles Sorel, the author's enemy), a tiresome bore, and Pancrace, "a young squirt who got there by sheer chance." Javotte asks Pancrace to lend her the book he used to learn how to talk the way he does, so that she can talk like a book as well, and Pancrace gives her his copy of *Astrée*. The giddy young girl is greatly impressed by Pancrace and falls in love with him, refusing to marry the stolid Bedout, wildly claiming that she could only possibly marry a gay blade in a plumed hat. She ends up, of course, seduced by the calculating young cad, just as Lucrèce is seduced by her Marquis.

Not perhaps immortal ficton, but it does reveal amusingly how strong flagrant self-interest was in those circles, and snobbery, and how the illusory world of romantic fiction and the imagined perfection of manners among the gentry impressed the simpler citizens. The road to social elevation seemed to pass through the ranks of the Précieuses.

But the administrators and civil servants were not so easily impressed; the lawyers and other trained officials ("hommes de robe") were by nature traditionalists, while their opposite numbers were the "hommes d'épées," the progressive forces of intelligence and open mind epitomized by Descartes, who despised the heavy pedantry of the past and its adhesion to precedent. We might be tempted to think of the old-fashioned bureaucrats as wholly opposed to new ideas, but in fact they were interested in Jansenism despite their Humanist training. In any case the crucial figure in this gradual evolution in morals and manners was the "gentilhomme," the man of cultivation and refinement who was to be the model for the men of business, finance, and the bureaucrats.

PART THREE

SECOND SECTION
ROYALIST POLICY, 1661–1702

When Mazarin died in March 1661, Louis XIV took over the reins of government; the period of personal rule began. Among his many problems was the press, which in the early days of journalism tended to revile and discredit the Crown and the old pieties, stimulating (or so the upper classes saw it) heresy and sedition by broadside and pamphlet. Patronage of writers was passing from the nobility to the world of commerce, Jansenism was splitting the Church, newsbooks were circulating briskly and supplying readers with all kinds of rumors and tales, true or false. To the government all this was sheer treason and insolence, and when Louis came to power young writers and journalists seemed to let loose a flood of outrageous new thought and freedom of expression, unheard of in previous reigns when writers were pious hacks like Monsieur Olier and the Community of the Holy Sacrament.

The book trade was depressed. The old days of booming exports of heavy theological works to a European market were over, and new directions in publishing were imperative. Small-sized books, quick and cheap to produce, would have to be the key to prosperity. Fearful of the risks, publishers were forced to hazard new titles, even if they were well aware that they would be pirated if they sold well. Soaring prices, unemployment, ambiguous legislation and the inadequate control over printing made any redress in the Guild impossible, divided as it was by conflicting self-interest. Even the leading publishers were hit by recession, and in addition to economic restraint the trade experienced political pressure from above. Reprisals against anyone showing Jansenist sympathies were severe: in 1657 Louis de Vendosme, a Huguenot, was sentenced to the Bastille simply on suspicion of having worked for Arnauld, and was joined there by Preuveray, a printer. And there were other cases. A consignment of books sent to Léonard by the Elzeviers was examined at the Customs post and found to contain copies of *Eclaircissement du droit et du fait de Jansenius*—Léonard was promptly jailed in the Bastille after going into hiding. Balesdens and Montausier interceded with Séguier, pleading that their bookseller did not know what books were sent to him, with the result that he was freed after fifteen days despite the accusations of enemies who maintained that he had forged documents for Fouquet in a lawsuit. After this it was Miles de Beaujeu's turn, and Desprez's, when damning evidence was found at their premises; and they had to wait a year before they won their liberty. Many Jansenists, both booksellers and printers, saw the inside of His Majesty's dungeons, and not only they but even Thierry, who in 1659 brought out a *Description du pays de Jansenie,* was accused, but had the benefit of help from the Chancellor. Muguet, though, was sent to prison in 1665 for publishing a pontifical Bull at the instigation of the Papal Nuncio. Noël, a Jansenist sympathizer, was flogged for publishing *Généalogie de M. le Prince,* Sébastien Martin was sent to the Bastille for a pamphlet condemned as offensive to the Crown, Jolybois was imprisoned for a mock panegyric on Mazarin, Rebuffé was flogged, Roger banished, and Rousseau, Barbote and Fossier sentenced to gaol for distributing unauthorized pamphlets.

It was a grim time, with the whipping post, prison and banishment, instruments of oppression in the background, but illicit printing went on unchecked. Le Petit found a printer (Louis Piot) for his indecent *Escole des filles,* to which the respected engraver Chauveau contributed a frontispiece over a Leyden imprint; and Rebuffé's two sons printed Le Petit's other scandalous book, *Bordel des Muses,* which would have led him to the stake had he been caught. Anti-royalist pamphlets were in constant circulation blaming the King's advisers, and a scurrilous literature mocked and exposed the decadence of Louis' Court. The *Histoire amoureuse des Gaulles* and its sequel, *France galante,* were read everywhere, accusing the King by name. Bookstalls and hawkers were regularly searched for the offending material, and printers suffered the Bastille in some numbers, like Bussy-Rabutin. The Queen vainly ordered the Bishop of Valence to buy up all copies of the *Histoire amoureuse de Madame* in Holland and put a stop to further publication. Charles Patin was caught with copies of the book, which he was probably about to sell through the underground, and the unfortunate man was sentenced to the galleys for life. The French ambassadors in The Hague and London mounted a diplomatic offensive against the sale and distribution of anti-monarchist propaganda; in the United Provinces burgomeisters were asked to destroy incriminating matter; Spain and the Spanish Low Countries were asked to do the same. In Paris the Lieutenant of Police was very busy—two of Elzevier's agents, Ribou and David, were arrested in 1669 for trafficking in banned literature, and suffered imprisonment.

It was a delicate time for a monarch concerned to consolidate royal prestige. He could not afford to be embarrassed by the printed word but had to secure absolute control over what was published. From this there emerged two connected policies initiated by Colbert: more effective legislative repression and more efficient policing of the trade.

CHAPTER I

ROYALIST PROPAGANDA

A DISORDERLY PRESS was intolerable to the King and his Ministers. The first most urgent task was to persuade writers to support the Crown, because they would be needed to promote royal prestige by competent propaganda. Mazarin, Richelieu and Séguier had all pursued policies aimed at royal aggrandizement and Colbert was a worthy successor.

1. Writers: the King's Servants

Colbert had close connections with the writers whom Mazarin had patronized and it was probably he who asked Costar, the official Historiographer in 1655, to draw up a list of writers who would merit subsidies; another obvious choice to advise on writers to recruit into the King's service was Chapelain, the Court poet. A letter of Chapelain's dated 18 November 1662 gives us an idea of the planned program of monarchist propaganda envisaged by the First Minister: the outstanding events of the reign were to be commemorated with medals bearing legends composed by the most adept writers; poets and historians would be employed to praise the institution of the monarchy in extravagant language, and panegyrics, memoirs and histories of the reign would be written. Monuments with appropriate inscriptions would be set up, tapestries woven with themes glorifying the King, frescoes and engravings planned with the same objective in view.

Colbert was sensitive about literary propaganda, and attached great importance to the post of Historiographer, desiring him to make notes every day on events with the ultimate intention of publishing a narrative history of the reign. Pellisson was appointed to this critical post after the King refused to accept Perrot d'Ablancourt, a Protestant, and after Pellisson's death, Racine and Boileau were approached to fill the position. Yet still there was no sign of publication and a list was requested of 90 possible writers who could combine their efforts to produce something. Thousands of livres were paid to the fortunate hacks willing to take it on, itself an indication of the value of the work in the eyes of the Establishment. It was Richelieu's original policy more systematically organized by Colbert, and another of Richelieu's schemes, the Académie Française, was given a new lease of life. Colbert introduced a tally which each member would use as evidence of his attendance at their meetings, which did a lot to encourage attendance (absenteeism could be construed as an insult to the King). When Séguier died, Louis himself consented to be Patron of the Académie, and Colbert created the "Petite Académie," the embryo of what later became the Académie des Inscriptions et Belles-Lettres, whose principal object originally was to design standards for medallions. But the Académies were the perfect base for experimental science, theory and technical research; invention was encouraged and in 1666 the Académie des Sciences was established to coordinate this work and plan a huge encyclopedia of arts and sciences, as authoritative as the great dictionary of the Académie Française.

Colbert was the mastermind, the overseer of literary activity, with a close interest in the first European scientific journal, the *Journal des Savants,* from its birth in 1665, and superintending the payment of effective publicists like Donneau de Visé, author of *Mercure galant.* It is hard to assess the results of this campaign. No doubt some of the foreign scribes he dragooned into his service were disgusted in the end by the motives behind it, and it is doubtful if their efforts added much to the royal aura, but by a widespread mixture of bribery and honors the absolutist State did ensure a degree of docility in the writing profession. Careerists were easily snared, and as sole patron of letters the King controlled the purse and the prospects, but it rested on an insecure basis and when royal funds declined late in the 17th century, writers sought other patrons.

2. The Royal Library and the Imprimerie Royale

Colbert also controlled two other institutions reflecting renown on the monarch, the Royal Library and the Imprimerie Royale, the royal publishing house. He put them to the same use as the scribblers in the King's cause. When he began his Ministry the Library had only 16,756 volumes in its stock, and that was largely due to the exertions of Richelieu, Mazarin and Séguier, who were as careful to increase their own collections as their master's. Colbert was a practical user of libraries and knew the value of a good information source; he appointed a team of librarians and specialists to reorganize and expand the acquisitions policy and improve facilities. His brother Nicolas was appointed Keeper in 1657, and in 1661, Superintendent of Buildings. To facilitate tighter control over the now rapidly growing library Colbert had it transferred from the Rue de la Harpe to a site near his own residence, and there he assigned Carcavy, Clément and Clairambault the task of complete restructuring and reorganization of the great collections.

The library was first enriched by the acquisition of the Comte de Béthune's private library, which Queen Christina of Sweden had hoped to buy for 100,000 écus. Further rare manuscripts (358 volumes of them) from Trichet du Fresne's collection, treasures from Gaston d'Orléans, hundreds of Fouquet's books, and Mentel's magnificent personal library all swelled the total. Negotiations were put in train for Mazarin's huge library, and a decree of the Privy Council in 1668 authorized exchange of some books between the Royal Library and Mazarin's, as a result of which the Royal Library acquired several thousand books and 2,000 manuscripts at negligible cost. Documents and historic archives were searched for and a collection of medallions was added, together with abbé de Marolles' engravings, the basis of what is today the famous Cabinet des Estampes.

Colbert's policy of centralization led to the Royal Library becoming a major asset to the nation, an instrument of national culture, and it had grown to a total of 40,000 volumes by 1681. On Colbert's death, Louvois assumed control of the Library and appointed Bignon as Director, with Louis Colbert, Nicolas Colbert's nephew, as Keeper. Carcavy, one of the three specialists appointed to plan the reorganization, was replaced by abbé Gallois and then by Thévenot, and Clément worked on the Catalogue of Printed Books. Books poured into the Library from agents in England, Italy, Holland, Sweden, and even Turkey. The Dépôt Légal regulations by which one copy of every new book was sent to the Royal Library were strictly enforced, and facilities for study were offered to scholars in 1692. Louvois was as concerned for the wellbeing of the Library as Colbert, and planned its removal to purpose-built premises on a commodious scale in the Place Vendôme. In 1691 work began on the Librarian's residence, but Louvois's death and a financial crisis forced the work to be abandoned. The Royal Library was finally installed in its present premises in the 18th-century part of the building, the old Palais de Mazarin.

The Imprimerie Royale was less busy in 1661 than it had been earlier and apart from occasional books, was chiefly occupied with publication of the great edition, the "Byzantine du Louvre," the series of Byzantine historians which was coming out at steady intervals. But the great de luxe editions were seen as an outmoded emblem of prestige, and Colbert had individual presentation copies of books made as prime examples of superior French book production, another expression of French *haute culture* and nationalism. He authorized the continuation of the Byzantine project, though money was tight, and discontinued any other work that was not directly related to the King's interest, though he did sponsor scientific publications in physics and natural history by members of the new Académie des Sciences. But, as Colbert saw it, that was not the main purpose of the Imprimerie, which was to promote the grandeur of the Crown using all the processes available, typography, illustration, illuminated manuscripts even, to emphasize with graphic skill the King's military successes or the magnificent fêtes held at Versailles. Print helped to multiply grandiose copies of books and portfolios depicting monuments, paintings and tapestries, all devoted to the imaging of kingship. The *Cabinet du Roi* was manufactured at the Imprimerie—sumptuously bound folios of engravings personally signed by the best artists of the day—Audran, Edelinck, Mellan, Chauveau, Silvestre and Sébastien Le Clerc—on exquisite paper with a feather-light type specially designed to harmonize with the illustrations. At a time when the book trade was having to produce mean little books without many illustrations, it was an affront.

3. *The King's Printers*

Just as the Imprimerie published the choicest examples of the typographic art, so the King's official printers under Colbert's direction were turning out work complimentary to the royal person. Laudatory epistles, official versions of campaigns, official Acts were the constituent material. During the Fronde the title King's Printer fell into disrepute when any printer or bookseller could secure a certificate dubbing him "official printer" to such-and-such a Prince or Guild, and he would so describe himself in the books he printed. But from 1661 order was introduced into the chaos and a decree stipulated that the King alone had the right to personal printers, and nominated specifically Antoine Estienne, Sébastien Cramoisy, Pierre Rocollet, Pierre Le Petit and Jacques Langlois as having the right to print "all business signed by the Secretaries of State, Privy Council proceedings, royal enactments and anything appertaining to the King's service." In 1662 Sébastien Huré II succeeded Antoine Estienne and Damien Foucault succeeded Rocollet; they in turn were succeeded by Léonard and Coignard. Others who had the title were Jacques Langlois II, who kept his father's title (1678), Guillaume Desprez, a Jansenist (1686) who replaced another Jansenist, Pierre Le Petit, and in 1687 Etienne Michallet obtained the same favored post after Mabre-Cramoisy's disappearance (and he had inherited the post from his grandfather Sébastien Cramoisy in 1669). By the end of the century Jean-Baptiste Coignard II, Jacques Langlois III, and Théodore Muguet had all succeeded their fathers as King's Printer—nepotism was the natural order of things. Jean Anisson from Lyons, a Director of the Imprimerie, also assumed the role of royal printer from Michallet, another printer from Lyons.

Five or six King's Printers divided the work between them, supplying sufficient copies for the King's use and putting the rest on sale. During Colbert's Ministry orders and regulations proliferated, and the administration grew to such proportions that a printing works had to be established at Versailles to cope with increased production; this made the lucky inheritors wealthy and their business sought after. When the Minister Fouquet fell, he owed Cramoisy nearly 10,000 livres for various ordinances issued at his command, and 1,500 livres for different printing jobs, and Cramoisy asked Colbert for 19,870 livres owing him for various deliveries. The State owed Léonard more than 50,000 livres in 1706. The higher the rank, the bigger the debt. In the age of absolute monarchy the role of King's Printer was of renewed importance, and Government preferred to act through respected and trusted firms rather than simply good printers, because they wanted loyal intermediaries to carry out the King's wishes in those areas it was vital to control—political, religious and literary.

4. Religious Propaganda

Before the Revocation of the Edict of Nantes a concerted effort was made to reconvert French Protestants to the Catholic faith, and a press campaign backed by monetary inducements was launched throughout France. A Sinking Fund for the Reconversion of Heretics was started from the revenue derived from vacant livings, plus one-third of the proceeds from livings occupied from the beginning of the year. The press campaign was directed by Paul Pellisson-Fontanier, an ex-Protestant, a friend of Mlle. de Scudéry, Secretary of the Académie Française and a royal historiographer. He was of the opinion that the best way to make sincere and lasting converts was to provide missionaries with books to enrich religious experience once the converts were back in the fold. A list of 52 titles was drawn up, mostly consisting of the standard catechisms and books of devotions: the

Catéchisme ou Instructions pour les nouveaux convertis sur les points principaux de la religion, the *Imitation de Jésus-Christ,* the *Introduction à la vie dévote,* Amelote's translation of the New Testament, the Psalter, and liturgical works to help Calvinists understand afresh the sacraments and rites of the Catholic Church.

Pellisson commissioned a printer, Clémentet, to do the work, and he in turn enlisted fifteen of the major Paris publishers with monopolies in the relevant titles. The wheels began to turn and in less than eighteen months between October 1685 and January 1687 more than a million books were delivered. Michallet alone had 30,000 translations of the Gospels and Epistles printed, 30,000 copies of the *Imitation* and 160,000 translations of the New Testament. Muguet and Léonard were almost as busy, and 147,632 translations of the New Testament, 126,000 of the Psalms, and 128,057 of the *Imitation* were ready for distribution by the King's agents.

Clémentet could not keep up with the wagon-loads of books arriving at his office each day—his accounting system broke down and he relied on the booksellers increasing their orders as necessary. They too were overwhelmed and called in assistance from Rouen, Châlons and Lyons, even appealing to printers in the Low Countries, which led to difficulties at the borders when the books were stopped for Customs examination. It meant financial risks for printers and booksellers. Clémentet paid out 381,736 livres to his suppliers in 1687, but he owed them at least another 700,000 livres; when an inquiry was held it was found that despite their promise to do so, publishers had not reduced the price of their books by one-third, and as they had many of them printed and bound at lower cost in the provinces, they were making huge profits. The price of each book was reduced, and Léonard received only 140,000 livres instead of the 215,623 he asked, Muguet 152,096 livres instead of 278,771, despite which cuts the publishers were paid in total 536,000. Official publishing in a national drive of this kind was a profitable business, and all part of the concentration of the trade in the interests of the ruling clique. The Sinking Fund for the Reconversion of the Protestants was one more arm in that collaboration between Government and publishers to their mutual advantage.

CHAPTER II

THE GOVERNMENT TACKLES
THE BOOK TRADE

IT WAS ONE THING for the Government to use the book trade to promote its policies; it was quite another to regulate it effectively. If the autocracy in power wished to ensure the banning of books that were a challenge to its authority and encourage books that were impeccably orthodox in religion and politics, tight surveillance of all publishing was essential.

1. Fewer Printers

Censorship was a police matter and Colbert set up a Police Council to keep watch and a strict record of the trade's activities. In 1666 a census of Paris printers was taken and 216 presses counted in 79 printing shops. There were only 222 journeymen and 69 apprentices, only enough to man half the presses; in 21 shops there were no journeymen, the owners themselves finding it better to work for other master printers. To supervise things, a special Commissioner from the Châtelet was assigned to the University precinct and the Palais, where most of the trade was concentrated. Colbert had declared that "scandalous libels and other forbidden literature must be suppressed, printers reduced to manageable numbers, and letter types marked in some way and their sale forbidden to unauthorized persons." Vitré, Cramoisy and Ballard had submitted reports on the feasibility of such plans. The Lieutenant Criminel intervened at a meeting of the Police Council to announce that two newsbook-sellers had been caught, and one flogged, the other sentenced to banishment, to which Colbert replied, "It is of the utmost urgency that illicit gazettes be stopped. While they were held to be of little account in Italy they were taken as gospel truth in the Netherlands. What an intolerable nuisance they were!"

The report by the three leading publishers was studied by La Margerie, the member of the Council with responsibility for the press, and he reported that the general conclusion was: too many printers, making control difficult; moreover, most printers were ignorant and destitute. The Guild should be forbidden to accept any more to the mastership pending new regulations. Colbert returned to a favorite theme: "We must forbid the casting or sale of any types without the express permission of a magistrate, and an inventory of type founts should be compiled to enforce high standards—only the best could be sold. Not only should there be a ban on any new freemen in the Guild but also on those who have not fulfilled the entry requirements." Commissioners were appointed to scrutinize the Statutes and regulations governing the Guild, and there was to be an accredited list of master printers, and a ban on new masters and on new founts.

La Marguerie prepared a report on the printers in business, revealing that 86 were on his books, "26 of whom were incapable of printing, and 16 were old offenders." He was reticent on Colbert's policy towards type founders, pointing out that they wished to continue working and if squeezed, would probably take their skills abroad, "a grievous loss, not easily replaceable." He then outlined a scheme for the new regulation of the trade: only apprentices of 16 or over were to be accepted; they were to know Latin and be able to read Greek. Printers were forbidden to print without a licence and must possess at least two presses; they were to operate within the University precinct and not outside it without permission. Official colporteurs were to be reduced to 12.

The minutes of the meeting give no indication how the scheme was received but there must have been further inquiries into offending printers, because La Marguerie reported that Le Petit, Gentil, Sébastien Martin and Langlois, all of whom were mixed up in the Arnauld controversies, had been pardoned; others, Noël, Preuveray, Fossier,

Rebuffé's widow, Roger, Rousseau and Barbote would be expelled. The matter of type foundries was again discussed, the majority agreeing with La Marguerie that if the type founders were threatened they would leave for England or Holland. When Séguier awoke from his usual torpor at meetings he asked what each Councillor thought about the present situation. Colbert told him what *he* thought:

> M. Colbert said that the first idea the Council had mooted was to reduce the number of printers by excluding the poorly skilled. He was planning a complete revision of the Statutes governing the trade and would visit all the printers, and from the knowledge gained he would frame a set of workable rules. He was convinced that because type was at the bottom of the whole problem he would forbid the casting of any types until proper regulations were made. There was no call to allow type founders a completely free hand without effective controls, and something had to be done within the next 7 or 8 days. The Lieutenant Criminel will check all printers' and booksellers' credentials and prepare for enforcement of strict control—without that, it would be impossible to guarantee the good regulation of French printing. The Estiennes and Vascosans were held in high esteem and their type was the finest in the world, their books the most correct. But Holland was now ahead in this respect, with more elegant type, better quality paper, and that was all the more reason for insisting on reform of abuses in the French trade. When the King ordered that there was to be no more gilding on carriages and buildings, it meant that a great many craftsmen were aggrieved because they made a living out of it, but it was done for the public good, which meant everyone's good.

This spirited rhetoric was to convince the Council to adopt rigorous measures, as he wanted, and to override La Marguerie who was sympathetic to the type founders and printers. La Marguerie added hastily that he had a plan prepared for the trade and said that a number of printers specializing in official publications had suggested they work from the College des Quatre Nations; and if other printers were banned from printing that kind of material, this would help limit the spread of seditious literature since pamphlets and posters would be in fewer hands. "And that would be a monopoly. There is no need to restrict public liberty in that way, but they could be confined to an area which could be covered in two hours. The best printers must be retained, the others banned. Even if the choicest printers have only one press and some of the less competent have two, preference must be given to the most capable."

Other Minutes have not survived but in 1667 a decree forbade any recognition of master printers who knew no Latin or could not read Greek letters; it required two presses in each workshop, and ordered the Lieutenant Criminel to pay a visit of inspection to printers' workshops. In conformity with resolutions passed at a meeting on 10 February 1667, the following printers were ordered to close their workshops: Alexandre, Roger, Denis Langlois, Sassier, Preuveray, Rebuffé, Noël, Jolybois, Négo, Lesselin, Journel, Rousseau and Barbote. The Police Council then took a decision to limit printers to 30, which immediately provoked protests from the rest, who presented a "Humble Remonstrance" to the Chancellor, denouncing the Commissioners who took advice only from influential publishers who already enjoyed too much monopoly. They pointed out that there were three members of the Cramoisy family in the list of 30, two Vitrés (who had only one press), two Martins who were related to Cramoisy, one of whom had been in trouble with the authorities, Le Prest had never printed any properly licensed books, Coignard had been arrested for taking on ten apprentices in one year, Le Petit was a Jansenist, and Cellier had dubious connections with Jansenists and Calvinists.

We do not know if in fact the favored 30 were allowed to print after this, but yet another scheme was prepared to regulate the trade and yet another decree from the Privy Council (October 1667) reaffirmed all previous orders, regulations and edicts, and declared: "No printer, bookseller or binder may print or sell a book without licence and without the express permission of the chief magistrate of the locality on pain of corporal punishment." A list of printing workshops and bookshops was to be forwarded to Chancellor

Séguier. Draconian measures to try to combat a deteriorating economic and political situation.

Controls were hard to implement in the provinces, where there might not even be a trade guild, and a ban on new candidates for master's status would have met with opposition from local Parlements who tended to support local enterprise and resent intrusion from Paris. In the capital, near the seats of power, Guild Syndics were more pliable, and by a decree of 16 December 1666 masterships were banned for 17 years, during which period only two printers, Gabriel Martin and Laurent d'Houry, and five rich and influential booksellers were admitted master by special decree or lettre de cachet. A widow could continue a business but the son could not inherit—equipment was sold to other printers. Booksellers could not open a new shop and binders were forbidden to operate a printing press.

Such constricting conditions fueled antagonisms within the trade's various branches—booksellers and printers, printers and binders. The binders, who were often booksellers as well, could profit, but booksellers who wanted books bound cheaply had to employ journeymen on the quiet, because no new master binders were allowed. Workmanship consequently deteriorated, and trade relations worsened when a binder tried to open a printing shop and was ordered to shut it—a step which only provoked more outrage among binders. They accused printers and booksellers of using unqualified workmen as binders, and a group of 36 journeymen-binders demanded that they be admitted to mastership, a move denied by decree of the Privy Council, and the binderies of Jouvenel and Rémy were closed after a decree forbade binders selling books. This fight was essentially between master booksellers who wanted to keep binding and printing in their own hands, and the large wholesale booksellers and publishers who sought access to large, efficient binderies and therefore supported the efforts of journeymen-binders to be allowed more masterships in their own trade since this would make such specialized binderies more practicable.

There were only 63 printers in Paris in 1679, 16 fewer than in 1666, and by 1683 there was more contraction when the government took further action. A decree recognized that 68 booksellers and 35 master printers had died since 1666 and authorized 31 new master booksellers and four master printers. The number of Paris printers was restricted to 36, each of whom had to possess at least four presses, and until the number stood at 36 (at that moment it was more) no new master printers could be admitted. Only sons-in-law of masters could be candidates for mastership, and master booksellers could only exercise the craft of printing if they had been apprenticed to that trade. Binders were excluded from the Guild and subject to special restrictions; any who were in business as booksellers had to choose between the two trades. Again there were protests. Booksellers feared that fewer printers would mean higher printing costs, and there were angry reactions from the expelled binders. Parlement was not inclined to ratify the decree and contested some of the provisions, but in March 1685 issued a confirmation of the decree, reaffirming the provisions of the 1618 Statute. This declared that all existing master printers and booksellers on 30 August 1685 might continue in their trades—bookselling, printing and bookbinding, and two binders were to be nominated as Assistants in the Guild administration.

Parlement was obliquely resisting the Crown through the Guild, and the Privy Council acted swiftly in a decree signed by Colbert quashing the ruling by Parlement and forbidding further action. The press was clearly a sensitive issue and very much in the forefront of Ministers' minds. A year later the Chancellor promulgated a new set of Statutes in the form of a royal edict which the Parlement was ordered to ratify immediately and without revision. The Crown forced its will upon the trade, reduced the numbers of practicing booksellers and printers, continued to limit new admissions to mastership, and finally expelled bookbinders from the Guild; as the proletariat of the trade they were a potential source of agitation, and dangerous in the eyes of France's ruling clique.

2. Colbert and the Paper Trade

Papermakers were in difficulties at this time because of the high costs of production, and Colbert's policy of expansion of trade made him turn his attention to a commodity he knew to be an important component of the nation's economy. He appointed a Commission to study the matter, consisting of the publishers Mabre-Cramoisy (Director of the Imprimerie Royale), Léonard, and Le Petit; the printers Vitré, Rondet and Mercier; and two paper merchants, Le Goux and Vengangueil. Their report revealed that half of the 400 paper mills in France were closed. France had previously supplied more than 150,000 reams annually to Spain alone, more than 200,000 to England and more than 40,000 to the Low Countries, but paper duties had drastically reduced the export trade to 30,000 reams a year. Unsold stocks were mounting in the paper warehouses, and there was competition from Genoa which, according to Vitré, could supply Spain, Italy, England and Holland, while the Dutch were building their own mills on the Meuse. Gaultier, a papermaker from Angoulême, received permission from the King of Spain to open 16 paper mills in the Spanish Netherlands, with various exemptions from taxation, "a large shed" in which to dry the paper, and a chateau to live in. France had to encourage the papermaking industry, not kill it with heavy duties.

Colbert accepted that the trade was hampered and agreed to an abatement of duty, varying from place to place, but war broke out with Holland and military adventures had to be financed; despite resistance to any more duties the Privy Council imposed a charge on all paper and parchment, at first exempting printing paper and paper for export. But then the exemptions were dropped and commissioners moved into printing workshops, checking on paper and taxing all paper bought after the date of the new impost. Duty varied from 100 sols for reams of 5 lbs weight to 30 livres for reams of 20-50 lbs, a much heavier rate than before, which could only spell ruin to the industry and so to the book trade. Guild Syndics and representatives of the papermakers sought an audience with Colbert at Versailles, warning him that the trade would be "annihilated," and some modification was agreed—printing paper used for licensed books was exempted, and paper for export was to carry the old duties. But the trade was not satisfied with this and claimed that licensed books only amounted to one–eighth of the books printed in Paris, most business being in primers, books of hours, prayerbooks, catechisms and similar standard lines. Further concessions were made and exceptions were extended to include specially authorized books, new editions, engravings, maps and playing cards, but the duty was kept on official documents and "other pamphlets." Colbert was authorized to tell the Guild that "the King has a special regard for their art and was pleased to abolish the duty on paper; that they were to continue printing as usual and strive to do it as perfectly as possible. The King would grant them his protection whenever it was needed." Colbert added that he would do the same. The new tariff was abolished in 1674 but the earlier stamp duty on paper was retained.

The details are significant only in that they show clearly Colbert's views on trade policy: he was not so candid about his underlying motive, which was to put a stop to anti-monarchist pamphleteering. He had found it difficult to control type foundries, and indeed printing, so was trying an attack on another, fundamental front: paper. His problem was to devise a tariff that would not injure "good" (i.e., conformist) literature. As a mercantilist par excellence Colbert knew if he killed the French paper industry it would be fatal to the French economy as a whole, and so he first made some concessions and then capitulated to economic realities. But other political and international factors were affecting French trade: the infamous Revocation of the Edict of Nantes (1685) had the immediate effect of driving skilled Protestant craftsmen and women out of France to settle in England and Holland, bringing their invaluable skills with them, including papermaking. Folly was heaped on folly in the last years of Louis XIV when even heavier taxation was imposed, virtually extinguishing the once prosperous industry.

3. Licensing and the Concentration of the Book Trade

Licensing and censorship had been a feature of publishing since the 16th century and successive Chancellors had tried to make the system work more efficiently. Séguier appeared to have achieved some success at the end of his long life when permits to publish had to be sought from either a local judge (in Paris the Lieutenant of Police) in the case of short books of a few pages, or from the Chancellor himself in the case of new books. All manuscripts had to be submitted to the Chancellor, who sent them on to the various censors with the name of the censor on the title page. This routine, part of the Bureau de Sceau's responsibilities, was known as a "committal." The censor wrote his report which was presented to the Court of the Bureau de Sceau by a Secretary of State, with the Patent ready for the Chancellery seal to be affixed or not as the case may be. The Chancellor pronounced the term of the licence, which depended on the importance of the book, and the costs incurred in publishing, the manuscript being filed in the Chancellery until the book appeared. A copy of the book had to be sent to the Chancellery to be checked against the original manuscript, to ensure that no unauthorized material had crept in. Laborious but apparently foolproof.

Evasions, however, there were, such is the ingenuity of the human spirit. Verse anthologies would have a few extra poems slipped into the printed version, which made them ultimately notorious in the eyes of authority and subject to even greater scrutiny. Even an eminent writer like Bossuet had to submit all his work to the censor, and a decree of 1682 made all preliminary matter (prefaces, dedications, etc.) subject to submission along with the text. While licensing was an effective form of control over undesirable publications, it was in practical terms a form of monopoly granted to a publisher in a title and naturally provoked hostility from publishers who were excluded from best-selling titles, which in turn encouraged piracy. The struggle which broke out over the question of extension of licences, or "privilege," we have described, and the edict of 1657 which affirmed that the extension of a licence could only be granted if the book in its new edition had been increased by at least one-third. In essence the dispute was about earning a living, difficult enough to do in a country governed by repressive autocracy, and the restrictions greatly unsettled the trade. The fight against monopolies continued, stirred by the resentment at the facile renewal of licences to publishers favored by government.

Colbert's reactions to this anarchy can be imagined, and we can perhaps see a hint of his intrusion in a decree of the Council of State (10 May 1662) about Sébastien Martin's unauthorized reprint of Du Ryer's translation of Strada's *Histoire de la guerre des Flandres,* which Courbé had the rights in. Four Councillors of State were charged with the duty of deciding what was fair to both parties, "And to secure proper regulation on behalf of His Majesty." The Councillors were Rouillé, Morangis, Verthamont and Boucherat.

This posed afresh the question of licences and their continuation. There was clearly no desire in the Council of State to extend monopolies, and La Marguerie was evidently opposed to it, but the most privileged—and most esteemed at court—defended their point of view vigorously. Eventually, after Josse, a Parisian, brought an action against Berthelin, a Calvinist from Rouen, for piracy of Beuvelet's *Méditations,* a ruling confirmed the Declaration of 20 December 1649. This, together with a decree of the Council dated 14 August 1663, confirmed the Compagnie des Usages' monopolies, recognized licences already granted, but forbade any new books to be printed without licensing under the Seal, and agreed that extension of copyright after expiry would be granted for just one year. It also forbade the licensing for publishing older authors' work unless it was considerably revised.

The door was now wide open for anyone wishing to have privilege in old books; most books published in the years 1660–66 remained the property of those who had published them for the first time; on the other hand, licences for revised editions of ancient texts forbade their pirating under pretext of "revision." When licences for old editions expired, those publishers who benefited from that became masters of the works concerned. Hence, thanks to royal protection, while Josse could retain his monopoly of Beuvelet's works, Huré and then Léonard also did well out of their hold on Granada's big-selling *Catechism* and Busée's *Méditations;* and they had a monopoly of François de Sales.

It was a matter of genuine concern: in Lyons publishers

were anxious about the trade restrictions, and in Rouen there was a long tradition of cheap reprints of expired titles which the policy of licence-renewal hampered badly. Privileges were rewards for good behavior, which the authorities claimed were "in the interests of good publishing." After a fire at Montaigu College, Le Petit secured a 50-year renewal of all his monopolies including Arnauld's works, translations of Luis de Granada, the missal and offices for Holy Week, the Psalms, the Story of the Old and New Testaments, Senault's books, and Greek and Latin primers—a hugely profitable trawl. Exclusive monopoly in Augustine's works was granted the Maurist order as a means of encouraging sound theology, and Muguet the publisher was granted a 50-year extension of his licence. Pralard, who had undertaken to publish volumes of Hippocrates and Galen, was granted an extension of his licence in them and for other major works including the Tridentine Catechism and *City of God*. Michallet secured a 25-year licence for Innocent III's *De contemptu mundi* on condition that he reissue it in a richly decorated edition, and for other devotional literature— Bonnefons' *Epîtres et Evangiles pour toute l'année,* and works by La Puente and abbé d'Abelly.

At the same time Sercy, Le Compte, Josse, Léonard and Couterot enjoyed many favors and it is hardly surprising that Lyons publishers demanded an end to such favoritism. The protests were in vain, though by the end of the century Chancellor Pontchartrain made such prejudicial practices more generally applicable. It seems clear that the Government was guided by a desire to encourage the publication of scholarly works, and publishers specializing in that kind of product were concentrated in Paris; they thus had an advantage over more distant competitors, but provincial publishing was put into a difficult position. The Statutes forbidding a publisher to operate outside the town in which he lived, and tight state control seemed against natural justice in the sense that it favored Paris firms who were much more expensive than provincial publishers, and once a publisher enjoyed an exclusive monopoly in a book he tended to raise its price. We shall see later what the consequences were.

4. La Reynie and the Policing of the Book Trade

Whatever measures were adopted, "mauvais livres" were still on the market, and still stricter police surveillance was imposed under the direction of La Reynie, Lieutenant of Police from 1667 to 1697, in close liaison with the Privy Council. Ruthless suppression was his policy, the Châtelet his fortress, the source of all law enforcement in Paris. He began by banning the sale of type to anyone other than master printers, and required the Guild to maintain a register of all deliveries; when a printing workshop closed, La Reynie saw to the disposal of its equipment. In 1670 he forbade sales of type, presses and other equipment without the permission of a magistrate, and specified that the material had to be delivered in the presence of Guild Syndics and two Assistants who certified the sale on a signed declaration. Transport of presses anywhere outside the original shop was closely supervised even when it was for government work (movement always worried the authorities), and presses in private houses, convents or colleges were totally forbidden.

Street hawkers, not without reason, had always been under suspicion and the number of their licences was reduced to 12, but La Reynie wanted tight supervision of bookstalls on the Pont Neuf and adjacent quays and hoped to confine the trade to a restricted area, but by the Sixties the trade was too diffuse to confine within the Palais or University quarter and firms established as far away as St. Séverin and along the road to the Rue Dauphine could not be uprooted. The Pont St. Michel and Quai des Augustins were included in the authorized districts.

La Reynie was severe on infringements of regulations—workers were under almost daily supervision in person by Commissioner Delamare, a man of energy and very cultured, but detested by the trade. In the Guild, Syndics and Assistants were elected in La Reynie's presence after careful initial selection and with government approval. The risks attendant on the publishing of banned books were so heavy that it was not worth the effort except for pamphlets set up hurriedly by candlelight at night. But banned books continued to circulate in Paris, imported from the provinces or from abroad. Articles 19 and 21 of the Statute of 1618 laid down that every consignment, case, bale or parcel of books entering Paris had to be kept pending a visit of inspection by a Guild Syndic or Assistant, yet despite repeated decrees this regulation remained a dead letter and banned books could be had fairly easily. Colbert asked La Reynie if books from Holland could not simply be banned in their entirety, but La Reynie was opposed to this "because a lot of valuable books are imported from Holland and good books are desirable wherever they come from"—the remark of an educated man! The ceaseless effort by government to crush undesirable material went on: a judgment of the Châtelet dated 3 September 1663 reminded everyone that when a consignment of books arrived, it had to be inspected by Guild officials at the Guild offices, not at "private houses," on Tuesdays and Fridays. This rule was in force until the end of Louis XIV's reign.

CHAPTER III

THE RESULTS OF CROWN POLICY: THE ARTIFICIAL PROSPERITY OF THE PARIS BOOK TRADE

T HE CONSEQUENCES OF repressive policies can best be gauged by glancing at the following table of printing presses and workshops in operation, 1644–1701:

Workshops with . . .	1644	1666	1679	1692	1694	1701
9 presses or more	—	—	1	5	4	1
8 presses or more	—	—	1	—	1	1
7 presses or more	1	—	2	—	—	—
6 presses or more	—	2	2	2	4	6
5 presses or more	5	8	8	5	7	4
4 presses or more	8	7	14	15	5	16
3 presses or more	11	18	14	11	13	12
2 presses or more	33	39	18	13	12	11
1 press or more	17	5	3	—	—	—
Total presses	**180**	**217**	**220**	**201**	**186**	**195**
Total workshops	**75**	**79**	**63**	**51**	**46**	**51**

The policy led to a reduction of only about one-fifth the number of presses, a small proportion when it is recalled that many of them were used only occasionally, and the squeeze on workshops meant that the little men went out of business.

In 1644 there were 257 journeymen and 94 apprentices; in 1666, 234 journeymen and 69 apprentices; in 1691, 214 journeymen and seven apprentices; in 1701, 339 journeymen and 41 apprentices. Masters making their returns would be torn between concealing the number of unauthorized workmen they employed and the need to prove they were doing enough business to stay open. There was more concentration of workers in the later period; in 1701 one printer employed more than 21 persons, two printers between 16 and 20, and two had between 11 and 15 men. The 1701 figures on personnel are much higher and could be taken to mean that the trade was flourishing, but included are journeymen who were in firms without work—11 at Muguet's for example. Others may have magnified their business to impress the Chancellor; some apprentices might have been included in the figures for journeymen, because the 1692 figures suggest a severe recession, yet it is known that apprentices were omitted in the returns that year to conciliate journeymen who wanted their numbers cut.

While the small businesses disappeared there was no great increase in very large firms, but the numbers of workmen engaged suggests that there was more specialization as between pressmen and compositors, and while only three printers were capable of printing in Hebrew and Greek, all of them possessed a good range of type founts, a fact supported by their inventories: some had type weighing 15,000–20,000 lbs, which suggests great resources in quantity and quality, as is reflected in the high standard of book production in Paris around the year 1700. Government strictness or natural evolution?

1. Crafts associated with printing

More evidence is available about associated crafts—the type founders, engravers, printsellers—than was available in the earlier part of the century. Figures survive of consignments of type dispatched from the Paris foundries—131 between 1680 and 1696, mostly to printers north of the Loire, only one to Bordeaux and Marseilles, two to Lyons, and none to Toulouse or Grenoble, whose printers would deal direct with Lyons. Two of the consignments were not signed for, five were from booksellers dealing in second-hand books, ten were from printers who had foundries, the remaining 114 were cast in four of the big Paris foundries: Cottin, Le Bé, Cot and Sanlecque. The big four had been buying up the little men, and by the 18th century many more had ceased operations. There was no sign of any innovations in punch cutting or engraving; most founders were content to preserve the materials they had. In the last years of the 17th century the Imprimerie Royale took the initiative and introduced new designs for letters which owed a lot to the art of calligraphy.

Copper engravers and print dealers had always had close relations with printers, and were often related by marriage. Hortemels, a bookseller, had a son and daughter who were engravers and married into the Cochin family; François, called de Chartres, was a printer's son-in-law and his son Nicolas was a bookseller and printseller; Marie, Pierre and Denys Mariette the same; and Mabre-Cramoisy, whose uncle Nicolas Loir was painter to the King and a member of the Académie Française, was commissioned with his uncle to print engravings for the Cabinet du Roi. Yet the late 17th century was a poor period for engraving as the elaborate frontispieces in theological works went out of fashion along with the pictures in devotional books and the inflated compositions illustrating epic poems or scenes in romantic novels. There were no successors to Bosse or Chauveau who had done so much to enhance the art of the book. Le Clerc did some work and Ertinger enjoyed a brief success, but apart from some books depicting architecture or voyages and travels there was nothing of any distinction. A single picture, the frontispiece in a book, was all a publisher could afford. Pitau, a second-rate engraver, asked 300 livres for engraving a picture by Simon François of Joseph carrying the infant Jesus into Egypt (1665); Van Schuppen wanted 110 livres for a picture of the Blessed Marguerite of Lorraine, probably a hastily executed plate for a holy picture selling cheaply, and later he was asking 530 livres for engraving Moricet's portrait of the Duc d'Angou. Beaufrère, another minor artist, received 300 livres in 1662 for an engraving of the same august features. Pitau is also recorded as having received 250 livres for 200 copies of a portrait of the Bishop of Senlis, and 2,000 livres in 1669 for a portrait of the King, after Le Febvre.

Why did illustrations get rarer? Though a single portrait, which could be sold separately as a print, did not appreciably add to the cost of production, fully illustrated books were very expensive to produce; but also one senses a change. As we enter the age of Academicism in painting, the Baroque extravaganzas of Bosse and Chauveau seemed wholly improbable, and although lacking in the passionate imagination of their predecessors, the late 17th-century minds were more interested in individual psychology—hence the predominance of the portrait. Even La Fontaine's Fables were not illustrated, but then his contemporaries saw primarily a moral lesson in their pages.

The final separation of bookbinders from their fellows in the trade put them in a ghetto. They had their own Guild run by four Wardens, with only a few dozen members. Some binders were in a big way of business, others one-man concerns, some did no gilding but contracted this out to gilders not in the trade. Standards were higher in Paris than in the provinces, and work done for a sophisticated clientele, but even here taste was changing: the de luxe editions with intricately filleted patterns gave way to plain morocco, with perhaps a family crest on the covers. Again there is that feeling of retrenchment and recession typical of the age of Louis XIV.

2. Booksellers: small and medium-sized firms

Government policy towards booksellers was not as rigorous as it was towards printers but only one apprentice a year could attain his freedom, and when bookbinder-booksellers were forbidden to practice as booksellers, the bookshops of Paris dropped from 400 in 1660 to 253 in 1701. Most shops were near the University, the traditional location, but the

Palais was the center of fashion, and we might look at a typical bookseller of the time, Antoine Quenet, to try to estimate the kind of business he did.

He was the son of a binder-bookseller, Robert Quenet, who sold ephemeral literature on the Pont Neuf when he began his career, like so many others. When he was made free of the trade in 1653 he opened a bindery and bookshop, and when the two trades were forcibly separated he chose to continue bookselling on the retail side—he did no publishing—and his stock was of modest proportions, valued at 2,355 livres, including Vitré's Bible, Arnauld's *Fréquente communion,* a Davity, some stock devotions, Busée's *Méditations,* and Granada's and Senault's works.

Others were hardly better off. Antoine Robinot and Claude Nivelle on the Rue St. Victor occupied two wretched little rooms whose stock amounted to fewer than 1,000 books, including the *Imitation,* Holy Week prayers, the Gospels and Epistles, Busée, the Confessions and Soliloquies of St. Augustine and hundreds of Hours. In most cases the little shops belonged to widows with limited stock or printers who retailed other men's publications as an extra, but two firms are of unusual interest: Guillaume Le Bé, the famous type founder whose celebrated collection of punches and matrices was valued at only 4,853 livres, also had a paltry bookstock, prayerbooks, Fathers, illustrated books, dictionaries, Bibles in pictures, 80 "Théâtres d'animaux," 400 pictures of animals, 25 packets of grocers' and apothecaries' stationery and 6 packets of booksellers' stationery. And Le Bé was not the only one to augment his income by the sale of cheap, popular lines. Antoine Raffle, another small bookseller, was primarily a printer, with two presses; when he died, formes were in place ready to print an almanac, a spelling book (the types, according to the inventory, "well worn"), an arithmetic book and prayerbooks. His stock, valued at 2,799 livres, included dozens of the usual saints' lives, 450 copies of the *Imitation,* Gospels and Epistles, 630 copies of "Good thoughts," games and playing cards, comedies, songs, model speeches, handwriting manuals, the Cries of Paris (56 dozen), Life of St. Catherine and St. Alexis (114 dozen), *Promenades d'amour* (50 dozen), *Malice des femmes* (90 dozen), reams of "Confessions of a good woman," and old-fashioned tales, *Huon de Bordeaux, Richard Sans Peur, La Belle Hélène, Gargantua, Til Eulenspiegel and Charlemagne.*

Fascinating proof of the extent to which popular literature was available in Paris, most of the titles above came from Febvre of Troyes, the home of mass reading matter. To judge by the stock on display it was carefully planned, very similar to other retailers who dealt with Febvre, one of Troyes' most prolific printers, who with Jean Musier and then Jacques Rivière supplied a ready market with reams and reams of popular matter.

More capital was available in the late 17th century: Eloy Elie, admitted to mastership in 1664, was bookseller to the Ursuline Order in the Rue St. Jacques and the Guild of the Daughters of St. Geneviève in the St. Victor district, with licence to print their prayerbooks and the works of Bérulle, St. Teresa, and St. John of the Cross. He had a stock of literally thousands of Hours, catechisms and spiritual classics, the *Imitation,* translations of the Gospels and Epistles by Simon Martin, and Maxims of the Saints. Antoine Cellier, a Protestant who earned royal favors when he was reconverted, left a well-equipped workshop in 1684 valued at 4,296 livres, in which were formes of standing type for books of Hours, his specialty, and a bookstock worth 7,360 livres comprising Bibles, New Testaments, Psalms and a range of controversial literature.

Another typical bookshop was that of Etienne Lucas, a binder who also published Protestant books—the Psalms and the New Testament in French were his specialty. He had a stock of 16,074 books in 1676. Le Febvre, another one, had 14,708 books in 1699, mostly religious classics; and Charles Angot, husband of Marie Josse, daughter of Georges I and second wife Elizabeth Chappelet, who rose to be a Syndic in the Guild and was a publisher with licences for a range of profitable titles, had a stock of 10,474 in 1694. His business was almost in the same category as the big firms which sold their own publications, like Anne Guillery, Pierre de Bats's widow, who had a stock valued at 19,334 livres and specialized in Hours and Benedictine service books. Jean

Couterot was among the aristocrats of the trade with a stock valued at 28,000 livres which he sold to Jean Vilette.

3. Booksellers: medium and large firms

Three-fifths of the books published in Paris between 1670 and 1700 were produced by some twenty firms. There was no fundamental change in the structure of the trade but a tendency to regroup, as if Crown policy, rather than consciously encouraging any concentration, was content to avoid too much fragmentation. Among the leading firms were new names—Léonard (a Fleming); Muguet, Michallet and Anisson from Lyons; and descendants of the older firms, Coignard, Thiboust, Thierry and Edme Martin II. Muguet was originally a printer, and Le Petit, Léonard, Michallet, Desprez and Simon Besnard were seeking to acquire a printing shop, which must have been seen as a prerequisite of success in the trade, and would certainly square with Colbert's avowed policy of creating large publishers independent of individual printers whose closed-shop policy kept prices high.

Most of the larger firms specialized in the predictable lines: religious and literary matter of average price, leaving the more expensive publications to the six largest publishers. They tended to have their shops in the Palais—about 40 at the beginning of Louis' reign, either within the precincts and galleries of the Palais itself or in adjacent streets, the Rue de la Calende, Rue de la Pelleterie, Rue de la Vieille Draperie and Rue Dauphine. Guillaume de Luynes was a big name there, publisher of the leading writers of the previous generation and profiting from his monopoly in Corneille's plays. Charles de Sercy specialized in landscape gardening, a fast-growing fashion, and books on hunting; Guignard specialized in history and etiquette, books aimed at the new citizens ambitious for social elevation. Le Gras had a stock of landscape gardening, hunting, etiquette and the works of Descartes, which proves him very much à la mode. Two other tradesmen, Claude Barbin and Louis Billaine, immortalized in Boileau's poetry (*Lutrin,* song 5, and *Satire,* number 9), had more personality than their dull colleagues.

Barbin, the illegitimate son of Concini's financial secretary, was apprenticed to Etienne Richer in 1641, and later had a bookstall on the quays selling risky pamphlets and political lampoons during the Fronde. His influential connections may have helped him to his mastership in 1654 and after a period of inactivity, he is back in business in 1659 with a new edition of *Recueil des portraits et éloges en vers* by Mlle. Montpensier and others. His establishment was in the sixth arcade of the Great Hall of the Palais opposite the door of Sainte Chapelle, and catered for every fashion. It was Barbin to whom La Rouchefoucauld sent the manuscript of his famous *Maximes* for publication, and Madame La Fayette chose him to publish her *Princesse de Clèves* and other novels. Ménage was another of his authors, and he published the mysterious *Lettres de la religieuse portuguaise,* the *Conjuration des Espagnols* by St. Réal, the first edition of La Fontaine's *Fables,* works by the Chevalier de Méré, and St. Evremond's *Oeuvres Mêlées.* More, he was the publisher of the greatest names of the day—Racine, Molière, Boileau, de Furetière. After 1685 he published fewer contemporary masterpieces but kept to authors of high caliber: Cousins' *Histoire d'Occident,* Varillas, Maimbourg, who had broken with Cramoisy, and Perrault's Fairy Tales, one of the last titles he ever produced. He sold his enormously valuable and varied stock a few years before his death in 1695 for 40,000 livres, including 360 copies of the 4-volume *Fables* of La Fontaine with a third share in it, 496 copies of Molière's works with a third share, 360 copies of Racine's plays with a half share, 1,200 copies of La Rochefoucauld's *Réflexions* with a third share, 500 copies of *Princesse de Clèves* with sole copyright, a one-third share in Boileau's works, the complete rights in Varillas and in Dacier (a translator), with thousands of copies of their works, a one-third share in Mézeray's *Histoire* with hundreds of copies, 400 copies of St. Evremond's works with sole rights, and 75 copies of La Quintinye's *Instructions pour les jardins fruitiers et potagers* with a third share.

Louis Billaine and Denis Thierry II were collaborators with Barbin but were not in the fashionable market. Thierry had premises in the Rue St. Jacques, was the regular printer to the Palais booksellers and their principal stockist in the University quarter. His main concern was publishing for the Franciscans, from which lucrative contract he made enough money to sell the franchise to Edme Couterot II for 37,400 livres. He must have been one of the richest tradesmen in Paris, with a bookshop in the second arcade at the Palais and another in the Rue St. Jacques near St. Benedict's church. He was sole publisher to the Benedictine Order in France and so had charge of the monumental works of scholarship the Maurists were bringing out: the *Acta sanctorum ordinis Sancti Benedicti,* the great edition of St. Anselm, Mabillon's *Vetera analecta* (1681) and his *Re diplomatica.* Billaine was a cultivated man about town, did not disdain the delights of the tavern, was well acquainted with Greek, Latin, Spanish, and Italian, and his catalog lists an impressive range of material including Luc d'Achery, Mabillon, Labbe's *Bibliotheca bibliothecarum,* La Mothe Le Vayer's *Traité de l'amour,* Corneille's *Théâtre,* and La Fontaine. He traveled abroad extensively on business, opened branches outside France, bequeathed the one in Rome to his agent, Crozier, and was more involved in the international trade than any other bookseller of his time. He issued bulky catalogs of second-hand books he had bought in Italy, Germany, Holland, Flanders and England on a wide range of subjects, including history, literature, and science in several European languages.

The significant feature of the two businesses just described is their emphasis on the *contemporary:* new authors, new subjects, modern languages. Once more we have proof, this time from business, of the marked change in the spirit of the age, from an outmoded system of thought to a recognizably modern age. But the devotional impetus was not spent. While the Palais supplied matter for progressive minds, the old Rue St. Jacques was up to its ears in the old conventional piety. Georges Josse I, a shareholder in the Compagnie des Usages, was a specialist in spiritual literature, issuing Beuvelet's *Méditations,* Father Audiffet's *Heures* and other little devotional books for the Carmelites and other nuns. His two sons, Georges and Louis, inherited a business worth 40,000 livres, and when Mabre-Cramoisy went into liquidation they bought up his copyrights in service books and prayerbooks and took over publication of Bouhours and other Jesuit authors. When Georges II died in 1694 his stock was valued at 67,000 livres.

Another similar firm was that of Edme Couterot who published liturgical works for various religious Orders, the Minims, Capuchins, and Recollects, and amassed a stock of 50,000 books, but the leading name in this field was Etienne Michallet, originally from Lyons; he was apprenticed to Siméon Piget and Le Petit in 1633 and incredibly spent over forty years in the trade before being admitted master in 1676, yet had from some source or other tacit approval to open a shop and start publishing. His titles began to appear in 1671: Menestrier's *Art du blason,* Bernier's *Abrégé de la philosophie de M. Gassendi,* Thévenot's *Recueil de voyages,* La Bruyère's *Caractères,* Vauban's *Ingénieur français* and Lémery's *Chymie,* with books on geometry, architecture, the art of fortification, and medicine (particularly Madame Fouquet's *Recueil de remèdes*)—heavy emphasis on science as well as the safe lines in devotions. He had copyrights in Abelly's works, and Boudon and Bonnefons and La Puente's *Méditations,* and was King's Printer after Mabre-Cramoisy died in 1687, as well as being the Jesuits' official publisher, particularly of the works of Nepveu, Alleaume, Texier, Guilloré and Crasset. When he died in 1702 his widow asked Alexandre Delespine 70,000 livres for the stock, which largely consisted of small-sized books modest in both format and price.

The publishers at Port-Royal, of course, were the promulgators of Jansenist doctrines: Le Petit issued countless editions of Arnauld, of Lancelot's grammar, Royaumont's Bible, Sacy's translations of the Scriptures and Jansenist liturgical books. When a fire at the Jansenist college at Montaigu destroyed his stock he was able to rebuild it so completely that eleven years later it was estimated at the fantastic sum of 100,000 livres. Next, André Pralard, Antoine Chrestien's son-in-law, was admitted master in 1669 and enjoyed powerful patronage, bringing out not only works by the Oratory Fathers like Malebranche, Lamy the mathematician, and Father Quesnel, but also Ellies Du Pin, the many translations of Augustine made by Antoine Arnauld, and others by Le Maistre de Sacy. Most devoted of the Jansenist publishers was Guillaume Desprez, identified with Pascal, publisher of his *Lettres provinciales* and *Pensées*. He, too, made a fortune and left a stock of 226,437 books and no fewer than ten presses.

The conclusion from all this would seem to be that business success was intimately related to the sale of French books and concentration on a specialist clientele; publishers brought out their own titles rather than stocking a range of other firms' imprints. We know something about the clientele but we would like to know far more than we do about the customers for the "modern" books—it would help us analyze the effect of new thought on the social classes of late 17th-century France. All we have is evidence (which is all too self-evident) from Couterot and Josse, and Desprez's surviving records show that he had only two correspondents abroad, de l'Orme in Holland and Crozier in Rome. Those firms' devotional list found customers in the Orders who were then engaged in evangelical work, sponsoring a lot of titles which the same publishers would be pleased to put out at a corresponding profit as well as personal zeal.

4. The Leading Booksellers

Six firms could be described as "grands libraires." Three we have mentioned, Billaine, Le Petit and Desprez; the other three were Sébastien Cramoisy, Fédéric Léonard and François Muguet.

Cramoisy was the dominant force in Paris publishing for years, and in the period 1669-1687 the firm was controlled by Sébastien Mabre-Cramoisy from a magnificent residence in the Rue St. Jacques, on the very spot where his grandfather Nivelle had hung out his sign, the Three Swans, many years before. He was Director of the Imprimerie Royale, "Prototypographer" to the King, sole printer of paper money, official printer to the Church of Paris—in short, the head of his profession. He married the daughter of a wealthy goldsmith, niece of Nicolas Loir, the King's Painter, and in 1670 reorganized the Compagnie des Usages, that nest of privilege, and prepared a lengthy catalog of his publications to promote his huge stocks of material. He could always rely on Jesuit backing, was publisher of Bouhours' and Maimbourg's popular books, and as King's Printer had a monopoly of publications emanating from the Court—the principal preachers for example, whose sermons were staple reading among devout members of the upper classes. He was the natural choice as publisher of orthodox works, Chanut's *Histoire du Concil de Trente,* Rapin's histories and Huet's works, but did not rest on these laurels, aware that in future booksellers would have to lean towards the modern schools, particularly "progressive" subjects in French.

But his fortunes gradually declined. He failed to rebuild the Compagnie des Usages in a way that would stay, because of course it meant Monopoly to his competitors who were not enjoying the privileges, and they went on pirating his prayerbooks. After 1684 the old firm failed fast. He had to buy up the old stock of the Imprimerie Royale, costly, extravagant books that did not sell, and retail them at half price, a process that occupied years and weakened his standing. All his best-selling lines were promptly pirated (Lyons publishers issued more copies of Maimbourg's popular histories than Cramoisy himself) and the high standards he insisted on only made him uncompetitive—he sold only 60 copies of a book by Maimbourg in one year and lost 18,000 livres on that one title. He died in 1687 and his widow, Françoise Loir, was forced to liquidate the firm at the famous sign of the Three Storks in 1698.

Fédéric Léonard was first apprenticed to Moretus and then to Billaine. Son of Marie de Medici's and the Duchess of Orleans' bookseller in Brussels, although a foreigner he cleverly managed to be admitted master in 1653 on payment of 400 livres to Guild funds. He began by purchasing Jean Petitpas' stock for 95,000 livres and Sébastien Huré's much larger stock together with the title King's Printer. After that his career was assured. Specializing in devotional books and with a monopoly of François de Sales's works, he had a profitable market, and once nominated as official printer and publisher to the Clergé de France after the much respected Vitré, his influence in ecclesiastical circles was confirmed.

He was in due course official publisher to the Dominicans, Cistercians and Praemonstratensians, and, as if all this was not enough, he was appointed printer to the King for all matters relating to War, Finance, and the Mint. He was also Parlement's official printer. To prosper this shrewd Fleming must have learned the subtle art of currying favor in high places. With Chapelain's help and by agreement with Elzevier he secured control of the profitable series of classics *ad usum Delphinum,* was much respected by Bossuet and Huet, and was a protégé of Montausier. His books were of first–rate quality and he would commission artists of the caliber of Philippe de Champaigne and Edelinck, and employed a typographer to advise on design, François Le Cointe. His Flemish connections must have accounted for his success in the Netherlands, and he was instrumental in introducing the Jansenists to Elzevier; he introduced Richard Simon's work into France and kept close links with his old patron Moretus, whose agent he was in Paris, responsible for running their headquarters there. A man with many irons in the fire, he brought new dynamism to the trade. His stock was worth 150,000 livres, his printing shop 7,000 livres, and his debtors owed him 60,000 livres, 33,000 of which was owed by the King and his Ministers for government commissions. Only Cramoisy was on a larger scale.

François Muguet was the third of the giants. After marrying his employer's niece he was admitted master in 1658, and after inheriting Deshayes's press, made it the best in Paris. He was King's Printer in 1661 and printer to the Archbishop of Paris, published works by Baluze, Colbert's librarian, and benefited from that scholar's financial backing when he was in need. That contact may explain the business he had from the Maurists when Billaine retired, and because he had undertaken some of their expensive scholarly productions, *Capitulaires et ordonnances de St. Maur,* Godeau's *Histoire de l'Eglise,* Marolles's *Semaine sainte* and others, he was assigned their copyrights and made his fortune. In 1684 he succeeded Léonard as printer to the Clergé de France, opened another press at Versailles in the hôtel de Seignelay, and published Amelote's translation of the New Testament. When he died his presses were valued at 9,793 livres, and his bookstock at 87,824 livres.

And we might also discuss another firm's success, after Muguet—the Coignards. Jean-Baptiste I was son of master printer Charles Coignard and was born in Paris in 1637. He married Philippe Tompère whose father owned a printing shop, and by 1658 he was a master printer at the Sign of the Golden Bible in the Rue St. Jacques, an Assistant in the Guild in 1671, King's Printer in 1678, and by 1687 a Guild Syndic and official printer to the Académie Française. He was an exceptionally skilled printer and typographer, a proof corrector par excellence, and kept his presses fully occupied. He was a considerable publisher and left 66,002 livres at his death. His widow and son, Jean-Baptiste II, made a profit of 30,000 livres between 1690 and 1694. With Muguet they were fully able to finance such massive undertakings as the first *Dictionnaire de l'Académie française* and *Antiquitates Constantinopolitanae,* something the Government recognized by granting Jean-Baptiste continuation of the copyright of Moreri's Dictionary, which brought him a fortune sufficient to endow his daughters richly, so much so that the Coignards were among those singled out for attack on grounds of abuse of privileges in 1720.

5. *Paris and the Book Trade*

Nationally and internationally Paris was an important center of the trade. Small businesses dealt with local trading, either in cheap literature from Troyes or second-hand books and other material of modest price, and the Palais bookshops had clients in Holland and other countries abroad as well as their local middle-class customers. Couterot, Josse, Desprez and Léonard have left lists of their customers, from which we know that Couterot and Josse had no connections outside France, that Couterot chiefly did business with the religious Orders, and that Josse worked for the Carmelites, Ursulines and their Orders of nuns. Desprez had business in the same region of France as Couterot and Josse; like the type founders these three firms did most of their business north of the Loire, with some in the South West, and Desprez had a branch in Rome and an agent in Amsterdam—we might have expected more signs of international links in the case of a man like Desprez. Léonard was different, a man whose business stretched across national boundaries to Rome, Germany, Flanders and Amsterdam, and with more contacts south of the Loire than north. Our documents reveal that none of these men had any liabilities outside Paris; the sums their few debtors owe them are negligible, and they seem to have been in debt only to papermakers. On the other hand, the Crown and Bourvalais, the tract publisher owed Léonard 50,000 livres. What did that signify?

The inventories of the four men show that they stocked their own publications rather than others', that their range was limited, and many titles had been marketed for a long time; Léonard alone had a decent range of foreign titles on offer. The conclusion must be that Couterot, Josse and Desprez put their effort into marketing their own publications in France, and Léonard was in the international market. What is surprising is the poor return on the heavy capital investment.

Catalogs give us more insight into their wares. For example: *Catalogue des livres imprimez à Paris chez le Veuve de Jean-Baptiste Coignard et chez Jean-Baptiste Coignard fils* (1690, 10pp., Quarto); *Catalogue des livres imprimez à Paris chez Edme Couterot* (1694, 8pp., Quarto); *Catalogue des livres de Guillaume Desprez* (1675, 8pp., Octavo); *Catalogue des livres imprimez chez François Muguet* (n.d., 23pp., Octavo). Cramoisy's *Bibliographia Cramosiana* was much larger than these slender volumes, each a list of the publisher's own publications alone. Other catalogs included their own and other publishers' titles, e.g., *Catalogue des livres imprimez et qui se trouvent à Paris chez Louis Josse, libraire et imprimeur de Son Eminence Monseigneur le Cardinal de Noailles* (1706, 4pp., Quarto), which has a section headed *Livres d'assortiment,* books from Lyons and Cologne. Another is a subject catalog: *Catalogue des livres anciens et nouveaux composés ou traduits en faveur de ceux qui s'appliquent à la médecine, chirurgie, pharmacie ou chymie.* They were also for local consumption in Paris.

Thomas Jolly (Jacques Dallin's son-in-law and Simon Besnard's partner) issued a series of catalogs of foreign books; Louis Billaine put out complete catalogs by country—

Italy, Spain, England, and by subject—theology, history, literature; Jean de La Caille, who wrote the *Histoire de l'imprimerie parisienne,* issued a catalog to announce his debut as a bookseller; in 1680 Antoine Cellier included large numbers of German books in his list; Jean Boudot, another newcomer and partner of Edme Martin's widow, was also strong in foreign works. All these names appear in an issue of the newly-founded *Journal des Savants* as sources of modern books from abroad, an indication of the growing complexity of the book world. In Martin and Boudot's *Catalogus librorum omnium qui reperiuntur parisiis in bibliopolo Viduae Emundi Martini et Joannis Boudot,* many works are pre-1600 and many post-1600. Boudot, who makes no distinction between old and new books, was an importer who traded with nearly every country in Europe except Spain (which would trade with Lyons rather than with Paris). As the dates get nearer in time the network widens to include more foreign countries doing business with Paris, first the Spanish Low Countries, then the United Provinces after 1630, and England after 1670. The Protestant north is overtaking the Catholic south, and Germany makes an extraordinary recovery after the Thirty Years War.

Now to compare the Paris catalogs with their foreign competitors. The *Catalogus librorum Petri Van der Aa* (Leyden, 1705) comprised 318 titles, 61 in French, and nearly all printed in Holland; another catalog (Gausse and Alberts, The Hague, 1714) lists 100 titles, 31 in French and all printed in The Hague, Amsterdam, Leyden and Rotterdam. The Dutch were evidently very interested in French books, although some Dutch publishers were agents of Paris firms, e.g., *Catalogue des livres de Hollande, de France et autres pays étrangers qui se trouvent présents dans la boutique d'Adrien Moetjens, et encore plusieurs autres, le tout à prix raisonnable* (Moetjens, The Hague, 1700, 276pp.). Of 815 titles in Latin, 188 were published in Amsterdam, Paris second with 107; of 3,510 titles in French, 1,312 came from Paris, 141 from Lyons, 558 from Amsterdam, 201 from Brussels and 248 from Cologne. There were only 208 Flemish, 132 Italian, 32 Spanish and 31 German titles. Places of publication were:

Paris	1,426 titles
Amsterdam	838 titles
The Hague	306 titles
Cologne	294 titles
Brussels	233 titles
Lyons	172 titles
Leyden	157 titles
Antwerp	153 titles

Leers, the foremost Rotterdam publisher, brought out a number of catalogs dated 1691–1706, and from them it seems that Latin was still the first language of scholars (7 out of 10 titles); a quarter came from central Europe and a quarter from France, a moderate number from the United Provinces and Switzerland, very few from England or the Spanish Low Countries. Latin was still the language of learning but French was now rapidly taking its place. Before the war between France and Holland and her allies there was considerable exchange of stocks between France and other countries, but Louis XIV's expansionist adventures closed frontiers, and by the end of the 17th century the Paris book trade is in severe recession.

Evidence of the growth in international book supply comes from two interesting notebooks from England, those of booksellers Thomas Bennet and Henry Clements of Oxford, partners in a big printing conger. They tell us that when books were exchanged they were paid for either in cash or kind, with a 20% discount, and that these two gentlemen traded with Leipzig, Frankfurt, Rotterdam, Brussels, Utrecht, Lyons and Paris, though mostly with Protestant countries; and Customs registers for the years 1697–1703 reveal that the two were important middlemen between the continent and England, and in fact dominated the trade in northern Europe.

The War of the League of Augsburg (1688–1697) interrupted trade between France and Holland, with unhappy consequences for Paris, as surviving evidence proves. The bookseller Hortemels died in 1691, worth 52,677 livres and possessing numerous copyrights; his correspondence reveals extensive relations with booksellers in Holland, Leyden (143 letters), Brussels, Lille and other towns in Flanders (104 letters), 26 letters from London and more from Nuremberg, Stettin, Frankfurt and Strasburg, with hundreds from all over France, from Rome and Montreal! Six months after his death his widow made a list of his creditors: Claude and Jean-François Dupuy, Godard and Cousin, papermakers; Léonard, Muguet and Barbin, booksellers; Rondet and Journel, printers; and Edelinck, from whom he had commissioned a portrait of Descartes for Baillet's biography. His effects were sold to pay off his debts. Such was fortune's wheel at this time. Next, Marie-Thérèse Martin separated from her husband, whose creditors included her mother-in- law, seven or eight booksellers, a printer and a binder, a locksmith, a stockbroker, a King's Councillor, and others. The debts amounted to 40,000 livres; his assets, including money owed him from booksellers in England, Holland, Germany, Italy and Flanders, amounted to 7,516 livres. Bills negotiated before the War were now of no value and Marie-Thérèse declared that books he had thought "sure and profitable" were affected by the present crisis and he could only lay his hands on 8,200 livres. He was a victim, she said, of "the present bad times," and she asked for more time to pay off his debts. It was agreed that they be repaid in six-monthly instalments.

Claude Cellier was forced to meet his creditors and had to surrender his possessions, a bankrupt, in 1696; François Muguet met disaster and had to auction his stock in 1697; in 1698 Simon-Barthélemy Bénard met his creditors—papermakers, booksellers and printers—who declared that "Bénard has suffered grievous losses because of the present war which has been so mischievous to trade. He failed to meet his costs and other expenditure necessary to his business, added to which he was engaged in a ruinous lawsuit with the Privy Council." He was therefore granted eight years in which to clear his debts, so as to avoid his own bankruptcy and the "loan of the debt he owed them."

Henri Lambin, another case, was imprisoned in the Petit Châtelet for debt; in 1701 Michel Courtois suffered the same fate, and in 1703 Nicolas de Vaux asked for time to pay his debts, but all to no avail. The Glorious Century, so-called, was for publishers nothing but a catalog of commercial disasters and bankruptcies. But to some it was by no means unprofitable, as we shall see.

6. *The Social Milieu: a Closed World*

As we saw earlier, one of the Crown's objectives in its dealings with the trade was to reduce the number of master booksellers and printers, and it pursued its objective ruthlessly; yet, in spite of that and the rigorous regulations of 1666–67, some managed to reach the status of master. In the period 1670–1700, 162 masters were admitted, 19 sons-in-law and only 59 apprentices. What was the social background of these people? Only 205 names were registered in the years 1666–1700, fewer than one-third of those in the period 1631–1665. Career prospects were drastically reduced. Of 168 apprentices, 10 were sons of masters in the Paris trade, 7 were sons of masters in the provinces, 27 the sons of minor officials, 6 of doctors, 12 of merchants in business in Paris, 4 were Masters of Arts. The majority were sons of masters either in the book trade or other trades, and it is likely that inside aid was needed if any promotion was envisaged. Manpower via the normal apprenticeship system must have been radically cut, and we find trained journeymen doing apprentices' work, and a new category, the "allouée," or day-wage laborer, to do the unskilled work.

For the lucky few who could remain in the trade, prospects improved, as we can judge from marriage contracts dated 1671–72, before the drastic regulations of 1666 had their effect. Seventeen out of 376 contracts relate to journeymen printers, booksellers and binders, with dowries varying from 60 to 600 livres (even 1,000 in one or two cases). Nineteen contracts were in the names of master printers and booksellers, though that title may not have been authorized in all cases, which might explain why a dozen of them had dowries of less than 1,000 livres. Eight cases involved dowries of between 2,000 and 8,000 livres. From such meager evidence it is hard to draw firm conclusions but it is interesting to note that the future wife of Gilles de Courbé brought only 150 livres as her dowry, and Francois Giffart's bride 800. Eight other cases showed significantly larger sums: Marguerite Lucas, a bookseller's daughter, was worth 2,000 livres to Francois Guichard, a publisher of Sancerre-en-Berry; Marie Jacquin, bookseller's daughter, brought 3,500 livres to Francois Gourrault, a master surgeon; and when Elizabeth Gourrault married Jean Verger; Catherine Couterot, the lawyer Charles de St Germain; and Marie Bourgin, Gilles Blaisot, they contributed 8,000 livres.

No figures survive from the end of the century but there is little doubt that there was wealth in the oligarchy of firms which controlled so much of the trade. In 1676 Le Petit gave a daughter 16,000 livres on her marriage to the captain of a regiment, and his other daughters made good matches; his sons became Secretaries to the Crown. In 1688 Muguet gave his daughter a dowry of 24,000 livres, and he could count two printers, a doctor of theology and a lawyer among his children, while two other daughters married lawyers. Desprez gave 25,000 livres to his daughter in 1696, 25,000 to a second daughter in 1701, and 19,000 to a third in 1709, and he owned houses in the Rue St. Jacques and Rue des Lombards, a small property in Vitry, another in Houilles and a vineyard in the Bezons region. Léonard's daughter received a dowry of 10,000 livres in 1678 when she wed Herbin, Controller of Finance, and his son Fédéric II, 120,000 livres in silver and merchandise when he married the daughter of a rich businessman in 1682. Fédéric I and II bought the Château de Boispréau near Malmaison, and the son's property was worth one million livres in 1709. In the early 18th century further evidence proves that the publishers Desprez, Coignard and Dezallier were each worth 400,000 livres.

For some it was a fortunate time, and royal policy paid dividends for the happy few. The early 18th century saw signs of an approaching recovery.

CHAPTER IV

THE RESULTS OF ROYAL POLICY:
LYONS TO AMSTERDAM

OLBERT'S LEGISLATION was designed to discourage publication of "bad" books, that is, anything hostile to the monarchy or established religion, and as a consequence clandestine printing became riskier in Paris. But what of provincial and foreign publishing?

1. The Provincial Book Trade in Ruins

Lyons, traditionally the most important publishing center outside Paris, was now in a perilous condition after the Thirty Years War, which killed its market in Germany, and as a consequence of economic depression. War between France and Spain affected Lyons more than Paris, but after the end of the Thirty Years War Lyons booksellers were back in Frankfurt prospecting for markets and restoring trade links with Italy and Spain. Despite Moretus' withdrawal from international trading, which injured Lyons, two of its biggest publishers, Borde and Arnauld, had great wealth in 1706, over 180,000 livres, and two others, Boissat and Remeus, were exporting classic works of Spanish theology to Antwerp, Amsterdam, Hamburg, Geneva and Basel in the 1660s, and distributing books from those cities throughout France and Spain. Girin and Riviere concentrated on domestic markets, and Mayer on Germany.

But the greatest name in Lyons publishing was Anisson. He succeeded Horace Cardon, a Lyons magistrate, and with his sons Jean and Jacques and his partners Posuel and Rigaud, he headed the firm for many years exploring overseas markets in Italy and Spain and sending his son on business to Germany and the Netherlands. In 1677, a time when such an enterprise was thought the height of folly, the Anissons published a 27-volume *Bibliotheca Patrum,* the last and largest work of its kind. In Spain they fought a bitter commercial war with competitors, especially Moretus, and to keep their market they did not scruple to pirate Moretus's publications, copying title-pages, frontispieces, and imprints too. Anisson was just as aggressive in Italy, where his enemies accused him of lowering standards to cut costs and steal markets. Lyons publishers were often in difficulties—in 1669 Boissat was deeply in debt, owing 80,977 livres to 38 creditors in a number of countries; in the words of the deposition, "the said debts were not paid because of a failure of business due to neglect by his associate Georges Remeus who made several trips abroad without properly accounting for the business he transacted, with consequent disorder in his affairs. Books published by the said Boissat remained unsold because of plague in Germany and war between France and Spain; some consignments of books were seized by corsairs, and there was no compensation for such losses. . . ."

Boissat's creditors accepted a compromise plan and he continued in business. Another Lyons partnership that faced bankruptcy was Girin and Rivière, in debt for 110,000 livres. A passage by an official named d'Herbigny in 1697 about the decline of the Lyons trade is instructive:

> Only two firms now trade abroad, mainly with Spain and the Spanish Indies, who do no printing, partly because of their natural lethargy and partly because paper is scarce and expensive in Spain, having to be imported from Genoa and La Rochelle. The only books printed there are Spanish or Italian works on law and Scholastic theology, so that it is a good potential market, but books must be reasonably priced because the Spaniards publish books quite cheaply themselves. Lyons suffers because of the duties publishers have to pay on the raw materials, which militates against cheapness of the product, hence Spain tends to import from Venice or Genoa where prices are lower. The last two cities have taken over the Lyons trade in Spain and

> Lyons publishers claim that until 30 or 40 years ago they
> enjoyed exemptions from duty which Paris now enjoys.

This was an exaggeration—d'Herbigny was pleading for
better conditions, but in fact Paris had to pay more for its
paper than Lyons because it was farther away from the paper
mills of Angoulême or the Auvergne than Lyons was from
the mills of Beaujolais and Auvergne, but Lyons was at a
disadvantage when it came to exporting books and trading
with Geneva. Certainly the latter looked for the cheapest
paper and its work force was paid lower wages than in Paris,
if we are to believe a memorandum of the Paris booksellers
which records 36 to 40 sols a day as the rate for a compositor
in Paris as against 16 to 18 sols in Lyons. On the other hand,
extensions of copyright enjoyed by Paris publishers deprived
Lyons firms of older material, while new works were rare in
Lyons; thus publishing there was starved for copy.

Lyons felt strongly about its handicap: the distance from
the source of power and privilege in the capital and the
source of its business, the writers, most of whom lived in
Paris. So why not establish a branch in Paris? The examples
of Muguet and Michallet would serve to show how successful
enterprising Lyonnese firms could be in Paris, and the
Anissons also followed their example. No effort was spared
to convince scholarly circles in Paris of the necessity of
welcoming a firm with 600,000 livres' capital to Paris, despite
the fact that Paris publishers all too rightly feared that the
Anissons would be agents for Lyons firms and so contribute
to the ruin of Paris firms by retailing material at lower prices.
To conciliate the "gens de lettres," Jean and Jacques
Anisson collaborated with Du Cange on a Greek glossary, a
formidable task from which Parisian publishers had recoiled.
Then Jacques Anisson became guide and go-between for
Mabillon when he toured Italy in search of manuscripts and
texts to edit, while other members of the Anisson clan tried
by every possible means to rush the barriers raised against
them by their Parisian rivals. In 1681 Jean Anisson, through
Colbert's intercession, asked the King for permission to set
up in Paris, but La Reynie, the police chief, opposed it; two
years later Jean's brother-in-law, Posuel, tried again, but in

vain. In 1685 abbé Féret, Posuel's uncle and an official in the service of the Archbishop of Sens, bought Posuel a place as bookseller to the local court, but this scheme also failed. However, Jean Anisson eventually managed to get into Paris by the main entrance, nominated Director of the Imprimerie Royale in place of Mabre-Cramoisy, a triumph that came too late to help Lyons publishing survive there, since Anisson in his role as Lyons representative on the Council for Commerce simply became more and more completely absorbed into the affairs of the capital.

In such circumstances it is quite obvious that piracy was bound to flourish. Verdussen's correspondence from Antwerp is filled with plans designed to frustrate Lyons piracies, but it was the Paris publishers who were the main target. For example, they retaliated against a Lyonnese established in Paris, called Berthier, who had injured them in some way, by pirating some of his books with the help of an accomplice in Cologne, and when Guillaume Desprez launched Le Maistre de Sacy's translation of the Bible they immediately pirated it in Liège, Luxemburg and Brussels, using Godard as their agent. The Lyonnese waged continual war against extension of copyrights which they felt were an abuse of privilege, and this in turn led to endless litigation by which they hoped to secure new legislation. But such methods could only alienate a Government so authoritarian as the one in power, and the only way for the Lyons firms to survive was by clandestine publishing of forbidden books or of current favorites under false imprints. Every profitable book first printed in Paris was duly reprinted in Lyons with a fake address.

Paris, of course, reacted angrily, complaining they had to bear the high costs of publishing, including paying for the manuscript, while Lyons could easily duplicate the book more cheaply, as if copyright didn't exist. All attempts to suppress the illicit trade failed, for the simple reason that there just was not enough time and energy to spare searching premises, and if pressure grew heavy the Lyons men would enlist the aid of monks, traditionally printers' allies, and hide out in monasteries; it was easy to conceal contraband books or find that keys had been lost when spies from Paris arrived to look for offending material. In such conditions it was useless for the Government to frame legislation to help Lyons when its fundamental policy ran counter to a healthy book trade.

It was the same in other places. Rouen practically existed on pirating other people's books, and with so many Protestants in the town it was a stronghold of opposition to the Crown. Printing forbidden books was almost a tradition, and a regular feature of its trade was the importation of banned books from the anti-Catholic Low Countries. In Champagne there was a flourishing trade in cheap literature centered on Troyes, just the kind of printed matter that aroused the government's deepest suspicions (hawkers and pedlars' packs could contain anything) and was very difficult to monitor. Other towns, Châlons, St. Menehould and Rheims, were in close touch with Dutch publishers and imported the same "mauvais livres" as the men of Rouen. Paris was becoming very like a city under siege.

2. Dutch Publishing Takes the Lead

The enervating effect of Colbert's reactionary policy was to kill a good percentage of the French book industry, and as always happens in a fiercely competitive market economy, other rival businesses will make up the gap. In the circumstances it was the Netherlands which took advantage of the depression in France; the Elzeviers infiltrated the French market with their attractive pocket editions, of high quality physically and intellectually, produced at modest prices and with guaranteed academic standards. Classical texts were systematically revised by professors at the University of Leyden, the most up-to-date publications of their kind, but even firms of this caliber were prepared to pirate anything appropriate to keep their branch bookshops supplied in Paris, and of course they fed the underground anti-monarchist movements with a lively trade in pamphlets attacking Louis XIV's Court, a traffic the French Government was helpless to suppress. As more victims of despotism left France for exile in the Low Countries, so more trade skills and crafts were at the disposal of Dutch firms. The

Jansenists were among the first to leave France, Arnauld living in Mons for the last fifteen years of his life, constantly on the move whenever danger threatened and inspiriting his old comrades in France with vigorous pamphleteering. Gerberon and Quesnel, former friends of his, eventually joined him and continued the struggle after Arnauld's death in 1694. The Spanish Low Countries were a haven for French Jansenists until Philip V restored order there in the early 18th century.

But these men played only a secondary role in the areas that interest us. The vast majority of publications in French printed abroad were the work of Protestant exiles, products of their intelligentsia at universities, particularly the Calvinists, who maintained constant communications with each other. Foreign students came in great numbers to Leyden, Sedan, Saumur and Geneva as part of their *peregrinatio academica* to sit at the feet of celebrated teachers. The lectures they heard were very different. The seat of orthodox Calvinism was Geneva but there were as many deviations and conflicts over the problem of Grace in the Protestant camp as in the Catholic, and there was particular concern over Socinianism. Whereas Geneva was rigid in its orthodoxy, requiring its ministers to sign the *Consensus Helveticus,* the Netherlands was much more tolerant, though the Calvinist Church was the official one. However, the Remonstrants kept to their more liberal interpretation, rather as the Catholics in Utrecht remained solidly orthodox while their Archbishop, Neercassel, and the clergy were overtly Jansenist. And Jews were permitted to practice their religion.

For these reasons the Netherlands, like England, was an obvious place of asylum—St. Evremond spent his exile in both countries, and Elie Saurin, a minister from Embrun, ended his days in Delft after being hounded from France for refusing to kneel before the Sacrament. There he met Labadie, a convert from the Jesuits and now a minister at Middelburg, whose mystical works were so influential, refusing to sign the Confession of Faith or accept the discipline of the French churches in the Low Countries. Despite having been persecuted himself, Saurin turned on Labadie and secured his suspension, but at least Labadie was allowed to live on there, and he opened a printing shop in Amsterdam to publish his mystical books.

Sometimes refugees came to Holland not from France but from Geneva, as did Jean Le Clerc, and his uncle Etienne de Courcelles before him, to join the Remonstrants. And it was at about that time that the great ordeal began for French Protestants. In 1681, after the Académie at Sedan was suppressed, Pierre Bayle was summoned to Rotterdam by an old pupil who had been promised by his uncle, the powerful Alderman Adriaan van Paets, that he would found a school. There the young emigré taught for twelve years and attracted to the school his old master and his colleague Jurieu from Sedan. In October 1685 the Revocation of the Edict of Nantes was passed, forbidding any Protestant who refused conversion to remain in France—they were to leave within a fortnight. It was the resulting flood of refugees that constituted the nucleus of an incredibly intellectual society.

The emigration affected Holland largely, but a great many went to England (with their pastor, Pierre Allix), to Altona in Denmark and to Berlin, and always the churches were a unifying factor, helping the immigrants conserve their language and culture, although in England they tended to assimilate to the native language and culture. In Holland they remained French in mind and tongue, and they were most numerous in that country, hoping always for a return to their native land; so, despite the welcome accorded them by the friendly Dutch, they were always anxious to know what was happening at home—hence the publication of so much pamphlet literature, and the gazettes. Skilled controversialists and well informed, the Protestant ministers began to express themselves not in books of piety or collections of sermons but in appeals to the French at home and in political attacks on Louis XIV; shades of opinion varied considerably vis-à-vis the King, and theology provided lush pastures for endless quarrels and debates, with Pierre Jurieu at the center of the most intolerant party. He issued anathemas on all who failed to think as he did, and pursued from parish to parish any ministers he suspected of being Socinians.

The place of refuge was soon more like an assembly of strong characters, full of energy and enterprise, typical of the

Protestant ethos, and given that they were numbered in hundreds of thousands, it is no surprise that French publications should expand considerably outside France. London and Berlin sheltered several French publishers but the heart of the exiled trade was in the Low Countries, which had of course a long printing tradition, and it was there that the most critical steps in the history of ideas and of the future of literature were taken.

One such exiled publisher was Henry Desbordes, one of the media men of his day. He was in business in La Rochelle, Niort and Saumur, definitely a Reformer, and his family were printers to the University of Saumur after it was founded by Duplessis-Mornay, publishing the work of learned Protestant professors, Louis Cappel, an Orientalist, Tanneguy Le Fèvre, La Place and Moyse Amyrault. But Desbordes was not quite orthodox enough and published a little book called *Liberti de sancto amore epistolae theologicae* with a fictitious imprint, "Irenopolis," offensive to orthodox Protestantism at Saumur, and was prevented from issuing any more copies, although he had smuggled some into Holland. His bookshop was closed because he had printed a program of studies which failed to meet the strict requirements of the university authorities, and in 1682 he was actually jailed, moving on to Amsterdam after regaining his liberty. He opened another shop there and waited for news from France with the other French refugees in that city, and through various contacts managed to acquire a copy of *Mercure savant* every month. He found his real métier when he met Pierre Bayle, a literary journalist of uncommon quality, and launched a paper that was very characteristic of the new ethos—*Nouvelles de la République des Lettres,* one of Europe's first critical journals.

Desbordes published a good deal of sectarian and controversial matter but also a fine illustrated edition of La Fontaine's *Fables* (2 vols., 1685, with engravings by Romeyn de Hooge) and, surprisingly, Richelieu's *Testament politique* (it is not known how the manuscript came into his hands).

Another refugee family, the Huguetans, had been closely connected with Protestant thought since its first years in 16th-century Geneva, the Low Countries and Germany.

Jean Huguetan had been an adviser to Gustavus Adolphus and was a leading Lyons publisher, and Jean-Antoine Huguetan specialized in monumental Patristics, with Ravaud. Jean Huguetan's three sons, Marc, Jean-Henri and Pierre, went into exile after the Revocation, running between them a very prosperous business specializing in atlases and portfolios of engravings, with exports to England and commerce throughout the Netherlands and Europe; and they published many service books under false imprints. Details of their credits are enough to indicate the scale of their business: Delgas, their agent in London and Oxford, owed them 10,000 florins, and Olenschlager of Frankfurt owed 14,107 florins. Their shops in Leipzig, Leghorn, Lisbon and Alicante had stocks with a total value of 30,000 florins, and their credit in Italy stood at 34,879.90 francs; in Germany 14,344 marks; in England £90,213; in Portugal 4823.82 Reis; and in France, Spain and Flanders, 37,801.14 florins. Their shares stood at 100 (or 150,000 florins).

An agreement dated 1702 shows that Jean-Henri had an office in London and Pierre one in Amsterdam, each with a share of 400,000 florins in the business, which represents resources from something far beyond bookselling, and was in fact from brokerage and trade in precious stones and wool. Pierre made a profitable marriage to the daughter of an Amsterdam burgomeister and Jean-Henri married Maurice Marguerite de Nassau, illegitimate daughter of the House of Orange. The King of France wanted to elevate him to the peerage and he died "Comte d'Empire et Danemark," a centenarian with a colossal fortune.

Because of their wide-ranging contacts, publishers on this scale were a vital element in the March of Mind, or, to use the vogue phrase of that day, the "Republic of Letters." The little world of Dutch and French emigré intellectuals was able to reach its peers in Berlin, Trèves, Copenhagen and Geneva through the medium of print, and also leading thinkers in the Catholic world. Bayle was in touch with many of them for contributions to his periodical, Magliabecchi in Florence, Dacier in France, the mathematician Ozanam, and Baluze, Colbert's librarian, who advised the Huguetans on publishing the correspondence of Jean and François Hotman, and offered general advice like, "Theodoretus has not yet received the attention he deserves and ought to be published in a decent edition. It is useless to attack St. Augustine for fear it will be prejudicial to your compatriot Muguet," and so on.

In the realm of ideas there were no barriers between Catholic and Protestant, as a letter from Papenbroeck makes clear. He was head of the Bollandists and worked in Amsterdam. Dissatisfied with his Flemish publishers, who made him publish his *Actions de Juin* at his own expense, and even more dissatisfied with the Spanish Inquisition, he gave his reply to them to a Protestant publisher. And again, Father Hardouin writes to the Huguetans:

> I have found you to be in every way sincere in the business I have transacted with you; you have always acted in good faith. I would now ask your discretion and trust in certain matters which make it impossible for me to use my name.

The Huguetans were an essential link between Paris and Amsterdam, and from their base in London made a significant contribution to the new freedom of thought, part of the shift in the center of gravity from the south to the north of Europe. And here Rainier Leers was of crucial importance. He was a Dutchman—one of Harvey's publishers (*Circulation of the blood*)—and assumed control of the family business in 1673, while his young son Arnout II was at The Hague publishing new and topical French books. Rainier married Cornelia Brand, an Arminian minister's daughter, and was in touch with Pierre Bayle when he came to Rotterdam. When the latter was out of work Rainier employed him as a corrector of the press, and while Bayle was editing the *Nouvelles de la République* for Desbordes it was Leers who published most of his scientific works. When Bayle stopped working on the *Nouvelles* he supervised the *Histoire de la vie et des ouvrages des savants,* which his friend Basnage de Beauval had given Leers to publish.

Bayle was a considerable figure in the diffusion of new scientific and historical studies, at the center of a network of correspondents, chiefly refugee scholars, whose work he passed on to Leers, who included Jansenist work by Arnauld and Quesnel on his list, and Malebranche was another of his authors. The Leers firm was better situated at Rotterdam for the export trade than the Amsterdam booksellers and he was in close touch with Berlin, via Hamburg, and had branch bookshops in Leipzig and Frankfurt, Geneva, Oxford, Cambridge and Edinburgh. He is a focal point in the world of Protestant science and letters; Dutch scholars write to him asking him to obtain books for them, and send him their manuscripts; Leibniz writes from Hanover asking him to market his *Codex diplomaticus;* the abbé Chèvremont writes from Brussels offering to share a monopoly he has been granted for business in Lorraine; Nicolas Hartsoeker writes from Paris asking him to send copies of his books to London, Copenhagen, Germany and Stockholm because he has not the means to do so from France. Father Bouhours writes from Paris:

27 November 1699

I am happy the parcel arrived safely. I will send you the rest on two conditions: 1. That you do not tell Josse I have sent you anything. 2. That you do nothing to hinder the sale. Soon you will receive a MS which will be exclusively yours to print as soon as you can. I do not know what you mean when you say that you only mean to please me—I would like to do business with you and I will save you expenses in carriage of letters and other writings as far as I can.

It will be a great pity if we cannot be sure of receiving what you publish. I will look for your publications here; you look to yours. A young friend of mine, named Chardon, has gone to Holland, nephew to M. Chardon the lawyer whom you may know. If you see him you might ask him something for me as I haven't the courage to ask him myself. He promised to bring me Jurieu's *Traité historique* and I will be happy to have the *Christianisme éclairci.* . . . No work has been done on the new edition of Bussy's letters but they ought to be edited by me—I will notify you of the time and place. A book has come out here called *Entretiens sur les contes*

de fées et sur quelques autres ouvrages du temps, well
written in a style like that of *Réflexions sur les défauts
d'autruy.* Since my friend Bussy and myself are treated
harshly in it I have written a sharp criticism of the book
and sent it to M. de Laubre, who printed Bussy's
letters. I don't know if he will get a licence for it but at
the risk of boasting I think I can say I have never written
anything with more relish. I am better after my illness
and I know at my age I can have but a few years
left. . . .

I am your servant,

De Charmont
[In another hand:] Father Bouhours

Leers' problem, as with so many of his colleagues, was to
find out how many of his publications actually found their
way into France. They could always be slipped in under cover
but it was more of a challenge to send them openly. If Dutch
publishers used false imprints they risked a rupture with their
business contacts in France, and yet, to avoid a complete ban
on their books, they had to tread delicately. After the
Revocation a tariff war broke out between France and
Holland, and as a consequence Dutch printers lost a big
market in France; but when bankruptcies began in Paris,
writers were disturbed at the threat to their livelihood and
Bossuet wrote to the Chancellor, Pontchartrain, asking for
some amelioration. We have comments on the situation from
Quesnel, writing to Du Vancel that "Reynier Leers, a
Rotterdam bookseller, has received a permit to export 20
bales of books to France and he is going there to discuss a
resumption of trade while a French publisher is to visit
Holland for a similar purpose. Leers has instructed M. David
(i.e., Arnauld) to send a letter recommending M. Damboise
(i.e., Arnauld de Pomponne)."
    The Chancellor authorized the importation of "useful"
books, and Leers conducted delicate negotiations to secure
permission for Bayle's great dictionary to be admitted into
France. He evidently won Pontchartrain's confidence because he concluded an agreement with Bignon under which

the Bibliothèque Nationale would receive certain books it
needed from Holland, and Clément, the Keeper of the
Library, was corresponding with Leers about missing manuscripts on the Jansenist controversy which had been stolen
from the Library and removed to Holland.

All of which attests a reasonably close contact between the
book trade in Paris and abroad, and not necessarily a hostile
one since books were being regularly shipped out and in
under various contracts, and Dutch booksellers frequently
went to Paris, clearly on good terms with quite orthodox
French publishers. The Crown, as a matter of high policy,
preferred to maintain contacts and negotiate rather than to
suspend business.

3. *"Ghost" printers and fictitious imprints*

Foreign printers went in for pirating of profitable lines and
false imprints, on a considerable scale; imaginary names and
addresses were common and the Elzeviers notorious, using
the name Sambix (a family of booksellers and calligraphers
who had long since died out) and, at their Amsterdam
branch, the "Jacques le Jeun" pseudonym. But the most
outrageous of all was "Pierre Marteau, Cologne," first used
by Jean Elzevier at Leyden in 1660 in a dangerous book
called *Recueil de diverses pièces servans à l'histoire de Henry
III;* it was used again in *Recueil de quelques pièces nouvelles
et galantes* (1663), *Mémoires du Mareschal Bassompierre*
(1665), *Histoire du Cardinal de Richelieu* (1666), *Histoire
amoureuse des Gaules* (1666), *Carte géographique de la Cour
et autres galanteries* (1668), and *Bupanie, histoire amoureuse
de ce temps* (1669). The titles are sufficient indication of
Marteau's scope. There were many other imitators: "Jacques
le Sincère," "Robert le Turc," "Jean le Blanc," "F. Revels,"
all from "Cologne," all pornographic or political, and any
other printers risking further reprints of the same stuff simply
repeated the same false imprints.

More seriously, Genevan printers who wished to enter the
Spanish market at Lyons' expense used Lyons imprints on
theological works which would have had no future in Spain
with Genevan imprints, and Lyons did the same when it tried

to oust Moretus from the Spanish market. And Lyons and
Rouen had no hesitation in using Paris imprints, even blandly
printing the text of the licence describing the penalties for
piracy!

Such complicated provenance gives bibliographers problems today. Authors lie concealed under the cloak of
anonymity or a pseudonym in cases where they had no hope
of authorized permission to publish, or in some cases they
affected to despise authorship as vulgar. Occasionally books
were published without the author's consent, and sometimes
an author would give his copy to a publisher but would
reserve to himself the rights in a reprint if the first edition
proved successful. A great many books and pamphlets for
the years 1670–1700 lack an author's or publisher's real
name, and the practice of pirating other people's work makes
identification even more hazardous: when dates themselves
are suspect (a pirated edition would repeat the date of the
original edition) there is often a confusion about the dates of
various editions. Much more work needs doing to clear up
ambiguities in this fascinating and perplexing period. Printers' ornaments and devices can help identify a book but even
these can be traps since pirate printers would naturally use
the original ornaments and devices, as they did when copying
Elzevier's books—his sphere and buffalo head and siren were
easily imitated. Signatures could vary from one workshop to
another, and advertisements are an indicator, but the
amount of patience required to establish the authentic
sequence can be guessed! Yet it is essential that such work be
done if we are to understand fully the literary, political and
publishing history of this turbulent epoch. Research in the
19th century was thorough enough for us to be able to
identify a work published in the Low Countries or in France,
but virtually nothing has been attempted in the vast field of
clandestine publishing or the French trade in pirate books
and pamphlets. Lyons firms copied the ornaments in the
Paris books they pirated, and it has been shown by a close
analysis of typography and ornament that many well-known
authors first saw the light of print in Lyons. No doubt a lot
more important information could be discovered about the
Rouen and Châlons trade, but a team of investigators would

be needed to unravel it. Here we would underline one major conclusion: that the prosperity enjoyed by Paris was more apparent than real and that the ultimate effects of a policy of repression were to stimulate an active underground press inside and outside France.

CHAPTER V

THE FINAL OUTCOME

NEITHER COLBERT NOR HIS SUCCESSOR Pontchartrain was able to keep out "undesirable" books from abroad or to wholly suppress them in France. Pedlars and newsbook-sellers continued in their dubious trade in spite of the strictest censorship, and the Government was its own prisoner in a sense, because it could never make up its mind which views in any controversy it could afford to admit when it could not foresee the consequences. The greater the fears within the Court, the more absurd the measures to gag authors and publishers, and respected figures like Bouhours, Nouet, Maimbourg, Fénelon and even Vauban came under suspicion, their work banned. Yet under the noses of the police an illicit press flourished, as if in conditions so restrictive that nearly everyone in the trade might come under threat, it was tempting to generate prohibited matter almost on principle, as the astonishing case of Savreux, the bookseller sympathetic to the Jansenists, who was found to have a huge stack of proscribed literature in one of the towers of Notre Dame!

After the Revocation, controls were tight and lists of books seized at the gates of Paris are impressive proof of the huge underground traffic swirling about the capital. In 1694 a journeyman printer employed by the widow Charmont-Rambaut of Lyons was hanged in the Place de Grève alongside an official of the Guild, Larcher, for printing and selling *Scarron apparu à Madame de Maintenon et les reproches qu'il lui fait sur ses amours.* Searches were made in various towns near the Flemish border, inns and taverns in Bondy and La Villette were watched for the arrival of parcels of suspect books, and Customs officers were rewarded on the discovery of forbidden books. To judge by the number of confiscated books, a very large number must have succeeded in entering Paris, and the stricter the surveillance, the more ingenious the methods used to circumvent it. Passions rose, and in his last years Le Roi Soleil was the object of universal hatred.

1. Pontchartrain and Bignon

Two men were responsible for the reforms now in view: Pontchartrain and Bignon. Pontchartrain was physically small, with a keen intelligence and lively mind, born into a family of great distinction—son of a President of the Chambre des Comptes, he was himself a councillor in the Cours des Requêtes and First President of the Britanny Parlement at a very difficult period. Later, Controller of Finance Le Pelletier had recalled him as one of his aides, intending him as his successor. One of Pontchartrain's most delicate tasks was the financing of the War of the League of Augsburg, and his skill led him to enjoy many royal favors. A Minister and Secretary of State at Court, in the Royal Household and the Ministry of Marine, he experienced all the exigencies of government before relinquishing the Department of Finance to Chamillart when he was chosen to be Chancellor in succession to Boucherat. From that moment he was concerned with the book trade and everything connected with literary culture, and was well aware of the press's potential in society and understood the absolute need to control it. Likewise, as a man of cultivation he showed great interest in the Academies as a feature of royalist prestige, and was closely concerned with the elections to membership. Too busy to devote himself to this side of his responsibilities, he delegated them to his nephew, the abbé Bignon.

Jean-Paul Bignon was born in 1662, grandson of a famous Advocate General, son of Jérôme Bignon II, Keeper of the Royal Library and Councillor of State, and originally intended for the Church, because he was the youngest and was short-sighted and in delicate health. He distinguished himself in the Congregation of the Oratory as a fine preacher, and in scholarship as the rival of Fléchier,

Bourdaloue and Massilon. His ambiance was one of learning, theological and scientific, and he shone, but his dissolute ways effectively prevented him from climbing the ecclesiastical tree. Instead, Pontchartrain gave him a government post, Secretary of State in the Royal Household, which gave him oversight of the Academies. He was nominated President of the Academy of Sciences and in the following year member of the Académie Française, then of the Académie des Inscriptions, King's Confessor and a Deputy in the Assemblée du Clergé. Soon after, he was given responsibility for the book trade (1699) in a department set up for that purpose, the Bureau de la Librairie. As a Privy Councillor he could bring into the highest councils of state all questions concerning the state of the press, and in 1719 he was appointed Grand Master of the Royal Library.

Such were the two men whose actions we will study. There was a difference in their character: Pontchartrain, a devoted servant of the King, withdrew into a religious retreat after his wife's death. Bignon, as lively minded as his uncle, was until his death in 1743 in regular correspondence with the intelligentsia of Europe. His letters and his policies reveal a man of a quite modern cast of mind, sceptical and scientific, not unlike Fontenelle. Bignon was a transitional figure, working always for the glory of the monarchy, yet aware of the virtues of tolerance, and willing to make concessions where practicable.

2. *The Inquiry into the Book Trade, 1701–02*

Bignon saw that while the book trade was docile enough in Paris it was otherwise in the provinces, and more discipline was needed to keep proper control over commerce with foreign booksellers. He tried to apply the policy of fewer presses to the provincial firms which was already in operation in Paris, and a decree of 1700 required a census of all presses presently working in France. Workmen had to fill in a questionnaire, proprietors of printing shops had to detail the presses they owned, the books they had printed in the previous year, the types they used, details of their apprentices and journeymen, the books in their shops. Everyone had to write out a summary of his career, giving the name of the master under whom he had served his apprenticeship, and any other masters he had worked for as an itinerant.

When this mass of information was received it was digested under various headings and preserved in two Registers for ready reference in the Bureau de la Librairie. Each printer's speciality was known to the authorities and any overlaps could be noted when it was time to launch another plan to reduce numbers of presses. After three years' study, action came in the form of a decree stipulating how many presses each town could have, which meant the closure of workshops and a ban on new ones until a stated output was guaranteed. Likewise, no new master printers could be admitted without approval of the Privy Council.

3. Licensing

Licensing had long been a means of control and previously the Chancellor had required that permits ("privileges") had to be authorized before printing anything, with the right to extend them reserved to him, even for "old" books—but if any older books had not been assigned to specific printers they were available for printing by anyone, subject to a local magistrate's consent. This area had been shrinking for some time because successive Chancellors had refused even reprints of older texts when a new edition was proposed by another publisher. Traditional works of scholarship which needed revision (a matter of French prestige) would be favored by the Chancellor and licences readily granted, but many little books, standard texts and liturgical books did not require permission or licence to reprint and were of course a regular source of income to humbler printers.

To Pontchartrain and nephew Bignon this was a loophole, and they decided to act, at least to regularize the position. Any religious books or textbooks could be printed anywhere in the Kingdom if they were in the public domain, on the authority of a local magistrate, but where there was need for a Patent order under the Seal—as for books of Hours—then a local permit was not in order. As so often in the Ancien Régime, practice varied and it was not until 1701 that a decree came into effect clearly stating that no printer or bookseller may print or seek to have printed any book without a licence under the Great Seal, confirming a decree of 1667 which forbade the printing of booklets of more than two leaves in Cicero type without a licence from the local magistrate and approval by a capable person selected by the said judge. Articles 3 and 4 ratified the principle of local licensing and general permits which carried different scales of charges. The general permit was valid throughout France and the holder could collaborate with booksellers anywhere, for which a full fee was charged; a local permit allowed a book to be printed only in the petitioner's locality, the fee being one-third that for a general permit. Finally there were permits which did not confer copyright in a title or prevent anyone else printing it at will—these cost 5 livres.

A cumbrous system, typical of the whole creaking bureacracy under Louis XIV, which classified even licences into three complicating kinds—general, local, and limited.

4. Censorship

The destruction of the Chancellery archives makes it impossible to tell how Bignon set to work in practice to ensure that the legislation was obeyed, but there is no doubt that his Bureau de la Librairie brought a degree of administrative reorganization into the book trade, and the heavy hand was felt in censorship of books which had to be registered in Bignon's Bureau. The manuscript was submitted to the Office of the Censor, who would give a decision after a delay of anything up to six months. If approved, the terms of the approval were entered in the Register with the Censor's name, and if rejected, reasons were given but the Censor's name omitted. The Registers of the Bureau are invaluable to the historian and tell us that there were no fewer than fifty-six censors employed from 1699 to 1704, chiefly academics and people of superior rank with a specialty: Bourdelot for medicine and physics; Charpentier for languages; Clairambault and d'Hozier for history; Dacier for history, Greek literature and drama; Cousin for history and numismatics; Filleau des Billettes for philosophy, law and literature; Dodart for medicine; Ellies Du Pin for Scripture and Church history; Fontenelle for history, geography, politics, architecture, and music; abbé Gallois for sacred history and science; La Hire for astronomy and architecture; Mansard for architecture; Pirot for religious matters; abbé Renaudot for poetry, Hebrew, devotional literature; Varignon for philosophy and science; abbé Vertot for morals and history.

Bignon required considered judgments from the censors, and the Registers contain many shades of opinion about the manuscripts under review, often cautious and neutral: "I find no reason to forbid publication"; sometimes positive: "this work will be most useful" or "will help the average layman considerably"; occasionally fulsome, as in the comment on Malebranche's *Conversations chrétiennes:* "worthy of the sincere piety, sublime genius and high reputation of the author." In rare cases approval was granted without scrutiny (Bossuet was in this category, but by no means all bishops were), frequently copy would be passed after alterations had been made, and sometimes the Chancellor would withold permission despite a favorable verdict by the censor. Rejections were for predictable reasons: the Government did not like the politics of the book; superstitious books, e.g., *Divers moyens et instructions pour le soulagement des hommes dans leurs peines et leures travaux* by Father Guichard of the Oratory, because "the author appears to favor superstitious practices," and "it is a trivial work." Prophecies were banned, as in *L'almanach journalier pour l'année 1705*—"the author predicts different temperatures and indicates lucky and unlucky days as if for a fact." Anything erotic or scandalous was banned, like *Prince Doria, histoire galant* by Pardon, which dealt with incest, and political or religious satire was on dangerous ground, as in the *Politique universelle ou Entretiens curieux sur le ministre du Cardinal de Richelieu,* which "includes a chapter dealing too harshly with Cardinal Richelieu and too freely with religion." The *Idée d'un règne doux et heureux ou Relation du voyage du Prince de Montferand en l'île de Mondeby* was "a completely vain conception" and the author had indulged in "violent satire against the clergy."

In matters of religion and science the Censor often reproached the author for unsound opinions: Le Clerc's *Système du monde fondé sur l'Ecriture sainte* was criticized for not taking modern physical theories into account; Platel's *Synopsis totius Cursus theologici* because it held too stubbornly to the doctrine of Papal Infallibility; the *Opera Sancti Augustini de gratis in ordinem analyticum reducta* because "the author confuses Augustine and Jansen"; *La Vie, les maximes de piété et quelques lettres* by Fournet, a Dominican, because it was "filled with fantastic tales and smacked too much of Madame Guyon's style." In some cases the Censor banned a book because it might foment faction, for example *Réflexions critiques sur la métaphysique de M. Degoumer,* which "contains some novel ideas too extreme for the present age." Most likely to pass muster were safe, orthodox views which provoked no questioning or argument; Jansenism, Quietism or extreme Gallican or Ultramontane positions were frowned on in the religious field, and anything with a Cartesian bias in science.

Politics was of course a very delicate subject. Sieur Alary's pamphlet explaining a *Prophétie . . . publiée en 1609 sur la naissance miraculeuse de Louis le Grand* was judged "too dangerous in present circumstances," and so was *Réflexions politiques sur les conspirations de Brutus contre César, de Pison contre Héron et des Pazzi contre les Médicis* by Eustache le Noble in 1702. Boisguilbert was forbidden to print his *Traité de la nature, culture police, commerce et interest des grains, tant par rapport au public qu'à toutes les conditions d'un état* because "it is no part of the author's duty to instruct Ministers concerned with the framing of the Corn Laws."

Works thought unworthy of publication were dismissed. Du Four's *Fondments de la médecine ancienne, nouvelle ou réformée* was tersely described as "worthless," most of it "lifted from other books," and J. B. Masson's *Nouveau tarif général pour le secours des payements de toutes les espèces de monnaies de France* was thought to be too close to a book by Barrème. Even a collection of carols was rejected as "badly put together, unworthy of the Mystery they celebrate, and the tunes are too secular." A manuscript entitled *Apologie de Louis le Grant sur l'anéantissement du calvinisme* was called "praiseworthy" but "it should have dealt more justly and with less confusion." And manuscripts were rejected on grounds of literary merit, like Forteville's essay, *Vie d'un cavalier religieux,* "which read like a crude provincial's attempt to write." One Pichot offered a romantic novel called *Amours convertis,* only to have it dismissed because "the verse is vile and the prose even worse," and *Cantiques au Saint Esprit* suffered the same fate: "the poem has neither rhyme, reason nor decent spelling."

Pierre Bayle remarks in a letter that Pontchartrain ordered his censors to pass nothing unless it was of "use"—this at a time when novels and banal devotional tracts were proliferating—and the Censors' Registers confirm this. Little wonder that writers with a taste for freedom sought asylum in the Netherlands.

Even when they had obtained a licence, authors and publishers had not finished with the Government: the book had to be registered with the Stationers' Guild. Until 1698 a summary version of the licence was entered alongside the book's title, but after that date the full text of the licence had to be written out so that no clause could be conveniently overlooked. Then publication was authorized and the prescribed number of copies deposited under the terms of the Dépôt Légal. Guild Syndics and commissioners from the Châtelet inspected printers' premises, every consignment of books imported from abroad was opened in the Guild offices (Guild records show that this was carried out to the letter), lists of books for confiscation were drawn up and the books destroyed by the Lieutenant General of Police. Pirated copies were often seized and sent to the original licence-holder. The apparatus of control was total and yet it still failed to stifle the flow of "mauvais livres" from abroad, even when a decree of 1710 ordained that books could enter France only through certain prescribed towns, Paris, Rouen, Nantes, Bordeaux, Marseilles, Lyons, Strasburg, Metz, Rheims, Amiens and Lille.

When this, too, failed, Bignon knew that something more flexible had to be tried. If trade was to be maintained at profitable levels he would have to permit open business with Dutch publishers. But that is another story.

5. *Royalist propaganda*

Pontchartrain and Bignon were not autocratic bigots but convinced royalists who tried to bring more efficient methods into the publishing world in the interests of the Crown. Events were against them. As cultured gentlemen from a privileged background they were genuinely concerned about France's contribution to contemporary literature and scholarship, and encouraged the Benedictines in their great historical work on the sacred sources. Pontchartrain took a deep interest in the Academies and engineered elections to insure that the best brains served on them. He revived the flagging fortunes of the *Journal des Savants* by making it an official organ, and conferred the title "Director General of Letters" (or as St. Simon called him, the "Moderator") on his nephew Bignon, with a commission to reform and revitalize the Academies by better administration. The Académie des Sciences and Académie des Inscriptions were given new Statutes and membership was limited to forty; ten were state dignitaries, ten were scholars paid a salary, ten were "research assistants" and ten, associate members. A scheme to commemorate Louis XIV's reign with a series of medallions was a project for the Académie des Inscriptions and a new policy was devised for the Académie des Sciences, to study applied rather than pure science. A commission of three "technologues" was set up to start work on a compendium of technical programs which eventually led to Diderot's seminal *Encyclopédie;* the plates used in that publication were copies of the engravings designed for the first official publication, a project outlined in Colbert's time with the intention of providing an elaborate description of all the arts, sciences and techniques. The "technologues," Nicolas Jaugeon, Father Truchet and Filleau des Billettes met regularly in Bignon's town house in 1693 and thereafter. It was essentially the work of the "Jaugeon Commission," continued by Réaumur from 1708, that paved the way for the superb *Encyclopédie* years later.

They began with a survey of "the art that preserves all other arts," namely printing, with extended studies of papermaking and bookbinding. The art of letter designing was fully described, with a detailed analysis of the proportion of each letter based on the careful examination of early works, tracing the evolution of types, but not neglecting the magnificent calligraphy of their own day. The geometrical basis of letters was later fundamental to the study of typography, and the theoretical work inspired action inside the Imprimerie Royale under its Director Jean Anisson. He compiled an inventory of the types and punches kept in the Imprimerie at the Louvre, which revealed that no new work had been done for fifty years. Granjon's famous Grecs du Roi were rediscovered after having been almost forgotten, and Anisson ordered new punches engraved based on designs by Jaugeon in harmony with contemporary taste, for use in the "Histoire métallique de règne de Louis XIV." Grandjean was the engraver, cutting four magnificent alphabets based on proportions worked out by the King's calligraphers. A team of artists prepared the ornamental designs and medallions for the portfolio, and Racine, Boileau and Charpentier wrote the text. Despite all the troubles of the time, this crowning achievement was published in 1704, a triumphant collaboration between the Imprimerie Royale and the Académie des Inscriptions: *Médailles des principaux événements du règne de Louis XIV,* printed in a new fount by Grandjean, a model for later type founts and the direct forerunner of modern-face type. French typography experienced a rebirth thanks to Pontchartrain and Bignon.

PART THREE

THIRD SECTION
PRINT AND PEOPLE IN
THE LATE 17TH CENTURY

To summarize the story to date: in the first half of the 17th century a religious revival encouraged printing and the trade benefited from the potent surge of evangelism inspired by the Counter Reformation. Priests and scholars in the old Humanist tradition published a great range of work, scholarly and pietistic, which flooded the book market and helped the traditional Faith survive the storms of the Reformation; debate was strident but the climate of thought reasonably liberal. Later the climate changed for the worse, wars brutalized the partisans of both sides, and the State was merciless in its assumption of absolute power. The Age of Richelieu and Séguier was the age of thought-control, opinion to be heard had to be Catholic and Royalist, everything to the contrary suppressed and public opinion manipulated in the interest of the Crown. By mid-century there was revulsion against political and economic oppression, manifested in a series of crises which erupted in the factious troubles of the Fronde uprising, and reflected in the book trade. Printers flouted government decrees; bread was more important than official coercion, and the Crown took steps to reassert its authority through an efficient police and a huge official bureaucracy. Docile printers and publishers were favored by the State, the rest suffered if they showed rebellious tendencies. The struggle between Crown and book trade continued, motivated not only by the need to earn a living that was made impossible by restrictive legislation but also on philosophical grounds; booksellers were often in the forefront of progressive thought.

This Section is devoted to the actual books published in the last thirty years of the 17th century, contrasting them with the equivalent production described in the first part of this work. The obvious change was the increase in foreign books printed for the Paris market, chiefly from the Netherlands. Paris publishers had been decimated by oppressive legislation, the trade in the provinces almost extinguished for the same reason. It was a period of economic depression.

And the book was evolving physically from the old folio, suitable for a scholar's lectern in his study, to the pocket-sized octavo for the non-specialist, from the ponderous "Summa" so dear to the Scholastics of a previous age to the "Epitome." Endlessly reiterated received ideas based on a veneration for precedent were challenged by new empirical facts, generalizing Montaigne succeeded by investigative Descartes. The age of reason was replacing the age of reverence. Our analysis of book production can proceed under headings familiar to modern eyes.

CHAPTER I

RELIGION

JUDGING BY THE SURVIVING BOOKS in the Bibliothèque Nationale, religious literature accounted for 41% of all publishing in Paris for the period 1666–1700, a figure that would have been much higher if so many commonly used prayerbooks and devotions had not perished. The heavy folio of theology and the literature of spirituality of the early 17th century had been for a quite different kind of reader. By the later 17th century most works of religion were in French, whether they were Scripture, liturgy, Patristics or devotions, a fact which does not simply mean that a vernacular tongue had taken the place of traditional scholar's Latin, but that theologians were no longer addressing other specialists, but the laity, or the educated classes among the laity. Even the controversies are less obscure and technical, the devotional exercises more direct and didactic, their derivation more clearly Scriptural—it is quite simply the influence of Protestant thought and practice. Religious literature in the 17th century was of oceanic proportions but it is possible to discern the main currents.

1. Spiritual literature: Return to the Wellsprings of Religion

By 1665 the monumental works typical of the Counter Reformation had ended with the last massive Papal edition of the Vulgate, the Louvain Bible and the great edition of the Fathers in 22 volumes published by Anisson of Lyons. The emphasis later in Paris was on inexpensive books of manageable size, with a bigger public in view. Bible studies were advancing towards acceptance of texts in the native tongue; abbé de Marolles published a French New Testament and

numerous Commentaries, Paraphrases and Epitomes foreshadowed a total translation of Old and New Testaments.
The monks of the Oratory and the Jansenists were working
on French translations of the whole Bible, and in 1666 two
versions of the New Testament appeared, Amelote's and
Sacy's (Jansenist). Amelote was responsible to Séguier for
reading manuscript translations of the Bible and no doubt
offered his own as a slap to the Jansenists who were not
allowed to publish their version in France but instead
brought it out in Rome, then in the Spanish Netherlands.
Though Amelote's translation had some success it was the
Jansenist version which caught the popular imagination,
despite its patchwork origins, a mixture of Vulgate and
Syriac texts with commentaries by the Fathers. There was a
partisan flavor to it and the episcopate asked for Papal
condemnation, which was readily forthcoming. Jansenist
partisans Barbier d'Aucour, Le Roy, Nicole and Arnauld
defended it in a pamphlet war against the Jesuits, to the
benefit of sales since the publicity sold more than 5,000
copies within six months, in a range of formats from quarto
down to tiny 24mo in French, Latin and even Greek—as a
contemporary comment put it, "In fine typography for the
rich, in ordinary letters for the poor, with notes for learned
readers, without notes for the layman." It appears beside
Amelote's Bible in some 17th-century library catalogs, from
which we must conclude that the Church had to accede to its
existence. Next came the Old Testament: Sacy translated it
and, with Séguier gone, his successor, aware of the enthusiasm which greeted the Mons New Testament, granted it a
licence and Desprez published it in 32 octavo volumes
between 1672 and 1693, with a commentary intended to
explain the literal and spiritual meanings based on the
Fathers and later commentators. At last the Scriptures were
available in French to the ordinary reader, and the large
number of pirated versions is proof of their instant popularity.

The liturgy was next. Although the Roman liturgy had
been adopted in some dioceses in the 17th century there was
a movement to reform breviaries and missals and emphasize
the independence of the Gallican church by issuing a revised

French use. Archbishop de Péréfixe appointed a Commission to reform the Paris breviary, with the result that what can only be described as Protestant influence again affected the text: more Scriptural passages were introduced instead of traditional formulae, Christ was given more prominence than the saints, and anything contemporary theologians thought purely legendary was omitted; the old hymns were replaced by metrical chants and the phrase *ad romani formam* omitted from the title page. The missal was then revised and other breviaries were recast in more scriptural terms, but in the words of the Cluniac breviary (1685), "nothing that does not derive from ancient authority, nothing not taken from Holy Scripture." In fact there was a strong Gallican strain in all the newly revised service books, and Neo-Latin poets of the Santeuil School and Father Jean Commire contributed verses. French sentiment was vindicated. When the missal was translated in French in 1661 by Voison it had an effect comparable with the new Bible translation, and when he published an Office for Holy Week with the Mass in French it brought about a revolution in religious practice. Mass was less a devotion to be routinely observed, more a communal act at the center of religious life.

Paraphrases and the Bible in pictures were in steady demand, particularly Le Bé's old woodcuts and Girard's Biblical scenes, and when Nicolas Fontaine, de Sacy's friend, composed a text, new pictures were cut after Flemish models to accompany it. The *Histoire du Vieux et Nouveau Testament representée avec des figures . . .* was intended as a stopgap until Sacy's translation was ready, but its popularity continued until the 19th century as the standard illustrated Bible for children. The Psalms came out in translation and with commentaries, Quesnel prepared an edition of the Gospels (suggested by Vialart, Bishop of Chalons) with commentaries, and a complete New Testament was issued under licence for books of pastoral instruction, with the title *Le Nouveau Testament francais avec réflexions morales sur chaque verset. . . .* The book was eventually condemned by the Pope.

It is not easy to estimate the readership for this kind of material but there were hundreds of thousands in circulation.

How did the average Catholic respond to it? Booksellers' catalogs give us some idea, and we will examine them later.

Even the texts of the Church Fathers were turned into French. Godefroy Hermant translated St. Basil's *Ascétiques* and John Chrysostom's *Traité de la Providence;* Cousin translated Eusebius's History of the Church and *Discours pour exhorter les paiens à embrasser la religion chrétienne.* Nicolas Fontaine translated *Réflexions . . . sur la vie de Jésus-Christ* by St. Augustine, St. Basil's *Lettres,* Cassianus' *Conférences* and *Institutiones,* Clement of Alexandria, Gregory the Great (*Pastoral*), Gregory of Nazianza (*Sermons*), John Chrysostom, and Leo the Great (*Sermons*). Tertullian and Cyprian were always in season and when Jansenism was at its height the Fathers who had most to say about Grace, the burning issue, were of most interest—Augustine and Chrysostom, especially Augustine's *Confessions.* Again, emphasis was on a return to the sources.

2. *Meditation and the Spiritual Life*

The sheer volume of devotional literature is what strikes one—for the publishers it was a bonanza. The writers in the older Humanist tradition—Richeome, Binet, Barry, Camus, Yves de Paris—were losing their grip; a few classic names were still read—St. Teresa, François de Sales, the *Imitation of Christ;* Granada, Rodriguez and La Puente were still in print and translations of the Northern school of mystics were common; Hayneuve, Bonnefons, Busée and St. Jure had a large following. The main feature in all this is the abundance of literature in French and the subtlety and profundity of the experience offered to the reader, and readers were clearly profoundly affected by it. There was Father Huby's *Pratique de l'amour de Dieu,* Father Guilloré's *Conférences spirituelles* and *Maximes spirituelles pour la conduite des âmes,* and books by Nouet. Surin, the exorcist of Loudun (for whose dealings with Mother Jeanne des Anges he suffered death), was the most famous, unquestionably one of the leaders of the school of French mystics. His works were only available in manuscript for years, but once published they were continually reprinted—the *Cantiques spirituels* and

Catéchisme spirituel. Another mystical work of outstanding merit was Bernières-Louvigny's *Chrétien intérieure* (14 reissues, 1661–74, revised by the Capuchin Louis-François; Edme Martin estimated he had sold 30,000). Boudon wrote many little books on the spiritual life, all twenty-seven of them eagerly read not only in France but throughout Europe.

Didactic literature was plentiful, too, written for people in all walks of life, fathers, widows, students, young women, rich, poor, the main theme being the abandonment of worldly ambitions and the search for perfection. Meditation, prayer, texts for daily spiritual exercises—there was a whole range of material to choose from: Father Maillard's *Méditations sur chaque verset des Evangiles de l'année;* Father Crasset's *Méthode d'oraison* . . .; abbé Rolduc's *Jour evangélique en trois cent soixante six véritez;* and Beuvelet's *Méditations* were all in the tradition of Bérulle, founder of the Oratory. Quesnel's *Prières chrétiennes en forme de méditation* were Jansenist, and Father Brignon revised and refreshed Buseé's *Meditations.* All the major Orders had their own paths of prayer in French for the faithful Catholic anxious to enrich his interior life, and he or she could turn to works by Capuchins, Augustinians and Benedictines.

The list is not complete at this point. The upper classes, laity and clergy planning a retreat, a Christian facing death, the layman striving toward the unitive life of the divine nature—all were abundantly served. Lives of the saints were as popular as ever, but not the traditional ones; rather, lives of more recently canonized individuals; the old cults lost their appeal, there is less Mariolatry, a purer form of devotion with classics of meditation, Malaval, Piny, Madame Guyon, possibly due to the attacks on superstition mounted by the opponents of Catholicism.

There were not so many collections of sermons; those that did appear were designed as models for clergy who lacked their own inspiration. Great performances of public oratory on national occasions or at a grand funeral would be put into print, but that was an arm of State propaganda; pulpit oratory is more strenuously concerned with the saving of souls—Vincent de Paul, François de Toulouse, Jean Eudes and others developed a clear and eloquent style suited to their intensely moralistic yet practical purposes. Large audiences attended their missions to hear Senault, Bossuet, Fléchier, and Séraphin the Capuchin preach repentance, and their books would be read as a program of study to follow. It could be said that prior to 1670, reading was done primarily to find spiritual nourishment, after that date because of its literary quality. Whatever the precise nature of its appeal, missions, seminaries, country priests, city curés, monks and bishops were hard at work in the name of the Church, instructing, elevating, converting. The atmosphere was that of a teaching ministry equipped with books of all kinds including the most basic. Each school and each diocese had its own catechism, and thousands were distributed in Paris alone, from substantial ones of several hundred pages for priests, to short summaries for ordinary members of the congregation, sometimes prefaced by an ABC. Tracts were once a familiar sight, but have now all vanished like so much of this huge output, and to gain some idea of the enormous industry which accounted for so much of the trade in evangelistic and didactic literature we depend on publishers' records.

3. The Evidence from Publishers' Catalogs

On the whole the books which were the armory of the evangelical movement we call the Catholic Revival were planned on simpler lines than the "religious" books of earlier times, both in style and physical format. Because they were slimmer they were more elusive, making it almost impossible to compile comprehensive bibliographies—there was just too much and most of it disappeared. For an accurate picture we need to consult publishers' catalogs, usually designed with a particular clientele in mind, so that a reasonably clear picture of the various clienteles and different schools of thought can be deduced. Below are some typical catalogs:

Catalogue des livres de Michel Le Petit et Estienne Michallet (1675): a modest list of liturgical books, with a bewildering variety of Hours in the smallest sizes, 12mo, 18mo, 24mo, 32mo and 48mo, "Hours of the Mission," "King's Hours," "King's Hours with vignettes," "Red and black," some in

French, some Latin, some in verse, all "newly printed." Folio Bibles in French, the Louvain New Testament, Gospels and Epistles in 12mo and 24mo, and Father Lubin's *Office de la Semaine Sainte.* Otherwise his stock was either theology in Latin or devotional literature in French: the *Imitation,* a *Combat spirituel,* some of John of the Cross, François de Sales's *Méthode pour la confession et la communion,* Borromée's *Instruction,* Rodriguez's *Perfection.* Some of his authors were a little passé: Barry's *Méditations* were written for an earlier generation and centered on Festivals of the Virgin, but he had more contemporary authors, too: Bonnefons's *Livre de vie* in several different sizes, evidently popular; Boudon's *Dieu seul, Amour de Jésus au Saint Sacrément, La dévotion aux anges,* and books by Father Le Jeune. Catechisms were clearly in demand because Michallet listed a great number: *Institutions chrétiennes, Enfant catéchismé* and others; prayers for use on various needful occasions were also a feature of his stock: *Manuel des prières avec les exercises de piété* is typical, in French or Latin.

Twenty-five years later Michallet's stock had passed into the hands of Delespine, one of the most prosperous businesses in Paris, and although he sold mathematical books and authors like La Bruyère, his speciality was devotional matter: the *Imitation,* St. Gertrude, St. Mechtilde, Jesuit authors, prayers for the dying, sermons by Texier, Courbon, 19 little books of piety by Boudon. Not much in the Scriptural line except Royaumont's Bible and copies of the Vulgate with Latin commentaries, few Patristic works, and only one book on the Mass, *Prières pendant la Messe.*

Desprez's *Catalogue des livres* (n.d.) was different, as we might expect from a Jansenist sympathizer. As the publisher of Sacy's translation of the Bible he naturally had a huge quantity in Latin and French, sold either as a whole or in separate Books. The *Imitation* he could offer in various sizes, octavo (4 livres), 12mo (45 sols), 24mo (25 sols). Bossuet figures prominently, but only his anti-Protestant works; Pascal one would expect to see, and St. Cyran, while Nicole's *Traité de morale* was then fashionable. All these pro-Jansenist works were supported by an array of Augustine's works, with Arnauld's translation of the *Confessions* (4 livres with Latin text; 40 sols without), the *Soliloquies* and the *Méditations*. Moralistic and spiritual works, for the most part with a practical bent, always with a firm Scriptural basis, typical of Jansenism, and stress on Penance and Communion, fundamental tenets of their doctrine, but few saints' lives—too much flavor of superstition. Instead, Lives of the Desert Fathers by Arnauld, and of other Early Fathers by Godefroy Hermant. The classics of mysticism were on sale: Tauler, St. Teresa, John of Avila, and Cardinal Bona's *Guide du ciel*. In all, the library of a Jansenist, though some authors like Quesnel were missing because Desprez had no licence to publish them; they belonged to other publishers. Such was the game of "privileges."

Another catalog is Urbain Coustelier's *Catalogue des livres, des feuilles ecclésiastiques, séculières et sentences comme aussi des instructions et billets de dêvotion propres pour les missions* (n.d.). The two sections were books and pamphlets, the books filling the first 30 pages. No folios, some theology and Patristics, a Louvain Bible, commentaries on the Bible, and devotional works, St. Jure's *Connaissance de l'amour de Dieu,* Bail's *Théologie affective,* de Sales, Granada, Bérulle, Caussin's *Cour sainte,* some quartos, then a mixed group of spiritual classics, Gertrude, Catherine of Siena, Rodriguez, Bourgoing, St. Teresa, St. Françoise, St. Ursula, Vincent de Paul, Bérulle, Mother Jeanne Absolu, Madeleine de Jésus, and a selection of funeral orations and homilies, the *Pédagogue chrétien,* the *Artisan chrétien,* the *Parfait missionaire* and Turlot's *Catéchisme.* Most of the books were of small size, octavo, 12mo, 16mo or 24mo, and there was a lengthy list of liturgical and didactic books, books for those contemplating a retreat and books for the use of "bons curés." The pamphlet section had the same professional reader in mind, with *Principaux devoirs d'un bon curé* (2 sols, 6 deniers), *Recueil de l'explication des principales parties de l'office divin* (7 sols, 6 deniers) and *Méthode pour administrer la sainte communion au peuple* (2 sols, 6 deniers) typical titles.

Appeals to economy were made. Fifty of the pamphlets listed could be had for 6 livres as a parcel, or 5 livres if made into a book with the stock title *Le parfait ecclésiastique,* and maxims for every day of the year, "15 of these pamphlets, each with 48 maxims, for 30 sols" (Latin or French). Another sheet contained *Sentimens de l'Ecriture Sainte tirez des Pères sur l'amour du prochain* (2 sols, 6 deniers without pictures; 2 sols, 10 deniers with pictures).

Tracts were a favorite form of propaganda, and sold by the hundred. *Instructions en petits billets propres aux missions* could be had in batches of a hundred, a dozen, or singly. Another such was the *Abrégé des principaux mystères de la foi* (30 sols per hundred), and there were notes on the sacraments, the tonsure, the sign of the cross, holy water, Christian conversation. Sins were under attack in *Avis charitable aux jureurs et blasphémateurs, Danse, Ivrognerie, Romans, Sales peintures et images, Médisance* and other amiable follies. Other leaflets of pious content intended for mass consumption were:

La Couronne de S. Sacrement de l'Autel	15 sols
Les Quatre fins derniéres de l'Homme enrichi de figures en taille-douce	10 sols
Dieu te regarde et tu n'y pense pas	3 sols
Les Avis de S. Therèse de Jésus	2 sols 6 deniers
Instruction chrétienne et pratique de piété pour le commun peuple	2 sols 6 deniers
Points principaux de la Noblèsse chrétienne	2 sols 6 deniers
Les prières du matin et du soir	1 sol 3 deniers
Trente-trois manières différentes d'honorer le Saint Sacrément	1 sol 3 deniers
Echo sur le Très Saint Sacrément de l'Autel	1 sol 3 deniers
D'autres petits écritaux	5 livres
Images morales	3 livres
Le Secret d'apprendre l'Oraison mentale	1 livre 3 deniers

Three further titles suggest that the whole list was intended for the clergy rather than the laity: *Des clercs déguisés ou de l'habit clérical; Mauclères ou des mauvais ecclésiastiques* and *Des prêtres décolez.*

This was the missionary literature of the age, long predating the secular equivalent today, our "animateurs culturels"! It clearly demonstrates the earnestness and anxiety with which a revival was broadcast to the masses during a troubled century. From the cloister and the study a new kind of press propaganda went out into the street, but it was but a phase; the Bibliothèque Nationale catalog of 1742 shows religious books dwindling in numbers after 1680, a sense of anti-climax, of disenchantment. There are no more devotions. The Age of Enlightenment (i.e., Rationalism) is at hand.

4. Theology: a Pyrrhic Victory

Traditional theology and canon law were still a substantial part of publishers' output but like the evangelical and devotional literature it was changing direction. In the writers Pascal called the "Neo-Thomists" there is still a strong trace of Scholasticism, but they belonged to the South, Bordeaux, Lyons or Grenoble, possibly because they were for the Mediterranean market, but more probably because academic theologians in Paris were more interested in a new, "positive" theology, more in line with contemporary issues. The Catholic-Protestant conflict was by now wearisome and a desire for clarity and simplification made both sides confine their debate to essentials.

The nature of the Eucharist was the first. Aubertin, a Protestant minister, wrote a treatise affirming that there was no justification for the doctrine of Transubstantiation in Scripture or in the Fathers until 600 A.D. He combined notions of truth and historical fact, he claimed, and denounced the "deviation" of Catholic dogma. Catholic theologians Daillé and Paul Ferry reaffirmed the validity of the historical argument, refused to base their case solely on Scripture, and restored the dispute to a place familiar to the combatants, the authority of the Early Church. Jansenists attacked the Protestant position in a massive work entitled *Perpetuité de la Foy de l'Eglise catholique touchant l'Euchariste contre le livre du Ministre Claude,* signed by Antoine Arnauld to lend it weight, together with two other works,

Préjugez légitimes contre les calvinistes (1671) and, in 1675, *Traité de l'unité de l'Eglise,* followed by *Prétendus réformés convaincus de schisme* in 1684. Catholic attacks increased, sometimes with restraint, sometimes aggressively, writers like Nicole, Arnauld, Le Maistre, Father Anselme de Paris, Ellies du Pin, Germain, Jacques Boileau and Denis de St. Marthe exploiting the historic argument, while Maimbourg, Pellisson, Ferrand and Fénelon centered on the official dogmas about the Eucharist and the validity of the Church. Bossuet directed the struggle in perfect harmony with Nicole and Arnauld, publishing his *Exposition de la doctrine de l'Eglise catholique sur les matières de controverse* in 1670, frequently reprinted, and in 1678 the *Conférence avec M. Claude;* in 1683, the *Traité de la Communion,* followed in 1688, after the Revocation of the Edict of Nantes, by *l'Histoire des variations des Eglises protestantes.*

The Government took advantage of the campaign to print thousands of booklets for distribution in the Protestant areas and was a great support to the writers and publishers who showed zeal for the reconversion of lapsed Catholics in the years between 1683 and 1686. But the Protestant pastors held fast, though often surrounded by their enemies, and Claude and Jurieu replied to all the attacks under great pressure. Catholic apologists allowed some liberty to their Calvinist opponents who exploited the internal quarrels of the Church against Jansenist penetration. Printers in Paris and Rouen put out the first editions of controversial texts which were then reprinted in Amsterdam and Geneva, but gradually, in the face of such persistent persecution, Protestants found it harder and harder to secure printers in France. Eventually, in 1685, to the sound of the eulogies written by hack poets in the King's pay, the last of the French Protestants sought refuge abroad, to continue the struggle from Holland, and indeed to go over to the attack.

The Catholic case had been put by a coalition of orthodox Jansenists, Gallicans and Ultramontanes, and as soon as the Revocation of the Edict of Nantes took effect—a pyrrhic victory—the coalition broke up, and the old Gallican quarrel restarted. Baluze, a disciple of Marca, published *De concordia sacerdotis et imperii,* which was placed on the Index in

1664, and learned theologians put out medieval texts in a laborious attempt to present their case; Mabillon's edition of St. Bernard served to remind people of the conflict between the founder of the Cistercians and Pope Eugenius III, and a collection of medieval writings published by Clousier seemed to prove that reformation of the See of Rome was demanded long before the Protestants. Father Thomassin, who had written the *Dissertation sur les Conciles* at the request of the Papal Nuncio, ended by pleasing no one and having his book suppressed.

The French experts in Canon Law were never so busy, but the only result was inflamed opposition. The French episcopate was in deadly conflict with the Papacy, and despite the Government's efforts it was unable to conceal the mutual antagonism from the public because it flared into print in a pamphlet war, much of the material published under its nose in Paris. Profiting from Madame de Longueville's death (she being the powerful patron of Jansenist Port-Royal), Harlay, Archbishop of Paris, and Father La Chaise went on to the attack, and Arnauld had to leave Paris, give up his meetings with followers in the Faubourg St. Jacques, and retire to Fontenay-aux-Roses. Eventually he feared for his safety and felt it impossible to escape the long arm of the State, leaving France for the Spanish Netherlands, where he hoped to find support.

Paradoxically, at just the same moment two doughty champions of Orthodox Catholicism also had to leave France: although Nicole was concentrating on his devotional books and did return to France, Arnauld never again went back. He was part of a group of supporters, with Gerberon and Quesnel, and led a wandering life between Mons, Brussels and Catholic Holland, free to expound his doctrines and publish his pamphlets with impressive effect.

The conflict with Innocent XI took a sharp turn at the same time when that Pope excommunicated the Marquis de Lavardin for placarding walls in Rome with Gallican propaganda. Louis XIV immediately had the *Protestation de M. le Marquis de Lavardin, ambassadeur extraordinaire de France à Rome* prepared and distributed in France and abroad, which provoked further replies from Italy, many translated into French and circulating in Paris. Talon, the Advocate General, published a violent indictment of the Pope as a statement of the Monarchist case, which was translated into Italian and Latin and intended clearly as part of France's policy in Europe. The tone of such international exchanges abruptly altered: it was now deliberately inflammatory against the Pope, and the last named was in the form of a dialogue, *Cibisme,* a warning shot. Nothing was overlooked in the struggle against the Pope—hacks were readily employed by His Most Christian Majesty, Louis, defender of the Faith, to attack the morals of the Supreme Pontiff. Not the most edifying spectacle—a new phase was entering the Catholic Reformation.

New quarrels were faithfully reflected in the pamphlets pouring from the Paris presses: the Quietist argument, debates about the Immaculate Conception, on the absurd excesses in Mariolatry. While the King could not hinder the Jansenists and even allowed the Protestant the right of reply, he was primarily concerned with works designed to reconvert heretics. Bossuet was in tight control and no manuscript submitted had a hope of publication without the censor's approval. Orthodoxy reigned supreme by coercion, censorship and the banning of any opposing ideologies, at least in Paris. It was otherwise outside France's borders. Before deciding how effective Louis' policy was, we need to find out how successfully foreign books and pamphlets penetrated the Paris market.

CHAPTER II

LITERATURE

1. The Classics

MORE GRAMMARS AND TEXTBOOKS were published from 1640 to 1680, mostly for student use in the Jesuit colleges and for young Jansenists at Port-Royal. Mabre-Cramoisy, Bénard, Thiboust and Esclassan were the specialists in this material and issued revised editions of Clénard's Greek grammar, Labbe's Latin primer, and the inevitable Despautère (with Codret's and Behourt's). Their lists were completed with Pajot's and Tachard's dictionaries, with books on rhetoric and Greek and Latin verse. Yet even here French was creeping in, and the Jesuits were quick to respond to the trend by annotating their Latin grammars in French. In 1642 Father Condren wrote a textbook for adult students of Latin with explanations in French, *Nouvelle méthode pour apprendre avec facilité les principes de la langue latin,* and Nicolas Mercier wrote his *Manuel des grammariens.* As always the Jansenists were ahead of their time and led the way in new methods of language teaching. *Nouvelle méthode pour apprendre facilement et en peu temps la langue latine* (1644) was followed by a shorter version in 1654, then a *Nouvelle méthode pour apprendre la langue grecque* (1655) by Lancelot. In 1657 came Arnauld and Lancelot's *Grammaire générale et raisonnée* and in 1662, the *Logique de Port-Royal.*

The new textbooks were a pattern for years to come. Bretonneau, Meslier and L'Oeuvre based their grammars on the Port-Royal model, but Jesuit textbooks continued with the conventional tables of declensions and conjugations, while Jansenist grammars had original pieces in verse and prose with French translations to serve as models. Even in the purely educational field the antagonists clashed. Jesuits preferred explanation and learning by rote, whereas Jansenists pioneered modern methods, introducing students to the actual literature, moving from the known to the unknown by example, teaching Latin and Greek by rendering texts into French, not guessing that this would eventually turn the two classic languages into dead, literary languages as opposed to the spoken language of scholarship.

So popular were the Port-Royal manuals that teachers at the Oratory and the University used them, quite possibly encouraged by the Dauphin's tutors, Bossuet, Huet and Montausier, who used Arnauld's methods. To facilitate the Dauphin's studies, Montausier prepared texts in which each word was given in the right order for ready translation into French. The best linguists and historians were employed by Colbert for the instruction of the Prince, and Montausier and Huet learned from their experience as his private tutors: they edited a series of classical texts with parallel French translations, extending to some forty books in the series, published by Léonard.

Latin and Greek, then, for a new generation, literature not for verbal communication, as Latin had always been, and for a wider public than the professional students. Not only the literature of the classical period—the poets and dramatists—but historians and philosophers, especially Cicero, whose Letters and Speeches were a great favorite in the age of Baroque imagination and the epistolary form so cherished; Seneca's and Pliny's letters were also avidly read. Aristotle's *Poetics* and *Rhetoric* were his most fancied works, and the comic playwrights—Aristophanes, Plautus and Terence, translated by Madame Dacier—satisfied sophisticated playgoers, while her husband's rendering of Sophocles sold well. Poetry was a challenge to translators, with La Valterie tackling both the *Iliad* and the *Odyssey,* and Houdar de la Motte translating passages from the *Iliad* into French. Anacreon and Sappho were translated by Régnier-Desmarais, and Longuepierre translated Anacreon and Bion and Moschus's *Idylls.* In Latin, Lucretius by Baron Des Coutures, Ovid by Thomas Corneille, Virgil and Horace

were all put into French; Michel de Marolles and the Sieur de
Segrais were best known for their Virgil.

The new kind of interest shown in the Classics came from
a new kind of reader, the phenomenon known as the
"honnête homme," a different animal altogether from the
Schoolmen and erudite theologians. He sought to be cultured in general terms, to acquaint himself with the classical
culture which was the basis of Western thought and morality;
to him the badge of refinement was a knowledge of poetry,
the Neo-Latin poetry then in vogue. Given this new impetus,
the Classics were reborn and circulated in the heads and
hands of the literati, who wanted nothing to do with liturgical
Latin or the rhetoric of the narrow classroom tradition.

2. Modern Languages

Equally there was a quickening of interest in modern
languages. Port-Royal was using new textbooks of its own
creation, the *Nouvelle méthode* series that soon ousted
Oudin's standard grammar. Italian was in fashion and from
Port-Royal came a similar textbook, *Nouvelle méthode pour
apprendre facilement et en peu de temps la langue italienne,*
soon followed by others for a variety of modern languages
and designed to teach spoken, not simply a literary idiom (by
Catanusi, Duez, Lanfredini, Lieutaud, Veneroni, Grassy),
and Oudin's French-Latin dictionary was revised. German
now made its first appearance as a language for study in Jean
Perger's *Grammaire allemande et française* (1665) and
Heim's *Nouvelle méthode pour . . . la langue allemande.*
Perger brought out a revised version of his grammar with a
new title, *Véritable et unique grammaire allemande* (1681),
and one Léopold devised a grammar with a modern ring to it,
L'art de parler allemand.

As to their readers, Port-Royal was catering for the man of
the world who wanted to add foreign languages to his assets,
and there is stress on the value of conversational ability,
which betrayed some weaknesses when the dialogue, well
suited to a gentleman of high estate, was of little use to a
businessman wanting to trade with his opposite number in a
foreign country. But French and other vernacular tongues

and the phrase books aimed to help conversational fluency are a clear indication that a new age has arrived. There was hardly any interest in English, though English publishers brought out useful phrase books and handbooks on the rudiments of the French language; French was on the way to becoming the *lingua franca* of Europe and the little books produced in England were intended to give some guidance with pronunciation, emphasizing once more the spoken rather than the written language. English and German had not yet acquired the status enjoyed by Italian and Spanish as literary media.

Foreign texts were unfailingly accompanied by a parallel version in French when they were published, and increasingly masterpieces of foreign literature came into print. Spain was the unquestioned leader here. The classics of Spanish spirituality were always in print, and in an age when the "dialogue" was so fashionable, moral fables, discussions on the position of women in society, we find, for example, Vives' *Dialogues* and his *Introduction à la sagesse* great favorites. Balthasar Gracian's *Homme de cour*—ancestor of the "honnête homme"—was done into French by Amelot de la Houssaye and helped shape this ideal in the idiom of the time. Novels were sure of instant success: Dutch and French provincial publishers profited by regular reprints of *Don Quixote,* Quevedo's *Visions,* and Scarron's *Nouvelles* (popular in Paris and in Spain); Charles Cotolendit put out a revised translation of Cervantes' *Novelas* and Filleau de St. Martin another one of *Don Quixote.* Parisian readers were supplied with French versions of Dona Maria de Zayas' *Novelas* and Perez de Montalvan's *Semaine* in 1684; and Lesage published his collection of Spanish plays in 1700 and a version of *Don Quixote* in 1704. Spanish fiction and drama were the main inspiration for French readers and writers, and Spanish exploration of the world fascinated them, as did their monarchy, which was so closely bound up with the French royal house. French translations of Spanish history were published in the Netherlands, Fléchier brought out his *Histoire du Cardinal Ximenes* in Paris, and Varillas two of his works about the policies of Spanish kings, with one on the life of Charles V of particular interest.

Italian was a close second. *Pastor fido* was translated by abbé Torche (1664–6) and Tasso's *Aminta* (1666) and Castiglione's *Galatea* and *Perfect courtier* reaped profits. Briencour translated Machiavelli; Le Maçon, the *Decameron;* Scudéry, Marini's *Calloandre;* Catanusi, Petrarch's erotic verses, and in 1662 President Nicole translated Canto I of Marino's *Adonis*. Vincent Sablon rendered Tasso's *Gerusalemme Liberata* into French; Perrault, Tassoni's *Sceau enlevé*, and Madame de Gomez, *Orlando Furioso*. Gherardi's collection of Italian drama was frequently reissued after its first appearance in 1695.

Not much that was new in all this, but the numbers of grammars published indicates a wide public in France wishing to get to grips with original texts, and indeed being well provided with them, as well as the French versions.

German literature made little impact, only Puffendorf appearing in French, though Spinoza was available in Holland but not in France. As for contemporary English writers, one might have expected a good number to be available in Paris, since English literature was of superb richness and variety at this time, but it was virtually non-existent in France, either in the original or in translation, probably because of religious bigotry. The Low Countries were the distributors of English books—the Protestant Netherlands—and we shall look at them later.

3. French Literature

Three categories of books were sold in this field: language textbooks, literary works, and critical theory. Grammars were for use in learning how to translate Latin into French rather than as a study of French, which was not yet taught in schools as a subject in its own right. Typical were Delbrun's *Liaisons de la langue française avec la latine* and Scipion Roux's *Méthode nouvelle pour apprendre aux enfants à lire parfaitement bien le latin et le français*. The Port-Royal grammars did analyze French on a logical system, not simply as a key to classical languages, but they had little influence at first.

Most books on French as a language were for the serious

reader with a taste for linguistics. Such were St. Martin's *Remarques sur les principales difficultés de la langue française;* Bérain's *Nouvelles remarques sur la langue française; Nouvelles observations,* or Alemand's *Guerre civile des Français sur la langue; Mots à la mode* and Tallemant's *Remarques et décisions de l'Académie Française.* Other grammars were intended for foreigners interested in the finer points of the language, for example, *Essay d'une parfaite grammaire de la langue française* by Father Chiflet (1659), which was so successful that it was kept in print not only in Paris but also in the Spanish Netherlands and, unusually, was a standard textbook in colleges and among fashionable society. The first official move to establish a proper lexical basis for French was the *Dictionnaire de l'Académie française,* begun by the printer Le Petit in 1677 and finished by Coignard in 1692, but so full of errors that it was finally destroyed. Coignard published a second revised edition of 1,000 copies, and in 1696 a third edition of 1,500. Export of the Dictionary was forbidden, but Huguetan brought out a pirated edition in Holland (with Coignard's connivance, it would seem), and since the conditions attaching to its copyright forbade all other French dictionaries, the dictionaries compiled by Furetière and Richelet had to be published abroad.

Poetry was fashionable in the mid-17th century but waned in the 1670s; Boileau commented, "Burlesque or comic poetry was much appreciated from the early 16th century to about 1660, and then it died," though it could be said that it lasted another decade or so, as figures prove; the discrepancy is probably due to reprints of works already known. Heroic poetry died out in the late 1670s and revived in the period 1666–75 thanks to Boileau's genius in this form, which prompted retorts from his many enemies. As for religious poetry, the decline is marked, despite the current taste for prose piety. La Fontaine was the only poet of any stature writing in the 1670s, his contemporaries satisfied to turn out verse of ringing banality, sycophantic praise of the King with an eye to a career at Court. In the words of Paul Hazard (*La crise de conscience européenne*): "Poets (i.e., the French and English writers of the period 1680–1715) they were not.

Their ears were shut to the glory of words, their souls had lost any sense of mystery. . . . They were interested only in demonstrating theorems, and when they wrote verse it was like geometry. Poetry died when it was invaded by Mechanistic ideas, and lost its true direction, its raison d'être. There was a crowd of versifiers, but after La Fontaine's death no other poet in France."

Drama was in some ways analogous to poetry. The great vogue for reading plays was in the years 1630–50, especially tragedy and tragicomedy, then there was a falling off: 63 new plays were published from 1661 to 1675, but only 33 from 1676 to 1690. Racine was not reprinted as frequently as Corneille and their successors were writing feebler stuff as the century progressed—inspiration had gone. There were some comedies in the final decade, three times as many comedies as tragedies, but mostly one-act plays, almost certainly printed clandestinely. As in every other genre a success here meant instant pirating; the *Précieuses ridicules* was pirated four times in 1660 alone, and six times between 1674 and 1698, *Tartuffe* nine times in 1669 and a dozen times more from 1671 to the end of the century. This was a problem for any successful publisher at a time when contraband publishing was almost a way of life, a situation which had worsened since the early years of the 17th century.

Fiction supplies yet another illustration of conditions in the trade. Literary historians tend to suggest that a vast number of novels was published in the late 17th century, a view that requires modification. Fiction was a profitable part of publishing in the 1658–1680 period but was then hit by the trade depression of 1685–1700, improving spectacularly in the last year or two. Once again it is hard to distinguish between the novels printed in Paris and those printed (and pirated) in Holland, or indeed to know which came from Paris and which from underground printers in general. R. C. Williams's *Bibliography of the 17th century novel in France* shows that a great many French novels were printed illictly.

The appearance of the novel underwent a change in 1660; after the multi-volume saga (cf. La Calprenède's *Faramond*) the small pocket-sized novel of relatively few pages came out, coining the word "nouvelle." Subject matter changed, too, with a hint of its fashionable appeal in titles which included words like "galante," "amant," "amours," and the location is always exotic—Granada, Morocco, Turkey, Persia, Calabria. Another vogue was for the "histoire" and "historique"—Williams lists 150 titles in which those words are used in the period 1670–1700. A Cologne imprint usually meant pornography; Amsterdam or The Hague, novels by Protestant refugees (Isaac Claude, Isaac de Larrey, Mlle de La Roche-Guilhem); in all other cases they were anonymous works smuggled into France. There was still an odor of disgrace about novel-writing, hence the cloak of anonymity assumed by society wits of the day who indulged the hobby, Le Noble, Madame de Villedieu or Madame De La Fayette. They might hope for one or two reissues in Paris, no more, and perhaps more reprints in the Netherlands, but this kind of light romance was only occasionally a success, an example being the *Princesse de Montponsier* (15 reissues in Paris, two in Lyons). We might take it as significant that so much reading of shallow fiction was done at a time of severe economic and political strain.

Speeches and letters were staple fodder for the upper classes, a Classical tradition, speeches printed after delivery on public occasions or often as propaganda. The death of a king would provoke countless funeral orations, but advocates' speeches in the courts were not thought worthy of print, though Bossuet's were eventually published in 1772, many years after his death. After 1670 there was a great increase in published sermons, which would accord with the contemporary taste for devotional literature, and priests or monks on missions would want them as models. Funeral orations on the grandest state occasions were, of course, extended opportunities for royalist propaganda (there is an exhaustive list in the catalog of the Bibliothèque de l'Arsenal). The most admired preachers of that day are now quite forgotten: Fromentières, La Rue, Cheminais and Father Le Jeune, but rarely did any of these orations see more than one edition, which suggests that there was no great public interest, only the self-interest of a ruling clique pursuing its own aims.

The art of letter writing was first given systematic expres-

sion by Guez de Balzac, who published his letters when he
thought them worthy of preservation, and found them
popular with readers. Other authors were more modest,
their correspondence appearing posthumously—Chevreau,
Gombauld, Tristan l'Hermite. One collection published c.
1650 was widely read and admired as a pattern, the *Recueil
de lettres nouvelles de Messieurs Malherbe, Colomby, Boisrobert, Molière*, since the properly conceived epistle was seen
as a perfect vessel of style. Translations of Latin letters were
common, a new genre for imitation, like the fictitious letter
best represented in Puget de la Serre's *Secrétaire à la mode*,
in print until 1700, another witness to the importance of
literature as education for the "honnête homme." Manuals
of style and polite conversation were plentiful in this artificial
society (Du Bosc, Patru, Richelet, Vaumorière, Milleran, Le
Pays) and the great Ur-text on this was Aristotle's *Rhetoric*,
adapted to suit the French language. Father Lamy wrote his
Art de parler, to be found in every drawing room; Oudart de
Richesource, a professor of Rhetoric, wrote a *Masque des
orateurs* (1667) and *Méthode des orateurs* and *Rhétorique de
barreau* (1668); Rapin wrote *Réflexions sur l'usage de
l'éloquence de ce temps;* Boissimon, *Beautez de l'ancienne
éloquence*, and Fénelon composed his famous *Dialogues sur
l'éloquence*, which goes to prove that this was an age of civil
servants, lawyers, officials of all kinds with a shared respect
for style.

Prose was superseding poetry, French was replacing Latin,
realistic comedy ousting baroque tragedy; practical literature
was preferred to démodé romance, didactic and program-
matic treatises on the subjective life of the spirit, and for
these salutary purposes a new clarity was forged, governed
by precise rules, not only in the literary realm but also in the
social and moral spheres.

4. The Moralists

Books on "how to succeed" were a feature of the age, but
whereas in earlier days it was the courtier or cavalier who was
the model of social excellence, now it was the "gentleman."
Quantities of books giving advice on behavior poured from

the presses between 1680 and 1700: abbé Gérard's *Caractère de l'honnête homme,* Vincent's *Caractères de l'honnête homme,* Goussault's *Portrait de l'honnête homme* were typical. We know that elementary books on manners were used in schools, but none have survived, and the success of a book like Courtin's *Nouveau traité de la civilité qui se pratique en France,* written for adults, indicates how important matters of address, expression, and the turning of a compliment must have been to the social climber. Advice to young people and their parents was readily available, often in the form of conversations between father and son, and we may suppose that such books were the pot-boilers of their day as well as a qualification by which the author secured a post as private tutor. Whenever a new Dauphin is ready for his formal education, books appeared giving advice on the education of a Prince (rather as books appear today as a follow-up to educational programs on television). Novelists like Préchac, courtiers like Callières, and needy hacks like Sorel and Guéret were ever alert to market a primer on the art of social intercourse. The *Art de plaire dans les conversations* by Vaumorière and Mlle. de Scudéry's *Conversations morales* were endlessly reprinted, sure of a wide and worldly audience.

Most of that audience was female. The earnest desire for education and schooling in taste evinced by women of the middle classes was frequently touched on by moralists like Fénelon, Poullain de la Barre, La Chétardie, Presidente de Noinville, Du Puy, de la Chaise, in a long-running contemporary debate about women's position in society. Bossuet asserted the superiority of men, other writers dealt with conjugal relations or household management. Moralists mocked or denounced the ways of the world, the depravity of high society, lewdness, excessive luxury, even dancing and frivolous pastimes. There was a growing awareness of what we would call psychology—a natural consequence of the interest in social relationships and behavior—and its most perfect expression was La Rochefoucauld's great work, *Réflexions ou sentences et maximes morales.* It was first published in 1665 and reprinted twice in the same year; Barbin published it five times between 1666 and 1693, and when the initial copyright expired in 1672 it was immediately reprinted in Lyons and Rouen, later reissued in Lyons in 1685 and 1690, in Toulouse in 1688, and pirated in the Netherlands in 1676, 1679 and 1692. There were six printings in Paris, six in the provinces and three in Holland, with one of unknown origin—sixteen in all, a total of some 25,000 copies.

Pascal was even more successful. His *Pensées* was first published by Desprez in Paris (1669) and reprinted four times the following year, once in 1671, more in 1672, in 1678 (twice), 1683 and 1686. Maire, Pascal's bibliographer, cites two other piracies in 1670, three Lyons editions (1675, 1679, 1687), one in Rouen (1675) and six in Amsterdam (1677, then two in 1688, 1694, two in 1699). That amounts to twelve impressions in Paris, two unidentified, four provisional and six Dutch—twenty-two in all, amounting to about 30,000 copies.

Another work, now little known but very popular in its day, was Nicole's *Essais de morale*. It went into eight official impressions and a vast number of pirated imprints which have never been properly identified. Finally, La Bruyère's *Caractères:* the first edition was soon exhausted and was followed by eight official impressions and a cataract of foreign and provincial piracies, which started a fashion for the "character" book, spreading to England and other European countries.

CHAPTER III

THE HUMAN SCIENCES

1. Theology and church history: the beginnings of modern scholarship

PARIS HAD BEEN TRADITIONALLY the center for the publication of Patristic studies and comprehensive editions of the Church Fathers, and at the close of the 17th century was still associated with that kind of scholarship. Cossart, a Jesuit, edited a 16-volume series, *Sacrosancta concilia* (1671–72), later revised by Hardouin at the request of the Assemblée du Clergé, in 1685. The Maurists were the last scholars to maintain this tradition, their abbeys throughout France seats of deep learning in Patrology and Ecclesiastical History as they labored at their exhaustive editions of the Fathers. Thirteen volumes of the *Spicilegium* (1655–77), five volumes of the *Bibliotheca ascetica* (1661–64), an edition of St. Basil's *Liber regularum* (1662), of St. Anselm (1675), Cassiodorus (1672), St. Ambrose (1686–90), St. Augustine (11 vols., 1687–1700), St. Jerome (1693–1706) and Le Nourry's *Apparatus ad bibliothecam maximam* (1694–97) were just some of their works, erudite and sweeping in scale, unmatched by any other body of men. The work proceeded despite difficulties, though behind it was support at the highest level, approving and encouraging publications which could only redound to the national glory. But they were never reprinted. The world which this kind of learning had once so nobly served was contracting with every passing decade.

The archivist's skill was developing as charters and other documentation were brought into play for the writing of church history or histories of the various Catholic Orders.

Here the abbey of St. German des Prés was a center of busy research: Mabillon edited the *Acta sanctorum Ordinis Sancti Benedicti analecta* and *Museum italicum;* Dom Ruinart compiled the *Acta primorum martyrum sincera* and edited Gregory of Tours's *History.* Baluze edited a selection of documents, *Miscellanea* and *Capitularia regum Francorum,* and Du Cange's two dictionaries are still in use today: *Glossarium infimae et mediae latinitatis* and *Glossarium mediae et infimae graecetatis.*

It was the start of modern historical research based on surviving written evidence. Father Anselme de St. Marie wrote a *Histoire de la maison royale de la France,* Father Quétif wrote the first literary history of the Dominican Order, and Le Nain de Tillemont, a Jansenist, published *Mémoires pour servir à l'histoire ecclésiastique des six premiers siècles.* It was the age of the great Byzantine series of Greek Fathers prepared for printing by the Imprimerie Royale, of Cotelier's *Ecclesiae Graecae monumenta* and of Cousin's translation of Eusebius's history of the early church, of the *Annales ecclesiastici Francorum* by Le Cointe, and Du Pin's huge *Bibliothèque des auteurs ecclésiastiques.* There was a readership for this, still, in a society so deeply reverencing the past and where precedent counted for everything in any dispute, a society of clerics who spoke to each other in terms they all understood (even across the religious divide) and who shared a keen taste for research into the minutest points of doctrine, whatever the labor involved.

The Orders were nothing if not partisan in their histories, Benedictines defending themselves against calumnies alleged by other Orders to a degree which sounds merely absurd to modern ears when it centered upon the validity or otherwise of relics they stubbornly cherished—were they true or false? Rules were drawn up to detect fakes, and deployed when necessary, as in the ludicrous case of the holy tear preserved by the Benedictines of Vendôme, allegedly taken by an angel from Christ's eye. Mere monkish quarrels these, but they touched on sensitive areas, chiefly the antiquity and authenticity of their Order, much as noble families disputed lineages. Out of this misplaced self-righteousness nevertheless came a rationale for the proper validation and study of records, known as Diplomatic, demonstrated by Mabillon in his *De re diplomatica,* published after his controversy with the Jesuit Papenbroeck. In the field of archive studies it was the equivalent of the *Discours sur la méthode,* feared as an equivalent threat to the Faith, too critical in its questioning of hallowed traditions. Like abbé Thiers, Mabillon was attacked for being too critical.

Critical methods were applied to Scripture to clear up points of doctrine and confirm the validity of the Church's teaching. Huet wrote his *Demonstratio evangelica* in 1679 to prove the truth of the Christian religion through the fulfillment of prophecies, and in his *Situation du Paradis terrestre* tried to locate Heaven on a map, a quaint exercise but this *kind* of attention paid to various aspects of belief and original authorities marks a change of attitude. In the Protestant world the Bible was under fine scrutiny and a chronology of events (the historical method) was attempted for the first time, which inevitably aroused deep feelings. Walton's Polyglot Bible stirred a good deal of controversy and Richard Simon's attempt to assign actual authors to the Books of the Old Testament raised alarm, intensified by another critical work, Paul Pezron's *Antiquité des temps retablié,* which claimed the world was older than the Hebrew text might suggest.

But Pezron's book launched fierce controversy and reveals how scholars—the objective minds of the time—were intrigued by such problems, and one by one a whole series of manuals designed to elucidate Scripture came out: Bernard Lamy's *Harmonia sive Concordia IV Evangelium,* in which he tries to work out a chronology for the events of Christ's life, using the evidence of John and Matthew; then in 1696 came an *Apparatus Biblicus,* an improved version of the *Apparatus ad Biblia* published in Grenoble in 1687, an attempt to clear up the many difficulties that came from reading the Bible. In 1690, Ferrand, a lawyer, published his *Summa biblica* with the same aim, followed in 1697 by d'Herbelot's *Bibliotheca orientalis.* The indefatigable Ellies Du Pin brought out *Prolégomènes sur la Bible* in 1699, and

Dom Petit-Didier his *Dissertations . . . sur les livres de l'Ecriture.* In 1693 Richard Simon had published a *Dictionnaire de la Bible* at Lyons with a modern approach, and soon Father Lelong produced a *Bibliotheca Biblica,* and Dom Calmet his huge treatises on the Scriptures. A new form of exegesis was emerging in which ordinary believers might take part, not only the theologians who had conducted those weighty and malignant debates in the days of the Reformation.

2. New Attitudes to History

Not only was there a golden age of scholarship in the field of French religious research at the close of the 17th century; it could also be seen in the fresh examination of Greek and Latin texts from antiquity, but not in ancient history or in French history. True, the fashion for collecting coins and medals did prompt some new approaches, and Le Nain de Tillemont, Du Cange and others paved the way for more modern work on Greek, Roman and Byzantine history, yet only two works that could be described as monumental, glorifying the monarchy, came out in Louis XIV's time: Anselme de Sainte Marie's *Histoire généalogique de la Maison de France* and Baluze's *Capitularia regum Francorum.* That is somewhat surprising.

Louis, despite Colbert's strenuous efforts, was unable to follow up the earlier generation of historiographers— Dupuy, Godefroy, the Du Chesnes and St. Marthes. In fact the next two recruits to the task were poets, Racine and Boileau, and their assignment was not to recount the great deeds of Louis' ancestors but to concentrate on Louis himself. It is not without significance that Varillas, after twenty years of work among the documents in the Bibliothèque du Roi, chose instead to compile more or less romantic narratives, and Father Daniel, who was to have written a history of France, after spending just two hours in the royal archives, fled!

The point is probably that traditional methods and the new spirit of critical inquiry were at odds, to the detriment of the former, and the reader of history, the honnête homme, wanted a more scientific approach, something clear and positive in place of the wearisome repetitions, the predictable obscurities of the old-style pedants. Educated readers would have been taught the elements of history at college, usually church history with a smattering of "universal" history: Urbain Chevreau's *Histoire du monde,* Torsellini's *Histoire universelle traduite de Latin,* Lelevel's *Entretiens sur l'histoire de l'univers* or Bossuet's *Discours sur l'histoire universelle.* The history of Greece and Rome was taught from translations of the classical historians Livy, Plutarch, Tacitus, Herodotus, and French history was mediated through little books like Saunier's *Abrégé de l'histoire de France, Histoire des rois de France,* La Mothe Le Vayer's *Introduction chronologique à l'histoire de France,* Bonair's *Sommaire royal de l'histoire de France* and others of similar content. The slim volumes would contain pictures of kings and work towards a triumphant climax, to inspire the student, whether at college or in his own home; the first "Groundwork of History" series.

Genealogy, the history of the great French nobility, of Byzantine emperors, of heresies (Arian, Nestorian and Albigensian), of Luther and Calvin, were all creditably written and testify to a large, well-informed and receptive readership. Conspiracies, then as now, were of abiding interest to readers, forerunners of the historical novel, and politicians, statesmen and rebels committed their memoirs to paper, though the leaders of the Fronde uprising were banned from print. Louis' ambitions abroad stimulated an interest in foreign affairs and a crop of books dealing with the history of adjacent countries, but the greatest work of history was being written daily by the King, and royalist propaganda never ceased to emphasize it. Foreign policy was summarized in printed letters circulated under the official imprimatur, important documents and treaties were published, all to the glory of the King. Newsbooks carried laudatory comment and the *Mercure galant* blazoned the exploits of the French armies, listing officers who had died of wounds and individual exploits. Poets celebrated the grandeur of the reign and pompous folios offered extravagant plates depicting battles, grandiose architecture and the personalities of the Court.

But reaction was setting in. The average intelligent reader wanted something more realistic, and factual reference books made their first appearance: the *Bibliothèque des auteurs ecclésiastiques,* the *Bibliothèque des auteurs, Dictionnaire de la Bible, Dictionnaire des arts et des sciences, Grand dictionnaire historique.* Bayle's *Dictionnaire historique et critique* showed what an impressive weapon an objective view of history could be in helping demolish royalist myth-makers. Even the King's Ministers were drawn into radical new practice when they ordered the Académie des Sciences to prepare the dictionary of arts and crafts; though they did not realize it, they were preparing the way for the Encyclopédists.

3. Law publishing

Law had to evolve, just as History did, and Canon Law was developing a new, more positive drive. When a country is governed by an established church there is a call for books on ecclesiastical law to settle the interminable disputes between Orders or between the State and the Holy See. Statutes, synodal decrees, Acts passed by the Assemblée du Clergé were the staple of many publishers; revenues, vacant livings, tithes and emoluments were subject to acrimonious disputes and provided lawyers with a satisfactory income. The basis of all such law was the *Corpus juris canonici,* reprinted in 1687, but by that time the trend was towards manuals for law students and popular treatises of interest to the informed layman, if we may trust the evidence in the Bibliothèque Nationale catalog. Roman law was of minimal interest apparently in the last quarter of the 17th century, although Justinian's *Institutes* were kept in print in French at the Imprimerie Royale, and Pithou's commentaries. The old school represented by Cujas was dead. Theophilos' *Institutes* were translated from Greek into Latin. Customaries continued to sell, presumably because they were used as basic reference works, and they did reflect an interest in the practical application of law which so characterized the age, as did the many new manuals for practicing attorneys which began to replace the heavy theoretical tomes and worship of precedents which so preoccupied Humanist lawyers.

Legislation was proliferating in this age of swelling bureaucracy, courts were promulgating scores of decrees and ordinances, making large profits for booksellers like La Feuillade, and the mass of law needed editing and publishing for reference. Louet's collection of decrees of Parlement, and Guénois and others' editions of royal ordinances were kept continually revised, and a new law journal was launched by Guéret, the *Journal du Palais,* to help lawyers keep abreast. This body of work foreshadows the publication of the royal Acts in the 18th century.

4. The New Geography

Geography took on a new lease of life as a result of new exploration and empire building. Jean Le Clerc's *Théâtre géographique du Royaume de France* was a landmark in the early 17th century, with works by cartographers Tassin, Boisseau and the Sansons, and while cartography was growing more sophisticated, there was a greater demand for accuracy in recording new discoveries abroad as well as more detailed plans of cities and regions at home. The French were pioneering in cartography on a global scale.

The advance of science in astronomy and military engineering improved cartographic techniques (determination of longitude, for instance) and under the guidance of the Académie des Sciences new maps were produced on scientific lines, including the first modern atlas of France and maps of regions by newcomers like Nolin, Jaillot, de Fer and Guillaume Delisle.

The *Neptune français* (volume 1) was published in 1693, a happy collaboration between cartographers, hydrographers, marine engineers and scientists in the Académie, providing a complete description of the French coastline and neighboring countries for navigators, especially naval officers. The work was under royal patronage and marked the end of a long period of Dutch supremacy in this field, though in this case the engraver was Dutch. Gazetteers and guides were much in vogue, easily carried in small octavo format, and although they were oriented on the Holy Land—almost like supplements to Bible study—there were others designed to show "division of the earth" or "knowledge of the globe," compiled by geographers and used as teaching aids in schools. Descriptions of France for travelers, descriptions of cities, lists of useful addresses and maps of towns were all making their debut.

Travels in France and other European countries were much read. An account of the grand tour made by Balthasar de Monconys with his pupil, the young Duc de Chevreuse, through France, Portugal, the Netherlands and Germany was published in no fewer than three different cities, Paris, Lyons and Amsterdam and while this was being eagerly read, a similar narrative, Claude Jordan's *Voyage historique de l'Europe,* was a great favorite, with Italy and Spain still the countries of most interest to Frenchmen (as in Comtesse d'Aulnoy's *Voyage d'Espagne*), though Samuel Sorbière's *Relation d'un voyage en Angleterre,* banned by the censor in England, did well in the bookshops. There was clearly a fascination with distant lands, Guyana, Cayenne, Louisiana, the struggles of various European powers for supremacy in the West Indies, but less interest in America than in Richelieu's time. Canada was an industry of its own, though narratives of Jesuit activities there dwindled with the decline in religious excitement; the demand had shifted to factual descriptions of the country and its resources. Turkey, the mysteries of the harem, Barbary pirates, the fate of Christian slaves, punitive expeditions by the French fleet in the Mediterranean and tales by missionaries, merchants and explorers provided a high percentage of Parisians' recreational reading. Once again the literature reflects the age, emphasis being on description (or sensation) with no space devoted to the sufferings of the missionaries—there is a more secular spirit in the writing of this new cosmography.

By the late 17th century the Far East lends its enchantment and it was here that the exertions of the Jesuits made news: their persecution in Japan, the dispatch of Jesuit mathematicians and astronomers to Peking by Louis XIV, the exchange of ambassadors between France and the King of Siam. And the earliest signs of the passion for Orientalism appears in the interior decor of the rich.

The Muslim world, Constantinople, the Middle East, Persia and India, exercised much fascination as a theme of escape and exoticism. Pierre Martino (*l'Orient dans la littérature française*) has shown how important the year 1660 was, the time when Colbert was in the ascendant and when a massive collection of voyages and travels in the Middle East was published by Thévenot. Paris booksellers no longer had to depend on foreign publications when writers like Thévenot, Tavernier (*Turkey, Persia and the Indies*), the Chevalier Chardin, de la Haye and Caron, and François Bernier's *l'Histoire de la dernière révolution des états du Grand Mogul* fulfilled the curiosity of readers.

French expeditions to Madagascar were the subject of numerous accounts, no doubt inspired by the Government, but it was the Far East that seized the imagination, especially the Jesuits' adventures in new and unknown territories, which despite their persecution in Japan continued in Indo–China, Siam and China. Many contributing factors brought these distant scenes close to home: the work of Father Alexandre of Rhodes, the appointment of French "apostolic vicars" to the Far East by the Company of the Holy Sacrament, the exchange of ambassadors between the King of Siam and the King of France, the dispatch of French Jesuit mathematicians and astronomers. So it need not surprise us if publications with Oriental themes began to issue from Paris: Chinese culture and history made impact in works like *China. . . . illustrata* by Father Kircher, which were also printed in Amsterdam, as was Father Martini's *De bello Tartarico* and his famous *Histoire de la China*. And Cramoisy brought out a series of narratives by Thévenot, illustrated with remarkable engravings based on sketches done on the spot, while abbé Bernou translated Father Magalhaens' *Nouvelle relation de la Chine*. Father Couplet produced his *Tabulae chronologicae* and *Confucius Sinarum philosophicus* and Father Le Comte brought his readers up to date with *Nouveaux mémoires sur l'estat present de la Chine*. Finally, Father Le Tellier brought out his *Défense des nouveaux chrétiens et des missionaires de la Chine*. . . .

Paris, the citadel of the Jesuits, was also the base from which the doughty Fathers issued their detailed narratives and polemics about China in the last two decades of the 17th century. After 1695 censorship increased severely (to the detriment of Paris publishers), with the inevitable result that books appeared with false imprints, which makes it hard to determine provenance. Nonetheless, seeds had been planted in the very heart of Louis' kingdom which no censorship could blight.

CHAPTER IV

SCIENCE

1. Military Science

VERY FEW TECHNICAL BOOKS in our sense of the term existed, but the kind of military expertise expected of officers in the army had to be catered for, as well as the technical aspects of their recreational pursuits. Hunting was the traditional sport of the officer class, and Jean de Franchière's *Fauconnerie* and Du Fouilloux's *Vénerie* were for fifty years best-sellers; farriery and horsemanship went naturally together with such aids as William Cavendish's *Nouvelle méthode pour dresser les chevaux* (the vogue word "méthode" was a guarantee the book would be modern), Samuel Fouquet's *Modèle du parfait chevalier*, Delcampe's *Noble art de monter à cheval*, and Imbotti's *Ecuyer français*.

For the young ambitious officer textbooks on military arts were abundant, with titles like *Devoirs de l'officier d'artillerie, Devoirs militaires des officiers d'infanterie et de cavalrie*, Louis de Gaya's *L'art de la guerre* and *Art militaire pour l'infanterie*. Weapons and explosives were treated in such manuals as *Pratique de la guerre contenant l'usage de l'artillerie, bombes et mortiers*, the *Art de jeter les bombes* and St. Rémy's *Mémoires d'artillerie*. Naval architecture and hydrography were important sciences at a time of imperial expansion overseas, and on land fortification was the key to military strategy, as in Chastillon's *Art universel des fortifications* (1665), La Fontaine's *Nouveau traité de fortification*, Milliet de Chasles' *Art de fortifier, défendre et d'attaquer les places*, and Du Breuil's *Art universel des fortifications*, replacing Du Four. Other authors were Du Fog, Blondel, Manesson-Mallet, Bernard, de Fer and Ozanam.

563

The vanity of the military caste was stoked up in such works as *Vray théâtre d'honneur et de noblesse,* a history of armorial bearings and jousting, and in other books praising the art of dueling. Heraldry was in demand by the new generation of upstart nobility, along with emblem books and gorgeous plates illustrating pomp and ceremony and allegorizing the "homme d'épee," the gallant swordsman. Even at a time when commoners were entering the army, the old Renaissance ideal of the warrior in Roman military garb was exploited, but now he is depicted stoutly defending a fortress, symbol of current military theory.

The reorganization of the army by Le Tellier and Louvois, the creation of a powerful navy by Colbert, and Vauban's influence on fortification and siege tactics were the inspiration behind the textbooks used in military academies; a professional army on modern lines had to replace the dashing cavaliers.

2. Treatises on Fine Art

In the arts the same processes were at work. The influence of Academies of Painting and Architecture inspired the writing of textbooks on perspective for architects, painters, sculptors and engineers. Jean Cousin's *Traité de Pourtraiture* was widely studied and a new translation of da Vinci's treatise on painting was published, with plates after Poussin. Other standard works of the period were Du Fresnoy's *Art de la peinture,* Roger de Piles' *Conversations sur la connaissance de la peinture, l'Abrégé de la vie des peintres,* and *Dialogues sur le coloris.*

Books on architecture multiplied from a dozen in the years 1600–40, and fifteen from 1641 to 1670, to over thirty from 1671 to 1700. Blondel's three folios, *Cours d'architecture* (1675–83), and Aviler's *Architecture pratique* were central to the study, and the five main orders of architecture received their due in *Principes de l'architecture, de la sculpture, de la peinture et des autres arts qui en dépendant* by Félibien. Modern canons of the arts (now often dismissed as "Academicism") sprang from this new platform of thought, and concomitant with the arts of symmetry and pure form was the new venture in landscape gardening.

We must emphasize at this point the role of the copper engraving as a crucial factor in the encouragement of the esthetic spirit in this era, as print dealers like Tavernier, Nicholas Langlois and Mariette made reproductions of paintings and tapestries available to a wide public. Pictures of objets d'art, fireplaces, ornamental locks, goldsmiths' work, embroidery, paneling—all helped create the climate of taste. Bosse, Stella and Dorigny in particular were active in the genre; Israel Silvestre produced engravings of Paris and its chateaux, Jean Le Pautre published three volumes of architectural plates, Langlois put out a 2-volume quarto edition of a book of a similar kind, completely à la mode, and Stella's pupil Charmeton did the same. Jean Marot, an architect, drew pictures of fireplaces, funeral monuments, ceilings, friezes and moldings for publication and Nicholas and Alexis Loir engraved carriages, wheelchairs, pedestal tables and fans. Ladame published the work of Bresville, a master locksmith, and a school of engravers were reproducing Bérain's designs.

Thus the period was much stronger in the Fine Arts than the earlier part of the century, and there seems to have been a definite aim behind the sumptuous volumes: to determine a code of rules and canons of taste, but also to glorify a hierarchical society and its aristocratic luminaries—above all, the King.

In a decree dated 22 December 1667, Louis initiated a program of propaganda through art: "It is the King's desire that engravings be made of plans and elevations of the royal residences, of paintings and sculpture, tapestries and classical statuary therein, and of plants and animals of every species, and all subjects of interest and curiosity." The engravings were to be numerous enough to warrant a volume of them each year, what was called the Cabinet du Roi, in the Bibliothèque Royale, a magnificent series of unparalleled splendor depicting fêtes, like the *Courses de testes et de bagues faites par le Roy et par les Princes en l'année 1662* and *Plaisirs de l'île enchantée*. The Gobelin tapestries were superbly reproduced in a masterly portfolio entitled *Devises pour les tapisseries du Roy où sont representez les quatre élémens et les quatre saisons de l'année* and *Tableaux du Cabinet du Roy au nombre de XXII et les statues et bustes antiques au nombre de XVIII avec leurs explications.* Others depicted the fountains, grottoes, groves and labyrinth at Versailles, and the Hôtel des Invalides.

The Cabinet du Roi had a serious scientific intention and was the inspiration behind a great many botanical, zoological and scientific works. The whole enterprise, directed by Perrault, was a tribute to Academicism at its best and made a profound impression on the artistic and intellectual life of the nation, but for Colbert it was ultimately a question of prestige, not scientific or practical utility, hence the lack of illustrations referring to mechanical arts. The epoch of the Roi Soleil was definitely not oriented towards technology.

3. Medicine and Natural History

Here too the trend is away from the ponderous folios favored by the Renaissance and towards ordinary sized books, wholly new, in French, and of modest length. New formats coincided with new advances and techniques in medicine and curative pharmacy, the result of discussions on the efficacy of various drugs, or about Harvey's discovery of the circulation of the blood and Pecquet's "chylifères." Descartes's book *Homme* (1664) brought on a crisis in medical circles and consequently textbooks tended to be more specialized, dealing with single aspects of disease: fever, the function of acids, anatomy, the blood. Dionis, Director of the Royal Garden, was keen to propagate new ideas. Chemistry was making strides, with six books on the subject appearing between 1660 and 1675, one with the intriguing title, *Chimie charitable et facile en faveur des dames.* Pharmaceutical recipes become more specific and scientific—new pharmacopoeias published included Charas's *Pharmacopée royale* and one favored by Paris apothecaries, Louis Pénicher's *Collectanea pharmaceutica.* In 1694 Pierre Pomet published the *Histoire générale des drogues,* based on samples he had collected during his travels abroad. Nicolas Lémery's *Traité universel des drogues* (1698) was a standard manual for years.

Little books were written as aids to the sick: Guybert's *Médecin charitable,* St. Germain's *Médecin royale,* and Dubé's *Médecin des pauvres,* and even a selection of books on beauty culture, a subject also dealt with by Kenelm Digby. La Martinière, an early experimenter, wrote the *Naturaliste charitable* in 1666, a little book of personal hygiene, and while her son was in prison Madame Fouquet compiled numerous books of receipts and remedies, all of which proved successful.

An important contribution to natural history was *Mémoires pour servir à l'histoire naturelle des animaux,* monographs on different animals, and botanical works included a translation of Grew's *Anatomy of plants* and a *Mémoires . . . à l'histoire naturelle des plantes,* Tournefort's *Eléments de botanique* and *Histoire des plantes qui croissent aux environs de Paris.* The experiments made by Robert Boyle and by Leeuwenhoeck were well known and in great demand, and the New World shows up in Plumier's *Description des plantes d'Amérique.*

Once again the most prominent work in this field was done by protégés of the King; the Crown exerted considerable influence over the sciences as part of its public strategy, and progress by any other route was inconceivable.

4. Occult Sciences

Until about 1630 books on what we might call the occult sciences, including alchemy, came out in a steady stream, then there was a falling off until 1650, a recovery in the next quarter-century, an abrupt fall between 1676 and 1680, and a further rise. Though caution is needed in assessing the data, in the early 17th century there was much prediction and popular astrology, and by the end more strictly scientific works, issued in thousands of little books, but of course this may simply be the accident of survival.

Certainly there is passionate interest in a Great Universal Cure, Potable Gold, the Philosophers' Stone, Transmutation of Metals. Divination and astrology were of perennial interest to the public—Belin's *Traité des Talismans* was first published in Paris in 1658, reprinted in 1664, 1671 and in 1709 with another work entitled *Poudre de sympathie.* In 1660 came Pagan's *Astrologie Naturelle* and *Discours physique sur l'influence des astres selon la méthode de M. Descartes* (1671 and 1674), and in 1690 Giuseppe del Terzis's *De gradu horoscopanti,* soon followed by Guynaud's *Concordance des prophéties de Nostrodamus . . .* (1693, 1709).

Most of these were published by d'Houry, a bookseller operating in his own house as a specialist in medicine and science. Many learned accounts of "occult" science appeared in the respectable scientific *Journal des savants,* which was based on Cartesian principles. The old theories of the interconnection between microcosms and macrocosms was debated, and Jerome Vitalis of Capua, in his book *Lexicon mathématique, astronomique et géometrique,* presented astrology as any other experimental science. François Placet argued in his *Corruption du grand et du petit monde* that men's sins reverberated in the Great Macrocosmos. Significantly Vulson de la Colombière, a Marshal and a specialist in ceremony and its inner allegorical meaning, the organizer of fetes, and Chief Herald, compiled a *Traité des songes et des visions nocturnes* (1646, repr. 1659, 1671, 1690, 1698).

One new feature was the occasional critique of theories once accepted as true without rational grounds. Malbec de Tresfel denounced the charlatans who recommended certain herbs as sure cures if prepared at precise times in accordance with the stars (in his *Abrégé des théories et des véritables principes de l'art appelé chymie*). Jacques de Billy's *Tombeau de l'astrologie judiciaire* and Jean-Baptiste Denis' *Discours sur l'astrologie judiciaire* refuted the basis of astrology.

But it was not until 1680 that an overt attack was made on entrenched superstitions by Thomas Corneille and Donneau de Visé in their comedy *La Divineresse,* aimed at a famous female charlatan, La Voisin, and a comedy, *Comète,* attributed to de Vise but which Fontenelle had a large share in—the play ridiculed the terror inspired by a recent comet. In 1682 Pierre Bayle published an anonymous paper in which he proved that comets had no connection with terrestrial disasters. Later, Fontenelle delivered a shattering blow with his *Histoire des oracles,* involving religious arguments, always dangerous.

In sum, even the better informed reader in this age held to his faith in occultism, and argument about demons and their role in prediction was by no means over; it was a superstitious age.

5. The Rise of Modern Science

Mathematics was the symbol of the new rationalism, and books on the calculus and geometry appeared in greater numbers. The practical bias of the age was seen in the growth of commercial arithmetic: Legendre's *Arithmétique en sa perfection* was for bankers and tradesmen, first published in 1663 (12th edition, 1705); d'Irson's *Arithmétique universelle* was almost as popular, and Barrème (a protégé of Colbert) wrote *Livre facile pour apprendre l'arithmétique de soy-même et sans maistre* and other manuals of accountancy for clerks, book-keepers and lawyers. Other practical skills which found their way into instructional books were land surveying, perspective, and the art of erecting sundials. Savary's *Parfait négociant* reached its 7th edition by 1713.

Mathematics split into several branches and textbooks were written for college students by both Jesuit and Jansenist teachers (the *Nouveau éléments de géometrie* was partly written by Arnauld himself). Projective and analytical geometry, infinitesimal calculus and physics were all taught, and the first conjectures about gravity, percussion, falling bodies, cold and heat, magnetism, optics and the Cartesian theory of animal mechanisms. Since the invention of the telescope, astronomy had been fashionable, and observations by amateurs were the subject of papers privately circulated; Paris Observatory was opened and when Jupiter's satellites were discovered, books and even posters were issued on the subject. Star catalogs made their first appearance (Edmund Halley's Supplement to Tycho Brahe's catalog) and in 1681 the Imprimerie Royale sponsored the first volume, of *Tychonis Brahe thesaurus observationum astronomicarum.* The second volume, sponsored by Picard,

Colbert's protégé, never appeared. Navigation was assisted by an annual *Connoissance des temps ou Calendrier et Ephéméride du lever et du coucher du soleil et de la lune,* beginning 1679.

These publications were for specialists, but the educated public was keeping up with science by reading simplified accounts of new theories like the *Entretiens sur las pluralité des mondes.* In the final thirty years of the 17th century there is a distinctly modern feel about scientific writings, and its impetus came from the State, a typical work being *Mémoires mathématiques et de physique tirée des registres de l'Académie des Sciences,* compiled by scientists of the Paris Observatory. It was the embodiment of the contemporary ethos—progress under the aegis of the Crown.

6. Cartesianism

The spirit of the age could be summed up in the word "Cartesian," and although Descartes's theories were subject to censorship they were nevertheless broadcast with the help of sympathetic publishers. The epoch-making *Discours de la méthode* was first published in Leyden by Jean Mair in 1637, not only under licence by the Dutch government but by royal licence granted at Mersenne's request. One has the feeling that Descartes wanted his daring new ideas to be exposed on the Palais bookstalls where theologians looked for their reading matter, and wanted to control the printing of his book and the readership for it; he retained 200 copies under the contract signed with his bookseller, and those he sent to his fellow savants at home and abroad with whom he felt an affinity. Those who could not read French were supplied with a Latin translation, done by a refugee in Holland called Etienne de Courcelles with Descartes's approval and published in Amsterdam by Elzevier in 1644. His next work, *Meditationes de prima philosophia,* was published in France by Soly (1641), with a preface addressed to the Dean and Faculty of Theology at the University of Paris, and though it was protected by royal licence it was not "authorized" in a way that pleased the theologians of the Sorbonne, who attacked it so severely that he had his next book, *Principiae philosophiae,* published in Amsterdam (Elzevier, 1644). In 1647 he permitted a translation into French by his friend abbé Picot (Paris, Le Gras, 1647) and later authorized a translation by Clerselier and the Duc de Luynes of the *Meditationes.* In 1649 his *Passions de l'âme* was published simultaneously in Paris and Amsterdam.

Descartes appeared to be trying to avoid open confrontation in his home country while insuring a wide readership through the good offices of a famous publisher—Elzevier. By acting with a degree of circumspection he would not antagonize the Jesuits and he might even hope that they might adopt an attitude of benevolent neutrality, possibly even teaching his philosophical principles in their colleges one day. Certainly he was granted a royal pension in 1647 and his followers were free to publish his work posthumously in France. Clerselier published a selection of his letters, Bobin, Girard and Henri Le Gras published *Le Monde,* Angot published *l'homme,* and Poisson of the Oratory edited the *Mécanique* (1668). In 1656 a Life of Descartes was published by Pierre Borel. In 1658 and 1660 the *Discours* was published in Paris, the *Méditations* reprinted in 1661 and 1673, the *Passions de l'âme* reprinted in 1650, 1664 and 1679, and the *Principes* in 1659, 1660, 1668 and 1681. Descartes's disciples were free to publish their own work—for example, Jacques Du Roure's *Philosophie divisée en toutes ses parties . . .* (1654), and in 1662 from Port-Royal, the *Logique ou l'art de penser,* which owed much to Descartes's ideas. In 1666 came the *Discernement du corps et de l'âme* by Géraud Cordemoy, and in 1669 Rouvière's *Nouveau cours de médecine* and his *Physique,* and also Rohault's *Entretiens sur la philosophie,* which expounded Descartes' doctrines to a Parisian audience with great effect. In 1674 Le Bossu published the *Parallèle des principes de la physique d'Aristote et de celle de Descartes* and Malebranche his *Recherche de la vérité,* which reached its fourth edition in 1678.

Not only was Cartesian philosophy fashionable in the Paris salons but in a disguised form it infiltrated the teaching in the colleges. It began, however, to meet with official resistance; when in 1663 most of Descartes' work was placed on the Index "until it be corrected," it made little impact in France, and the Government felt obliged to forbid a funeral oration over his coffin when it was brought to Paris in 1667. In 1671 the Archbishop of Paris formally instructed the University that the King forbade the teaching of any doctrine other than its own official system as laid down in the Statutes and ordinances; only fear of ridicule (especially from writers such as Boileau) prevented President Lamoignon from issuing a decree in the name of Parlement. Government suppression continued: Lamy of the Oratory was warned at the University of Angers, and in Caen the Faculty of Theology withheld degrees from anyone whose thesis showed influence by Cartesian theories. Maurists, Genovéfains and Oratorians all returned to traditional philosophy, but even this did not satisfy Royalty, and in 1685 the King once more forbade the teaching of either Descartes' or Gassendi's doctrines, which were condemned again in 1691 when eleven "Propositions" taught in Paris colleges were singled out for attack.

Not surprisingly Malebranche found it hard to obtain approval for his book *Recherche de la vérité* and was forced to find publishers in Holland for his other works or else bring them out secretly, and yet Fontenelle was bold enough to publish openly his *Entretiens sur la pluralité des mondes* in 1685. Regis was forced to wait until 1690 before his philosophy course was sanctioned, and was allowed to publish it only if there was no mention of Descartes in the title. In such a climate of hostility to new thought Descartes' opponents rushed into print condemning his work, a typical example being the Jesuits Rochon and Pardies' *Lettre d'un philosophe à un cartésien et ses amis* (Paris, 1672, reprinted 1683), though their second work hinted at some sympathy with the new philosophy. La Grange of the Oratory published his *Principes de la philosophie contre les nouveaux philosophes Descartes, Rohault, Regis, Gassendi, le Pere Maignan,* and the Jesuit Le Valois (under the pseudonym La Ville) put out his *Sentiments de M. Descartes touchant l'essence et les proprietes des corps opposés à la doctrine de l'Eglise et conformés aux erreurs de Calvin sur le sujet de l'Euchariste.* Then, in 1689, Pierre-Daniel Huet published *Censura philosophiae Cartesianae* and Father Daniel his *Voyage du monde,* which provoked a further battle of the books, ancient and modern. The old world was trying to shut out the new.

The very ferocity of the reaction shows that Cartesianism was gaining ground, and in fact a good number of school-books and many publications for the intelligent layman were infected with Cartesian thought. One such, *Philosophia vetus et nova,* attributed to abbé Colbert but really by Du Hamel, was eclectic in its coverage, and Flamel's *Medulla aristotelica* listed Aristotle's errors; other books of the day owed much to Cartesian theories (e.g., Pourchot's, the last in the 17th century, and Dagoumer's, first in the 18th), and if more had survived there is little doubt they would reveal a debt to Descartes. By 1700 Cartesianism had triumphed, and even the semi-official organ, the *Journal des Savants,* devoted a good deal of space to his theories. Some of the new books written to introduce them to a wider audience have interesting titles: *Entretiens sur ce qui forme l'honnête homme et le vrai savant, l'Entretien sur les sciences et les arts* and *Méthode d'étudier les sciences et la philosophie.* By this time newer theories evolving from Descartes and rendering some of his conclusions obsolete were already appearing in print elsewhere, but France, in the grip of a vigilant censorship and with a powerful lobby upholding traditional prejudice, was no longer the cradle of philosophical and scientific progress.

CHAPTER V

NEWS AND INFORMATION

1. Broadsheets and Yearbooks

AN APPETITE FOR NEWS was a marked feature of city life in Louis XIV's reign. Accounts of disasters and supernatural wonders had been common since the 16th century and Bayle's scorn for those who were in dread of comets suggests that such marvels still circulated in the 17th century, though the credulous were probably to be found in rural areas rather than the city. Posters were a familiar sight on town walls, debating religious or political issues or even arguing lawsuits. Acts, decrees, regulations, taxation laws were posted up as a matter of routine, and Louis XIV was at pains to publish Open Letters detailing his diplomatic and military successes this way. The sheer quantity of the material can be gleaned from Corda's 10-volume *Catalogue des factums et autres documents judiciaires antérieures à 1789,* published by the Bibliothèque Nationale, yet it was not here that things changed but in the development of almanacs. At first they were large, with a crude woodcut of the King in a posture suggesting glory or conquest, and a calendar and predictions. Others were booklets with blank spaces and lists of feast days, phases of the moon and prognostications, forerunners of all the pocket reference books of our day. There was an *Almanach d'amour* and an *Almanach des belles,* and in 1677 the first edition of the long-running *Almanach de Paris,* which was launched to counteract the kind of simple-minded almanacs published in the provinces announcing that "it had nothing to do with the supernatural which no one can know about." This was the start of the annual digest and the yearbooks which are now so common.

The official lists also began here. Lists of the King's household, of State officers, the *Etat de France,* 1644, annually from 1649, official directories and calendars were seen as an essential part of government records until the Revolution: the *Liste générale de tous les officiers du Châtelet de Paris* and the *Almanach ou calendrier pour l'année* (1688), retitled *Almanach royale* in 1700, were typical. The *Calendrier de la Cour* (75,000 copies published by Collombat) began life in 1700, and one of the first directories was the *Adresses de la ville de Paris;* an early *World of learning* was published by the Académie des Sciences, called *Connaissance des temps.*

We have come a long way from the simple almanacs and shepherds' calendars of the street pedlars, but there is a direct lineage from a few elementary dates, feast days and seasonal facts to the annual digests of statistics so beloved by present-day bureaucrats.

2. Periodicals

The "periodical" was born during the Fronde troubles, originally as Letters in prose or verse or "Mercuries" addressed to a dignitary in the form of a chronicle of recent events. When peace returned, the *Muse historique* appeared (1665), giving fashionable gossip and news of high society with some literary items and political commentary; it was copied quickly by other printers with an eye to a cheap profit and quick return: *Muse héroï-comique au Roi, Muse royale à Madame la Princesse Palatine* published by a bookseller named Lesselin, the *Muse Dauphine,* and Robinot's verse epistles addressed to the King and Queen, all fulsomely royalist.

Donneau de Visé, who lampooned the tribe of newsmongers in his comedies, himself started the *Mercure galant* (1672). Like others it began as a chatty chronicle of events at Court, accounts of fêtes, notices of new plays and books, and some original material—sonnets, madrigals, even prose fiction. He knew his readers and supplied what every courtier felt he needed to keep up with his peers, a digest of current affairs and the satisfaction of cultural curiosity which the Précieuses had made fashionable for at least thirty years. Letters from readers were a regular feature of Donneau's paper, and there was no problem over a licence since he and his collaborator, Corneille, were acceptable to the Establishment, the paper was easily watched, could be relied on to support the government and gave no trouble. The fugitive press was the headache, appearing irregularly and from different quarters, easily produced and hard to find. The *Mercure galant* gave much space to the Army and its successes, listing the gentry who had left home to serve and stressing old-style heroics by the daring cavaliers, a rewarding press exercise for Donneau because he was given a pension of 6,000 livres, really a State subsidy.

In 1672 the first official record of proceedings in Parlement started, the *Journal du Palais,* continuing for twelve years, but when Colletet tried to launch his *Journal de la ville de Paris* in 1676, his enterprise was thwarted by a decree in Council. An attempt to communicate news of progress in medicine was short-lived—Nicolas de Blégny's *Nouvelles de toutes parties de médecine* was finally killed off by a similar decree after surviving from 1679 to 1685.

The outstanding journal was the *Journal des Savants,* which began life in 1665. The idea of a bibliographical journal goes back as far as Mézeray but only came to fruition when with Colbert's support a young member of the Parlement, Denis de Sallo, undertook the editorship, only to be forced out when his sympathies were thought to be too Gallican. He was followed (by Chancellor d'Aligre's orders) in the editorial chair by abbé Gallois (too lazy) and abbé La Roque (too boring). When Bayle and Le Clerc started a rival periodical from the safety of Holland an attempt was made to revitalize the *Journal* under Cousin's editorship, and some lost readers were won back in the first years of the 18th century when Chancellor Pontchartrain gave it semi-official standing, with Bignon as editor calling on his wide circles of specialist censors to contribute articles in their respective fields. It was another move by the Crown to control the press, yet despite that imposed conformity its quality improved and it had an increasing readership at home and overseas, its authority respected and its success measured by its many imitators.

But the freest and most puissant expression of uncoerced opinion on political, cultural and scientific questions was in Holland, where many of the French intelligentsia were in exile. Copies of the physically slight but intellectually influential gazettes and "news" serials slipped through the posts into France—it was impossible to exclude them—and such periodicals as the *Nouvelles de la République des Lettres* and the *Bibliothèque Universelle* helped widen Frenchmen's horizons, limited by Louis's despotism, and gave them a representative picture of Europe and the problems of international politics, screened or distorted by the French censorship.

CHAPTER VI

WHAT ELSE THEY READ

P UBLISHERS WHO ENJOYED the King's favor or were patronized by powerful Ministers of the Crown could be relied upon to issue only the most acceptable material, from which we might erroneously conclude that the Counter Reformation and Absolute Monarchy had between them triumphed in France. By no means. The underground press was at all times very active, as the various lists recording books seized after raids make quite plain.

1. Catholic Controversies

A great many books and pamphlets were published abroad, out of reach of the Paris censors, and among them were Jansenist publications stubbornly protesting their case and keen to convey their message back to France. They originated in Amsterdam, published by the Elzeviers under false imprints, but the counterblast really began when Arnauld, the leader of the schismatic sect, left France for good in 1679. He saw himself as a defender of Catholicism in such anti-Protestant pamphlets as *Le Calvinisme convaincu de nouveau de dogmes impies, Préservatif contre le changement de religion,* and *Véritable portrait de Guillaume Henry de Nassau, nouvel Absalon, nouvel Hérode, nouveau Cromwell, nouveau Néron,* characteristic of his passionate polemicism. He was a champion of vernacular translations of Scripture, a consistent supporter of Church versus King, attacked Jesuits on all possible occasions, and continually asserted that Jansenism was a mere bogy, not a heresy, to the Catholics who opposed him. What interests the student of the clandestine press is the ease with which he wrote and disseminated

578

his unorthodox views, which were later taken up by two of his closest disciples, Gerberon and Quesnel, who influenced public opinion in France strongly in favor of the Jansenist position, opinion which fed on the two classic statements of their case, the *Lettres provinciales* and the *Morale pratique des Jésuites.*

Other religious literature from the fringe aimed itself at the worldliness of proud prelates with titles like *Jésuite sécularisé, Moine sécularisé,* and *Rasibus, ou Le procès fait à la barbe des capucins par un moine défroqué.* Guy Patin's *Lettres* contributed to a growing feeling of anticlericalism in France and as we survey the spread of rational criticism directed at the Church through underground channels, it is clear that the Revocation of the Edict of Nantes was a policy disaster. Far from marking the ultimate victory of the French Counter Reformation, it was the start of a great wave of reaction against Church and State which finally engulfed both in 1789.

Other exiles who exercised considerable influence from their haven abroad were Malebranche and Richard Simon. The former was a born pedant, with nothing of the rebel in him, but was introduced to Cartesianism when he picked up a copy of Descartes's *Traité de l'homme* in a bookshop. From that moment he devoted himself to the rewriting of orthodox theology in Cartesian terms, a delicate operation, but his *Recherche de la vérité* was instantly successful and provoked royal anger against the Cartesians. He followed it with two others, *Conversations chrétiennes* and *Méditations sur l'humilité et la pénitence,* which were on open sale in Paris though the first had to be printed covertly in Lyons because Molin the printer had neither official nor the author's permission. Yet the same book was published in Brussels apparently with the author's connivance; it was a perplexing time. Malebranche issued his books from a number of foreign places, Rotterdam, Amsterdam, Cologne and Antwerp, a man with a deep sense of mission who was determined that his words should reach his compatriots back home from beyond their walls. His books were shown no mercy by the Paris Chancellery, who alerted the Customs and the Stationers Guild to be on the watch for the detested works. In

Rouen and at the city gates of Paris, 100 copies of Malebranche's *Méditations sur l'humilité et la pénitence* were seized and the Dutch edition frozen, while in Lyons his *Conversations chrétiennes* were published under a false imprint by Antoine Molin. Possibly the manuscript had been taken to the publishers' by a third party who wanted to profit but also hoped for some fame, though it is known that Malebranche approved a revised edition when it was published in Brussels the same year by Fricx.

Nothing was quite clear-cut in an age when imposition of the law was not easy; Malebranche felt he had to accept more responsible involvement, and allowed the abbé Catelan to commission Daniel Elzevier in Amsterdam to bring out his *Traité de la nature et de la grace* for Arnauld's attention. And once he had taken that decisive step he had Blaeu of Amsterdam put out an edition of 3,000 copies of *Méditations chrétiennes* and *Traité de morale,* using Balthasar d'Egmond as a conventional imprint, in Cologne. Then, like so many others, he had recourse to Leers of Rotterdam to issue most of his attacks on Arnauld, especially *Entretiens sur la metaphysique et sur la mort.*

A man, then, of phlegmatic, even pacifist temperament, but convinced that he had a mission to deliver a message to clarify theological problems by Cartesian principles of "method," he used printers on the periphery of the French publishing world, a practice which does not appear to have worried him. The Government's attitude towards him seems ambivalent. They did nothing to hinder the success of his *Recherche de la vérité,* nor did they take any action against the *Conversations chrétiennes,* but such was not the case when the philosopher tackled the problem of Grace in his *Traité de la nature et de la grace.* Harlay, Archbishop of Paris, was delighted with the blow struck at Arnauld, but Bossuet urged Arnauld on the quiet to reply to it, and the Holy Office was alerted at the same time, probably by the Jesuit Ricci.

It would appear then that the Chancellor frowned on any toleration of Malebranche. As we have seen, his pamphlets against Arnauld were watched for and, on the 16 July 1683, the *Méditations*—published by Denis Thierry, Guild Syndic no less—were ordered to be seized. They were stopped dead in Paris and more were seized in Rouen; Malebranche made efforts to secure a lifting of the ban, but without any success, and was forced to lend out copies of his own to friends. Yet things did improve: while the Dutch copies were frozen, others appeared in Lyons with the help of the author of some little tracts, who offered them for sale "without hindrance but also without any noise."

From that time Malebranche's works were under some restriction and the author said to his friend Francois Lamy, when he was about to publish his *Entretiens sur la métaphysique et sur la mort,* that the book would be of more use to foreigners than to his own people because there was little chance of it being available in France. But his "persecution" was a little more flexible: Lamy, who lived in the Meaux diocese, took it upon himself to present a copy of *Entretiens* to Bossuet, who was quite happy with it. Soon negotiations went ahead for the publication of *Recherche de la vérité* and other works by its author in France, and their circulation does not appear to have suffered through any search and seizure, and in fact benefited by the publicity.

Richard Simon was another case: a man of profound perceptions and a clarity of mind which fitted him to expound the Bible from a sound historical and linguistic standpoint, appropriate to an age of dawning science but unlikely to recommend him to the orthodox. His first major work, *Histoire critique du Vieux Testament,* brought a charge of blasphemy against him since it challenged the foundation of the Faith, yet it was sanctioned by the Sorbonne, and Sainte Marthe, Superior of the Congregation of the Oratory, authorized it. Billaine, the publisher, thought it good publicity to issue a table of contents abroad as a kind of prospectus, but it fell into Bossuet's hands, was condemned by the Privy Council and 1,300 copies were confiscated. Elzevier published it in Holland and Simon kept prudently under cover, wary of the powers threatening him and hiding under a multitude of pseudonyms, but continuing his work. Three of his seminal studies came out in Rotterdam, published by Leers: *Histoire critique du texte du Nouveau Testament, Histoire critique des versions du Nouveau Testament* and *Histoire critique des commentaires du Nouveau*

Testament, and despite every obstacle, hundreds of copies were sold in Léonard's bookshop in the center of Paris without the Government making any move against them.

2. *Politics: Underground Literature*

The one fact which prompted the great outpouring of French books published outside France was the Revocation of the Edict of Nantes and the migration of French Protestants; naturally a large proportion of those books were on religious themes, including Biblical exegesis, since many émigrés were Calvinist scholars specializing in Oriental studies. There were books about the Jews, collections of sermons by exiled pastors, books on Morals or Mysticism by prolix authors, La Placette, Antoinette Bourignon, Pierre Loiret and Labadie, former Jesuit, but the surprising point is the diversity of views—controversies and tracts of every sect. At the center of the conflict was Jurieu, who appeared to think his mission was to root out deviations—Arminianism or Socinianism, and he blamed successively Aubert de Versé, Papin, Jaquelot, Philippe Legendre, Elie Saurin, Jean Le Clerc and Pierre Bayle. Though many of their works were clearly not welcomed in France yet, La Placette's writings were known and widely read, and *De veritate religionis christianae* by Grotius, and Jacques Abbadie's *Traité de la vérité de la réligion chrétienne* (admired by Madame de Sévigné, Bussy-Rabutin and Montausier) were watched for at the gates of Paris. And in addition to these, great numbers of books were written for the benefit of Catholics as well as for the Protestant sects. Blows and counterblows were exchanged in print, with the militants Arnauld, Nicole, Bossuet and Father Maimbourg in the van. Bayle's reply to Maimbourg's history of Calvinism was publicly burned in the Place de Grève and Police Chief La Reynie placarded Paris with 2,000 posters condemning it, the outcome of which was unprecedented publicity for Bayle.

Alongside the controversial matter, pamphlets attacking the policies of Louis XIV proliferated and there was much airing of Huguenot sufferings, but quite clearly there was divergence of opinion among the exiles. For the student of the period the difficulty is to determine the origins of the various manifestos, since most of them went into innumerable reprints: quite obviously, some (Jurieu's *Lettres pastorales* and *Soupirs de la France esclave* for example) were primarily intended for the New Converts, while most of the others addressed to French Catholics appear to have been aimed at home consumption within Louis' kingdom.

Political and military events were followed with keen interest by exiles gleeful at the spectacle of an unseemly quarrel between two such hated representatives of the old order as Louis XIV and Pope Innocent III, and they were happy to intervene with comments on the contradictions within Catholicism. The crowning of William of Orange as King of England was a decisive act in changing attitudes toward absolute monarchy. Jurieu, head of the orthodox Calvinists, justified the coup d'etat, invoking the principle of the people's sovereignty, but the moderates saw dangers in the Republican cause. When Larroque and Pierre Bayle issued their famous *Avis aux réfugiés sur leur prochain retour en France*, huge controversy broke out. In this atmosphere we can understand that on the one hand events could prompt some zealots to see the fulfillment of Biblical prophecy, and on the other hand an opportunity to make money out of newsmongering.

The gazettes were a recent invention and popular in Holland, and Dutch gazette-writers saw big possibilities in the French market as early as 1639; by 1667 the French, working among exiles abroad, began to make their own contribution: La Font was one, working for Amsterdam news sheets, and in Leyden and St. Glain, and remembered as the translator of Spinoza's *Tractatus theologicopoliticus*. After the Revocation of the Edict of Nantes new names appear: Aubert de Versé, Flournois, and Lucas, who came from a line of Rouen printers and was an intimate of Spinoza; another such was Tronchin de Breuil, one of Colbert's and Claude Jordan's aides. A new feature was the insertion into gazettes of sheets called "lardons," a kind of stop press, blank pages for the late insertion of news or of later commentary the journalist dare not include at source. At the same time periodicals of the same stripe as the *Mercure*

Galant were started, the most important the *Mercure Historique et Politique* founded by Courtilz de Sandras and later edited by Jean Rousset; others were the *Courrier véridique ou l'Anti-Rousset,* Jacques Bernard's *Histoire Abrégée de l'Europe,* the *Lettres Historiques* of Henri Basnage and Jean Du Mont, Lucas's *Quintessence de nouvelles,* de Sandras's *Elite des nouvelles de toutes les cours d'Europe* and Gueudeville's *Esprit des cours de l'Europe.*

The violence of tone so prevalent in the journals suggests that they were designed for French refugees in Europe generally, and Bayle said to Lenfant in 1685: "As for the gazettes, they are of limited interest here, I can tell you; their main purpose is to be read abroad."

One of the French ambassador's duties was to complain to the Dutch authorities about the calumnies regularly printed in the gazettes published for the consumption of French subjects at home, but the complaints had little effect because the news sheets were not issued with the consent of the Dutch government, but were the responsibility of the local towns where they were printed. A local decree would be issued closing down the press but the editor and assistants would simply move to the next town until the furor died away. One indignant French official wrote in 1670: "they will go without anything except their beloved gazettes, which come into France by the cartload and in ships of all shapes and sizes." The mutual hostility between France and Holland guaranteed against any effective action being taken by the Dutch when they sympathized with so much of the contents.

Another popular piece of reading-matter was the scandal-sheet. Bussy-Rabutin wrote a scurrilous satire called *Histoire amoureuse des Gaules,* a thinly disguised account of the libidinous life of the French Court, and soon imitators followed in troops. The Government tried to suppress them and copies were seized wherever possible; even Daniel Elzevier received a solemn warning from Paris. Joly, secretary to Colbert de Croissy, French ambassador in London, was hurriedly sent to Utrecht to buy back 1,500 copies of *Amours de Madame,* and Pralard and other Paris publishers had to do the same. Patin, another publisher of high society scandals in Paris, was forced into exile, but all of Colbert's efforts and those of his Police Chief failed to halt the flood of pornography. According to Antoine Bruneau, some printers' assistants were actually executed and others sent to the galleys in 1694 for publishing *Ombre de Scarron,* a book decorated with a picture of the Place des Victoires. Instead of the statues which were actually in the Place, the illustration depicted the four women who had shared the King's bed: Mlle. de la Vallière, Mlle. de Fontange, Madame de Montespan and Madame de Maintenon, all holding the King captive in chains. Dutch and German satirical prints and pamphlets vilified Louis, accusing him of cruelties to Protestants and of creating a despotism. He was likened to the Beast in the Apocalypse, ridiculed and lampooned openly or indirectly, and as his reign drew to a close the chorus of vilification grew louder. Absolutism in France was the target of abuse in the rest of Europe, the French seen as slaves of a hated regime.

Erotic and pornographic novels and memoirs poured out, written and distributed by exiled anti-monarchists, fellow-spirits with a grievance. Gregorio Leti, the nephew of an Italian prelate, was converted to Calvinism and lent his fertile pen to descriptions of Papal scandals and lengthy "histories" which were widely read. One of his collaborators was Courtilz de Sandras, a man of impeccable background and captain of a regiment, who was cashiered. He began writing romances, and read the market shrewdly, detecting an avid interest in current affairs and among the unsophisticated a permanent curiosity about the aristocracy. With his connections he was able to mix a popular potion compounded of fact and fiction in his thrilling stories of military life and the Court, and was rewarded with immense popularity. He wrote under cover of anonymity, which makes it difficult to know which titles are his, but between 1683 and 1686 he probably was responsible for *Mémoires contenant divers événements remarquables arrivés sous le règne de Louis le Grand,* which contrasted the deeds of the young King with the years after 1661 when he came under Colbert's influence. Among other titles were *Conquêtes amoureuses de Grand Alcandre dans les Pays-Bas, Histoire des promesses illusoires depuis la paix de Nimègue, Conduite de la France depuis la paix de Nimègue.* He was ambiguous in his attitudes, attacking Court morals but defending French foreign policy. In 1686 he founded the *Mercure historique et politique* and there is a suspicion that he was subsidized by royal funds because his stance was royalist in politics, but his speciality was the spicy "mémoire," always an unfailing hit with the Paris bourgeoisie. He handed over the editing of his journal to a refugee, Rousset de Missy, in 1689. His *Remarques sur le gouvernement du Royaume durant les règnes de Henri IV surnommé le Grand, de Louis XIII surnommé Dieudonné, le Grand et l'Invincible* was a non-political work, chiefly anecdotes and fake biographies with fanciful political manifestos, owing little to reality. He criticized Colbert's mercantilist policies, and the Comtes de Rochefort, Turenne, Fabert and d'Artagnan contributed picaresque and highly colored accounts of their lives. The author-adventurer's aim was of course to earn money rather than to discuss serious politics, and he prudently lived for several years in Holland, doing business with printers and booksellers who specialized in clandestine work, and produced leaflets for such publishers as André of Luxemburg and Godard of Rheims who gave him away to the authorities, so that he spent some time in the Bastille. A record of the man and his exploits survives in a letter written by a government agent to d'Argenson, police chief in Paris:

> There is a military man in Paris about 55 years of age who is making a nice living selling pernicious books. His name is Montfort de Courtile and he lives with his wife, brother and sister-in-law, who sell his manuscripts to booksellers, and his books are then sold at the Palais, on the Quai des Augustins and in all the principal Paris bookshops. Quite a lot of pedlars hawk his stuff around. He compiles histories and has written "political testaments" of the late M. Colbert, M. de Turenne and M. Louvois, and has been mixed up in this business for 25 years and even spent a year in the Bastille in 1698 or 99. Clerc thinks he was sentenced to banishment but he has a house in the country near Sens and lives in Paris. . . . He often visits Holland to arrange for the printing of his books and seems able to import them secretly into

France. His sales are huge and he gets his books bound
by a binder named Robert near Puits-Certain. He says
he gets secret orders for binding and that Courtile is
protected by a Commissioner—his wife boasts of it. The
name of the Commissioner is Delamare.

Delamare may well have been protecting Courtile under
orders from higher authority; there was a curious ambiguity
about the case, repeated in other cases. Eustache Le Noble,
Procurator General in the Metz Parlement, was forced to
leave the country after scandals connected with Colbert, and
had been a royalist pamphleteer concocting vehement
denunciations of Innocent XI and William of Orange with
equal impartiality. His regular monthly series entitled *Pierre
de touche politique* enjoyed an enormous circulation, with
issues of 6,000 not uncommon. This kind of publication was
unlicenced, but was not hounded unless it created a diplomatic incident. It was even a useful form of political
influence, not necessarily embarrassing to the French Court.
Le Noble was another equivocal character, imprisoned for an
offence but allowed to continue his useful work from prison
and then to escape to carry on effective propaganda for the
royalists in such tracts as *Travaux d'Hercule* (1693–94) and
Nouveaux entretiens politiques (1702–09). We know that
d'Argenson sent him one écu each week while he appeared
to denounce him officially. The French Government were
trying to fight their enemies with their own methods, clear
proof of a policy of segregation, keeping the dissidents
outside the walls yet employing underground devices to
satisfy Parisian taste for the forbidden.

CHAPTER VII

THE LITERARY WORLD

1. Paris

PARIS BY THE LATE 17TH CENTURY was a very large city. The old ramparts had been demolished, and on the Left Bank wide tree-lined boulevards linked the Mail de l'Arsenal with the Cours-la-Reine and Champs Elysées. Fashionable society promenaded here as if Paris were already the center of the world. Large squares were planned and built, including the Place Royale and Place Dauphine in Henri IV's time and the Place des Victoires and Place Louis-le-Grand in Louis XIV's reign, and two bridges, the Pont-Marie and Pont-Royal, were built opposite the Tuileries after the Pont Neuf was completed. They were of stone, and the old houses lining the Pont Neuf were demolished to enable traffic to move more easily. The great building program was yet another—perhaps the most important— manifestation of royal power, asserting the supremacy of the King in unambiguous terms. The Palais was the main headquarters of the Administration and Judiciary. The Luxembourg Palace, built between 1615 and 1620, was the embodiment of the Queen Mother's power, Marie de Medici, and her wish to be seen as occupying a modern town residence more in keeping with contemporary taste and more practicable than the old Louvre. Buildings for members of the Royal Family were constructed under the direction of Androuet du Cerceau, Métezeau, Le Mercier and Le Vau. Colbert greatly expanded the whole program after 1661 with the Apollon Gallery with decorations by Le Brun, the Louvre colonnade, the Observatory and the Gobelin tapestry factory, as well as great triumphal arches to the glory of

588

the King. After 1680 money was scarce for use on grandiose schemes but the Dome of the Invalides was erected over the great hospital and home for old soldiers retired from the victorious armies of Louis (by that time he was showing more interest in Versailles).

New churches, convents and hospitals in Paris testified to an energetic program of ecclesiastical activity which came with the Catholic Counter Reformation. The taste was Baroque, sumptuous interiors, altars and huge statuary dominating the naves of new and old churches. It seemed to reflect royalist pretensions. Town houses were increasingly fashionable, built by the *nouveaux riches,* and space for residential expansion was made in the Marais and Ile-Saint-Louis. Speculators moved in and money was made, notably by the leading publisher, Cramoisy and his relatives. The ultimate in fashionable addresses was the Place Royale and houses sprang up with courtyards in front and delightful gardens at the rear, inhabited by the nobility and higher ranks in the Government; families as ancient as Guise or Montmorency, Argenson and Boucherat had their seats in this exclusive district, and gentry of lower rank owned more modest houses or apartments there. The district from the Louvre to St. Eustache and the Hôtel de Soissons was similar, and the vicinity of Rue St. Thomas de Louvre, between the Louvre and the Tuileries, numbered many aristocrats' dwellings, the Maison Rambouillet being the most famous. Richelieu gave this district its distinctive character when he built a large palace and garden on the line of the ancient fortifications, an example followed by other Ministers from Mazarin to La Vrillère, from Lionne to Séguier, from Colbert to Louvois, all of whom took advantage of the cleared site to build their own luxurious mansions in the area today occupied by the Bibliothèque Nationale.

Nor did the Right Bank have a monopoly of new buildings; when the Luxembourg was built the Concini and Condé families, so closely allied to the Queen Mother, built their own magnificent edifices nearby, and the Faubourg St. Germain was divided up after Queen Marguerite's death, when her palace was demolished and on that site more new town houses were built, the best known being Nevers, de

Guénégaud, Conti, Créquy, Lauzun, Morstein and Chamillard, an aristocratic roll of honor to help keep up the tone of
the sector where foreign royals lodged on their way through
Paris.

Apartments and tenements for the increasing population
of bourgeoisie were built at a speed which must have seemed
breathtaking to contemporaries. The actual population is
hard to estimate but it was probably around 550,000, and yet
the large number of booksellers must make us wonder, in an
age when a best-selling title might only manage some scores
of sales in a town of similar size today, what was it about the
readership 300 years ago that ensured such a big market?
One reason is that Paris concentrated its educated and
prosperous classes in a fairly small area, a market readily
accessible and dense. Open the *Almanach Royal* for the year
1705: therein are listed all officers and ranks in society from
least to greatest, from Privy Councillors in the great town
houses, 37 in number, to the Maîtres des Requêtes, an
important court, and we note that they lived either in the
Marais, the St. Germain district or near the Palais-Cardinal,
and there were 88 of them including 21 secretaries, clerks and
bailiffs. There were 164 lawyers in the King's service and
after them come the First President, 9 Vice Presidents, 49
Councillors in the Great Council, the Procurator-General
and his 13 deputies, and ten Secretaries. After them come
the Chancellery officials, and we know from an edict of
March 1704 that no fewer than 340 King's secretaries were
employed at Court.

After the royal officials come the officials connected with
Parlement: 25 Presidents, 181 Councillors, 20 Gens du Roi,
a dozen clerks; the Cour des Comptes has 13 Presidents, 78
Members, two representatives of the King; the Cour des
Aides has 8 Presidents, 43 Members, one Advocate General,
as well as numerous secretaries and clerks. Other Departments of State employed numbers of officials, all living in
Paris whether at the Châtelet, the Hôtel de Ville or in the
intricate network of tax offices. A formidable total, but in
addition there were innumerable petty officials appointed to
administer the law: notaries, agents, brokers, advisers on a
range of subjects, judicial and commercial. There were also

101 doctors of medicine. If we add to the 1,500 civil servants all the many ancillary professions associated with administration, mostly legal, the final figure is about 2,500. This is the most privileged class in Paris and all of them will have of necessity a private library. To this already impressive figure add the many lesser figures on the fringes of the state bureaucracy, plus the vast population of monks and clergy, and the number of potential readers can be seen to be very large. There must have been a vigorous intellectual life.

Education had expanded since 1600, as the *Livre commode des adresses de Paris pour 1692* (by Nicholas Blégny under the pseudonym "Du Pradel") reveals. Under the heading *Première instruction de la jeunesse* (available apparently in all districts of Paris), we learn there was "a master and mistress in charge of the petty schools under the direction of the Precentor of Paris whose responsibility it is to teach children of both sexes the Catechism and prayers, to teach Latin and French and the elements of reading and writing and arithmetic." After this stage children were taught by "experts in Scripture, Spelling and Arithmetic." If they wished to aspire to greater heights, then "In the University and in many suburbs and other districts there are Masters of Arts who will take lessons, hear Latin and Greek repeated and can teach Philosophy and Mathematics." The pages that follow list dozens of such establishments.

The compiler of the *Almanach,* Blégny, was a partisan of the Precentor and no admirer of charity schools, so they are omitted, although the previous fifty years had seen a great many more run by the Sisters of the Infant Jesus, the Brothers of Christian Doctrine, the Daughters of Charity (the Grey Sisters), the Sisters of Martha, the Brothers of St. Antoine and the Tabourin Brothers, with help from the Community of the Holy Sacrament. Elementary education was making great strides.

In the Humanities (Rhetoric and Philosophy) the Collège Louis-le-Grand, administered by Jesuits, was training thousands of students, and colleges under the aegis of the University were reorganized—Harcourt College, Plessis, Navarre, Marche, Montaigu, Lisieux, Beauvais, Cardinal-le-Moine, Grassins and others, and particularly the newly-founded Collège des Quatre-Nations. In addition, the religious Orders had "collegial houses" within the University framework where their novices could study.

In the higher reaches of education, advanced theology was available at Navarre, jurisprudence in the law schools of the Rue St. Jean-de-Beauvais, and medicine in the Collège des Médecins on the Rue de la Bucherie. Nineteen lecturers at the Collège Royal taught Hebrew, Greek, Mathematics, Philosophy, Latin Speaking, Medicine, Surgery, Anatomy, Pharmacy, Botany, Arabic, Syriac and Canon Law, and lessons in surgery, anatomy, chemistry and botany were given in the Royal Gardens; in the Rue des Cordeliers there was a school of surgery. And there were other educational opportunities. Under the heading "Mathematics" Blégny adds: "MM. Cassini, de la Hire, Couplet, Sédillot and Cusset of the Royal Academy of Sciences (with apartments in the Royal Observatory for their astronomical work) are Professors of Mathematics." Other Professors, including Ozanam, Lieutaud and Blégny the Younger, taught at home, and La Hire gave public lectures at the Académie d'Architecture on the art of dressing stone. Although there is no mention of accountancy or book-keeping, there is no doubt they were also taught. The complete education of an "honnête homme" included other subjects and the biggest attraction was the *Nobles exercises pour la belle éducation*. The academies and riding schools offering this well-rounded program had been reduced to two, but "the salaried instructors are generally divided between them" and the teaching included Mathematics, Arms Drill, Horsemanship, and Dancing. There were plenty of dancing masters and drill masters, and history and geography tutors, and language teachers are listed for Italian, Spanish, German, English, Turkish and Arabic; often they were authors of language manuals.

Blégny completes the picture with an account of seminars and meetings: "There is a meeting every evening at M. Ménage's in the Cloisters, Notre Dame, where all kinds of subjects are discussed"; M. de Villevant, Master of Petitions, "welcomes distinguished scholars for debates on a variety of subjects." The Orientalist d'Herbelot arranged meetings of the same kind at 7 o'clock every evening, the Marquis de Dangeau every Tuesday afternoon, abbé de La Roque every Thursday afternoon, and Chassebras de Bréau every Saturday afternoon. The Académie Française met three times a week in the old Louvre and members of the Académie des Sciences every Wednesday and Saturday in the Bibliothèque Royale. The Société Royale de Médecine met every Sunday in Blégny's house, the Académie d'Architecture met every Monday afternoon and the Académie de Peinture et Sculpture had teaching programs. From all this evidence it would seem that intellectual life in late 17th-century Paris was dominated by the official classes, what La Bruyère called "The Town." Churchmen had their own circles, from the scholars of St. Germain-des-Prés to the professors who taught in the Seminaries. Presiding above all was the aristocratic culture of the Royal Court.

The other reference book of the period, *Etat de la France* (3 vols, 1702), gives details of the upper echelons of society and churchmen: noblemen, gentry and clerics in the hierarchy at Versailles, and other dignitaries with their little Courts—Condé at Chantilly, for instance—but many had a place in Paris too, where they would spend much of the year. The capital was in effect draining off the nation's minds, and most of the writers lived there.

2. The Writers

Author-publisher relations afford us insights into the cultural state of that society and the economics which underpinned it. Fewer than two hundred new books were published annually, but they covered a wide range of subjects, each a microcosm. Medicine, to take an example, attracted both genuine practitioners and quacks with specifics for all diseases. The Law included the jurist-theoreticians and practicing magistrates, all busily commenting or refining further on legal precedents. Architects and art historians wrote about their specialist interests, catering to a taste which grew on what it visibly saw being constructed on all sides in Paris. Military engineers wrote textbooks for a more technically-minded army. Geographers, dictionary-compilers, authors of the latest Neo-Latin poetry, mathematicians were all satisfying a market. The technical experts and members of the Académie des Sciences were in the van of progress, extending the frontiers of knowledge in a range of subjects from horticulture to farriery, from cooking to topiary, from accountancy to bridge-building. Of the traditionalists, clergy and laity wrote on their two main subjects as of old, Religion and Literature.

Incredible as it may seem to us today, one of every two authors was in the church, and in the highest ranks: Bossuet, Fléchier, Huet and Fénelon were prelates who succeeded Bérulle, Camus, St. François de Sales and Richelieu, and there was less spirituality and more controversy from their pens. Benedictines of St. Maur were working on the last scholarly editions of the Fathers at the end of the century, and Dominicans and Capuchins were not so prolific. Lamy and Malebranche were the most popular authors, with Maimbourg, Daniel and Bouhours, the Jesuit historians and men of letters. Churchmen in the later period possibly put more effort into pastoral work than into writing, but a new feature was the number of abbés writing, not many for the greater glory of the Church, and their backgrounds were varied. Abbé Dangeau was born a Calvinist and received back into the Church, went on a mission to Poland and was an agent of Pope Clement XI, having spent the early part of his life in the army. He bought himself a post as King's Reader, secured a number of livings and entered the Académie Française. He wrote several textbooks on geography, grammar, spelling, weapons, and almost anything he felt would be useful, a journeyman of letters, dependable when asked for something by his publishers.

Lower down the scale were men like Jacques Testu de Belleval, a Court preacher who rose to be abbé de Belleval and prior of St. Martin, and owed everything to his tact and adaptability. He was a favorite among the Court ladies, from Madame de Sevigné to Madame de Montespan and the Duchesse de Richelieu, and his output was relentlessly pious: Christian poetry, moral tracts, Christian maxims, thoughts on preaching, and a *Lettre escrite à une personne qui, apres avoir longtemps douté sa vocation avait enfin pris la décision de se faire religieuse.* Altogether insipid, he retired but returned to the Court at Versailles hoping for a bishopric, but Louis judged him shrewdly and refused it.

Other clerics owed their success to a talent for preaching; abbés Pure, Cassagnes and Cosin, targets of Boileau's satire, were of that kind. First necessity was to curry favor with a nobleman, then approach the King: Fléchier was successively a private tutor to the Caumartin family, Monausier's retainer, then tutor to the Dauphin, then his chaplain and so on to higher things. Others owed their advancement to extra-ecclesiastical factors. Gaspard Abeille, a gifted conversationalist, acted in and wrote tragedies and was secretary to the Maréchal de Luxembourg; abbé Claude Boyer, a member of the Académie Française, wrote twenty-two plays, though manifestly without talent. Others were adventurers like Charles-Claude Genest, a clerk in Colbert's department who tried his luck in the West Indies, was taken prisoner by the English and became French tutor to an English nobleman; after he was freed, his knowledge of horses helped him to the post of equerry to the Duc de Nevers. He later took holy orders, went to Rome on a mission and when he returned was taken up by notables like Pellisson, Bossuet, Malézieu and Madame de Thianges, de Mortemart and Montespan; he was eventually appointed abbé of St. Vilmier before quitting the Court at Sceaux.

Genest must have been highly intelligent to win the support of Bossuet, but many of the authors-turned-abbés made a respectable reputation simply by writing popular versions of arcane subjects. One Gédéon Pontier was of this breed, his main claim to fame a *Cabinet de la bibliothèque des grands,* a mishmash of truisms. The unfortunate man was bitingly portrayed by La Bruyére:

> He seizes paper and pen without a single thought in his head and says, 'I'm going to write a book.' Mind you, he has no need to write a book apart from the pittance it will bring him. Useless to beg him to take up joinery or be an honest wheelwright because he hasn't served an apprenticeship in any useful art. So let him be a copyist, proof corrector, anything but a writer! No, he

wants to write and publish, and since no one ever sends a blank sheet to the printer's he has to scribble something on it, anything at all: that the River Seine flows through Paris, that there are seven days in the week, that it is raining. And because this was not contrary to public order or religion or to the State (after all, he was only helping to dilute good sense or habituate readers to tasteless trash), the censor passed everything he submitted, it was printed and to the eternal shame of our contemporaries, reprinted!

It would be misleading to take at face value the titles by which lay writers described themselves; better to take a cross-section of general works (i.e., those not dealing with specialist subjects) and trace the careers of their authors. In a random sample of 70 books, 12 of the authors were nobles, 32 lawyers, and seven doctors. The nobles were not writing for gain—La Rochefoucauld, St. Evremond, Bussy- Rabutin—but filling up their idle hours, and their books consequently came out under a pseudonym or without their consent or after their death. The duc de Luynes signed his pious little works "Antoine de Laval," the Marquis de l'Hospital and *grandes dames* who wrote novels were usually discreet about it, though there were bolder spirits, the toast of their giddy set who wrote out of devilment or because it was a talent they wanted to show off: Mme. de Villedieu, the Comtesse d'Aulnoy, the Comtesse de Murat, the Comtesse de La Suze, and Mlle. de La Force.

It was not considered good form at Court to indulge in a literary career, though the Chevalier de Méré put his name to his books about how to acquire social poise. Most writers were from the lesser gentry or the civil service, very often lawyers. Pierre and Thomas Corneille were lawyers; Nicolas and Gilles Boileau were law clerks in the Parlement; La Fontaine followed his father's career as Director of Waters and Forests in Château-Thierry; La Bruyère, like his father, was Collector of Revenues for the city of Paris. Chapelain was a notary's son who hoped to be a doctor; abbé d'Aubignac and Charles Perrault, lawyer's sons. Examples could be multiplied. For most it was a matter of patience, because security meant making a good match or buying a lucrative post; only the most dedicated would not accept that kind of solution, as Racine did not. The Church was another form of insurance if they could find a good living, because it offered them the freedom to write and the possibility of advancement.

Then there were the freebooters, the real men of letters, often connected with the theatre: Noël Lebreton, Sieur de Hauteroche, would not entertain a judicial career but went off to Spain, later joined a theatrical company in the Marais, acted in the Hôtel de Bourgogne and retired in 1684. Dancourt was a lawyer before he went on the stage, married an actress and later began to write plays. In most cases a breakthrough into the literary world was impossible without backing, as in Quinault's case, a baker's son who gained entry to the household of the Duc de Guise through an introduction by his master, and once he made his name married a rich widow, bought himself a post as King's valet de chambre and was made an equerry.

Campistron, another playwright, came from a slightly higher social level, son of a Procurator General, and through Racine was brought to the notice of the Duchesse de Bouillon, dedicated an opera to the Duc de Vendôme and found an assisted passage to the Duke's service as his secretary. Racine's own career is a brilliant illustration of the power of innate talent to carve itself a niche in the most exalted circles, but whether lay or ecclesiastic, writers' lives were very similar, as Claude Fleury's demonstrates. He began as a young lawyer, a conscientious worker welcomed into President Lamoignon's household where he met Bossuet, who recognized sound character and good learning and helped him enter the Church and the Court. He was later a tutor to the Princes of Conti, in place of Lancelot who lost the job because he was unwilling to take his pupils to see comedies. Fleury's career shone ever more brightly when he took over the education of the young comte de Vermandois, the legitimate son of Louis XIV and Mlle. de la Vallière, was made abbé of Loc-Dieu, helped Bossuet to administer his diocese and was nominated Sub-Tutor to the Duc de Bourgogne, which post greatly facilitated his task of writing histories of the church and books about education. He was later confessor to Louis XIV.

These few examples show that abbés or writers all belong
to the same breed, men with a zest for life and able to turn
their experience to good account, doing well with a little
encouragement and patronage. Tutor, secretary, librarian,
any such post was a push in the right direction, and once
ensconced in a great house the vital contacts which ensured
promotion would come. If possible, secure a comfortable
post at Court, by flattery, a dedication, or native ability, get
a church appointment, a place in an Academy or on the
pension list—all were avenues to be explored, essential at a
time when royalties to an author were non-existent. Favor by
an aristocrat (a Condi, a Conté, a Bouillon or Luxembourg)
or the monarch himself was the ultimate objective, the tip of
the tree which grew out of the soil of humiliation. There was
no other source while authors were so little regarded (La
Bruyère witnesses to this); and once again this leads us to
consider the question of authors' rights.

In 1665 booksellers secured rights in the books they
published, and that right could be extended in time. From
then on copyright had a commercial value which was
negotiable, it raised the status of their list and for the first
time made authors think about *their* rights. Hitherto, when
an author brought his manuscript to a bookseller the
risks—according to the bookseller—were all his, and his
likely profits were compromised by the relatively short time
his copyright ran, usually less than ten years. When rights
were granted *in perpetuo,* as the Crown preferred in
pursuance of its policy of tight control, then this reflected on
the author, who saw it as a token of his work's real worth,
and so he would ask a higher price for his manuscript or a
bigger share in the profits, while the bookseller would argue
the hazards he faced and the losses he sustained because of
piracies. Boileau reminds us of this:

> I know a fine spirit without crime or shame
> Whose work a just tribute can earn for his name,
> But puzzled am I by those authors so bold
> Who fight shy of glory and much prefer gold
> —(*Ars poétique,* IV)

That was the view of the traditional high-minded author who thought emoluments vulgar. Here is Guéret in 1669:

> You won't believe how commercially-minded booksellers and playwrights besmirch the honor of the profession. Hardly anyone writes for love of it; money is the mainspring of nearly all the books you see.

In 1699 abbé de Villiers explained how things were:

> Authors think up a title and with nothing more in mind they'll offer it to a bookseller if he will give them money for it. The title will be cunningly devised to have snob appeal which will impress the bookseller. The price is based on the bulkiness of the book: 30 pistoles for a 12mo which will sell for 30 sous. A deal is struck. The bookseller advances money or a promissory note. . . .

The bookseller's point of view is expressed in a pamphlet of 1685 explaining why books published in Paris are dearer than in Lyons:

> In former times authors contributed to the cost of printing from money they earned by way of their pensions or from State subsidies for propaganda work. If they were not able to help with money, at least they did not demand it. Today things are very different: whether from want or greed or some other reason, writing is now just a means to earn a living.

Change was on the way and new techniques in the trade helped it come about. Style was changing from the obscurity and erudition of the past to a clarity and elegance which made French literature a model for other literatures and brought in a wider readership. La Bruyère had many imitators, there was a big rise in novel reading, the cult of the "gentleman" encouraged more curiosity and so wider reading, and the epistolary art flourished as part of the educated person's equipment. More and more people from all walks of life tried writing, and slowly the utility book made its way: information, potted culture, practical manuals were bringing traditional culture to a wide range of people hitherto excluded.

Details of authors' contracts are not easily found but we have some idea of their situation. We know of Pierre Corneille's debts, and that Racine did well from his books. Sometimes an author could make a lot of money—abbé Jean Richard received 16,000 livres for his 6-volume *Discours moraux;* Sacy and his successors earned 33,000 livres for their translation of the Bible; Barbin gave Varillas 1,500 livres for each of the 20 books of his poem *Hérésie* (Varillas boasted of having made 12,000 livres from his booksellers). The huge profits made by booksellers out of Counter Reformation propaganda for converts made authors want to join the lucrative market. Louis Ferrand is such a case. He wrote a Latin paraphrase on the Psalms and copyrighted it, negotiating with Pralard, a bookseller, for a half share on promising to add a French translation. It was agreed that he would not reclaim more than half the profits accruing to him, and either party would accept an extension of the copyright only if profits were shared. In 1685 Pralard received an order for a big consignment of Psalms already translated by Macé, a curé, and Ferrand then hoped to circumvent Pralard by offering 1,000 livres to Lambin to print the Psalms without telling him about his contract with Pralard, and then clinching a deal with yet another bookseller, Léonard, who gave him a lump sum. Both Lambin and Léonard sought a new copyright, which Pralard opposed, but as a result of his sharp practice Ferrand secured a better deal from Pralard which anticipated larger profits:

> We the undersigned have agreed as follows: M. Ferrand and M. Pralard consent to the sharing of the copyright in 'Psalms of David in Latin and French' translated by M. Ferrand, in this wise: M. Ferrand is to have one half of the 10,000 copies printed, and I am to have the other half after the costs of printing, binding and other work has been reimbursed in the sum of 5,463 livres. With regard to the other copies designed for the New Converts, I am to have two-thirds and M. Pralard the remaining one-third. Whatever copies M. Pralard sells to individual customers in his shop or to booksellers in

> the provinces will be shared between us in accordance with the agreement of 1683 made before Langlois and his colleagues. To this M. Pralard agrees and abides by all the above. Signed in duplicate 27 March 1686.

From the bookseller's point of view a hard bargain, but he may have feared he would be excluded from a profitable publishing venture because he was a Jansenist, and he had to keep in mind Ferrand's good standing with the Department of the Privy Seal, an important department of State for a stationer. Another author who made a nice profit from the New Convert propaganda was abbé Martignac, whose surviving contract with Muguet and Pralard shows that one-third of the profits were for him. Thomas Corneille could impose his will on Coignard over the publication of his *Dictionnaire des arts et des sciences* and *Dictionnaire universel géographique et historique* for half the profits. And profits could be large, as in Corneille's case or in Sacy's Bible, but most books were a modest investment from which authors received proportionately modest fees. Playwrights would get more from an actors' company than from publishers—Ribou gave Molière only 2,000 livres for *Tartuffe* and Molière's widow had only 1,500 livres for seven of his plays. La Fontaine received 600 livres for his *Psyché* and Corneille's *Critique du Sertorius* fetched 200 écus in 1663.

Pierre Le Boeuf made his publisher, Nicolas Bessin, promise to pay him 55 livres when half his manuscript was finished, and the same sum for a *Catalogue de diverses sortes de plantes avec quelques observations touchant leur usage.* In 1666 Tallemant sold his translation of Plutarch's *Lives* in 6 volumes, 12mo, for 726 livres, and a little later Thomas Guyot, a college regent, received 2,400 livres payable in 6-monthly installments of 150 livres for his translation of Virgil's *Bucolics,* Plautus's *Captivi,* a new edition of Cicero's *Letters* and a translation of Virgil's *Georgics.* In 1690 Coignard's widow paid André Félibien 1,500 livres for the revision of his book *Principes de l'architecture, peinture et sculpture,* and in 1701 Nicolas de Vaux gave the abbé de Hauteserre 500 livres and 50 copies of his *De jurisdictione eccleisiastica.*

The surviving accounts relating to one particular author, Claude Fleury, tell us a lot about the finances of writing. In 1686 he contracted with his publisher to assign him the copyright of *Traité des études* for 500 livres, 50 copies of the first and second editions, and 100 of the third. The next year he secured the copyright of *Devoirs des maîtres et des domestiques* and *Soldat chrétien,* which the publisher, Aubouin, had bought for 16 livres in the Chancellery. Fleury then made another agreement (he owed the publisher 649 livres, 4 sous) under which he was to receive 300 livres for the first edition of *Devoirs.* On 1 October 1690 Fleury ceded his copyright in the first volume of *Histoire ecclésiastique* in return for the discharge of a debt he owed the publisher—25 écus, 100 vellum copies and 19 bound in morocco. Later Fleury received 100 copies of his next book, *Moeurs des Israelites,* from another publisher, Clousier, plus 200 livres payable six months after publication.

The figures are not so large when we remember how established Fleury was as a writer, but the evidence makes it clear that authors' rights had increased substantially since the position fifty years before. As La Bruyère put it:

> We pay the tiler for tiling a house; we pay a workman for his time and materials; oughtn't we to pay an author for what he thinks and publishes? And if it's good, oughtn't we to pay him handsomely?

Publishers claimed they had to take account of piracies when computing book prices and that kept prices high, while they had no guarantee that their own copyrights would be respected. True enough, any book with sales appeal was liable to piracy by unscrupulous booksellers, and in the words of a document of the time:

> To recoup his outlay on a book the publisher must reason thus: if I were certain that the book would not be pirated and that provincial booksellers would take only my published copies, then I could get rid of 6,000, 8,000 or 10,000 copies and get back 300 or 500 pistoles I paid the author; each book would cost only 10 sols and I could sell it to the public for only 40 sols, but because I

> have to confine my sales to Paris—2,000 or 3,000 at
> most—each copy costs 30 or 40 sols and I have to
> charge 3 livres, 10 sols or 4 livres for a book.

But in fact the commercial morality of publishers, whether
in Paris or the provinces, was no higher than that of their
pirate foes, and the literature of the period is strewn with
references to books published without the author's consent
or manuscripts acquired in underhand fashion. Molière had
to watch the bookseller Jean Ribou very carefully when he
tried to engineer a share in *Précieuses ridicules*—in fact sole
privilege in it. Wealthy writers were prepared to publish at
their own expense, and sometimes authors were directly
concerned in the sale of their books when they espoused a
cause, as the Jansenists did, or took advantage of the right
connections, as Gervais a Capuchin did when he had a
selection of his sermons published at his brother's expense
and sold them to his fellow Capuchins.

A new source of revenue was journalism. Renaudot and
Donneau de Visé must have been sure of regular subscriptions and a clientele when they launched the *Gazette* or
Mercure Galant or *Journal des Savants* without dependence
on bookseller-middlemen. If an author had an eye on a
specific market he would dispense with middlemen and use
street pedlars, as Le Noble did with his pamphlets and news
sheets, or Blégny in his medical journalism and other doctors
and popularizers, Lémery, Thuillier, Pomet, Cusac and
Tardy. This kind of practice was confined to ephemeral
work, but booksellers strongly resisted any infringement of
their sacred rights and would only accept authors' copyrights
if the books were marketed through proper trade channels.
The war against pirates was unending: in 1682 Blégny's
books published over a false imprint ("Widow Pasdeloud")
were seized, and when Le Pelletier sold his *Instructions pour
l'attention de toutes sortes d'expéditions en Cour de Rome*
from home, it was condemned by a decree of the Privy
Council. But the very practices prove a strong wish on the
part of authors to be freed from irksome trade restrictions,
though their hopes were premature. The new practice of
publishers obtaining subscriptions began at about this time,

and some authors who probably thought they could do that as well as their publishers were indignant. Blondel wrote a comment on it in *Mémoire sur les vexations qu'exercent les libraires et les imprimeurs de Paris* (1725) which rails against the baseness of booksellers and asks why authors cannot benefit from the profits of their own work, a campaign which was later brought to a successful conclusion by Diderot.

CHAPTER VIII

ACCESS TO BOOKS

1. The Great Collectors

IN THE NEW TOWN HOUSES built for the prosperous bourgeoisie and aristocrats of Paris, rooms and galleries were planned to house books, either because it was *comme il faut* or from a genuine interest. Books were in fine bindings, chosen with exquisite taste to consort with other objets d'art in the same room, a matter of conspicuous display, socially impressive. Blégny's directory lists 120 "collections of curiosities" and 26 "women of taste," presumably proved by the excellence of their collections. The list includes nobility, businessmen, civil servants and some quite modest citizens, and their specialties were statues, prints, drawings, bronzes, coins, medals and even shells. When books were also present they were there as specimens, but there were many individual libraries—76 in all, totaling 10,000 volumes.

Many libraries have since disappeared or been merged with others, especially scholars' and booklovers' collections belonging to owners not themselves very wealthy. Among the most famous collections were those of Dupuy and Mentel, which went into the Royal Library, and Mazarin, a real bibliophile, bought 10,000 books from Naudé. The Patin, Balesdens and Clément libraries suffered dispersal, as did the famous Petau collection of priceless MSS; Fouquet's was sold after his condemnation, and the Mesgrigny and Molé libraries, too. The de Thou library was sold, the manuscripts to Colbert, the books to Président Ménars. Condé's books were kept in his Paris mansion before being taken to Chantilly, but other

Ministers were not so attached to books: Cardinal Du Camboust de Coislin was so little interested in the splendid legacy inherited from his grandfather Séguier that he let the books go and the manuscripts went to the Royal Library. Le Tellier and Louvois were scarcely booklovers either, but the other Le Tellier, Charles-Maurice, Archbishop of Rheims, published a catalog of the books he possessed, which had come from the Imprimerie Royale, and in 1700 gave most of his manuscripts to the Royal Library. But there was no greater bibliophile than Colbert. His library was already famous in 1662, his objectives threefold: to have copies of unpublished documents of value; to assemble manuscripts and original plays; to buy early printed books from all over Europe. The purpose was to provide a huge resource for statesmen and politicians and be a mine of basic materials for writers. Carcavy was appointed Director, succeeded by Baluze, and Clément and Clairambault were Sub-Librarians, and Colbert watched the progress of his library with keen interest. When he died in 1683 he had amassed a treasure- house which was bought by Louis XV for 300,000 livres.

Ministers, Secretaries of State, Privy Councillors and other officials possessed private libraries, of which the aristocracy of the legal profession, Loménie de Brienne, Boucherat, Foucault, Phélypeaux, Fieubet, Caumartin, Hector de Marle, and Charles Hénault were the most outstanding. President de Harlay collected books, medals and coins in his house in the Cour de Palais, later bequeathed to the Jesuits, and Lamoignon installed a library and a librarian (Baillet) in his great mansion at Angoulême, scene of brilliant gatherings.

The Bignon family was at once more scientific and Cartesian in character and their library in the Rue des Bernardins reflected this. When abbé Jean-Paul Bignon was appointed Head of the Publishing Bureau in the Chancellery he used his position to enrich his collections, sending to Holland for books from all parts of Europe. The de Mesmes family took only a superficial interest in their collection, which was later dispersed in 1706 at the same time as the Bigots' library.

Other notable libraries were those of the Talons, Vyon d'Herouval, relatives of Lamoignon, and Cousin, the scholarly President of the Chambre des Comptes who was ready enough to accept a post as royal censor. And yet others adorned their homes with rich private collections—notably Presidents Dorieux, de la Proutière, Séguin, Tambonneau and Lambert, who figure on the walls of galleries filled with paintings and precious objects.

Of 76 private libraries in Blégny's list, 45 belonged to the aristocracy of the civil service, a tradition which persisted into the 18th century, when the search for manuscripts grew even more difficult and early printed books took their place; hence, at the close of Louis XIV's reign, wealthy people went in for art, retreating from the book as an object for collecting—all this before the age of the "limited edition" (that degenerate form of bibliophily), which had not yet been conceived. Lower down the scale, doctors, lawyers and clerics collected books, drawings and prints, and literary men like Ménage, Justel, Thévenot and Launoy, and journalists Sallo and Jean Gallois looked for novelties. Scholars such as Gaignières, obliged in their research to consult documents, ended by adding relevant works of art or—like Marolles and Rousseau—looking for old master drawings.

In all, the activities of all these collectors were later editions of the old Humanists, and their libraries and galleries are the foundation of our present-day public collections; quite often the manuscripts they acquired ended up in the Royal Library, but more often they went to the libraries of religious orders. Jean de La Haye left 6,000 volumes to the Franciscans, Michel de Masle's and Richelieu's went to the Sorbonne, Henri Du Bouchet's to the St. Victoire abbey, where Tralage's also went. Ménage and Huet sent theirs to the Jesuits, Le Tellier to St. Geneviève and the geographer Baudrand to St. Germain des Prés. Monasteries often had well-appointed rooms to house books, cabinets of coins and medals, and paintings. The Sorbonne had a gallery built in 1648 with a ceiling painted by Sanson Le Tellier, the gallery 38 metres long and 10 metres wide. Mazarin's palace had a sumptuous gallery 58 metres × 10 metres with a high vaulted ceiling famous in its day. The Sorbonne's library room turned out to be too small when Richelieu's books came its way; the Abbey St. Victor had 18,000 books in 1684, St. Geneviève 20,000 books in the late 17th century, and 45,000 thirty years later; the Jacobins in the Rue St. Honoré owned 20,000 volumes in 1727, the Augustinians 18,000 and the Maison Professe of the Jesuits 20,000 in 1721. The totals had grown consistently since Father Jacob compiled his bibliography; books and book collectors had grown considerably between the years 1630 and 1720.

The figures also reveal how the field of knowledge was expanding in all subjects and how difficult it was for a rich man to have all he required. Richelieu may have foreseen this when in his will he gave instructions that his library be made "public," though nothing came of it. Henri Du Bouchet bequeathed his collection to the canons of St. Victor, but with a clause requiring them to make the books available to writers and literary men: they opened the library from 7 to 11 on Monday, Wednesday and Saturday, and 2–5 in the afternoons. The Bibliothèque Mazarine opened for use in 1691 on Monday and Saturday mornings and afternoons in accordance with the Cardinal's wishes, and visiting scholars were allowed access to most private libraries. A new age was dawning.

2. Personal Libraries

As for the lower orders, our information about their reading comes from the inventories made on their decease, as we saw in the earlier chapters of this book, but oddly there is less information in the latter half of the century than the first half, because it was more than ever customary to list only the costlier items, and so we have left to us a deceptive picture when many thousands of commonplace books which formed the real staple of reading matter are unrecorded. The books of most interest to us were dismissed as "a devotional work," "a history," "a comedy," and miscellaneous books were described as "a parcel." Of 49,000 titles mentioned, only 18,500 were given in detail in one extant group of inventories; in a further 100 cases the titles were mere abridgments; hence any conclusions must be tentative.

Below is a table based on the 200 inventories examined:

	0–20 books	*21–100*	*101–500*	*50l–1,000*	*1,000 +*
Ecclesiastics		3(1)*	11(8)	3(3)	2(2)
Artisans, merchants	10(4)	10(2)	2(1)		
Architects, artists	1	3(2)	2(1)		
Citizens	2	7(1)	2(2)		
Notaries	1(1)	2	1(1)		
Lawyers		1	8(8)	3(3)	3(4)
Members of Parliament		4(2)	11(9)	3(3)	
King's secretaries	1	1	2(1)		
Judiciary officials	1	4(1)	2(1)		
Finance officers	3(1)		5(2)	1(1)	
Councillors of State	1(1)	1(1)	4(3)	1(1)	
Gentry	6(4)	15(5)	15(5)	1(1)	5(5)
Court officials		5(1)	4(1)	1(1)	
Others	9(1)	6	4(1)		
Total	**35(12)**	**62(16)**	**73(44)**	**13(13)**	**10(11)**

*The figures in parentheses refer to the 100 inventories described in greater detail.

Apart from churchmen and doctors, the rest are divisible into three main categories: artisans, merchants and citizens; officials; gentry and courtiers. Artisans, merchants or citizens rarely owned more than 100 books, not usually described in detail because of their low value. Officials, Privy Councillors and Members of Parlement had good personal libraries, and—a new development—the nobility and some courtiers had the largest collections.

Let us now look at the works most clearly defined in the 100 inventories, beginning with Religion and primarily the theological works which were prevalent before 1670:

Bible	88
Commentaries	
Maldonado	10
Cornelius a Lapide	5
Jansen	10

Hours	7
Breviaries	21
Missals	8
Offices of the Church	5
Fathers of the Church	
Ambrose (Works)	9
(Life)	2
Athanasius (Works)	8
(Life)	2
Augustine (Works)	43
(Life)	5
Basil (Works)	12
(Life)	2
Bernard (Works)	8
(Life)	4
Clement of Alexandria	0
Cyprian	5
Cyril	4
Gregory the Great	17
Gregory of Naziana	3
Gregory of Nyssa	3
Hilary	4
John Chrysostom (Works)	20
(Life)	10
Jerome	15
Tertullian (Works)	16
(Life)	2
Bibliotheca Patrum	3
Achery, *Spicilegium*	5
Josephus	39
Nicephoros	6
Zonaras	6
Eusebius	10
Baronius	20
Aquinas	18
Bellarmine	13
Becanus	7

The Bible is much more in evidence than it ever was in the early 17th century and it was not uncommon to own more than one copy, which might be the Vulgate, the Paris or London Polyglots, or new translations, usually the Jansenist from Port-Royal. The Fathers were in quarto or octavo formats and in French, very different from the great folios in Latin or Greek which typified the early 17th century. The large number of Aquinas's works is due to a revival of

Thomism; the Neo-Thomists and Ultramontane partisans of the Counter Reformation have entirely disappeared. France has become thoroughly Gallican. The table below lists more recent theology and church history as well as traditional Gallican works:

Chronologies	28
Histories of the Popes	16
Histories of the Council of Trent	29
Maimbourg, *History of Heresies*	33
Recent ecclesiastical history	37
Pragmatique Sanction	7
Traité des libertés de l'Eglise gallicane	19
St. Marthe. *Gallia Christiana*	4
Official publications of the Clergé de France	10
Mémoires issued by the Clergé de France	7
Theological treatises	13
Petau	5
Thomassin	15
Apologetics	14
Bossuet	30
Fénelon	9
Richard Simon	10
Jansen, *Augustine*	5
St. Cyran	18
Arnauld	35
Arnauld d'Andilly, *Lettres*	5
Nicole	21
Pascal	16
St. Amour, *Journal*	5

The obvious feature is the rapid spread of books by recent French theologians, particularly Maimbourg and Bossuet, who were fashionable, and of course the Jansenist classics are well represented.

Devotional Literature and the Spiritual Life

Lives of saints	30
Lives of the Fathers	11
L'imitation de Jésus Christ	16
Denis the Carthusian	5

Luis de Granada	24
La Puente	8
Rodriguez	8
St. François de Sales	17
Caussin	14
St. Jure	5
St. Teresa	15
Life of Jesus	11
Lives of individual saints	41
Senault	6
Prayers for Holy Week	15
Année chrétienne	16
Année sainte	5
Moral theology	13
Catechisms	13
Beuvelet, *Méditations, Instructions*	6
Singlin, *Instruction chrétienne*	9

Lives of the saints and of the Fathers are still the favorites but there is more interest in modern biographies than in traditional hagiography. Luis de Granada, Teresa, and the *Imitation* were still an influence, but it is under a new, Jansenist impulsion because the writers just cited were translated into French at Port-Royal and widely distributed from there. In many of the inventories there was strong Jansenist bias, and in the parcels described as "devotional books" there was a great quantity of religious matter.

Greek and Latin Classics

Aristophanes	5	Aesop	7
Aristotle	39	Herodotus	17
Catullus	5	Hippocrates	6
Caesar	13	Homer	11
Cicero	39	Horace	23
Demosthenes	12	Juvenal	11
Diodorus Siculus	7	Livy	26
Lucian	11	Lucan	7
Martial	11	Sallust	3
Ovid	22	Seneca	32
Petronius	11	Suetonius	7
Plato	9	Tacitus	21
Plautus	12	Terence	17
Pliny	21	Thucydides	14
Plutarch	28	Virgil	27
Polybius	8	Xenophon	7
Quintilian	7		

Plutarch, Seneca and Cicero were still in the lead, followed by the historians and then the poets. Classical culture was a close second to Christianity, and, as the next table shows, philosophy, both ancient and (increasingly) modern:

Aristotle	39
Plato	9
Philosophical studies (various)	14
La Chambre, *Caractère des passions*	7
Gassendi	6
Descartes	25
Rohault	9
Malebranche, *Recherche de la Vérité*	8

Science was represented by these categories:

Agronomy	5
Botany	15
Zoology	8
Pharmacopeias	8
Geography	15
Atlases	23
Architecture	31
Fortification	13
Philostratus' Tables	19
Bosio, *Roma subterranea*	10
Commercial arithmetic	7
Geometry	9

Botany and pharmacy were the new sciences, and there was interest in the many new manuals of geometry and arithmetic.

General and National History

Davity	17
Ancient history and annals	21
Pasquier	23
Serres	9
Dupleix	12
Du Chesne	10
Mézeray	28
Daniel	4

Histories by Reign

Charles VI	10
Charles VII	4
Louis XI	5
Charles VIII	5
Charles IX	5
History of the dispute between Boniface VIII and Philip the Fair	9
Maimbourg, *History of heresies*	33
Varillas	14
Aubigné	6
Davila	26
Thou	20
Godefroy, *Cérémonial*	11
St. Marthe, *Histoire générale de la France*	13
Vulson de la Colombière	6

Mémoires

Froissart	7
Commines	10
Du Bellay	5
Castelnau	7

Local History

Paris	18
Burgundy	9
Brittany	8
Provence	6

Letters

Ossat	9
Du Perron	8

Biographies

Montmorency	5
Turenne	5
Richelieu	20
Mazarin	6
Coligny	9

Politics

Machiavelli	8
Bodin	10
Grotius	10
Le Bret	8
Campanella	3
Silhon	5
Marca	5
Geography	15
Atlases	23
Ancient history	28

History and Geography of Foreign Countries

Holy Roman Empire	10
England	23
Spain	26
Netherlands	33
Italy	37
Malta	10
Peloponnese	5
Moscow	5
Turkey	59

Voyages and Travels

General collections	35
Africa	11
Far East	29
America	6

The taste for history was widespread, a by-product of the global exploration of the time as European powers contended for new territories overseas. Local, national, monarchical history, and biographies of eminent persons were all part of a thirst to understand the expanding world. Note the many owners of atlases, mainly the great Dutch ones, by Ortelius, Hondius or Blaeu, the great interest in the Far East, in Turkey and in North America.

We have already noticed the phenomena of periodicals, yearbooks and dictionaries, the materials of a small reference library. The table below shows their distribution:

Dictionaries

Vaugelas, *Remarques sur la langue française*	7
Ménage, *Dictionnaire étymologique de la langue française*	7
Richelet, *Dictionnaire français*	5
Furetière, *Dictionnaire universel*	6
Moreri, *Le grand dictionnaire historique*	19
Bayle's Dictionary	8
Dictionnaire de l'Académie Française	5
Du Cange	8
Dictionnaire français-latin-grec	35

Periodicals

Journal des Savants	11
République des Lettres	7
Ouvrages des Savants	8
Bibliothèque universelle	7
Mercure français	7
Mercure galant	7
Etat de la France	10

In the table below grammars and dictionaries are grouped with the works they helped people read, by language:

Spanish

Dictionaries and grammars	5
Cervantes	1
Góngora	1
Lazarillo de Tormes	1
Quevedo	1
Montemayor	1
Unspecified "parcels"	3

Italian

Dictionaries and grammars	18
Petrarch	7
Boccaccio	4
Castiglione, *Cortegiano*	1
Ariosto	12
Tasso	7
Marini	4
Unspecified "parcels"	11

German

Dictionaries	7
Unspecified "parcels"	3

English

Various	2
Unspecified "parcels"	1

Italian was of more interest than Spanish, and German shows an increased readership.

The final table shows the relative popularity of French writers:

Guez de Balzac	16
Boileau	5
Corneille	17
Desmarets de St. Sorlin	13
La Bruyère	6
La Calprenède	10
La Fontaine	12
La Mothe le Vayer	13
Le Moyne	6
Le Noble	9
Marolles	8
Molière	15
Life of	2
Racine	6
St. Evremond	6
Scudéry	10
d'Urfé	5
Voiture	8
Pleas	21
Parcels of stories	20
Parcels of funeral orations	4
Parcels of comedies	9

A much larger crop of native writers than in the period 1600–1660; the classical French critics and writers are in the collections of all social classes, with Molière and Racine in the lead. And in those "parcels" there must have been many novels.

Libraries differed in content and size. Commeau, a lawyer, had 3,500 books in 1685, including nearly 1,200 folios and more than 1,000 quartos, total value 2,422 livres 5 sols, a great proportion of his wealth. He had 340 folios of theology and church history, and several Bibles including the Paris Polyglot, the Latin Bible published by the Imprimerie Royal, and English translations. He had Toledo, Maldonado and Estius's commentaries; a complete set of the Fathers and the *Maxima Bibliotheca Patrum* (Lyons, Anisson, 1677); a set of the Church Councils and the Louvre Byzantine edition of the Greek Fathers; Eusebius, Josephus, Baronius's *Annales*, the *Annales Cisterciennes*, the *Bibliotheca Praemonstratensis*, *Gallia Christiana*, *Acta sanctorum*, *Ordinis sancti Benedicti*, and Labbe's *Chronologie*. Other huge tomes were the *Annales ecclesiastici Francorum*, the *Mémoires* and *Procès-Verbaux des Assemblées du Clergé de France*, St. Cyran's works and St. Amour's *Journal*. The Fathers were also in quarto, and so was d'Achery's *Spicilegium*. Amelote's translation of the New Testament, Baluze and Jean de Launoy's works were in octavo and 12mo. A heavily traditional collection with little devotional literature: Caussin's *Cour sainte* in the folios, 10 volumes of Luis de Granada and St. Cyran's Letters in a parcel which may have contained other spiritual books.

The law was Commeau's special concern: 1,200 law books, 449 folios and 420 quartos, including such choice sets as Antonio Agustin's *Antiquae collectiones Decretalium* and *Epitome juris pontificii, De concordia sacerdotii et Imperii, Pragmatique Sanction* and Barbosa's *Libertés de l'Eglise gallicane* in the field of Canon Law. In Civil Law he had Godefroy's *Corpus juris civilis,* Azon's *Somme,* Guy Pape's *Decisiones* and standard authorities like Alciat and Cujas. A host of other names testified to the completeness of this personal library—Choppin, Tiraqueau, Coquille, Peleus, Charondas Le Caron, Le Bret, Loyseau, Bacquet, Bernard Automne, and Joly's *Conférences des ordonnances,* Néron's *Edicts et ordonnances des très-chretiennes roys* and many collections of decrees.

Non-ecclesiastical history accounted for 750 volumes, 200 folios, the rest in quarto. Greek, Latin and Byzantine historians, histories of England, Flanders, all the major French historians (de Thou, Davila), genealogists and local historians. Very little travel. Philosophy and Humanists were not much in evidence: the standard classical authors with Petrarch, Marsilio Ficino, Justus Lipsius and Gassendi. Medicine and natural science were reasonably well represented, with Hippocrates and Galen, Dioscorides, Cardan, Du Laurens, Agricola's *De re metallica,* Scaliger's *De causis planetarum,* Caesius's *De mineralibus,* Ptolemy, Morin's *Astrologia gallica,* a trigonometry, and Blondel's textbook on architecture.

This was the complete traditional library of a supporter of the status quo. He had what the well-equipped jurist would need to have, even the profusion of local histories being probably related to their customaries. Not the slightest interest in literature—for this literal-minded pedant the imagination was probably a snare, and contemporary writers did not exist. His library could as easily have been for a jurist of fifty years earlier.

Another big library, different from Commeau's, was that of Toussaint Rose, marquis de Coye, King's Councillor, Secretary to His Majesty's Cabinet. Bibles he had but no commentaries; no Fathers and no theology. A *Vie des saints, Imitation, Cour sainte,* and Madame Hélyot's *Vie des Pères hermites* and a parcel of devotional books. Religious history included Josephus, the General Councils, the Louvre Byzantine, Pallavicino's *History of the Council of Trent,* Maimbourg's *Hérésies.* In Canon Law, the *Corpus juris civilis* and standard works on feudalism, customaries and royal legislation, Grotius's *De jure belli.* There was a great deal of history: Belleforest, Mézeray, de Thou, Davila, Chalcondyle's *Histoire des Turcs,* Du Chesne's *Histoire d'Angleterre,* and a lot of genealogy.

He had some architecture, Fournier's *Hydrographie,* Bosio's *Roma subterranea,* natural histories of plants, Bauderon's *Pharmacopée,* thirty volumes of medicine, atlases, travels, a Koran in Arabic, some modern philosophy—Gassendi, La Chambre, Rohault, Bacon and Galileo.

What gives his library an individual look is the literary component: Erasmus' *Adages,* Ronsard, Du Bartas, Balzac,

Ménage's *Origine de la langue française, Fables choisies* (which could be La Fontaine's), Desmarets' *Clovis* and *Ariane,* La Mesnardière's *Poétique,* nine volumes of *Palmerin d'Olive* and three parcels of "stories." He was evidently a literary student because he had sets of the *Mercure galant, Mercure hollandais, Orlando inamorato,* Gongora, Spanish comedies and other Spanish and Italian books. A much more eclectic collector than Commeau and more interested in the contemporary scene.

A final example from the major private libraries: the Comte de Morstein, a Senator and Grand Treasurer of Poland. He had several Bibles including Le Jay's Polyglot but no commentaries, Isaac La Peyrère on the Pre-Adamites; Richard Simon's critical works on the Old and New Testaments; Augustine alone of the Fathers, a *Vie des saints, Guide des pêcheurs, Introduction à la vie dévote,* La Puente, François de Sales, lives of Vincent de Paul, St. Catherine of Bologna. A little theology: Thomassin's *Traité des fêtes* and Huet's *Demonstratio evangelica.* Church history: the Louvre Byzantine, *Gallia Christiana,* Burnet's history of the Anglican church, Bossuet, the *Provinciales* and the *Morale des Jésuites.* On law, only Grotius' *De jure belli.* A good deal of literature: Boileau, Petrarch, and Tristan l'Hermite, Boccaccio, Tasso, Della Crusca's dictionary, *Astrée,* Scudéry's *Almahide,* and eleven "comedies" unnamed. A great many scientific works, natural histories in French and other languages, Bochart, Malpighi, Dodart, Perrault, Alsted's *Encyclopedia scienciarum,* Lémery's *Chimie* and books on mathematics. Aristotle, Hobbes, Gassendi, twelve volumes of Descartes and Spinoza's *Tractatus varii* made up the philosophy.

History was well represented: Davila, de Thou and all the major French historians, and histories of other countries (but no local history), sixteen volumes of pamphlets, works on heraldry, genealogy, numismatics. Blaeu's atlas was there with other maps, the Elzevier "République" series about various countries, Dapper's books on exotic lands in Africa, China, America and, nearer home, Hungary and Spain. At his home in Montrouge he had beautiful gardens and his esthetic interests are clearly brought out in such bibliographical treasures as the *Tableaux de platte peinture,* Thibault's *Académie de l'épée,* Marolles's *Temple des Muses,* Valdor's *Triomphes de Louis XIII,* the Entry of the King and Queen into Paris in 1660, and albums based on the Cabinet du Roi. He had a large collection of prints depicting Rome, engravings by Dürer and Lucas van Leyden, Teniers' *Théâtre des peintures,* da Vinci's *Della pittura,* an Alberti, and de Félibien's *Entretiens sur les vies et les ouvrages des plus excellens peintres.* He also had studies of architecture: Vitruvius, Androuet Du Cerceau, Le Muet, Marot and others, the *Academia tedesca della architectura, scultura et pittura* by Joachim von Sandrart, and treatises on fortification. Views of palaces, gardens, topographies by Blaeu and Mérian, the works of Silvestre and Pérelle, albums of decorative designs, of fountains, foliage, paneling, grotesques, carriages, urns, epitaphs, flowers, goldsmiths' patterns, scrolls, fireplaces, portraits which must have enhanced the appearance of his library room. Here, clearly, was a collector the very antithesis of dull old Commeau.

Other personal libraries were not so extensive. Charles Amelot (1694) was an abbé and prior of St. Trinité at Beaumont-le-Roger. Among his 500 books were several Bibles, breviaries, many folio volumes of the Fathers, theology including Maldonado's *De sacramentis,* Petau and Morin. Father Labbe's edition of the Councils and a history of the Council of Trent were alongside Church history which included Baronius, Dupuy's history of the Boniface-Philippe le Bel dispute, the *Libertés de l'Eglise gallicane* and Father Alexandre's *Histoire ecclésiastique.* His devotional material included de Sales, St. Teresa, Luis de Granada's *Mémorial* and *Guide des pêcheurs,* Nouet's *Méditations,* and lives of Thomas à Becket and Cardinal Commandon. He had a history of the Jesuits, Hermant's lives of the Fathers and "all the works of Port-Royal." He had an *Iliad,* a Virgil, a Juvenal, a Terence, Seneca, Lucian (in translation), Cicero's *De officiis,* Propertius and Xenophon. In his library stood two large globes (one by Coronelli) and "27 maps on taffeta," and he had a history of Mexico and travel book on Siam. Perhaps the most personal touch was a group of books which betray a peculiar interest—Bourju's *Cours de philoso-*

phie, Bodin's *République,* Machiavelli's *Prince,* Balzac's *Prince,* Fontenelles's *Lettres diverses de M. le chevalier d'Her* . . . and fifteen volumes of the annual *Etat de la France.*

That library makes an interesting contrast to Joseph Petit's, a curé in the parish of St. Roch who had the same number of books. Jean de la Haye's translation of the Bible, a complete collection of the Fathers, Perron's *Histoire évangelique,* various commentaries on Scripture, Richard Simon's *Réponse aux théologiens de Hollande, Corpus juris canonici,* Fleury's *Institution du droit ecclésiastique* and the works of Thomassin were the foundation of his theological library. More recent theology included the Jansenist *Augustinus,* St. Cyran's *Instruction chrétienne,* Neercassel's *Amour pénitent,* Chamillard's *Défense des religieuses de Port-Royal.* Other polemics were Rancé's *Conduite chrétienne* and Bossuet's militant tracts. Petit was devout, to judge by his big collection of spiritual books—the *Introduction à la vie dévote,* St. Jure's *Homme spirituel,* Letourneux's *Année sainte,* and lives of saints. Manuals on consolation for the sick and dying remind us that he was a busy parish priest, and he offered advice to women for he had Fénelon's *Education des filles* and *Devoirs des maîtres et des domestiques* by Fleury. His piety on the whole had a marked Jansenist tinge.

He was not strong on secular literature: a Logic, a Greek grammar, Italian and Spanish grammars, a treatise on the sphere and another on manners and courtesy, Amelot's *Homme de cour,* and some books on teaching. He did possess Descartes's *Passions de l'âme* and Huet's *Censura philosophiae cartesianae,* and a work on metaphysics, which betokens an interest in contemporary thought. The collection indicates a man of evangelistic temperament whom one might expect to be drawn to the Jansenist school, and of a liberal tendency reflected in a wide choice of reading within the religious framework of his age. Not at all unusual.

Now for a typical member of the officer class, Louis de Lapara, Lieutenant General, Governor of Montdauphin and Chevalier of the Order of St. Louis. History and geography are his subjects. He had Moreri's Dictionary and Davity's

Etats et empires, a short history of Louis XII's reign, two histories of Holland, one of Germany, La Croix's *Etat présent de l'Empire ottoman,* a great many memoirs, especially of the late Wars of Religion, and biographies of the Duc d'Epernon, the Duc d'Alba, the Duc de Guise, Queen Elizabeth I of England, Richelieu, Mazarin, Condé and William of Orange. He had a few pamphlets, Le Noble's *Esprit de Gerson* and the annual *Etat de la France.*

We see here the military man puffed up with *la gloire* and narratives of Louis XIV's victories, sieges, plans of fortresses, Freitag, Blondel and Vauban's books on fortification and geometry for engineers. He also had a *Description de la Morée,* a travel book about the East, Petronius and Theophrastus, Le Noble's *Ecole des sages,* Sir William Temple's works, Machiavelli, Boursault's *Lettres,* Rabelais, La Fontaine, *Télémaque* and St. Evremond's works. A varied collection with very little on religion, except Le Noble's *Dissertation sur la date de naissance de Jésus Christ* and *Sources de dévotion.*

A very individual library such as many of his rank and profession had, for example the Comte de Mélingue who died of wounds at Malaga in 1704 and left Cicero's *Letters,* a translation of Petronius, Montaigne's *Essays,* little books on morals and history, Richelieu's *Testament politique,* Fontenelle's *Dialogues sur la pluralité des mondes,* Lucretius's *De rerum natura,* a life of Mahomet, Tasso's *Aminta,* a biography of Queen Elizabeth and lives of various painters. The Comte was indubitably an "honnête homme."

Finally, two lawyers: René-Roland Le Vayer, Seigneur de Boutigny et de la Chevalrie, a member of the Parlement and of a family well known in France (the one La Mothe Le Vayer belonged to), and Toussaint Fournier, Sieur de Morlat. First, Le Vayer.

He had 600 books, 150 of them folios, all of them listed in detail. Nearly half were law books but few were on Roman law. There were several editions of the *Corpus juris civilis,* Theodosius's Code, Cujas and Mornac's commentaries, not much Canon Law, a Dictionary of Civil and Canonical practice, and a work on ecclesiastical emoluments. He had a large collection of customaries, decrees, ordinances and pleas (notably those of Patru, Le Maistre, Marion and Expilly), in fact a strictly technical library quite unlike lawyers' collections in the earlier part of the century. And it was the same for religion: no traditional commentaries on the Bible, no theology but an arsenal of Bibles, a Louvre quarto, Vitré's 7-volume translation, Sacy's 10-volume translation, Royaumont's Bible, Le Bret's *Histoire de l'Ancien et Nouveau Testament.* Letourneux's *Année chrétienne;* Precepts on the Christian life, a Martyrology, Pascal's *Provinciales* and *Pensées,* and a new book by Abbadie. Otherwise there were only a few traditional spiritual works, the *Imitation,* Luis de Granada's Catechism and Caussin's *Cour sainte.* He had some Church history: two histories of the Council of Trent by Sarpi and Pierre d'Orléans' *Histoire des révolutions d'Angleterre,* with Leti's *Nipotismo di Roma* and a history of the Crusades. Secular history included histories of France, Strada's *Histoire de la guerre de Flandres,* a history of Holland, and biographies of Elizabeth I of England, Charles V, Turenne, 18 volumes of Varillas, a life of Richelieu and his *Mémoires* and *Testament.*

Geography was among his interests. He had maps by Sanson, Ortelius' *Theatrum orbis terrarum,* Fournier's *Hydrographie,* and accounts of voyages to America, Africa and China (in this he was typical of his time). Once again there is an individual quality about his books: Erasmus, Montaigne, Grotius's *De jure belli ac pacis,* La Mothe Le Vayer, Cyrano de Bergerac, Cureau de la Chambre, St. Evremond, a book about the Sybilline oracles, Guy Patin's letters and some bound volumes of the *Journal des Savants.* In pure literature he was well supplied: Montemayor's *Diana, Lazarillo de Tormes,* Petrarch's works, Boccaccio, Ariosto, Boccalini, Malherbe, La Fontaine, Scarron and the *Virgile travesti,* novels including *Clélie* and *Télémaque,* grammars, La Fontaine's *Fables,* Corneille and Molière.

This lawyer came from a literary background, so it is not surprising to see such a good selection of belles-lettres or to note that his taste is very like that of men in public life who were seen as models of general culture, a feature of social life now important in Paris society but not reflected in Commeau's library, which had all the hallmarks of a bygone age.

Toussaint Fournier had but few books, fewer than 200, nearly all in a pocket-sized format, though with a number of folios, chiefly law textbooks by Cujas, Bacquet and Du Moulin. He owned Pasquier's *Recherches de la France,* Cardinal d'Ossat's *Lettres,* Guicciardini's *Histoire d'Italie,* Bodin's *République,* Descartes's *Homme,* Justus Lipsius's *Politique,* a travel book about Jerusalem, Godefroy's *Cérémonial,* Du Perron's *Ambassades* and oddly enough, some books in German. Among the small-sized books were a *Loi des douze tables,* Justinian's *Institutes, Paratitla in IX Codicis Justiniani,* a Paris customary, a book on money, an Edict on Waters and Forests, Le Bret on Jurisprudence, a Hippocrates, Horace, Plutarch, Suetonius, a Greek and Latin dictionary, a French grammar, a book on horse riding, Las Casas' *Découverte des Indes occidentales,* Melanchthon's *Chronicles,* two issues of the *Mercure galant,* Bassompière's *Mémoires,* Aimoin's *De gestis Francorum,* books on politics, Bacon, Machiavelli, Méré's *Conversations,* St. Réal's *Césarion,* a life of Molière (possibly Grimarest's), Desmarets's *Alaric,* Bordelon's *Remarques ou Réflexions critiques, morales et historiques sur les plus belles . . . pensées . . . des auteurs anciens et modernes* and his *Belle éducation.*

He had little relating to orthodox religion: an Old Testament, a history of the Council of Trent, Labbe's chronology and Abbadie's *Vérité de la réligion chrétienne,* which suggests a modern, secular man with close interests in new thought.

The libraries of the people we have just described belonged to men of rank and privilege, and were created in a more or less structured way; but now let us glance at some tiny collections with just a handful of books. Firstly, someone who was positively of the upper class, the Marquis de Vilette, a Lieutenant General of Marines. His books were all in a small room (his dressing room) adjoining his wife's bedroom, and we find there Bayle's Dictionary, a book about plants,

Sully's *Mémoires,* a treatise on War, Descartes's *Des météores,* vol. 1 of Sacy's Bible, and seven 12mo volumes of devotions. They might all have been just a selection from his grand country house to ornament a room in his Paris residence or provide bedside reading.

Antoine Hurlon, Sieur de Pennemont was a Gentleman in Ordinary to the King and an important person, but he too could muster only one book at his Paris address: an illustrated *Histoire du Vieux et du Nouveau Testament.* Charles-Hilaire Piet, Seigneur de Beaurepaire, had only one Bible and two parts of Davity's *Etats et empires du monde;* and lower down the social ladder, Guillaume de Riberolles had a book by Furetière, Moreri's dictionaries, Pomet's *Histoire générale des drogues,* a Pliny and a portfolio of the *Entrée triomphante du Roi.*

In the often small collections belonging to women there was almost invariably a number of devotional books. Charlotte de Nonpar de Caumont La Force, wife of Gabriel, Comte de Lauzun, had Godeau's New Testament, the *Imitation,* the Psalms, a work on Dying, and two books of Hours. Marguerite Archambault possessed the *Fleurs des saints* in two folios, Bernières-Louvigny's *Chrétien intérieur,* an *Explication des cérémonies de la messe* and fifteen other little books of piety including one on how to prepare for death. And we have evidence from other inventories that women's collections were of this kind as a rule; e.g., Elisabeth Rousseau, Marie Herbin (Jean-Baptiste Chevallier's wife), Germaine Crouzet, wife of a Paris citizen, Guillaume Riche.

Three citizens have also left evidence of their personal taste, which proved to be devotional with a leaning towards history; their names: Charles Santeuil, Jérome Esnault and Martin Le Jumentier. A bonnet-maker, Claude Labbe, read Pliny, Tacitus, Josephus and some history; Claude Artus, a watchmaker, had 35 "little books," mostly "stories"; Lecoeur, a wine merchant, had a slightly bigger library—four folios, a *Fleur des saints,* a Bible, a Roman history and Royal Ordinances, and 34 "little books on different subjects, mostly devotional." Marguerite Bain, wife of a grocer,

Philippe Andrieux, owned thirty books "of different sizes, history and devotional books bound in vellum and calf."

Etienne Fromager, a master painter and gilder, had "twenty books of different sizes, some in calf, some vellum, mostly devotions and history of design"; Marie Loppin, wife of a painter and varnisher, left a "walnut shelf with two devotional books worth 40 sols"; Anne Fontaine, wife of a wine merchant and master sculptor, "a small cupboard with two glass panels and a carved bracket, containing 23 books in a variety of subjects, worth 15 livres"; Anne Deperroy, wife of a gilder, "seven volumes in quarto and 12mo vellum covered, mostly old devotional books, and a *Vie des saints* in two volumes, worn."

People of the artisan class, it would seem from our evidence, were of marked piety when they were book-owners, but on the whole, master tradesmen and merchants did not go in for books.

3. *Other Sources*

In some classes of society books were conspicuous by their absence, notably among the older aristocracy (who may have admitted a few bookshelves just for show), petty officials, and tradesmen, but it is futile to be definite about a subject which only yields us partial evidence. Some very famous people who certainly had personal libraries have left no trace of them, and in the humbler classes wills did not always survive—in any case they frequently left no wills. If we want a real picture of popular culture, the culture based on ballads, street literature, romances, almanacs and tracts of the kind distributed by the thousands in the parishes, we have to look elsewhere. Ephemeral printed matter of the cheapest, most disposable kind was appearing day by day while those ponderous folios were being turned by the learned and professional classes, and to understand its place in French history and society in the 17th century then we must find out as much as we can about it.

A synodal Statute from Châlons-sur-Marne lists the manuals priests were supposed to have, and throws light on what must have been daily practice in many parishes all over France. The priest should be equipped with: Molina's *Instruction des prêtres,* a *Vie des saints,* Granada's *Guide des pêcheurs,* Beuvelet's *Méditations,* John Chrysostom's work about the priesthood, the *Imitation* in Latin, de Sales's *Introduction à la vie dévote* and a good Ceremonial, say the *Missionaire oratoire.* It is laid down that those who cannot give out copies to parishioners must give alms to the poor. Priests were expected to meditate on Beuvelet's words or La Puente, Granada or Busée when rising or on going to bed, to say the catechism at eight or the Exhortations for the following Sunday, and to study cases of conscience in "Toledo, Navarre, Binsfeld, Bonald and Du Metz." At four in the afternoon they were to continue their morning studies or open a book of devotions. The bishop also stipulated that "parishioners should at all times have in their houses, wherever someone can read, a catechism, a life of saints, Granada's *Guide des pêcheurs, Bon Laboureur, Pédagogue chrétien,* the *Imitation,* de Sales's Conduct of Confession and Communion, and the little book called *Pensés-y-bien.* Any or all of these can be read to the family at least on Sundays and Feast Days with attention and devotion."

Further, he adds, "Insure that there is a book of piety in every house in the parish, in the vulgar tongue (the titles given above are perfectly suitable), which can be read in the church porch every Sunday and on Feast Days after Vespers or at some suitable time of day for a quarter of an hour by the schoolmaster or devout person. As your judgment permits, you could even enjoin your communicants—those who can read—to buy copies of the undermentioned books as an act of penitence." Beneath is a summary list of approved books: "A small library of books for ecclesiastics published by Jacques Seneuze, printer to the Bishop, at reasonable prices." Another bookseller, Thierry, had leaflets printed advertising new books, particularly Sermons. We know that M. Olier, curé of St. Sulpice, had set up a small bookstall near his church door to sell books which will answer Protestants, atheists and freethinkers, "hoping that where once superstitious books and magic were sold, everyone might find a remedy for poisonous doctrines and a preservative against vice" (*Life of M. Olier*). He was careful to examine the books he offered for sale, "to make sure they did not contain anything contrary to faith or morals." In 1672 Muguet published an *Avis donnez aux confesseurs par St. Charles Borromée, archevèque de Milan, imprimez par le commandement de Monsoigneur l'archevèque de Paris pour les missionaires de son diocèse* which is a most astonishing document. It instructs priests to keep a register on cards, one for each family, arranged by district, street and signboard, with information as to how often "each parishioner reads his devotional books; it should preferably be every day but at least on Sundays and Feast Days." This is very like proof that the reading of approved literature was incumbent on all the faithful.

So much for prescribed piety. What of the street literature carried in colporteurs' packs, both official and illicit? Troyes was the town which produced most of it, beginning with Nicolas Oudot, who reprinted cheap copies of the old fairy tales and Gothic romances of chivalry dating back to the 15th century and earlier, using battered woodcuts. His business prospered and he had many imitators in Troyes, Normandy and Lyons after 1660. No trouble finding clients in country or city, because pedlars visited hamlets and cottages, and on the bridges and streets of Paris a roaring trade was done. We know from the evidence of leaflets surviving from the time of the Fronde uprising that they were in great demand in Paris, where booksellers kept in close contact with the street literature specialists of Troyes—witness the quantities of material published by Oudot. They put out a New Testament under Promé's imprint in 1628 and a yearly almanac of Commelet's, then under Gervais Clousier's imprint, the *Nouveau et parfait mareschal royal* (1655), a regular feature of their "Bibliotheque Bleue," and in 1657 the *Voyages et observations du Sieur de La Boullaye Le Goux*, the *Voyages du Sieur Vincent Le Blanc* (1658) and *Mihi et musis— Geographie historique unique et particulière*. The Oudots also published a Rouen edition (1660) of ten volumes of *Cassandra* for Courbé, *l'Histoire de la grande isle de Madagascar* for

Pierre Bienfait, and either in association with Antoine Raffle or on his behalf, the *Apothicaire charitable* by Guybert, the *Bastiment des receptes* and a *Grande Bible des Noels tant vieils que nouveaux.*

Such titles are proof that some of Paris's leading booksellers were closely associated with printers who were in the street pedlar trade; there is no doubt that the latters' publications did a brisk business in Paris, and furthermore Nicolas Oudot, son of the Troyes printer of the same name, was apprenticed to Sommaville on 8 October 1659 and was made free on 25 November 1664. On the 29 January following he was registered as a master printer and announced his marriage to Promé's widow, who was in business at the beginning of the 18th century distributing the little blue books from her shop in the Rue de la Vieille Boucherie, all from the presses of her brothers Jean and Jacques at Troyes.

More evidence comes from the Febvre family, their colleagues and compatriots. Claude, son of Jacques Febvre, in business from 1621 to 1649, worked for eleven years with Jean Hénault before taking over from his father, who did not specialize in that kind of work. His brother Denis married Anne Bouillerot, from a well-known printing family in Paris, and Jacques II, Claude's son who succeeded him, was apprenticed for six years to Ravenot, Charles Coignard and Jean de La Caille.

Undoubtedly such alliances must have accounted for the prevalence of street literature from Troyes, at least from the mid-17th century. For the late 17th century we have Antoine Raffle's will, and he was certainly concerned with the Oudots in publishing "Bibliothèque Bleue" books. At his death Raffle left formes already set up for an "almanac des postes," for an elementary treatise on spelling, arithmetic, and prayers; there were also some wood blocks, "very old, called 'dominoes'," and letters for captions. So, we can see that Raffle himself printed these little booklets. His accounts show connections with Febvre of Troyes and reveal details of nearly 4,000 dozen and 100 reams of packmen's literature.

In detail, the material embraced many types of literature: the usual devotional titles, Bibles and New Testaments,

Bible in Pictures, Epistles and the Evangelists, Psalters, Becanus' *Somme* (perhaps a little surprising), Hours, Augustine's *Confessions,* Arnauld d'Andilly's *Lettres,* Busée's *Méditations,* Father Lenfant's *Vie des saints, Pédagogues chrétiens,* the *Imitation,* the inevitable *Pensez-y-bien,* Boudon—all by the dozen, the last two by the hundred. In addition there were *Châtiment des enfants,* ABCs, Rudiments, *Traité de l'orthographe,* arithmetic, songs, carols, "livres de civilité," *Sécretaire de la Cour, Cabinet d'éloquence,* life of the Three Marys, St. Catherine and St. Alexis, St. Brigid, St. Anthony, life of Jesus, the *Trépassement de la Vierge, Confession de la bonne femme,* prayers for forgiveness, the *Quatre fins de l'homme.* He also had romances of a traditional kind: *Pierre de Provence, Huon de Bordeaux, Belle Hélène, Charlemagne, Fortunatus, Griselda, Maugris d'Aigremont, Til Eulenspiegel, Gargantua, l'Aventurier Buscon,* and Quevedo's *Visions.* Hundreds of plays: *Marianne,* the *Cid* (51 dozen), Scarron's *Jodelet.* Satires: *Vierbaguet, Gratelard, Gringolet, Paris burlesque, Tombeau de la Mélancolie.* Medical remedies, popular recipes, astrology: *Ecole de Salerne, Histoire des songes, Miroir d'astrologie, Médecin charitable, Apothicaire charitable, Petit Albert, Bâtiment de recettes.* Finally, recipes for jams, gardening books, Cries of Paris, the "Danse des Maccabées," along with thousands of games, to do with war, the world, women, Cupid, and inn signs.

Finally two documents help reveal Jacques Febvre's operations. When Raffle died Febvre was anxious to find another business partner and contacted Jean Musier, with whom he contracted to sell (on 28 May 1696) a ream of "square" paper for 3 livres, a ream of the Rudiments for 3 livres, 10 sols, one hundred Psalters for 17 livres, *Huon de Bordeaux,* lst and 2nd Parts at 14 livres the dozen, *Danse macabre* for 18 livres the gross, and *Mélusine* at 40 sols the dozen. On 9 January 1703 he signed another contract, with François Rivière, granting him the exclusive output of his press at a slightly higher price but allowing him to sell most of the said titles less 10 sols. The Febvres were by no means the main publishers in Troyes: the Oudots did business with Paris on a greater scale, and so it leads us to draw the conclusion that there was considerable penetration of the Paris market by these little popular booklets, and therefore that the "livres d'histoires" and other packets of unspecified materials were of just this kind, alongside the devotional literature.*

---

*The *Catalogue des livres qui se vendent en la boutique de la Veuve de Nicolas Oudot* is an invaluable source of information on popular literature in the early 17th century. She offered "Entertaining books, popularly known as the Bibliothèque Bleue and sold books of Hours called Longuettes, alphabets, etiquette books, devotions for school use. She goes on to announce: 'Several kinds of devotional books for children, carols and canticles, ancient and modern, lives of saints. All kinds of books, many newly printed. Comic sketches are being looked for though they are not on the current list. New titles are regularly added and soon one will appear which is of particular value to families and even to nuns because of its uplifting tone. Further search for canticles will be made with all speed. . . . Books such as *Pédagogue chrétien, Trompette du ciel* and the Gospels and others from Rouen are available'." The stock was evidently extensive, educationally and spiritually, a quite substantial syllabus in cheap form. This is a testimony to the transition from an oral to a print culture.

CONCLUSION

U P TO THE YEAR 1643 the fortunes of the book trade fluctuated; the years from 1643 to 1672 were a turning point when a long period of political and economic crisis was followed by a sharp rise in productivity, reaching a maximum between 1664–71. Smaller books by then were in the majority, smaller in physical size, no doubt a response to the economies demanded by a fiercely competitive market, yet one feels that it also reflects a shrinking of the spirit, a malaise which would indeed be a reflection of the historical period. The age was at first expansive, then it recoils into recession.

From that generalization everything follows: there were two phases in the French Counter-Reformation, firstly the weighty literature of erudition in which ponderous theoretical disputes took form alongside little didactic books of piety, instruments of the missionary societies offering spiritual sustenance in an effort to revive the Faith, and also helping publishers make a living in compensation for the very restricted market represented by the folios of recondite theology. Latin was giving way to vernacular languages in scholarly works, particularly in Medicine, where the traditional Humanist treatises based on Classical sources were rivaled by little practical books. Law was no longer the paramount subject now that the old tendency to cite and observe only precedent was passing away. There was a wave of translations and more awareness of new approaches to old problems, a resort to the press to present new viewpoints, notably by Jansenists. Pamphleteering was almost a profession, especially at times of political crisis, as in the Fronde uprising. There were passing fashions in political, literary

PRINT, POWER, AND PEOPLE

and geographical subjects—Richelieu's Canadian policy, and later, activities in the Far East. Satire and burlesque sold well in turbulent and distressing periods, and moralizing replaced the old conventional piety as the century wore on into the long reactionary years of Louis XIV's reign, the period which has come to be called the crisis of the European conscience, when a formal religious sensibility was changing into something more objectively critical and rational.

Tempting though hypotheses might be, we have to remember that all conclusions about book production and a reading public depend on *surviving* books, and so can only be partial and tentative. To check any tenable hypotheses we need to test the evidence of surviving books against other sources. And we find that where it is available, the documentary evidence confirms the testimony of the actual books. Printers and booksellers were a communicative breed and left not only their business records but a great deal of official memoirs and other matter relating to their daily commerce, often litigious because they were engaged in life and death struggles to survive. We can read their private letters, listen to the publisher Vitré recalling nostalgically the golden days of the early 17th century and offering his own no doubt biased reasons for the decline in the trade, or Léonard explaining in 1670 why the big books do not sell any more. A snatch of dialogue between two Lyons printers which survives preserves a complaint about lack of copy, and so illustrates the tight economic climate and probably tight censorship of their day more than many a learned article centuries later. All the evidence tends to show that economic and intellectual consequences of a mighty transition from expansion to depression are soon made plain in the publishing trade. Statistics do not say everything; the simple reaction of men and women alive at the time is more important than cold figures for analysis. And overarching all else was the threat of coercion from the two all-powerful agencies then controlling people's lives, the religious and the civil.

The Church was supreme and exercised her power instinctively rather than in any contrived way, especially in the period from the death of Henri IV to the end of Louis XIII's reign, a time of unparalleled influence and prosperity for the Church, both materially and morally. Men and women flocked to join the religious Orders, and huge gifts of money poured in with happy consequences for the Paris book trade, busy supplying armaments for the new Church Militant. But the Church was not monolithic and was full of contradictions in its doctrines, its policies vis-à-vis Rome (the wearisome Gallican-Ultramontane quarrel), and the place of spirituality and mysticism in the life of the flock. Although fertilized from Spain and Italy, the French Catholic Renaissance had its own personality, a basic thrust grounded on direct study of the Early Fathers of the Church; it mistrusted Neo-Scholasticism and Neo-Thomism. The rapidly growing libraries were steeped in Gallican literature and there is little doubt that Jansenism stems from that, as the shelves testify abundantly. And later 18th-century thinking was deeply influenced by Jansenist thought.

Yet the Church was declining in the face of a more powerful monarchy; quite discernibly the University Faculty of Theology and the Assemblée du Clergé, which once struck fear into dissenters, have markedly less influence. As in many other matters, Henri III and his Ministers paved the way for royal absolutism when they first moved to censor books, though there was then relative prosperity and little incentive to unrest in the trade. Under Richelieu and Séguier royal authority is convincingly established. While the trade in printed books prospered in Paris the European trade was suffering from the Thirty Years War, and with no market outlets there was overproduction and unsold stocks. From this state of anarchy came the policy of surveillance and absolute control, to suppress subversive printing and concentrate production more efficiently, and the Crown's anxiety in the face of a deteriorating political situation is understandable. After Richelieu's death his policy was called in question, there was evidence of division in the Church over the Jansenist party, and the explosion of "Mazarinades," those potent political pamphlets aimed at Mazarin and the Establishment, turned the first twenty years of Louis XIV's reign into a virtual free-for-all. Contracts, agreements, licences were ignored, Catholic publishers used any copy they could get to help sales while Protestant publishers in Holland, better equipped and with more energy, came back into the French market, thus compounding an already dangerous situation.

Which leads us to the age of Colbert. His policy was to restore order, efficiency and monopoly, which in theory was admirably suited to the government for obvious reasons; unfortunately, hard economic facts only encouraged the self-interest of printers and publishers. While royal ascendancy ruled in Paris under the shadow of Court and Chancellery, it was weak in the rest of the country. Moreover, Louis' aggressive diplomacy led to wars with his neighbors, and like many autocrats before and after him he failed to silence growing discontent, which flowed into underground channels and kept up continuous opposition to him. Hence Bignon, appointed to tighten up control of the trade (he resembled the typical "philosophe" of the 18th century), was forced to apply censorship flexibly; it would not work in any other way. So, the King and his Ministers had to tolerate a book trade that was closely bound up with the nation's economic health. But what of the principal actors in the drama—the readers?

It is extremely difficult, even now, to describe the reading public in any detail or assess the influence their reading had on them. How does reading affect attitudes? Even in our own day it is hard to be sure; despite endless surveys, firm conclusions are almost impossible. It is even more difficult to estimate reading habits and their effects in the 17th century, but perhaps certain points may be made.

The classic question is, of course: *Who* read? Or rather, Who read what? The evidence of a good library can tell us something, but we have to remember that a well stocked library was itself a gesture towards the cultural conventions of the time, and those with access to libraries were often those whose respect for the traditional symbols of education and tradition were acquired in their youth at college or university, strongholds of tradition. In the period we have been surveying those readers would be the professional classes and the aristocracy; the artisan and merchant classes would be excluded. What did the last-named actually read, barred as they were by lack of education from using the libraries which were the preserve of the administrative and ecclesiastical castes? They had affection for simple pictures with a text—almanacs and calendars, woodcuts of saints or kings, simple story books, pious uplift, perhaps practical aids for their trade. What we call "street literature," the mass of ephemeral ballads, sensational broadsides and chapbooks, has mostly disappeared, but as we showed in the last chapter, there was a thriving industry based on Troyes and Rouen, which must mean that in their own unsophisticated way the great unlettered masses enjoyed a more "lettered" culture than we guess. But it is only in the 18th century that "popular" literature becomes really varied; most of the romances would have been for women of high social rank and not for the peasantry. Tabarin and Bruscambille wrote their humorous pieces not for some huge popular audience but for their friends in the civil administration at the Palais; though written for fun the material is quite sophisticated and not aimed at the shopkeepers of the Rue des Lombards. And "country" pedlars looked for their customers in the towns and the middle ranks of society, concentrating on places where there was no bookshop, not as a rule in humble cottages where in all probability no one could read. The same would apply to Paris as to any other town.

Change came, slowly and gradually in the later years, when elementary education reached more people after the upheavals of civil war, and a simple reading public was created for crude tracts and pious leaflets. It was evolution of a kind, yet there was a great gulf between readers of street literature and traditional users of "real" books. Reading then as now was a badge of class, the privilege of an elite, and even in that world there were two cultures, that of the civil servant and that of the cavalier, what the French called the "gens de robe" and the "gens d'épée." The first were the lineal descendants of the old Humanists, the people who made the professions possible, revitalized by the fresh thinking forced upon the Church by the need to confront Protestant dissent. The Counter Reformation was formal and logical, with a respect for the past, especially for authority, and the complex hierarchy of officials serving

Church and State had innate reverence for degree and subordination, essential to their philosophy, entrenched in their learning. The literature they wrote and read was theological rather than "spiritual," which would be too individual and subjective to suit the pedantic and cautious lawyer and cleric, and certainly theoretical rather than practical, designed for academics rather than the average reader. A pedantic Humanism worshipping precedent and authority, hence in Biblical studies with a strong preference for the Fathers, who represented "good learning," impeccable erudition more to the convoluted taste of a 17th-century scholar than the simple texts of the Scriptures.

This meant that Philosophy held a central place in their hearts, and in literature the classical formalists like Plutarch, Seneca and Cicero, a lawyer if ever there was one. History was paramount in the "Human sciences" as they called them, and there was an interest in Memoirs, compounded by the tensions and preoccupations of religious strife and the growth of new, dynamic heresies. The histories that claim most readers are those which reflect a national psyche damaged by the stresses of challenge and reaction brought on by Protestantism and the struggles between the French monarchy and the Papacy. There is a consistent backward-looking trend which quite fails to discuss contemporary problems, social or scientific, in the printed books of the day. The servants of the vast bureaucracy seem obsessed with the past, as if to reassure themselves of respectability, or as if the mystical literature of the time were subjective, transient, not to be trusted.

Quite different attitudes are found in the aristocracy, especially those close to the Crown, the Privy Councillors, the heads of the Judiciary and the Ministers in charge of the economy. For them the new scientific spirit—as we hope to have proved in these pages—was everything. It gave them new hope, not only intellectually but socially. Cartesianism liberated thought from the past and created new forms of expression, new expertise. Descartes's letters clearly reveal which way he felt the future would go, even though so many of his contemporaries preferred to cling to older modes of thought out of a need to feel secure.

The old aristocracy and the cavalier class were the products of an earlier tradition for which the printed word did not exist; when it did impinge more on them later on, if we read the evidence of the libraries correctly, they seemed to prefer the literature of sensibility. There is a definite feeling among the gentry and the military caste (where they are readers) for the spontaneous and the open-minded, in contrast to the pedantry of the lawyers and bureaucrats. We know which of these tendencies eventually triumphed; the old formalism gradually dissolved under the acid of a vigorous curiosity, as if the old-fashioned "homme de robe" gave way to the buoyancy and drive of the "homme d'épée," finally emerging as the "honnête homme." This last type was the product of economic circumstances from which we can never fully escape, and there is no doubt that just at the moment when the mind was changing direction, economic necessity forced physical changes in the printed book. The New Reason found concrete expression in books of smaller, more convenient size, as if the book trade was engaged in a general stocktaking before starting on new lines.

Europe divided North and South, with consequent effects on France, which was not insulated from the rest of the world. Venice had been the center of gravity of the book trade in the western world until the beginning of the 17th century, but by the end the Netherlands had beaten Venice not only in the wool trade but in publishing. The Protestant North had the effect of consolidating Catholicism in Southern Europe, but Catholicism lost its impetus. Thriving Protestant trading cities like Amsterdam and Leyden, which owed their prosperity to many factors, not least the wars of religion, had to find markets other than Germany, which had been ruined in the Thirty Years War, and they turned to France, as did Geneva and London, whose roles at this time must not be underestimated. At that very moment, coincidence or not, the initial inspiration of the Catholic Reformation was exhausted, and Jansenism exposed some intrinsic contradictions, a further embarrassment to the Church.

The time was ripe for a new beginning, for new modes of thinking, calling upon the reasoning faculties to solve problems. It could be called the dawn of the Age of

Criticism, the Enlightenment. The Bible is subjected to new critical examination, there is more objective examination of hallowed superstitions, nothing taken for granted. New research into fundamental physics begins, from Descartes to Newton, and on the surface of the globe geographical exploration extends to its very circumference, all part of a new inquiring spirit which is no longer the preserve of a small circle of approved scholars but increasingly draws in a wider interested public. Naturally the leading spirits are ahead of the rest, but in France there seems to be paralysis, a nation gripped by outworn pieties, respect for degree, encouraged by its King to remain so, in reaction against modernism. Paris in the late 17th century was like an embattled citadel of absolutism under siege by hostile batteries from without.

And all the time the printed word was crucial because the book was always more than an instrument of information and instruction—it was a persuader, and though inevitably in a hierarchical age addressed to a minority of readers, it was an index of change on the way. Perhaps it charted changes of emphasis rather than any deep underlying continuity in a society which was more stable than it appeared. Above all else, what strikes the student of a changing society, whether attitudes towards the King or religion or popular superstitions, is the slowness of change, the sheer inertia. The history of the book is a minority history in a society which was still primitive as far as the majority of the people were concerned, still primarily an oral culture, but it was the minority which had the future in its hands. That is the message with which this long story ends.

SOURCES AND BIBLIOGRAPHY

MANUSCRIPT SOURCES

A. Bibliothèque Nationale

Archives of various relevant institutions in 17th-century France are of course the essential basis of any study of the printed book at that time. Chief among them are the Chambre Syndicale des Imprimeurs et Libraires Parisiens; the Inspection de la Librairie et de la Bibliothèque Royale, now preserved in the Cabinet des Manuscrits. M. R. Estivals used them, not without some difficulty, for his two studies: *Le Dépôt Légal sous l'Ancien Régime de 1537 à 1794* (Paris, 1961) and *La statistique bibliographique de la France sous la Monarchie au XVIII siècle* (Paris, The Hague, 1965).

1. The archives in the Department of Manuscripts of the Bibliothèque Nationale, from which only one is cited here: Archives 34. Copyright register of the Royal Library from 1694 to 1721.
2. MSS 21813–22050, now called the Chambre Syndicale archives (17th and 18th centuries), which were originally from there but also contain other related materials from the Bureau de la Librairie. H. Omont compiled an inventory published in the *Bulletin de la Société de l'Histoire de Paris,* v. 13, 1886, pp. 151–9, 174–184, and recorded in the *Bibliothèque Nationale. Catalogue général des MSS français. Ancien petit fonds français,* Nos. 20065–22884. Paris, 1898. They are bundles of legal documents now bound, and registers of the Chambre Syndicale. Among the latter are:
MS français 21837: apprenticeship indentures, 1606–1672.
MSS français 21842–21843: masterships, 1617–1671 and Minutes of various meetings.

MS français 21845, fol. 218. Books registered at the Stationers' Guild (Communauté des Libraires et Imprimeurs).

MSS français 21855–21856: Resolutions of the Communauté des Libraires et Imprimeurs.

MS français 21872: register of the Communauté de St. Jean l'Evangélist, 1586–1742.

MSS français 21897–21898: register of books forwarded to the Chambre Syndicale by the Customs, August 1697/98; 2 January 1600–30 Sept., 1701.

MS français 21930: Books seized by the Syndics and Assistants, 1698– .

MSS français 21938–9: Books submitted by their authors to the censors, with remarks of the censors, 1696–1704.

MS français 21943: Books sent by printers and publishers to the Communauté, 1626–1689.

MSS français 21944–21948: Register of copyrights assigned to the Chambre Syndicale by the Chancellor.

3. MSS français 22061–22102: The Anisson collection, named after its first owner. Essentially the archives of the Inspection du Librairie but includes some from other sources, e.g., the Dépôt Légal and a number of others which are not here cited. The Collection has been most carefully inventoried by E. Coyeque, *Bibliothèque Nationale. Inventaire de la Collection Anisson sur l'histoire de l'imprimerie et de la librairie principalement à Paris (MSS français 22061–22193)*. (Paris, 1900, 2 vols.). Below we list only those documents which were of particular value:

MSS français 22061–22062: Book Trade Regulations, 1513–1740 and 1563–1751.

MS français 22064: Apprentices and journeymen, 1539–1787.

MS français 22065: Masterships.

MS français 22071–22072: Copyrights and licences, 1475–1764.

MS français 22074: False imprints.

MS français 22081: Searches of printing shops, 1542–1786.

MS français 22082: Regulations relating to paper, 1524–1772.

MS français 22115: Billposting and hawkers, 1560–1776.

MS français 22117: Typefounding and engraving, 1583–1764.

The above is enough to indicate the types of materials in the archives: Guild (Communauté) registers, and legal dossiers. The long series of bibliographical registers covering certain aspects of book production in the 18th century only begin at the end of the 17th and so were not of sufficient utility for our purposes.

Other archival sources

MS français 7054: Documents from La Reynie's office—accounts and invoices relating to payment of editors of books for the New Converts (1684–1686).

MS français 8118: Minutes of the Police committee, 1660 and 1667.

MS français 9511–9512: Account book of abbé Claude Fleury.

MS français 11768: Documents relating to the book trade.

MS français 14127: Inquisitions into authors who have written histories of France commissioned by royalty, arranged by the reigns during which they lived. (Extracted from the Epargne Registers in the Chambre des Comptes. La Roque. Bibliothèque de la Chancellerie.)

MS français 16746: fol 402: "Paper consumption by the Paris printing trade." Report by Antoine Vitré, c. 1665. Fol. 412: Memo about the translation and publishing of the Royal Bible in French. (Harlay Collection.)

MS français 16753–16754: Printing licences (Registre du Sceau), 1635–1651, 1653–1664. (Séguier-Coislin.)

MS français 17341: fol. 38: Memorandum re Denis Langlois, printer, prisoner in the Bastille.

MS français 17345: fol. 9: Interrogation of Denis Langlois by Dreux Daubray, 24–25 July 1657.

MS français 17395–17411: Correspondence from Sebastien Cramoisy, Antoine Vitré and Pierre Rocollet to Chancellor Séguier.

MS français 17563: Chancellor Séguier. Various documents. In fol. 107, Census of Paris printers, 15 October 1666.

MS français 17566: Memoranda about printing addressed to Chancellor Séguier.

MS français 18600: Files of documents from the Séguier-Coislin collection, chiefly relating to press censorship, Bible translation and accounts of the Imprimerie Royale, 1640–1647.

MS français 18624, fol. 484: Disbursement from Office of the Privy Seal.

MS français 21739–21750: Police files on the book trade from Commissioner Delamare's archive.

New MSS français, 399–400: Report on the book trade in France under Chancellor Pontchartrain. Statements by printers, publishers and binders from all parts of the kingdom, edited by Jean-Paul Bignon, Privy Councillor and Head of the Book Trade Bureau and Royal Library, 1700–1701.

New MS français 2511: Document relating to Jean Anisson and the Imprimerie Royale, 1691.

New MS français 5843: Original documents relating to the Imprimerie Royale, 1669–1783.

New MS français Colbert MSS 110; fol. 275: Letter from Cramoisy to Colbert.

Joly de Fleury 26, 339, 591 and 1682: Documents about printing.

B. Archives Nationales

Documents relating to the book trade and censorship in the 17th century are in Series K and KK (royal accounts) and Series M and MM, especially the Archives of the University of Paris, E, O^1, V^5, V^6, X, Y and Z^{1A}, and additional material is in the Archives Notariales. Specially noteworthy are Series Y, X and V in the Châtelet Archives.

Archives Notariales. The main sources here are:

a. Book trade people: Etudes 1: 129–130, 159–166. II: 106, 143–189, 225. III: 471, 546–572. IV: 96–107. VI: 166, 167. VIII: 586, 589–636, 720. XI: 82–155. XII: 5. XIII: 3, 11, 41, 107. XVI: 85, 274. XVII: 23–28, 186–207, 484. XVIII: 171, 172, 258, 318. XIX: 357, 443, 486–498, 526. XXI: 197. XXIII: 266, 335–352. XXVI: 27. XXVIII: 2. XXIX: 21, 179–185. XXXIII: 124, 297–304. XXXIV: 118, 143. XLIII: 3–197. XLV: 65–68. XLVI: 122. XLIX: 356–437. LI: 349. LIV: 307, LVII: 61, LX: 12, LXIV: 168. LXV: 27, 104, 126. LXVI: 104. LXIX: 100. LXX: 182, 224. LXXII: 5. LXXIII: 348. XC: 98. XCI: 240, 540 bis. XCIII: 55. XCVII: 8. XCVIII: 372. C: 372, 449, 451. CII: 50, 138. CV: 780–805. CVI: 13. CIX: 69–221. CX: 94, 100, 102, 105, 110. CXV: 90, 119, 195, 256. CXVI: 77. CXXI: 10, 41. CXXII: 20–26.

b. Personal libraries.

Etudes I–VII; IX–XIII, XV–XVI, XVIII–XXI, XXIV, XXVI, XXVIII–XXX, XXXIII–XXXVI, XLI, XLIII, XLV, XLIX, LI–LIV, LXVI–LXVII, LXXIII, LXXV, LXXXI, LXXXVI–

LXXXVII, XC, XCI, XCVIII, CV–CVII, CIX–CX, CXII–
CXIII, CXV, CXVIII.

C. *Other Libraries and Depositories*

1. **Paris.**
Bibliothèque de l'Arsenal (Archives de la Bastille). See
particularly F. Ravaison. *Les Archives de la Bastille,* Vols. I–XI
(1659–1710). (Paris, 1866–1901), and F. Funck-Brentano. *Les
Lettres de cachet des prisonniers de la Bastille, 1659–1789.* (Paris,
1903).
  Bibliothèque Mazarine (MSS 4205–4217).
  Bibliothèque de la Sorbonne. Catalogue (Chevillier).
  Bibliothèque de l'Institut de France (MS 1870).
  Bibliothèque St. Geneviève. Catalogue (Daunou).
  Bibliothèque Historique de la Ville de Paris (MS 10474).
2. *Provinces.*
  Bibliothèque Municipale de Rouen (MS Leber 341).
  Lyons.
  Archives du Rhone (Series B).
  Archives de la Ville (FF 261 and FF 146).
  Archives de la Communautè des Libraires de Lyon (HH 98 and
    608).
  Archives de la Côte d'Or; Haute Garonne, l'Ardèche, l'Aube
    and Vauciuse.
3. *Foreign Archives.*
  Archives of the Plantin-Moretus Museum, Antwerp. Nos. 187;
    921–967—documents relating to the Frankfurt Fair, 1610–
    1644. Nos. 142–3, 147–51, 294–300—Moretus correspon-
    dence. Nos. 76–7, 526, 591—Letters addressed to Moretus.
    Nos. 129, 133, 188, 410–12, 496–8, 759–61—Moretus ac-
    counts.
  Rotterdam. Gemeente Archief.
  Leyden. Gemeente Archief.
  Amsterdam. See M.M. Kleerkooper and M. P. Van Stockum.
    De Boekhandel te Amsterdam, voornamelik in de 17e eeuw
    (The Hague, 1914) and I. H. Van Eeghem. *De Amsterdamse
    Boekhandel, 1680–1725* (Amsterdam, 1963. 4 vols.)
  Geneva. City Archives.
  Vatican. Archives (MS Lat. 8192, 8016, 3076, 3539).

PRINTED SOURCES

Early legal documents

Lettres patents . . . pour le règlement des libraires, imprimeurs et relieurs de ceste ville. vérifiés en Parlement le 9 juillet 1618 (Paris, P. Mettayer, 1618.) B.N. F. 23610 (723). 1621 ed. B.N. F. 13020 and R. 8309.

Recueil des status et règlements des marchands libraires, imprimeurs et relieurs . . . de Paris, divisés par titres (Paris, Julliot, 1620.) B.N. F. 13019.

Lettres (patentes) obtenues par aucuns des imprimeurs et libraires de Paris en l'année 1649. B.N. F. 2361 (52), and H. 5001.

Conférence des statuts accordez par le Roy à la Communauté des imprimeurs et libraires de Paris en l'année 1683. B.N. F. 12983.

Edict . . . pour le règlement des imprimeurs et libraires de Paris . . . 21 Aoust 1686. B.N. F. 16584, 20229.

Edict . . . pour le règlement des imprimeurs et libraires de Paris (pour le règlement des relieurs et doreurs de livres). B.N. F. 26444 and 47012.

Code de la librairie et imprimerie de Paris . . . Conseil d'Etat du Roy le 28 fèvrier 1723. B.N. F. 26319 and 31862.

Deeds. See *Bibliothèque Nationale. Département des Imprimés.*

Catalogue des factums et autres documents antérieurs à 1790 by Auguste Corda, and continuations. (Paris, 1890–1905. 7 vols) Publishers' Catalogues. See Bibliothèque Nationale Catalogues for all lists preserved in that library.

Early Bibliographies (17th–18th centuries)

Draud, Georg. *Bibliotheca classica sive Catalogus officinalis quo singuli singularum facultatum ac professionum libri in quavis fere lingua extant. . . . recensentur* (Francfort, 1611).

———. *Bibliotheca exotics . . . La bibliothèque universelle . . . contenant le catalogue de tous les livres qui ont été imprimés ce siècle passé aux langues françoise, italienne, espaignolle et autres.* (Francfort, 1610).

Lipen, M. Bibliotheca realis. (Francfort, 1679–1685, 6 vols.)

Jacob, (Father) Louis. *Bibliotheca gallica universalis. Catalogus omnium librorum per universum regnum Galliae annis, 1643–1653.* (Paris, 4 vols).

———. *Bibliotheca parisiana. . . . 1643–1650.* (Paris, 5 vols.)

La bibliographie française et latine de Paris, janvier–avril 1678. 4 fascicules.

La Croix du Maine, François and Du Verdier, Antoine. *Les bibliothèques françoises.* (Paris, 1772–3. 6 vols.)

Bibliographies compiled by religious Orders

Lelong, Father Jacques. *Bibliotheca sacra.* (Paris, 1723). A bibliography of the Bible.

———. Supplement. (Halle, 1778–1785).

———. *Bibliothèque historique de la France.* (Paris, 1768–78, 5 vols.)

Fabricius, Johann Albert. *Bibliographia antiquaria.* (Hamburg, 1760, 2 vols.)

———. *Bibliotheca latina.* (Venice, 1728, 2 vols.)

———. *Bibliotheca latina.* (Leipzig, 1773–4, 3 vols.)

———. *Bibliotheca graeca.* (Hamburg, 1790–1809, 12 vols.)

Other Subjects

Herigone, P. *Cursus mathematicus.* (Paris, 1644). The bibliography.

Albert, Antoine. *Dictionnaire portatif des prédicateurs français.* (Lyons, 1757).

Hérissant, L.A.P. *Bibliothèque physique de la France.* (Paris. 1771).

Lenglet-Du Fesnoy, Nicolas. *Méthode pour étudier l'histoire.* (Paris, 1772, 15 vols.)

———. *Histoire de la philosophie hermétique.* (Paris, 1742, 3 vols.)

———. *Méthode pour étudier la géographie.* (Paris, 1768, 10 vols.)

Author Bibliographies

Du Pin, L. E. *Bibliothèque des auteurs ecclésiastiques du 17 siècle.* (Paris, 1708, 7 vols.)

Ceillier, R. *Histoire générale des auteurs sacrés et ecclésiastiques. (Paris, 1729–1783, 23 vols.)*

Baillet, A. *Jugement des scavans sur les principaux ouvrages des auteurs.* (Paris, 1685–6, 9 vols.)

Nicéron, Jean-Pierre. *Mémoires pour servir a l'histoire des hommes illustres dans la République des lettres avec un catalogue raisonné de leurs ouvrages.* (Paris, 1727–45, 43 vols.)

Goujet, Abbé Claude-Pierre. *Biblothèque françoise au Histoire de la littérature françoise.* (Paris, 1740–56, 18 vols.)

Catalogue des livres imprimés de la Bibliothèque du Roy: Théologie, 1739–42, 3 vols.; *Belles Lettres,* 1750, 1 vol.; *Jurisprudence,* 1753, 2 vols.

Modern bibliographies (19th–20th centuries)

Brunet, Jacques-Charles. *Manuel du libraire et de l'amateur de livres* (Paris, 1860–65, 6 vols.)

Index Aureliensis Catalogus librorum sedicim saeculo impressorum, A-Aosta. (Baden Baden, 1962–). In progress. A rearrangement of existing printed catalogues and therefore incomplete.

Spain.

Palau y Dulcet, Antonio. *Manual del librero hispano americano.* (Barcelona, 1948–1965, 20 vols.) In progress.

Great Britain.

Pollard, A.W. and Redgrave, G.R. *A Short-title catalogue of books printed in England, Scotland and Ireland and of books printed abroad, 1475–1640.* (London, 1926).

Wing, Donald. *Short-title catalogue of books printed in England, Scotland, Ireland, Wales and British America and of English books printed in other countries 1641–1700.* (New York, 1945–48, 2 vols.)

Italy.

Michel, P. H. and S. *Répertoire des ouvrages imprimés en langue italienne au XVII siècle conservés dans les bibliothèques de France.* A–B (vol. 1); C–D (vol. 2). In progress. 1967.

Incunabula.

Renouard, Philippe. *Imprimeurs et libraires parisiens du XVI siècle,* vol. 1: ABADA–AVRIL (Paris, 1964).

Baudrier, Henri. *Bibliographie lyonnaise.* (Lyons, 1895–1921, 12 vols.)

Thomas, H. *Short-title catalogue of books printed in Spain and of Spanish books printed elsewhere in Europe before 1601 now in the British Museum.* (Paris, 1921).

Thomas, H. *Short-title catalogue of books printed in France and of French books printed in other countries from 1470 to 1600 now in the British Museum.* (London, 1924).

Thomas, H. *Short-title catalogue of Portuguese books printed before 1901 now in the British Museum.* (London, 1940).

Johnson, A. F. and Scholderer, V. *Short-title catalogue of books printed in Italy and of Italian books printed in other countries from 1465 to 1600 now in the British Museum.* (London, 1956).

Johnson, A. F. and Scholderer, V. *Short-title catalogue of books printed in the German-speaking countries and German books printed in other countries from 1455 to 1600 now in the British Museum.* (London, 1962).

Johnson, A. F. and Scholderer, V. *Short-title catalogue of books printed in the Netherlands and Belgium and of Dutch and Flemish books printed in other countries from 1470 to 1600 now in the British Museum.* (London, 1965).

Catalogue général des livres imprimés de la Bibliothèque Nationale. In progress.

Specialist Bibliographies

RELIGION

Bible.

Darlow, T.H. and Moule, H.F. *Historical catalogue of the printed editions of Holy Scripture in the library of the British and Foreign Bible Society.* (New York, 1963, 4 vols.)

Sailly, L. de. *Etude bibliographique du Nouveau Testament de Mons et des impressions du libraire Migeot de 1664 à 1703.* (Mons, 1926).

Van Eys, W. *Bibliographie des Bibles . . . en langue française des XV et XVI siècles.* (Geneva, 1900, 2 vols.)

Liturgy.

Bohatta, H. *Bibliographie des breviere, 1501–1850.* (Stuttgart, 1963).

Weale, W. H. and Bohatta, H. *Catalogus missalium ritus latini ab anno MCCCCLXXIV impressorum.* (London, 1928).

Patrology.

Hurter, H. von. *Nomenclator litterarius, 1564–1663* (1907); *1664–1763* (1913). *Dictionnaire de théologie catholique.* (Paris, 1903–1965, 17 vols.)

Mischelitsch, A. *Kommentatoren zur Summa Theologiae des Thoma von Aquin.* (Graz, 1924).

Jansenism.

Colonia, D. de. *Bibliothèque janseniste.* 4th ed. (Brussels, 1740).

Willaert, L. *Bibliotheca Janseniana Belgica.* (Paris, 1949–51).

Quietism.

Bremond, H. "Essai de bibliographie quiétiste" (In *Documentation d'Histoire,* 1910, pp. 291–98 and 447–57).

Protestantism.
Haag, E. *La France protestante.* (Paris, 1846–59, 10 vols.)
Spiritual Literature.
Dagens, J. *Bibliographie chronologique de la littérature de spiritualité. Les sources, 1501–1610.* (Paris, 1952).
Dictionnaire de spiritualité ascétique et mystique. (Paris, 1932–) In progress.
De Backer, A. *Sainte Thérèse en France au XVII siècle, 1600–1660.* (Louvain, 1966).
Benedictines.
Tassin, R. P. and Martène, E. *Histoire littéraire de la Congrégation de Saint-Maur.* (Paris, 1770).
Robert, Ulysse. *Supplément.* (Paris, 1881).
Berlière, U. *Nouveau supplément.* (Paris, 1908–32, 3 vols)
Albareda, A. *Bibliografia de la Regia Benedictina.* (Montserrat, 1933).
Dominicans.
Quétif, J. *Scriptores Ordinis Praedicatorum.* (Paris, 1719–34, 3 vols.)
Franciscans.
Bernardinos a Bononia. *Bibliotheca scriptorum Francisci Capuccinorum.* (Venice, 1747).
Wadding, L. *Scriptores Ordinis Minorum.* (Rome, Sbaraglia, 1806).
Godefroy de Paris. *Les frères Mineurs Capucins en France.* (Paris, 1937, 3 vols.)
Ubald d'Alençon. "La spiritualité franciscaine." (In *Etudes Franciscaines* v. 40, 1927.)
Lexicon Capuccinum. (Rome, 1951)
Carmelites.
Villiers, C. de. *Bibliotheca carmelitana.* (Orléans, 1752; repr. 1927).
Jesuits.
De Backer, A, and Caravon, Auguste. *Bibliothèque de la Compagnie de Jésus.* New ed. (Paris, 1890–1909, 9 vols.)
Oratory.
Batterel, L. *Mémoires doméstiques pour servir à l'histoire de l'Oratoire.* (Paris, 1902–5, 4 vols.)
Bonnardet, E. *Essai de bibliographie oratorienne.* 7 année, no. 25, janvier 1937, p. 46–50.
Ingold, A.M.P. *Essai de bibliographie oratorienne.* (Paris, 1880–2, 2 vols.)
St. Sulpice.
Bertrand, A. L. *Bibliothèque sulpicienne.* (Paris, 1900, 3 vols.)

Canon Law.
Artonne, A., Guizard, L. and Pontal, L. *Répertoire des statuts synodaux des diocèses de l'ancienne France.* (Paris, 1963).
Camus, M., and Dupin, J. *Lettres sur la profession d'avocat.* 4th ed. (Paris, 1818).
Literature.
Lanson, G. *Manuel bibliographique de la littérature française moderne.* (Paris, 1921).
Cioranescu, A. *Histoire de la littérature française du XVII siècle.* (Paris, 1965–8, 3 vols.)
Tchemerzine, A. *Bibliographie d'editions originales et rares d'auteurs français des XV–XVIII siècles.* (Paris, 1927–34, 10 vols.)

INDIVIDUAL AUTHORS

Boileau.
Magne, E. *Bibliographie générale des oeuvres de N. Boileau-Despréaux et de Gilles et Jacques Boileau.* (Paris, 1928).
Corneille.
Picot, E. *Bibliographie cornélienne.* (Paris, 1876).
Le Verdier, P. and Pelay, E. *Additions à la bibliographie cornélienne* (Rouen and Paris, 1908).
Galileo.
Cinti, D. *Bibliotheca Galileiana.* (Florence, 1957).
Grotius.
Termeulen, J. and Diermanse, P. J. J. *Bibliographie des écrits imprimés de Hugo Grotius.* (The Hague, 1950).
Jurieu.
Kappler, E. "Bibliographaie chronologique du ministre Jurieu (1637–1713)" (In *Bulletin de la Société d'histoire de protestantisme français,* v. 84, 1935, pp. 391–440).
Madame de La Fayette.
Aston, M. "Essai de bibliographie des oeuvres de Mme de La Fayette." (In *Revue d'histoire littéraire de la France,* 20 année, 1913, pp. 899–918).
La Fontaine.
Rochambeau (de). *Bibliographie des oeuvres de La Fontaine.* (Paris, 1911).
La Rochefoucauld.
Marchand, J. *Bibliographie raisonné de La Rochefoucauld.* (Paris, 1948).
Molière.
Lacoix, P. *Bibliographie molièresque.* 2nd ed. (Paris, 1875).

Guibert, A. J. *Bibliographie des oeuvres de Molière publiées au XVII siècle.* (Paris, 1961, 2 vols. Supplément, 1965.)

Montaigne.

Richou, G. and Delpit, J. *Inventaire de la collection J. F. Payen et J. P. Bastide.* (Bordeaux, 1877).

Pascal.

Maire, A. *Bibliographie générale des oeuvres de Blaise Pascal.* (Paris, 1925–7, 5 vols.)

Etienne Pasquier.

Thickett, D. *Bibliographie des oeuvres d'Estienne Pasquier.* (Geneva, 1956).

Pibrac.

Pibrac, R. de. *Catalogue des ouvrages et éditions de Guy du Faur, seigneur de Pibrac.* (Paris, 1901).

Ronsard.

Seymour de Ricci, R. *Catalogue of a unique collection of early editions of Ronsard.* (London, 1927).

St. Amant.

Lagny, J. *Bibliographie des éditions anciennes des oeuvres de Saint Amant.* (Paris, 1960).

Scarron.

Magne, Emile. *Bibliographie généralle des oeuvres de Scarron.* (Paris, 1924).

Georges and Madeleine de Scudéry.

Mongrédien, G. "Bibliographie des oeuvres de G. et M. de Scudéry." (In *Revue d'histoire littéraire de la France,* 1933 and 1935.)

THEATRE

Horn-Monval M. *Répertoire bibliographique des traductions et adaptations françaises du théâtre étranger du XV siècle à nos jours.* (Paris, 1958–67).

THE NOVEL

Williams, R. C. *A bibliography of the XVII century novel in France.* (New York, 1932).

Baldner, R. W. *Bibliography of seventeenth century French prose fiction.* (New York, 1967).

POETRY

Lachèvre, F. *Bibliographie des receuils collectifs de poésie publiés de 1597 à 1700.* (Paris, 1901–22, 4 vols.)

Toinet, R. *Quelques recherches autour des poèmes héroïques-épiques français du XVII siècle.* (Tulle, 1899).

MORALISTS

Toinet, R. "Les écrivains moralistes au XVII siècle: essai d'une table alphabétique des ouvrages publiés pendant le siècle de Louis XIV, 1638–1715." (In *Revue d'histoire littéraire de la France,* 1916, pp. 570–610; 1917, pp. 296–306, 565–675, 1918. pp. 310–320, 655–671; 1926, pp. 395–407.

HISTORY

Bibliothèque Impériale. *Catalogue de l'histoire de France.* (Paris, 1855–1932, 23 vols.)

Bourgeois, L. and André, L. *Les sources de l'histoire de France. Le XVII siècle (1610–1715).* (Paris, 1913–1935, 8 vols.)

GEOGRAPHY, TRAVELS

Atkinson, G. *La littérature géographique française de la Renaissance. Répertoire bibliographique.* (Paris, 1927; supplément, 1936).

Bibliothèque Nationale. Départment des Imprimés. *Catalogue de l'histoire d'Asie.* 1 vol.

———. Départment des Imprimés. *Catalogue de l'histoire d'Afrique par G. A. Barringer.* 1 vol.

Bibliothèque Nationale. Département des Imprimés. *Catalogue de l'histoire de l'Amérique et de l'Océanie par G. A. Barringer.* 5 vols.

Anagmine, E. "L'Italia vista da viaggiatori francesi del sec. XVII." (In *Nuova Rivista Storica,* v. 21, 1937. p.1–)

Cordier, Henri. *Biblioteca sinica. Dictionnaire bibliographique des ouvrages relatifs à la péninsule indochinoise.* (Paris, 1912–32, 4 vols.)

Foulcher-Delbosc, R. *Bibliographie des voyages en Espagne et en Portugal.* (Paris, 1896).

McCoy, J. *Jesuit relations of Canada, 1632–1673.* (Paris, 1937).

Marion, S. *Relations des voyageurs français en Nouvelle France.* (Paris, 1923).

Martino, P. *L'Orient dans la littérature française au XVII et au XVIII siècle.* (Paris, 1906).

Pouliot, L. *Etudes sur les relations des Jésuites de la Nouvelle-France, 1632–1672.* (Montreal, 1940).

Sabin, J. *Dictionary of books relating to America.* (Amsterdam, 1961–2, 29 vols.)

Stillwell, M. B. *Incunabula and America, 1450–1800.* (New York, 1961).

Streit, R. and Didinger, J. *Bibliotheca missionum.* (Munster, 1916–8, 11 vols.)

SCIENCE

Caillet, A. L. *Manuel bibliographique des sciences psychiques ou occultes.* (Paris, 1913, 3 vols.)

Bibliothèque Impériale. Département des Imprimés. *Catalogue des sciences médicales.* (Paris, 1857–73, 2 vols.)

Choulant, L. *Handbuch der Bücherkunde für die ältere Medecin.* (Leipzig, 1841).

———. *Bibliotheca medico-historica.* (Leipzig, 1842).

Dechambre, A. and Raige-Delorme. *Dictionnaire encyclopédique de la Médecine.* (Paris, 1864–89, 100 vols.)

Guitard, E. H. *Manuel d'histoire de la littérature pharmaceutique.* (Paris, 1942)

Pauly, A. *Bibliographie des sciences médicales.* (Paris, 1874).

Salander, H. *Bibliotheca Walleriana.* (Stockholm, 1955, 2 vols.)

CHEMISTRY, PHYSICS, NATURAL HISTORY

Duveen, D. J. *Bibliotheca alchemica et chemica.* (London, 1949).

Ferguson, J. *Bibliotheca chemica.* (London, 1954, 2 vols.)

Nissen, C. *Die Botanische Buchillustration.* (Stuttgart, 1951).

Pritzel, G. A. *Thesaurus litteraturae botanicae.* (Leipzig, 1872.)

Quinby, J. *Catalogue of botanical books in the collection of Rachel McMasters Miller Hunt.* (Pittsburgh, 1958).

Le Coanet, M. "Les traductions françaises d'Euclide." (In *Revue française d'histoire des sciences,* 1957, p.38–)

Houzeau, J. C. and Lancaster, A. *Bibliographie générale de l'astronomie.* (Brussels, 1882–9. 2 vols.)

BOOK ILLUSTRATION

Bibliothèque de la Ville de Lyon. *Livres à figures du XVII siècle. Catalogue d'exposition par G. Couton, J. Jehasse et H. -J. Martin.* (Paris, 1965).

Canivet, D. *L'Illustration de la poésie et du roman français au XVII siècle.* (Paris, 1957).

Duportal, J. *Contribution au catalogue général des livres à figures du XVII siècle, 1601–1633.* (Paris, 1914).

Praz, Mario. *Studies in seventeenth century imagery.* 2nd ed. (Rome, 1964, 2 vols.) Vol. 2 is a bibliography.

Tchémerzine, A. *Répertoire des livres à figures rares et précieux édités en France au XVII siècle. (Paris, 1933).*

ALMANACS AND STREET LITERATURE

Grand-Carteret, J. *Les almanachs français.* (Paris, 1896).

Mongrédien, G. "Bibliographie des oeuvres du facetieux Bruscambille." (In *Bulletin du Bibliophile,* 1926, pp. 373–84, 422–30).

———. "Bibliographie tabarinique." (*Bulletin du Bibliophile,* 1929).

Saffroy, G. *Bibliographie des almanachs et annuaires . . . du XVI siècle à nos jours.* (Paris, 1959).

Seguin, J. P. *L'information en France avant le périodique.* (Paris, 1964)

JOURNALISM

Hatin, E. *Bibliographie historique et critique de la presse périodique française.* (Paris, 1866).

———. *Les Gazettes de Hollande et la presse clandestine aux XVII et XVIII siècles.* (Paris, 1865).

MISCELLANEOUS

Catalogue d'une très importante collection de livres d'architecture, recueils d'ornements. (Paris, 1914).

Cockle, M. J. *Bibliography of military books up to 1642.* (London, n.d.)

Guiffrey, J. "Traités du XVII siècle sur le dessin des jardins et la culture des arbres et des plantes." (In *Mélanges offerts à M. Henry Lemonnier,* Paris, 1913, pp. 224–47).

Mouchon, J. *Supplément à la bibliographie des ouvrages français sur la chasse.* (Paris, 1953).

Thiébaud, J. *Bibliographie des ouvrages français sur la chasse.* (Paris, 1934).

Vicaire, G. *Bibliographie gastronomique.* (Paris, 1890).

BIBLIOGRAPHY

A. History of The Printed Book

GENERAL

Audin, M. *Somme typographique.* (Paris, 1947–9, 2 vols.)
Centre International de Synthèse. "L'Ecriture et la psychologie des peuples." (*XXII Semaine de Synthèse,* (Paris, 1963).
Dahl, S. *Histoire du livre de l'Antiquité à nos jours.* (Paris, 1960).
Dainville, F. de. "Pour l'histoire de l'Index." (In *Recherches de science religieuse,* v. 43, 1954, pp. 86–98).
Dictionary catalogue of the history of printing from the John M. Wing Foundation in the Newbery Library. (Boston, 1961, 6 vols.)
Dronnkers, E. *Catalogus der bibliothek van de Vereeniging ter Bervordering van de Belangen des Boekhandels, Amsterdam.* (The Hague, 1920–65, 7 Vols.)
Escarpit, B. *La révolution du livre.* (Paris, 1965).
Febvre, L., and H. J. Martin. *L'Apparition du livre.* (Paris, 1958). Translated as *The coming of the book* by David Gerard (London, 1976).
Flocon, A. *L'Univers des livres: étude historique des origines à la fin du XVIII siècle.* (Paris, 1961).
Fournier, P. S. *Manuel typographique.* (Paris, 1766, 2 vols.)
Grolier, E. de. *Histoire du livre.* (Paris, 1954).
Presser, H. *Das Buch vom Buch.* (Bremen, 1963).
Printing and the mind of man. A descriptive catalogue . . . ed. J. Carter and P. H. Muir. (London, 1967).
Renouard, A. C. *Traité des droits d'auteur dans la littérature, les sciences et les beaux-arts.* (Paris, 1838, 2 vols.)
Steinberg, S. H. *Five hundred years of printing.* (London, 1966).

FRANCE—GENERAL

Actes du cinquième congrès national de la Société française de littérature comparée. (Lyons, May 1962). *Imprimerie, commerce et culture.* (Paris, 1965).
Bollème, G., Ehrard, J., et al. *Livre et société dans la France du XVIII siècle.* (Paris, 1965).
Brun, R. *Le livre français.* (Paris, 1948).
Centre Lyonnais d'Histoire et de Civilisation du Livre. *Cinq études lyonnaises.* (Paris, 1966).

Chauvet, P. *Les ouvriers du livre en France, des origines à la Revolution de 1789.* (Paris, 1959).

Duportal, J. *Etude sur les livres à figures édités en France de 1601 à 1660.* (Paris, 1914).

Estivals, R. *Le dépôt légal sous l'Ancien Régime, de 1537 à 1791.* (Paris, 1961)

———. *La statistique bibliographique de la France sous la Monarchie au XVIII siècle.* (Paris, 1965).

Falk, H. *Le privilège de librairie sous l'Ancien Régime.* (Paris, 1906).

Kolb, A. *Bibliographie des Französischen Buches im 16 Jahrhundert.* (Wiesbaden, 1966).

Lanette-Claverie, C. *L'Enquête de 1701 sur la librairie dans le royaume.* (Thesis, Ecole des Chartes).

Lepreux, G. "Les trois premiers siècles de l'imprimerie en France." (In *Union Syndicale et Fédération des Syndicats des Maîtres Imprimeurs en France. Bulletin Officiel,* Christmas 1926, pp. 1–108.)

Lepreux, G. *Gallia typographica ou Répertoire biographique et chronologique de tous les imprimeurs de France depuis les origines de l'imprimerie jusqu' à la Revolution.* (Paris, 1909–14, 7 vols.)

Maittaire, M. *Historia typographorum aliquot Parisiensium vitas et libros complectens.* (London, 1717).

Martin, H. J. "Les Benedictines, leurs libraires et le Pouvoir." (In *Mémorial du XIV centenaire de l'abbaye de St Germain-des-Prés,* Paris, 1959, pp. 273–287).

Mellotée, P. *Histoire économique de l'imprimerie.* Vol. 1: *L'imprimerie de l'Ancien Régime, 1439–1789.* (Paris, 1905).

Mémoire sur les vexations qu'exercent les librairies et imprimeurs de Paris, ed. L. Faucou. (Paris, 1879).

Michon, L. M. *La reliure française.* (Paris, 1951).

———. "A propos des grèves d'imprimeurs à Paris et à Lyons au XVI siecle." (In *Fédération des Sociétés Historiques et Archéologiques de Paris et de l'Ile-de-France, Mémoires,* 1953, pp. 103–115.)

Milkau, F. *Handbuch der Bibliotheks-Wissenschaft.* Vol. 1: *Schrift und Buch.* (Wiesbaden, 1952).

Néret, J. A. *Histoire illustré de la librairie française.* (Paris, 1953).

Pottinger, D. T. *The French book trade in the Ancien Régime, 1500–1791.* (Cambridge, Mass., 1958).

Reusch, H. *Der Index der verboten Bücher.* (Bonn, 1883, 2 vols.)

Syndicat National des Editeurs. *Monographie de l'Edition.* (Paris, 1967).

Thoinan, E. *Les relieurs français, 1500–1800.* (Paris, 1893).

Weigert, R. A. "L'Illustration française dans la première moitié du dix-septième siècle." (In *Le Portique,* no. 5, 1947).

PARIS

Adhémar, J. "La Rue Montorgueil et la formation d'un groupe d'imagiers parisiens au XVI siècle." (In *Vieux Papier,* 1954, no. 167, pp. 25–33.)

Bernard, A. *Histoire de l'imprimerie royale du Louvre.* (Paris, 1867).

Bibliothèque Nationale. *L'Art du livre à l'imprimerie nationale, des origines à nos jours.* (Paris, 1951).

Chevillier, A. *L'Origine de l'imprimerie à Paris. Dissertation historique et critique.* (Paris, 1694).

Delalain, P. *Les libraires et imprimeurs de l'Académie Française de 1631 à 1793.* (Paris, 1907).

———. *Etude sur la librairie parisienne du XIII au XV siècle.* (Paris 1891).

Dumoulin, J. *Vie et oeuvres de Fédéric Morel, imprimeur depuis 1557 jusqu'à 1583.* (Paris, 1901).

Giraudet, D. *Une Association d'imprimeurs et de libraires de Paris réfugiés a Tours au XVI siècle.* (Tours, 1877).

Hauser, H. *Ouvriers du temps passé.* 5th ed. (Paris, 1927).

Howe, E. "The Le Bé family." (In *Signature* 8, 1938).

Jammes, A. *La Reforme de la Typographie Royale sous Louis XIV: le Grandjean.* (Paris, 1961).

Jammes, A. and Veyrin-Forrer, J. *Cinq siècles de typographie nationale.* (Paris, 1958).

———. *Les premiers caractères de l'Imprimerie Royale. Etude sur un specimen inconnu de 1643.* (Paris, 1958).

La Caille, J. de. *Histoire de l'imprimerie et de la librairie ou l'on voit son origine et son progrès jusqu'en 1689.* (Paris, 1689).

Lepreux, G. "Antoine Estienne, premier imprimeur ordinaire du Roi." (In *Bibliographie Moderne,* 1907, nos. 4–5).

———. *Contribution à l'histoire de l'imprimerie parisienne.* (Paris, 1909–14). From *Revue des Bibliothèques,* 1909–1914.

———. "Une Enquête sur l'imprimerie de Paris en 1644. (In *Bibliographie Moderne,* 1910, pp. 5–36).

Lonchamp, P. "Un libraire au XVII siècle: Claude Barbin." (In *Bibliographie Moderne,* 1914, pp. 10–39).

Lottin, P. *Catalogue chronologique des libraires imprimeurs de Paris.* (Paris, 1789).

Martin, H. J. "Guillaume Desprez editeur de Pascal et de Port-Royal." (In *Fédération des Sociétés Historiques de Paris et de l'Ile-de-France. Mémoires,* 1952, pp. 206–8).

———. "L'Edition parisienne au XVII siècle." (*Annales,* 1952, pp. 303–18).

———. "Un grand éditeur parisien au XVII siècle: Sébastien Cramoisy." (In *Gutenberg Jahrbuch,* 1957, pp. 179–188).

———. "Ce qu'on lisait à Paris au XVI siècle." (In *Bibliothèque d'Humanisme et Renaissance,* vol. 21, 1959, pp. 222–30).

Morison, Stanley. *L'Inventaire de la fonderie Le Bé selon transcription de Jean-Pierre Fournier.* (Paris, 1957).

Omont, H. "Un document relatif à la fondation de l'Imprimerie nationale." (In *Bulletin de la Société de l'histoire de Paris et de l'Ile-de-France,* 1887, pp. 187–8).

Poche, Jean. (pseud. of Pierre Deschamps). *Quelques adresses de libraires, imprimeurs, relieurs, marchands . . . du XVII siècle.* (Paris, 1899).

Reed, G. E. *Claude Barbin (c. 1628–1698).* Thesis. (Brown University, 1964).

Renouard, A. A. *Annales de l'Imprimerie des Estiennes.* (Paris, 1843).

Renouard, Ph. *Les fondeurs de caractères et leur clientèle de province à la fin du XVII siècle.* (Paris, 1900).

———. *Documents sur les imprimeurs, libraires . . . ayant exercé à Paris de 1450 à 1600.* (Paris, 1901).

———. *Répertoire des imprimeurs parisiens, libraires, fondeurs de caractères et correcteurs d'imprimerie depuis l'introduction de l'imprimerie à Paris jusqu'à la fin du XVI siècle.* (Paris, 1965).

Thévenin, L. "Un libraire de Port-Royal: André Pralard." (In *Bulletin du bibliophile,* 1961, pp. 18–38).

Tromp, E. *Etude sur l'organisation et l'histoire de la Communauté des libraires et imprimeurs de Paris, 1618–1791.* (Nîmes, 1922).

Vicaire, G. and Pichon, J. *Documents pour servir à l'histoire des libraires de Paris 1486–1600.* (Paris, 1895).

FRENCH PROVINCES

Audiat, L. *Essai sur l'imprimerie en Saintonge et en Aunis.* (Paris, 1879).

Audin, M. "Les grèves dans l'imprimerie à Lyon au XVI siècle." (In *Gutenberg Jahrbuch,* 1935, pp. 172–189).

———. "L'imprimerie à Lyon." (In *Revue du Lyonnais,* 1929, pp. 1–122).

Beaupré, H. *Recherches historiques et bibliographiques sur les commencements de l'imprimerie en Lorraine.* (Nancy, 1945).

Bonnet, E. *Les débuts de l'imprimerie à Montpellier.* (Montpellier, 1895).

Bory, J. T. *Les origines de l'imprimerie à Marseille.* (Marseille, 1858).

Brincourt, J. B. *Jean Janon et ses fils: leurs oeuvres.* (Sedan, 1902).

Caillet, M. *L'oeuvre des imprimeurs toulousiains aux XVI et XVII siècles.* (Toulouse, 1963).

Clément-Janin. *Les imprimeurs et libraires dans la Côte-d'Or.* 2nd ed. (Dijon, 1912).

Danchin, F. *Les imprimés lillois, Répertoire bibliographique de 1594 à 1815.* (Lille, 1926–1931, 3 vols.)

Dauphin, V. and Pasquier, E. *Imprimeurs et libraires de l'Anjou.* (Angers, 1932).

Davies, N. Z. *Protestantism and the printing workers of Lyons.* (Thesis. Ann Arbor University, 1959).

Desgraves, L. *Etudes sur l'imprimerie dans le Sud Ouest de la France aux XV, XVI, et XVII siècles.* (Amsterdam, Erasmus, 1968).

———. "Bibliographie des ouvrages imprimés par Guillaume Millanges, 1625–1649." (In *Bulletin de la Société des Bibliophiles de Guyenne,* Bordeaux, 1961).

———. "Bibliographie des ouvrages imprimés par l'imprimeur bordelais Jacques Millanges, 1620–24." (In *Revue Historique de Bordeaux et du Département de la Gironde,* 1957, pp. 279–83).

———. "Supplément." To entry above.

———. "Bibliographie des ouvrages imprimés par Simon Millanges, Bordeaux 1961." (In *Bulletin de la Société des Bibliophiles de Guyenne*).

———. "Supplément." To entry above.

———. "Second supplément." Bordeaux, 1964. (*Bulletin de la Société des Bibliophiles de Guyenne*).

———. "Les 'Bulletins d'Information' imprimés à Bordeaux aux XVI et XVII siècles." (*Bulletin de la Société des Bibliophiles de Guyenne,* Bordeaux, 1964).

———. *Les Haultin.* (Geneva, 1960).

———. "Les ouvrages pedagogiques imprimés à Bordeaux aux XVI et XVII siècles." (In *Actes de l'Academie Nationale des Sciences, Belles-Lettres et Arts de Bordeaux,* 4th series, v. 19, 1963).

Ducourtieux, P. *Les Barbou imprimeurs à Lyon-Limoges-Paris, 1524–1823.* (Limoges, 1895–8).

Ducourtieux, P. and Bourderey, L. *Une imprimerie et une librairie à Limoges vers la fin du XVI siècle.* (Limoges, 1896).

Duthilloeul, H. R. *Bibliographie douaisienne.* (Douai, 1835).

Frère, E. *Manuel du bibliographie normand.* (Rouen, 1858).

Gauthier, P. J. *Recherches sur les anciens mâitres imprimeurs châlonnais.* (Châlons-sue-Marne, 1913).

Labadie, E. *Notices biographiques sur les imprimeurs et libraires bordelais des XVI, XVII et XVIII siècles.* (Bordeaux, 1900).

La Bouralière, A. de. "L'imprimerie et la librairie à Poitiers pendant le XVII et le XVIII siècle." (In *Bulletin et Mémoires de la Société des Antiquaires de l'Ouest,* 1905, p. 331).

Lacaze, L. *Les imprimeurs et libraires du Béarn, 1552–1883.* (Pau, 1884).

Lhote, H. *Histoire de l'imprimerie à Châlons-sur-Marne.* (Châlons-sur-Marne, 1894).

Maignien, G. *L'imprimerie, les imprimeurs et les libraires à Grenoble du XV au XVIII siècle.* (Grenoble, 1884).

Marchand, J. *Une Enquête sur l'imprimerie et la librairie en Guyenne, mars* 1701. (Bordeaux, 1939).

Morin, L. *Histoire corporative des artisans du livre à Troyes.* (Troyes, 1900).

Pellechet, M. *Notes sur les imprimeurs du Comtat Venaissin et de la Principauté d'Orange.* (Paris, 1887).

Perrod, M. *Répertoire bibliographique des ouvrages franc-comtois imprimés antérieurement à 1790.* (Paris, 1912).

Poyet, P. *Essai de Bibliographie limousine.* (Limoges, 1862).

Simons, J. *Bibliographie douaisienne des ecrivains de la Compagnie de Jésus.* (Douai, 1896).

Trénard, L. *Commerce et culture: le Livre à Lyon au XVIII siècle.* (Lyon, 1953). (*Albums du Crocodile,* juillet-août 1953).

Ventre, M. *L'imprimerie et la librairie en Langedoc au dernier siècle de l'Ancien Régime, 1700–1789.* (Paris, 1958).

Vingtrinier, A. *Histoire de l'imprimerie à Lyon.* (Lyon, 1894).

GERMANY

Benzing. *Die Buchdrucker des 16 und 17 Jahrhunderts im Deutschen Sprachgebiet.* (Wiesbaden, 1963).

Der Deutsche Buchhandel in Urkunden und Quellen hrsg. von Hans Widmann unter Mitwirkung von H. Kliemann und B. Wendt. (Hamburg, 1965, 2 vols.)

Goldfriedrich, J. and Kapp, F. *Geschichte des Deutschen Bucchandels.* (Leipzig, 1886–1903, 4 vols.)

Schwetschke, G. *Codex nundinarius Germaniae litteratae bisecularis.* (Halle, 1850, 2 vols.)

BELGIUM

Bergmans, P. *Les imprimeurs belges à l'étranger.* (Brussels, 1932).
Bibliothèque Nationale. *Anvers, ville de Plantin et de Rubens. Catalogue de l'exposition organisée à la galerie Mazarine (mars-avril 1954).* (Paris, 1954).
Bibliothèque Royale de Belgique. *Le Livre en Brabant jusqu'en 1800.* (Exposition, Brussels, 1935).
Clair, C. *Christopher Plantin.* (London, 1960).
Dermuhl, A. and Bouchery, H. F. *Bibliographie betreffende de Antwersche drukker.* (Antwerp, 1938).
Histoire du livre et de l'imprimerie en Belgique des origines à nos jours. (Brussels, 1930–34, 6 vols.)
Lepreux, G. *Les imprimeurs belges en France.* (Paris, 1910). (From *Bulletin du Bibliophile*).
Mémorial des journées Plantin. (Antwerp, 1956).
Plantin, C. *Correspondance,* ed. M. Rooses et J. Denucé. (Ghent, 1883–1918, 5 vols.)
Rooses, M. *Christophe Plantin.* 2nd ed. (Antwerp, 1893).
Sabbe, C. *L'oeuvre de Christophe Plantin et de ses successeurs.* (Brussels, 1937).
Verdussen, *Briefwisseling van de gebroeders Verdussen,* ed. M. Sabbe. (Antwerp, 1923–36, 2 vols.)

SPAIN

Defourneaux, M. *L'Inquisition espagnole et les livres français au XVIII siècle.* (Paris, 1963).
Hazanas Y La Rua, J. *La imprenta en Sevilla.* (Seville, 1945–49, 2 vols.)
Perez Pastor, C. *Bibliografia Madrilena.* (Madrid, 1891–1907. 3 vols.)
————. *La imprenta en Medina del Campo.* (Madrid, 1895).
————. *La imprenta en Toledo.* (Madrid, 1887).
Sanchez, J. *Bibliografia Aragonesa del siglo XVI.* (Madrid, 1913–14, 2 vols.)
Sierra Corella, J. *La censura de libros y papeles y los indices y catalogos espanoles de los prohibidos y expurgados.* (Madrid, 1947).

GREAT BRITAIN

Blagden, C. and Hodgson, N. *The notebook of Thomas Bennet and Henry Clements, 1686–1719.* (Oxford, 1956).

Blagden, C. *The Stationers' Company: a history, 1403–1959.* (London, 1960).

Clair, C. *A history of printing in Britain.* (London, 1965).

Dictionary of printers and booksellers in England, Scotland and Ireland and of foreign printers of English books, 1557–1640. (London, 1910).

Handover, P. M. *Printing in London from 1476 to modern times.* (London, 1960).

Plant, M. *The English book trade.* 2nd ed. (London, 1965).

Plomer, H. *Dictionary of the printers and booksellers who were at work in England, Scotland and Ireland from 1668 to 1725.* (London, 1922).

ITALY

Ascarelli, F. *Tipografia cinquecentina italiana.* (Florence, 1953).

Berberi, F. *Paolo Manuzio e la Stamperia del Popolo Romano.* (Rome, 1942).

Brown, H. F. *The Venetian printing press.* (London, 1891).

Dorez, L. "Le Cardinal Marcello Cervini et l'imprimerie à Rome, 1520–1550." (In *Mémoires de l'Ecole française de Rome,* XII, 1892, pp. 289–313).

Fumagalli, J. *Lexicon typographicum Italiae . . . ristampa xerografica completata da tre supplementi con indici cumulativi.* (Florence, 1966).

Petitmengin, P. "A propos des éditions patristiques de la Contre-Réforme: le 'Saint-Augustin' de la Typographie vaticane." (In *Recherches augustiniennes,* vol. IV, Paris, 1966, pp. 199–251).

Renouard, A. A. *Annales de l'imprimerie des Alde . . .* (Paris, 1834).

Vichi, A. M. G. *Annali della Stamperia del Popolo Romano, 1570–1598.* (Rome, 1959).

NETHERLANDS

Bergmans, G. S. *Nouvelles études sur la bibliographie Elzevirienne.* (Paris, 1897).

Burger, C. P. "Amsterdamsche boeken op de Frankforter mis, 1590–1609." (In *Het Boek,* 23ste deel, 1935/36, pp. 175–194).

————. "De Amsterdamsche uitzever Cornelis Claesz, 1578–1609." (In *De Guldenpasser,* 9 Jhr., 1931, pp. 59–68).

Davies, David. *The world of the Elzeviers, 1580–1712.* (The Hague, 1954).

Enschede. *Fonderies de caractères et leur matériel dans les Pays-Bas du XV au XIX siècle.* (Haarlem, 1908).

Hellinga, W. G. and La Fontaine Verwey, H. de. *In officina Joannis Blaeu.* (Amsterdam, 1961).

Kossman, E. F. *De Boekverkoopers, notarissen en cramers op het Binnenhof.* (The Hague, 1932).

Kruseman, A. C. *Aantekeningen betreffende den boekhandel van Noord-Nederland in de 17 en 18 eeuw.* (Amsterdam, 1893).

Ledeboer, A. M. *Alfabetische list der Boekdrukkers Boekverkoopers en uitgevers in Noord-Nederland.* (Deventer, 1872).

Moes, E. W. *De Amsterdamsche Boekdrukkers en uitgevers in de zestiende eeuw.* (Amsterdam, 1896–1907, 2 vols.)

Rahir, E. *Catalogue d'une collection unique de volumes imprimés par les Elzevier et divers typographes hollandais du XVII siècle.* (Paris, 1896, repr. 1965).

Stevenson, E. L. *Willem Janszoon Blaeu, 1571–1638.* (New York, 1914).

Van Biema, E. *Les Huguetan de Mercur et de Vrijhoeven.* (The Hague, 1918).

Van Eeghen, I. H. *De Amsterdamse boekhandel, 1680–1725.* (Amsterdam, 1960–7, 4 vols.)

Willems. *Les Elzevier. Histoire et annales typographiques.* (Brussels, 1880).

PORTUGAL

Anselmo, A. J. *Bibliografia das obras impresas em Portugal no seculo XVI.* (Lisbon, 1926).

Barbosa Machado, D. *Bibliotheca lusitana.* (Lisbon, 1741–1759, 4 vols.; repr. Farnborough, 1965–8).

SWITZERLAND

Bonnant, G. "La librairie genevoise au Portugal du XVI au XVIII siècle." (In *Geneva,* nouvelle série, v. 3, 1955, pp. 183–200).

————. "La librairie genevoise dans la péninsule ibérique au XVIII siècle." (*Ibid.,* 1961/62, pp. 103–124).

Chaix, P. et al. *Les livres imprimés à Genève de 1550 à 1600.* (Geneva, 1966).

Chaix, P. *Recherches sur l'imprimerie à Genève de 1550 à 1564.* (Geneva, 1954).

Gaullieur, E. H. *Etudes sur la typographie genevoise du XV au XIX siècle et sur les origines de l'imprimerie en Suisse.* (Geneva, 1855).

Geisendorf, P. F. "Lyon et Genève du XVI au XVIII siècle; les foires et l'imprimerie." (In *Cahiers d'Histoire,* publiés par les universités de Clermont, Lyon, Grenoble, v. V, 1960, pp. 65–76).

Kleinschmidt, J. R. *Les imprimeurs et libraires de la République de Genève.* (Geneva, 1948).

B. Other Useful Works

Adam, A. *Théophile de Viau et la libre pensée française en 1620.* (Paris, 1936).

———. *Histoire de la littérature française au XVII siècle.* (Paris, 1948–56, 5 vols.)

———. *Vie et oeuvres de Descartes; étude historique.* (Paris, 1910).

Agréables conférences de deux paysans de St. Ouen et de Montomorency sur les affaires du temps, ed. F. Deloffre. (Paris, 1961).

Allain, E. *L'instruction primaire en France avant la Révolution.* (Paris, 1881).

Allier, R. *La Cabale des dévots, 1627–1666.* (Paris, 1903).

Aragonnes, C. *Madeleine de Scudéry, reine du Tendre.* (Paris, 1934).

Argenson, R. Le Voyer, Cte de. Notes. (Paris, 1866; Rapports inédits . . . Paris, 1891.)

Ariés, Philipe. *L'enfant et la vie familiale sous l'Ancien Régime.* (Paris, 1960).

Arnaud, A. *Oeuvres publiées par G. Du Parc de Bellegarde and J. Hauteface, avec notice biographique par N. de Larrière.* (Paris, 1775–83, 43 vols.)

Ascoli, G. *La Grande Bretagne devant l'opinion française.* (Paris, 1930, 2 vols.)

Astruc, C. "Les manuscrits grecs de Richelieu." (In *Scriptorium,* v. VI, 1952, pp. 3–17).

Atkinson, G. *Les relations de voyages du XVII siècle et l'évolution des idées. Contribution à l'étude de la formation de l'esprit du XVIII siècle.* (Paris, n.d.)

———. *The 'extraordinary voyage' in French literature before 1700.* (New York, 1920).

Aubery, L. *Histoire du Cardinal-Duc de Richelieu.* (Paris, 1660).

Aubineau. *Notices littéraires sur le XVII siècle.* (Paris, 1859).

Auvray, P. and Monfort, F. "Richard Simon, d'après des documents inédits ou peu connus." (In *Oratoriana*, 1960, pp. 46–69).

Babelon, J. P. *Demeures parisiennes sous Henri IV et Louis XIII.* (Paris, 1965).

Bady, R. *L'homme et son 'institution' de Montaigne à Bérulle, 1580–1625.* (Paris, 1964).

Bagrow, L. and Skelton, R. A. *Meister der Kartographie.* (Berlin, 1964).

Baillet, A. *La vie de M. Descartes.* (Paris, 1691).

Balmas, E. "L'inventario della biblioteca di Racine." (In *Annali della Facoltà di Economica e Commercio in Verona dell'Università degli Studi di Padova, 1964/65,* série I, vol. I, pp. 411–472).

Bar, F. *Le genre burlesque au XVII siècle. Etude de style.* (Paris, 1960).

Barnes, A. *Jean Le Clerc et la République des Lettres.* (Paris, 1938).

Baroni, V. *La Contre-Réforme devant la Bible.* (Lausanne, 1943).

Bassompierre. *Journal de ma vie. Mémoires de M. de Bassompierre,* ed. Chanterac. (Paris, 1870–77, 4 vols).

Bataillon, M. *Erasme et Espagne.* (Paris, 1937).

Battifol, L. *Le Louvre sous Henri IV et Louis XIII.* (Paris, 1930).

Baudry de St Gilles d'Asson, Antoine de. *Le journal de M. de St Gilles,* ed. E. Jovy. (Paris, 1936).

Bayle, P. *Pensées diverses sur la comète,* ed. A Prat. (Paris, 1912, 2 vols.)

Beall, C. B. *La fortune de Tasse en France.* (Eugen, 1942).

Bedel, C. "La pharmacie au XVII siècle." (In *XVII Siècle,* no. 30, Janvier 1956, pp. 25–43 and 46–61).

Bellanger, Justin. *Histoire de la traduction en France (auteurs grecs et latins).* (Paris, 1903).

Bénézit, E. *Dictionnaire des peintres, sculpteurs, dessinateurs et graveurs.* (Paris, 1903).

Bergougnoux, L. A. *L'esprit de polémique et les querelles savantes . . . Marc-Antoine Dominicy, 1605–1650. Ses protecteurs, ses amis, ses adversaires.* (Paris, 1936).

Berthelot du Chesnay. "Les missions de St Jean Eudes." (In *XVII Siècle,* no. 41, 1958, pp. 328–48).

Berthelot du Chesnay. "La spiritualité des laïcs." (In *XVII Siècle,* no. 62–3, 1964, pp. 30–46).

Bertrand, J. *L'Académie des Sciences et les académiciens de 1665–1793.* (Paris, 1869).

Berty, A. *Histoire générale de Paris. Topographie historique du vieux Paris.* (Paris, 1866–97. 6 vols.)

Beugnot, B, *Jean-Louis Guez de Balzac: bibliographie générale.* (Montréal, 1967).

Bibliothèque de la Ville de Lyon. *Livres à figures du XVII siècle français.* (Lyon, 1964).

Bibliothèque Nationale. *Fontenelle, 1657–1757.* (Paris, 1957).

Bibliothèque Nationale. *Malherbe et les poètes de son temps.* (Paris, 1955).

Birn, R. "Le *Journal des Savants* sous l'Ancien Régime." (In *Journal des Savants,* 1965, pp. 15–35).

Blanchet, L. *Campanella.* (Paris, 1920).

Blet, P. *Le Clergé de France et la monarchie. Etude sur les assemblées générales du clergé de 1615 à 1666.* (Rome, 1959).

Blum, A. "Louis XIV et l'imagerie satirique pendant les dernières années du XVII siècle." (In *Archives de l'Art français,* VII, 1913, pp. 172–286).

Boas, M. *Robert Boyle and seventeenth century chemistry.* (CUP, 1955).

Boase, A. M. *The fortunes of Montaigne: a history of the Essay in France, 1580–1669.* (London, 1935).

Bodin, J. *Le Colloque . . . des secrets cachés des choses sublimes.* (Paris, 1914).

Boislisle, A. de. *Paul Scarron et Francoise d'Aubigné.* (Paris, 1894).

Boissier, G. *L'Academie Française sous l'Ancien Régime.* (Paris, 1909).

Boissonade, P. *L'industrie du papier en Charents et son histoire. (Ligugé, 1899).*

Bonnafé, E. *Dictionnaire des amateurs français au XVII siècle.* (Paris, 1884).

Bonnerot, J. *La Sorbonne.* (Paris, 1927).

Bontinck, F. *La lutte autour de la liturgie chinoise aux XVII et XVIII siècles.* (Louvain and Paris, 1962).

Bossuet, J. B. *Correspondance . . . Nouvelle édition . . . par Ch. Urbain et E. Lévesque.* (Paris, 1900–25, 14 vols. and 1 vol. of tables).

Boucher, F. *Le Pont-Neuf.* (Paris, 1925, 2 vols.)

Bouette de Blémur, J. *Eloges de plusieurs personnes illustres en piété de l'Ordre de St Benoit.* (Paris, 1679).

Bouillier, F. *Histoire de la philosophie cartésienne.* (Paris, 1854, 2 vols.)

Boulet-Sautel, M. et al. *Les débuts de la presse française: nouveaux aperçus.* (Goteborg, 1951).

Bouquet, H. L. *L'Ancien collège d'Harcourt et le lycée St Louis.* (Paris, 1891).

Bourchenin, E. *Etude sur les académies protestantes en France au XVI et au XVII siècle.* (Paris, 1882).

Bourgeon, J. L. "L'Ile de la Cité pendant la Fronde." (In *Paris et Ile-de-France. Mémoires publiées par la Fédération des Sociétés Savantes de Paris et de l'Ile-de-France,* v. XIII, 1062, pp. 23–144).

Bourgoin, A. *Un bourgeois de Paris lettré au XVII siècle: Valentin Conrart et son temps.* (Paris, 1863).

Bournet, L. *La querelle janséniste.* (Paris, 1924).

Brasillach, R. *Pierre Corneille.* (Paris, 1938).

Bréhier, H. "Le developpement des études d'histoire byzantine du XVII au XX siècle." (In *Revue d'Auvergne,* janvier-février 1901).

Bremond, H. *La querelle du Pur Amour au temps de Louis XIV.* (Paris, 1914).

———. *Histoire littéraire du sentiment religieux en France depuis la fin des Guerres de Religion jusqu'à nos jours.* (Paris, 1936, 12 vols.)

Brissaud, J. B. *Cours d'histoire générale du droit français public et privé.* (Paris, 1904).

Broglie, E. de. *Mabillon et la société de St Germain-des-Prés au XVIII siècle.* (Paris, 1888, 2 vols.)

Broutin, P. *La Réforme pastorale en France au XVII siècle.* (Paris, 1956, 2 vols.)

Brown, H. *Scientific organization in XVII century France, 1620–1680.* (Baltimore, 1934).

Brunot, F. *Histoire de la langue française des origines à nos jours.* (Paris, 1906–48, 11 vols.)

Brunschvig, L. *Descartes et Pascal lecteurs de Montaigne.* (New York and Paris, 1944).

Buisson, F. *Dictionnaire de la pédagogie et d'instruction primaire.* (Paris, 1887, 3 vols.)

Busson, H. *La pensée religieuse française de Charron à Pascal.* (Paris, 1933).

———. *La religion des classiques, 1660–1685.* (Paris, 1948).

Callières, J. de. *La fortune des gens de qualité et des gentilhommes particuliers.* (Paris, 1663).

Les Caquets de l'accouchée, ed. E. Fournier. (Paris, 1856).

Cauchie, M. "La réglementation du commerce des livres en 1649." (In *Documents pour servir à l'histoire littéraire du XVII siècle,* Paris, 1924, pp. 83–5).

Caullery, M. *La biologie au XVII siècle,* no. 30, 1956, pp. 25–44.

Cerf, M. "La censure royale à la fin du XVII siècle." (In *Communications,* 1967, no. 9, pp. 2–27).

Certeau, M. de "'Mystique' au XVII siècle: le problème du langage 'mystique'." (In *Mélanges H. de Lubac,* 1964, v. 2, pp. 267–291).

————. "Les oeuvres de Jean-Joseph Surin." (In *Revue d'Ascétique et de Mystique,* 1964, v. 40, no. 4, pp. 443–76; 1965, v. 41, no. 1, pp. 55–78).

————. "Politique et mystique: René d'Argenson, 1596–1651." (In *Revue d'Ascétique et de Mystique.* janvier-mars 1963, pp. 45–82).

Ceyssens, L. "La publication de l' 'Augustinus' d'après la correspondance de Henri Calénus." (In *Antonianum,* XXXV, pp. 417–8).

Chapelain, J. *Lettres . . . publiées par P. Tamizey de Larroque.* (Paris, 1880–3, 2 vols.)

Chatelain, U. V. *Le Surintendant Fouquet, protecteur des lettres, des arts et des sciences.* (Paris, 1905).

Chaunu, P. *La civilisation de l'Europe classique.* (Paris, 1966).

Chauviré, R. *Jean Bodin, auteur de la République.* (Paris, 1916).

Chérot, H. *Etude sur la vie et les oeuvres du P. Le Moyne, 1602–1671.* (Paris, 1887).

————. *Trois educations princières dix-septième siècle.* (Paris, 1896).

Chesneaux, J. *Le Père Yves de Paris et son temps.* (Paris, 1946, 2 vols.)

————. *L'Apologétique en France de 1580 à 1670: Pascal et ses précurseurs.* (Paris, 1954).

————. "Problèmes et difficultés de l'humanisme chrétien." (In *XVII Siècle,* nos. 62–3, 1964, pp. 4–29).

————. "L'Humanisme chrétien du XVII siècle à la lumière d'ouvrages récents." (In *Studi Francesi,* no. 18, 1962, pp. 414–40).

Cioranescu, A. *L'Arioste en France des origines à la fin du XVIII siècle.* (Paris, 1939, 2 vols.)

Clair, P. *Louis Thomassin, 1619–1695. Etude bio-bibliographique.* (Paris, 1964).

Clément, L. *Henri Estienne et son oeuvre française.* (Paris, 1899).

————. *La police sous Louis XIV.* (Paris, 1956).

Cognet, L. *Crépuscule des mystiques, Bossuet, Fénelon, Tournai.* (Paris, n.d.).

————. *De la dévotion moderne à la spiritualité française.* (Paris, 1958).

————. *Antoine Godeau, évêque de Grasse et de Vence, un des premiers membres de l'Académie Française.* (Paris, 1900).

————. *La spiritualité moderne.* v.1: *l'essor, 1500–1650.* (Paris, 1967).

Cohen, G. *Ecrivains français en Hollande dans la première moitié du XVII siècle.* (Paris, 1920).

Colbert. *Lettres, instructions et mémoires . . . publiées par Pierre Clément.* (Paris, 1868, 10 vols.)

Colloques. Cahiers de civilisation. *Croissance d'une capitale.* (Paris, 1961) (Etudes de R. Dion et al.)

Conservatoire National des Arts et Métiers. *Catalogue de l'exposition Histoire et prestige de l'Academie des Sciences, 1666–1966.* (Paris, 1966).

Coornaert, E. *Les français et le commerce international à Anvers fin du XV-XVI siècle.* (Paris, 1961, 2 vols.)

Corblet, J. *Origines troyennes de l'Institut des Filles de la Croix.* (Paris, 1869).

Cordelier, T. *Madame de Maintenon.* (Paris, 1955).

Cordonnier, Ch. *Les Filles de la Croix despuis leur fondation jusqu'à nos jours.* (Paris, 1922).

Couton, G. *La vieillesse de Corneille, 1658–1684.* (Paris, 1949).

Couton, G. and Martin, H. J. "Une source d'histoire sociale: le registre de l'état des âmes." (In *Revue d'Histoire Economique et Sociale,* 1967, v.45, no. 2 pp. 244–53).

Crooks, E. J. *The influence of Cervantes in France in the XVII century.* (Baltimore, 1931).

Crozet, R. *La vie artistique en France au XVII siècle, 1598–1661. Les artistes et la société.* (Paris, 1954).

Cubells, Mme. "Le Parlement de Paris pendant La Fronde." (In *XVII Siècle,* no. 35, 1957 pp. 171–201).

Dagens, J. "Hermétisme et cabale en France de Lefèvre d'Etaples à Bossuet." (In *Revue de litterature comparée,* janvier-mars 1961, pp.5–16).

————. *Bérulle et les origines de la Restauration catholique, 1575–1611.* (Paris, 1952).

Danville, F. de. *Cartes anciennes de l'Eglise de France.* (Paris, 1956).

————. "Collèges et fréquentation scolaire au XVII siècle." (In *Population,* 8 année, 1957, p. 473).

————. "Effectifs des collèges et scolarité aux XVII et XVIII siècles dans le Nord-Est de la France." (In *Population,* 10 année, 1955, pp. 455–488).

————. "L'enseignement des mathématiques dans les collèges de

France des XVI et XVII siècle." (In *Revue d'Histoire des Sciences*, v. VII, 1954).

―――. "L'enseignement des mathématiques au XVII siècle." (In *XVII Siècle*, no. 30, 1956, pp. 62–68).

―――. "L'évolution de l'atlas de France de Louis XIII." (In *Ministère de l'Education Nationale. Comité des travaux historiques. Actes du 87 Congrès National des Sociétés Savantes*, Paris, 1963).

―――. *La géographie des humanistes*. (Paris, 1940).

―――. *La langage des géographes*. (Paris, 1964).

―――. *La naissance de l'humanisme moderne*. (Paris, 1940).

―――. "Le premier atlas de France: le Théâtre françois de M. Bouguereau, 1594." (In *Actes du 85 Congrès National des Sociétés Savantes*, Chambéry-Annecy, 1960. Session de Géographie, Paris, 1961, pp. 1–50).

Darricau, R. "La spiritualité du Prince." (In XVII *Siècle*, 1964, no. 62–3, pp. 78–111).

Daumas, M. "La vie scientifique au XVII siècle." (In *XVII Siècle*, no. 30, 1956, pp. 110–133).

David, M. V. *Le débat sur les écritures et l'hieroglyphe aux XVII et XVIII siècles*. (Paris, 1965).

Davy de Viriville, A. *Histoire de la botanique en France*. (Paris, 1954).

Dedouvres, L. *Le Père Joseph Du Tremblay. Notice biographique d'après le Sieur de Hautebresche. Essai bibliographique*. (Angers, 1889).

Dedouvres, L. *Le Père Joseph. Etude critique sur ses oeuvres spirituelles*. (Angers, 1901).

―――. *Le Père Joseph polémiste, ses premiers écrits, 1623–1626*. (Paris, 1895).

Deelder, C. *Bijdragen voor de Geschiedenis van de Rooms Katholikien kerk in Nederland*. (Rotterdam, 1888–92, 2 vols.)

Dejob, Ch. De l'influence du Concile de Trente sur la littérature et sur les beaux-arts chez les peuples catholiques. *Essai d'introduction à l'histoire littéraire du siècle de Louis XIV*. (Paris, 1884).

Delassaut, G. *Le Maistre de Sacy et son temps*. (Paris, 1957).

Delattre, P. *Les établissements de Jésuites en France depuis quatre siècles*. (Enghien, 1940–1957, 4 vols.)

Delaunay, P. *La vie médicale aux XVI, XVII et XVIII siècles*. (Paris, 1935).

Delavaud, L. *Quelques collaborateurs de Richelieu*. (Paris, 1915).

Delcourt, Marie. *Etude sur les traductions des tragiques grecs et latins en France depuis la Renaissance*. (Brussels, 1925).

Delisle, L. *Le Cabinet des Manuscrits de la Bibliothèque Impériale (Nationale).* (Paris, 1868–81, 4 vols.)

Deloche, M. *Autour de la plume du Cardinal de Richelieu.* (Paris, 1920).

———. *La Maison du Cardinal de Richelieu.* (Paris, 1912).

Deloffre, F. *La Nouvelle en France à l'age classique.* (Paris, 1967).

Demante, G. "Histoire de la publication des livres de Pierre Du Puy sur les libertés de l'Eglise gallicane." (In *Bibliothèque de l'Ecole des Chartes,* 1 série, v. V, 1843–4, pp. 585–).

Depping, G. B. et G. *Correspondance administrative sous le règne de Louis XIV.* (Paris, 1850–55, 4 vols.)

Derathe, R. *Jean-Jacques Rousseau et la science politique de son temps.* (Paris, 1950).

Descartes, R. *Oeuvres,* ed. Ch. Adam et P. Tannery. (Paris, 1964–5, 13 vols.)

Deschamps-Juif, M. "L'historiographe André Du Chesne, 1584–1640." (In *Ecole Nationale des Chartes. Position des thèses soutenues par les élèves de la promotion de 1963,* pp. 45–9).

Desgraves, L. "Aspect de la controverse entre catholiques et protestants dans le Sud Ouest entre 1580 et 1630." (In *Annales du Midi,* 1964, pp. 153–187).

Desmolets, P. N. *Mémoires de littérature et d'histoire.* (Paris, 1749).

Dethan, G. *Gaston d'Orléans, conspirateur et prince charmant.* (Paris, 1959).

Devreese, R. *Bibliothèque Nationale. Département des Manuscrits. Catalogue des manuscrits grecs. II: Le Fonds Coislin.* (Paris, 1945).

Deyon, Pierre. "La production manufacturière dans la France du XVII siècle." (In *XVII Siècle,* nos. 70–71, 1966, pp. 47–63).

Dhotel, J. *Les origines du catéchisme moderne d'après les premiers manuels imprimés en France.* (Paris, 1967).

Dibon, P. *L'enseignement de la philosophie dans les universités néerlandaises à l'époque pré-cartésienne.* (Leyden, 1954).

———. "Le refuge Wallon précurseur de Refuge Huguenot." (In *XVII Siècle,* 1967, nos. 76–7, pp. 53–74).

Dock, M. C. *Etude sur le droit d'auteur.* (Paris, 1963).

Documents du Minutier Central concernant l'histoire littéraire rassemblés et publiés sous la direction de J. Moniont et J. Mesnard. (Paris, 1960).

Doncieux, G. *Un Jésuite homme de lettres au XVII siècle, le Père Bouhours.* (Paris, 1886).

Donze, R. *La grammaire generale et raissonnée de Port-Royal.* (Berne, 1967).

Doublet, G. *Godeau, évêque de Grasse et de Vence.* (Paris, 1911–13).

Doucet, R. *Les bibliothèques parisiennes au XVI siècle.* (Paris, 1956).

Doutrepont, A. "La dédicace littéraire à l'époque classique en France." (In *Académie Royale de Belgique. Bulletin de la Classe des Lettres et des Sciences Morales et Politiques,* 5 serie, XXIV, 1938, 5, pp. 148–182).

Drouhet, Ch. *Le poète François Mainard, 1583?–1646.* (Paris, 1909).

Dubé, W. *Bérulle et les protestants, 1593–1610.* (Paris, 1966).

Dubois-Quinard, C. *Laurent de Paris. Une doctrine du Pur Amour en France au début du XVII siècle.* (Rome, 1959).

Du Breul, J. *Théâtre des antiquités de Paris.* (Paris, 1612).

Dubu, J. "La condition sociale de l'écrivain de théâtre." (In *XVII Siècle,* no. 31, 1958, pp. 341–9).

Dulong, G. *L'abbé de St Réal. Etude sur les rapports de l'histoire et du roman au XVII siècle.* (Paris, 1922, 2 vols.)

Duplessis d'Argentré, C. *Collectio judiciorum de novis erroribus.* (Paris, 1728–36, 3 vols.)

Dupont-Ferrier, G. *La vie quotidienne d'un collège parisien. Du Collège de Clermont au Lycée Louis-le-Grand. I. Le collège sous les Jesuites, 1563–1762.* (Paris, 1921).

Dupront, A. *Pierre-Daniel Huet et l'exegèse comparatiste au XVII siècle.* (Paris, 1930).

Duval, E. *La vie admirable de soeur Marie de l'Incarnation.* (Paris, 1647).

Egger, M. *L'Héllenisme en France.* (Paris, 1869, 2 vols.)

Engel, C. E. "Connaissait-on le théâtre anglais en France au XVII siècle?" (In *XVII Siècle,* no. 48, 1960, pp. 1–15).

———. "Henri Justel." (In *XVII Siècle,* no. 61, 1963, pp. 18–30).

Escarpit, R. *Sociologie de la littérature.* (Paris, 1958).

Escole, L' paroissiale ou la manière de bien instruire dans les petites escoles, par un prestre d'une paroisse de Paris, (Paris, 1654).

Espiner-Scot, J. G. "Le cercle de Henri de Mesmes." (In *Mélanges Lefranc,* Paris, 1936).

———. *Claude Fauchet, sa vie, son oeuvre.* (Paris, 1938).

Evans, W. H. *L'historien Mézeray et la conception de l'histoire en France au XVII siècle.* (Paris, 1930).

Fabre, A. *Chapelain et nos deux premières académies.* (Paris, 1890).

Fage, R. *La vie à Tulle au XVI et au XVII siècles.* (Paris, 1902).

Fagniez, G. *La femme et la société française dans la première moitié du dix-septième siècle.* (Paris, 1929).

———. "L'opinion publique et la polémique au temps de Riche-lieu." (In *Revue des Questions Historiques,* LX, 1896, no. 2, p. 466).

———. "L'opinion publique et la presse politique sous Louis XIII." (In *Revue d'Histoire Diplomatique,* XIV, 1900, pp. 352–401).

Féret, P. *Le Cardinal Du Perron: orateur, controversiste, écrivain.* (Paris, 1877).

———. *Un curé de Charenton au XVII siècle.* (Paris, 1881).

———. *La Faculté de théologie de Paris et ses docteurs les plus célèbres.* (Paris 1900–1907, 5 vols.)

Ferraize, J. *La vie admirable et digne d'une fidèle imitation de la B. Mère Marguerite d'Arbouze dite de St. Gertrude.* (Paris, 1628).

Ferté, J. *La vie religieuse dans les campagnes parisiennes, 1622–1695.* (Paris, 1962).

Feugère, A. "Le movement religieux dans la littérature du XVII siècle." (In *Revue des Cours et Conférences,* XXXVII, 1, 1937–8, and XXXVIII, 2, 1938).

Flachaire, Ch. *La dévotion à la Vierge dans la littérature catholique au commencement du XVII siècle.* (Paris 1916).

Fleury, M. and Valmary, P. "Les progès de l'instruction élémen-taire de Louis XIV à Napoléon III." (In *Population,* 12 année, 1957, no. 1, janvier-mars, pp. 71–92).

Floquet, A. P. *Bossuet, précepteur du Dauphin.* (Paris, 1864).

Fohlen, Mme J. "Dom Luch d'Achery, 1609–1685 et les débuts d'érudition mauriste." (In *Revue Mabillon,* 1967/8, passim).

Fontanon, A. *Les edicts et ordonnances des rois de France depuis Louis VI dit Le Gros jusqu'à présent.* (Paris, 1611, 3 vols.)

Fosseyeux, H. *Les écoles de charité à Paris sous l'Ancien Régime et dans la première partie du XIX siècle.* (Paris, 1912).

Fouqueray, H. *Histoire de la Compagnie de Jésus en France des origines à la suppression, 1528–1762.* (Paris, 1910–25, 5 vols.)

Francois de Sales. *Oeuvres* . . . ed. Dom B. Mackey et P. Navatel. (Annecy, 1892–1964, 27 vols.)

Franklin, A. *Histoire générale de Paris. Les anciennes biblio-thèques de Paris.* (Paris, 1867–76, 3 vols.)

———. *Histoire de la Bibliothèque Mazarine et du Palais de l'Institut.* 2nd ed. (Paris, 1901).

———. *La Sorbonne, ses origines, sa bibliothèque, les debuts de l'imprimerie à Paris et la succession de Richelieu d'après des documents inédits* . . . 2nd ed., Paris, 1875.

———. *La vie privée d'autrefois.* (Paris, 1887–1900, 27 vols.).

———. *Précis de l'histoire de la Bibliothèque du Roi aujourd'hui Bibliothèque Nationale.* 2nd ed. Paris, 1875.

Fromilhague, R. *La vie de Malherbe. Apprentissages et luttes, 1555–1610.* (Paris, 1954).

Fulton, D. "Printings of 'Le Prince'." (In *Bulletin of the New York Public Library,* 1959, pp. 318–9).

Funck-Brentano, F. and Estrées, P. d' *Figaro et ses devanciers.* (Paris, 1900).

———. *La Bastille des comédiens. Le For L'Evêque.* (Paris, 1910).

Gaquère, F. *Pierre de Marca, 1594–1662, sa vie, ses oeuvres, son gallicanisme.* (Paris, 1932).

Gaquère, F. *Le dialogue irénique: Bossuet-Leibniz. La réunion des Eglises en échec, 1691–1702.* (Paris, 1966).

Garnier, J. *Systema bibliotheca Collegii Parisiensis Societatis Jesu.* (Paris, 1678).

Garreau, A. *Monsieur Henri-Marie Boudon et le secret de l'Ecole française.* (Paris, 1967).

Gastaldi, Vittoria. *Jean-Pierre Camus, romanziere barocco evesco di Francia.* (Catania, 1964).

Gaston, J. *Les images des confréries parisiennes avant la Révolution.* (Paris, 1910).

Gazier, A. *Blaise Pascal et Antoine Escobar.* (Paris, 1912).

———. *Histoire générale du mouvement janséniste des origines jusqu'à nos jours.* (Paris, 1922, 2 vols.)

Georges, E. *St. Jean-Eudes.* (Paris, 1936).

Gérard-Gailly, E. *Un Académicien grand seigneur et libertin au XVII siècle: Bussy-Rabutin, sa vie, ses oeuvres et ses amis.* (Paris, 1909).

Ghellinck, J. de *Patrologie et Moyen Age.* v. III. (Brussels and Paris, 1948).

Gibral, F. *Bernard Lamy. Etude biographique et bibliographique.* (Paris, 1964).

Gillot, H. *La querelle des anciens et des modernes en France.* (Paris, 1914).

———. *Le règne de Louis XIV et l'opinion publique en Allemagne.* (Nancy, 1914).

Glasson, E. *Histoire du droit et des institutions de la France.* v. VIII. *Epoque monarchique.* (Paris, 1908).

Godefroy de Paris. *Les Frères Mineurs capucins en France. Histoire de la province de Paris.* (Paris, 1937–50, 2 vols.)

Goubert, P. *Louis XIV et vingt millions de Français.* (Paris, 1966).

Goyet, T. *L'humanisme de Bossuet.* v.1: *Le goût de Bossuet.* v.2: *l'humanisme philosophique.* (Paris, 1965).

Grange de Surgères. *Répertoire historique et bibliographique de la 'Gazette de France' depuis l'origine jusqu'à la Révolution, 1631–1790.* (Paris, 1902–5, 4 vols.)

Grise, C. M. "Towards a new biography of Tristan l'Hermite." (In *Revue de l'Université d'Ottawa,* avril-juin 1966, pp. 294–316).

Guéranger, P. *Institutions liturgiques.* 2nd ed. (Paris, 1878–85, 4 vols.)

Gueudré, M. C. "La femme et la vie spirituelle." (In *XVII Siècle,* nos. 62–3, 1964, pp. 46–77).

Guibert, J. de *La spiritualité de la Compagnie de Jésus. Esquisse historique,* (Rome, 1953).

Guiffrey, G. et Laboulaye, E. *La propriété littéraire au XVIII siècle. Recueil de pièces et de documents.* (Paris, 1859)

Guiffrey, J. *Artistes parisiens des XVI et XVII siècles. Donations, contrats de mariage, inventaires.* (Paris, 1915).

Hainsworth, G. *Les novelas ejemplares de Cervantes en France au XVII siècle.* (Paris, 1933).

Harisse, H. *Le Président de Thou et ses descendants.* (Paris, 1905).

Hauréau, B. *Hugues de St. Victor. Nouvel examen de l'edition de ses oeuvres. Deux opuscules inédites.* (Paris, 1859).

Hautecoeur, L. *Histoire de l'architecture classique en Europe.* II. *Le règne de Louis XIV.* (Paris, 1942, 2 vols.)

Hazard, P. *La crise de conscience européenne, 1680–1715.* (Paris, 1935, 3 vols.)

Héfélé, C. J. *Histoire des Conciles,* v. IX. (Paris, 1931).

Hendricks, D. "Profitless printing: publication of the Polyglot (Antwerp, Paris, London)." (In *Journal of Library History,* 1967, vol. 2, no. 2, pp. 98–116).

Hennebert, F. *Histoire des traducteurs français d'auteurs grecs et latins pendant le XVI et le XVII siècle.* (Ghent, 1858).

Hermant, G. *Mémoires . . . sur l'histoire ecclésiastique du XVII siècle, 1630–1663,* ed. A. Gazier. (Paris, 1905–1910, 6 vols.)

Holmes, C. E. *Eloquence judiciaire de 1620 à 1660 reflet des problèmes sociaux, religieux et politiques de l'époque.* (Paris, 1967).

Huijben, J. "Aux sources de la spiritualité française du XVII siècle." (In *La Vie Spirituelle,* XXV, 1930, pp 113–139; XXVI, 1931, pp. 17–46 and 75–111; XXVII, 1931, pp. 20–42 and 94–112).

Huijben J. et Debongnie, P. *L'auteur ou les auteurs de l'Imitation.* (Louvain, 1957).

Humbert, F. "Un temoignage sur la recherche des coordonnées géographiques." (In *La Revue Française d'Histoire des Sciences,* IV, 1933, pp. 18–21).

Ierni, F. G. "Paris en 1596 vu par un Italien," trad. G. Raynaud. (In *Bulletin de la Société de l'Histoire de Paris et de l'Ile-de-France,* v. 12, 1885, pp. 164–170).

Irsay, S. d' *Histoire des universités françaises et etrangères.* (Paris, 1955, 2 vols.)

Jacquinet, P. *Les Prédicateurs du XVII siècle avant Bossuet.* (Paris, 1885).

Jammes, A. "Louis XIV, sa bibliothèque et le Cabinet du Roy." (In *The Library,* 5th series, vol. XX, no. 1, March 1965, pp. 1–12).

Janmart de Brouillant, L. *L'Etat de la liberté de la presse en France aux XVII et XVIII siècles. Histoire de Pierre Du Marteau imprimeur à Cologne.* (Paris, 1888).

Joly, C. *Traité historique des écoles épiscopales et ecclésiastiques.* (Paris, 1678).

Jordan, N. "Théodore Godefroy, historiographe de France, 1580–1649." (In *Ecole Nationale des Chartes. Position des thèses soutenues par les élèves de la promotion de 1949.* Paris, 1949, pp. 91–95).

Jourdain, Ch. *Histoire de l'Université de Paris au XVII et au XVIII siècle.* (Paris, 1892).

Julien Eymard d'Angers. "Le Renouveau du Stoicisme en France au XVI siècle et au début du XVII siècle." (In *Association Guillaume Budé,* VII *Congrès, Actes,* pp. 122–153).

Jurgens, M. et Maxfield-Miller E. *Cent ans de recherches sur Molière.* (Paris, 1963).

Kerviler, R. de *Le Chancelier Pierre Séguier.* 2nd ed. (Paris, 1875).

———. "La presse politique sous Richelieu et l'academicien Jean Sirmond, Paris, 1877." (Extracted from *Correspondant,* CII (1876), pp. 943–969 and 1083–1098).

Kerviler, R. de and Barthélemy, E. de *Valentin Conrart, Premier Sécretaire Perpétuel de l'Académie Française. Sa vie et sa correspondance.* (Paris, 1881).

Labrousse, E. *Inventaire critique de la correspondance de Pierre Bayle.* (The Hague, 1961).

———. *Pierre Bayle.* I: *Du Pays de Foix à la cité d'Erasme.* II: *Héterodoxie et rigorisme.* (The Hague, 1963–4, 2 vols.)

————. "Le refuge hollandais: Bayle et Jurieu." (In *XVII Siècle*, nos. 76–77, pp. 75–94).

La Bruyère. *Oeuvres*. New ed. (G. Servois). (Paris, 1912, 3 vols.)

Lachèvre, F. *Etienne Durand poète ordinaire de Marie de Medici, 1585–1618*. (*Bulletin du Bibliophile*, 1905).

————. *Le procès du poète Théphile de Viau*. (Paris, 1909, 2 vols.)

Lafuma, L. "Le Duc de Roannes et le Code Louis XIV." (In *XVII Siècle*, no. 64, 1964, pp. 54–67).

Lagny, J. *Le poète St. Amant, (1594–1661)*. (Paris, 1964).

————. *Bibliographie des éditions anciennes des oeuvres de St. Amant*. (Paris, 1961).

Lallemand, P. *Histoire de l'éducation dans l'ancien Oratoire de France*. (Paris, 1889).

Lanson, G. "Etude sur les rapports de la littérature française et de la littérature espagnole au XVII siècle, 1600–1680." (In *Revue d'Histoire Littéraire de la France*, 1896, p. 45– and 321–; 1897, p. 61– and 180–, and 1901, p. 395–).

Lapadu-Hargues, F. *Recherches sur l'imagerie de piété au XVII siècle, mémoire dactylographié*.

Laplanche, F. *Orthodoxie et prédication. L'oeuvre d'Amyrant et la querelle de la grâce universelle*. (Paris, 1965).

Le Revière, J. de *Histoire de la vie et des moeurs de Marie Tessonière, native de Valence en Dauphiné*. (Lyon, 1650).

Larocque, J. *La plume et le pouvoir au XVII siècle*. (Paris, 1888).

Larroumet, G. "Le public et les écrivains au XVII siècle." (In *Revue Bleue*, 1887, pp. 143–150).

Lathuillère, R. *La Préciosité. Etude historique et linguistique*. (Paris, 1967).

Latourette, G. de *Théophraste Renaudot d'après les documents inédits*. (Paris, 1884).

Lawton, H. W. "Notes sur J. Baudoin et ses traductions de l'anglais." (In *La Revue de la Littérature Comparée*. VI, 1926, pp 673–81).

Lebeau, E. "La bibliothèque musicale des éditeurs Ballard." (In *XVII Siècle*, nos. 21–2, 1954, pp 456–562).

Lebègue, R. "Les correspondants de Peiresc." (In *Les Anciens Pays-Bas*, Brussels, 1943).

————. *La poésie française de 1560 à 1630*. (Paris, 1951, 2 vols.)

————. "Les traductions en France pendant la Renaissance." (*Actes du Congrès Guillaume Budé*, Strasbourg, 1933).

Leblanc, P. *Les Paraphrases françaises des Psaumes à la fin de la période baroque, 1610–1660*. (Paris, 1960).

Leblanc, Y. "Les Enluminures de Le Maître de Sacy." (In *XVII Siècle,* no. 321, 1956, pp. 475–501.).

Leclercq, H. *Mabillon.* (Paris, 1957, 2 vols.)

Ledos, E. G. *Histoire des catalogues des livres imprimés de la Bibliothèque Nationale.* (Paris, 1936).

Leiner, W. *Der Widmungsbrief in der französischen Litteratur, 1580–1715.* (Heidelberg, 1965).

Lelong, J. *Discours historique sur les principales éditions des Bibles polyglottes.* (Paris, 1713).

Lemarchand, G. "Crises économiques et atmosphère sociale en milieu urbain sous Louis XIV." (In *Revue d'Histoire Moderne et Contemporaine,* v. 14, 1967, pp. 244–266).

Lemasne-Desjobert, M. A. *La Faculté de Droit de Paris aux XVII et XVIII siècles.* (Paris, 1966).

Lenoble, R. *La géologie au milieu du XVII siècle.* (Paris, 1954).

———. *Mersenne et la naissance du mécanisme.* (Paris, 1943).

———. "La representation du monde physique à l'époque classique." (In *XVII Siècle,* no. 30, 1956, pp. 6–24).

Léonard, E. G. *Histoire générale du Protestantisme.* (Paris, 1961–4, 3 vols.)

Leprince, N. T. *Essai historique sur la Bibliothèque du Roi.* (Paris, 1856).

L'Estoile, P. de *Journal . . . pour le règne d'Henri IV et le début du règne de Louis XIII.* (Paris, 1948–60, 3 vols.)

Letourneau, G. *La mission de J. J. Olier et la fondation des grands séminaires de France.* (Paris, 1906).

Leturia, Pedro de "Lecturas asceticas y lecturas misticas entre los Jesuitas del siglo XVI." (In *Archivio Italiano per la Storia de la Pietà* II, 1953).

Levi, A. *French moralists. The theory of the passions, 1585–1649.* (OUP, 1964).

Levi-Valensi, J. *La médecine et les médecins français au XVII siècle.* (Paris, 1933).

Lipsius, Justus. *L'Autobiographie.* (Ghent, 1889). Extract from *Messager des Sciences Historiques de Belgique,* v. LXIII, 1889.

———. *Correspondance inédite . . . conservée au Musée Plantin-Moretus.* (Antwerp, 1964).

Loisel, A. *Institutes coutumières.* New ed. (M. Reulos). (Paris, 1935).

Longworth-Chambrun, S. "La vogue de Shakespeare au Grand Siècle." (In *Revue Hebdomadaire* 7, 1924, pp. 463–476).

Louis le Grand, 1563–1963. Etudes, souvenirs, documents. (Paris, 1963).

Lovering, S. *L'activité intellectuelle de l'Angleterre d'après l'ancien Mercure de France, 1672–1778.* (Paris, 1930).

Lyon, G. *La philosophie de Hobbes.* (Paris, 1893).

Macpherson, H. *Censorship under Louis XIV, 1661–1715.* (New York, 1920).

Magendie, M. *La politesse mondaine et les théories de l'honnêteté en France au XVII siècle, de 1600 à 1660.* (Paris, 1925).

———. *Le roman français au XVII siècle, de l'Astrée au Grand Cyrus.* (Paris, 1932).

Magne, E. *Le coeur et l'esprit de Madame de La Fayette.* (Paris, 1927).

———. *Madame de La Fayette.* (Paris, 1926).

———. *Le plaisant abbé de Boisrobert.* (Paris, 1909)

———. *La vie quotidienne au temps de Louis XIII.* (Paris, 1942).

———. *Voiture et les origines de l'Hotel de Rambouillet, 1597–1635.* (Paris, 1611).

———. *Voiture et les années de gloire de l'Hotel de Rambouillet, 1635–1648.* (Paris, 1912).

Maintenon, Marquise de. *Madame de Maintenon institutrice,* ed. E. Faguet. (Paris, 1887).

Male, E. *L'art religieux après le Concile de Trente.* (Paris, 1932).

Malebranche. *Oeuvres complètes,* ed. A. Robinet. (Paris, 1958–67, 20 vols.)

Mandrou, R. *Introduction à la France moderne. Essai de psychologie historique, 1500–1640.* (Paris, 1961).

———. *De la culture populaire aux XVII et XVIII siècles: la Bibliothèque Bleue de Troyes.* (Paris, 1964).

Mangenot, E. *La Vulgate de Sixte-Quint.* (Lille, 1913).

Marmier, J. *Horace en France au XVII siècle.* (Paris, 1912).

Marsan, J. *La pastorale dramatique en France à la fin du XVI et au commencement du XVII siècle.* (Paris, 1905).

Martimort, A. G. *Le Gallicisme de Bossuet.* (Paris, 1953).

Martin, H. J. "Un polémiste sous Louis XIV: Eustache le Noble, 1643–1711." (In *Ecole Nationale des Chartes. Position des thèses soutenues par les élèves de la promotion de 1947.* Paris, 1947, pp. 85–91).

Martin, V. *Le Gallicanisme et le Réforme catholique.* (Paris, 1919).

———. *Le Gallicanisme politique et le Clergé de France.* (Paris, 1929).

Martino, P. *L'Orient dans la littérature française au XVII siècle et au XVIII siècle.* (Paris, 1906).

Masson, A. "Le Chancelier Séguier bibliophile." (In *Bulletin de la*

Société des Bibliophiles de Guyenne, v. XXXVI, 1967, pp. 67–86).

———. "Mazarin et l'architecture des bibliothèques au XVII siècle." (In *Gazette des Beaux-Arts,* décembre 1961, pp. 355–366).

Mathorez, J. "A propos d'une campagne de presses contre l'Espagne à Paris." (*Bulletin du Bibliophile,* 1913).

———. "Notes sur Maître Guillaume, fou de Henri IV et de Louis XIII." (*Bulletin du Bibliophile,* 1911).

———. "Mathurine et les libelles publiés sous son nom." (*Bulletin du Bibliophile,* 1922).

———. "Rapports intellectuels de la France et de la Hollande du XVII au XVIII siècle." (In *Journal des Savants,* 1921, pp. 157–168).

Matoré, G. *Histoire des dictionnaires français.* (Paris, 1968).

Mélèse, P. *Un homme de lettres au temps du Grand Roi: Donneau de Visé, fondateur du 'Mercure Galant'.* (Paris, 1936).

———. *Le théâtre et son public à Paris sous Louis XIV, 1659–1715.* (Paris, 1934).

Mémoires des intendants sur l'état des generalités dressés pour l'instruction du duc de Bourgogne, ed. A. M. de Boislisle. (Paris, 1881).

Mersenne, M. *Correspondance, publiée par Mme. P. Tannery.* (Paris, 1932–67, 10 vols.)

Mesnard, J. "Pascal à l'Académie Le Pailleur." (In *La Revue d'Histoire des Sciences.* v. XVII, 1963, pp. 8–9).

Mesnard, P. *L'essor de la philosophie politique au XVI siècle.* (Paris, 1951).

———. "Du Vair et le Néo-Stoicisme." (In *La Revue d'Histoire et de Philosophie,* 1928, pp. 142–166).

———. *Histoire de l'Académie Française.* (Paris, n.d.)

Metzger, H. *Les doctrines chimiques en France du début du XVII à la fin du XVIII siècle.* v.1. (Paris, 1923).

Meuvret, J. "Les idées économiques en France au XVII siècle." (In *XVII Siècle,* nos. 70–71, 1966, pp. 3–19).

Meyer, A. de "Les premières controverses jansénistes en France au XVII siècle." (In *XVII Siècle,* nos. 70–71, 1966, pp. 3–19).

Meyer, K. A. de *Paul en Alexandre Petau en de geschiedenis van hun handschriften.* (Leyden, 1947).

Millaud, J. "La vie et l'oeuvre de Dom Luc d'Archery, religieux bénédictin de la Congrégation de St. Maur, 1609–1685." (In *Ecole Nationale des Chartes. Position des thèses soutenues par les élèves de la promotion de 1952.* Paris, 1952, pp. 79–82).

Molé, M. *Mémoires,* ed. A. Champollion-Figeac. (Paris, 1855–57, 4 vols.)

Molhuysen, P. C. *Bronnen tot de geschiedenis der leidsche Universiteet.* (The Hague, 1913–1919).

Mols, R. *Introductin à la démographie historique des villes d'Europe,* v. 2. (Louvain, 1955).

Mongrédien, G. *L'Affaire Fouquet.* (Paris, 1956).

——. *Cyrano de Bergerac.* (Paris, 1964).

——. *Précieux et précieuses.* (Paris, 1963).

——. *Recueil des textes et des documents du XVII siècle relatifs à Molière.* (Paris, 1968).

——. *La vie de société aux XVII et XVIII siècles.* (Paris, 1950).

——. *La vie littéraire au XVII siècle.* (Paris, 1947).

——. *La vie quotidienne sous Louis XIV.* (Paris, 1950).

Montalant-Bougleux, L. A. *J. B. Santeul ou la poésie latine sous Louis XIV.* (Paris, 1855).

Morgan, B. T. *Histoire du Journal des Savants depuis 1665 jusqu'en 1701.* (Paris, 1855).

Morin, P. *Opuscula et epistolae,* ed. J. Quétif. (Paris, 1675).

Mornet, D. "Comment étudier un auteur de troisième ou de quatrième ordre." (In *Romanic Review,* XVIII, 1936, pp. 204–16).

——. *Histoire de la littérature française classique, 1660–1700.* (Paris, 1947)

Mours, S. *Le Protestantisme en France au XVII siècle, 1598–1685.* (Paris, 1967).

Mousnier, R. *L'assassinat d'Henri IV, 14 mai 1610.* (Paris, 1964).

——. "Comment les Français du XVII siècle voyaient la Constitution." (In *XVII Siècle,* nos. 25–26, pp. 9–36).

——. "Etudes sur la population de la France au XVII siècle." (In *XVII Siècle,* no. 16, 1952. pp. 527–542).

——. "L'évolution des institutions monarchiques en France et ses relations avec l'état social." (In *XVII Siècle,* 1963, nos. 58–59, pp. 57–72).

——. *Histoire générale des civilisations.* 3rd ed. *Les XVI et XVII siècles.* (Paris, 1961).

——. "Les idées politiques à Paris pendant La Fronde." (In *Bulletin de la Société d'Histoire de Paris,* 1957–1959, a. 84–86, pp. 43–5).

——. *Lettres et mémoires adressés au Chancelier Seguier, 1633–49.* (Paris, 1964, 2 vols.)

——. "L'opposition politique bourgeoise à la fin du XVI et au début du XVII siècle: Louis Turquet de Mayerne." (In *Revue Historique*, 1955).

―――. *Paris au XVII siècle*. (Paris, 3 fasc.)

―――. *Progrès scientifiques et techniques au XVIII siècle*. (Paris, 1958).

―――. *La vénalité des offices sous Henri IV et Louis XIII*. (Rouen, 1945).

Mouy, P. *Le développement de la physique cartésienne, 1646–1712.* (Paris, 1934).

Musée historique lorrain, Nancy. *Jacques Callot et les peintres et graveurs lorrains du dix-sèptieme siècle*. (Nancy, 1954).

Namer, E. *Documents sur la vie de Jules-César Vanini de Taurisano*. (Bari, 1966).

Naudé, G. *Advis pour dresser une bibliothèque présenté a Mgr. le Président de Mesme*. (Paris, 1627).

―――. *Jugement de tout de qui a été imprimé contre le cardinal Mazarin depuis le sixième janvier jusqu'à la Déclaration du premier avril mil six cent quarante neuf*. s.1.n.d.

Neveu, B. *Un historien à l'école de Port-Royal: Sébastien Le Nain de Tillemont, 1637–1698*. (The Hague, 1966).

Neveu, B. "La vie érudite à Paris à la fin du XVII siècle d'après les papiers du P. Léonard de St Catherine." (In *Bibliothèque de l'Ecole des Chartes*, CXXIV, 2, pp. 432–511).

Nicolet-Brousset, M. "La condition de l'homme de lettres au XVII siècle à travers l'oeuvre de deux contemporains: Ch. Sorel et A. Furetière." (In *La Revue d'Histoire Littéraire de la France*, 1963).

Observatoire de Paris. *Catalogue de l'exposition Institut de France, Académie des Sciences, troisième centenaire, 1666–1966*. (Paris, 1965).

Olivier-Martin, F. *Histoire de la coutume de Paris*. (Paris, 1922–29, 2 vols.)

Omont, H. "Catalogue des manuscrits de Jean et Pierre Bourde-lot, médecins parisiens." (In *La Revue des Bibliothèques*, v.1, 1891, p. 81–).

―――. *Missions archéologiques françaises en Orient aux XVII et XVIII*. (Paris, 1902).

―――. "La Collection Byzantine de Labbe et le projet de J. J. Suarès." (In *Revue des Etudes Grecques*, 1904).

―――. "Du Cange et la Collection Byzantine du Louvre." (In *Revue des Etudes Grecques*, 1904).

Optat de Veghel. *Benôit de Canfield, 1562–1610, sa vie, sa doctrine et son influence*. (Paris, 1949).

Orcibal, J. *Le Cardinal de Bérulle: évolution d'une spiritualité.* (Paris, 1965).

———. *Louis XIV contre Innocent XI. Les appels au futur concile de 1688 et l'opinion française.* (Paris, 1949).

———. *Louis XIV et les Protestants.* (Paris, 1951).

———. *Les origines du Jansénisme. II: Jean Duvergier de Hauranne, abbé de St. Cyran et son temps, 1581–1638.* (Louvain, Paris, 1947).

———. *Le procès des maximes des saints devant le Saint-Office.* (Rome, 1968).

———. *La rencontre du Carmel thérèsien avec les mystiques du Nord.* (Paris, 1959).

Pannier, J. *L'Eglise réformèe de Paris sous Louis XIII, 1610–1621.* (Strasbourg, 1922).

———. *L'Eglise réformée de Paris sous Louis XIII de 1621 à 1629 environ.* (Paris, 1932, 2 vols.)

———. *L'Eglise réformée de Paris sous Louis XIV.* (Paris, 1931).

———. "Le Salon de Madame Des Loges." (In *L'Eglise réformée de Paris sous Louis XIII.* Paris, 1922).

Paschini, P. *Cinquecento romano e riforma cattolica.* (Rome, 1958).

Patin, G. *La France au milieu du XVII siècle, 1648–1661, d'après la correspondance de Gui Patin.* (Paris, 1901).

Peignot, G. *Dictionnaire critique, littéraire et bibliographique des principaux livres condamnés au feu, supprimés au censurés.* (Paris, 1806, 2 vols; repr. 1966).

Pellisson, P. et Olivet, P. J. d' *Histoire de l'Académie Française,* ed. Ch. L. Livet. (Paris, 1858, 2 vols.)

Penrose, B. *Les nouveaux horizons de la Renaissance française.* (Paris, 1952).

Perceveaux, P. "Trévoux et 'sa' principauté au Grand Siècle." (In *Communications* 1967, no. 9, pp. 2–27).

Perrens, F. T. *Les mariages espagnols sous le règne de Louis XIV et la régence de Marie de Medicis.* (Paris, 1869).

Petitmengin, P. "A propos des éditions patristiques de la Contre-Réforme: le 'St Augustin' de la Typographie Vaticane." (In *Recherches Augustiniennes,* v.IV, 1966, pp. 199–251).

Peyre, H. *Qu'est ce que le classicisme?* (Paris, 1942).

Pic, P. pseud. de G. Steinheil. *Guy Patin.* (Paris, 1911).

Picard, R. *La carrière de Jean Racine.* (Paris, 1956).

———. *La poésie française de 1640 à 1680. Poésie religieuse; epopée; lyrisme officiel.* (Paris, 1964).

Picot, G. *Cardin Le Bret et la doctrine de la souveraineté.* (Nancy, 1948).

Pilorget, R. "Les problèmes monétaires francais de 1602 à 1689." (In *XVII Siècle* nos. 70–71, 1966, pp. 107–130).

Pinot, V. *La Chine et la formation de l'esprit philosophique en France, 1640–1740.* (Paris, 1932).

Pintard, R. *La Mothe Le Vayer, Gassendi, Guy Patin: études de bibliographie et de critique.* (Paris, 1943).

———. *Le libertinage érudit dans la première moitié du XVII siècle.* (Paris, 1943, 2 vols.)

———. "La littérature et le goût au seuil de l'époque classique." (In *XVII Siècle,* nos. 50–51, 1961, 1–2, p. 57).

———. "Pour le tricentenaire des Précieuses ridicules. Préciosité et classicisme." (In *XVII Siècle,* nos. 50–51, 1961, pp. 8–20).

Pinvert, L. "Sur l'opinion que le XVII siècle a eue du XVI." (In *Bulletin du Bibliophile,* 1910, pp. 205–15, 461–7).

Plattard, J. "Un chapitre de l'histoire de la langue française. Où et comment les étrangers séjournant en France au XVII siècle apprenaient le français." (In *Revue des Cours et Conférences,* 1936/37, pp. 497–507).

Poète, M. *Une vie de cité: Paris, de sa naissance à nos jours.* (Paris, 1924–31, 3 vols.).

Polin, R. *La politique morale de John Locke.* (Paris, 1960).

Poullain de la Barre, F. *De l'éducation des Dames pour la conduite de l'esprit.* (Paris, 1674).

Pourrat, P. *La spiritualité chrétienne.* (Paris, 1926–8, 3 vols).

Poutet, Y. "A propos d'un ouvrage très rare de la Bibliothèque municipale de Bordeaux ('L'escole paroissiale')." (In *Bulletin de la Bibliothèque de Guyenne,* janvier-juin 1963, pp. 27–50).

Prat, J. M. *Maldonat et l'Université de Paris.* (Paris, 1856; repr. 1963).

Préclin, E. et Jarry, E. *Histoire de l'Eglise depuis les origines jusqu'à nos jours, fondée par A. Fliche et V. Martin, 19.* (Paris, 1955, 2 vols.)

Quemada, B. *Introduction à l'étude du vocabulaire médical, 1600–1710.* (Paris, Besançon, 1955).

Quesnel, P. *Pasquier Quesnel et les Pays-Bas.* Correspondance publ. avec introduction et annotations par J. A. C. Tans. (Groningue, Paris, 1960).

———. *Un janséniste en exil. Correspondance de Pasquier Quesnel,* ed. Mme. A. Le Roy. (Paris, 1900, 2 vols.)

Radouant, R. *Guillaume Du Vair, l'homme et l'orateur.* (Paris, 1907).

Rahir, E. "Saisie de livres prohibés au XVII siècle sur Guy Patin et Ch. Patin son fils." (In *Bulletin du Bibliophile,* 1924, pp. 198–202).

Rancé, A. J. *De Thou, son Histoire universelle et ses démêlés avec Rome.* (Paris, 1881).

Raoul de Sceaux. *Histoire des Frères Mineurs capucins de la Province de Paris, 1601–1660.* v.1: *1601–1625.* (Blois, 1967).

Ravaisson, F. *Archives de la Bastille. Documents inédits recueillis et publiés par F. Ravaisson.* (Paris, 1866).

Raynaud, M. *Les médecines au temps de Molière.* (Paris, 1862).

Rebelliau, A. *Bossuet, historien du Protestantisme.* (Paris, 1891).

Reesink, H. *L'Angleterre et la littérature anglaise dans les trois plus anciens periodiques de Hollande de 1684 à 1700.* (Paris, 1931).

Religion, érudition et critique à la fin du XVII siècle. (Paris, 1967).

Reulos, M. *Etude sur l'esprit, les sources et la méthode des Institutes coutumières d'Antoine Loisel.* (Paris, 1935).

Reure, O. C. *La vie et les oeuvres de Honoré d'Urfé.* (Paris, 1910).

Reutter de Rosemont, L. *Histoire de la pharmacie à travers les âges.* (Paris, 1931).

Reynier, G. *La femme au XVII siècle, ses ennemis et ses défenseurs.* (Paris, 1929).

Richard, M. *La vie quotidienne des protestants sous l'Ancien Régime.* (Paris, 1966).

Rigault, H. *Histoire de la querelle des Anciens et des Modernes.* 2nd ed. (Paris, 1959).

Rohault, J. *Oeuvres posthumes,* ed. Clerselier. (Paris, 1682).

Rou, Jean. *Mémoires inédits et opuscules,* ed. Waddington. (Paris, 1857).

Rouvier, J. "Naissance du droit international au XVII siècle." (In *XVII Siècle,* nos. 58–59, 1963, pp. 40–56).

Saint-Germain, J. *La Reynie et la police au Grand Siècle d'après de nombreux documents inédits.* (Paris, 1962).

———. *La vie quotidienne en France à la fin du Grand Siècle.* (Paris, 1965).

Saint-Simon. *Mémoires,* nouvelle édition par A. de Boislisle. (Paris, 1930, 2 vols.)

Sainte-Beuve. *Port-Royal.* (Paris, 1840–59, 5 vols).

Samfiresco, E. *Ménage polémiste, philologue, poète.* (Paris, 1902).

Samsami, N. *L'Iran dans la littérature français.* (Paris, 1936).

Sandys, J. E. *A history of classical scholarship.* Vol. 2: *From the revival of learning to the end of the 18th century.* (CUP, 1908).

Sayous, P. A. *Histoire de la littérature français à l'étranger depuis le commencement du XVII siècle.* (Paris, 1853, 2 vols.)

Scherer, J. *La dramaturgie classique en France.* (Paris, 1959).

Schmidt, H. A. P. *Liturgie et langue vulgaire.* (Rome, 1950).

Schutz, A. H. *Vernacular books in Parisian private libraries of the sixteenth century according to the notarial inventories.* (Chapel Hill, n.d.)

Secret, F. *Les Kabbalistes chrétiens de la Renaissance.* (Paris, 1963).

Sée, H. *Les idées politiques en France au XVII siècle.* (Paris, 1923).

Seguin, J. P. *L'information en France avant le périodique: 517 canards imprimés entre 1529 et 1631.* (Paris, 1964).

Sella, D. "L'industrie lainière à Venise." (In *Annales,* 12 année, no.1, janvier-mars 1957, pp. 29–45).

Serouya, H. *Spinoza, sa vie, sa philosophie.* (Paris, 1947).

Sicard, A. *Les études classiques avant la Révolution.* (Angers, 1886).

Simon, R. *Histoire critique du Vieux Testament.* (Rotterdam, 1685).

Snoeks, R. *L'argument de la tradition dans la controverse eucharistique.* (Louvain, 1951).

Snyders, G. *La pédagogie en France aux XVII et XVIII siècles.* (Paris, 1965).

Somaize; Dictionnaire des précieuses, ed. Ch. Livet. (Paris, 1866).

Sonnet, M. *Statuts et réglements des petites écoles de grammaire de la ville, cité, université, fauxbourgs et banlieues de Paris.* (Paris, 1672).

Sorel, Ch. *Histoire comique de Francion,* ed. E. Roy. (Paris, 1924–31, 4 vols.)

Sourches, L. F. de Bouchet, Marquis de. *Mémoires du Marquis de Sourches sur le règne de Louis XIV,* ed. Cosnac, Bertrand et Portat. (1882–93, 14 vols.)

Steinmann, J. *Richard Simon et les origines de l'exégèse biblique.* (Paris, 1960).

Storer, M. E. *Un épisode littéraire de la fin du XVII siècle. La mode des contes de fées, 1685–1700.* (Paris, 1928).

Strowski, F. *St. François de Sales.* (Paris, 1898).

Surin, J. J. *Correspondance,* ed. M. de Certeau. (Paris, 1966).

———. *Guide spirituel,* ed. M. de Certeau. (Paris, 1965).

Sutcliffe, F. E. *Guz de Balzac et son temps. Littérature et politique.* (Paris, 1959).

Tabuteau, R. *Deux anatomistes français: Les Riolans.* (Paris, 1929).

Tallemant des Réaux, G. *Historiettes,* ed. A. Adam. (Paris, 1960).

Tapié, V. L. *Baroque et classicisme.* (Paris, 1957).

———. "Comment les Français du XVII siècle voyaient la Patrie." (In *XVII Siècle,* nos. 25–26, 1955, pp. 37–58).

Targe, M. *Professeurs et régents de collège dans l'ancienne Universitè de Paris, XVII–XVIII siècles.* (Paris, 1902).

Taton, R. *L'oeuvre mathématique de Girard Desargues.* (Paris, 1951).

———. *Histoire générale des sciences publiée sous la direction de René Taton.* v.2: *La science moderne de 1450 à 1800.* (Paris, 1958).

———. *Enseignement et diffusion des sciences en France au XVIII siècle,* sous la direction de R. Taton. (Paris, 1964).

———. *Les origines de l'Académie Royale des Sciences.* (Paris, 1966).

Terrebasse, H. de *Antoine de Pluvinel Dauphinois, 1552–1620.* (Lyon, 1911).

Tessier, D. *Diplomatique royale français.* (Paris, 1962).

Thorndike, L. *A history of magic and experimental science.* v. VIII. (New York, 1964).

Thuau, E. *Raison d'Etat et pensée politique à l'époque de Richelieu.* (Paris, 1966).

Timbal, P. C. "L'esprit du droit privé au XVII siècle." (In *XVII Siècle,* nos. 58–59, 1963, pp. 31–40).

Tooley, R. V. *Maps and map-makers.* (London, 1949).

Tortel, J. *Le préclassicisme français.* (Paris, 1952).

Trenard, L. *Commerce et culture. Le Livre à Lyon au XVIII siècle.* (Lyon, 1953).

Truchet, J. "La substance et l'éloquence sacrée d'après le XVII siècle français." (In *XVII Siècle,* no. 29, 1955, pp. 309–29).

———. "Bossuet et l'éloquence religieuse au temps du Carème des Minimes." (In *XVII Siècle,* 1961, nos. 50–51, p. 64–).

Ubald d'Alençon. "La spiritualité franciscaine." (In *Etudes fransiscaines,* v. XXXIV, 1927, pp. 276–96, 338–51, 449–71, 591–604).

Urbain, Ch. "Notes sur l'histoire de la défense de la Déclaration de 1682." (In *Bulletin du Bibliophile,* 1882, pp. 49–62, 106–121).

———. "Louis de Lesclache, 1600?–1670." (In *Revue d'Histoire Littéraire de la France,* 1894, pp. 352–8).

———. *Nicolas Coeffeteau, dominicain, évêque de Marseille, un des fondateurs prose français, 1574–1623.* (Paris, 1893).

Uri, I. *Un cercle savant au XVII siècle, François Guyet.* (Paris, 1886).

Vaganay, H. "Pour la bibliographie des éditions françaises de Du Bartas." (In *Bulletin du Bibliophile,* 1928, pp. 311–313, 398–400).

Van Deursen, T. *Professions et métiers interdits. Un aspect de l'histoire de la Révocation de l'Edit de Nantes.* (Groningen, 1960).

Vanel, J. B. *Les Bénédictines de St Germain-des-Près et les savants lyonnais.* (Paris, Lyon, 1894). (Extract from *La Revue du Lyonnais,* 1893/94).

Van Malssen, P. J. W. *Louis XIV d'après les pamphlets répandus en Hollande.* (Paris, 1937).

Van Schoute, J. P. "Les traducteurs français des mystiques rhéno-flamands et leur contribution à l'élaboration de la langue dévote à l'aube du XVII siècle." (In *Revue d'Ascétique et de Mystique,* 1963, pp. 319–337).

Van Tieghem, P. *Répertoire chronologique des littératures modernes.* (Paris, 1935).

———. *Histoire littéraire de l'Europe et de l'Amérique, de la Renaissance à nos jours.* (Paris, 1941).

Vauban. *Projet d'une Dîme royale suivi de deux écrits financiers,* ed. E. Coornaert. (Paris, 1933).

Vaucaire, R. *Etude sur Habicot, sur l'anatomie et la chirurgie de son temps.* (Paris, 1891).

Vernières, P. *Spinoza et la pensée français avant la Révolution.* (Paris, 1954).

Vissac. *De la poésie latine au siècle de Louis XIV.* (Paris, 1862).

Vivarez, H. *Les étapes du progrès: Barrême arithméticien et poète.* s.l., 1909.

Voeltzel, René. *Vraie et fausse église selon les théologiens protestants français du XVII siècle.* (Paris, 1956).

Watson, R. A. *The downfall of Cartesianism, 1673–1712.* (The Hague, 1966).

Weigert, R. A. *L'époque Louis XIV.* (Paris, 1962).

Wickelgren, F. L. *La Mothe Le Vayer, sa vie, son oeuvre.* (Paris, 1937).

Wildenstein, G. "Le Goût pour la peinture dans les cercles de la bourgeoisie parisienne autour de 1700." (In *Gazette des Beaux-Arts,* XLVIII, 1956, pp. 113–195).

Willaert, V. *Histoire de l'Eglise depuis les origines à nos jours.* (Paris, 1960).

Withmore, P. J. S. *The Order of Minims in seventeenth century France.* (Paris, 1967).

Woodbridge, B. *Gatien de Courtilz, Sieur de Verger. Etude sur le précurseur du roman réaliste en France.* (Baltimore, 1925).

Zuber, R. *Les "Belles infidèles" et la formation du goût classique: Perrot d'Ablancourt et Guez de Balzac.* (Paris, 1968).

INDEX OF PERSONAL NAMES

691

INDEX OF PLACES

ABOUT THE AUTHOR

Henri-Jean Martin is a distinguished French historian of the celebrated *Annales* school, President of the Institut du Livre, and Professor at the Ecole des Chartes. Previously he held the post of Principal Keeper of the libraries of Lyons and later was a Senior Librarian at the Bibliothèque Nationale, Paris. His other major works include *L'Apparition du livre* (Albin Michel, 1958), in collaboration with Lucien Febvre, translated by David Gerard as *The Coming of the Book* (NLB, 1976) and *Histoire et pouvoirs de l'écrit* (Perrin, 1988). Under his direction, in collaboration with Roger Chartier, the monumental history of the French book trade, *Histoire de l'édition Française* (Promodis, 1982–1987) is recognized as a landmark in the history and sociology of the book.

ABOUT THE TRANSLATOR

David Gerard was Senior Lecturer in Bibliographical Studies, College of Librarianship Wales. In addition to *The Coming of the Book,* Gerard has translated another of Professor Martin's works, *Literature for the Masses During the Ancien Régime,* and has published *Libraries and the Arts; Libraries and Leisure;* and *Libraries in Society*—as well as two professional autobiographies, *Shrieking Silence* (Scarecrow, 1988) and *Primrose Path* (Elvet Press, 1991).